The Writers' Table

A menu of poetry and prose

TABLE 42 PRESS

Published in 2024 by FeedARead.com Publishing

First Edition

A CIP catalogue record for this title is available from the British Library.

MAN CHE STER
A UNESCO City of Literature

CHORLTON Book Festival

Contents

Introduction

Chorlton Writers' Café started as a series of workshops led by local authors Jackie Kay, Rosie Garland and Martin Griffin during Chorlton Book Festival. The workshop founder, Jo Somerset, was convinced that this area of Manchester contained a wealth of untapped literary talent, and she devised the café format as a mechanism to unleash this underground reservoir. After the first series of workshops, the café group found its home at Benito Lounge in the neighbourhood's busy shopping street.

Writers are an isolated species, busying away in their own burrow. This post-lockdown initiative brought people together in real life in a buzzing café. Providing a space to toil alongside each other on their work-in-progress contradicts that isolation and creates community. We are grateful to Benito Lounge's wonderful staff for serving hot and cold drinks to the weekly writers' table while all the brain cells are churning.

The opening poem evokes the surroundings and the writers' silence. Everyone gets on with their own work, and apart from some informal buddying, there is no sharing or critique at the sessions. This means there is no judgement. Which also means that writers join at any stage of their writing journey – from complete beginners to self-published poets and established authors. As time passed, people shared their successes in competitions, poems in literary journals and novelists who gained publishing deals.

After nearly two years of meeting every Tuesday morning, Café members became curious about each other's work. Was there enough merit to interest readers beyond the group? Chorlton Book Festival offered to support an anthology of writing from the writers' table at Benito Lounge, and this became the title of the book.

Of course, anthologies do not arrive fully formed. This volume is the product of considerable collaboration. Lucy Power thoughtfully unified the disparate creative contributions, with other group members planning, editing, proof reading and illustrating.

This mix of stories, poetry and life writing demonstrates the rich mix of creativity that formed the vision for the Writers' Café. While perusing the variety of pieces, readers might imagine the combination of silent concentration and background buzz that inspired the writing. Maybe some will start a writers' café of their own.

Margo Singer

Chorlton Café Writers

Who are they?

These anonymous vintage portraits, vibrantly painted, stacked high upon the café walls, gazing down on us?

Censorious, provocative glances studied indifference and genuine curiosity as if alive.

Music piping in the background, softly buzzing conversations nearby, cutlery tinkling, tantalizing aromas of coffee blend with the scents of food as the morning progresses.

Aspiring writers hunched over scribbling notebooks, all silent, but for the constant tip tap of keyboards and pens, feverishly absorbed in writing *our* stories, poems, memoirs, and novels.

Who are we?

Do they wonder at us, totally engrossed, perched near the High Street window where the buses, vans, and shoppers scurry past and the world goes by.

In our corner by the large plate glass view we are lost in our concentration, enjoying our own individual, imaginative worlds.

Precious time – a little oasis in a busy convoluted world.

Anne Delargy

Silverdale

Silverdale, oh my God Silverdale!
Our first – and last – camping trip.
It was a long, long journey: buses,
Trains and walking; like snails
With our houses on our backs.
When we got there, it was almost dark.
I pitched the tent in a soggy field,
Trekked off to buy food
At the camp shop, only to find,
When I returned, the stove wasn't working.
High winds, driving rain, sea a long way out:
A Northern English summer.
When the rain eased up,
We walked on the huge beach
In the dark. You loved it,
So many, many smells,
Little rock pools of delight.
Returning, deliriously happy,
Your rolled on your back
In the sodden grass.
Oh, the stench! Fox shit,
The worst smell in the world.
Impossible to sleep,
or even breathe

Beside you,
I dragged you to the bathroom,
Where you were barred from entry.
The most hangdog of all dogs,
You cowered under the shower outside
And I carried you back inside my coat,
Shivering and shaking.
Zipped into my sleeping bag,
I thought you'd die of cold,
I thought I'd choke to death,
Crushed up with Pepe Le Pew.
When the light finally came,
On another cold and rainy day,
I saw your flailing paws had
Ripped a rent in the tent.
I love you, Rex, I really do.
But I'm never going camping
Again in Silverdale with you.

Sharon Richards

The Runaway

It was near the end of Doctor Who and he was having a massive fight with the Cybermen and I had to answer the door and miss the best bit ’cos my brothers are bigger than me and they pushed me off the sofa to make me do it and I’m only six and a quarter so I’m the littlest and they call me Short Arse and it’s not fair.

A fat woman stood on the doorstep. When she smiled down at me, her cheeks went round and sticky-out like a hamster’s.

‘Do you own a rabbit?’

I nodded. I know it’s rude not to speak when a grown-up asks you a question because, every time my brothers do it to Mum, she says, ‘You can stop playing the snotty, silent teenager right now, young man.’

I’ve got four brothers, so she says that a lot.

But I did it to the lady ’cos I was annoyed about Dr Who, and anyway, Mum always tells me not to talk to strangers.

‘Thank goodness!’ the fat lady said. ‘I’ve just seen one out on the street, and I wondered if it belonged here.’

The lady’s chins wobbled when she spoke and it made me want to laugh, even though I was missing Dr Who.

‘Okay...’ I closed the door.

‘Rolo’s got out again!’ I shouted.

I dragged my shoes from underneath the big pile behind the front door and sat on the mat to put them on. Why does Mum buy me lace-ups when she knows I can't do them?

By the time I'd given up trying with my laces, the Dr Who music was playing at the end and I'd missed it.

'Come and help me find Rolo!' I shouted dead loud to my brothers, but they'd already started killing zombies on the Xbox, so they ignored me. They ignore me most of the time. Sometimes they stop ignoring me, but then they call me 'Retard' instead, like when I can't do my shoes properly.

Mum came out of the kitchen.

'A lady's seen Rolo outside, Mum. He's got out of the run.'

'Where outside?'

'Dunno.'

We went and stood on the doorstep and looked up and down our street.

If you go out of our house and turn right, there's a canal. I know that's turning right because my teacher told me that right is the hand that I write with. If you go the other way, that's left because left is the hand that's left over.

But don't go left from our house—it's dangerous. Left is the big main road what's got four lanes of traffic. It's never quiet. Even if I wake up in the middle of the night, I can still hear the lorries. They make the whole house shake. I always wake up loads of times.

Mum did a big sigh. 'Bloody rabbit! It could be anywhere; I've got no idea where to start.' She looked to the right, towards the canal and then left, to the main road, but she didn't move off the doorstep.

She took a pink vaper out of her pocket and took a big puff. It smelled lovely.

'Watermelon and raspberry,' she said.

That's the one I'm going to get when I'm older.

After some more puffs and some more looks up and down, she said, 'Maybe he'll just come home by himself, eh?'

Come home by himself? I wish Dad would come home by himself, but he's got a new family now, and all I've got is a stupid, stinky rabbit that wees in the same place where he sleeps in his hutch. I did that too when Dad left, but it was by accident. Rolo wees in his bed on purpose.

That's why Mum got me Rolo—'cos Dad left us. She read out a notice in the paper shop window, '*Rabbit free to a good home*', and got all excited. But I wasn't excited because I never, ever wanted a rabbit. I wanted a hamster. I've wanted a hamster all my entire life since I was a baby. I'd call him Fluffy and I'd keep him in my bedroom and make him do tricks and he wouldn't smell, even though Mum says they always do. But she wouldn't buy me one 'cos they cost twenty-five pounds in the pet shop, and you have to buy them a cage and a wheel as well, but the free rabbit came with a free hutch too, so she got me that instead.

I bet Dad would never have got me a rabbit—he'd have bought me a hamster. I started to cry, but not about the hamster.

'Don't get upset, love; we'll find him.'

She looked a bit like she was going to cry too. She looks like that a lot since Dad went. She crouched down in front of me and smiled. I could tell she was making herself do it.

'Listen,' she said; 'if we don't find him, how about we get you that hamster you're always on about?'

'Really?'

Just then, over her shoulder, I spotted Rolo's white tail bobbing left—straight towards the big main road. Two huge lorries thundered by.

I looked up at Mum. 'It's okay, Mum; I know where he is!'

I took her hand and dragged her along after me.

And I ran and ran and ran, as fast as I could.

Right, right, right. All the way to the canal.

Josh Lonsdale

Hermit

Your sallow cheeks, puddling the grounds,
deflated balloons long after the party is over.

Neck loose like a defeated clothesline
unhinged and beaten by the winds.

Old shepherd, gumming your sheep to death,
only clouds live beyond your beak.

Dragging your belly through the dirt,
mistaking toes for local mirages.

Snuffed torches, the false memory of speed,
your failures strewn like toppled pawns.

You hope this will not be your legacy:
the charlatan 'individual' now divided.

But nobody remains who can draw the days
where you fit into the palm of a hand.

Juliet Goldbart

South Island NZ: Another Country

We drove down a steep road to the village in the mist. By the time we had parked, the rain was falling steadily and the mountains all but invisible. Small groups of people, cagoule-clad, clustered in the cafes and on street corners.

"Huh! It's just like Keswick in the rain." I said.

The next morning, however, the sky was a brilliant gentian blue. The glacier sparkled high above us, giving truth to our motel's name of Bella Vista. We walked up, and up, to the glacier viewpoint, along sun-dappled paths, past tree ferns and head-high flax, past spiky Fierce Lancewood and tall Rimu. This forest felt primeval, dense, damp and disconcerting. We walked in silence but heard the clear song of the bell bird. Then we spotted dainty little fantails, dancing along beside us, eating insects thrown in the air as we walked. As they flew, they spread their pretty wings and tails and we laughed. This land is strange; strange and beautiful.

Lucy Power

The Squirrel Lament

They chopped down all the trees on Wordsworth Street.
The chainsaw men left drifts of wooden snow,
and brutal stumps, and glaring light and heat;
they felled each tree just like a domino.
Branch by branch, for clear views of the stars,
they vanished vintage trees with no disease,
left silent leafless roads, and sapless cars,
and made the squirrels homeless by degrees.
They replaced trees with plants that don't need care,
(new ornamental dwarf varieties),
with no space for a squirrel anywhere.
Like crowded boats of displaced refugees,
or the shrinking icebergs of the polar bear,
the squirrels have no place in tiny trees.

Cal Park

Another time

The burglars are loud. High. Bold.

Curled up on the sofa, reading, Jaya must have fallen asleep. The sound of glass smashing jolts her awake, and she sits up, hugging her pyjamaed knees, fully alert now.

Hide, she tells herself, pulling up the fluffy grey blanket from around her feet, until it covers her whole body. Her chest heaving with panic, she wills herself to lie still.

A Saturday night, and no TV or music playing, just a single reading light left on from before it had got dark. *Better, or worse, if they know I'm in?* Too risky to find out.

What if they hear me breathing?

Clutching her phone, Jaya slides to the floor, then scuttles across the corridor, crab- like, to the nearest room, Kaiden's. Diving under his bed, she wriggles on her belly through the sharp-edged boxes, piles of clothes and abandoned tech. *Kaiden.* She imagines him ambling through the front door, headphones on, still not speaking to her after their row.

I've got to tell Kaiden. 'Don't come home, stay away.' He won't listen though. He'll come to help me. Won't he?

The voice on the other end is too loud.

'Emergency services. Which service do you require?'

'Police,' she whispers. 'Now.... please.'

What was that number you could press after you dialled 999? The one that let the call handler know it was too dangerous to speak? She'd circulated it on Facebook, for God's sake. *Think.*

Burglars. Address. Alone. Do it.

A voice, not hers, whispers the necessary words. She closes her eyes. *Did the men hear her?* Drawers slamming. *Keys.* They must be looking for car keys. *I lost the car in the divorce* she wants to say. *Unlucky.*

Where would Kaiden have gone? *I'm not a kid, ok? Back off, will you?* Fine. Done. Excellent. She hadn't asked.

She taps her phone, reeling again at the screen's sudden brightness.

'**Burglars. Called police stay away**.' She texts, wincing at the grammar.

Her phone screen lights up immediately. *Oh, thank God, he's got the message,* Jaya thinks, breathing again.

'Kaiden has notifications silenced' comes the reply.

Fuckssake! Suddenly she's furious. *What does that even mean? 'I like hear you, but I like, don't? How's that working for you? Or me, or anyone who's having a, like, EMERGENCY AND ACTUALLY NEEDS TO CONTACT YOU?*

How long will the air last down here, amongst the dusty boxes under Kaiden's bed? And... are those *dirty* clothes that she can smell? Pressed tight against the wall, Jaya realises she's hiding behind The Box, the large battered cardboard one containing Kaiden's football medals, flimsy trophies, his threadbare toy rabbit, his cub scout uniform, his games, his jagged drawings. His life. *Their life.* Kaiden had thrown the whole lot out, no longer seeing a need for any of it. Jaya had actually gasped to find it all in the outside bin, so casually discarded. She remembers sitting slumped on the doorstep, clutching the box, a sharp pang of recognition accompanying each item as she carefully lifted them out, one treasure at a time. She'd lingered especially over the wide-eyed photos of Kaiden aged six. Those photos were crumpled up now, that beautiful smile contorted. She'd quickly gathered everything back in the box, and stashed it away under Kaiden's bed.

It's not that deep, she imagines Kaiden saying. *You have no idea*, she thinks.

Suddenly, she misses Sparky, their dog. Not that Sparky was ever really intimidating enough to scare off burglars, even in his younger days. Jaya can just imagine their little terrier barking like crazy though, giddy with excitement to see strangers in the house, and her here, under the bed, playing the 'come find me' game like Kaiden used to do.

What if I die here, now? Amongst these trophies that aren't even mine?

She can just imagine Kaiden rolling his eyes at that.

The burglars are crashing around in the living room now. Their boots stomping on her faded Indian rug, a precious souvenir from when she last went travelling, two decades ago. She hears a rip, as the TV is yanked from its socket.

Can you die from fear? *She died as she lived... how? Hiding? Keeping quiet?* No, she's said plenty, too much even, at times. Lots has been left unsaid though, except in her head. She's a mediator after all, trained in the art of negotiation. Brilliant in many, many situations. Just not at home, it seems, where it matters most.

Oh God, they're here, in Kaiden's room, now. From under the bed, Jaya can hear the men breathing, muttering, can smell their sour smell. They're wearing black trainers, not boots, she sees now, now that their feet are so close to her, she can barely breathe.

Has she fainted or fallen asleep? In the haze, she hears Sparky barking frantically, desperate to reach her.

'Good boy!' she calls. 'Here, Sparky!'

Then, from the front door, the crackle of a police walkie talkie, 'Something something clear,' it sounds like.

It's over, she thinks. *Thank God.* Slowly, cautiously, she begins to slide herself out from under the bed. Suddenly, there's nothing but snarling; a flash of teeth into flesh, her flesh, a cry, blood everywhere, then hot, white pain. *Not Sparky.* Then, a torch beam dazzling her eyes, as a man's voice commands the dog,

'Kaiser! DROP!'

Then, that same voice on the police radio, 'Ambulance!' The dog sitting now, still barking excitedly. A uniformed arm reaching in, under the bed, a strong hand gently pulling Jaya out.

Later, in hospital, coming round from the anaesthetic, Jaya sees first a bunch of garage flowers on her bed, then Kaiden's worried face leaning in, breaking into a smile.

'You alright Mum?'

Jaya smiles.

'Yeah,' she says slowly. 'I'm fine.'

'Police fella brought them.' Kaiden says, indicating the flowers. 'I know, carnations, eh? *Loser*!'

Kaiden grins, and briefly squeezes Jaya's hand.

'*Starving!*' he says. 'You got any food?'

And Jaya laughs, full of love for this boy, for this life, right here.

Mary Cohen-Lavarello

The Mummy Mafia

They don't all drive the same buggy
They don't need to
They don't all join the same classes
They don't want to

Mummy Mafia they don't sleep
Sleep is history - they just eat
Mummy Mafia have your back
Hunting cake down like it's crack

No special handshake needed
For introduction
There with spares for babycare
Before you've asked them

Mummy Mafia they don't sleep
Sleep is history - they just eat
Mummy Mafia have your back
Every problem has a hack

They'll rock your pram or buy your caffeine
Share each hard-won knack for napping
They'll sympathise and if you cry
They never need to ask you why

Mummy Mafia they don't sleep
Sleep is history - they just eat
Mummy Mafia have your back
Chuck your pillows, join our pack

Jean Thompson

The peace of silence

Elsa stopped speaking the day after her 85th Birthday. It wasn't because of a medical or psychological trauma or catastrophe; she just decided to stop speaking. She had thought about it the day before, on her actual birthday, but being basically a kindly and thoughtful woman, she thought that it would be churlish if she didn't say thank you to all her relatives and friends for their cards and presents.

Naturally her concerned family whisked her off to the doctor, who looked puzzled and referred her to hospital for further investigation. Had she lost her hearing they asked the doctors? Had she had a stroke, they wondered? Was she suffering from depression?

All the time, Elsa smiled co-operatively, but still did not speak. She was examined and prodded, scanned and intruded upon over a period of weeks and months, but still she did not speak

'Well,' the specialists said knowledgeably, 'your mother appears to be able to hear alright. She does not seem to be depressed or suffering from any psychiatric disorder that we can identify. There is a condition called elective mutism, but it is unusual for it to start at this late stage in life. Has your mother suffered any emotional trauma perhaps?'

The concerned family scratched its collective head but could not think of anything that could have caused this strange and frustrating state. Eventually everyone gave up their investigations, and reconciled themselves to the fact that if they wanted to know anything from Elsa, they would have to have plenty of paper and pencils to hand. Fortunately, Elsa had not stopped writing, as the various doctors had discovered, so some form of communication was still possible,

After a while, the various family members stopped expecting her to reply even by writing, and Elsa was left more or less in peace to consider her life so far, and how the next few of her years might be. It was easier all round for them not to have to try to communicate meaningfully. They checked she could still cope in her home, went shopping for her, made sure she was eating properly, took her for outings even, and went on chatting among themselves, and left her blissfully alone.

Elsa took a metaphorical deep breath and relished the fact that she did not have to try to talk any more. She had stopped speaking, which is not in itself the same as talking, and had her mind free to think. She felt she had stopped talking many years ago, or rather people had stopped really conversing with her, and so this step of her not speaking was not such a big one as others assumed.

As a girl and a young woman she had talked very rarely, never quite knowing what to say, and believing that on those occasions when she tried to say something, she was either ignored or looked at somewhat askance. She felt that she had never quite got it right.

Elsa tried to remember why she had not been happy talking when she was a child and a young girl. She was naturally a quiet rather timid girl, with a mother who did not encourage her to be outgoing. She was the girl who was going to be her mother's support. Her other sisters and brothers, and there were several of them, did well at school, studied at college and even university, had careers, but not her. She was the proverbial mother's help, and because she was a quite a biddable girl, she accepted this lot. She could have rebelled, but that did not occur to her. She wanted to be a 'good girl', she wanted to be seen as a great help. She was quiet in looks as well as manner, dressed plainly and sensibly and generally merged into the background. Did the circumstances mould her, or was she happy to fade into the background because of the way she was made?

'Elsa,' said one or other of her sisters, 'do you not want to get married and have a family of your own? Or have a career as we are doing?'

'Oh,' she would invariably reply, 'I am happy being here, helping mother to look after father and all of you. I suppose I will never get married.'

But marry she did. Much later in life, after her mother and father had died, her sister persuaded her to go to a gardening class, as a way of getting out of the house. Any friends she had had in the past had long ago married and moved away, or were busy with their children. She had always taken delight in the garden, and found it soothing and rewarding. But what happened at the gardening class? Surprise to everyone, she met Tom who shared her love of growing things. His interest in her gardening experiences became an interest in her, then something more, and much to everyone's amazement, they married. Elsa was in her late thirties by then, and no-one was more surprised than her, and, secretly and privately, delighted when children came into their life in quick succession.

As she had nurtured her garden, so she nurtured and nourished her children. She took delight in their development, and talked and talked to them. Now in this self-chosen silence, she could remember more clearly the part the spoken word had played in her life. The magic of talking to her children, even before they were probably old enough to understand. Talking to them as they walked round the shops, talking to them as they walked to school, talking to them always as they sat at home. No mobiles, no technological intrusions into conversation in those days. And her children in turn loved talking. They excelled at it. Elsa liked to think that was her gift to them.

She had never talked so much in her life before, and as she talked she grew in confidence. She became adept at negotiating her way round tricky situations, and was respected for it. She forgot she was that quiet, shy and uncertain girl she had thought she was, and believed she was able, confident, outgoing. But that young girl was still in there, waiting to take over again whenever there was a situation Elsa felt she could not control. The confident persona was just that, a persona that could easily be shaken.

She and Tom got along well, not passionately but comfortably enough. A kind man, who accepted her as she was, and was caring to her and their children. Even though they started a bit late in the process by the standards of the day, they had two children, both healthy and seemingly well adjusted, and a source of contentment to their parents. Every now and then, when Elsa felt that familiar shiver of insecurity, she wondered if she could have been different. Could she have rebelled against the way of life that was imposed upon her in her younger years?

'I am very lucky,' she told people. 'A good husband and two lovely children. What more could anyone want.'

What more indeed?

Time went on, the children had children of their own. Tom was lost, mourned appropriately and decorously, but her life more or less still as it had always been. Instead of talking to her children, she talked to her grandchildren, and they seemed to like her tales of a life they could not identify with.

Often they would initiate their conversations.

'Tell me grandma, how it was when you were young?'

'Grandma, do you remember the war? What happened to you then?'

She talked, and they listened. When did that stop? When her talking became just speaking that no-one really listened to.

So, here she was, 85 years old, and realising that no-one was actually listening to her anymore. All those years of the effort she made to build up her conversational skills and repertoire now not worth much at all. So, that little bit of flinty determination that had always been there lurking, took over and she decided she would stop talking, stop making that huge effort. She was tired of being the 'good girl'.

The more she didn't talk, the more time and space she had to think. To confront things that she had long hidden by the effort of talking. There was no-one that she needed to make that supreme effort for anymore. Grandchildren adults themselves now, with a vocabulary and means of communicating that were alien to her. What could she give them by mere words?

Now her conversations were all in her head. From the moment she stopped speaking, the more meaningful her words became. Delivered only to her and for her, they did not have to be moderated by thinking what the other person might want or need to hear.

When she saw her next door neighbour, she was able to think and say, if only to herself,

'What a silly woman wearing that outfit. How old does she think she is? She looks ridiculous, trying to compete with her own daughter.'

When the dog from across the road was digging in her garden, she said gleefully to herself,

'That dog's a real pest. No-one in the road likes it. How good it would be if someone got rid of it.'

When her bossy son-in-law came to see her and tried to offer his advice about what she should do with the house or her savings, she smiled kindly, and nodded and said to herself,

'If you think I am going to listen to a word you say, you are very much mistaken. You want to take control of my money. You think I can't manage my affairs anymore. Well, you can wait as long as you like, but my money will stay with me until I am gone, and then it will go to my daughter, your wife, and my son. I will arrange things so you won't be able to get your hands on it. Ha, see how you'll like that.'

And still she smiled affably, so he thought he might have made his point, and he went home easier in his mind.

How liberating it was to let years of reasonableness and well-mannered behaviour go, if only in her mind! On the day after her 86th birthday, her daughter took her to see her newly born great grandchild, a girl to be called Elsa like her. Her granddaughter looked at her affectionately and said,

'I am glad you came to see us, grandma. What a shame you won't be able to tell her the stories you told us when we were little and sing her the songs.'

Elsa looked at the tiny baby they had put on her lap, and wondered at this new addition and remembered all the times in the past she had talked and been listened to.

'Well, my dear,' she said, in a voice none the weaker for not having been heard for a year, 'I would not be too sure about that if I were you.'

Stephen Raw

Ward 12

One hot-water caddy, paper cups, tea bags and rich tea biscuits.

One large card with hand-painted sunflower.

One tall, yellow pedal-bin.

Four stacked green plastic chairs.

One comfy wooden chair with squishy sound when sat on.

One mobile phone charging cable.

One white board with green hand-written words: 'D&F as tolerated'.

One cantilevered pay-for tv: off.

One bar of lavender soap on white sink.

Eight silk flowers in a black vase.

Six fresh sweet peas smuggled past nurses.

Too many sarcastic 'Get Well Soon' cards blu-tacked to the walls.

One hospital bed with quivering air mattress.

One 'Z-bed' for overnight vigils.

Unnumbered paper towels for dabbing countless tears.

One partner of four decades with shallow breathing.

Sharon McCarthy

Sixth sense

I write to make sense of myself,
what I see, hear, taste, touch and smell.
Sometimes it's all a bit too much,
like being cornered in some paintballing hell.
Hit one, my sense of pride,
nowhere to hide.
Hit two, my sense of duty,
you can be too kind.
Hit three, my sense of justice,
impossible for all.
Hit four, my sense of humour,
a difficult one to call.
Hit Five, my pride,
too strong to override.
Hit six, my common sense,
to know when it's time to quit
before I take another hit,
in this game of self reflection and introspection.

Jo Somerset

I would like to revisit the notion that

men make their own history

'even in an age unlike our own, / Someone will remember who we are.' (Sappho, *Stung with Love*)

even though some women like
Ban Zhao squeezed their noses in
and others like *Sappho* wrote
history in poetry,

'History is really about....man, giant-sized, seen against the background of the entire world, universalized in his conflict with destiny, the gods, and the cosmic order.' (Herodotus, *The History*)

because *Herodotus* – a poet – wrote
about wars, and Sappho portrayed
society (love), he was called a
historian
and she wasn't.

Women are invisible, although

'The said Alison Device sayth, that ....her grandmother...did advise her to let a devil or a familiar appear to her.' (Thomas Pott, *Discovery of Witches)*

enslaved peoples are more invisible,
since women's voices appear in male-
inscribed accounts of *witch trials* but
there's no
voice in the record of a slave's sale.

So men in charge made their own
history - common-sense, but not
understood until someone says it,

like the wipe-out of Jewish people
wasn't
wholly grasped until it was named,
with boundaries, and substance
colouring in the Holocaust with
ineffable gruesome detail.

Men make history within the confines of
their worldview. Is that why it's all battles
and conquering?

'Reporter: What do you think of Western civilisation?
Gandhi: I think it would be a good idea.'
(Graffiti on a New York city wall)

Edward Said refers to *"Western civilisation"* as 'an ideological fiction' rooted in
'the history of conquest, immigration,'

war and domination,

and now as a woman I'm trying to change the tune.

Pax Europaea - the period of relative peace since World War Two in which the EU played a major role.

It's wrong to say we've had seventy years
of peace. The *Pax Europaea*, which I
now revoke, hides warlike savagery

- by war I mean military actions
where people are bombed and killed -

In Europe many people were bombed
and killed in this time and beyond our
continent we've interfered, so more
people were bombed or killed, and
further afield our allies bombed and
killed with our compliance.

So less peace talk and more dead talk,

give voice to the perished, the
persecuted, the buried, the desecrated,

the lands raped, tribes obliterated and
cultures maimed,

'"Know thyself," said Socrates. "Know thyself," said Sappho, 'and make sure that the Church never finds out.'" Jeanette Winterson, *Art and Lies*.

and read Gramsci, who encouraged
'knowing thyself',

roll back the blanket of European
smugness, false humility and amnesia
and uncover ugly bugs, give names
and narratives, unearth stories from
the seething mass, inject sideways
knowledge, apply intellect

'Here's the redress that's long been owed/Here's the first step on the road.' Jackie Kay, 'Flag Up Scotland, Jamaica'.

acknowledge our debts (like *Glasgow
University*

'the wise ones/... /whispered about empires /..../their destiny/to crumble and fall.' Inua Ellams, 'Tusk'.

and *Manchester Museum*)

to understand how globalisation
overwhelmed the world.

Clem Herman

Leavings

It was still dark when the train departed. Frost glistened on the bare branches as they sped through the quiet countryside, the track winding its way northwards. The small heater under the seat gave off a warm stream of air and Anna tucked her feet in closer, wrapping her scarf tight. Every now and again, she jolted forward as the train drew to a halt, at the familiar little stations. Through the steamed windows, she could make out the silhouettes of travellers boarding with their bags.

By the time they arrived at the port, the sky was brightening and small shafts of light were visible through the clouds. The foot passengers stood huddled against the biting wind. Anna clutched her rucksack close and shuffled her way behind them up the metal gangway. There was hardly a soul on deck, but she decided to stay outside, and settled down on a whitewashed bench, sheltered from the wind at the back of the boat. No matter how many times she had made this journey to and from the mainland, there was still the same sense of anticipation as they set off, a feeling of connection with all those who had crossed back and forth before, either seeking adventures, fleeing from hardship, or returning as she was today. Anna was easily seasick, and already the sounds and smells began to unsettle her stomach. She remembered her grandmother's advice to watch the horizon, and kept her eyes focused on where the sky met the sea in the distance, feeling the rise and fall of the swell. Her grandmother's own perilous childhood journey across the choppy North Sea remained a scar, a haunting down the generations, its impact ebbing and flowing like a breaking wave.

The sun broke through about halfway across. A lone gannet following the boat dipped up and down, gliding close to the surface of the swell in hope of a morsel of fish. Anna turned her face upwards and watched the clouds hastening across the sky. She took in a deep breath of cold crisp air and felt an unexpected moment of peace. The sea had suddenly calmed; the waves although still choppy were now just a gentle sway and her nausea subsided. Turning to the west, Anna saw a sliver of dark appearing above the indigo line of the horizon. The first sight of land was always a delight, the familiar shapes gradually emerging as they approached the rocky coastline. Down below on the deck, men in hi-vis jackets were preparing for landing, hauling ropes onto the pulleys, the hum of the engines punctuated by the clanking of steel and thump of metal chains.

Later, as she sat in the warm kitchen, her hands wrapped around a hot steaming mug of tea, Anna started to tell her mother about the journey, trying to break the tension that sat like a block of granite between them.

'The best bit is when you see the land ahead and the shapes of the hills slowly reveal themselves like strange animals emerging from the sea,' she mused wistfully. But her mother's attention was elsewhere, not listening.

'You should have a bowl of soup,' her mother told her. 'It's what you always want after a journey.'

This is what she does, thought Anna, *telling me what I want. She never asks*. The cabbagey odour from the stove rekindling her nausea.

'I'm OK for the moment mum, let's just sit and drink our tea.'

'...and how long are you staying this time?' her mother's eyes avoiding Anna's, her gaze focused instead on the large painting at the back of the room. Anna looked over at the picture. It was one of her favourites, the wild waves crashing against the rocks, and the dark brooding sky beyond, the looming sense of menace always expressed so strongly in her mother's work. Anna noticed the lines around her mother's eyes, and with a jolt realised she was getting old. She glanced down at the hands fidgeting anxiously on the tablecloth. Always stained with remnants of paint, they were beginning to look gnarled like old oak.

‘Oh, I don’t know, just a couple of days.’ Anna tried to keep her voice calm and steady, ‘I’ll need to get back.’

‘I’m sure Sandy would like to see you’, she heard her mother say, and her heart sank. *Why did she always have to bring him up?*

Sandy had been Anna’s best friend growing up and by the time they were in their teens everyone assumed they would be together forever, but for Anna it was Sandy’s family she was most drawn to. She had often stayed over with them up in the village, in the warm and bustling household, playing games and messing about in the fields. The Sutherlands had been on the island for generations, and Sandy’s cousins and relatives seemed to be scattered across every village. Such a contrast with the isolated cottage, where she and her mother lived, overlooking the cliffs, the rocks tumbling down to the turbulent water below. Those stunning views gave her mother inspiration for her stormy paintings, the studio with its wide windows, crammed with easels, oils, brushes and half-finished paintings. Sandy and Anna, best friends forever. But that was before Fiona, and before everything changed.

Anna remembered how her crush on Fiona had been sudden and furious, an all-consuming passion. At first it had surprised her, and she tried to brush it away, but the pounding heart and blushes did not lie. And after they’d kissed that first time, Anna knew for sure: *what* she was, *who* she was. Fiona insisted they keep it secret, scared of how their friends would react, insisting they only meet up when no-one was around. Feeling desperate, Anna had confided in Sandy, but he’d gone and told another boy and the gossip had spread like wildfire. Fiona denied that anything had happened, accusing Anna of making it all up. After that Anna had withdrawn into her books, nursing the pain of rejection and humiliation, biding her time till she was able to leave for college on the mainland.

‘I haven’t seen Sandy for years,’ said Anna coldly, ‘he more or less avoided me after what happened with Fiona.’

‘Such a shame. He was such a nice boy, so kind and …’

'Er, not really,' interrupted Anna, 'he was too spineless to stand up for me, and afraid all the others would call him gay too.'

'Well, I always thought you'd end up together.' Anna felt the sting of her mother's words and took a deep breath, suppressing her simmering anger.

'Let's go for a walk down to the river,' she suggested quietly.

They took their usual route. The path down to the river was muddy and strewn with soggy leaves. The trees now bare against the pale grey sky, a few yellowed leaves still clinging on courageously despite the icy wind. There was a restlessness in the air, the staccato of crows cawing, and the creaking of the empty branches in the gusts of wind. The rhythmic sound of their boots crunched on the ground. Anna had instinctively linked her arm through her mother's as they entered the wood to stop her slipping, but now the physical contact felt awkward, and she let go. Ahead she could see the line of trees converge where the path emerged into a clearing. They walked on in silence till they reached the little stone bridge that took them over the brook and turned right to follow the path.

From a distance you could see the resemblance between the two women, the same tall frame and lilting walk, and the sharp angular chin, although Anna was taller by a few inches, and her shoulders wider in her winter coat, collar turned up against the cold. Her mother still wore her old khaki Barbour jacket, sensible and practical for all seasons.

'You know I had no choice, I just had to get away after everything.' Anna's voice broke the silence like a sharp knife, startling her mother who looked up at her. She felt her mother's hand touch her on the arm and tried not to flinch.

'I know, I know,' she heard her mother say, 'but it was hard for me too, you've no idea how I wept after you'd gone.'

Anna hesitated before responding, not wanting to lash back and descend into a squabble. *It was not about you,* she wanted to say, *you did not support me, and you clung on to your fantasy of what you wanted me to be. I could not live like that.* But she said none of that.

‘I do miss our walks,’ she said instead.

‘You know I only wanted what was best for you,’ said her mother after a long pause. ‘I should have known better after what happened to me.’

‘You mean … when you first came to the island?’ asked Anna hesitantly, surprised at this sudden intimacy.

She knew the reason that her mother had moved up to the island all those years ago, but they hardly ever spoke about it. Anna had met her grandparents only a handful of times. She had a memory of a trip down south when she was about twelve and they’d met in the big department store in town. That’s when her grandmother had told her about watching the horizon, her eyes glazing over as she recalled her childhood journey on the train and boat from Nazi occupied Vienna, when she’d had to leave her own parents behind to their terrible fate. Anna’s mother had grown up in the shadow of this knowledge, always present as a burden and a responsibility, knowing she was never enough and could never fill the void that seemed to envelop her parents, despite the busy bustle of their lives.

‘When I first came here,’ began Anna’s mother, ‘I was young, full of the wonder of you, my new baby, and this wild and beautiful place. I had found my spiritual home and wanted you to be free, living in the outdoors, in nature.’

‘I could never go back to my parents,’ she continued, her voice wavering a little as she spoke. ‘Your grandfather had made that clear when he cut his jacket collar on the day I left. That’s a thing they do when someone has died, and it was his way of saying I was dead to him. There was no way back after the shame of being pregnant and unmarried, and the life I had chosen away from their community.’

‘Oh’ said Anna, shocked. ’I didn’t know that … about the jacket collar I mean.’

There was a silence, broken only by the rustle of branches overhead.

'But that's all in the past,' said her mother. 'We have a good life here, don't we?' her face turned up to look at Anna, searching for reassurance.

Anna sighed. She understood why her mother's fury and sadness had been funnelled into her wild and turbulent paintings, why they were so moving to those who saw them with their power and passion.

'Yes, *you* have a good life here, mum,' she said, 'but this is not the place for me anymore.'

The rain was starting now, just a few soft drops, but the sky had turned dark, and it would not be long before the storm whipped up.

Anna hesitated a moment, then decided not to push things further. It was enough that they were together, walking.

'Let's go home now,' she said quietly, 'I quite fancy a bowl of soup.'

She linked her arm through her mother's, and they quickened their pace, turning left at the river to see the choppy water as it meandered downwards, bubbling over the rocks. A solitary dipper bobbed up and down on a rock, echoing the movement of the river. Then it was gone in a flash. The two figures, hunched against the rain, turned back up the hill.

Sam Tovey

Unspent Love

What is grief?
Unspent love,
Towards those above.

A heart full
Of memories and dreams,
Of what could have been,
And moments in between,
Full of love as vast as the deep blue seas.

Now it's stored deep
in the chambers of my heart,
Some days it pulls me apart,
As if the pieces are there,
Like a shattered work of art,
With one piece lost;
A missing part.

And I ask,
Will this grief ever cease?
There is no worse pain,
There is no release.

Grief has no expiry date.

Yet in time's embrace,

It might abate.

Though, never a constant state,

For grief is love and love is fate.

The love I have will have to wait.

Juliet Goldbart

A Doubtful Silence

When the boat engine stops, there is, at first, silence. Almost immediately we hear the birdsong; then, as our ears learn to listen, the rush of waterfalls and tiny wavelets hitting the boat's hulls. I think of John Cage's 4′33″. Is there ever total silence? Was that his point?

In the almost-silence, the beauty of the landscape is quite overwhelming. The wind has dropped, and the lake is an obsidian mirror reflecting snow-tipped mountains, clouds, deep green forest and the intense blue sky. We breathe deeply. The air is cool despite the sunshine, and I feel my heart rate slow.

When the boat engines restart, a storm of camera clicks invades our ears. We rush to capture the vision, but the absence of sound is elusive. How can you capture absence, except as a fragile memory?

Josh Lonsdale

No Thing

Nothing with wings allowed.
You and the new food under a glass,
locked away in a see-through display

anything over-limbed and over-the-limits.
Service of sentence. The displaced subject
becomes object of attention. Fully wrapped

around the one limb given, the lifelong grip
clinging to mother's unbled fountain.
When will you learn to let go?

The air so close you bump your head.
Waking is a shrinking aperture of light
and your eyes are shrivelled periscopes.

Once you had such vision. To see beyond
your taxed horizon. The landscape unseating
and sorting through skins, unable to withstand

a fixed position. The spirit entangled in self-
fellatio, eternally speeding toward punctured
release without end in sight.

Where once you brought the living world
into you, now your slingshot tongue rests
unused: for no winged things are allowed.

Stephen Raw

Storm Kathleen, 8th April 2024

A green ramp, with gorse yellow teeth,
lowers to reveal frenzied sea.
Metal scrapes on concrete jetty –
wind, wind, wind it shrieks.

As unwitting witnesses
we testify to skippering of the highest order.
Hurriedly abandoning the ferry
we leap the waves,
just the good side of safe and step on to the island.

Twenty-three involuntary members of the bereavement club
gather in sunshine –
toddlers, the very pregnant, the old, the first-timers.
We set a course for Iona's hilltop.
Walking carefully, with the rucksack cargo:
whisky,
tumblers,
a dram of water,
    – ashes.

Across wet grass, wet rocks,
the party reach the cairn –
one, in particular, recollects past broadcasts.
Today's undertaking calls for precious ash
be exposed to Kathleen.
Wheeling away on release –
a soaring more than scattering –
the dusty cloud strikes out north,
still sailing on the wind
while whisky is poured like communion wine.
Summoned by love to do this in remembrance of her.

Speechless.

Crossing the Sound,
the climb,
a group photo,
a cautious descent,
become fresh lines of
loving memories,
looking loss in the eye,
fixing a distant view.

Lindy Newns

Last Day of the Holiday

Alice lets her rucksack fall with a thud to the floor, fumbles for the light switch. The bulb fizzes, then goes out with a tiny pop. She turns the bedside lamp on but it doesn't help. It's still dark with the blinds closed and the air's dusty and heavy. All she wants to do is get a shower, lie down on the bed and go to sleep. It's stuffy and hot; she tries to open the window but it's painted shut. Marty insisted on this place. It was cheap and that's important to Marty but means there is no air conditioning. Alice sighs. She sits and feels the pine frame of the bed under her thighs. She falls backwards and shuts her eyes.

"Alice? Alice? Did you check the mattress?"

He knows she didn't. She's not going to either. Let the bugs have their way. If there *are* bugs. There've been no bugs so far. Except mosquitoes. She hears him scrabbling about in his rucksack to find the mosquito repellent. *Jesus.* That drives her mad too – the constant searching for wallet, glasses, cap, whatever he has put at the bottom of his bag and cannot find. Once, twice, three times a day.

But okay - he needs to find the repellent and probably the cream as well or he'll not be able to sleep, which means that neither will she. His skin is raw where he's been bitten. The mosquitoes have gorged on him every day for ten days in spite of the chemical lemon reek which trails after him. She feels sorry for Marty but the sound of his scratching gets on her nerves and his peeling skin offends her. She tells herself, "*It's not his fault, it's not his fault,*" but she can't stop herself blaming him.

He can't find the spray and starts to empty his rucksack methodically, lining up clothes, suntan lotion, sunglasses, guidebooks next to her on the bed. She wants to sweep her arm and knock it all onto the floor.

He finally finds the repellent and sprays it thickly around the room before beginning the inspection. Every place they stay, he opens the wardrobes and drawers, looks under the bed and behind cupboards then checks the toilet, taking out his pack of sanitisers, wiping carefully round the toilet seat, the basin, the shower tray.

A grubby, dark motel on the outskirts of Athens, just for one night, and he'll get his flight back home. She has another two weeks. Alone. She doesn`t care where she goes after she is rid of him, as long as there's sun and she is free. She should have ditched him a year ago, but he lost his mum and she hadn't the heart.

She's tired, that's the trouble. And spooked because of the heat. She'd thought drinking would help. It hadn't.

She sits up. What is he even looking for? Dust? Cockroaches? Loose change?

"Just checking."

She rolls her eyes, pulls off her sandals and shorts and lets herself fall back onto the bed, feels sleep catch her in its amiable embrace.

"Don't you want a shower?"

"Thought I'd wait for you."

She could feel him hesitating by the bed. Looming.

"Are you hungry?"

"No."

"I could go to that café and get you a cold drink. Some fruit?"

"No." She grits her teeth. Please God he doesn't touch her.

The door to the wardrobe creaks. The trouble is, he loves her and that makes her somehow responsible for him. And aren't all relationships a compromise? Maybe she is being too harsh. She hears herself telling her best friend about the holiday, listing all the irritations and hears them say it. Too harsh. He cares for her, has done nothing at all to hurt her.

But he is like a badly treated dog that can be beaten and ignored and treated badly, still offering a paw, whining a little, putting its head on your lap until you give up and pat it.

She feels sweat collecting along her hairline; the room is suddenly much hotter. She wonders about going down to a bar and knocking back a large ouzo, but today on the bus she caught the sour smell of aniseed and alcohol seeping from her pores; she is still a little drunk from lunch. She hasn't been completely sober all holiday.

His fault. If he was not so needy and so precise and so pink and blistered.

She hears the crumpling of a pack of tissues. A slight squeak as he wipes the basin. The toilet seat going up with a clunk.

Sleep lifts her gently towards the ceiling.

"Oh God!"

The panic in his voice jolts her fully awake.

"What is it?" She sits up.

"Look – look!"

She looks at the bedside cabinet. The drawer he is pointing into. A bible, and a blue thin plastic bag, the kind that all the supermarkets in Greece use.

"It's just a bag."

"It moved!"

She thinks she sees it move.

"Well what is it?"

"I don't know."

"Look."

"Can't you?"

She realises that he thinks it may be a spider or a mouse. Maybe it's the way they scutter but more likely to be because his mother was frightened of both and fear is catching.

It smells. She stretches out her hand. Marty moves away, putting her between him and the drawer. He has a phobia about birds too. If it's a bird and it flies up out of the bag, he will panic.

It can't be a bird. Or if it was, it's dead

She touches the plastic bag and gently takes hold of it, pulls it up and out of the drawer and looks inside.

"It's a loaf of mouldy bread. Look."

Marty looks. He is immediately indignant.

"Disgusting. It stinks. I'll go and complain to reception."

"Don't. Leave it. I'll put it in the bin, see."

"I don't want it in the room."

"Put it outside in the corridor."

"They'll think it's ours."

"Bloody hell. Does it matter?"

It did. Marty takes the bag and leaves to find somewhere to throw it away.

Alice lies back down on the bed. She looks at the ceiling for a moment, and then finds herself laughing. A loaf of moudly bread! Her eyes close.

"Aren't you going to have a shower? I checked it."

She opens her eyes, takes a deep breath. He smells of soap and mint, and once she had loved him for that.

She forces herself up, sleepwalks into the shower.

Anne Delargy

Mermaids in my basement

Don't get me wrong,
I love this little house.
It's cosy and convenient,
Nestled between nice neighbours
And handy for the shops.
But underneath it,
I long to find
A secret underground world
Of caves and caverns
And swimming holes,
With seaweed dripping
From the ceilings, full of
Cavorting dolphins and
Bellowing monsters and
Mermaids singing.

Jean Thompson

Mosaics

464

Thomas had counted the small coloured pieces, and there were 464. Thomas liked numbers. Numbers always stayed the same. You could move them around, add them up, take them away, divide and multiply, but numbers were numbers. He was good at numbers, they said at the place they called school.

Thomas looked at the space between the small coloured pieces, and knew that if the empty space had been filled in, there would have been 489 pieces.

The person called mum and the person called dad were talking about the coloured pieces. They did not talk about how many pieces there were; Thomas knew that they were not interested in numbers like him. The person mum and the person dad talked a lot. They used words all the time. Thomas didn't talk. He could remember talking and using words when he was very little, but he didn't really understand what words meant, and when he did say words to people, they didn't seem to understand him, so he just stopped talking. He liked numbers better. Words in his head were OK, he used words in his head a lot, and he heard the words other people said, and sometimes he understood what the words meant, especially if they were using words about things he was interested in, but he no longer said the words out loud.

Sometimes, people tried to make him say the words out loud. They would say

"Talk to us Thomas", "tell us what you want" or "tell us what you mean".

But Thomas didn't.

When he used to try that, the words he said didn't make people know what he wanted, or what he meant, and that made him angry and confused. When that had happened, he used to scream out loud, to try to get them to hear the words he was saying. When he had done that, 'the mum' used to have drops of water coming out of her eyes, and she had the sort of face that Mrs Davies at that school place called sad. Thomas had been told that sad was not a good thing to be, so he stopped saying the words.

When he was at the school place, the person they called his teacher and the person they called his helper didn't make him say words. They knew that Thomas didn't say words. The person they called his teacher had a name. It was Miss Henderson. If you added the letters of Miss Henderson up, it was 152. Thomas knew that letters had numbers. In the place school, there was a picture on the wall of the letters. Underneath each letter there was a number. A was 1 and Z was 26. Thomas always liked to add up the numbers of the letters in words. Letters could be A or a, and Z or z, but the numbers would always be the same. That was why Thomas liked numbers. They were always the same. The person they called his helper had a name as well. It was Mrs Davies. Her number was 110.

Sometimes the person mum took him to another place to see a person called Dr. Appleby, and a person called Helen. Dr Appleby's number was 99, but he knew that the words could also be DOCTOR Appleby, and then his number was 152, which was the same as Miss Henderson. Thomas thought Dr. Appleby was not the same as Miss Henderson, so he thought that Dr. Appleby's number should always stay as 99. Dr Appleby and Helen always tried to get Thomas to use words, so Thomas did not like to go to see them in the big building that smelled of wet earth. Dr. Appleby and Helen talked to mum and used an interesting word; autism. Thomas had seen the word autism written down. It was interesting because he did not know many words that ended in 'sm'. Autism's number was 83, and if you added 8 and 3 together, that was 11, which was one of Thomas's favourite numbers.

Thomas thought that mum did not think the word autism was interesting, because she had a look on her face that Mrs Davies had said was sad.

Thomas liked the place school best of all. He knew what would happen there, and he could listen to the words other people used without being made to use words himself. Now the person dad was using words to him.

'Can you see all these little pieces Tommo? This is what they call a mosaic.'

Sometimes the person dad used the word Tommo to Thomas. Thomas's number was 76. Tommo's number was also 76, and that was how Thomas knew that Tommo was the same person as Thomas. Sometimes other people called him Tommy or Tom, but then the numbers were not 76, so Thomas did not think they were the same person. Dad was still using words about the pieces.

'A mosaic is a picture made up of lots of little pieces of glass or stone.'

Mosaic was an interesting word. Thomas had not heard that word before. Its number was 79. Thomas was not sure what it meant when dad talked about a mosaic being a picture. Thomas did not think the little pieces of stone could be a picture. A picture did not have all the thin spaces and gaps running across it. A picture was in a book, or on a wall, not on the ground in 464 pieces (or 489 if there were no empty space).

He knew that the person mum and the person dad were looking at each other and their faces looked like the faces Mrs Davies showed him and said they were happy, or smiling. Thomas did not like to look at people's faces because they changed all the time, and sometimes the words they used were not the same as the looks on the faces. Also, if he looked at people's faces, they would look back at his face, which Thomas did not like. Even though he did not look at peoples faces, he knew when people were looking at each other, or looking at him.

The mum and the dad were saying words to each other now. Mrs Davies said that when people said words to each other and back again, it was called a conversation. Sometimes dad said words to Thomas like,

‘Three hundred and thirty-five add two hundred and forty-seven take away one hundred and thirty-two divide by nine.’

He would give Thomas some paper and a pencil and Thomas would write down 50. He did not know if that was a conversation.

Sometimes his mum would say words like,

‘What would you like to eat Thomas.’

Thomas did not say anything then, because there were too many numbers to work out quickly enough. His mum then just gave him something that she knew he would eat. Sometimes she had given him things he did not want to eat, and he had screamed, so she heard him that he did not want that to eat, and did not give it to him again.

The words that mum and dad were saying to each other were making them smile and have happy faces. Thomas did not know why they were happy because the mosaic was **not** a picture, and the dad had said that it was.

Dad was saying,

‘Mosaics are a bit like life really, tiny fragments which mean nothing on their own, but together make up something wonderful. Some pieces are dark colours, and some pieces are bright colours. You have to have the dark bits to show up the bright bits.’

Mum said some words back, so Thomas knew it was a conversation.

‘You can be quite a philosopher, can’t you.’

They put their hands together, the dad’s hand and the mum’s hand. This was interesting to Thomas. He did not like to put his hand with anyone else’s. When he was very little, people had tried to put their hand together with his hand, and he had screamed, so they didn't do it now. Miss Henderson and Mrs Davies didn't make him do that.

Mum and dad had started to walk away. They were leaving the mosaic. Thomas did not want to go because he had not finished with the numbers. He still had some numbers to add up and divide and take away. He knew that when they walked away from things, they wanted him to go with them. In his head he said the words,

'Don't go yet, Thomas is not ready.'

He did not say the words aloud because they would not have heard him.

Thomas screamed.

Rose M Cullen

Seanathair

When the knock came
His heart pounded
As loudly as the pounding at the door
A knocking which would be answered
Or boots would follow
Splintering wood and more besides

He had known this day would come
Was he ready?
The baby cried
His wife cradled the baby and would not look at him
Was she ready?

Knocking, knocking like his knees
He smiled grimly
It must be done
They should not enter with their hob-nailed boots
He must open the door
Not an inch or a quarter
But all the way
Stand on his own threshold full fronted

And then, desperate moment
Yes
There was one, *Thank Christ*
One whose liquid grey eyes
Crinkled at the edge
Had cried, had laughed joyfully
He saw that man and only that man
'Can I say goodbye to my wife?'
A moment across time
Caught in amber
The man with the grey eyes nodded
'Be quick about it.'

He legged it then
My seanathair
Out the back
Over the wall

They returned
The Black & Tans
With kerosene and matches
But the women were ready
With their din of dustbin lids
And buckets of water

A wife and children
Walked out unscathed

Out the back
Over the wall
He would not have been
My seanathair
(My mother not yet born)
Were it not for that man
With those crinkled eyes.

Jean Thompson

What's in a name?

That's parents for you. When they decide on a name for their child, they think it's fun or trendy or heaven forbid even cute to give them a name like Minnie. Of course, it could have been worse. They could have chosen one of the longer forms like Winifred, Wilhelmina, Hermione, Clementine or even Minerva. Doesn't bear thinking about.

My parents' friends thought the name Minnie was lovely. Ha! They didn't have to go to school with a name that all the kids only knew as the sidekick of Mickey Mouse fame. To add insult to injury when my little brother was born he was given the name Michael, but no-one except our parents ever called him Mickey. No, he was called Michael, Mike when he was older or even Mikey, but all of those seemed to slip under the radar of other children. No, only I was forever known as a girl mouse loved by Walt Disney. Whenever school had a dress-up day, or book character day, how amusing it was to dress me up in a red dress and headband with white spots. It was lucky that my mother was never able to track down yellow shoes to fit me.

I could almost have understood my father choosing the name, after all he was called Donald, but what was my mother thinking of? Was she called Daisy or Clarabelle? No, she had the very reasonable name of Elizabeth or Liz.

'Why did you call me such a silly name?' I asked throughout my childhood.

'Oh, it's a lovely name. It was a bit different, and we thought it was sweet,' was the only answer I got. Sweet indeed.

But even worse was the response,

'Don't worry about what other children say, they're only jealous.'

Sam Tovey

I am who I am

I was told to hide a part of me,
To keep it tucked away unseen,
For fear of what they'd think or say,
If they knew where my ancestors lay.

Not just the colour of my skin,
But the land that my forebears lived in,
A place that carries weight and meaning,
With different ideas often convening.

My elders knew the pain firsthand,
Of racism, abuse, and reprimand,
And so they warned me, "Don't expose,
Your true heritage: don’t disclose!"

So I would say I'm from elsewhere,
And hide my Pakistani world with care,
But in doing so, I felt a loss,
As if part of me came at a cost.

Disconnected from my roots,
And the ancestors who paved the route,
To bring me to this world of mine,
To live, to love, and to define.

So now I choose to break free,
From the chains of my history,
To embrace the beauty it retains,
And all the richness it contains.

I won't be silenced or hide away,
For who I am is here to stay,
And my heritage will always be,
A vital part that makes up me.

Carole Belfield

The Fairy Godmother

A dank rainy night in Manchester.

A dark doorway.

Tommy, tossing in a damp sleeping sack set on cardboard, mutters at demons invading his sleep.

The Fairy Godmother shakes the rain off her wand, holds it up, and kicks at an empty bottle.

'Gotcha!' she mutters. Shaking Tommy, she whispers in his ear, 'Eejit, wake up, you've got one wish.'

'Whazzat?' Tommy shields his eyes from the dazzling wand.

'Come on you, I haven't got all night.'

He tries to focus his eyes and hitch himself up. It's that fuckin' FG again. Young, jeans, pink hair? Where's the sparkly frock? Is he dreaming?

'What d'ye want?' he says.

'You heard.'

'Well,' he stammers, 'a lickle 'ouse? A lass?'

'That's two. Make your mind up.'

''Ouse, then.'

FG rolls her eyes. 'You don't want much do you?'

Tommy's in no mood to argue, ''ow about one of them flats out Ancoat's way?'

FG purses her lips.

‘A fuckin’ room then?’

FG waves her wand around, says nothing.

Is she tekkin him for a ride?

Seeing she’s getting nowhere, FG flounces off. Tommy watches her weave down the alley, probably off to pester some other poor sod. Every fuckin’ doorway. He closes his eyes.

He’s still tossing and dozing when his shoulder's shaken again. What now, them bizzies? Worse, was it them bastards as beat ‘im up?

A hand pulls back his sack. Another light shines in his face. ‘Come on Tommy. Wake up man, you’ll catch your death in this weather.’

Tommy, properly awake now, terrified, grabs the nearest bottle by its neck, smashes it against the wall, waves it unsteadily at the light.

‘Put that down, you’ll cut yourself. It’s me, Sal, from The Mission. I’ve got you a room at Narrowgate, they’ll sort you out.’

Words fall on deaf ears, ‘Go away y’ bastard or I’ll stick this on y’.’ Tommy staggers up, legs snarled in his sack. He waves the bottle around. Falls against Sally.

Seconds later, blood on the pavement.

The FG glances back, tuts, turns off her wand and fades into the brickwork.

Lucy Power

Less Home

Rough sleeper sinks deeper
into city cracks, wrapped
in misery. Padded
nylon sack of nothing,
trapped in timeless pocket.

Locked out, no socks,
pock-marked, guards cardboard
cold bed, cold back, rocks back,

rock like marble dignitary, frowning
from his pedestal: 'I did good things here.
Honour me!'
The wet man honours
no-one and no thing, except
his empty Starbucks cup.

Accept my hard-earned
golden nugget quid and
be grateful, be quiet,
be lost and invisible.

The hordes walk by,

to here, and there, to hear

the man request a meal

deal. Big deal. *How can we know*

you won't spend it on drugs?

Better you starve and freeze to death,

than we fund your habit

of not quite coping.

You aren't roping us in

to this old-fashioned narrative

of blessing the meek

and reluctant less fortunate.

For you shall not inherit the earth.

Cal Park

Significant Day Number One Thousand and Ninety-Six

'Always dress your best,' my Grandad used to say. 'Because when you wake up in the morning, you never know whether it will be a significant day or not.'

But I did know. For me, every single day that I no longer woke up in the same house as Craig was a significant day. That's a grand total of one thousand and ninety-five significant days so far.

'Never take your freedom for granted, people.'

I forget if it was Grandad, or Nelson Mandela who said that. It was the sort of thing Grandad would say, even though he never left his horrible partner. And, until today, neither had Mum. But, today, Significant Day Number One Thousand and Ninety-six, I get off the bus as usual, and I'm walking to work when I see her.

'Mum? Mum, it's me!' *That's her, Mum! After all this time.* I look around, cautiously. *Finally, she's on her own!* My heart leaps. She must have tracked me down, found out where I work. I knew she would, one day. *When she can, when it's safe.* That's what I'd told myself, day after day, for one thousand and ninety-five days.

It's my turn to be brave now, but I can't stop shaking. Suddenly, with a ferocity that almost drowns me, I'm flooded with old childhood fantasies; me standing up to Craig, man to man, knocking him out and rescuing Mum. *One day,* I used to say to myself, *When I'm as tall, and strong as you. When I'm brave enough.*

Mum looks different. Her hair's shorter, darker too. *Why did she cut her hair?* Three years is a long time. My hair's much longer now, I know Craig would hate it. *I've started shaving and everything, Mum. I've got so much to tell you!*

I've been working out too, at night, secretly, so my cousins won't laugh at me. Also, what else am I going to do while everyone else is asleep?

In my dreams, Mum and I are back living together, just the two of us, like the old days, before Craig came into our lives. I'm five years old again, and we're in our cocoon, lying there in her bed, singing songs and telling stories. Mum never liked the dark either. Being with her was like keeping the lights on; we both felt safe. Eventually we'd have to go to sleep, of course. But every night, before she closed her eyes, Mum would pull me close, and whisper in my ear, in a funny American accent,

'Tomorrow's looking good, kid.' And I'd giggle, partly because it tickled, but also because it made me happy. It was something else my Grandad used to say, apparently. Not sure where he got that from, probably from one of those black and white movies he used to be glued to, I imagine. Grandad knew every line, and he'd whisper the words along with the movie, like a mantra, a prayer, almost, come to think of it.

'Tomorrow's looking good, kid.'

For the last few years that I lived under Craig's regime, it was mostly me, saying it to myself, in the dark. Before that though, in 'BC (before Craig)' times, if Mum was sad or quiet, as she could often be, I'd whisper it in her ear. I couldn't always tell if she'd heard me or not. 'Sweet dreams', I sometimes added, in case she'd fallen asleep.

But this isn't a dream. Mum is right there, in front of me, in the flesh. That slight stoop she has. That same dark blue woollen coat, old-fashioned now, I think, suddenly, and those big scared eyes looking down at the pavement.

She's seen me first, and she's walking away. Wait, what? *She's turning away.* I can't breathe. *No, no no.* Is he watching her? I look around quickly, then I can't help myself. I catch hold of Mum's arm to stop her.

'Wait!'

I see the look of fear in her eyes and I let go, ashamed. *I'm just like him. She's turning away from me. Me!* She can't seem to look at me. I feel like a crazy person. I want to jump up and down in front of her, waving my arms, waving those table tennis bats, or whatever they are, bringing in the plane. *You're safe to land now. It's me, Sam, your boy, just...taller.* Mum keeps looking over her shoulder. She's trying to tell me something. *This must be it, the plan, finally.* I knew this day would come. And I'm ready. A man now, just about.

'I can't do this, I can't do this,' she gabbles, still not looking at me. And she scuttles off. I know she's terrified of what Craig will say if he finds out she's seen me.

At night, when I close my eyes, I can still hear him telling her,

'Me or him, your choice.'

But Craig isn't there.

'Mum, it's me.' Tears are streaming now. *This can't be it.*

Can you have night terrors in broad daylight? That's what this feels like, one of Mum's night terrors. The nights she'd wake up screaming, running around, thinking there was someone in the house. Sometimes, she'd think I was the intruder. One time she shook me, like she thought I was going to kill her. I had to be ready. Ready to help her back into bed, to stroke her hair, to bring her back from wherever the terrors had taken her.

Her night terrors stopped when Craig moved in. And mine began. I was seven, and I'd always slept in her bed. I needed her there to go to sleep. She was often asleep in the day. Medication will do that; I learnt that pretty young. Scary every time though, trying to wake her up, praying and praying that she hadn't died and left me on my own with him.

Until then, night time was our time. If Mum went to bed, I went too, whatever time it was.

One night before Craig moved in, I remember waking up and shouting for her. *Where was she*? I felt around for her in the bed, shocked by the realisation that I was alone here, in my own bed somehow, and not hers. I got up, padded down the corridor to her room, and was half climbing into bed beside her when a man, Craig, I later learned, grabbed my arm, pinching my skin, until my breath caught in my throat. He spun me back round, and shoved me towards the door.

'Mum?' I pleaded. I saw her eyes open wide, full of concern, then close again quickly, playing dead. *This won't last.* I consoled myself. *In the morning, when I tell her that he hurt me, she'll end it,* I thought.

The next day, I showed her the mark on my arm, where Craig had grabbed me. She rubbed it better, like she always would, but stopped and walked away when I started the,

'He's horrible Mum, he's mean and...' At first, I thought she hadn't heard me, so I hopped off the stool I was on, and followed her across the kitchen where she was frying eggs. 'Mum, he hurt me!'

'It's time you slept in your own bed, Sam.' said Craig, coming into the kitchen and heaving himself into a chair.

'But. I always...'

I looked appealingly at Mum. 'Tell him. That's how we go to sleep.' Mum looked across at Craig.

'Craig's right, Sammy. You're seven now, you're not a baby anymore.'

My whole world changed that day. With Craig, came order – we actually had food in the house now - but with order, came rules, endless rules.

For a start, I wasn't allowed to go to anyone's house, except Aunty Jane's. Aunty Jane was Mum's older sister. They didn't always get along. Aunty Jane was more forceful, she spoke her mind, which Mum hated. Predictably, they fell out over Craig.

'He's isolating you.' Aunty Jane told her. 'Can't you see that? He *wants* us to fall out.' Mum stopped speaking to her sister soon after Craig moved in. Aunty Jane pleaded to still be able to see me though, and I guess it suited Craig that I wasn't always there. I'd stopped asking to go to friends' houses ages ago. Craig always said no, and anyway, it had become double-edged, seeing other kids' lives, and how their parents took an interest in them, in me, even. So yeah, Craig's rules. When I got in from school, as soon as I'd eaten, I'd have to go to my room. As a punishment for I don't know, breathing, or literally anything, my bedtime was brought earlier and earlier. Those summer nights were long, when I was eleven, and alone in my room, imagining my friends playing out. When all my electronics were taken off me, I'd read. Then Craig would catch me reading and snatch my torch off me. I'd wait until I heard him downstairs, then take out the other, secret torch I'd hidden under the mattress. Yeah, I wish.

Once, coming back from Aunty Jane's, I saw Mum in the kitchen window. I grinned and waved at her.

A look of anxiety, or was it pain? crossed her face. She opened the door, and straight away I could smell cookies baking.

'Hey you made cookies! Are they ready yet?' I said, taking off my coat and heading towards the kitchen. But Mum was gesturing urgently with her eyes for me to go upstairs.

'Best get up there, quick.'

I didn't understand the rush, but I saw the look on her face and I knew it wasn't worth arguing. Miserably, I started trudging up the stairs. As I climbed up, I could hear laughter. Craig? Doing an impression of a normal person? Then I saw Craig's family coming through from the kitchen, our kitchen, into the lounge, our lounge, laughing and joking. *I'm here, I live here too!* I wanted to scream at him, at all of them, but I just fell onto my bed sobbing.

Later, I started drawing. One night, Craig came to my room, and found the ghoulish cartoons I'd drawn of him.

'I'll deal with you in the morning,' he said, in a low, cold voice. 'Stay in your room.'

I couldn't bear it, the thought of waiting all night for his punishment. That's when I crept down, picked up the phone and whispered to Aunty Jane to come and get me. She'd been waiting. Standing ready, like I am now.

'Mum!' I sprint after her. 'It's ok. I'm ok. Are you ok? Has he done anything?'

Mum shakes her head, still not looking at me. Her coat has come open and I see her belly protruding. *She's pregnant,* I think, stunned. *No!*

Suddenly I understand. *Not now.* I tell myself. If Aunty Jane had tried to take me away on any other day, I wouldn't have gone with her either.

'It's ok,' I say, 'I'm fine. I got a job. Did you know that? I'm going there now. At the Esso garage, that one, down there on the left. Every day except Mondays, 5 til 9, after college, that's where I am, where I'll be, if you need me, I mean.' I'm gabbling now.

'They've put me on the tills. I'm actually quite good, getting the hang of it anyway. So, you take care yeah? I love you. I'll see you soon yeah?'

Mum nods, her eyes full of tears. She's walking off again, her head down.

I call after her, 'Hey Mum?'

She turns around quickly. 'I can't, Sam' she says. 'Not... yet.'

I force a grin through the tears.

'I know. How's tomorrow looking though?'

'Tomorrow's looking good, kid,' she whispers, and then she is gone.

Anne Delargy

Poets

When you're not allowed to speak,

To use straightforward honest words

That's when the metaphors appear.

We have no other choice.

We don't say the name

Of our Country any more,

We don't raise our flag.

Instead we draw watermelons and write,

"They buried us, not knowing

That we are seeds."

We don't talk about our land any more.

Instead we sing, "Our olive trees have been here

Planted firm and deep in this good earth,

For a hundred generations."

We don't mention our houses any more,

Stolen or destroyed.

We just hold up the ancient keys

That show our right to return.

We don't recite the names

Of our dead babies now.

We simply say

"She was the soul of my soul."

Only the poets will survive

This catastrophe.

As they did the last

And all the ones before that.

Because now every single one of us

Every – single – one

Has become a poet.

Sam Tovey

Melting Pot

I'm a Sunday Roast at 3pm,
And a biryani when the clock strikes ten.

A Bollywood scene when afternoon turns night,
Homes Under the Hammer in the morning light.

Wear salwar kameez on Christmas Day,
And my Carhartt jacket to the local café.

I'm from Surrey in a job interview,
And from Pakistan when I've got nothing to lose.

My identity is my responsibility,
I'm the epitome of my society,
British, Pakistani, or in between,
I have a choice on how I want to be seen.

Juliet Goldbart

Calcutta 1987: a city love affair

I arrive in April, probably a mistake. Leaving the plane, a tidal wave of heat assaults me, the humidity shocks me. Smells assail my nostrils; aviation fuel laden with something over-ripe, hot and earthy. Befuddled by the long journey and time difference, I queue for immigration in a winding polyglot crowd.

A young man in uniform holds up a card with my name. Smiling, he takes my suitcase and I follow him to a beige jeep, emblazoned with a red cross and the organisation's name. The jeep has no seatbelts. I sit in the front and hold tight to a handle on the dashboard.

We travel as fast as the chaotic mass of traffic permits, skirting motorbikes carrying mum, dad and a toddler, passing young boys herding goats towards the city, passing men by the side of the road selling cauliflowers and animal hides stretched out on the red earth. Images sear into my consciousness. My knuckles are white, but I am too dazzled for fear.

Eventually, we park outside a glass-fronted hotel, set back from the road. At reception, I am given a large key on a brass fob and an envelope. I thank the driver who hands my suitcase to a turbaned man who shows me silently to my room.

After a cold shower, I lie on the bed watching the ceiling fan rotate lazily, lifting the heavy air, then open the letter. It contains a timetable for my work at the specialist school and an invitation; my host will meet me at the hotel at six to take me to her home for dinner.

Dinner is fun, though my jet-lagged eyes droop. My host, Mrs K, is charming. We are joined at the table by D, her young son. Each time Mrs K leaves the table, D shows me how people eat with their hands in different regions of India. Soon, there is rice all round his plate and a turmeric coloured sauce running up his right arm. Mrs K expresses indulgent horror and sends him off with his ayah. “He is delightful.” I assure her, and we exchange smiles.

The following morning, and each weekday, I am collected by the jeep driver and a jolly group of teachers who live north of the hotel. In the morning I observe their classes, in awe of their skill in handling the children. Their equipment is battered and old fashioned, but serviceable. The children experience a wide diversity of disabilities, and each has an individual programme of education and physiotherapy.

In the afternoons, I teach sessions on cognition and communication. Each evening I re-write my planned lectures, the better to match my theory with the school staff’s practice. I stand at the front, a dull wren beside their jewel plumage. Lizards scurry across the far wall, but if I am caught watching, my class will shriek and jump on their chairs. The practical activities I have devised to enliven the lectures seem unfamiliar, but when Mrs K and her deputy role-play teacher and student, there is laughter and soon everyone is joining in.

The jeep returns me to the hotel before taking the teachers home. We are a wilted, sweaty band, but off-duty now. I ask about the strange scallop-shaped decorations apparently hand-slapped onto every concrete surface. They confer in Bengali, seemingly embarrassed, then explain that it is cow dung, collected and dried for use as cooking fuel by street dwellers. I smile in appreciation of both the ingenuity and the teachers’ frankness.

In the early evenings I walk, too wired to rest or eat. My route takes me alongside the Maidan, an enormous park, the lungs of the city, past the massive white frontage of the Indian Museum to the glamorous Oberoi Hotel, I continue along Park Street where street sleepers congregate to wash at the pump and back via the Oxford bookstore on Park Street. In 1987, there are few Europeans walking in the city and I attract many half glances and a few open stares, but I feel perfectly safe.

Dusk is brief at this latitude, and it is soon dark. Back at the hotel, I order a papaya and lime with a *nimbu pani* (fresh lime and soda water), no ice. I am careful to wash the fruit with sterilised water and my hands with soap. I eat the fruit and swallow my antimalarials; the taste is bitter against the sour of the nimbu pani.

I plug in a mosquito coil. Through netted windows I look down over the city. The sky is too polluted for stars, but the ground is lit by thousands of cooking fires, their flames releasing the smell of burning dung into the sky. I take a deep breath. The city has captured my heart.

Jo Somerset

History-Shmystery

Historiography is an ugly term for something that simply means all the words that have been written about history. From those multiple strings of words, a competent knitter would produce a vast sweater, unwearable by any human: a surging sea of colours slashed with zig-zags and curlicued clashing patterns flowing along complex paths. Finding the neck-hole would be straightforward for classic historians like Trevelyan, but not if the postmodernists got hold of it. "For what is a neck?" Foucault might ask. And if we don't know what a neck is, how could our diligent knitter create a hole for it?

As for the arms! Raglan or drop-shoulder sleeves, ribbed cuffs or dolman style? This historiographical sweater would wave like an octopus, each flailing arm proclaiming its uniqueness, its essential truth. Thin or baggy, long, three-quarter or short, garishly patterned or elegantly plain, every arm would claim their special place in the annals of sweater-dom, relating to, yet distinct from, all other sweaters ever knitted world-wide in a thousand years.

Did I say that historiography is *all* the words written about history? That's bunkum. It's actually all the words *published* by academics - let's call them **historians**. There are other words about the past, but they don't count. These writers aren't historians, they are **novelists.**

Would it advance our understanding of history if we mixed up the scholarly and the fictional? After all, the earliest historians like Herodotus in Ancient Greece and his Chinese equivalent Sima Qian were not historians at all, but poets or astrologers. Note that women are conspicuous by their absence. However, Pope Joan can't have been the only woman in centuries past to achieve her ends by concealing her gender, so it is safe to say that some pre-modern historians were probably women. Others collaborated with their father/brother/husband to create the History that bore his name. If we haven't heard of these women, it is nothing to do with lack of scholarship and everything to do with patriarchy.

There's a conflict between narrative, interpretive and postmodern handling of history. Last century, telling history moved from the chronological narrative mode to a model which attributed meaning to historical facts, rather than simply relating a series of events, an approach introduced by E.H. Carr in *What Is History?* (1961). Post-second world war civil rights movements added voices of oppressed minorities, women, working class and colonized peoples. Observing the world from these different viewpoints fed the postmodern hunger for deconstruction. New Historicism at last enriched the mix of who could talk about the past by juxtaposing contemporaneous literary and non-literary texts to reach deeper understanding of eras being studied.

Would juxtaposing history and fiction show that authenticity is itself inauthentic if its boundary is limited to people in universities? Would perspectives from other writers give history a crisper meaning, by bringing the past to life through stories?

Juggling and jumbling in this way might jiggle the threatening stasis. I can't agree with Francis Fukuyama that we have reached the 'end of history'. Future generations might make sense of the present by examining the past from many angles; knitters grasping time in its shape-shifting fluidity from yarn to garment to unravelled formless heaps. The future doesn't deserve to be left with a mess of stitches, time racing in and out of the gaps, accompanied by rapid clicking of needles and slow, exasperated sighs lubricated with sweat of the brow and saliva of expletives.

However, muddying the water between fact and fiction, between truth and untruth, can be unhelpful in this 'post-truth' era. Questioning whether certain events like the Holocaust actually happened needs stamping on. But the knitter needs to follow a new pattern, a form of narrative along the story-telling spectrum which fuses facts and diverse voices with meaning.

While spinning the words about history into a yarn and knitting them into a garment is not a practical project, weaving words into a cogent, intelligible whole is the writer's craft. If allowing a wider variety of voices to talk about history allows us to see who and what we are in these confusing times, and even prevents blunders to which we humans seem so prone, then this is indeed a worthy project. There is no time like the present, but at the same time, time slips away into the past. Let's sit forward and see where the fusion takes us.

which must have been designed by Poiret. Her dark eyes perused the interior of le Dôme and landed on the artists' table where her languid gaze lingered until one of the men—the toad—leapt up and offered his seat. She nodded in acknowledgment.

The group held their breath; was this vision known to one of their party?

That did not appear to be the case, she had simply chosen to join them. Her name was Anna Moore.

'… from the west of Ireland, where thunderous waves lash the shore.' She offered. An Irishwoman then, though her French was fluent and spoken like a native. A voice low and lilting, but truth be told she said little beyond that brief introduction. She had no need, Babette decided; Anna's beauty said everything that needed to be said.

From the first, Babette felt a chill and sensed something unnatural, something that was dead within this woman's eyes even though they sparkled and shone like diamonds. The company were transfixed. Gertrude leant towards Anna with unabashed interest. The men reminded Babette of dogs around a bitch in heat with their tongues hanging out and their tails wagging furiously.

After a short while Anna declared that she proposed to sit for one of the artists—but only one. Their mouths fell open in a sigh of expectation. She rose to leave. In passing, the Irishwoman placed a hand on Guilbert's shoulder. 'You shall be my bright arrow.'

Guilbert smiled triumphantly—not least at this loose translation of his name.

Then the vision was gone leaving only the trailing wisp of a dream. Babette caught the far-away look in Guilbert's eyes and at once felt her heart break into a thousand glittering shards.

On Monday, Babette climbed the narrow stairs to Guilbert's small attic studio, she came armed with fresh baguettes and knocked at his door ready to resume her pose for the latest canvas; one in which she featured as the Madonna. A sweet irony she felt as she nursed the secret in her womb. *Today.* She thought. Perhaps *today* would be the day to tell Guilbert that he would soon be a father and that they should look for a place where they might all live together. Guilbert peered through a crack in the door with ill-disguised irritation.

'Babette … what are you doing here? I did not send for you. I cannot be disturbed.'

Babette frowned, he had never before spoken to her in so curt a manner, his words sharp as pinpricks, 'Guilbert?'

'You must leave. I cannot, I must not be disturbed.' He glanced behind him.

Through the gap Babette caught sufficient glimpse of the Irishwoman, half-naked. Their gaze connected and a slow smile crept across Anna's features whilst her eyes remained hard and cold as obsidian.

'You still need to eat, Guilbert!' Babette thrust the baguettes through the door and turned on her heels.

A week passed. Babette's certainty that her lover would call for her slipped into an anxious hope and then, by the end of the second week, gave way to an abject despair. Girding herself for a confrontation, she returned to the studio. She could hear voices from within but there was no response to her knock, even when she pounded on the door panel and raised her voice in a desperate plea.

'Guilbert!! I must speak with you! Open the door!'

The concierge rattled her cane against the banister and called up from the floor below demanding that the noise cease immediately.

Babette's head fell forward against the door panel, 'Please Guilbert …' she whispered. 'I know you are in there.'

As she made her way from the building Babette questioned the concierge, 'Have you seen him? Is he alright?'

The old woman waved her away, 'It's the last time I am taking in artists—they are nothing but trouble!'

Babette paid a visit to Gertrude at Rue de Fleurus and was invited into the salon. In the fortnight and more since the night at Le Dôme the Steins had not seen Guilbert. Neither had they encountered the mysterious Irishwoman again but they had learned something.

'Her countrywoman, Eileen Gray, visited with us and she tells me that the poet Mr Yeats believes this Anna Moore to be an incarnation of The Leanan Sidhe.' Gertrude smiled wryly.

'She?' Babette was confused.

'An Irish fairy apparently. Mr Yeats has a passion for fairies and sees them at the bottom of every garden.'

'Is she sitting for Guilbert, as promised?' Leo interjected breathlessly.

'We should very much like to see the painting when it is finished. Perhaps, to purchase it.' Gertrude's eyes gleamed at the prospect.

Babette refused the offer of coffee and proceeded with haste to the home of Bracque. She paced his rooms feverishly voicing her concern for her lover, biting her fingernails and clawing at the back of her hands. Georges seized her by the shoulders and looked with concern into her eyes. 'Babette, dearest girl you must stop torturing yourself. Guilbert will come back to you.'

'Can't you speak with him?'

Georges smiled kindly, 'It is a madness of the moment. This woman has placed a spell on him—it could have been any one of us!'

'That's it—a spell! She has bewitched him.' Babette wrung her hands, 'I knew it, I knew it from the moment I laid eyes on her. She is a devil. What can I do Georges?'

Bracque shrugged in his easy way, 'Perhaps you could pray.'

Babette lingered on the street in Montmartre outside the warren of artist quarters where the poorest lived and where the toad had his atelier, painting on cardboard when he could not afford canvas. The sun was high in the sky and beads of sweat trickled down her spine. She felt faint and a little nauseous. She needed to lie down but grasped a lamp post instead.

It was in this state of desperate fatigue that Picasso found Babette and half carried her into a cramped and cluttered room which smelt of fried onions. A corpulent woman pressed a glass of cool water into her shaking hands.

'Is she alright, Fernande?' Pablo asked with concern.

'Pregnant. That's it, ain't it dearie?' The woman chucked Babette under the chin and smoothed the damp strands of hair from her brow.

Babette nodded, feebly.

'Guilbert—does he know?'

Babette shook her head then looked towards the toad. 'Have you seen him? Can you speak to him? He shuts the door in my face.' She sobbed, suddenly overwhelmed, 'I fear … I don't know—I am afraid.'

Picasso sneered, his eyes aflame, 'It's her, the beauty. He is her *bright arrow.* More of a prick I should say!'

Fernande dug him in the ribs, 'Pablo, enough, the girl needs help. Guilbert cannot simply desert Babette in her present condition. We must speak with him, knock some sense into that thick artist head of his—and I know all about that!' she glared at Picasso.

'Thank you, thank you!' Babette pushed herself up from the bed, revived by the offers of assistance.

Picasso rapped loudly on the door. Below, the concierge was muttering a litany of complaints.

'Guilbert, open up!' the Spaniard cried.

In a moment of silence, they heard a thud from within.

'Something is wrong—I feel it!' Babette wailed.

Fernande nodded, 'You must break down the door, Pablo.'

'Really!'

'Yes, now!' Fernande demanded.

The concierge called up, 'Who will pay? Someone must pay!'

Picasso took a deep breath and heaved his shoulder to the door. He winced at the impact and then charged again. This time it gave way and he stumbled through the opening, swiftly followed by Fernande who was clutching Babette by the hand.

They looked about at the general chaos of the studio. A low moan arose from the corner. Guilbert was slumped on an old chaise covered in drapes.

Babette gasped to see the pallor of his complexion, the thin shrunken cheeks and chapped lips. His eyes were glazed and he shivered uncontrollably.

'Guilbert!' she screamed.

Fernande shouted to Picasso, 'Hurry—go and get a doctor at once!'

'She has left me …' Guilbert's voice was low and strained, features wracked with sorrow.

Babette stroked his brow. He grasped at her hand, 'Find her … you must find her.'

Babette flared to fury, 'It is that demon, that witch who has done this to you!'

A painful sound rattled in Guilbert's chest.

'Guilbert don't leave me!'

The young artist shook his head and with effort he spoke, 'I cannot die—look, she has made me immortal …' His eyes glistened for a moment as though he had a vision of heaven. With that, the breath left his body for the last time.

'Guilbert!'

Fernande shouted impatiently to Pablo, 'The doctor, you oaf! At once!'

But Picasso remained frozen in front of a large canvas, it was covered in angular blocks of vivid colour and strange shapes, an eye like a cyclops. He was awestruck.

'It is magnificent. A masterpiece.'

Babette pushed passed him and grabbed a canvas knife. With a ferocious howl and a sweeping violent movement, she began to slash at the painting, this way and that, until it lay in orange, green and red ribbons at her feet.

Josh Lonsdale

Exploded View

We can move in reverse or speed forward;
the hardest is to stay with the scene.

Learned *that* in the dark room
tenderly feeding the projector

we can warp the timeline
but never break the chain of events,

the artist has to die

here

there

or anywhere

we so choose

without instruction

in how to chart success

without evidence

to back up the claim.

Take a vacation

attempt to find it elsewhere

an indeterminate of deafening

the otherside

of the clam,
sealed as a widower's lips

a pause without eager resume

that's all one ever craved for

wishful thinking
in exploded view.

Carole Belfield

The Birthday Present

The main characters:

The Twins, Fran and Dan.

Bobby, Our Dog — has a few words of English such as, 'cheese,' 'walkies' 'fetch'

The Best Toys, Bunny Rabbit and Jingle Bear—they speak English and Dog in voices too high-pitched for humans to hear.

Mum

Our Nana

Names have been altered to protect the innocent

Bunny Rabbit and Jingle Bear were sitting on the sofa chatting with Bobby the Dog.

'Bobby, did you know it's The Twins' birthday on Sunday?' asked Jingle in his best posh Dog accent.

'When's that?'

'Tomorrow.'

'Bow, wow! How old are they?'

'Nine, same as us,' said Bunny. 'We were all born on the same day.'

'What? What? Wow! That's really old,' growled Bobby

'Are you getting them a present?' asked Jingle.

'Dunno. What can I give them? I'm only a dog.' He thought for a few moments. 'I've got a new chewy. They could have that I suppose.'

'I'm not sure they'd like that,' Bunny said, winking at Jingle.

Bobby went to his basket for a think and fell asleep. He dreamed about birthdays. When he woke up he had a plan. He trotted over to where Bunny and Jingle were fighting over the TV remote control, each wanting to watch different programmes.

'Hey guys, I've got an idea. I found a massive bone in the garden. It would make a great birthday present for The Twins. What's not to like about a good bone?'

The Best Toys looked at one another. They knew The Twins wouldn't want some old bone but Bobby was only a baby and they didn't like to upset him.

'Go for it, Bobby,' they said, and left it at that.

'Do you want to come and see it?' Bobby barked.

'I suppose,' said Bunny glancing out of the window to see if it was raining.

'Give us a lift then,' said Jingle.

Bobby grabbed their fleecy arms in his teeth and trotted to the back door. It was ajar, so he squeezed through.

'Where is it then?' Bunny was grumpy he wanted to watch TV.

'I dragged it behind the shed. It's huge.'

Bobby propped The Best Toys carefully against the shed wall while he scrabbled around the back, his bottom and tail wagging furiously as he dragged out the big bone. The Best Toys imagined it would be an ordinary doggy bone, but what Bobby pulled out from behind the shed was as big as him and not like any bone they'd ever seen before.

‘Are you sure that’s a bone?’ said Jingle. ‘It looks more like a stone to me.’

‘Duh! Of course, it is. Dogs smell bones, right?’ Bobby was getting cross now.

‘You can’t give it to The Twins in that state. It will have to be cleaned.’

‘Don’t worry. I’ll give it a good licking.’ Bobby growled.

‘Well don’t go chewing it or they’ll think it’s second-hand,’ advised Bunny.

Bobby looked longingly at the big bone stone but promised not to gnaw it.

Bunny said, ‘Take us back now, Bobby, there’s a programme on the TV we want to watch. It’s about sub-atomic particles.’ (Not that they would understand a word of it, but The Best Toys liked things that were smaller than they were.)

Bobby got on with cleaning up the bone. It took him ages, but he was pleased with the result. He pushed the whopping thing back behind the shed, ready for the big day.

When it arrived, The Twins had loads of presents. In the afternoon all Those Cousins arrived for a party. Bobby, who hadn't had a chance to give the twins his present, sat watching for an opportunity. While the children scoffed a cake the size of a small, chocolate flying saucer, he went into the garden and dragged out the present. It took a long time to get it into the house. His teeth hurt by the time he dropped it at The Twins’ feet.

He barked, ‘Bow Wow, look what I’ve got you for your birthday. Fantastic, eh?’

The Twins and Those Cousins all stared down at the bone.

'Mum, Mum, come and see what Bobby's just dragged in,' shouted Dan.

'No need to yell, and you, Bobby, stop that barking right now,' said Mum.

She looked down at the bone, 'Goodness! Where did you get that, Bobby? Is this what you were digging up when I shouted at you to leave the daffodils alone?' Mum knelt down for a closer look. 'Nana, come and see this.'

Our Nana was tidying up the kitchen. She came into the living room wiping her hands.

'Mm,' she said, 'you know, kids, this bone isn't from any animal from around these parts.'

'It looks like a vertebra,' said Fran. They had been learning about skeletons at school. Dan said nothing. For once he agreed with his twin.

'Let's take it to the museum and see what they have to say about it,' said Our Nana.

The next Saturday, the family, including Bobby and the Best Toys, went on the train to Leeds. The Twins took turns in carry the box in which the big bone nestled in a clean towel. At the museum they showed the man on the reception desk what was in it.

'I think we'd better take you to the curator in charge of Palaeontology. Follow me,' he said.

So, they all trouped off behind the man who carried the box as if it contained newborn baby. He led them down the stairs, along a corridor until they came to a big wooden door.

Dan poked Fran in the ribs, nodding his head at the brass nameplate. 'Do you get it?' he giggled, reading out aloud, 'Ms. Dinah

Sawduss, Head of Palaeontology,' and burst out laughing, 'Dinah Sawduss!'

Jingle looked at Bunny, who shook his head. He knew Bobby would never understand the joke. There was no point in translating.

'I think you might want to take at look at this Ms. Sawduss,' said the man ushering them into a musty room full of bones. Bones were on tables, on the shelves, in see-through plastic boxes. Pictures of bones hung on the wall, and books about bones were piled up on a chair.

Ms. Sawduss, a tall woman with a silver dinosaur brooch pinned to her white coat said, 'Come in, come in. What have we got here?'

And that's how come, several weeks later, the archaeology team arrived at The Twins' home, where they carefully sliced up the lawn. They stacked the grass in one corner, and began digging. By week three, they had unearthed more bones, each bigger than the last. The lead expert, Mr. Neil Down, was a friendly man with white frizzy hair and a stripy jumper. He kept The Twins up-to-date with the finds, and took time out from the dig to go to the school to explain things to the children

'The bones we have found are from the tail of an exceedingly large dinosaur. We don't know which one until we've completed the dig,' he told them.

They were all incredibly excited. The Twins became very popular at their school. Of course, the dig was all thanks to Bobby. He didn't mind. Everyone made a fuss of him at the school gates. He swelled with pride at the thought of the important gift he had given The Twins. He loved them as much as he loved The Best Toys.

When news of the find got out, a steady stream of visitors came to see the dig. They included a camera team from the television, and a journalist from The Guardian newspaper. The dig was big news.

By week four, next-door's garden was dug up. More bones were found. By week seven it had moved to next-door-but-one's lawn at the end of the road. By the autumn Mr Neil Down's team was digging up the railway station car park.

One afternoon Bobby joined The Best Toys on the sofa. They had some exciting news.

'Guess what Bobby. They've found something exciting at the station.'

Bobby growled, 'What? What?'

'The dinosaur's head. They've now got an almost complete skeleton.'

'Crikey, how do you know that?'

'The Twins couldn't stop talking about it when they came back from school,' said Jingle.

'It's the biggest dinosaur ever found,' said Bunny

'One no-one has ever seen before,' said Jingle

'No, it isn't.'

'Yes, it is.'

'How do you know?'

'I heard Mr Neil Down talking about it.'

'Stop arguing and tell me what else you know,' growled Bobby. 'Show some respect. Remember who found it.'

'Sorry Bobby,' they muttered.

On the twins' tenth birthday the whole family including Bobby, was invited to the Natural History Museum in London to celebrate the hanging of the new find. The Best Toys were stuffed in backpacks, because The Twins were too old now to admit they still loved them, though they still cuddled them in bed.

A muffled voice from Fran's rucksack said, 'Did you know Bobby, they had to close the museum for months?'

'What? What? How do you know, Jingle?' Bobby barked.

'We heard Our Nan explaining it to the Twins. She told them they had to wire the dinosaur bones together, then suspend them from the ceiling of the museum,' said Bunny, his voice stifled by a large packet of crisps in Dan's backpack. 'We heard The Mum say the hall was massive, almost as long as a football pitch.'

'Crikey,' barked Bobby, 'I hope no bones fall on our heads.'

In the enormous hall, the dinosaur was concealed under a huge curtain. There were many photographers and TV crews there.

The Lord Mayor got up on a platform and said into the microphone, 'I am proud to be here today to unveil this most important contribution to the museum's collection. It is all thanks to Bobby the dog.'

On and on went the speech. Hearing his name mentioned frequently, Bobby barked with excitement. It was some time before Fran could calm him down with his Favourite Treat.

'I wish he'd stop talking and take off the cover,' said Fran. The Best Toys who had both struggled to get their heads out of the backpacks agreed. Bobby was too busy with his Favourite Treat to notice, when the Lord Major drew back the curtain with a flourish. Cameras flashed and there were gasps all round as the onlookers saw above their heads, the world's biggest dinosaur. No one had ever seen anything like it before.

About a third of the way along its tail a card dangled from a blue ribbon. Dan picked up Bobby to show it to him.

> 'Bobby,' he said, 'it says, *This important discovery adds to what we know of Dinosaurs. It is the result of careful excavation by Bobby the Dog.'*

Of course, Bobby didn't understand a word, but Bunny, his head still poked out of the backpack translated for him.

On the wall were pictures of the dig and a large photograph of Bobby, The Twins and The Best Toys. Beneath the pictures was an information sheet. It described what the dinosaur would have looked like, what it would have eaten, and how it had hunted for its dinner.

Fran carried Bobby over to look at all the pictures.

'Look, there's a track where our road runs today,' she said. 'I bet it was made by dinosaurs.'

Jingle explained it all to Bobby who barked, 'Not a house in sight. Where did Dogs live in those days?'

'I don't think dogs hadn't been invented back then,' said Jingle.

'What? What?' barked Bobby.

The Twins had been invited to name the new dinosaur. After a lot of argument, they chose, BOBDANAFRANOSAURUS. A big brass plaque with this name on it, hangs on the wall of the Natural History Museum. Of course, privately, Fran tells her pals it's called, BOBFRANADANOSAURUS.

You should take yourself down to London and take a look at it. You'll be amazed.

Mary Cohen-Lavarello

Let's Go Home. Mum's Dead And All The People Are Dead

a girl had told her Dad.

My phone reporting this to me

and simultaneously

where best to buy a country home.

Sharon McCarthy

Forgive Again and Again

Forgiveness is like a kiss on the lips
that creates a flutter
like a butterfly does
but its brevity leaves
a lasting longing
at the moment
that it turns to dust
just as
at the close of day
so the butterfly must.
Thus begins again the pursuit of trust
that will lead to forgiveness
again and again,
as we must.

Jo Somerset

Seeds that grow

Spring 1989.

Plumes of cigarette smoke rise above fourteen women sitting on grey foam blocks in the Gay Centre. They are sucking and puffing their anxiety into the room.

*

There was a mother who accepted her daughter's lesbian identity but said, *I'm sad that you'll never have children. You'd have been a great mum.*

There was you considering adoption but the barriers to being designated 'acceptable parents' were too huge.

There was a gay guy at work who'd said, *I'm jealous of lesbians who have children. I'd love to be a father.* Where there's a willy, there's a way. But he was too scared to get an AIDS test, and that was a deal-breaker.

There was a yellow book glaring on your table: *Getting Pregnant Our Own Way: A Guide to Self-Insemination.* Your mother's jaw tightened and belly burned as she sneaked a look inside. She said nothing to you, her daughter. The knowledge she'd swallowed silently smouldered during the following months, despite the powerful antacids she gulped every day.

*

At the Gay Centre, some guys who've volunteered as donors hand their questionnaires over. They're willing to share for free. In their world, *property is theft*, so they'll ejaculate and give it away, without owning any person who grows as a result. They're cool with that.

In the ten years since the world's first test-tube baby was born in Oldham in the UK, there are now hundreds like her. During this decade, 'assisted reproduction' is travelling from maverick science to mainstream medical procedure.

Out there, the Human Fertilisation and Embryology Bill is presented to Parliament. In here – *we're here because we're queer* – you're nurturing a secret branch of embryology, planning your own fertilisation without attracting attention. There's been enough about 'Lesbiangrad or Gayville?' in the Manchester Evening News recently. You just want to get on with your lives, which includes creating life.

You're bucking the patriarchy. You don't care about regulation; you know what you're doing. You want a child. Simple. You don't need medics invading your privates, poking and prodding, pricking and pushing. No-one fusses like that about a traditional fuck. You're doing the same thing without the fuck.

*

A few months later.

"Oh!" you shriek when you pull the little stick out of its chemical and see that it's bright blue.

"Exciting!" crows your brother.

"Omigod!" says your mother. "I can't say I'm pleased."

You want your child to know they were wanted and were conceived with love. You don't – can't – imagine how they will feel.

*

1995. Five years have passed.

Your son is five. It's clear from his height and physique which donor 'clicked'.

Your boy climbs into your bed. The alarm's gone off. You're groggy and warm.

"Mum. Did I have a dad in the first place?"

"No, you've always had two mums. A nice man called Andrew gave us his sperm so we could make a baby. That's called a donor, which means a giver. What do you think of that?"

"Int'resting."

*

Years go by. 2006.

The lanky boy, six-foot four, strides past trees in full leaf, their roots bulging up paving stones which threaten to trip him. As he passes a tall man walking towards him, their eyes meet on the same level.

Wait, thinks the boy, a few paces further on. He turns. *Are you Andrew?* The man stops, faces the boy, says *yes*. The boy stammers something to do with sperm or donor, he can't remember afterwards, and the man goes, *Oh yeah, how are you doing?* They shake hands. The man says, *Do you want to go for coffee?* and the boy says, *No, I'm late, I've got to go. Good to meet you,* and lopes off along the dappled pavement.

*

Today, 2024.

That LGBTQ+ centre has been rebuilt for The Proud Trust, on the very spot where I chose a questionnaire that contained a seed into the future.

Sharon McCarthy

Lockdown Shopdown

Bring me jam ham and cheese,
whichever type,
You pick it please.
Bread that's brown but bereft of seed
and a block of butter, with added salt,
I'm in need.
Cake of any kind,
I'm a bit partial, you'll find.
Smoothie would be groovy and passata non grata
for my pasta I would approvy.
Alas I almost forgot that stuff for Mad Maz,
my crazy, lazy, one-eyed cat.
Whiskas, I believe, plus anything lovely and luscious
that's going to be delicious.

Yes, but what about chorizo for that savoury t- reat,
and don't forget some crackers;
I'll throw in charity shop maracas.
Manchego prego for that Iberian fuego
to warm your heart at dusk.
How about eggs and bacon?
Prerequisites for Sunday brunch,
unless I'm mistaken?

A copy of The Guardian?
Or will you wait for The Observer?
Then I can pop into Barbican for delights further.
Hillaire Belloc springs to mind whenever I look at these rhymes.

You are more akin to The Bard himself;
I will aspire to your skills,
as I peruse each shelf!
Guardian, I will be
of all those aforementioned delights you
so kindly agree to deliver to me;
Excepting the eggs and bacon,
of which I boast plenty.
Bard I am not, but Bardot I might concede,
as I flatter myself err my powers to seduce
and pleasure bequeath.

Oh good,
I'm delighted you have these provisions already,
As long as I can keep my handle bars steady
I will cycle round to your door
shortly after 4.

If you are having Bardot
I'm Zsa Zsa Gabor!

Off you must venture,
but don’t dilly dally too far
else I’ll have to fetch you
in my car,
AKA Rita,
as in Red headed Lolita,
1940s et al.

Yes, you are more like Rita than Brigitte,
energetic, vivacious and petite;
more ripple than twirl.
Alors,
merci mademoiselle de la nourriture,
I’ll invite you to dinner when Lockdown is no more.

Rose M Cullen

Who let the Dogs Out

We arranged to meet at the swings. Two o'clock.

'Make it tooth hurty.' Jason interjected, 'To be on the safe side.'

I groaned, 'I'll be asleep by then.'

'No, you won't.'

He was right. I wouldn't get a wink. Also, he'd promised to bring a bottle of wine. 'Mum and Dad won't miss it; they've joined another one of those wine clubs.'

Over his garden fence, Jason had overheard their neighbour Mr Brody discussing what went on in the park after dark. 'No word of a lie' Mr Brody had said to his mate, 'Private WhatsApp group, they've invited me to join.'

What went on in the park at night became something Jason wanted to talk about all the time—that and which schools we'd be off to after the summer.

'It's called dodging innit?' I offered.

'Dogging, you numpty.' Jason scoffed.

I imagined all these people bringing their poodles, pit bulls and terriers to the park in the middle of the night. Maybe the dogs joined in with whatever went on. There was something called 'doggy style', according to Jason. He was full of useful information. He showed us video reels on his phone. Lots of grunting. Sol was shocked. He'd never seen porn before. Neither had I, but I wasn't going to let on in front of Jason, never mind be wussy about it.

Jason offered to send us the link. Sol was like, *no way, if my mum finds it ...!* Jason smirked, said his parents never checked anything.

He sent the link to me but I deleted it straight away. It wasn't that my dad nosed into everything I was doing, it was just that if he did find something like that, I don't know, then he would be 'disappointed'. There was just me and my dad, you see. Sometimes I'd come in and he'd be at the kitchen sink trying to peel potatoes with tears running down his cheeks. We had a freezer full of easy-peasy dinners for those sorts of nights.

When he overheard Mr Brody talking about it again and mentioned a date Jason came up with the idea of checking out the dogging for ourselves.

Our local park has a play area, football pitches, a few flowerbeds that the volunteers look after but there are also woods at the back. Not just a few trees but a country park with a proper nature trail with a boardwalk over the parts that get muddy when it rains. There's even a couple of ponds. When I was little, me and Mum went up there on expeditions to catch tadpoles. Sol came too sometimes. Mum talked about lifecycles, not just tadpoles, all sorts of things you could find living in the woods. She was a conservationist. Sol's dad came to collect him from our house one day and he laughed out loud when he saw our posters for the Green Party in the window. Sol had told him that mum was a Conservative.

The dogging was supposed to happen in the car park where the nature trail began. Jason said we should loop through the woods to keep out of sight. It was well after two thirty and we were still waiting for Sol. Jason texted again. I shivered, it was July but the night was cold and I only had a T shirt under my bomber jacket. There weren't any clouds, just a full moon; one of those ones that looks so close you wonder why there isn't a moon base up there already. I took another glug from Jason's bottle, it was a red wine: I didn't particularly like the taste but it made me feel sort of warm and fuzzy and seemed to calm my nerves.

'Might know Sol'd be a wussie baby!' Jason snorted, reaching for the bottle before I finished it all off. 'Let's go.'

I hung back, 'Give him another minute.' 'He's not coming.' 'Maybe he didn't wake up.'

Jason laughed, 'Wet the bed more like. Come on—we'll miss all the shagging.' There was a gleam in his eye. I could see he was jittery, full of energy, raring to go. 'Or are you chicken too?' He glanced over his shoulder throwing out the challenge.

I followed.

The moon was so bright that we didn't need a torch to cut through under the overhanging trees. As we neared the car park, we could tell that something was going on, like an electricity in the air—or maybe it was just the way my heart was thumping. We saw a glimmer of light. Jason stretched his hand out behind to bring us to a halt and then a finger to his lips. I could hardly breathe never mind make a sound. We should keep low and circle the area, he suggested, like we were reconnaissance for a secret mission—which I suppose we were. The light from the interiors of several vehicles which were parked up threw a group of dark figures into silhouette. Others hung back in the trees. I felt an awkward lump forming in my throat. If we were caught, we would be in big trouble. Jason was straining to catch sight of the 'action' as he called it but we dare not approach any closer. I could sense his excitement, the thrill of something forbidden, whatever was going on inside each of the three cars involved in the event.

Over to my right I heard the click of a lighter as a shadowy figure lit up a cigarette and, in that moment, I caught sight of the man's features. My eyes widened, Jason's dad.

Jason was so busy switching on the video on his mobile that he didn't notice. He was zooming in on the nearest car hoping to catch sight of something despite the dark. I imagined him in the High School playground ready to establish himself as one of the Top Boys showing off his 'porno collection'.

I heard a soft gasp from him. Even with the dim interior, the face of a woman in a skimpy black corset was suddenly clearly outlined. A groan escaped Jason, or something more like a sob. That's when his dad spotted us.

Next thing we were both running full pelt back through the trees, crashing through the undergrowth.

I didn't stop until I made it back across the playground and into the maze of streets which led to my front door. I fumbled for the key. My mind was doing cartwheels, the semi-naked image of Jason's mum was on a frenetic loop. I scarcely realised that the lamp in the hall was lit until Dad rushed towards me.

'Ricky! Where've you been? I've been out of my mind. I've called the police!'

I could see the terror in his eyes and tears smarting behind them.

I flung myself at him and wrapped my arms around him. He grabbed my head and shoulder and pulled me into a tight embrace.

I learnt two things that night. One was that when Dad couldn't sleep, which was often, he would come and sit in my bedroom to watch me sleep; it comforted him. That's when he discovered I wasn't there.

The second thing I learnt was that I was in no rush to learn about sex; growing up could wait.

Mary Cohen-Lavarello

Relentless

You're doing it right
if your baby's alive
meeting its milestones
and seeming to thrive

but when up in the night
getting flushes of ire
as your baby won't sleep
and your arms are on fire

because three hours of rocking
have not lulled this boy
your breasts feel deflated
the tears start to cloy.

Blind-groping for options
for endings, for sleep
weighing up if it's worth
a short break for a weep.

Is this doing it right?

This unwilling faith?

Is each step in the dark

the right one to take?

I know that the answer's

to soak up each breath

to savour his softness

content on my chest

but I've savoured my socks off

it won't fill the night

perhaps sometimes crying

is doing it right.

Stephen Raw

Memory-Spaces

For Margaret

Your youngest's partner announces
a grandchild, avocado-shaped.
Before you stop celebrating
the baby is already the next fruit size bigger.
They simply cannot stop growing.
Will they fill your memory-space with stories
    of their birth,
    of their weight,
arguments as to whom they resemble the most?
Maybe you?

Were they knitted from the self-same
stardust as you are now?

Time is up on your ride.
But look – the carousel does not slow down,

no tender handover,

no 'please be careful' as you dismount.

The merry-go-round of matter never stops.

Surrounding love rallied to help you alight

in those final days

as your fruit-size grew backwards.

A succulent peach now a pip.

Stardust works like this.

For a spell it masked your grace –

the self-same beauty your unborn grandchild

    has reclaimed.

Sharon Richards

FOR SALE BY AUCTION

Lot 1: New arrival to family of nine. Perfect condition. Female. Unwanted gift.
All bids considered. **No reserve.**

Lot 2: One childhood. Damaged. In poor / neglected condition.

Lot 3: An assortment of teenage years. Distressed. False front. Several blemishes.

Lot 4: One state education. Excellent condition, several later, more modern, university additions. **No reserve. Auctioneers estimate £40,000-50,000 of student debt.**

Lot 5: One marriage. Brand New. Perfect condition. Matching inlays of hope and optimism.

Lot 6: One mother's body. 34 years old. Framework good. Some marks. Condition commensurate with age and usage. **Heart sold separately.**

Lot 7: One mother's heart.
Item no longer available for sale.

Lot 8: One marriage. Evidence of affair. Significant damage. Visible attempts at restoration. Some cracks still evident.

Lot 9: One Marriage. Item disassembled into two halves.

Lot 10: One Decree Nisi with matching Decree Absolute. Mint condition. Lifetime guarantee. Buyer can expect many years of happy use.

Lot 11: One career. Impressive example of its type. Integral glass ceiling.

Lot 12: One middle age. Some slight sagging. Significant evidence of empty nest syndrome.

Lot 13: Selection of miscellaneous items from the 'New Lease Of Life' school of designers. Very desirable.
Includes hobbies, travel, good friends, much-loved second husband, grandchildren and genuine happiness.

Lot 14: One old age. A wonderful example. Genuine patina. Mounted on a solid base of second spouse/soulmate. Flanked by loving children and grandchildren .

Lot 15: Stockpile of treasured memories. Jumbled. Uncatalogued. Some evidence of dementia. Several parts missing.

Lot 16: One peaceful death. Superb example. Quite rare. Set off with loved-ones. Ornate display box.

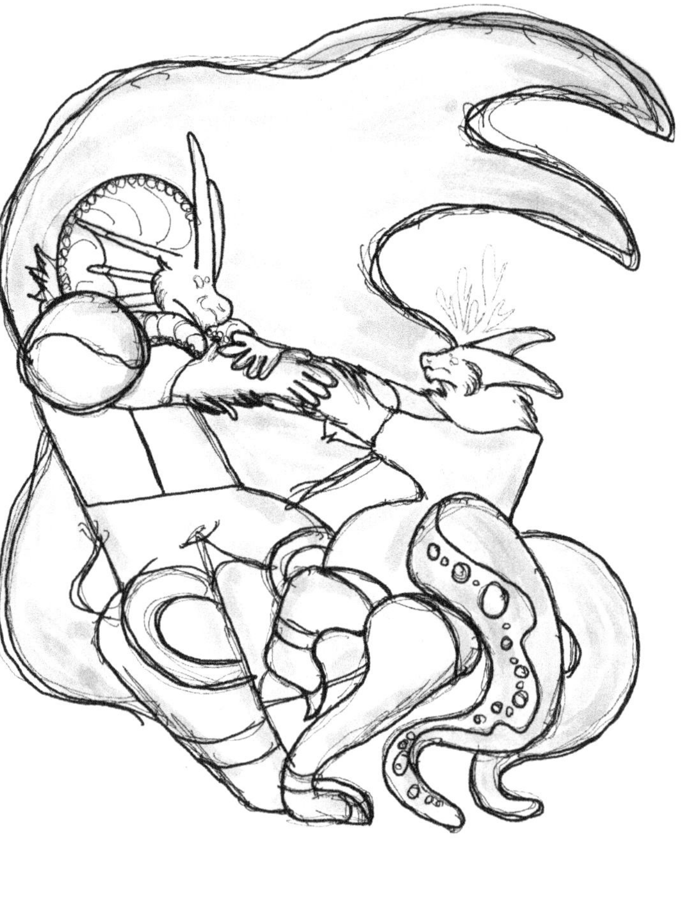

Acknowledgements

'Seanathair' by Rose Cullen was first published in *The Buzzin Bards: A Manchester Poetry Anthology,* Local Gems Press 2019

'Mermaids in my basement' by Anne Delargy was first published in *Mermaids in my basement,* Amazon 2021

'Silverdale' by Anne Delargy was first published in *Rex My Love,* Amazon 2021

'Less Home' by Lucy Power was first performed at Poppycock's *Magic Mothers* (tiny GLOBAL productions) album launch, Carlton Club, Manchester 2024

'Last Day of the Holiday' by Lindy Newns was first published in *Strand,* issue 12, February 2021

'FOR SALE BY AUCTION' by Sharon Richards received a Highly Commended award in the King Lear competition 2023

'The Peace of Silence' by Jean Thompson, submitted as 'Elsa's Year of Silence', received a Highly Commended award in the King Lear competition 2023

Biographies

Carole Belfield

Around ten years ago I wrote my first novel. It was rubbish. Since then, with help from writing groups, I've written short stories, flash fiction, amusing tales for children, and novels in genres as wide ranging as Historical Adventure, Coming of Age and Romance. I've made no serious effort to publish but was picked up by an agent interested in my 'Northern' novels, one of which was short-listed for a Northern Writers Award.

Mary Cohen-Lavarello

Mary Cohen-Lavarello is a Co-mother of a toddler and a Paediatric doctor. She is from London but thinks Chorlton is probably the best place in the world to live. She loved writing poems as a child, but since medical school has written them to process some of the grim realities of disease. During maternity leave, the Writers' Cafe was a weekly break from her son, but she ended up writing poems about him anyway.

Rose M Cullen

Rose M Cullen has written for the stage, including the RSC and Contact Theatre, and the screen. Short stories have appeared online and in anthologies. Her debut novel, *The Lucky Country*, was published in 2021 and *Black Water* in 2024. *Harlequin is Dead,* the first of a historical crime fiction series, set in the London theatre world of the 18th century, will be published by Sapere Books in 2024. Rose can be found at https://rmcullenauthor.wordpress.com/about/

Anne Delargy

I was born into an Irish Catholic family of avid readers and wrote my first poem when I was six.

I especially love spiritual and religious poetry - Blake, Herbert, Rumi, Raabia.

I became a Muslim in 2005 when I was living in Crete and working in the Synagogue there.

I have published two books of poems: *Rex my love* (jointly with my beloved dog) and *Mermaids in my Basement.* Both available on Amazon.

Famya Faraz

Famya, a character designer and illustrator artist, is inspired by fantasy animation, manga and novels. She has a unique style, working both traditionally and digitally to create something special through character design and interactions. The same is true of her writing which is inspired by fantasy and adventure.

Famya's use of colour also symbolises this special ability of craft, giving her audiences a feeling of nostalgia, whether through pastel and muted colour palettes or greyscale.

Juliet Goldbart

I would describe myself as a recovering academic! Having spent over 40 years co-authoring research papers, I am now trying to write fiction and creative nonfiction. Through my work, and since retiring, I have travelled widely. Describing my impressions and experiences of people and places has offered a bridge into a less formal style of writing, and Chorlton Writers group has given me the confidence to commit my disparate observations to print.

Clem Herman

Clem Herman is Emerita Professor of Gender and Technology at the Open University, and her research has been widely published in academic journals and books. She has recently become involved in creative writing following her retirement, and is experimenting with writing short stories, poems and radio plays. Born in Amsterdam and raised in London, she moved to Manchester in 1977 and has lived in Chorlton with her wife Deirdre for more than thirty years

Josh Lonsdale

Josh is a writer, illustrator, and general fool wandering toward or away from wisdom. He began his poetic experiments during the pandemic era – the fruit of which is a debut collection: *Inhaling the Exhausts of the Human Complaint* – and he is currently embroiled in the perilous quest of writing a novel. It's fair to say that he's doing his best to manage a lifelong compulsion to write that causes far more problems than it solves.

Sharon McCarthy

As a Teacher and Librarian my life has always embraced language and literature; it makes sense, therefore, that I write. I write for pleasure and pain. It is my insight into the best and worst that life has to offer. Those words are my companions on my journey of discovery whether they bring laughter or sorrow or understanding or compassion. They help me try to connect the individual with the rest of humanity. Some of these words will never leave my side, others will come and go as I struggle to make sense of my world, my allotted time and space, whether through poetry, fiction or nonfiction my writing comes from faith, trust and a sprinkling of fairy dust, courtesy of Peter Pan.

Lindy Newns

Lindy Newns regularly hosts Mostly Manchester Stanza group. Her poetry and flash fiction have appeared in Orbis, Acumen, Riggwelter, L'Ephemere, Popshot, and various anthologies including *Poems for Grenfell* and she is a regular reader at various open mics, including Chorlton's own Speakeasy at the Dulcimer bar.

Cal Park

I'm a psychotherapist and systemic practitioner with a strong interest in language, therapeutic writing and narrative therapy. In previous roles, I've written for radio, print and TV. Before that, I was a kid who preferred 'real' (and preferably funny) stories to fantasy.
I still don't get fantasy. As a writer I often take real emotions – fear, longing, joy, grief, as a starting point for my stories, which although fictitious, hopefully, emotionally, feel 'real.'

Lucy Power

I am a writer and musician living in Manchester. I originally trained as a visual artist, but more recently studied Creative Writing. My poems explore rural and urban situations peopled with diverse characters; I'm interested in making the hidden visible, elevating the everyday, and highlighting the overlooked. I perform at spoken word events, and my poems appear in various publications including Commonword, Flapjack Press and Morecambe Poetry Festival anthologies.

Stephen Raw

Stephen is a visual artist who turned to writing poetry as his wife was dying from pancreatic cancer last summer. He has been encouraged by the Writers group to go back over the disjointed lines he wrote at the time and give them shape. He lives in Chorlton.

Sharon Richards

I began writing when a neurological condition meant I could no longer continue my career as a clinical psychologist (I could no longer read either, but that's a long story).
I'm now a storyteller. It keeps me in printer paper and earned me a nomination for Cheshire Woman of the Year.
My YA books, *Pirates Out of Time* and *Deathly Inheritance*, were both shortlisted for the Cinnamon Pencil Mentoring Prize.
I'm currently tackling my first grown-up book.

Margo Singer

After training as a teacher of art and textiles, I co-wrote *Textile Arts: Multicultural Traditions* in 1989 and in 2007, *Textile Surface Decoration*, both published by Bloomsbury. After working as a volunteer at Elizabeth Gaskell House, I wrote *Passion and Propriety - Elizabeth Gaskell Dress and Textiles*, published by the Gaskell Society (also 2007). I am deeply interested in the history of art and textiles and am currently writing a novel set in 19th century Manchester.

Jo Somerset

Jo Somerset, founder of Chorlton Writers' Café, is an author and open mic performer. Her first novel *Mission: Find Mum* is published in September 2024 by Stairwell Books, closely followed by an adult picture book *Eating the Alphabet* (Inroad/Beaten Track, autumn 2024). In 2020 she won the Leanne Bridgewater Award for Innovation and Experiment at Salford University, where she completed a MA in Creative Writing. Jo is a trustee of Manchester Literature Festival. Insta: @jo.somerset

Jean Thompson

I guess I could be said to have been an intermittent writer in the past, when work and family commitments allowed for it.
Since retiring in 2007, I have been able to give more time to writing and am currently a member of 3 very different writing groups. Usually I write short stories, which are sometimes informed and influenced by my previous working experience as a social worker and child mental health practitioner.

Sam Tovey

I began writing poetry to unravel and process moments that have shaped who I am. In my poetry, I delve into the tapestry of identity and life's experiences, particularly in my 20s. With both British and Pakistani heritage, I spent many years suppressing parts of myself for fear of being perceived as an outsider. My poetry reflects the challenges inherent in striving for authenticity in our identities, illustrating the universal quest for self-discovery and growth.

Printed in Great Britain
by Amazon

47722996R00078

LECTURAS
Serie **Estética**
Director CHARO CREGO

TÍTULO ORIGINAL: *Ästhetik des Performativen*

Calle del Gobernador, 18
28014 Madrid
Tel.: 914 296 882
WWW.ABADAEDITORES.COM

diseño SABÁTICA

producción GUADALUPE GISBERT

ISBN 978-84-15289-18-0
IBIC AFKP
depósito legal M-26603-2014

preimpresión DALUBERT ALLÉ
impresión PUNTO VERDE, S.A.

ERIKA FISCHER-LICHTE

Estética de lo performativo

traducción
DIANA GONZÁLEZ MARTÍN
Y DAVID MARTÍNEZ PERUCHA

introducción
ÓSCAR CORNAGO

MADRID 2014
ABADA EDITORES
LECTURAS DE ESTÉTICA

Quiere la transformación. Oh, entusiásmate por la llama
dentro hay algo que se te escapa, que luce transformaciones;
aquel espíritu que proyecta, que tiene la maestría de lo terrestre,
nada ama tanto en la curva de la figura como el punto de inflexión.

Lo que se encierra en la permanencia ya es lo petrificado;
¿Vanamente se cree seguro al abrigo del gris anodino?
Espera, algo muy duro avisa a lo duro de lejos.
Ay... ¡se alza ausente martillo, prepara su golpe!

Al que como una fuente se derrama lo reconoce el reconocimiento;
y lo lleva encantado por la alegre, serena creación,
que a menudo concluye con el principio y comienza con el fin.

Todo espacio feliz es hijo o nieto de la separación
que ellos cruzan atónitos. Y Dafne, transformada,
quiere, desde que se siente laurel, que cambies en viento.

Rainer Maria Rilke
(trad. Eustaquio Barjau)

INTRODUCCIÓN
«En torno al conocimiento escénico»

Óscar Cornago
CSIC / Madrid

> Por fin el horizonte se nos aparece otra vez libre, aunque no esté aclarado, por fin nuestras naves pueden otra vez zarpar, desafiando cualquier peligro, toda aventura del cognoscente está otra vez permitida, el mar, *nuestro* mar, está otra vez abierto, tal vez no haya habido jamás *mar tan abierta*[1].

Con estas palabras saludaba Nietzsche a comienzos de los años ochenta del siglo XIX el nuevo horizonte de conocimiento que se abría al mundo; «por fin nuestras naves pueden otra vez zarpar» —decía el filósofo eufórico ante los nuevos retos del saber— en *La gaya ciencia*, la ciencia alegre, un proyecto de conocimiento (de filosofía) que tenía en su centro el cuerpo puesto en escena, un cuerpo que siente, que siente nostalgia, siente enfermedades, siente alegría y dolor... sobre todo dolor.

En la política, como en las artes o la ciencia, la Modernidad se ha vivido como un período de cierre de lo que venía de atrás y apertura de un tiempo nuevo, el final de una historia y el comienzo de otra..., nuevas preguntas, nuevas necesidades, nuevos presentes, otras posiciones ante el pasado, ante esa misma historia de la política, las artes y las ciencias. Sobre este cuestionamiento de sus propias bases epistemológicas se ha ido construyendo; lo esencial de la Modernidad, más allá de fundamentalismos de uno u otro signo, radica en el sentido de este movimiento, de este estar-pensándose. Ése es el gesto —físico— con el que Nietzsche se pone en escena, y poniéndose en escena *se realiza* como cuerpo que piensa, como inte-

1 Friedrich Nietzsche, *La gaya ciencia*, Madrid, 1988, p. 254.

lectual o como artista, en definitiva como persona que piensa y pensando hace, la teatralización del pensamiento.

El libro que presentamos, *Estética de lo performativo,* de Fischer-Lichte, editado por primera vez por la editorial alemana Suhrkamp en 2004 y traducido ya a varios idiomas, se sitúa dentro de esta tradición cultural y artística de la Modernidad. El amplio recorrido que se abre desde la Ilustración, pasando por el Romanticismo alemán hasta llegar a teorías más recientes es el horizonte frente al que se construye; desde ahí se propone otra forma de entender el fenómeno «teatral» y, en términos más generales, el hecho escénico.

Así se suceden a lo largo de estas páginas referencias clásicas, desde Diderot, Engel y Rousseau, Goethe y Schiller, Nietzsche o Freud, pasando por algunos de los pioneros de la sociología, la antropología y las teorías culturales contemporáneas, como James George Frazer, Robertson Smith, Emile Durkheim, Georg Simmel, Walter Benjamin, hasta autores de la II mitad del siglo XX, como Merleau-Ponty, J. L. Austin, Erving Goffman, Victor Turner, Maturana y Varela, Gregory Bateson, Paul Watzlawick, Gilles Deleuze, René Girard o Judith Butler, por citar sólo algunos nombres de campos diversos de los que se hace eco este estudio.

Todo esto ha abierto un campo de trabajo dentro de las Humanidades y las Ciencias Sociales que ha llevado a repensar las bases de la propia Estética como eje fundamental en el planteamiento de la Modernidad. Algunas de las referencias más recientes con las que dialoga Fischer-Lichte, no tan conocidas en el ámbito hispánico, como el estudio de Gernot Böhme, *Atmósferas. Ensayo para una nueva estética* (*Atmosphäre. Essays zur neuen Ästhetik*, 1995) o el de Martin Seel, *Estética del aparecer* (*Ästhetik des Erscheinen*, 2000), dan buena cuenta de estas nuevas líneas de trabajo marcadas por un llamativo tono escénico sobre el que nos queremos extender a lo largo de esta introducción.

Es esta mirada de largo alcance la que nos permite acordar con el autor de *La gaya ciencia* que efectivamente, a pesar del transitado paisaje cultural en el que nos situamos, hay algo que se vuelve a abrir, una aventura nueva para el cognoscente. Y este reto, que a pesar de los años sigue reformulándose como nuevo, tiene que ver con la escena, con el cuerpo y con la relación —en escena— con el otro. La condición de la Modernidad, es decir, el ser moderno, radica en la posibilidad de volver a repetir las palabras de Nietzsche, las mismas pero distintas; volver a afirmar la aventura del cognoscente, constatar una vez más que a comienzos del siglo XXI la empresa de pensar(se) en escena y desde la escena sigue siendo la misma que ha atravesado toda la Modernidad pero diferente, que el horizonte está abierto, que las naves pueden zarpar de nuevo.

El espacio abierto a partir de las propuestas teóricas de este volumen apuntan otras posibilidades de plantear la comunicación escénica y pensar el lugar de lo escénico, otro modo de entender al hombre-actor; de entender lo que ocurre en ese lugar de la «actuación» y cómo se desarrolla, y sobre todo la importancia —y la responsabilidad— para todo ello de quien está delante, el hombre-espectador, presente físicamente, mirando y sintiendo lo que pasa, o sea, lo que le pasa. A partir de esta perspectiva la dimensión estética, que ha sido hasta finales del siglo XX uno de los enfoques por antonomasia para estudiar el arte en sí mismo y éste como metáfora de la realidad, se entrelaza con una dimensión ética con la que todavía la teoría y la historia del arte, y en términos más generales la ciencia, no sabe bien qué hacer. Si la teatralidad es un mecanismo que remite a un afuera de lo que estamos viendo, la ética ilumina la otra cara de ese afuera, un más allá de las formas, las estéticas y los criterios artísticos, que los sostiene al tiempo que se sitúa en otro lugar.

El momento señalado como período de consolidación de esta perspectiva —vamos a llamarla «performativa»—, reflejo a su vez de transformaciones culturales que se han ido dando en ámbitos diversos, son los años sesenta y setenta, período en el que la performance se legitima como género artístico; una práctica que no por azar va a nacer unida a una intensa producción teórica y epistemológica. Sin embargo, la historia comienza siempre antes, y aunque en ciertos períodos los signos de cambio cobran mayor intensidad y las transformaciones se representan de manera más evidente, las evoluciones están ocurriendo constantemente. Por ello no es difícil encontrar antecedentes y precursores que antes de esas fechas ya anunciaban lo que estaba por venir, la diferencia, lo que siempre está viniendo.

Desde este acercamiento culturalmente complejo dialogan propuestas artísticas de épocas y géneros distintos, como obras y fenómenos culturales de los siglos XVIII y XIX, pasando por referencias centrales en el teatro del siglo pasado como Gordon Craig, Eisenstein, Reinhardt, Piscator, Grotowski, el Living Theater, el Performance Group o Eugenio Barba, o más hacia el campo de la música, las artes de acción y el *body art* de la II mitad de siglo: John Cage, Marina Abramović, Joseph Beuys y el entorno de Fluxus, Chris Burden, Gina Pane, Michel Journiac, Herrmann Nitsch; hasta exponentes de la escena alemana más teatral de los años ochenta y noventa como Klaus Michael Grüber, Frank Carstoff, Heiner Goebbels, Christoph Marthaler, Christoph Schlingensief, Einar Schleef, al lado de otros nombres de diversa procedencia, unos bien conocidos en los circuitos internacionales, como Robert Wilson, Societás Raffaelo Sanzio o Coco Fusco y Guillermo Gómez Peña, junto a otros no tan conocidos como Cornerstone Theater o Angelus Novus.

No es una coincidencia que, a nivel metodológico, sean también los años sesenta y setenta cuando empieza a conformarse en el ámbito cultural y sobre todo universitario lo que comúnmente se conoce como «teoría», en aquel entonces en pugna con las metodologías historicistas. De aquel viejo debate entre teoría e historia, vamos a rescatar una frase de Foucault, de *Las palabras y las cosas*, un libro de 1966, en la que se afirma con una claridad difícil de rebatir que el Estructuralismo no es «un método nuevo», sino la «conciencia despierta e inquieta del saber moderno»[2]. Estas fueron las décadas del Estructuralismo, que luego el medio universitario iba a transformar en Postestructuralismo, los años de la Semiótica y las teorías sistémicas, de las teorías del caos y de la divulgación en las Humanidades de la física de micropartículas, los fractales, la ecología y el pensamiento de la complejidad.

2 Michel Foucault, *Las palabras y las cosas. Una arqueología de las ciencias humanas*, Madrid, 1968, p. 206.

Algunos de estos enfoques resuenan en este volumen; unas veces porque sus instrumentos de análisis se apoyan en ellos, otras, al revés, porque le sirven para tomar distancia frente a ellos, como es el caso de la Semiótica.

Pero más allá de debates de época, a nivel metodológico una de las aportaciones del trabajo de Fischer-Lichte ya desde aquellos años es el haber sabido cruzar la teoría con la historia, pensar la teoría desde su acontecer histórico, en movimiento, y mirar la historia a partir de un aparato teórico hecho visible, discutido y abiertamente expuesto en relación con un presente, académico, cultural y escénico, desde el que se escribe. Separar una cosa de la otra, hacer teoría fuera de la historia, o historia sin un enfoque teórico que saque a la luz los instrumentos que se están utilizando para mirar el pasado, son pretensiones que esconden lo que no muestran, aunque el tiempo en algunos casos las justifique. En el prólogo a la tercera edición de la *Semiótica*, en 1994, cuyo segundo volumen estaba dedicado a la evolución histórica de los sistemas de significación escénicos, Fischer-Lichte insiste en este aspecto: «las definiciones de teatro nunca se refieren a la 'esencia' del teatro», sino que son «consideradas como instrumentos en función de las distintas finalidades del análisis en el marco de una determinada teoría»[3].

La historia tampoco es cuestión de esencias, sino de movimientos; las esencias competen más bien al instrumental puramente teórico, es decir, una construcción abstracta, sobre la que se *fundamenta* un modo de mirar, un lugar desde el que colocarse frente a la escena (de la historia) y una actitud o potencia con la que sostener una actuación, desde un presente, en ese teatro de operaciones que es también el medio universitario. Y el sentido de la historia tiene que ver antes con la dirección de esos movimientos, hechos siempre desde un presente, que con el sentido de esos fundamentos que, en cuanto históricos, son también móviles.

3 Erika Fischer-Lichte, *Semiotik des Theaters. Bd. 1*, Fráncfort, 1994, p. 2.

Esto explica que este libro no sea sólo un estudio *fundamentado* teóricamente de un modo de entender el funcionamiento de lo escénico a partir de su dimensión performativa, sino que sea también, antes que eso o necesariamente al mismo tiempo, un libro en el que se apunta una historia, una historia de las artes escénicas en la Modernidad, sobre todo a partir de los años sesenta y setenta del siglo XX, y de los modos culturales que las han acompañado; aunque esta perspectiva histórica haya quedado más desarrollada en otros trabajos de la autora como su *Historia breve del teatro alemán* (*Kurze Geschichte des deutschen Theaters*, 1992) o el *Teatro desde los años sesenta. Las fronteras de la neovanguardia* (*Theater seit dem 60. Jahren. Grenzgänge des Neo-Avantgardes*, 1999).

Pero además de esta historia, siempre está la otra, la historia de la que se forma parte por el hecho de estar haciendo, en este caso, teoría o historia, o ambas al mismo tiempo. Todo hacer –podemos afirmar retomando la perspectiva de trabajo que aquí se expone– es además, en alguna medida, un hacer historia. Por eso este libro no sólo proyecta un relato de las artes escénicas, resultado de una metodología y una teoría singular cuyo análisis es el objeto central del estudio, sino que también forma parte él mismo de otra historia.

Esta otra historia se inicia también, no por casualidad, en aquellos años setenta, los años de la semiótica, que en el caso de Fischer-Lichte se concretaron en monografías como *Significado. Una hermenéutica y una estética semiótica* (*Bedeutung-Einer semiotischen Hermeneutik und Asthetik*, 1979), previas a los tres volúmenes de su *Semiótica del teatro*, de 1983, traducida al castellano por Arco-Libros en 1999, y llega hasta esta *Estética de lo performativo*, resultado a su vez de varios proyectos de investigación que se han ido sucediendo. Entre medias, a la altura de los años noventa, vendría el estudio de la teatralidad como paradigma cultural de la Modernidad e instrumento de análisis en las Humanidades.

El concepto de «teatralidad», no sólo como objeto, sino como modo de estudio, como forma de mirar, sirvió para poner en escena los mecanismos de producción de significados en su proceso de funcionamiento y el resultado de estos procesos, las representaciones, que hasta entonces habían ocupado el centro de la atención.

Este planteamiento «teatral» hizo posible tomar la distancia necesaria desde la que sacar a la luz lo que había alrededor de estos mecanismos semióticos, lo que los determinaba y sobre los que se construían, como el propio cuerpo del «actor», las mediaciones materiales o las formas de percepción, mediaciones que no se agotaban en esos procesos pero que los sostenían, y a cada una de las cuales Fischer-Lichte dedicó un volumen coordinado dentro de la serie *Theatralität*. Curiosamente, la cualidad de estos materiales que más va a interesar va a ser el hecho de que no se agoten en el mismo proceso de la comunicación artística y social.

El arco que se dibuja entre un momento y otro, entre el estudio de los signos y el enfoque performativo, deja ver algunos de los ejes que han guiado la evolución desde los años setenta, no sólo de lo que se ha ido estudiando en el campo de las Humanidades en cada momento, sino sobre todo de las metodologías que se han ido empleando, es decir, de las formas que ese estudio ha ido adoptando, de los modos de mirar o las formas –*despiertas e inquietas*, como diría Foucault– del saber moderno.

La posibilidad de los estudios teatrales como área de investigación y conocimiento –una línea de trabajo en cuyo desarrollo dentro del ámbito alemán y europeo Fischer-Lichte ha trabajado activamente–, y no sólo del teatro como aprendizaje de una técnica que se agota en sí misma convertida en espectáculo o de una historia desligada de las preguntas que en cada momento se plantea una sociedad, tiene que ver también con estas formas de saber que –nuevamente en los términos performativos de la *Estética*– son antes que nada unas formas de hacer y estar en la historia, de estar frente al otro, de situarse en un presente, escénico o académico, desde el que entender a través del pasado lo que ahora (nos) está pasando. Estas formas han ido cambiando a lo largo de la historia porque han ido cambiando los presentes desde los que se construye y se entiende esa historia, han ido cambiando las preguntas y las necesidades, han ido cambiando los contextos culturales y artísticos, las maneras de hacer política, el funcionamiento de la economía y los modos de plantearse el hecho social.

No es un azar que «teoría» y «teatro» compartan una misma raíz etimológica; hacer teoría como un modo de construir una forma de mirar, de tomar distancia para desarrollar una perspectiva de estudio (de representación), es un modo de estar en un presente, es una manera de ser histórico y dialogar con la historia desde un espacio y un lugar concretos, desde un aquí y un ahora, desde un cuerpo; acercamientos que no son en primer lugar abstracciones. La actualidad de un tema, da lo mismo si es la Antigüedad clásica o el arte industrial tardorromano, sobre el que Alois Riegl estableció algunas de las bases de la teoría formal del arte, no depende del tema sino del modo como se aborda, del lugar desde el que se mira, de la escena en la que nos situamos para mirar. La historia no se construye como acumulación de pasados, sino como sucesión de presentes desde los que se proyectan esos pasados. No atender a los primeros para ver solamente los segundos, centrar la mirada en cualquier pasado sin saber que se mira desde un presente, es una forma de mixtificación que ha pesado en la propia historia del teatro, metáfora donde las haya para entender el funcionamiento de la historia siempre representada.

Esta *Estética* ocupa un lugar preciso dentro de ese recorrido, marca una estación de llegada que es a su vez un punto de partida, unas expectativas de futuro, de futuro de las artes escénicas y también del estudio de las artes escénicas como proyecto de investigación, creación y conocimiento dentro del paisaje en movimiento que conforman las distintas disciplinas académicas; una propuesta de estudio que se hace en relación, por tanto, con otras disciplinas que desde ámbitos como la filosofía y la estética, la antropología, la sociología, la teoría de los medios o de las artes en general están pensando también cómo seguir entendiendo esos aspectos tan amplios, pero tan concretos a la vez desde el punto de vista de su materialidad, que configuran lo escénico, aspectos como las formas de estar presente, los modos de entender el cuerpo y la acción, las maneras de percibir y recordar, la relación entre distintas materialidades, entre el cuerpo que actúa, la palabra escrita o la imagen, o la influencia de todo ello en la construcción de los significados.

Este estudio se sitúa en este momento, lo asume y lo discute. Para ello traza una genealogía a lo largo de la Modernidad de un abanico de ideas que están en la base de este enfoque teórico y que marcan algunas de las diferencias del momento actual en el ámbito de las Humanidades y las Ciencias Sociales, como el concepto de lo performativo, en torno al cual gira una constelación de nudos teóricos y escénicos: presencia, comunidad, contacto, *liveness*, corporalidad, atmósferas, sonoridad, materialidad, autopoiesis o liminalidad, por citar sólo algunos de los elementos de una enciclopedia cultural que expresa nuestro tiempo. Con esta finalidad se ha perfilado el instrumental de análisis, abandonando viejas concepciones acerca del hecho teatral para colocarse en un presente delimitado no sólo por las prácticas que caracterizan la escena contemporánea, sino por metodologías y líneas de trabajo procedentes de otros campos.

Este libro es, por tanto, el resultado del cruce entre un cierto paisaje histórico, artístico y cultural y un aquí y un ahora, fundamentado teóricamente, desde el que se mira y se construye ese paisaje. En ese cruce entre lo que se mira y desde donde se mira surge un presente, un presente escénico, un lugar en el que situarse, que podemos calificar también de «teatral» en el sentido que le daba Antoine Vitez al teatro como brújula para orientarse en el espacio.

Este recorrido metodológico, que es fácil de seguir atendiendo a la evolución de las disciplinas académicas desde los años setenta, pero que no se restringe a lo académico, no es objeto de discusión explícito en este libro, pero sí lo ha sido en otros de la misma autora, donde la necesidad de actualizar el campo de los Estudios Teatrales o de las Ciencias del Teatro –traduciendo literalmente el término alemán Theaterwissenschaft– ha sido objeto de su trabajo, como en su reciente *Ciencias del Teatro. Una introducción en los fundamentos de la materia* (*Theaterwissenschaft. Eine Einführung in die Grundlagen des Fachs*, 2010).

El interés de Fischer-Lichte, directora durante las dos últimas décadas del Instituto de Ciencias Teatrales de la Universidad Libre de Berlín y miembro de varias instituciones de ámbito nacional y europeo dedicadas a la producción del conocimiento y las políticas científicas, por la evolución de los campos de saber y más concretamente del teatro como espacio de investigación ha guiado buena parte de su actividad profesional. Lo más sorprendente de este currículum es que no ha dejado de mirar no sólo la escena, sino desde la escena, de manera que ha llegado a situar el conocimiento y sus formas de producción en lo más frágil y lo más difícil de aprehender, en la experiencia sensorial, en lo que ocurre en un espacio cuando un cuerpo actúa frente a otro.

Terminar vinculando el conocimiento y el acontecer estético a un proceso escénico «indisponible» *(unverfügbar)*, una cualidad en la que se insiste a lo largo de estas páginas, quiere decir, al menos en lo que respecta a las artes escénicas, aunque no sería difícil considerarlo como paradigmático para el fenómeno artístico en general, que no hay una verdad del conocimiento que no pase por un aquí y un ahora concretos, que no pase por un presente escénico determinado por una serie de variables materiales que no son trasladables a ninguna otra situación; en otras palabras, el conocimiento depende del lugar, de la forma de estar en ese lugar, de los cuerpos que lo ocupan y el tipo de relaciones que se establecen entre ellos. El conocimiento es una cuestión física, como diría Nietzsche, y por ello ética, podemos añadir.

Y esto no sólo afecta al modo de plantear una discusión teórica, sino en primer lugar a los espacios donde se generan esas discusiones, es decir, al propio medio académico, como supo ver otro filósofo más contemporáneo lector del primero, Peter Sloterdijk, en su libro *El pensador en escena*, que ahora podríamos parafrasear como *el profesor en escena*, cuando afirma poniéndose la careta de Zaratustra «que no existe nada más indecente que la falta de energía que se presenta como ciencia», ni «nada más sospechoso que el miedo a la verdad que se hace pasar por conciencia crítica; y nada más falso que esa incapacidad de reconocimiento que se hace pasar por una facultad superior»[4].

Es desde este lugar *fundamentalmente* teatral, pero teatral en el sentido en que lo presentaba Nietzsche, no como marca de lo falso, sino como necesidad de verdad y por tanto de aconteci-

4 Peter Sloterdijk, *El pensador en escena. El materialismo de Nietzsche*, Valencia, 2000, p. 135.

miento (de esa verdad), que hay que entender la insistencia de Fischer-Lichte, aun a riesgo de producir disonancias estilísticas, en la exacta traducción de cada uno de los términos que conforman este nuevo panorama teórico. En el centro de este sistema de elementos teóricos está el concepto de «representación», como no podía ser de otro modo en esta historia *teatral* que viene de los años de la semiótica y el estudio de los sistemas de producción de significados. El concepto de representación es el convidado de piedra en esta tragedia del conocimiento que, como todas las tragedias, trata de la salvación, de la salvación no *en* la historia –que diría Benjamin, otra de las voces que resuenan en este relato–, sino *de* la historia; en este caso, desde el punto de vista metodológico, de la historia del conocimiento, que es también por exclusión la historia de aquello que tradicionalmente no ha formado parte de ella, no ya como objeto de conocimiento, sino como forma de conocimiento, como ha sido el cuerpo en tanto que posibilidad.

El término «re-presentación» remite a una realidad previa que se vuelve a hacer presente por medio de una mediación material, como la palabra o la imagen, organizada por medio de unos códigos. El fundamento de la representación, lo representado, lo que en la tradición metafísica se ha considerado su «verdad», queda siempre fuera. Salvar el conocimiento de la historia de la representación, o de la historia del teatro como representación, no es empresa fácil, supondría abrirse a la posibilidad de la experiencia como forma del conocimiento. Desde esta dificultad podemos entender las palabras de Nietzsche al comienzo de esta introducción, su euforia ante una tarea inagotable, la tarea de ser humano *–demasiado humano–* no a partir de la asunción de una identidad previa, como actor en una representación ya escrita, en el sentido tradicional de la vida como teatro, sino como proceso inmediato de realización (escénica), un proceso que sólo puede entenderse como un continuo estar-haciéndose en cada espacio, en cada situación.

No es una coincidencia que sea éste –«realización escénica»– el término por el que se ha optado en sustitución de toda una serie de denominaciones que remiten ya sea a una realidad previa al propio hacer escénico, como «representación», «puesta en escena», «trabajo de dirección», ya sea a un material fijado, ya acabado como «obra», «espectáculo», «performance», «pieza» o «drama». Algunos de estos términos, especialmente el de «representación», son los que habitualmente se hubieran utilizado para traducir el original alemán «Aufführung» (representación en el sentido de realización) o la forma verbal «aufführen» (representar en el sentido de realizar). En su lugar se ha preferido subrayar la dimensión performativa de esta palabra, trasladándola al castellano como «realización escénica», que es el término que se va a utilizar en todo el libro en contextos que en otros estudios habrían hecho esperar algunas de las opciones antes mencionadas.

En tanto que «realización escénica» el hecho teatral no puede ser entendido sino como aquello que se está haciendo en un escenario, es decir, frente a un público, durante un momento preciso, y lo que ahí está ocurriendo como resultado de unas acciones, de una organización del espacio y del tiempo, y sobre todo de la manera de relacionar unos elementos con otros, un proceso que se ha traducido como «bucle de retroalimentación autopoético» («autopoietische feedback-Schleife»). El sentido de este proceso, que no se puede entender sino como algo que *está pasando*, está sujeto a lo que pueda ocurrir entre estos elementos y al modo como unos afectan a otros, algo que en cada ocasión va a ser distinto. Ahí pasa algo de lo que no se puede disponer, que no se puede trasladar a otro lugar, ni traducir a un lenguaje; ahí pasa algo que se está escapando tan pronto como está sucediendo y que pertenece al orden de la experiencia. Ligar el sentido de un acontecimiento, de una obra o una acción, de una historia o una persona, a ese momento de pérdida, de inestabilidad y quiebra, de aquello que más allá del lenguaje, de sus signos y significados, sólo pertenece a la experiencia, es entenderlo como algo vivo, algo que siempre va a ser otra cosa distinta de un significado, de una historia, de una imagen o un texto.

El lenguaje de Fischer-Lichte es de una claridad llamativa, más aún cuando se aplica a cuestiones teóricas complejas. Sin embargo, en esta *estética de lo performativo* lo más valioso, paradójicamente, no deja de ser aquello a lo que se quiere llegar, como el propio hecho escénico, pero que inevitablemente se escapa, incluso a pesar de tanta claridad; lo que no está disponible a través de conceptos ni teorías, aunque sean éstos los que hagan posible, incluso con sus limitaciones –o mejor dicho, gracias a estas–, mirar hacia ese lugar. Una teoría es, igual que el teatro, una forma de organizar la mirada, y las teorías más valiosas, como las realizaciones escénicas –artísticas– más difíciles, son las que apuntan a un lugar que siempre se va a escapar porque siempre va a estar más allá o más acá de esa mirada, incorporándose en los cuerpos –valga la redundancia–, son las que se construyen desde los límites hechos visibles de estos cuerpos como máquinas de interpretar, y desde ahí permiten pensar –quiero decir: sentir– esa posibilidad de salvación, no en la historia, sino de la historia, de la historia de las representaciones o de la historia de las teorías, que es otra forma de representación. Para ello es necesario, volviendo otra vez al autor de *La gaya ciencia*, la valentía para detenerse «ante la superficie, los pliegues, la piel; admirar la apariencia y creer en las formas, los tonos, las palabras»[5], la valentía para ser profundos sin abandonar la superficie, sin abandonar la escena y el juego (de la escena), sin dejar de hacerse cargo –responsable– de lo que está ocurriendo, aquí y ahora.

5 Friedrich Nietzsche, *La gaya ciencia*, *op. cit.*, p. 159.

ERIKA FISCHER-LICHTE

Estética de lo performativo

I. FUNDAMENTOS PARA UNA ESTÉTICA DE LO PERFORMATIVO

El 24 de octubre de 1975 tuvo lugar un acontecimiento notable y digno de reflexión en la galería Krinzinger de Innsbruck. La artista yugoslava Marina Abramović presentó su performance *Lips of Thomas*. La artista dio comienzo a la performance despojándose de toda su ropa. Después, Abramović se dirigió hacia la pared posterior de la galería para clavar una fotografía de un hombre de pelo largo que se parecía a ella y la enmarcó en una estrella de cinco puntas. Desde allí se dirigió a una mesa cercana cubierta por un mantel blanco sobre la que había una botella de vino tinto, un tarro de miel, una copa de cristal, una cuchara de plata y un látigo. Se sentó en una silla junto a la mesa, tomó el tarro de miel y la cuchara de plata. Lentamente empezó a vaciar el tarro de un kilo hasta comerse todo su contenido. Después vertió vino tinto en la copa de cristal y lo bebió a pequeños sorbos. Repitió esta acción hasta vaciar la botella y la copa. Acto seguido rompió la copa con la mano derecha y la mano comenzó a sangrar. Abramović se levantó, se dirigió hacia la pared en la que había clavado la fotografía y, de cara a los espectadores, se rasguñó en el vientre una estrella de cinco puntas con una hoja de afeitar. De su carne brotó sangre. Entonces tomó el látigo, se arrodilló de espaldas al público bajo la fotografía y se azotó violentamente la espalda. Aparecieron marcas ensangrentadas. Seguidamente se tendió en una cruz hecha de bloques de hielo con los brazos bien abiertos. Del techo colgaba un radiador orientado a su vientre cuyo calor hizo rebrotar la sangre de la estrella de cinco puntas tallada en su carne. Abramović permaneció inmóvil tendida sobre el hielo, claramente dispuesta a prolongar su martirio hasta que el radiador derritiera el hielo por completo. Tras permanecer treinta minutos en la cruz de hielo sin hacer amago de irse o de interrumpir la tortura, algunos espectadores fueron incapaces de soportar por más tiempo su suplicio. Se apresuraron hacia los bloques de hielo, tomaron a la artista, la recogieron de la cruz y la apartaron de allí. Con ello dieron fin a la performance.

La performance había durado dos horas. En el transcurso de esas dos horas la performadora y los espectadores crearon un acontecimiento que difícilmente podía tener cabida o gozar de legitimación en el marco de las tradiciones, las convenciones y los estándares tanto de las artes visuales como de las escénicas. La artista no construyó ningún artefacto con las acciones que ejecutó; no creó ninguna obra con existencia independiente de ella misma, fijable o transmisible. No actuó como una actriz que interpreta el papel de un personaje dramático que come mucha miel, bebe mucho vino y se causa las más diversas heridas. El significado de sus acciones no era el de un personaje que se hiere a sí mismo, sino que, al realizarlas, Abramović se hirió de verdad. Maltrató su cuerpo forzando deliberadamente sus límites. Lo sometió a un exceso de substancias que, ingeridas en pequeñas dosis, pueden tener un efecto fortalecedor. En tal cantidad, sin embargo, producen indudablemente malestar e indisposición, síntomas que, curiosamente, la artista no dejó traslucir ni en la expresión de su rostro ni en sus movimientos. Además, se infligió lesiones tan duras que el público se vio obligado a poner fin a un dolor físico tan extremo. Pero la artista tampoco dio muestras de dolor: no se sorprendió ni gritó ni contrajo su rostro por el sufrimiento. Evitó mostrar cualquier indicio corporal que pudiera ser interpretado como evidencia de indisposición o padecimiento, sin permitirle en ningún momento al espectador saber con seguridad si se trataba de la expresión de un dolor verdadero o si, por el contrario, se trataba de un dolor sólo fingido. La artista se limitó a llevar a cabo acciones que transformaron visiblemente su cuerpo –ingirió grandes cantidades de vino y miel y le produjo lesiones visibles–, sin mostrar signos externos de los estados internos causados por ellas.

De este modo sumió al espectador en una situación irritante, de profundos desconcierto y desasosiego, en la que normas, reglas y convicciones hasta ese momento incuestionables parecían haber perdido su validez. En la visita a una galería o a un teatro valía tradicionalmente la convención de que el papel del visitante era el de observador o espectador. Quien visita una galería contempla las obras expuestas desde una distancia mayor o menor, pero siempre sin llegar a tocarlas. El espectador, en el teatro, observa lo que ocurre sobre el escenario sin entrometerse, incluso en momentos de gran emoción o implicación internas, como cuando un personaje (Otelo) se dispone a matar a otro (Desdémona), pues es plenamente consciente de que el asesinato es sólo fingido y de que la actriz que interpreta a Desdémona al final aparecerá ante el telón y, junto al actor que encarna a Otelo, hará la consabida reverencia. En la vida cotidiana, por el contrario, es común intervenir inmediatamente cuando alguien amenaza con herirse a sí mismo o a herir a otro, incluso aunque con ello uno ponga en peligro su integridad física, y hasta su vida o las de otros. ¿Cuál de las dos normas debería haber seguido el espectador en la performance de Abramović? Se hirió, en efecto, a sí misma y estaba dispuesta a prolongar indefinidamente su autotortura. Si hubiera hecho lo mismo en cualquier lugar público, probablemente el espectador no habría vacilado demasiado tiempo en intervenir. Pero en este caso, ¿exigía el respeto a la artista que se la dejara llevar a cabo lo que parecían ser su plan y su intención artísticos? ¿No se corría el riesgo de arruinar su «obra»? Y por otro lado, ¿era compatible con criterios humanitarios y con la compasión humana contemplar tranquilamente cómo la artista se infligía lesiones? ¿Quería relegar al espectador al papel de *voyeur*? ¿O pretendía ponerlo a prueba para saber hasta qué punto debía llegar para que algún espectador pusiera fin a su tortura? ¿Qué norma debe prevalecer en una situación como ésta?

En su performance, y con su performance, Abramović creó una situación en la que hizo oscilar a los espectadores entre las normas del arte y las de la vida cotidiana, entre postulados estéticos y éticos. Los precipitó a una crisis para cuya superación no podían recurrir a parámetros de conducta que todos pudieran reconocer y aceptar. Los espectadores reaccionaron, en primer lugar, mostrando justamente los signos corporales que la performadora se había negado a mostrar: signos que se podían inferir a partir de estados internos, signos del increíble asombro que suscitó mientras comía y bebía, o del estupor que causó al romper la copa de cristal con la mano. Cuando la artista empezó a tallar la propia carne con una cuchilla de afeitar, se pudo oír literalmente cómo los espectadores contenían la respiración debido a la conmoción. Cualesquiera que fueran las transformaciones que experimentaron los espectadores durante esas dos horas, transformaciones que se manifestaban visiblemente en su expresión corporal, desembocaron en la realización de una acción perceptible por todos que tuvo consecuencias perceptibles: pusieron fin a la tortura de la artista, y con ella a la performance.

Cuando en el pasado se hablaba del potencial transformador del arte, de su capacidad para transformar tanto al artista como a los receptores de la obra, se solía partir de una concepción del arte en la que al artista lo poseía la inspiración o en la que el receptor vivía una experiencia interior que, como al Apolo de Rilke, le gritaba: «tienes que cambiar tu vida». No obstante, es sabido que en todos los tiempos ha habido artistas que han maltratado su cuerpo. En leyendas o autobiografías de ciertos artistas se habla continuamente de problemas de insomnio, del consumo de drogas o de alcohol, de diversos excesos y también de autolesiones. Pero en esos casos, la violencia que los artistas ejercían contra su propio cuerpo no era presentada como arte ni tampoco era considerada así por los demás[1]. Prácticas similares les fueron, en el mejor de los casos, toleradas a artistas de los siglos diecinueve y veinte, que son los inspiradores de los actuales, aceptán-

1 El caso de Antonin Artaud es una excepción. No fue el escenario el lugar sobre el que puso en práctica su idea de un teatro de la crueldad, un teatro como peste, que depara la muerte o la curación, sino en su propio cuerpo, maltratado por las drogas y la aplicación de electroshocks.

dolas como posible fuente de inspiración para sus logros artísticos o como precio a pagar por la consecución de la obra, pero sin considerar que le añadieran nada a ésta.

Por el contrario, hubo –y hay– otros ámbitos culturales en los que las prácticas por las que personas se infligen lesiones y se exponen a peligros graves no sólo se consideran «normales», sino incluso ejemplares y paradigmáticas. Me refiero sobre todo a los ámbitos de los rituales religiosos y de los espectáculos de feria. En muchas religiones se atribuye a los ascetas, eremitas, faquires o yoguis un estatus espiritual especial, pues no sólo se exponen a privaciones y peligros inconcebibles para los demás mortales, sino que se infligen las más increíbles torturas. Mucho más asombroso es aún el hecho de que, en determinadas fechas, grandes masas se sometan a tales prácticas, como en el caso de la flagelación. Práctica individual o grupal de frailes y monjas desde el siglo once, la autoflagelación se ha retomado posteriormente en las formas más diversas: por una parte, por procesiones de flagelantes que, desde mediados del siglo trece y durante el catorce viajaban por Europa y realizaban sus rituales públicamente, a menudo ante una audiencia numerosa; y por otra, por comunidades de penitentes, muy extendidas sobre todo en los países de lenguas latinas, cuyos miembros se azotaban mutuamente en diversas ocasiones. En la procesión del Viernes Santo en España y en determinados lugares del sur de Italia, durante la liturgia de Semana Santa y la procesión del Corpus Christi, todavía hoy se mantiene la práctica de la flagelación voluntaria.

A partir de la descripción de la vida de los Dominicos del convento Unterlinden, cerca de Colmar, redactada por Katharina von Gebersweiler a principios del siglo catorce, sabemos que la flagelación voluntaria era una parte fundamental –cuando no la culminación– de la liturgia:

> Al final de las oraciones matutina y nocturna, las hermanas permanecían en el coro, se quedaban de pie y rezaban hasta que recibían la señal para emprender sus ejercicios de devota veneración. Algunas se atormentaban con genuflexiones mientras alababan a Dios. Otras, abrasadas por el fuego del amor divino, eran incapaces de

> contener las lágrimas, y las acompañaban con lamentos de devoción. Estaban allí sin moverse hasta que se colmaban con nueva gracia y hallaban a «aquél que ama su alma» (*Cantar de Salomón* I, 7). Otras, por su parte, atormentaban diariamente su carne con los más duros maltratos: unas con varas de abedul, otras con látigos formados por tres o cuatro correas anudadas, unas terceras con cadenas de hierro, y aun otras con flagelos provistos de espinas. En Adviento y durante toda la Cuaresma, las hermanas se dirigían a la Sala Capitular o a otros lugares de reunión tras las oraciones matutinas y magullaban sus cuerpos severamente con los más variados instrumentos de flagelación hasta que brotaba la sangre, tanto era así que el azote de los latigazos resonaba por todo el convento y ascendía, más dulce que cualquier otra melodía, hasta los oídos del Señor Dios de Sabaoth[2].

El ritual de la autoflagelación llevaba a las monjas más allá de su vida conventual y las trasladaba a un estado que poseía un potencial transformador. La tortura que infligían a su carne y la violencia que ejercían sobre su cuerpo operaban una perceptible transformación de su físico, que se hacía efectiva asimismo como proceso de transfiguración espiritual: «A aquellos que se acercaban a Dios por todos estos caminos se les iluminaba el corazón, se les purificaban los pensamientos, se liberaban de sus pasiones, se les aclaraba la conciencia y su espíritu se elevaba hacia Dios»[3].

La autoflagelación voluntaria, que inflige daño al cuerpo con el fin de conducir a una transformación espiritual, es reconocida todavía hoy por la Iglesia Católica como una de las prácticas para penitentes[4].

2 Jeanne Ancelet-Hustache, «Les 'Vitae sororum' d'Unterlinden. Edition critique du manuscrit 508 de la bibliothèque de Colmar», en: *Archives d'histoire doctrinale et littéraire du Moyen Âge* (1930), pp. 317-509, pp. 340 y s. Agradezco esta referencia a la obra de Niklaus Largier *Lob der Peitsche. Eine Kulturgeschichte der Erregung*, Múnich, 2001, pp. 29 y ss.

3 Ancelet-Hustache, «Les 'Vitae sororum' d'Unterlinden», p. 341, cit. por Largier 2001, *Lob der Peitsche*, p. 30.

4 Véase E. Bertaud, «Discipline», *Dictionnaire de spiritualité 3*, París, 1957, donde se

Un segundo ámbito en el que se aceptan las autolesiones y la exposición voluntaria al peligro es el de los espectáculos de feria. En ellos se llevan a cabo prácticas que, en «condiciones normales», implican graves lesiones. Sin embargo, a quienes las realizan, por ejemplo en los números en los que tragan fuego o espadas, o cuando se perforan la lengua con agujas, milagrosamente no les ocurre nada. Por otro lado, los artistas circenses ejecutan otras acciones extremadamente peligrosas que los ponen en peligro real, y en las que arriesgan incluso la vida. La maestría de este tipo de artistas se demuestra, pues, por su capacidad de afrontar el peligro. En pruebas como los ejercicios sobre el alambre sin red, la doma de fieras y el adiestramiento de serpientes, basta con que la concentración del acróbata o del domador se relaje una fracción de segundo para que el siempre acechante peligro se haga realidad: el acróbata cae al suelo, el domador es atacado por el tigre y el encantador de serpientes es mordido o estrangulado por ellas. Éste es el momento más temido por el público y al mismo tiempo el más febrilmente esperado, el momento al que, llegue a hacerse realidad o no, se orientan sus miedos más profundos, su fascinación y su curiosidad morbosa. En estos espectáculos lo esencial no es tanto la transformación de los actores, o incluso la de los espectadores, cuanto la exhibición de la singular fuerza física y mental de los artistas circenses, cuyo objetivo es asombrar y maravillar al público, precisamente el tipo de emoción por la que los espectadores de Abramović se sintieron atrapados.

La transformación de los espectadores en actores constituye la segunda peculiaridad de la performance de Abramović. A este

---

menciona que la autoflagelación, si se practica en las condiciones moderadas «en las que ellos las llevan a cabo», permite «acercarse con humildad al sufrimiento de Cristo durante su flagelación. [...] La práctica de la flagelación de ningún modo pertenece a la espiritualidad monástica primitiva o al primer cristianismo, en los que los auténticos ejercicios de penitencia, el ayuno, la castidad y la vigilia, estaban en la oración. La flagelación, por tanto, debe considerarse una práctica digna de atención, que se practicaba desde su popularización de mano de los Santos y que hoy constituye una parte fundamental de la vida religiosa» (p. 1310), cit. por Largier 2001, *Lob der Peitsche*, p. 40.

respecto pueden mencionarse ejemplos de distintos ámbitos culturales, como los rituales penales de inicios de la Modernidad. Como ha mostrado Richard van Dülmen, después de una ejecución pública los espectadores se apiñaban alrededor del cadáver para poder tocar su cuerpo, su sangre, sus miembros e incluso la soga con la que había sido ajusticiado. De ese contacto esperaban obtener la curación de ciertas enfermedades y, en un sentido más amplio, la garantía de su bienestar y de su integridad física[5]. Esta transformación del espectador en actor se realizaba con la esperanza de un cambio duradero en el propio cuerpo. Su fin era, así, completamente distinto del de la transformación que experimentó el espectador en la performance de Abramović, pues en este último caso no se trataba de la salud física del espectador, sino de la de la artista. Con las acciones que, por medio del contacto con la performadora, lo transformaron en actor, el espectador pretendía salvaguardar la integridad física de la artista. Por lo tanto, sus acciones eran consecuencia de una decisión ética orientada hacia otra persona, en este caso la artista.

En este mismo sentido, se diferencian también radicalmente de las acciones por las que los espectadores se transformaban en actores durante las *serate* futuristas, las *soirées* dadaístas y los «tours guiados» de los surrealistas de principios del siglo veinte. Pues en dichos casos se impelía a los espectadores a la acción mediante *shocks* sabiamente administrados. La transformación del espectador en actor se seguía, con un cierto automatismo, de la pauta de la escenificación y su realización estaba muy lejos de ser el resultado de una decisión consciente de los espectadores, según se puede inferir sin mayores dificultades a partir de los informes sobre ese tipo de actos y de los los manifiestos de los propios artistas. En su manifiesto «El teatro de variedades» (1913), Filippo Tommaso Marinetti, por poner un solo ejemplo, propone las siguientes estrategias para provocar a los espectadores:

5 Véase al respecto Richard van Dülmen, *Theater des Schreckens. Gerichtspraxis und Strafrituale der frühen Neuzeit*, Múnich, 1988, especialmente pp. 161 y ss.

> Introducir la sorpresa y la necesidad de reacción por parte de los espectadores de la platea, de los palcos y de la galería. Algunas propuestas a propósito: poner cola en algunos asientos para que el espectador, hombre o mujer, que permanezca encolado, suscite la hilaridad general. (El frac o la *toilette* dañada serán naturalmente pagados a la salida). –Vender el mismo asiento a diez personas: lo que implica embarazo, escaramuzas, altercados–. Ofrecer asientos gratuitos a señores o señoras notablemente maniáticos, irritables o excéntricos, que vayan a provocar alborotos con gestos obscenos, pellizcos a las mujeres u otros comportamientos extraños. Espolvorear los asientos con polvos que provoquen picores, estornudos, etc.[6]

Se trataba aquí, pues, de un espectáculo artístico en el que los espectadores se convertían en actores por el impacto del *shock*; además, el resto de los espectadores y los organizadores del acto los veían por momentos enfadados, irritados, risueños, enfurecidos, e incluso en otros estados de ánimo. En la performance de Abramović la transformación de algunos espectadores en actores suscitó emociones encontradas entre los demás espectadores: vergüenza, por ser demasiado cobardes para intervenir, enfado quizá, o acaso ira porque la performance hubiera terminado antes de tiempo y no se hubiera podido comprobar hasta qué punto estaba dispuesta a llegar la artista en su tortura voluntaria. Quizá también sentimientos positivos como alivio y satisfacción porque alguien se decidiera por fin a dar por terminado el suplicio, el de la performadora y probablemente el de algunos de los espectadores[7].

6 Filippo Tommaso Marinetti, «El teatro de variedades», en José A. Sánchez (ed.), *La escena moderna: manifiestos y textos sobre el teatro de la época de vanguardias*, Madrid, 1999, p. 119.

7 A eso mismo se refería la artista de performance Rachel Rosenthal cuando afirmó que «[i]n performance art, the audience, from its role as sadist, subtly becomes the victim. It is forced to endure the artist's plight emphatically or to examine its own response of voyeurism and pleasure, or smugness and superiority. [...] In any case, the performer holds the reins. [...] The audience usually 'gives up' before the artist.» Rachel Rosenthal, «Performance and the Masochist Tradition», en *High Performance*, invierno 1981/2, p. 24.

Independientemente de cómo pudiéramos juzgar las coincidencias y las diferencias tras un análisis pormenorizado, no se puede pasar por alto que la performance de Abramović presentaba rasgos tanto de ritual como de espectáculo, que oscilaba permanentemente entre su condición de ritual y su condición de espectáculo. Como ritual[8] causó la transformación de la artista y la de algunos espectadores, sin que ello tuviera como consecuencia, como suele ser el caso en los rituales, un cambio de estatus público o de identidad. Como espectáculo causó asombro y repulsa en los espectadores, les asustó y les incitó al voyerismo.

Una performance así escapa al alcance de las teorías estéticas tradicionales. Se resiste tenazmente a la aspiración de una estética hermenéutica: la comprensión de la obra de arte. En este caso se trata menos de comprender las acciones que llevó a cabo la artista que de comprender sus experiencias mientras lo hacía y las que suscitó en los espectadores. Es decir, se trata de la transformación de quienes participaron en la performance.

Esto no significa que para el espectador no hubiera nada que interpretar o que los objetos empleados y las acciones que se llevaron a cabo con ellos –y con respecto a ellos– no pudieran interpretarse como signos. La estrella de cinco puntas, por ejemplo, podría aludir a una gran variedad de contextos míticos, religiosos, culturales, históricos y políticos, sin dejar ni mucho menos de lado la posibilidad de interpretarla como referencia al símbolo de la Yugoslavia socialista. Cuando la artista enmarcó su fotografía con una estrella de cinco puntas y luego se talló otra igual en el vientre, el espectador pudo interpretar estas acciones como un signo de la ubicuidad del Estado, que constriñe al individuo con sus leyes, normas e injusticias, como signo de la violencia que ese mismo Estado ejerce sobre el individuo, y que se inscribe en su cuerpo. Cuando la performadora, sentada en la mesa cubierta con un mantel blanco, usó una cuchara de plata y una copa de cristal, el espectador pudo entenderlo como la reproducción de

8 Para el concepto de ritual, véase el capítulo sexto, apartado 3: «Liminaridad y transformación».

las condiciones de la vida cotidiana en un entorno burgués –aunque la exagerada ingesta de miel y de vino podía implicar tal vez una crítica a la sociedad de consumo y de despilfarro capitalista y burguesa. O quizá observara en estas acciones una alusión a la Eucaristía. Si se centraba en este contexto, el espectador podría haber interpretado la flagelación como una referencia al tormento de Cristo y a los flagelantes cristianos, pero si elegía otro, podía haberse asociado con castigos y torturas estatales, o incluso con prácticas sexuales sadomasoquistas. Asimismo, cuando la artista se tendió con los brazos abiertos sobre la cruz de hielo, el espectador probablemente lo asociara con la crucifixión de Cristo. Y su propia iniciativa de bajarla de la cruz quizá la entendiera como un modo de evitar la repetición de la muerte de Cristo como sacrificio, o como una recreación del descenso de la cruz. El espectador podría haber interpretado el conjunto de la performance como un acto de oposición a la violencia infligida al individuo por parte del Estado, en su nombre y en el de la comunidad, una violencia entendida no sólo en sentido político, sino también religioso. Una violencia, en fin, que él mismo se ve obligado a infligirse. En este caso, es probable que el espectador la hubiera entendido como una crítica a determinadas condiciones sociales, las que hacen posible que el individuo sea víctima del Estado y le obligan a ser víctima de sí mismo.

Tales interpretaciones, por más que puedan parecer plausibles en una reflexión posterior, quedan fuera del acontecimiento de la performance. Además, durante su transcurso, los espectadores no pudieron aventurarse a tales hipótesis interpretativas más que de manera muy limitada. Pues el significado de las acciones ejecutadas por la performadora no se limitaba a «comer y beber en exceso», «tallarse una estrella de cinco puntas en el vientre» o «autoflagelarse»; al contrario, las acciones realizaban exactamente lo que significaban. Constituyeron una nueva realidad, una realidad propia, tanto para la artista como para los espectadores, es decir, para todos los participantes en la performance. Esta realidad no fue solamente interpretada, sino que fue sobre todo y principalmente experimentada en sus efectos. Causó a los espectadores asombro, espanto, repulsa, repugnancia, malestar, vértigo, fascinación, curiosidad, compasión, agonía y les precipitó a realizar a su vez acciones constitutivas de realidad. Es de suponer que las emociones que se suscitaron, tan intensas como para que algunos de los espectadores finalmente se decidieran a intervenir, excedieron con creces las posibilidades de la reflexión y los esfuerzos de constitución de significado y de interpretación del acontecimiento. No se trataba de comprender la performance, sino de experimentarla y de enfrentarse a experiencias que, *in situ*, escapaban a la capacidad de reflexión.

De esta manera, la performance creó una situación en la que dos relaciones fundamentales tanto para una estética hermenéutica como para una estética semiótica fueron redefinidas: en primer lugar, la relación entre sujeto y objeto, entre observador y observado, entre espectador y actor. Y en segundo lugar, la relación entre la corporalidad o materialidad de los elementos y su signicidad, entre significante y significado.

Tanto para una estética hermenéutica como para una estética semiótica es esencial distinguir netamente entre sujeto y objeto. El artista, sujeto (1), crea la obra de arte como un artefacto separable, fijable, transmisible e independiente de sí. Dada esta primera premisa, un receptor cualquiera, sujeto (2), puede hacerla objeto de su percepción y de su interpretación. El artefacto fijable y transmisible, la obra de arte como objeto, garantiza que el receptor se pueda poner frente a ella una y otra vez, que descubra continuamente en ella nuevos elementos estructurales y que le pueda atribuir siempre significados nuevos y distintos.

La performance de Abramović no brindaba esta posibilidad. Como ya se ha mencionado, la artista no fabricó ningún artefacto, sino que trabajó sobre su propio cuerpo y lo modificó ante los ojos de los espectadores. En lugar de una obra de arte, que es independiente de la artista y de los receptores, Abramović creó un acontecimiento en el que todos los presentes se vieron involucrados. Este hecho implica que los espectadores tampoco tenían frente a sí un objeto independiente de ellos que pudieran percibir e interpretar una y otra vez de modo distinto. Tuvo lugar una situación *hic et nunc* en la que los presentes, que compartían un mismo espacio y tiempo, se convirtieron en cosujetos. Sus acciones desencadenaron reacciones psicológicas, afectivas, volitivas, energéticas y motoras que dieron lugar a su vez a otras acciones. Mediante este proceso, la relación dicotómica entre sujeto y objeto se transformó en una relación oscilante en la que las respectivas posiciones no se podían determinar ya con claridad ni se podían diferenciar netamente. Los espectadores que entraron en contacto con la artista para bajarla de la cruz de hielo ¿establecieron acaso una relación entre cosujetos? O, por el contrario, su intervención, realizada sin su requerimiento ni su consentimiento expreso, ¿convirtió a la artista en objeto? O planteado a la inversa, ¿no serían acaso los espectadores los que terminaron convertidos en marionetas y objetos de la artista? No disponemos de una respuesta clara y unívoca a estas preguntas.

La alteración de la relación entre sujeto y objeto está estrechamente vinculada con la transformación de la relación entre materialidad y signicidad, entre significante y significado. Tanto en la estética hermenéutica como en la semiótica todo se orienta a la consideración de la obra de arte como signo, de lo que no se puede colegir que pasen por alto la materialidad de la obra, muy al contrario, pues a cada uno de los detalles del aspecto material se le presta gran atención. Pero todo lo perceptible de ese aspecto material se considera como signo, y se interpreta en consecuencia: sea el grosor de las pinceladas y los matices específicos de color en una pintura, o el sonido, la rima y la métrica de un poema. De este modo, cada elemento se convierte en un significante al que se le pueden atribuir significados. Así, en la obra de arte no hay nada más allá de la relación entre significante y significado, sin perjuicio de que a un mismo significante se le puedan atribuir los más diversos significados.

Es cierto que en la performance de Abramović, el espectador podría muy bien haber llevado a cabo los preceptivos procesos de constitución de significado y haberle asignado el suyo a cada uno de los objetos y de los actos, como muestran las hipótesis de interpretación para un espectador ficticio mencionadas más arriba. De igual modo, es evidente que las reacciones físicas de los espectadores suscitadas al observar las acciones de Abramović no se pueden reducir a los posibles significados que esos mismos espectadores quieran atribuirles. Si cuando Abramović se rasguñó la estrella en la piel los espectadores apenas pudieron contener la respiración o sintieron náuseas, no se debió a que interpretaran tal acción como la inscripción de la violencia del Estado en el cuerpo, sino a que vieron brotar la sangre e imaginaron el dolor en el propio cuerpo, y esa percepción incidió directamente en su reacción corporal. La corporalidad o materialidad de la acción prevaleció en este caso claramente sobre la signicidad. Es decir, que la corporalidad o materialidad no ha de ser entendida como excedente físico en el sentido de un resto irredimible, «un resto terrenal que sobrellevar penosamente»*, pues no surge de los significados que se le asignan a cada acción. Es, al contrario, anterior a todo intento de interpretación que pretenda ir más allá de la autorreferencialidad de la acción. El efecto físico motivado por las acciones parece prevalecer en este caso. La materialidad del acontecimiento no llega a adquirir el estatus de signo, no desaparece en él, sino que produce un efecto propio e independiente de su estatus sígnico. Y puede que precisamente ese efecto –el corte en la respiración o la sensación de náusea– sea el que ponga en marcha el proceso de reflexión. Una reflexión que probablemente se dirija menos a los significados atribuibles a cada acción que a la pregunta de por qué una acción determinada ha desencadenado una determinada reacción. ¿Qué relación hay en este caso entre efecto y significado?

Por un lado, estos desajustes en las relaciones entre sujeto y objeto y entre los estatus material o corporal y el de significante, tal y como se proponen en la performance *Lips of Thomas* de Abramović, parecen establecer una nueva relación entre las categorías de sentir, pensar y actuar, en cuya investigación detallada entraremos más adelante. En cualquier caso, a los espectadores se les autoriza a actuar, a participar como actores.

Por otro lado, estos desajustes ponen en cuestión la distinción tradicional, precisamente en tanto que heurística, entre estética

* Johann Wolfgang von Goethe, *Faust II*, versos 11954 y ss. [Nota de los T.: distinguiremos a partir de ahora las notas de la autora de las de los traductores numerando las primeras y marcando con un asterisco las segundas].

de la producción, estética de la obra y estética de la recepción, y hacen que quede obsoleta. Pues si no puede hablarse ya de una obra de arte que exista independientemente de su productor y de su receptor, si en lugar de ella nos encontramos frente a un acontecimiento en el que todos los participantes están involucrados –aunque en distinta medida y con distinta función–, y si la «producción» y la «recepción» tienen lugar en el mismo espacio y tiempo, parece extremadamente problemático continuar operando con parámetros, categorías y criterios desarrollados en el ámbito de tres estéticas distintas. Como mínimo hemos de volver a examinarlas para comprobar en qué medida siguen siendo instrumentos idóneos.

Esta revisión parece especialmente urgente si tenemos en cuenta que *Lips of Thomas* no fue desde luego ni el único ni el primer acontecimiento artístico en el que las antedichas relaciones sufrieron una redefinición. A principios de los años sesenta se produjo en las artes occidentales un generalizado e insoslayable giro performativo[9] que no sólo tuvo como consecuencia un impulso de la misma naturaleza en cada una de ellas en particular, sino que condujo a la creación de un nuevo género artístico: el llamado arte de acción y de la performance. Desde entonces, las fronteras entre las distintas artes se han vuelto cada vez más tenues, se ha tendido progresivamente a la creación no tanto de obras de arte cuanto de acontecimientos, que se empezaron a realizar con llamativa frecuencia en forma de realización escénica*.

9 Para el concepto de lo performativo, de la manera que lo entenderemos aquí, véase el capítulo segundo.

* La estética de lo performativo de Fischer-Lichte, como se dedicará a explicar ella misma por extenso, se basa en una cierta comprensión del concepto de *Aufführung*, un término que en circunstancias normales traduciríamos sin más por 'representación', como cuando hablamos de una representación teatral u operística. Sin embargo, la carga teórica del término español, de la que está libre la voz alemana, y, más en segundo término, su polisemia, lo hacen incompatible con los supuestos teóricos mantenidos en este libro. La autora parte de que la *Aufführung* (que verteremos por 'realización escénica') no está al servicio de la expresión o de la exposición de ningún contenido dado previamente –en general, un texto dramático–, lo que convierte al término 'repre-

En las artes visuales el carácter de realización escénica predominaba ya en el *action painting* y en el *body art*, como ocurriría posteriormente también en las esculturas de luz y en las videoinstalaciones, entre otros. En ellas, o bien el artista se presentaba a sí mismo ante el público en la acción de pintar y exhibía su cuerpo, que previamente había caracterizado de un modo particular y/o con el que actuaba de manera singular, o bien se invitaba al observador a moverse por la exposición y a interactuar con los elementos expuestos mientras los otros asistentes observaban. La visita se convertía en muchos casos en la participación en una realización escénica: muchas veces se trataba además de experimentar la especial atmósfera creada en los distintos espacios que rodeaban a los visitantes.

Fueron sobre todo artistas visuales y plásticos, como Joseph Beuys, Wolf Vostell, el grupo Fluxus o los artistas del accionismo vienés quienes crearon en los años sesenta el nuevo género del arte de acción y de la performance. Desde principios de los sesenta hasta hoy mismo, Herrmann Nitsch lleva a cabo acciones consistentes en desollar y despedazar un cordero en las que no solamente los actores, sino también los demás participantes entran en contacto con objetos tabuizados en otros contextos, en ellas es posible además tener experiencias sensorialmente singulares. En las acciones de Nitsch los espectadores se involucran también físicamente, y se convierten en actores: se les rocía con sangre, excrementos, agua de fregar y otros fluidos, y se les da la oportunidad de chapotear en ellos, de destripar ellos mismos al cordero, de comer carne y de beber vino[10].

---

sentación' en inadecuado para transmitir su significado. Lo que en ella se produce es autorreferencial y constitutivo de realidad, y es además resultado de la intervención tanto de los actores como de los espectadores. Es justamente performativo, de ahí que tanto el sustantivo *Aufführung* como el verbo *aufführen* se correspondan con bastante exactitud con los términos ingleses *performance* y *to performe* respectivamente. Nos decidimos, pues, por 'realización escénica', a pesar de que no es de uso común –como sí lo es la voz alemana–, porque además de expresar con bastante exactitud el significado del término original conserva las nociones de actividad y de transitividad. Cuando el contexto lo aconseje usaremos meramente el término 'realización'.

También a principios de los sesenta los artistas FLUXUS comenzaron a realizar sus acciones. En su tercera acción, que tuvo lugar en el Auditorium Maximum de la Technische Hochschule de Aquisgrán el 20 de julio de 1964, téngase en cuenta la fecha*, y que llevaba el título *Actions / Agit Pop/ De-collage / Happening / Events / Antiart/ L'austrisme / Art total / Refluxus – Festival der neuen Kunst*, participaron los artistas FLUXUS Eric Andersen, Joseph Beuys, Bazon Brock, Stanley Brouwn, Henning Christiansen, Robert Filliou, Ludwig Gosewitz, Arthur Køpcke, Thomas Schmit, Ben Vautier, Wolf Vostell y Emmett Williams. En otra de sus acciones: *Kukei, akopee – Nein!, Braunkreuz, Fettecken, Modellfettecken* [*Kukei, akopee ¡No!, cruz parda, esquinas de grasa, esquinas de grasa modelo*], Beuys provocó un altercado que no se sabe bien si fue consecuencia del gesto mayestático de elevar horizontalmente sobre su cabeza una barra de cobre recubierta de fieltro o del vertido de ácido clorhídrico (las circunstancias exactas son inciertas si nos atenemos al testimonio de la fiscalía general en las indagaciones que se llevaron a cabo entre 1964 y 1965). Los estudiantes abordaron el escenario y uno de ellos le propinó a Beuys varios puñetazos en la cara; empezó a salirle sangre de la nariz y su camisa blanca quedó empapada en ella. Beuys, completamente cubierto de sangre, y en plena hemorragia, reaccionó sacando chocolatinas de una caja y arrojándoselas al público. Rodeado por un griterío enloquecido y por un tumulto de personas enardecidas, Beuys tomó un crucifijo con su mano izquierda y lo levantó implorante, sin moverse del sitio, mientras con su mano derecha también alzada parecía pedir calma[11]. Se trataba también en este caso de la definición conjunta

10 Véase al respecto Erika Fischer-Lichte, «Verwandlung als ästhetische Kategorie. Zur Entwicklung einer neuer Ästhetik des Performativen», en Fischer-Lichte *et al.* (eds.), *Theater seit den sechziger Jahren*, Tubinga/Basilea 1998, pp. 21-91, especialmente pp. 25 y ss.

* Se trata del vigésimo aniversario del atentado fallido contra Hitler que llevó a cabo Claus von Stauffenberg.

11 Véase al respecto Uwe M. Schneede, *Joseph Beuys – Die Aktionen*. Aspectos de la obra comentados y con documentación fotográfica, Osfildern-Ruit, 1994, especialmente pp. 42-67.

de las relaciones entre los participantes, y también en este caso el estatus de corporalidad o materialidad se impuso al sígnico.

En la música el impulso performativo llegó ya a principios de los cincuenta con los *Events* y *Pieces* de John Cage[12]. En este caso eran los más diversos acciones y sonidos, especialmente los producidos por los propios oyentes, los que daban lugar a un acontecimiento sonoro, mientras el músico, como fue el caso del pianista David Tudor en *4'33"* (1952), no tocaba ni una sola nota al piano. En los años sesenta fue aumentando el número de compositores que comenzaron a dar indicaciones a los músicos en sus partituras con el fin de que realizaran movimientos visibles para el público. El carácter de realización escénica de los conciertos (ya de por sí presente) empezó igualmente a ganar en importancia. Buena prueba de ello son los nuevos conceptos acuñados por algunos compositores, como el de 'música escénica' (Karlheinz Stockhausen), el de 'música visual' (Dieter Schnebel) o el de 'teatro instrumental' (Mauricio Kagel). Con ello se establecieron nuevas relaciones entre músicos y oyentes[13].

En literatura el impulso performativo no sólo se manifestó en lo intrínsecamente literario, por ejemplo, en la llamada novela laberíntica, que convierte al lector en autor al ofrecerle materiales que puede combinar a voluntad[14]. Este impulso también se manifiesta en la gran cantidad de recitales literarios en los que el público se congrega para escuchar la voz de un poeta o de un escritor. Un claro ejemplo es la espectacular lectura que Günter Grass hizo de su obra *El rodaballo* el 12 de junio de 1992 en el Thalia-Theater de Hamburgo, en la que fue acompañado por un percusionista. Pero

12 Véase *Untitled Event*, que tuvo lugar en el Black Mountain College en 1952, Erika Fischer-Lichte, «Grenzgänge und Tauschhandel. Auf dem Wege zu einer performativen Kultur», en Fischer-Lichte *et al.* (eds.), *Theater seit den sechziger Jahren*, Tubinga/Basilea, 1998, pp. 1-20.

13 Véase al respecto Christa Brüstle, «Performance/Performativität in der neuen Musik», en Erika Fischer-Lichte y Christoph Wulf (eds.), *Theorien des Performativen* (= *Paragrana*, vol. 10, cuaderno I), Berlín, 2001, pp. 271-283.

14 Véase Monika Schmitz-Emans, «Labyrinthbücher als Spielanleitungen», en Erika Fischer-Lichte y Gertrud Lehnert (eds.), *[(v)er] SPIEL [en] Felder – Figuren – Regeln* (= *Paragrana*, vol. 11, cuaderno 1), Berlín, 2002, pp. 179-207.

el público no sólo llena las salas en las que leen autores vivos, sino que gusta igualmente de asistir a lecturas de las obras de poetas muertos mucho tiempo atrás. Ejemplos destacados son la lectura que Edith Clever hizo de *La Marquesa de O* (1989), la que Bernhard Minetti hizo del cuento de los hermanos Grimm *Bernhard Minetti* (1990), o el acto *Homer lesen* [*Leer a Homero*], que realizó la compañía Angelus Novus en 1986 en la Künstlerhaus de Viena. Los integrantes de la compañía leyeron, por turnos pero sin interrupciones, los 18.000 versos de *La Ilíada* durante veintidós horas. En salas adyacentes había ejemplares de la obra, que invitaban a los oyentes, dispersados por todo el edificio, a la lectura individual. De esa manera se marcaba con claridad la diferencia entre leer el texto y escuchar la lectura pública, entre un leer como desciframiento del texto y un leer como realización escénica. Finalmente, la atención de los oyentes terminó dirigiéndose a la materialidad específica de cada una de las voces de los lectores –su timbre, su volumen, su intensidad, etc.–, cuya importancia se hacía especialmente clara en cada cambio de turno. La literatura se presentaba enfáticamente como realización escénica: cobraba vida a través de las voces de los lectores físicamente presentes y estimulaba la imaginación de los oyentes, igualmente presentes, apelando a sus sentidos. Las distintas voces eran mucho más que un medio para la transmisión del texto, precisamente porque, debido la alternancia, cada uno de los lectores le confería al texto su propio estilo e influía directamente sobre los espectadores independientemente de lo que leyeran. Además, la realización escénica estuvo condicionada por el factor tiempo: el prolongado lapso de veintidós horas no sólo modificó la percepción de los participantes, sino que también les hizo conscientes de tal modificación. El transcurrir del tiempo condicionó la percepción y, sobre todo, condicionó la posibilidad de hacer consciente la trasformación que se produjo en ella. Los participantes hablaron más tarde sobre la experiencia de transformación de sí durante la celebración del acontecimiento[15].

15 Véase al respecto Reiner Steinweg, «Ein 'Theater der Zukunft'. Über die Arbeit von Angelus Novus am Beispiel von Brecht und Homer», en *Falter*, 23, 1986.

También el teatro experimentó un impulso performativo en los años sesenta. Consistió sobre todo en una redefinición de la relación entre actores y espectadores. En el primer «Experimenta» (celebrado entre el 3 y el 10 de junio de 1966 en Fráncfort) se estrenó en el Theater am Turm *Insultos al público*, de Peter Handke, bajo la dirección de Claus Peymann. La idea era redefinir el teatro a partir de la relación entre actores y espectadores, legitimarlo no sólo en tanto que representación de «otro mundo». El teatro dejaba de entenderse como la representación de un mundo ficticio que el espectador observa, interpreta y comprende, y empezaba a concebirse como la producción de una relación singular entre actores y espectadores. El teatro se constituyó entonces como posibilidad de que aconteciera algo *entre* ellos. Para conseguirlo era sin duda esencial ese *algo* que ocurría entre ellos, y mucho menos importante –al menos en principio– *qué* fuera ese algo. En cualquier caso, no se trataba ya de la representación de un mundo ficticio o de la producción de una comunicación teatral interna, es decir, la comunicación entre personajes dramáticos, aquella a la que sólo se llega por medio de la comunicación teatral externa, la que tiene lugar entre el escenario y el público, entre los actores y los espectadores. Los actores hicieron algunos intentos y pusieron a prueba este nuevo modelo de relación dirigiéndose directamente al público con expresiones como «¡estúpidos!», «¡bestias!», «¡ateos!» o «¡ladrones!», y establecieron una relación singular con ellos por medio de movimientos corporales. Los espectadores, por su parte, reaccionaron aplaudiendo, poniéndose de pie, abandonando la sala, haciendo comentarios, subiendo al escenario y peleándose con los actores, entre otras cosas.

Todos los participantes parecían coincidir en que el teatro se caracteriza por una procesualidad específica: por las acciones de los actores, realizadas para producir una relación determinada con los espectadores, y por las acciones de los espectadores, con las que o bien dan su aprobación al tipo de relación propuesta por los actores, o bien la modifican o, en algunos casos, llegan incluso a emprender la búsqueda de otra que la sustituya. Se trataba, pues, de negociar las relaciones que habrían de darse entre actores y espectadores para constituir de ese modo la realidad del teatro. En ese proceso las acciones de los actores y las de los espectadores no tenían en principio otro significado que su propia ejecución. En ese sentido eran, pues, autorreferenciales. Y en tanto que autorreferenciales y constitutivas de realidad pueden ser denominadas, como todas las acciones descritas en los ejemplos citados hasta ahora, 'performativas' en el sentido de J.L. Austin[16].

La noche del estreno los procesos de negociación se llevaron a cabo de modo consensuado. Los espectadores asumieron el rol de actores, atrayendo con sus acciones y comentarios la atención de los actores y de los demás espectadores. Finalmente, algunos se negaron a continuar la negociación de las relaciones abandonando la sala, mientras otros terminaron llegando a un acuerdo con los actores y regresaron a sus asientos tras sus reiterados requerimientos. La segunda noche, por el contrario, se desató el escándalo. Los espectadores que subieron al escenario, y que querían participar, no aceptaron las propuestas de negociación por parte de los actores y del director para que depusieran su actitud. En vista de las circunstancias, el director interrumpió las negociaciones, intentó imponer su propia definición de la relación entre ambas partes y terminó expulsando a los espectadores del escenario[17].

¿Qué sucedió en este caso? Parece claro que los espectadores que irrumpieron en el escenario y el director Claus Peymann partían de premisas distintas. Peymann obró según el criterio de poner en escena un texto literario en el que se tematizaba la relación entre actores y espectadores. Pero en su opinión, de ello no se seguía la posibilidad de entender la realización escénica como una propuesta no simulada, sino real, de poner en cuestión la relación entre actores y espectadores. Y consecuentemente no estaba en condiciones de extraer, a partir de su montaje de un texto tan particular, conclusiones de esa naturaleza. Lo que hacía, en su opinión, al poner en escena la pieza, era crear una «obra»

16 Véase el capítulo segundo.

17 Véase al respecto Henning Rischbieter, «EXPERIMENTA. Theater und Publikum neu definiert», en *Theater heute* 6, julio de 1966, pp. 8-17.

que presentaba a los espectadores. Éstos, por su parte, podían expresar su aprobación o desaprobación a la propuesta por medio de aplausos, silbidos, comentarios, etc. Pero se les negaba el derecho a intervenir en la «obra» y a modificarla con sus acciones. Peymann entendió el abordaje del escenario por parte de algunos espectadores como una violación de los límites impuestos por él y como un ataque al carácter de obra implícito en su montaje que cuestionaba su autoría y su poder de decisión. Peymann se aferró, en definitiva, a la relación tradicional entre sujeto y objeto.

Los espectadores por el contrario concluyeron, a partir del aparente consenso de que el teatro se constituye y se define por la relación entre actores y espectadores, que en la realización escénica no se trataba de un tipo de obra en la que hay que considerar cómo se «traslada» un texto y de qué medios teatrales hay que servirse para ello, sino que se trataba de un acontecimiento que tenía por objeto la redefinición completa de la relación entre actores y espectadores y que, precisamente por ello, brindaba también la posibilidad del cambio de roles. Desde el punto de vista de los espectadores, la realización escénica sólo podía ser un éxito en tanto que acontecimiento si se les concedía protagonismo. La performatividad postulada por la realización escénica no podía llevarse a cabo por medio de acciones convencionales como el aplauso, el silbido o el comentario de los espectadores, sino que exigía una verdadera redefinición de relaciones cuyo resultado se concebía como abierto, y que por ello mismo debía ser capaz de conducir a un cambio de roles.

Mientras que la intervención de Peymann, desde su punto de vista, se había realizado para asegurar y restablecer la integridad de su «obra», para los espectadores expulsados del escenario la realización escénica había sido un fracaso como acontecimiento. En cambio, en la vanguardia teatral americana, en el Living Theatre de Julian Beck y Judith Malina, al menos desde *The Brig*, de 1963, o en el Environmental Theater de Richard Schechner y su Performance Group, fundado en 1967, la «audience participation» se convirtió en algo cotidiano. Los espectadores no sólo podían participar, sino que eran invitados expresamente a tocar a los actores y se les pedía incluso que no rehuyeran el contacto recíproco, con lo que se llegaba a realizar una especie de ritual comunitario, como ocurrió sobre todo en *Paradise Now* (Avignon, 1968), del Living Theatre, y en *Dionysus in 69* (Nueva York, 1968), del Performance Group[18]. La redefinición de las relaciones entre actores y espectadores consistió en estos casos en desplazar la preponderancia del estatus sígnico de las acciones y de los significados potencialmente atribuibles a ellas hacia su corporalidad específica y hacia los efectos de todo tipo que pudieran producir en el conjunto de los participantes: psicológicos, afectivos, energéticos y motores, así como hacia las experiencias sensoriales de gran intensidad que hacían posibles.

La difuminación de las fronteras entre las artes, proclamada u observada reiteradamente desde los años sesenta por artistas, críticos de arte, estudiosos y filósofos puede ser descrita también como giro performativo. Las artes visuales, la música, la literatura o el teatro tienden a partir de entonces a llevarse a cabo en y como realizaciones escénicas. En lugar de crear obras, los artistas producen cada vez más *acontecimientos* en los que no están involucrados sólo ellos mismos, sino también los receptores, los observadores, los oyentes y los espectadores. Con ello se modificaban las condiciones de producción y recepción artísticas en un aspecto crucial. La función esencial de dichos procesos ya no la desempeña una obra artística de existencia independiente, al margen de sus productores y receptores, una obra que surja como objeto a partir de la actividad del sujeto artístico, y que se confía a la percepción y a la interpretación del sujeto receptor. En su lugar nos las vemos con un acontecimiento al que pone en marcha y da fin la acción de varios sujetos: la del artista y la del oyente o espectador. Con ello se ha modificado igualmente la relación entre el estatus material y el sígnico de los objetos empleados y de las acciones ejecutadas en la realización escénica. El estatus material no es función del

18 Véase al respecto Julian Beck, *The Life of the Theatre*, San Francisco, 1972; Julian Beck y Julia Malina, *Paradise Now*, Nueva York, 1971; Richard Schechner, *Teatro ambientalista*, México D.F., 1988 y *Dyonisus in 69*, Nueva York, 1970.

sígnico, sino que se desprende de él y aspira a una existencia propia. Es decir, que el *efecto* inmediato de los objetos y de las acciones no depende de los significados que puedan atribuírseles, sino que tiene lugar al margen de cualquier intento de atribución de significado. En tanto que acontecimientos que presentan estas cualidades especiales, las realizaciones escénicas brindan la posibilidad de experimentar cambios en su transcurso, esto es, de transformar a todos los que participan en ellas: a los artistas tanto como a los espectadores.

El giro performativo en las artes difícilmente puede comprenderse con ayuda de las teorías estéticas tradicionales. Aun cuando puedan ser útiles en algunos aspectos, son incapaces de comprehender el aspecto crucial de este giro: la transformación de la obra de arte en acontecimiento, y la de las relaciones ligadas a ella: la de sujeto y objeto y la de los estatus material y sígnico. Y precisamente para poder dar cuenta de este fenómeno, para investigarlo y elucidarlo, es necesario el desarrollo de una nueva estética: una estética de lo performativo.

II. ACLARACIÓN DE CONCEPTOS

1. El concepto de performativo

El concepto de 'performativo' fue acuñado por John L. Austin, que lo introdujo en la terminología de la filosofía del lenguaje en el ciclo de conferencias *Cómo hacer cosas con palabras*, que dictó en 1955 en la Universidad de Harvard. La acuñación de este término tuvo lugar aproximadamente en la misma época en la que he localizado el giro performativo de las artes. Aunque Austin había empleado en trabajos anteriores el término 'performatorio' (*performatory*) de modo tentativo, terminó decantándose por la palabra 'performativo' (*performative*), porque «es más corta, menos fea, más manejable y porque su formación es más tradicional»[1]. En un ensayo elaborado un año después, «Emisiones realizativas», escribió sobre su nueva elección: «tienen ustedes todo el derecho a no saber lo que significa la palabra 'performativo'. Es una palabra nueva y una palabra fea, y acaso no signifique demasiado. Pero en cualquier caso hay algo a su favor, que no es una palabra

1 John L. Austin, *Cómo hacer cosas con palabras. Palabras y acciones*, Barcelona, 1998, p. 47 (nota 8).

profunda»[2]. El término deriva del verbo '*to perform*', 'realizar': «se 'realizan' acciones»[3].

Austin recurrió a un neologismo porque había hecho un descubrimiento revolucionario para la filosofía del lenguaje: que los enunciados lingüísticos no sólo sirven para describir un estado de cosas o para afirmar algo sobre un hecho, sino que con ellos también se realizan acciones, y que por lo tanto hay también, además de enunciados constatativos, enunciados performativos. Austin explica la peculiaridad de esta segunda forma de enunciación con ayuda de lo que llama 'performativos explícitos'. Cuando alguien al arrojar una botella contra el casco de un barco dice «bautizo este barco con el nombre de *Queen Elisabeth*», o cuando en una boda el funcionario del registro civil, tras preguntar a ambos cónyuges, pronuncia la frase: «les declaro marido y mujer», no está describiendo un estado de cosas previo. Por ello dichos enunciados no pueden ser subsumidos en las categorías de «verdadero» y «falso». Lo que ocurre con ellos es más bien que se crea un estado de cosas nuevo: el barco lleva desde ese momento el nombre *Queen Elisabeth*, y la señora X y el señor Y son desde ese momento un matrimonio. La proferencia de esos enunciados ha cambiado el mundo. Los enunciados de este tipo no sólo dicen algo, sino que realizan exactamente la acción que expresan, es decir: son autorreferenciales porque significan lo que hacen, y son constitutivos de realidad porque crean la realidad social que expresan. Son estos dos rasgos distintivos los que caracterizan a los enunciados performativos. Lo que los hablantes de las distintas lenguas siempre han sabido y han practicado de forma intuitiva lo formulaba por primera vez la filosofía del lenguaje: el habla tiene potencial para modificar el mundo y para transformarlo.

Los casos citados son sin duda ejemplos de un modo de hablar formular. Pero el solo uso de la fórmula no basta para

2 John L. Austin, «Emisiones realizativas», en L. M. Valdés Villanueva (ed.), *La búsqueda del significado*, Barcelona, 2000, p. 417.

3 *Cómo hacer cosas con palabras*, p. 47.

garantizar que el enunciado sea performativo. Para ello deben cumplirse una serie condiciones no lingüísticas, de otro modo el enunciado se malogra y se queda en mera palabrería. Si la frase «yo les declaro marido y mujer» no fuera proferida ni por un funcionario del registro civil ni por un sacerdote u otra persona expresamente autorizada para ello –como el capitán de un barco en alta mar–, o si fuera proferida en el marco de una comunidad que procediera mediante otro sistema, entonces no se darían las condiciones para unir a dos personas en matrimonio.

Las condiciones a cumplir para que un enunciado sea performativo no son, por lo tanto, sólo lingüísticas, sino sobre todo institucionales y sociales. La enunciación performativa se dirige siempre a una comunidad en una situación dada en la que alguno de sus miembros ha de estar presente representándola. En este sentido implica la realización de un acto social. Con ella no sólo se lleva a cabo la unión matrimonial, sino que al mismo tiempo también se realiza escénicamente.

En el desarrollo posterior de sus conferencias, Austin abandonaría la contraposición entre enunciados constatativos y performativos, y propondría en su lugar una división constituida por tres tipos de actos de habla: locutivos, ilocutivos y perlocutivos. Con ello quería aportar pruebas para demostrar que hablar es siempre actuar, que consecuentemente las constataciones también pueden tener éxito o fracasar, y que los enunciados performativos también pueden ser verdaderos o falsos[4]. Por lo tanto, es el propio Austin quien constata la inadecuación de su distinción entre enunciados performativos y constatativos. Como ha mostrado Sybille Krämer, la escenificación de este fracaso por parte del propio Austin puede ser entendida como un ejemplo que demuestra «la vulnerabilidad de todos los criterios definitivos y

4 Véase especialmente Shoshana Felman, *The Literary Speech Act. Don Juan with J.L. Austin or Seduction in Two Languages*, Ithaca/Nueva York, 1983; así como Krämer/Stahlhut, «Das 'performative' als Thema der Sprach- und Kulturphilosophie», en Erika Fischer-Lichte y Christoph Wulf (eds.), *Theorien des Performativen* (= *Paragrana*, vol. 10, cuad. I), Berlín, 2001, pp. 35-64.

la exposición de todos los conceptos definitivos a las incertidumbres, a los imponderables y a las ambigüedades propias de la vida real»[5]. Con ello Austin desvía su atención hacia el hecho de que justamente lo performativo es lo que pone en marcha una dinámica «que conduce a la desestabilización de la idea misma de esquema conceptual dicotómico»[6].

Este aspecto es de especial interés para una estética de lo performativo. Como se ha mostrado en los ejemplos de performances, acciones y otras realizaciones escénicas aducidos anteriormente a modo de introducción, son precisamente las parejas conceptuales dicotómicas del tipo sujeto/objeto o significante/significado las que pierden su polaridad y la nitidez de sus límites al ser puestas en movimiento y al empezar a oscilar. Aunque Austin, con razones de peso, haya certificado el fracaso de la dicotomía entre los conceptos de constatativo y performativo, ello no significa en ningún caso que cuestione la definición que ofreció cuando en un primer momento se refirió a los 'performativos explícitos'. Según ella, son actos lingüísticos autorreferenciales y constitutivos de realidad y como tales pueden tener éxito o fracasar, dependiendo sobre todo de condiciones institucionales y sociales. Sin embargo, como deja entrever su extensa y detallada teoría de los infortunios, su fracaso era para Austin el caso más interesante. Como otra de las características de lo performativo se podría señalar, por lo tanto, su capacidad para desestabilizar construcciones conceptuales dicotómicas, e incluso para acabar con ellas.

Austin emplea la noción de performativo exclusivamente en referencia a actos de habla. Ahora bien, su definición del concepto no excluye ni mucho menos su aplicación a actos físicos como los que se realizaron, por ejemplo, en *Lips of Thomas*. Muy al contrario, pues su aplicación casi se nos impone en este caso. Como he señalado anteriormente, se trata ciertamente de accio-

5 Krämer/Stahlhut, «Das 'Performative' als Thema der Sprach-und Kulturphilosophie», p. 45.

6 *Ibid.*, p. 56.

nes autorreferenciales y constitutivas de realidad (lo que, al fin y al cabo, siempre son las acciones), y por ello mismo capaces, de la manera que sea, de dar lugar a una transformación de la artista y de los espectadores. Pero, en este caso ¿qué podemos hacer con respecto al criterio para determinar el éxito o el fracaso? No hay duda de que la artista ingirió demasiado vino y miel de verdad, ni de que se hirió realmente con una cuchilla de afeitar y con un látigo. Igualmente indudable es que los espectadores terminaron con el tormento de Abramović cuando la bajaron de la cruz de hielo. Pero la performance ¿tuvo éxito o fracasó? ¿Cuáles son las condiciones institucionales cuyo cumplimiento o incumplimiento nos autorizaría a valorar la realización escénica como «lograda» o «fracasada»?

Como en este caso estamos ante una performance artística, cumple pensar en primer lugar en las condiciones que establece la institución arte. El lugar de su realización, una galería de arte, nos remite ya explícitamente a la institución arte, que en nuestro caso hace la función de marco en el que la realización escénica es llevada a cabo conjuntamente por todos los participantes. Pero ¿qué se infiere de ello? ¿Cuáles son los requisitos establecidos por la institución arte a principios de los años setenta, un momento en el que se acababa de poner en marcha, tanto desde su interior como desde sus márgenes, una redefinición y reestructuración de esa institución que avanzaba con gran pujanza? En este caso las condiciones institucionales no son tan claras e indiscutibles como en el del matrimonio o en el del bautismo de un barco. La institución arte, en cualquier caso, apenas puede ofrecernos criterios que permitan decidir de manera fundamentada si la intervención de algunos de los espectadores ha de ser valorada como un éxito o como un fracaso de la performance.

No bastaría de todos modos con ellos, ya que no nos podemos limitar al hecho de que la performance tuviera lugar en un marco legitimado por la institución arte. Como ya he mostrado, presentaba características tanto de ritual como de espectáculo. Surge, pues, la pregunta de hasta qué punto tuvo lugar en nuestro caso una transformación del marco «ritual» y del marco «espectáculo» en una performance artística. Así pues, cuando nos planteamos la pregunta del éxito o el fracaso, ¿en qué sentido hay que tener en cuenta el choque de estos marcos entre sí y con el marco «arte»?[7].

En todo caso, es evidente que la lista de condiciones a satisfacer para decidir si un enunciado performativo ha tenido éxito ofrecida por Austin, difícilmente se puede aplicar a una estética de lo performativo[8]. Pues, como muestra a las claras *Lips of Thomas*, uno de los factores importantes en este caso es precisamente el juego con los distintos marcos y sus colisiones, un factor de gran importancia para la transformación de los participantes. ¿Podemos considerar esa transformación como la clave para juzgar el éxito o el fracaso de la performance? ¿Quién podría arrogarse la

7 Sobre el concepto de marco, véase Gregory Bateson, «A Theory of Play and Phantasy» (1955), en *Steps to an ecology of mind*, Chicago, 2000, pp. 177-193 (esp. *Pasos hacia una ecología de la mente*, Buenos Aires, 1972), así como Erving Goffman, *Frame analysis: an essay on the organization of experience*, Nueva York, 1974 (esp. *Frame analysis. Los marcos de la experiencia*, Madrid, 2006).

8 «A.1) Tiene que haber un procedimiento convencional aceptado, que posea cierto efecto convencional; dicho procedimiento debe incluir la emisión de ciertas palabras por parte de ciertas personas en ciertas circunstancias. Además,
A.2) en un caso dado, las personas y circunstancias particulares deben ser las apropiadas para recurrir al procedimiento particular que se emplea,
B.1) El procedimiento debe llevarse a cabo por todos los participantes en forma correcta, y
B.2) en todos sus pasos»
Éstas son condiciones que, *mutatis mutandis*, han de cumplirse también para que un ritual tenga éxito, independientemente de que se lleven a cabo por medio de acciones lingüísticas o corporales, o con acciones de ambos tipos. No ocurre lo mismo con las dos últimas condiciones:
«Γ.1) En aquellos casos en que, como sucede a menudo, el procedimiento requiere que quienes lo usan tengan ciertos pensamientos o sentimientos, o está dirigido a que sobrevenga cierta conducta correspondiente de algún participante, entonces quien participa en él y recurre así al procedimiento debe tener en los hechos tales pensamientos o sentimientos, o los participantes deben estar animados por el propósito de conducirse de la manera adecuada, y, además,
Γ.2) los participantes tienen que comportarse efectivamente así en su oportunidad». (*Cómo hacer cosas con palabras*, p. 56).

capacidad de decidirlo? La pregunta por el éxito o el fracaso, al menos así planteada, parece mal formulada. Es por ello que el concepto de performativo, considerado en el marco de una estética de lo performativo, requiere una modificación.

Mientras que en la disciplina en la que surgió, la filosofía del lenguaje, el concepto de performativo ha perdido importancia, sobre todo después de la elaboración de la teoría de los actos del habla, es decir, con la divulgación de la idea del habla como acción, en la filosofía de la cultura y en la teoría de la cultura reapareció con pujanza en los años noventa. Hasta finales de la década de los ochenta, en los estudios culturales dominaba una idea de cultura muy influida por la expresión metafórica «cultura como texto». Tanto los fenómenos culturales concretos como las culturas en su conjunto se entendían como contextos estructurados constituidos por signos a los que se les podían atribuir significados. Consecuentemente, los más diversos intentos de describir e interpretar las culturas fueron denominados «lecturas». Según esta idea, la tarea principal de los estudios culturales consistía en descifrar e interpretar textos, preferiblemente en lenguas extranjeras casi incomprensibles, o en deconstruir, en el proceso de lectura, textos ya conocidos que eran releídos atendiendo a posibles subtextos.

En los años noventa se produjo un cambio de enfoque en la investigación. Se empezaron a tomar en cuenta los rasgos performativos de la cultura, que hasta ese momento habían pasado inadvertidos. Tales rasgos dan lugar a una manera autónoma de referirse (de modo práctico) a realidades ya existentes o que se tienen por posibles, y les confieren a las acciones y acontecimientos culturales un carácter de realidad específico que el modelo tradicional, centrado en la idea de texto, no comprehendía. La metáfora de «la cultura como performance» empezaba a ganar en importancia. En ese proceso fue necesaria la revisión del concepto de performativo para que incluyera de manera explícita las acciones físicas.

Sin remitir de forma expresa a Austin, Judith Butler introdujo en la filosofía de la cultura el concepto de performativo en su artículo de 1988 «Performative Acts and Gender Constitution: an Essay in Phenomenology and Feminist Theory»[9*]. En este trabajo se pretendía demostrar que la identidad de género no es previa en tanto que identidad, esto es, que no viene determinada ontológica ni biológicamente, sino que se entiende como el resultado de determinados esfuerzos culturales de constitución: «in this sense, gender is no way a stable identity or locus of agency from which various acts proceed; rather it is [...] an identity instituted through a *stylized repetition of acts*»[10]. Butler llama a estos actos 'performativ', «where 'performative' itself carries the double-meaning of 'dramatic' and 'non-referential'»[11]. Aun cuando a primera vista esta definición del concepto parece diferir considerablemente de la de Austin, las diferencias se minimizan tras un examen más atento. Tienen que ver sobre todo con el hecho de que Butler no aplica aquí el concepto de performativo a los actos de habla, sino sobre todo a acciones corporales.

Los actos performativos, en tanto que corporales, hay que entenderlos como 'non-referential' en la medida en que no se refieren a algo dado de antemano, a algo interno ni a una sustancia o a un ser a los que esos actos tengan que servir de expresión, pues no hay identidad estable, fija de la que pudieran serlo. La expresividad se presenta en este sentido como diametralmente opuesta a la performatividad. Los actos corporales denominados aquí performativos no expresan una identidad preconcebida, sino que más bien generan identidad, y ése es su significado más importante.

9 El artículo fue publicado en 1990 en el volumen *Performing, Feminism, Feminist Critical Theory and Theatre*, Sue-Ellen Case (ed.), Baltimore/Londres, 1990, pp. 270-282.

* Ha sido publicado también en español: J. Butler, «Actos performativos y constitución de género: un ensayo sobre fenomenología y teoría feminista», *Debate feminista*. 9.18, octubre 1998, pp. 296-314. La traducción de las citas será en cualquier caso nuestra.

10 *Ibid.*, p. 270. [«en este sentido, el género no es en ningún caso una entidad estable o un emplazamiento operativo del que procedan los diferentes actos. Es más bien [...] una identidad constituida por una *repetición estilizada de actos*»].

11 *Ibid.* [«donde 'performativo' conlleva el doble sentido de 'dramático' y de 'no-referencial'»].

También el término 'dramático' apunta a este proceso de generación: «By dramatic I mean [...] that the body is not merely matter but a continual and incessant *materializing* of possibilities. One is not simply a body, but, in some very key sense, one does one's body [...]»[12]. Esto significa que también el cuerpo, en su particular materialidad, es el resultado de una repetición de determinados gestos y movimientos. Únicamente este tipo de actos dan lugar al cuerpo como algo individual, sexuado, étnico y culturalmente marcado. Así pues, la identidad –como realidad corporal y social– se constituye siempre a través de actos performativos. 'Performativo' significa en este sentido, sin duda, como en Austin: constitutivo de realidad y autorreferencial.

El desplazamiento del enfoque de los actos de habla a las acciones físicas acarrea, sin embargo, consecuencias que justifican el establecimiento de una distinción importante en la definición de conceptos entre Austin y Butler. Mientras que para Austin el criterio más importante es el de «éxito» o «fracaso» y se pregunta, por lo tanto, por las condiciones funcionales para el éxito –algo que nos ha planteado una seria dificultad en el caso de la performance de Abramović–, Butler se pregunta por las condiciones fenoménicas de la corporización.

Apelando a Merleau-Ponty, que no considera el cuerpo únicamente como una noción histórica, sino también como un repertorio de posibilidades que estar continuamente haciendo realidad, es decir, como «an active process of embodying certain cultural and historical possibilities»[13], Butler explica el proceso de generación performativa de la identidad como un proceso de corporización *(embodiment)*. Lo define, por lo tanto, como «a manner of doing, dramatizing and *reproducing* a historical situa-

12 *Ibid.*, p. 273. [«Por dramático entiendo [...] que el cuerpo no es mera materia, sino una continua e incesante *materialización* de posibilidades. Uno no es simplemente un cuerpo, sino que, en un sentido crucial, uno hace su propio cuerpo»].

13 *Ibid.* [«un proceso activo de corporización de determinadas posibilidades culturales e históricas»].

tion»[14]. Mediante la estilizada repetición de actos performativos se corporizan determinadas posibilidades histórico-culturales y sólo así se generan el cuerpo, en tanto que marcado histórica y culturalmente, y la identidad.

Las condiciones en las que se realiza en cada caso el proceso de corporización no se limitan exclusivamente al ámbito del poder y de las capacidades del individuo –no se puede escoger de modo totalmente libre qué posibilidades se corporizan ni qué identidad se quiere adoptar–, ni tampoco están completamente determinadas por la sociedad –aunque la sociedad puede intentar imponer la corporización de determinadas posibilidades sancionando unas discrepancias que de todos modos no puede evitar totalmente. Es decir, que en el concepto de performativo propuesto por Butler también se percibe claramente su potencial, ya apuntado por Austin, para acabar de raíz con las dicotomías. En los actos performativos y con los actos performativos, con los cuales se constituye el género –y la identidad en general–, la comunidad ejerce violencia corporal sobre el individuo. Pero al mismo tiempo, en cambio, estos actos brindan sin duda la posibilidad de que en ellos, y con ellos, cada individuo se cree a sí mismo como tal –incluso aunque sea al margen de las ideas dominantes en la comunidad y pagando el precio de las correspondientes sanciones sociales–.

Butler compara las condiciones de corporización con las de las realizaciones escénicas teatrales, pues en ellas los actos con los que se crea y se realiza la pertenencia a un género «no son, sin duda, los actos de uno [mismo]». En ellos se trata más bien de una «experiencia compartida», de una «acción colectiva»; de hecho, la acción realizada es una acción en cierto sentido comenzada siempre antes de que un determinado actor aparezca en escena. Así, la repetición de la acción es un volver a poner por obra *(re-enactment)* y un volver a experimentar *(re-experiencing)* un repertorio de significados socialmente establecidos de antemano. En esos actos ni se inscriben códigos culturales en un cuerpo

14 *Ibid.* [«un modo de hacer, dramatizar y *reproducir* una situación histórica»].

pasivo ni los yoes corporizados preceden a las convenciones culturales que le dan significado al cuerpo. Butler compara la constitución de la identidad a través de la corporización con la escenificación de un texto dado de antemano. Pues de igual manera que un mismo texto se puede poner en escena de formas distintas y que los actores, dentro de las pautas del mismo, son libres de delinear e interpretar su papel de un modo nuevo y distinto, un cuerpo que posee un género específico actúa dentro de los márgenes de un espacio corporal limitado por ciertas normas y propone sus propias interpretaciones dentro de los límites de las instrucciones de la dirección de escena. Así pues, la realización de la identidad de género, o de cualquier otra, como proceso de corporización se lleva a cabo de forma análoga a la de una realización escénica teatral. En este sentido, las condiciones para la corporización pueden ser descritas y definidas de modo más exacto como condiciones de realización escénica[15].

La teoría de lo performativo, tal y como la esboza Judith Butler en este primer ensayo[16], al poner el énfasis en los actos performativos corporales y al concederles un gran peso a los procesos de corporización, parece estar cumpliendo el fin que la teoría de Austin había expresado como deseable con sus condiciones de éxito: encaminarse hacia una estética de lo performativo. No obstante, su concepto necesita una modificación en lo que atañe a nuestro contexto, como pondrá de manifiesto una somera revisión de la performance de Abramović.

Sin duda, la idea de cuerpo como corporización de determinadas posibilidades históricas es aplicable, y con provecho, al trato

15 A pesar de que la concepción del teatro de Butler es ya difícilmente compatible con la dominante en el teatro contemporáneo –algo que ella misma declara refiriéndose a Richard Schechner, aunque no extrae las correspondientes conclusiones para sus propias realizaciones escénicas–, ello afecta sobre todo a su comparación posterior entre los travestis en escena y los travestis en situaciones cotidianas, pero no a la relación entre condiciones de corporización y condiciones de realización escénica.

16 Ya en su libro *Gender Trouble*, que apareció poco después, llevó a cabo algunas modificaciones de importancia que contradicen las definiciones ofrecidas en su primer artículo. Esto vale igualmente para sus publicaciones posteriores.

que Abramović le dio al suyo. Abramović corporizó en el transcurso de su performance distintas posibilidades históricas, pero desde luego no sólo aquellas que representaban posibilidades vigentes en el momento histórico de su performance, sino sobre todo también aquellas que en su tiempo eran tenidas por meras posibilidades en el pasado, aunque algunas –como la flagelación– oscilaban entre posibilidades históricas (como la flagelación de las monjas) y presentes (como acciones de castigo o de tortura, o como prácticas sexuales sadomasoquistas). Sus actos performativos tampoco recrearon los modelos históricos mediante la mera repetición, sino que los modificaron decisivamente: la performadora no sufrió de modo pasivo toda la violencia, los daños y las torturas que se infligió, sino que fue en todo momento su instigadora activa. Tampoco estamos aquí ante una repetición de los actos performativos, como ocurre en la propuesta de Butler, en la que la repetición es esencial: cada acción realizada durante la performance de Abramović tuvo lugar una sola vez. Con respecto a la manera en que los entiende la definición de Butler, los procesos de corporización llevados a cabo tanto en *Lips of Thomas* como en otras performances, acciones y realizaciones escénicas teatrales necesitan una determinación más detallada o alguna modificación conceptual, sobre todo porque aquí estamos ante *re-enactments* estéticos y, en cierto sentido, diferidos. Butler, por su parte, apenas si hace referencia a procesos estéticos en sentido estricto, se centra fundamentalmente en acciones cotidianas.

Al explicar las condiciones de corporización como condiciones de realización escénica, Butler establece un interesante paralelismo entre su teoría y la de Austin (aunque siga sin hacer referencia explícita a ella). Ambos consideran la realización de los actos performativos como una realización escénica ritualizada y pública. Para ambos existe sin duda una estrecha y evidente relación entre performatividad y realización escénica (*performance*). En la misma medida en que las palabras '*performance*' y '*performative*' son derivaciones de '*to perform*', parece obvio que la performatividad conduce a la realización escénica, es decir, se manifiesta y se realiza en el carácter de realización escénica de las acciones performativas, como en la tendencia de las artes, tras el impulso performativo del que hablábamos, a realizarse en y como realización escénica; o en sus desarrollos, que han dado como resultado nuevas formas artísticas como el «arte de la performance» y la «acción artística», cuyos meros nombres son ya un signo inequívoco de su carácter performativo. Teniendo en cuenta esto, es legítimo colegir que, tanto en la teoría de Austin como en la de Butler, la realización escénica es la esencia de lo performativo, aunque ninguno de ellos use el término realización escénica en ningún momento.

De ahí que parezca oportuno fundamentar una estética de lo performativo en el concepto de realización escénica. Es decir, que a las teorías de lo performativo ya existentes habría que añadir una teoría estética de la performance o de la realización escénica.

Ahora bien, desde los años sesenta y setenta del siglo veinte han surgido gran cantidad de las más variadas teorías de la performance en el campo de las ciencias sociales, en particular en la antropología cultural y en la sociología. Hasta el punto de que hoy en día el de *performance* hay que entenderlo como «an essentially contested concept»[17]. En los estudios culturales el concepto se ha convertido en una especie de *umbrella term* [término abarcador], sobre cuyo uso se quejaba Dell Hymes ya en 1975 en los siguientes términos: «If some grammarians have confused matters, by lumping what does not interest them under 'performance', [...] cultural anthropologist and folklorists have not done much to clarify the situation. We have tended to lump what *does* interest us under 'performance'»[18]. Desde entonces la situación se ha vuelto todavía más confusa[19].

17 Marvin Carlson, *Performance. A critical introduction*, Londres/Nueva York, 1996, p. 5.

18 Dell Hymes, «Breakthrough into Performance», en Dan Ben-Amos y Kenneth S. Goldstein (eds.), *Folklore: Performance and Communication*, La Haya, 1975, p. 13. [«Si algunos gramáticos han confundido las cosas clasificando todo aquello que no les interesa en la categoría de 'performance' [...] los antropólogos culturales y los folcloristas tampoco han hecho gran cosa para clarificar la situación. Hemos tendido a agrupar todo lo que *no* nos interesa en la categoría de 'performance'].

19 Véase especialmente Jon McKenzie, *Perform - or else. From discipline to performance*, Londres/NuevaYork, 2001, que ofrece sorprendentes propuestas para el desarrollo sistemático del concepto de performance en los estudios culturales.

En vez de recurrir a algunos planteamientos desarrollados en los campos de la sociología, de la etnología o de los estudios culturales en general, me parece que en aras al desarrollo de una estética de lo performativo tiene más sentido partir de los que, hasta donde yo sé, son los primeros intentos de teorización del concepto de performance: los desarrollados en las dos primeras décadas del siglo veinte. Su objetivo era fundar una nueva disciplina académica en el campo del arte: los estudios teatrales.

2. El concepto de realización escénica

Cuando a principios del siglo veinte fueron fundados los estudios teatrales en Alemania y empezaron a extenderse como disciplina universitaria autónoma y como una nueva y necesaria rama de la teoría del arte, se produjo una ruptura con la idea de teatro que había preponderado hasta ese momento. Desde los intentos de literaturización del siglo dieciocho, el teatro se impuso en Alemania no sólo como una institución moral, sino también como una institución «textual». En las postrimerías del siglo diecinueve el carácter artístico del teatro pareció legitimarse casi exclusivamente por su relación con la obra de arte dramática, es decir, con el texto literario. De hecho, ya el propio Goethe en su texto de 1798 *Über Wahrheit und Wahrscheinlichkeit der Kunstwerke [Sobre la verdad y la probabilidad de las obras de arte]* había formulado la idea de que el carácter artístico del teatro residía en la realización escénica. Fue Wagner quien retomó y desarrolló esta idea en su escrito de 1849 *La obra de arte del futuro*. No obstante, para la inmensa mayoría de sus contemporáneos del siglo diecinueve, el valor artístico de la realización escénica lo acreditaba precisamente el texto representado. En 1918 el crítico de teatro Alfred Klaar escribió en el contexto de una polémica contra los entonces incipientes estudios teatrales: «El escenario únicamente puede mantener todo su valor si la creación literaria lo llena de contenido»[20].

20 Alfred Klaar, «Bühne und Drama. Zum Programm der deutschen dramatischen Gesellschaft von Prof. Max Herrmann», en *Vossische Zeitung*, 18 de julio de 1918.

Conforme a este criterio, el teatro se consideraba hasta entonces objeto de los estudios literarios. En cambio, el fundador de los estudios teatrales en Berlín, el germanista Max Herrmann, especialista en la Edad Media y la primera Modernidad, centraba su atención en la realización escénica. Defendía la necesidad de crear una nueva rama de la teoría del arte –los estudios teatrales– con el argumento de que lo que constituye el teatro como arte no es la literatura, sino la realización escénica: «[...] la realización escénica es lo más importante [...]»[21]. Herrmann no se conformaba con un mero cambio de papeles que resultara en la preponderancia de la realización escénica sobre el texto, sino que defendía el establecimiento de una oposición esencial entre ellos que terminara excluyendo su vinculación: «El teatro y el texto dramático [...] son, en mi opinión, [...] ya desde el origen, contrarios, [...] la evidencia de tal oposición es clara: el texto es la creación lingüístico-artística de una sola persona, el teatro es un logro del público y de quienes están a su servicio»[22]. Como ninguna de las disciplinas artísticas existentes incluía la realización escénica entre sus objetos de estudio, sólo se dedicaban a los textos y a los monumentos, hubo que crear una nueva. Así pues, los estudios teatrales se fundaron en Alemania como ciencia de la realización escénica.

La inversión de los términos texto y realización escénica, que Herrmann se proponía llevar a cabo para defender la creación de una nueva disciplina que se ocupara del teatro como realización escénica y no como texto, tuvo una interesante concomitancia en la creación de otra disciplina en el cambio de siglo: la creación de los estudios sobre los rituales. Mientras que en el siglo diecinueve existía una clara jerarquía entre mito y ritual, y se consideraba que el mito tenía primacía y que el ritual era meramente recreado, ilustrado o representado por él, a finales de siglo la relación entre ambos conceptos experimentó una inversión. En sus *Lectures on the*

21 Max Herrmann, *Forschungen zur deutschen Theatergeschichte des Mittelalters und der Renaissance*, Berlín, 1914, II, p. 118.

22 «Bühne und Drama», en *Vossische Zeitung*, 30 de julio de 1918. Respuesta al Prof. Dr. Klaar.

Religion of the Semites (1889) William Robertson Smith propuso la tesis de que el mito servía meramente como interpretación de un ritual y, consecuentemente, tenía un valor secundario. En su opinión la primacía debía ostentarla el ritual:

> En la medida en que los mitos consisten en elucidaciones del ritual, su valor es secundario, y puede asegurarse que en casi todos los casos el mito surge del ritual y no el ritual del mito. El ritual era algo invariable y el mito, en cambio, era variable; el ritual era obligatorio mientras que la creencia en el mito dependía de la fe de los creyentes[23].

El interés de los estudios religiosos debía pues centrarse en el ritual. Así, el principio fundamental de la religión sería la práctica y no la doctrina, no el dogma. La preponderancia de los textos religiosos, vigente hasta el momento sobre todo en las culturas protestantes, se ponía seriamente en cuestión. En sus investigaciones Smith se ocupaba esencialmente de los rituales de sacrificio, como los de camellos, por ejemplo, que eran frecuentes entre las tribus árabes según los informes de un autor del siglo cuarto d.C., de nombre Nilo, o en los rituales de sacrificio judíos según se presentan en el Antiguo Testamento. Smith interpretaba el sacrificio de camellos como una ancestral práctica totémica y elaboró una teoría según la cual había que entender al animal sacrificado como centro de un banquete comunitario. La realización conjunta de este acto, es decir, la asimilación corporal de la carne y de la sangre del animal sacrificado –de una divinidad, como la llama Smith adoptando el sentido que cobra en el totemismo–, uniría a todos los participantes por medio un lazo social indisoluble. El ritual antedicho instituye a la comunidad por primera vez como comunidad de comensales, de tal manera que del grupo que participa en el ritual surge una comunidad política. No es difícil percatarse de que estamos ante actos performativos, que son los que crean

23 W. Robertson Smith, *Lectures on the Religion of the Semites: The Fundamental Institutions*, Londres, 1894, p. 19.

aquello que realizan: la realidad social de una comunidad (de comensales).

La teoría de Smith sobre el sacrificio ha tenido una grandísima influencia no sólo en los estudios religiosos, sino también en la etnología, la sociología y en los estudios sobre la Antigüedad. El etnólogo James George Frazer reconoce su deuda con Smith en el prólogo a la primera edición de su libro *The Golden Bough (La rama dorada)*, de 1890, para el desarrollo de la idea principal de su libro: la concepción de un dios asesinado violentamente y resucitado. El sociólogo Emile Durkheim también se siente en deuda con Robertson Smith, pues afirma que sólo después de estudiar sus *Lectures* tuvo clara conciencia de la crucial importancia de la religión en la vida social[24].

Los argumentos para fundar las investigaciones sobre el ritual y los estudios teatrales se basan en premisas similares. En ambos casos se trataba de una inversión terminológica dentro de una jerarquía: entre mito y ritual, en un caso, y entre texto literario y realización escénica, en el otro. Es decir, en ambos casos se revocó la preponderancia de los textos en favor de la supremacía de la realización escénica. En esa medida puede afirmarse que es ya con la instauración de las investigaciones sobre los rituales y de los estudios teatrales –y no con el surgimiento de la cultura de la performance en los años sesenta y setenta– cuando se produce un primer giro performativo en la cultura europea del siglo veinte[25].

Jane Ellen Harrison, cabeza de los llamados ritualistas de Cambridge, un grupo de filólogos especializados en la Antigüedad, llegó al extremo de establecer una relación genealógica directa entre ritual y teatro que pretendía demostrar la prioridad de la realización escé-

24 Véase asimismo, sobre esta reversión de la relación entre ritual y mito, Hans G. Kippenberg, *Die Entdeckuny der Religionsgeschichte, Religionswissenschaft und Moderne*, Múnich, 1997.

25 No debe entenderse con esto que estemos ante el primer giro performativo en la cultura europea, sino más bien ante el primero del siglo veinte. Existe cierta controversia en la crítica académica sobre si teniendo en cuenta la indiscutible función cultural de las *cultural performances* en los siglos posteriores al invento y a la generalización de la imprenta, y hasta el final del siglo diecinueve, se puede hablar también de giro performativo en ese caso.

nica sobre el texto. En su extenso estudio *Themis: A Study of the Social Origin of Greek Religion*, de 1912, desarrolló una teoría sobre el origen del teatro griego a partir del ritual. Harrison partía del supuesto de la existencia de un ritual predionisíaco en el que se adoraba al *daimon* de la primavera, al *eniautos daimon*. El ritual dionisíaco se entendía, a su vez, como derivado del antiguo ritual del *daimon* de la primavera. Harrison se esforzó por aportar pruebas para demostrar que el ditirambo –del cual, según Aristóteles, surge la tragedia– no estaría recreando otra cosa que el canto de celebración del *eniautos daimon*, que es una parte esencial de este ritual. Gilbert Murray contribuyó al estudio de Harrison con su «Excursus on the Ritual Form Preserved in Tragedy». Remitiéndose a diversas tragedias, especialmente a las *Bacantes* de Eurípides –¡precisamente uno de los textos trágicos más tardíos!–, intentó demostrar que elementos como el *agon*, el *threnos*, el mensajero y la epifanía, los cuales según Harrison procedían del ritual del *eniautos daimon*, cumplían en la tragedia funciones similares a las que cumplían en el ritual.

La teoría de Harrison dejaba sin fundamento a la convicción de sus contemporáneos de que la cultura griega, con respecto a cuyo modelo y a cuyos parámetros modelaban la suya, había sido una cultural textual. A la luz de su teoría, los tan admirados textos de las tragedias y las comedias griegas serían la última consecuencia de las acciones con las que se realizaba un ritual en honor al dios de una estación del año. Primero sería el ritual, y a partir de él se habrían desarrollado el teatro y los textos escritos para ser realizados en él.

La teoría de Harrison, pese a que hoy se le da valor casi exclusivamente como hito de la historia académica, contribuyó decisivamente a sustentar la idea de un giro performativo. Lo único que le faltaba al concepto de realización escénica para convertirse en un concepto clave era una minuciosa fijación teórica. Herrmann se propuso realizar esa tarea en diversos trabajos entre 1910 y 1930.

Es significativo que Herrmann sitúe como punto de partida y piedra angular de sus reflexiones la relación entre actores y espectadores:

> El sentido originario del teatro [...] radica en que era un juego social –un juego de todos para todos–. Un juego en el que todos participan –protagonistas y espectadores–. [...] El público toma parte en el conjunto de manera activa. El público es, por así decirlo, creador del arte del teatro. Hay tantas partes distintas implicadas en la configuración de la fiesta del teatro, que es imposible que se pierda su esencial carácter social. En el teatro siempre se da una comunidad social[26].

Sólo porque se da la copresencia física de actores y espectadores puede tener lugar la realización escénica, es esa copresencia la que la constituye. Para que una realización escénica pueda tener lugar, actores y espectadores han de reunirse durante un determinado periodo de tiempo en un lugar concreto y hacer algo juntos. Al definir el sentido originario del teatro como «un juego de todos para todos», Herrmann define la relación entre actores y espectadores de un modo esencialmente nuevo. Los espectadores ya no son considerados observadores distantes o cercanos de las acciones que realizan los actores sobre el escenario y a las que ellos, sobre la base de sus observaciones, les atribuyen determinados significados, ni como intelectuales descifradores de los mensajes formulados con las acciones de los actores y a partir de ellas. No estamos ante una relación entre sujeto y objeto, ni en el sentido de que los espectadores conviertan a los actores en objeto de su observación, ni en el de que los actores como sujetos y los espectadores como objetos se enfrenten entre sí con mensajes innegociables. Por copresencia física se entiende más bien la relación de cosujetos. Los espectadores son considerados parte activa en la creación de la realización escénica por su participación en el juego, es decir, por su presencia física, por su percepción y por sus reacciones. La realización escénica surge, pues, como resultado de la interacción entre actores y espectadores. Las reglas que la hacen posible son entendidas como reglas de un

26 Max Herrmann, «Über die Aufgaben eines theaterwissenschaftlichen Instituts», conferencia del 27 de junio de 1920, en Helmar Klier (ed.), *Theaterwissenschaft im deutschprachigen Raum*, Darmstadt, 1981, pp. 15-24, p. 19.

juego que se negocian entre todos los participantes –actores y espectadores– y que pueden ser igualmente respetadas o quebrantadas por ambas partes. La realización escénica acontece *entre* actores y espectadores, es creada por ambos conjuntamente.

Probablemente Herrmann no llegó a esta definición de la singular *medialidad* del teatro basándose únicamente en reflexiones puramente teóricas o derivadas de la historia del teatro. Las realizaciones escénicas del teatro de su época debieron sin duda de contribuir también a ello. Fue sobre todo Max Reinhardt quien en sus montajes creaba una y otra vez disposiciones espaciales nuevas que obligaban a los espectadores a abandonar la posición de observadores propia de las salas de teatro clásicas, los llamados *teatros a la italiana*, y les posibilitaban nuevas formas de interacción con los actores. En *Sumurun* (1910), por ejemplo, Reinhardt extendió un *hanamichi* (una amplia pasarela empleada tradicionalmente en el teatro kabuki japonés) que atravesaba el patio de butacas de los Kammerspiele del Deutsches Theater de Berlín. De este modo los acontecimientos sucedían en medio de los espectadores. Reinhard hacía que sucedieran cosas en el escenario y en el *hanamichi* simultáneamente, de tal manera que los actores aparecían sobre el *hanamichi* justamente «at some vital point in each scene» [«en un momento crucial en cada una de las escenas»], como señaló críticamente un reseñista con motivo de su presentación en Nueva York[27]. Era pues inevitable que los espectadores que miraban a los actores que aparecían en el *hanamichi* se perdieran irremediablemente lo que sucedía sobre el escenario. Aquellos que, por el contrario, preferían seguir lo que ocurría en el escenario, se perdían las intervenciones de los actores en el *hanamichi*. De este modo, obligándolos a seleccionar autónomamente las impresiones sensibles, los espectadores se convertían en sentido enfático en «creadores» de la realización escénica. El juego de la realización escénica se llevaba a cabo según las reglas

27 «Why Lot's Wife Could not Have Sat out 'Sumurun'. The pedestrians on that bridge would have aroused her curiosity so that she would have turned into twenty pillars of salt». Crítica sin autor identificado, tomada del archivo del Theatermuseum de Viena.

establecidas de una parte por los actores (y el director) y de otra por los espectadores. Eran negociables.

La primera vez que esto se pudo aplicar de modo estricto fue en los montajes de *Edipo Rey* (1910) y de la *Orestíada* (1911) que el propio Reinhard realizó en el Circo Schumann de Berlín. En ellos el coro se movía continuamente entre el público, los actores aparecían por detrás, por delante y en medio de los espectadores de modo que, como comentó el crítico Siegfried Jacobsohn: «las cabezas de los espectadores [apenas] podían distinguirse de las de los figurantes, que se encontraban literalmente en medio del público»[28]. Y Alfred Klaar, que posteriormente recrudecería la polémica con Max Herrmann sobre la preeminencia del texto sobre la realización escénica, se quejaba al respecto de la *Orestíada* de:

> la distribución de la acción, delante, en medio, debajo y detrás de nosotros; esa incesante necesidad de cambiar el punto de vista; esa invasión del patio de butacas por parte de los actores, que con sus trajes ondulantes, sus pelucas y su maquillaje se aproximaban a nosotros; esos diálogos mantenidos a distancia; esos gritos repentinos desde cualquier rincón del teatro que nos sobresaltaban y desorientaban; todo eso dispersa: no alimenta la ilusión, la extingue[29].

En esta situación a los espectadores les era imposible ponerse en el lugar de mero observador, fuera distante, interesado o incluso apasionado. No les quedaba otro remedio que reorientarse continuamente tanto con respecto a los actores cuanto con respecto a los demás espectadores. La realización escénica acontecía en este caso literalmente *entre* actores y espectadores, y también entre los espectadores mismos. Reinhardt supo aprovechar de las más diversas maneras las singulares condiciones de medialidad logradas por medio de la copresencia física de actores y espectadores con la intención de hacer posibles nuevas relaciones entre ellos, de generarlas continuamente.

28 Siegfried Jacobsohn, *Das Jahr der Bühne*, vol. I, Berlín, 1912, p. 51

29 Alfred Klaar, *Vossische Zeitung*, 14 de octubre de 1911.

De acuerdo con su idea de que toda realización escénica *acontece* entre actores y espectadores, esto es, que no es ni fijable ni transmisible, sino fugaz y transitoria, a la hora de formular su definición de realización escénica Herrmann no se ocupó ni de los textos que se realizan ni de los artefactos que se emplean, por ejemplo, en los decorados. Mostró su rechazo, en efecto, a las pinturas de fondo del escenario, tanto si eran de estilo naturalista como si eran expresionistas –a pesar de que les reconocía en muchos casos valor artístico– y las tildó de «error de principio de consecuencias decisivas»[30]. A su juicio se trataba de elementos irrelevantes para el concepto de realización escénica. La singular y efímera *materialidad* de la realización escénica se constituye más bien a través de los cuerpos de los actores que se mueven en y por el espacio. «En el arte de la actuación [...] radica lo esencial del logro teatral», sólo él crea «la obra de arte auténtica y más pura que el teatro es capaz de producir»[31]. En este contexto a Herrmann parecen no interesarle mucho el personaje y el mundo ficticios creados por el arte interpretativo. Habla, antes bien, de «cuerpo real» y de «espacio real»[32], es decir, que no concibe el cuerpo del actor en el espacio escénico como mero portador de significado, como era habitual desde el siglo dieciocho, sino que se centra en la materialidad específica del cuerpo y del espacio. Son ellos los que contribuyen en mayor medida a la constitución de la realización escénica, y no meramente los personajes y los espacios ficticios creados en ella.

Tocante a este aspecto se encuentra igualmente un llamativo paralelismo en el teatro de Max Reinhardt. Los nuevos espacios teatrales que creó, por ejemplo, con el *hanamichi* o con el teatro-carpa del Circo Schumann, no estaban al servicio de la recreación de determinados lugares ficticios de manera novedosa. En tanto que «lugares reales» brindaban más bien a los actores nuevas posibilidades de aparecer en escena, de moverse por ella o, en un

30 Max Herrmann, «Das theatralische Raumerlebnis», en *Bericht vom 4. Kongress für Ästhetik und Allgemeine Kunstwissenschaft*, Berlín, 1930, pp. 152 y ss.

31 *Ibid.*

32 *Ibid.*

sentido más amplio, nuevas opciones interpretativas, mientras que a los espectadores les abría nuevas posibilidades de percepción y de experimentación.

Algo similar vale también en muchos casos para el arte interpretativo en los montajes de Reinhardt. Así, hubo reseñistas que criticaron tanto la realización escénica de la *Electra* de Sófocles, adaptada por Hugo von Hofmannsthal, y presentada en el Kleines Theater de Berlín en 1903, como las de *Edipo Rey* y la *Orestíada* por el protagonismo concedido a la corporalidad específica de los cuerpos de los actores, con el que acaparaban toda la atención y relegaban a los personajes a un segundo plano. Gertrud Eysoldt, que interpretaba a Electra, fue expresamente criticada por el desmesurado empleo de su cuerpo y por la descomunal intensidad de ese empleo. Con estas propiedades contravenía sobre todo las normas vigentes para la realización escénica de las tragedias griegas en lo concerniente a la «fuerza», al «decoro» y la «sonoridad». En su lugar aparecían «nerviosismo», «pasión desenfrenada» y «roncos bramidos»[33]. Con tales estridencias la actriz traspasaba la frontera entro «lo saludable» y «lo enfermizo» o «lo patológico». El «griterío, la agitación, el exceso de elementos espantosos, la distorsión y el descuido en cada línea»[34] y la «pasión desmedida hasta lo absurdo» sólo podían «calificarse de patológicos»[35]. Rechazaban los movimientos sin «medida» ni «discreción» de Gertrud Eysoldt por no estar al servicio de la recreación del texto, por remitir insoslayablemente a su propio cuerpo, y rechazaban igualmente por «insoportable» su transgresión «patológica», en la que veían la disolución de las fronteras del yo de la actriz, no las del yo del personaje[36].

También en los montajes de *Edipo Rey* y de la *Orestíada* muchos críticos deploraron el hecho de que los actores atrajeran la aten-

33 Fritz Engel en el *Berliner Tageblatt* del 31 de octubre de 1903.

34 Richard Nordhausen, crítica publicada en un medio no identificado, referencia tomada del archivo Theatermuseum de Colonia.

35 H. E. en *Freisinnige Zeitung* del 3 de noviembre de 1903 [no aparecen más que las iniciales del autor].

36 Véase la crítica de Paul Goldmann publicada en un medio no identificado, en el archivo del Theatermuseum de Colonia.

ción del espectador con la peculiar forma de emplear sus cuerpos. Esto valía por un lado para los extras, los «caminantes desnudos», que «se metían entre en la orquestra con antorchas, subían corriendo hacia el palacio por las escaleras y volvían al ataque como salvajes», y a quienes Siegfried Jacobsohn no supo encontrar ni función ni significado en el *Edipo*[37]. Alfred Klaar también se burló de su intervención en la *Orestíada*. Criticó severamente las «extrañas contorsiones de sus cuerpos y sus miembros que introdujo la dirección en el Esquilo de ayer», y se mofó de que «los caminantes con el torso desnudo cumplieran su cometido e hicieran, inclinados como estaban hacia el suelo, un alarde gimnástico digno de recordación»[38].

Las críticas se dirigieron, por otro lado, a la interpretación de los protagonistas. Jacobsohn se quejaba de que el tipo de entretenimiento fuera un «irritante espectáculo para masas educadas en corridas de toros»[39]. Como ejemplo de su espanto menciona la escena siguiente:

37 Siegfried Jacobsohn, *Die Schaubühne 46*, 17 de noviembre de 1910.

38 Alfred Klaar, *Vossische Zeitung*, 14 de octubre de 1911. Jacobsohn se quejaba de que aquellos caminantes no eran «ni fieles desde el punto de vista histórico ni elementos de un nuevo clasicismo», y llegaba a la conclusión de que era «un lamentable despilfarro de energía» y de que habían «querido ofrecer en el circo un concepto aproximado del teatro griego antiguo, un concepto que de todos modos no puede nunca ser más que una aproximación» (en *Die Schaubühne 46*, 17 de noviembre de 1910); Gilbert Murray, que había secundado las tesis de Jane E. Harrison, lo valoró, sin embargo, de un modo muy distinto. Él mismo había preparado la traducción para el montaje londinense del *Edipo Rey* por parte de Reinhardt. Se refiere así a los caminantes tocante al reproche de los críticos londinenses de que el montaje era «antigriego» *(unGreek)*: «Professor Reinhardt was frankly pre-Hellenic (as is the *Oedipus* story itself), partly Cretan and Mycenaean, partly Oriental, partly –to my great admiration– merly savage. The half-naked torchbearers with loincloths and long black hair made my heart leap with joy. There was real early Greece about them, not the Greece of the schoolroom or the conventional art studio» (cit. por Huntly Carter, *The Theatre of Max Reinhardt*, Nueva York, 1914, pp. 221 y s.). Obviamente, la manera de emplear el cuerpo en el montaje de Reinhardt concordaba completamente con las ideas de Murray –y Harrison– sobre la cultura griega como una cultura primordialmente performativa.

39 Siegfried Jacobsohn, *Das Jahr der Bühne*, vol. I, Berlín, 1912, p. 49.

> Cuando Orestes pretende golpear a su madre se limita a empujarla hacia fuera en la puerta del palacio, retenerla ahí y empujarla de nuevo hacia el interior del palacio después de una lucha dialéctica. Una vez dentro la persigue escaleras abajo hasta la pista, se enzarza allí con ella y forcejean hasta que la empuja muy lentamente de nuevo escaleras arriba. Es espeluznante[40].

En todos los casos aducidos, la singular manera en la que los actores empleaban su cuerpo les hacía tomar conciencia a los espectadores de sus propios «cuerpos reales». Los de los actores aparecían en escena menos como portadores de unos significados que sus movimientos y gestos tuvieran que transmitir para dar forma a un personaje dramático que para imponérseles a los espectadores en su marcada y patente carnalidad. Lo que para la gran mayoría de los críticos mereció una severa condena, fue, en cambio, para el resto de los espectadores, un elemento que contribuyó decisivamente al abrumador éxito de todos los montajes mencionados.

Max Herrmann procedió en su trabajo de fijación teórica del concepto de realización escénica con la misma radicalidad, si no con más, con la que Reinhardt lo puso en práctica. Desplazó el foco de interés del cuerpo como portador de signos –como expresión y trasmisor de determinados significados– al «cuerpo real», es decir, de su estatus sígnico a su estatus material. Mientras que los críticos partían de la idea de que la función del actor en la realización escénica era dar expresión con su cuerpo a los significados previamente establecidos en el texto y transmitírselos al espectador –poniendo el texto por delante de la realización escénica–, Herrmann excluía completamente la cuestión de la recreación de una realidad ficticia sobre el escenario y la de los posibles significados atribuibles a la apariencia externa de los actores y sus acciones. Esto puede tener que ver con el hecho de que ésas eran las únicas cuestiones que la crítica de teatro y la teoría de la literatura de entonces consideraban relevantes, pues se

40 *Ibid.*, pp. 49 y s.

daba por supuesto que su único objeto era la valoración del aspecto semiótico de una realización escénica. Así pues, hay muchos argumentos que sustentan la afirmación de que Herrmann, al igual que Judith Butler, consideraba la expresividad y la performatividad como conceptos mutuamente excluyentes. Así parece confirmarlo el concepto de realización escénica que desarrolló. Al convertir en el aspecto esencial de su definición tanto la copresencia física de actores y espectadores, que conjuntamente hacen que la realización escénica acontezca, como las acciones corporales realizadas por ambos grupos, y al centrar con ello su atención en un proceso dinámico, imprevisible tanto en su transcurso como en su resultado, margina la expresión y la trasmisión de significados previamente dados. Los significados que surgen en este proceso sólo pueden producirse en él y por él. Sin embargo, Herrmann no llegó a esta conclusión, al menos no expresamente. Por ese motivo, en su definición del concepto de realización escénica las reflexiones sobre su *semioticidad* específica, sobre su singular manera de generar significado carecen de relevancia.

Al entender la realización escénica como una «fiesta» y como un «juego» –como aquello que acontece entre actores y espectadores–, al describir su materialidad específica como efímera, como un proceso dinámico y no como un artefacto, Herrmann priva de fundamento al empleo del término «obra de arte» en el caso de la realización escénica –aun cuando él mismo, al defender la condición del teatro como arte autónomo, hable de la interpretación de los actores como la «auténtica», la «más pura obra de arte que el teatro es capaz de producir». Hay que tener en cuenta que el criterio imperante en su tiempo era el de que el arte estaba necesariamente ligado al concepto de obra. Visto desde la perspectiva actual, sin embargo, la definición de realización escénica de Herrmann excluye el concepto de obra. La realización escénica no adquiere, pues, su carácter artístico –su *esteticidad*– por la obra que supuestamente crea, sino por el acontecimiento que como tal realización escénica ejecuta. La realización escénica tal y como la entiende Herrmann da lugar a una constelación única, irrepetible, sobre la que la mayoría de las veces sólo se pueden ejercer una influencia y un control limitados, y en la cual ocurre algo que sólo puede acontecer de esa manera una vez –como no puede ser de otro modo tratándose del encuentro de un grupo de actores con un cierto número de espectadores de temperamentos, estados de ánimo, deseos, ideas y conocimientos distintos, en un determinado momento y en un determinado lugar–. En esa situación, a Herrmann le interesaban ante todo las actividades y los procesos dinámicos en los que ambas partes se implicaban.

Así, Herrmann considera la actividad «creativa» que despliega el espectador como «un furtivo revivir, una enigmática réplica del trabajo de los actores que se asimila no tanto por el sentido de la vista cuanto por el *sentido corporal (Körpergefühl)*, un secreto ímpetu interno que lo lleva a ejecutar los mismos movimientos, a reproducir el mismo tono de voz en su garganta»[41].

Con ello se insiste en que para la experiencia estética «lo más decisivo teatralmente» en la realización escénica es «la experiencia conjunta de los cuerpos reales en un espacio real»[42]. La actividad del espectador no se entiende como un mero ejercicio de su fantasía, de su imaginación –que es la impresión que se puede tener tras una lectura apresurada–, sino como un proceso físico. Este proceso se pone en marcha al tomar parte en una realización escénica por medio de una percepción que no realizan sólo el ojo o el oído, sino también el sentido corporal; que realiza, pues, el cuerpo entero de manera sinestésica.

Los espectadores reaccionan no sólo a las acciones físicas de los actores, sino también al comportamiento de los otros espectadores. Así, Herrmann señala que «siempre se encontrarán individuos entre el público que sean incapaces de revivir el logro interpretativo y que por el contagio anímico del conjunto del público, tan tremendamente propicio en otros casos, y tan poco propicio en éste, se termine abortando la posibilidad de que los individuos que sí estaban preparados revivan la experiencia»[43]. Con la metá-

41 Herrmann, «Das theatralische Raumerlebnis», p. 153. [Énfasis de la autora].

42 *Ibid.*

43 *Ibid.* La idea de Herrmann de una revivencia no sólo «anímica» y su defensa de la idea de «enigmática réplica del trabajo de los actores», y del «secreto

fora del «contagio» vuelve a dejarse claro que cuando hablamos de experiencia estética en el contexto de una realización escénica no la referimos a una «obra», sino a lo que surge a partir de aquello que acontece entre los que toman parte en ella. Por eso, en este caso, es más importante la emergencia de lo que ocurre que lo que ocurre, y aún mucho más importante que los significados que se le puedan atribuir. Que Abramović cortara repentinamente su propia carne con una cuchilla de afeitar tuvo más relevancia que el hecho de que se tallara una estrella de cinco puntas o que los posibles significados que pudieran atribuírsele a la estrella. Lo que afectó a los que tomaron parte en la realización escénica de Abramović, aunque fuera de muy diferente manera y en distinto grado, fue tanto *el hecho* de que ocurriera algo como ese *algo* que sucedió. Si Herrmann, al emplear expresiones como «revivencia interna», «vivencia compartida» o «contagio anímico» apuntaba a una transformación del espectador como resultado de la realización escénica, y en caso afirmativo, en qué medida lo pretendía, es algo que a partir de sus propias palabras no se puede ni afirmar categóricamente ni descartar.

En el fondo, el concepto de realización escénica de Herrmann implica una sustitución del concepto de obra por el de acontecimiento. Tanto una estética hermenéutica como la distinción heurística entre estética de la producción, estética de la obra y estética de la recepción son incompatibles con él. La específica esteticidad de la realización escénica estriba en su condición de acontecimiento.

El concepto de realización escénica de Herrmann, tal y como lo he reconstruido a partir de diversos escritos e intervenciones

ímpetu interno que lo lleva a ejecutar los mismos movimientos, a producir el mismo tono de voz en su garganta», encontró una base tan fascinante como sólida en la teoría de las llamadas neuronas espejo, que dieron a conocer en los años noventa del siglo veinte Vittorio Gallese y Alvin Goldman. En ella se habla de neuronas que suscitan en un observador de acciones un impulso para realizar esas mismas acciones, aunque en general el observador experimenta un bloqueo que le impide completarlas. Véase, de los mismos autores: «Mirror neurons and the simulation theory of mind-reading», en *Trends in Cognitive Sciences*, vol. 2, n. 12, diciembre 1998, pp. 493-501.

orales del autor –recogidas en apuntes de sus alumnos–, resulta en una ampliación del concepto de lo performativo *avant la lettre*, es decir, según ha sido posteriormente definido por Austin y por Butler[44]. La definición de Herrmann concuerda con las más modernas en la medida en que no entiende la realización escénica como representación o expresión de algo previo o dado, sino como el resultado de una creación genuina: tanto la realización escénica misma como su materialidad específica se producen únicamente en el proceso de ejecución por las acciones de todos los que toman parte en ella. El concepto de realización escénica de Herrmann va más lejos que el concepto de lo performativo de Austin y Butler en la medida en que hace hincapié en el cambio que durante la realización escénica se lleva a cabo en las relaciones entre sujeto y objeto, por una lado, y entre materialidad y signicidad, por otro. Sin embargo, se queda un poco atrás al pasar por alto el problema de la generación de significado en su transcurso. En suma, la aportación de Herrmann es especialmente interesante y prometedora para los propósitos de este trabajo, pues implica una sustitución del concepto de obra por el de acontecimiento en el contexto de los procesos estéticos, por más que no vaya acompañada de una referencia explícita a las posibles transformaciones. Como resultado de todo ello surge, pues, la sugestiva empresa de fundar una estética de lo performativo sobre el concepto de realización escénica.

Puesto que el desarrollo de esta estética parte del giro performativo llevado a cabo en las artes a partir de los años sesenta del siglo veinte, parece razonable abordar en primer lugar la cuestión de en qué modo o modos las propias artes han modificado desde entonces el concepto de realización escénica, y con él el de lo performativo. En la medida en que este trabajo se realiza decididamente desde el enfoque de la teoría del arte, tal procedimiento no necesita de ulteriores explicaciones. No se partirá por tanto de

44 Véase también Rudolf Münz, «'Theater –eine Leistung des Publikums und seiner Diener'. Zu Max Herrmanns Vorstellungen von Theater», en Erika Fischer-Lichte *et al.* (eds.), *Berliner Theater im 20. Jahrhundert*, Berlín, 1998, pp. 43-52.

la discusión de distintas teorías estéticas, ni se ofrecerán ejemplos provenientes del arte contemporáneo que las eluciden, las modifiquen o las refuten, según el caso. Su punto de partida lo constituirá, por el contrario, el *state of the arts*, al que confrontaremos con distintos enfoques teóricos.

Como se ha mostrado en el proceso de reconstrucción del concepto de realización escénica de Herrmann, puede ser productivo, por razones heurísticas, tratar por separado los aspectos que en la realización escénica en tanto que acontecimiento nos hemos encontrado mutuamente condicionados, inseparables y enlazados: su medialidad, su materialidad, su semioticidad y su esteticidad, sin perder por ello de vista su mutua implicación. Los cuatro capítulos siguientes estarán dedicados a la cuestión de en qué formas se han servido las artes desde los años sesenta de estos aspectos en sus realizaciones escénicas. Prestaremos especial atención a las realizaciones escénicas teatrales y a las del arte de acción y de la performance. A las primeras porque Herrmann desarrolló su concepto de realización escénica pensando en el teatro, y al arte de acción y de la performance porque con él y en él se ha producido la sustitución de obra por acontecimiento en las artes visuales.

III. LA COPRESENCIA FÍSICA DE ACTORES Y ESPECTADORES

Como ha mostrado Herrmann, la condición medial de la realización escénica radica en la copresencia física de actores y espectadores. Para que dicha copresencia sea posible, dos grupos de personas que funcionan como «actuantes» y «observantes» deben congregarse en un momento determinado en un lugar concreto y compartir en él un lapso de tiempo de sus respectivas vidas. La realización escénica tiene su origen en el encuentro de ambos grupos, en su confrontación, en su interacción.

En consecuencia, en una realización escénica rigen condiciones muy particulares respecto a la «producción» y a la «recepción» –por hacer uso una vez más de los términos tradicionales. Mientras que los actores realizan acciones –se mueven por el espacio, gesticulan, hacen muecas, manipulan objetos, hablan o cantan–, los espectadores observan sus acciones y reaccionan. Parte de esas reacciones puede muy bien producirse de manera puramente «interna», pero una parte al menos igual de importante la constituyen las reacciones perceptibles: los espectadores ríen alborozados, suspiran, se quejan, sollozan, lloran, patalean, se deslizan en sus asientos arriba y abajo, se echan hacia adelante con expresión tensa en el rostro o se reclinan relajados, aguantan la respiración y permanecen casi inmóviles; consultan repetidamente su reloj, bostezan, se duermen y empiezan a roncar; tosen y estornudan; hacen crujir papel de envolver, comen y beben;

murmuran o comentan en voz alta y de manera indiscreta lo que ocurre en escena, ovacionan, aplauden, silban o abuchean, se levantan, abandonan la sala con un portazo.

Reacciones de este tipo son perceptibles tanto para los demás espectadores como para los actores, que las sienten, las oyen o las ven. Esas percepciones resultan, a su vez, en reacciones perceptibles de los actores y de los demás espectadores. La interpretación de los actores pierde o gana en intensidad; aumenta el volumen de sus voces hasta ser irritantes o, por el contrario, cada vez más seductoras; se animan a añadir gags y otras improvisaciones o se saltan sus entradas o sus intervenciones; se acercan a la platea para interpelar directamente a los espectadores, para pedirles un cambio de comportamiento o que abandonen la sala. En el caso del resto del público, la percepción de las reacciones de los espectadores interpelados resulta en un aumento o en una disminución de su grado de participación, de su interés, de su tensión; la risa de unos puede hacerse más audible, llegando incluso a ser convulsa en casos extremos, mientras que otros quizá se atraganten con ella. También puede resultar en una mutua llamada al orden, en una pelea o en insultos entre ellos. Hagan lo que hagan los actores, sus actos tienen efectos en los espectadores, y hagan lo que hagan éstos sus actos tendrán igualmente efectos en los actores y en el resto de los espectadores. En este sentido se puede afirmar que la realización escénica se produce y se regula por medio de un bucle de retroalimentación autorreferencial y en constante cambio. De ahí que su transcurso no sea totalmente planificable ni predecible.

Esta indeterminación se había considerado desde finales del siglo dieciocho como una lacra, como una molestia que había que remediar a cualquier precio o, al menos, minimizarla. Para lograrlo se desarrollaron y probaron distintas estrategias. A finales del siglo dieciocho y durante el diecinueve se apostó, además de por la literaturización, por disciplinar al espectador. Se promulgaron normas para el teatro con la intención de prevenir el muy molesto y, por desgracia, a menudo contagioso «comportamiento indebido». Bajo amenaza de sanción se prohibió llegar tarde, comer, beber o hacer comentarios entre los asistentes durante la realización escénica. La invención de la iluminación de gas se utilizó para eliminar una de las principales fuentes de problemas: que los actores pudieran ver a los espectadores y, sobre todo, que éstos pudieran verse entre sí. Charles Kean experimentó desde los años cuarenta del siglo diecinueve con el progresivo oscurecimiento de la platea y Richard Wagner sumió al público en una oscuridad completa en el primer Festival de Bayreuth (1876). El propósito de todas esas medidas era impedir el bucle de retroalimentación: las reacciones visibles o audibles de los espectadores que, como tales, eran potencialmente molestas y debían transformarse en «internas», la idea era que se percibieran como mucho en tanto que internas. Como consecuencia de ello, se exigió y se fomentó la «empatía» del espectador, que fue conceptualizada y definida por Friedrich Theodor Vischer como un «acto de cesión anímica» *(Akt der Seelenleihung)*[1*]. Como sabemos por los repetidos escándalos teatrales de la época, sin ir más lejos el ocurrido con ocasión del estreno de la obra de Hauptmann *Antes de amanecer,* el 20 de octubre 1889, que había organizado la sociedad Freie Bühne de Berlín, estas medidas tuvieron un éxito modesto.

Cuando a principios del siglo veinte el director de teatro pasó a ocupar un primer plano en la actividad teatral, tuvo lugar un decisivo cambio de estrategia. A partir de ese momento, en vez de coartar las reacciones perceptibles de los espectadores se intentaba que se produjeran como consecuencia del empleo de determinadas estrategias escénicas. Es decir, que la dirección de teatro se ocupaba expresamente del comportamiento del espectador, y para ello había que organizar y dirigir el bucle de retroalimentación. Sergei M. Eisenstein formuló esta aspiración de forma especialmente concisa. Con ocasión de su montaje de la obra de

1 Cfr. Friedrich Theodor Vischer, «Das Symbol» (1887), en Friedrich Theodor Vischer, *Kritische Gänge*, vol. 4, Robert Vischer (ed.), Múnich, 1922, p. 435; Friedrich Theodor Vischer, *Ästhetik* (1846-1848), vol. 2, Múnich, 1922; Robert Vischer, «Der ästhetische Akt und die reine Form» (1874), en *Drei Schriften zum ästhetischen Formproblem*, Halle, 1927.

* Para comprender este concepto es importante que el lector tenga en mente el carácter ambiguo del verbo aleman *'leihen'*, que puede significar tanto 'prestar' como 'tomar prestado', una ambigüedad de difícil traslado a nuestra lengua.

Ostrovski *Todos los sabios son bastante sencillos* (1922/23), describió al espectador en su ensayo «Montaje de atracciones» (1923) ni más ni menos que «como el elemento básico del teatro» y definió la tarea de la realización escénica teatral como «dirigir al espectador en un sentido determinado (o a un estado de ánimo buscado)»[2]. Estrategias escénicas parecidas pueden rastrearse no sólo en los años veinte, especialmente en el teatro soviético y alemán, o en los años treinta, por ejemplo, en los *Thingspiele* de los nacionalsocialistas*. Los futuristas italianos ya las habían puesto en práctica, como demuestra el manifiesto «El teatro de variedades» citado anteriormente; un ejemplo aún más temprano serían los trabajos de Max Reinhardt. Su empleo del *hanamichi* y de las pistas del circo, así como los particulares métodos de escenificación que resultaban de su empleo de la corporalidad y la carnalidad de los actores, nos permiten reconocer su decidida intención de abrirle al espectador nuevos modos y perspectivas de percepción, y de llevarlo así a reaccionar, a su vez, de manera perceptible. Pero parece que las cosas no terminaron de salir bien en todos los casos. Así, un crítico escribe con ocasión del montaje de la obra de Erwin Piscator *Hoppla, wir leben!* [*¡Andá, si estamos vivos!*] (1927): «El tiempo dirá si las realizaciones escénicas de este tipo someten o no al espectador a un exceso de tensión física»[3].

El giro performativo en los años sesenta iba de la mano de una nueva actitud hacia la contingencia. Ésta no fue sólo aceptada de manera predominante como condición de posibilidad de las realizaciones escénicas, sino que fue saludada con entusiasmo. El

2 Sergei M. Eisenstein, «El montaje de atracciones (1923)», en S. M. Eisenstein, *El sentido del cine*, Madrid, 1999, p. 169.

* Los *Thingspiele* se consideran «la única contribución de los nazis al teatro en tanto que arte. El *Thing* era la asamblea tribal del pueblo teutón, y los *Thingspiele*, que tenían lugar al aire libre, eran una mezcla de "agit-prop" nazi, retreta militar, oratorio pagano y función de circo», Richard Grunberger, *Historia social del Tercer Reich*, Barcelona, 2007, p. 383.

3 Monty Jacobs, *Vossische Zeitung*, 5 de septiembre de 1927, cit. en Günter Rühle, *Theater für die Republik*, 2 vols., Fráncfort, 1988, vol. 2, 1926-1933, pp. 792-794, p. 794.

interés se centró expresamente en el bucle de retroalimentación como sistema autorreferencial y autopoiético[4] que no es susceptible de interrupción ni de control por medio de estrategias de montaje, y cuyo resultado final ha de ser de naturaleza abierta e impredecible. En ese proceso el interés se desvió de un posible control del sistema a su particular modo de autopoiesis. ¿De qué modo se influyen mutuamente las acciones y los comportamientos de actores y espectadores en una realización escénica? ¿Cuáles son las condiciones específicas que subyacen a esta mutua influencia? ¿Cuáles son los factores que condicionan su desarrollo y su resultado final? ¿Se trata realmente de un proceso estético, o es más bien social?

No es sólo que se hayan venido planteando preguntas de este tipo con respecto a las realizaciones escénicas, sino que éstas se realizan a menudo como experimento justamente para poder darles respuesta. La realización escénica no se entiende sólo como el lugar en el que las acciones y el comportamiento de actores y espectadores se influyen mutuamente, en última instancia de manera misteriosa, y en el que se negocian las relaciones entre ellos. Es también el lugar en el que se exploran el funcionamiento específico de esa influencia mutua y las condiciones y el desarrollo de los procesos de negociación. La tarea de la dirección consiste en desarrollar estrategias de escenificación con las que se pueda componer y producir una disposición experimental de los elementos con perspectivas de éxito. La dirección establece pautas que son decisivas para el funcionamiento del bucle de retroalimentación, intenta aislar y focalizar algunas variables y factores; otros, si no los elimina, sí los relega al menos a un segundo plano. Otras veces se concentra en la combinación de parámetros muy determinados.

La valoración de los resultados termina siendo, de todas formas, difícil. Los procesos de negociación no se desarrollan, por

4 Para el concepto de autopoiesis, como se emplea aquí y en lo que sigue, véase Humberto R. Maturana y Francisco J. Varela, *El árbol del conocimiento: las bases biológicas del entendimiento humano*, Santiago de Chile, 1984.

lo general, de la misma manera en distintas realizaciones de una misma escenificación, a menudo se observan incluso considerables diferencias, lo cual apenas permite manifestarse sobre ellas parcialmente. Por esa razón no ha de sorprender que en la mayoría de los casos no se pueda decidir de manera definitiva si se trata de un experimento mediante el que se está intentando explorar el funcionamiento del sistema autopoiético o si, en cambio, se trata más bien de un juego en el que se hacen malabarismos con sus distintas variables, factores y parámetros. De cualquier modo, lo lúdico del experimento y lo experimental del juego se refuerzan mutuamente.

Las estrategias de escenificación desarrolladas bien para la construcción de una disposición experimental de los elementos o bien como conjunto de reglas de juego, tienen como horizonte tres factores estrechamente relacionados entre sí: 1) el *cambio de roles* entre actores y espectadores, 2) la *formación de una comunidad* entre ellos, y 3) los distintos modos de *contacto* recíproco, es decir, la relación entre distancia y cercanía, entre lo público y lo privado o lo íntimo, entre el contacto visual y el corporal. Por más variadas que sean esas estrategias –dentro de un montaje, en los montajes de un director o los montajes de distintos directores–, siempre tienen algo en común: no sólo deben presentar y significar un cambio de roles, la formación y la disgregación de comunidades, la cercanía y la distancia, sino que tienen que conseguir que todos esos procesos se lleven a efecto. Al espectador no hay que ponerle ante los ojos simplemente el cambio de roles, la formación de una comunidad, la distancia o la cercanía, sino que hay que hacer que los experimente en su propio cuerpo como participante en la realización escénica.

1. Cambio de roles

Al referirme a la performance *Lips of Thomas* de Abramović, califiqué el cambio de roles como un fenómeno en el que la relación entre sujeto y objeto, que había estado vigente tradicionalmente en el teatro –y en las artes visuales en general–, se torna resbaladiza y escapa a cualquier intento de comprensión unívoca. ¿Se trata de una relación entre cosujetos o meramente de una actualización de la relación tradicional?

La pregunta por la participación del espectador surge en la mayoría de los casos de cambio de roles, sin que, no obstante, se haya dado con una respuesta clara. Asimismo, se han hecho propuestas en las que se enfatizan diferentes aspectos, cada uno de los cuales le ha conferido a la pregunta un peso distinto. Precisamente como motor de la dinamización y de los continuos desajustes en las relaciones entre sujeto y objeto, el cambio de roles se antoja particularmente adecuado para investigar en él el bucle de retroalimentación autopoiético que se establece entre las acciones y los comportamientos de actores y espectadores, y la influencia que tienen los unos sobre los otros.

A finales de los años sesenta y principios de los setenta Richard Schechner experimentó con su Performance Group con distintas formas de participación del espectador, y para cada una de ellas se centró en un parámetro distinto para la negociación de las relaciones entre performadores y espectadores. En la primera producción del grupo, *Dionysus in 69* (1968, una versión de *Las Bacantes* de Eurípides), se intentó establecer una relación equitativa entre cosujetos. Schechner menciona dos condiciones para el cambio de roles en el caso de los espectadores:

> First, participation occurred at those points where the play stopped being a play and became a social event – when spectators felt that they were free to enter the performance as equals. [...] The second point is that most of the participation in *Dionysus* was according to the democratic model: letting people into the play to do as the performers were doing, to 'join the story'[5].

5 Schechner, *Enviromental Theater*, Nueva York, 1973, p. 44 [«Primero, la participación tenía lugar en aquellos momentos en que la obra dejaba de serlo para convertirse en un acontecimiento social; cuando los espectadores se sentían con la confianza suficiente para involucrarse en la representación como iguales. [...] En cuanto al segundo aspecto, la mayor parte de la participación en Dionysus se efectuaba conforme a un modelo democrático: permitiendo que la gente entrara a la obra para hacer lo mismo que los actores, es decir, «inte-

El cambio de roles para los espectadores empezaba ya con la entrada en el teatro, para la que Schechner ideó una particular *opening ceremony* que había tomado de las descripciones de los ritos de iniciación que Arnold van Gennep había reflejado en *Los ritos de paso* (1909). Los espectadores podían participar en el ritual del nacimiento de Dioniso al comienzo de la realización escénica, en el de la muerte de Penteo después, así como en la danza bacanal con la que terminaba: «Together we make a community. We can celebrate together. Be joyous together. [...] So join us in what we do next. It's a circle dance around the sacred spot of my birth (Dionysus)»[6].

La escenificación de estos ritos se basaba fundamentalmente en las descripciones de ritos reales provenientes de distintas culturas. El ritual de nacimiento y de muerte, que constituía la parte central de la realización escénica, era una imitación del rito de adopción de los Asmat en Nueva Guinea. En la primera realización escénica los actores aparecieron en escena con muy poca ropa, las posteriores las realizarían completamente desnudos. Asimismo, los espectadores sólo podían asistir si estaban a su vez desnudos. Los hombres del grupo estaban tendidos en el suelo codo con codo mientras que las mujeres estaban de pie encima de ellos con las piernas abiertas y con el torso ligeramente inclinado hacia delante, de tal manera que se formaba un túnel que representaba «el canal del nacimiento». Al principio de la realización escénica el actor que hacía de Dioniso era empujado con rítmicos movimientos de cadera a través del «canal del nacimiento» y renacía como dios. En la muerte de Penteo este movimiento se repetía en la dirección opuesta. La realización escénica concluía con un rito de incorporación: performadores y espectadores formaban una procesión y abandonaban el espacio escénico, el lla-

---

grándola a la trama». Schechner, *El teatro ambientalista*, México D.F., 1988, p. 41]. [Trad. ligeramente modificada.]

6 «Juntos formamos una comunidad. Podemos festejar unidos. Gozar juntos. [...] Así que uníos a nosotros en lo que haremos ahora: vamos a formar un círculo alrededor del sacro lugar de mi nacimiento (Dioniso)». Schechner, *Dionysus in 69* [No se indica número de página].

mado Performance Garage, cuyas puertas estaban abiertas de par en par, y salían a las calles de Nueva York.

Schechner destaca especialmente dos aspectos en esta forma de participación del espectador: en primer lugar, hace hincapié en la relación entre cosujetos iguales («to enter the performance as equals», «according to the democratic model»). En segundo lugar establece una oposición entre el proceso estético del *play* y el *social event* en el que se convertía la performance por la participación de los espectadores.

Aunque las estrategias escénicas descritas tenían por objeto tratar a los espectadores como cosujetos, como *equals*, los espectadores se tomaban muchas veces libertades que convertían al performador en objeto: las performadoras sintieron repetidas veces que abusaban de ellas, que las estaban tratando como prostitutas[7]; un grupo de estudiantes secuestró al actor de Penteo para impedir su sacrificio a manos de Dioniso, lo que al performador (William Shepard) terminó acarreándole lesiones. Es decir, que la «liberación» de los espectadores y su conversión en cosujetos tuvo como resultado en algunas ocasiones que los espectadores liberados dominaran a los performadores y se produjeran contra ellos de forma violenta.

En producciones posteriores, Schechner probó otro modelo de participación del espectador en el que eran los performadores los que ejercían una cierta presión sobre los espectadores, intentaban manipularlos e incluso forzarlos. En *Commune* (1970-1972), que trataba sobre la guerra de Vietnam, concretamente sobre los incidentes de My Lai, un performador (James Griffith) escogió al azar a quince espectadores que debían entrar en un círculo en medio de la sala para hacer de los habitantes del pueblo de My Lai. En la mayoría de los casos los espectadores seguían las indicaciones sin objeción. Pero había algunos que se resistían. En esos casos el performador se quitaba la camisa y decía:

> I am taking off my shirt to signify that the performance is now stopped. You people have the following choices. First, you can come

7 Véase *Enviromental Theater*, p. 42 (esp. *Teatro ambientalista*, p. 40).

> into the circle, and the performance will continue; second, you can go to anyone else in the room and ask them to take your place, and, if they do, the performance will continue; third, you can stay where you are, and the performance will remain stopped; or fourth, you can go home, and the performance will continue in your absence[8].

Al espectador en cuestión se le ofrecían una serie de alternativas que en cualquier caso lo convertían en actor, incluso aunque permaneciera inmóvil era responsable de la interrupción de la performance. Con ello se le estaba negando la posibilidad de que escogiera la alternativa que había escogido: seguir observando como espectador los actos del performador sin exponerse. Se producía entonces una situación en la que las posiciones de sujeto y objeto ya no se podían diferenciar con claridad. ¿Quién ejercía en este caso la coacción y la violencia contra quién? ¿El performador, que pretendía hacer al espectador actor, o el espectador, que, con su resistencia a convertirse en actor, interrumpía la realización escénica e intentaba inducir a los performadores a continuar actuando en contra de sus planes y de lo que habían acordado de antemano? Cada uno de los participantes quería para sí la posición de sujeto, por lo que intentaba relegar a los otros a la posición de objeto. Este estado de cosas no se solucionó en absoluto en las largas conversaciones subsiguientes, sino que incluso se reforzó. Lo único que conseguían esas conversaciones era hacer más evidente el dilema en el que las reglas del juego establecidas en la escenificación de la realización escénica ponían a todos los participantes.

El desarrollo de este peculiar caso, que Schechner relata a partir de las anotaciones de su diario[9], nos abre una fascinante

8 *Ibid.*, p. 49 (esp. «Me estoy quitando la camisa para expresar que la realización escénica se interrumpe. Ustedes tienen las siguientes alternativas. Primero, pueden entrar al círculo y la función continuará; segundo, pueden dirigirse a cualquier persona que esté en la sala para que tome su lugar y, si lo hace, la realización escénica seguirá; tercero, pueden permanecer donde están y la realización escénica seguirá detenida; o, cuarto, pueden irse a su casa y la realización escénica continuará en su ausencia», p. 44) [Trad. ligeramente modificada].

9 *Ibid.*, pp. 49-54 (esp. pp. 44-49).

perspectiva sobre el funcionamiento del bucle de retroalimentación autopoiético. Al respecto, sin embargo, hay que tener en cuenta que el cambio de roles aumenta considerablemente la impredecibilidad del desarrollo de la realización escénica. Es decir, que al observar el bucle de retroalimentación en el contexto del cambio de roles, lo hacemos con una lupa de aumento. La negativa de cuatro de las quince personas escogidas por Griffith a entrar en el círculo y a convertirse en actores centró en ellos la atención de toda la concurrencia y así, paradójicamente, los convirtió en actores, lo quisieran o no. De ello resultó una contradicción performativa, pues con su negativa estaban llevando a cabo precisamente aquello que se querían negar a hacer. Fueron ellos quienes suscitaron la discusión. Participaron activamente en la negociación de relaciones y, ya en tanto que actores, insistieron en formar tomar parte en la realización escénica como espectadores. En el desarrollo posterior del proceso de negociación algunos performadores también exigieron, apelando al principio de equidad, ejercer su derecho a preguntarle a otra persona, esto es, a algún espectador, si estaba dispuesta a tomar su lugar y continuar con la realización escénica para poder ser libres ellos mismos de abandonar la sala. Dos performadores encontraron espectadores que se mostraron de acuerdo, pero expresaron sus reservas porque ni conocían sus respectivos papeles ni sabían cómo continuaba la realización escénica. La imprevisibilidad no hizo más que aumentar.

Tras tres horas de discusión, tres de los cuatro impugnadores decidieron abandonar la sala; después de que al cuarto le hubieran explicado los motivos por los que debía permanecer en el círculo, se declaró finalmente preparado para participar (quizá también porque su novia había tomado el papel de una performadora). La realización escénica, en palabras de Schechner, pudo entonces reanudarse –yo incluiría, sin embargo, las tres horas de discusión en ella y simplemente hablaría, por lo tanto, de su continuación–. Schechner hizo de apuntador de las dos espectadoras que debutaban como performadoras. La realización finalizó con el diálogo previsto en el texto y la subsiguiente procesión por las calles de Nueva York.

En ningún momento de la realización escénica se pudo prever qué dirección tomaría su desarrollo posterior. De la negativa de los cuatro espectadores no se seguía necesariamente una evolución determinada, sino una multiplicación de posibilidades. En este sentido la negativa a participar puede compararse con el famoso aleteo de mariposa que pone en marcha un proceso cuyo posterior desarrollo desencadenará o evitará un huracán. En cada momento del proceso de negociación era posible o pensable otra evolución, otro giro. Lo que surgió por mor del cambio de roles es aplicable en un sentido más amplio al bucle de retroalimentación: ni las reacciones de los espectadores son previsibles o completamente controlables ni lo son los efectos que tendrán sobre los actores y los demás espectadores. Aunque en muchos casos se pueda tratar de microprocesos apenas perceptibles y sólo accesibles para el observador a través de la lupa de aumento que es el cambio de roles, están presentes en toda realización escénica. La copresencia física de actores y espectadores, que constituye cualquier realización escénica, es la que pone en marcha estos procesos de manera irrevocable. Allá donde coincidan físicamente personas, las unas reaccionan a la presencia de las otras, aun cuando no sea siempre de manera perceptible por la vista o el oído. Se podría decir, parafraseando el conocido apotegma de Watzlawick, que no se puede no reaccionar a la presencia ajena*.

De ahí que en toda congregación de personas se dé siempre una situación social. Por eso es curioso que Schechner opusiera realización escénica a acontecimiento social cuando al referirse a la participación de los espectadores con ocasión de la realización escénica de *Dioniso* dijo: «the play stopped being a play and became a social event» [«la obra dejó de ser una obra y se convirtió en un acotecimiento social»]. Con esta contraposición entre realización escénica como un proceso estético y acontecimiento social Schechner pierde de vista la singular importancia

* La autora se refiere a uno de los axiomas de la teoría de la comunicación humana de Paul Watzlawick: «*Man kann nicht* nicht *kommunizieren!*», que podríamos traducir por «¡no se puede *no* comunicar!».

de la participación de los espectadores de la manera en la que el Performance Group la puso en práctica. Dinamizaba no sólo la relación dicotómica entre sujeto y objeto, sino también la relación tradicional entre acontecimiento artístico, en este caso teatral, y acontecimiento social. Además, hacía posible que los participantes fueran conscientes de que toda realización escénica es siempre un acontecimiento social, pues en ella estamos siempre, por imperceptiblemente que sea, ante una negociación o estipulación de posiciones y de relaciones, es decir, estamos ante relaciones de poder. En la realización escénica se hallan inseparablemente unidos lo estético y lo social o político. Esta vinculación no se debe necesariamente a que en ella se traten asuntos públicos o se defienda un programa político. Viene ya dada de antemano por la copresencia física de actores y espectadores, y está garantizada por ella. Es razonable pensar que el reconocimiento del vínculo indisoluble entre lo estético y lo político en una realización escénica se ha dado desde siempre, al menos de manera implícita. Éste puede ser uno de los motivos por los que en la Alemania del siglo diecinueve, por caso, el teatro no fuera reconocido como arte y fuera puesto bajo supervisión policial. Y también es sin duda uno de los motivos por los que las artes desde los años sesenta tienden a producir realizaciones escénicas en vez de obras. (Quizá ello explique también por qué la estética filosófica apenas se ocupa del teatro, pese a que el concepto de acontecimiento ocupa una posición prominente en ella). El cambio de roles, que sólo es posible por medio de la copresencia física, da al traste con la aparente dicotomía entre lo estético y lo político. Da lugar a que emerja la específica vinculación entre lo estético y lo político en la realización escénica, y ello independientemente de si se defiende que entre actores y espectadores hay una relación de cosujetos, de si se proyecta o se realiza tal cosa, o de si les brinda a actores y a espectadores posibilidades de manipulación mutua. Así pues, deja claro *y* permite experimentar que en las realizaciones escénicas lo estético es de consuno político, y que ambos dominios son inseparables.

Esta nueva visión, surgida a partir de los experimentos de finales de los años sesenta y principios de los setenta, constituyó el punto de partida para experimentos posteriores con el cambio de roles. En el año del quinto centenario del llamado descubrimiento de América por Colón (1992), los artistas de performance americanos Coco Fusco y Guillermo Gómez-Peña presentaron su performance *Two Amerindians Visit...* en distintos lugares: en plazas públicas, como el Covent Garden en Londres y la plaza de Colón en Madrid; en museos de arte y galerías, como en Irvine, Nueva York o Chicago; y en museos de ciencias naturales, como en Washington, Minneapolis y Sidney. La performance fue abordada como un experimento con el que los artistas pretendían demostrar la tesis de que el mero acto de percibir a otro es ya un acto político, y la de que en las culturas occidentales la mirada sobre los otros –y sobre uno mismo– está todavía hoy determinada por el discurso colonialista.

En cada uno de los lugares donde se hizo la realización escénica Fusco y Gómez-Peña «vivían» en una jaula dorada como amerindios sin descubrir, oriundos de una pequeña isla en el Golfo de México que los europeos –por motivos sin esclarecer– se habían olvidado de descubrir durante quinientos años. Llamaron a su tierra natal Guatinau y a sí mismos guatinaui. Ambos se vestían como amerindios de fantasía: Fusco llevaba una faldita de rafia y un sujetador de piel de tigre, un collar de garras enormes, unas gafas de sol y zapatillas deportivas. Gómez-Peña se había maquillado el rostro como una máscara de tigre –en irónica referencia al estereotipo del «fiero guerrero mexicano»–, y ocultaba sus ojos tras unas gafas de sol. Llevaba un gigantesco adorno en la cabeza, llamativamente engalanado, y tanto en su punta como sobre la frente mostraba dos imágenes de un jefe indio. Del cuello se había colgado unas vistosas joyas que le cubrían también el pecho. En las caderas se había atado un taparrabos fijado a la cintura con un cordón de perlas. Calzaba mocasines y había adornado sus pantorrillas con collares de perlas. Fusco y Gómez-Peña tenían atada una correa en el cuello. Los guardas que vigilaban la jaula los llevaban al retrete atados.

Ambos realizaban lo que llamaron sus «tareas tradicionales», que iban desde levantar peso, pasaban por coser muñecos de vudú y llegaban hasta ver la televisión y trabajar en el ordenador portátil. En la jaula había una caja en la que se podía leer que por una pequeña cantidad Fusco bailaría (concretamente música rap, como se vería más tarde), Gómez-Peña contaría auténticas historias amerindias (aunque se servía de una lengua inventada) y que ambos posarían con los visitantes para hacerse fotografías.

Ante la jaula había grandes paneles de información. El primero mostraba momentos álgidos de la historia de las exposiciones coloniales; el segundo exponía una falsa entrada de la *Enciclopedia Británica* sobre los «amerindios», así como un mapa convenientemente manipulado del Golfo de México.

Para hacer plausible su tesis sobre la visión colonialista, los dos artistas empleaban, entre otras, tres estrategias de puesta en escena. Primero escenificaban el discurso colonialista: su apariencia externa, sus actos y sus modos de conducirse corporizaban estereotipos del «mudo e incivilizado otro» al que los miembros de las culturas occidentales debían civilizar e interpretar, por el que tenían que hablar. Al mismo tiempo esta escenificación del discurso colonialista estaba estructurada de modo que incluía elementos que no sólo cuestionaban los estereotipos, sino que también cuestionaban de manera radical la exigencia de autenticidad, con lo que hacían imposible la percepción de la performance en el sentido del discurso colonialista, o como mínimo la dificultaban. En segundo lugar, para sus actuaciones escogieron marcos peculiares que en circunstancias normales condicionan la percepción de la performance, y que por ello son responsables de cómo será entendida: como performance artística (en galerías y museos de arte), como una suerte de exposición etnográfica (en el museo de historia natural) o como un acto de conmemoración del «descubrimiento» de América (en la Plaza de Colón de Madrid). Para un espectador atento, estas dos primeras estrategias posibilitaban que la performance no se percibiera a través de la visión del discurso colonialista, sino como un enfrentamiento con él. La tercera y más importante estrategia de puesta en escena estaba fundamentada en el cambio de roles. Los performadores asumían una y otra vez la posición de espectadores, algo que a éstos les pasaba a menudo inadvertido. Observaban el comportamiento de los espectadores, sus reacciones, sus comentarios y sus actos, después los anotaban y finalmente terminarían publicándolos. Para facilitar esa tarea, la performance se montaba de modo que fueran precisamente los artistas los que incitaran a los espectadores a que tomaran a su vez la posición de actores. Así, los espectadores se veían obligados a actuar si querían ver algo más que las denominadas actividades cotidianas. Y para ello tenían que pagar literalmente un determinado precio, un precio que no era únicamente la cantidad que tenían que satisfacer. Al preguntarles a los vigilantes si podían dar de comer a Fusco, al pedir guantes de goma para acariciar las piernas de Gómez-Peña, al querer informarse sobre si los protagonistas se aparearían en público en la jaula, al pagar la cantidad prescrita para alimentar a Fusco con un plátano, para verla bailar o para escuchar los incomprensibles relatos de Gómez-Peña, los espectadores realizaban acciones que captaban la atención tanto de los dos artistas como de los demás espectadores, acciones que los convertían en actores.

Los artistas, al observar a los espectadores que se habían convertido en actores, fueron capaces de diferenciar tres formas de percepción y de conducta:

1. La de los colegas artistas y las personas que se mueven en el ámbito de la cultura, que reconocieron la performance como algo artístico, y que, sin embargo, por motivos artísticos y morales, entre otros, criticaron a los artistas de manera abierta y pública *in situ*, y les reprocharon, por ejemplo, que engañaran al público al actuar como si se tratara de una exposición etnológica.
2. La de aquellos espectadores que entendían perfectamente el carácter de «juego de intercambio de roles», pero que aun así querían participar, por ejemplo, hombres o mujeres de negocios en Madrid o Londres que pasaban por casualidad, o visitantes de la galería en Nueva York, que dieron de comer a Coco Fusco un plátano y que querían fotografiarse con ella.
3. La de los espectadores que entendieron la performance, independientemente de su lugar de ejecución, como una especie de exposición etnográfica ante la que reaccionaron en algunos casos compasivamente y con protestas, y en otros con curiosidad y aprobación.

Los dos performadores se asignaron la posición de observadores distantes que habían creado una disposición experimental, controlaban su cumplimiento y observaban cómo se comportaban los «conejillos de indias» en las condiciones establecidas en el experimento. Los artistas, al crear, y aspirar a supervisar, unas condiciones que convertían a unos espectadores en objeto de observación de otros, estaban dándole la vuelta, desde su punto de vista a una posición establecida por el discurso colonialista: los espectadores tomaban, aunque en parte fuera inconscientemente y contra su voluntad, la posición de «salvajes» que son observados, fijados, controlados e interpretados por otros.

Cabe destacar, sin embargo, que los performadores escenificaban un juego de perspectivas, y con él la posibilidad de un intercambio permanente de posiciones: el rechazo de la visión colonialista por parte de los performadores, acompañada sin duda de una visión que los controlaba a ellos (la de artistas y funcionarios de la cultura); el cambio de puntos de vista entre performadores y espectadores en cuanto al juego, al «como si» (los hombres de negocios involucrados); la mirada cosificadora, y en parte sin duda compasiva, hacia los performadores como «salvajes incivilizados», algo que parecían confirmar los espectadores por su identidad de miembros de una cultura superior y civilizada (los *believers*); la mirada controladora y al mismo tiempo codiciosa (los acosos sexuales); la mirada vigilante de un grupo de espectadores sobre otro (los *non believers* sobre los *believers*); y por último, la mirada observadora, distante y no menos controladora de los performadores sobre los espectadores, que reafirmaba a los artistas en su convicción de la persistente virulencia del discurso colonialista en la cultura occidental, lo que los reafirmaba asimismo en su identidad en tanto que «otros»[10].

10 Véase sobre la performance Erika Fischer-Lichte, «*Rite de passage* im Spiel der Blicke», en Kerstin Gernig (ed.), *Fremde Körper. Zur Konstruktion des Anderen im europäischen Diskurs*, Berlín, 2001, pp. 297-315; Coco Fusco, «The oder History of Cultural Performance», en *The Drama Review* 38, 1 (primavera 1994), pp. 145-167.

Puede que desde el punto de vista de los dos artistas la manera en la que la performance trascurrió en los distintos lugares de ejecución y ante distintos espectadores confirmara su tesis inicial. Sin embargo, a la luz de las consideraciones que acabamos de hacer parece razonable abrigar ciertas dudas al respecto. Surge la pregunta de si cuando los performadores hablan de la mirada de un observador neutral no se tratará en realidad de una atribución *a posteriori*. Una idea que sugeriría que los artistas creían que les era posible liberarse del bucle de retroalimentación, lo cual entraría en contradicción con todo lo argumentado hasta ahora. Puede que la performance demostrara, e hiciera a todos los participantes experimentarlo, que el acto de percibir a otro es siempre un acto político, pues siempre conlleva atribuciones ajenas y propias, así como mecanismos de control. Esto no sólo era válido en el contexto de la realización escénica para la percepción de los artistas por parte de los espectadores –como sugería Fusco– o para la de los espectadores por parte de otros espectadores, también lo era para la percepción de los espectadores por parte de los performadores. Sus percepciones, las acciones vinculadas a ellas y su manera de comportarse ponían en marcha el bucle de retroalimentación de la influencia mutua y lo mantenían activo, lo que imposibilitaba prever el desarrollo de la realización escénica. Por eso mismo, parece problemático pretender interpretar las reacciones de los espectadores como la expresión de una mentalidad colonialista preexistente. La realización escénica parafraseaba y reescenificaba el discurso colonialista de una manera que daba lugar a discrepancias sustanciales, que las provocaba incluso –no sólo en lo que concierne a los detalles irónicos de la puesta en escena introducidos por los performadores, sino en lo que concierne a las acciones de aquellos espectadores que se avenían al juego interpretativo del «como si» o que, por el contrario, intentaban boicotearlo dirigiéndose a los artistas directamente por su nombre.

Tanto los actores como los espectadores intentaron servirse del cambio de roles para imponer su derecho y su capacidad para determinar tanto la percepción de los demás como el discurso en cuyo contexto situarla e interpretarla. Se pudo comprobar de forma fehaciente que lo estético era lo auténticamente político. La constante y activa dinamización de la relación entre sujeto y objeto que siempre se da en la realización escénica tenía lugar en forma de una especie de lucha de poder, como un constante cambio de posiciones entre performadores y espectadores. La realización escénica, y con ella el bucle de retroalimentación, transcurría como una lucha para ejercer un determinado poder de definición e interpretación que la artista, en *The Drama Review*, obra publicada una vez finalizada toda la serie de realizaciones escénicas, no sólo interpretaba desde su punto de vista, sino que también continuaba por otros medios.

En *Two Amerindians Visit...* los diversos marcos, que venían dados por los distintos lugares y ocasiones en los que se realizó, se revelaron como una importante estrategia de puesta en escena. Pues los marcos no sólo hacían posibles las diversas percepciones de la performance, sino que además brindaban a los espectadores otras posibilidades de convertirse en actores. Con la selección de los lugares en los que ejecutar su performance, Fusco y Gómez-Peña se decidieron por un procedimiento que permitía investigar la influencia de cada uno de los distintos marcos por separado.

Christoph Schlingensief, por el contrario, trabajó en sus producciones de los años noventa con el método de emplear en una sola realización escénica varios marcos distintos y hacerlos chocar entre sí. En su producción *Chance 2000 – Wahlkampfzirkus '98* [*Chance 2000 – Campaña electoral circense'98*], que montó en 1998, año electoral, en el Volksbühne de Rosa Luxemburg Platz de Berlín, era casi imposible para el espectador discernir en muchos momentos en qué tipo de acontecimiento se encontraba: ¿en una realización escénica teatral (en fin de cuentas se trataba de una producción del Volksbühne y se vendían entradas en taquilla)?; ¿en una función de circo (lo cual se podría inferir por el lugar elegido para la realización escénica, una pista de circo, y por el hecho de que los miembros de la familia de artistas circenses Sperlich efectuaran una serie de números)?; ¿en un *freak-show* (si es que se puede denominar así a la aparición de unos minusválidos en escena, a los que por momentos se trataba de forma sumamente grosera)?; ¿se trataba de un *talk-show* (pues en el transcurso de la realización escénica se *producían* distintos diálogos y entrevistas)?; ¿o era en un mitin político, en realidad la fundación de un partido (pues la pista se cubrió con listas y Schlingensief les pedía a los espectadores que se dirigieran a ella y se inscribieran en las listas como miembros del partido Chance 2000)? En muchas ocasiones parecían transcurrir simultáneamente dos o tres tipos distintos de evento. Una situación en la que los distintos géneros se comentaban unos a otros, reflexionaban los unos sobre los otros y se cuestionaban entre sí.

Así, por ejemplo, cuando muchos espectadores acudían a la pista para, siguiendo la petición de Schlingensief, inscribirse como miembros del partido –y poder así por fin decidir por sí mismos su destino político–, el actor Martin Wuttke se enfrentaba a ellos desde la tribuna que había encima de la entrada a la pista y los tachaba de masa conformista que sigue a su líder incondicionalmente, además les atronaba los oídos durante un cuarto de hora con un megáfono a través del que repetía la frase: «¡Yo soy el agente patógeno del pueblo y vosotros sois un plástico estresante autógeno!». Los constantes choques entre marcos y, como resultado de ellos, las permanentes rupturas del marco recién establecido, desconcertaban e irritaban visiblemente a muchos espectadores, lo que desencadenaba las más diversas reacciones, con las que se convertían una y otra vez en actores. Los choques y rupturas de marcos se revelaron como la más eficaz estrategia de puesta en escena para iniciar el cambio de roles: de espectadores a actores, pero también de actores a espectadores, y para aumentar exponencialmente la impredecibilidad del bucle de retroalimentación autopoiético.

La realización escénica constaba de una serie de números que no sólo eran presentados en una sucesión arbitraria, además la duración de cada uno podía abreviarse o prolongarse a discreción. Regía la regla de juego de que los actores tenían derecho a negarse en cualquier momento a ejecutar un número concreto, o que podían, si así lo deseaban, añadir o inventar números nuevos, lo cual implicaba la ruptura de los marcos «realización escénica teatral» o «función de circo». Este derecho se les garantizaba igualmente a los espectadores, que hacían uso de él con entusiasmo creciente. Cada vez que la negativa de un actor dejaba un hueco libre –en ocasiones incluso en mitad de un número–, los espectadores se presentaban en la pista con *su* número. Por regla general tanto Schlingensief como los otros actores se retiraban a asientos ubicados en la pista y observaban al espectador o a la espectadora en cuestión. En tales casos algunos espectadores aprovechaban para intervenir, como parte activa y en igualdad de derechos, en las negociaciones de las relaciones entre ambas partes, mientras Schlingensief los observaba, a veces parecía que para animarlos, aunque otras les cortaba bruscamente. A pesar de que Schlingensief estaba –salvo en contadas excepciones– presente durante toda la realización escénica y pretendía dar la impresión de querer controlar y dirigir su desarrollo, lo cierto es que con las reglas de juego establecidas era una tarea completamente imposible. Puesto que todos los actores y todos los espectadores tenían por principio derecho a intervenir en el transcurso de la realización escénica en cualquier momento, a todo el mundo le quedaba claro que el bucle de retroalimentación no seguía otro principio que el del azar. Como quiera y cuando quiera que un espectador interviniera o que un actor se negara a hacerlo, la realización escénica daba un nuevo e imprevisible viraje. Un viraje ante el que tanto Schlingensief como el resto de participantes tenían que reaccionar, lo que daba lugar a un nuevo viraje y así sucesivamente *ad libitum*, o hasta que se declaraba de manera arbitraria el final de la realización escénica. Puede llegar incluso a afirmarse que cada una de las realizaciones escénicas de *Chance 2000-Wahlkampfzirkus'98* no consistía en nada más que en poner por obra y hacer susceptible de experiencia, sobre la base del principio del azar, el funcionamiento del bucle de retroalimentación.

Los permanentes choques y rupturas de marcos creaban una y otra vez situaciones nuevas para los espectadores en las que no podían comportarse «de modo automático», es decir, no podían comportarse de modo adecuado a unas reglas establecidas dentro de un marco, sino que tenían que decidir qué marco era el válido para ellos. Cuando Schlingensief trataba de modo grosero a los minusválidos, que estaban en la pista además de él, de la familia de artistas circenses Sperlich, de los actores Martin Wuttke y Bernhard Schütz y de la llamada familia Schlingensief, tenían que elegir si querían referir el hecho al marco teatral, en el que la brutalidad sería tenida por meramente fingida, por un «como si», o al marco de la interacción social, en el que el ciudadano Christoph Schlingensief se comportaba de modo inadecuado con minusválidos. Quien se decidía por el marco teatral permanecía tranquilamente sentado en su asiento, quien lo hacía, por el contrario, por el de la «interacción social» intervenía en actitud de protesta.

Los choques y rupturas de marcos precipitaban a los espectadores no sólo a una *crisis*[11], porque estaban constantemente en una situación de incertidumbre sobre qué marco debía regir y porque les exigían tomar permanente decisiones, sino también porque los limites entre ámbitos, que los marcos habían delimitado de manera clara hasta ese momento, se difuminaban, si es que no habían sido suprimidos por completo. ¿Qué distingue una asamblea política de una realización escénica teatral? ¿Qué diferencia la fundación de un partido de una función de circo? ¿No se trata en todos esos casos de realizaciones escénicas en las que se negocian y se establecen las relaciones entre los participantes y en las que se ejecutan distintos tipos de «piezas artísticas»? ¿Acaso no se trata siempre de la relación entre actores y espectadores, de la pregunta por las condiciones para que alguien sea actor o espectador y por las consecuencias de ello?[12] ¿Quién está en condiciones de hacer que alguien se convierta en actor o en espectador? ¿Quién o qué confiere capacidad operativa?

11 Véase Irene Albers, «Scheitern als Chance: Die Kunst des Krisenexperiments», en Johannes Finke y Matthias Wulff, *Chance 2000. Die Dokumentation – Phänomen, Materialen, Chronologie*, Neuweiler, 1998, donde se interpreta *Chance 2000*, en el sentido de la etnometodología de Garfinkel, como un experimento de crisis, que la autora refiere principalmente a la perfecta escenificación de los medios de comunicación y de la política. El experimento desvelaría, pues, los mecanismos de esa puesta en escena y nos permitiría entorpecerlos de manera productiva. A mi parecer esa referencia no es, sin embargo, de primera importancia.

12 Véase Uri Rapp, *Handeln und Zuschauen. Untersuchungen über den theatersoziologischen Aspekt in der menschlichen Interaktion*, Darmstadt/Neuwied, 1973.

El cambio de roles incrementaba, pues, no sólo el grado de indeterminación de la realización escénica, también la imprevisibilidad del bucle de retroalimentación, y de un modo tan enorme que se hacía visible para todos. Además, hacía explícito su potencial político implícito. En el caso de Schlingensief el cambio de roles estaba planteado de tal manera que al espectador no sólo le posibilitaba esa experiencia, podía también, actuando, influir en el desarrollo de la realización escénica. A esta experiencia se llegaba pagando el alto precio de pasar por otras dos que se anulaban mutuamente. Por un lado, el espectador tenía que presenciar cómo el giro que le había dado a la realización escénica era desbaratado por las posteriores intervenciones de otros espectadores o de los actores. Por otro, los continuos choques entre marcos le permitían experimentar que él, independientemente de que hubiera intervenido y se hubiera convertido en actor a los ojos de los demás espectadores o de que se hubiera quedado en su asiento agobiado por la inseguridad o quizá buscando una distancia irónica, había influido con su conducta en la marcha de la realización escénica, que dependía de él la dirección que tomara el bucle de retroalimentación. El espectador experimentaba así al mismo tiempo su poder y su carencia de poder y se veía obligado a comportarse de alguna manera al respecto. Lo que es seguro es que no estaba en condiciones de anular el principio del azar, el que seguía el transcurso de la realización escénica. Únicamente podía, aunque de modo limitado, intentar utilizarlo a su favor.

Los tres ejemplos de cambio de roles aducidos proceden de contextos estéticos y políticos completamente distintos. Schechner fundó el Performance Group en un tiempo en que el teatro a la italiana, con su clara división entre actores y espectadores, y con el consecuente oscurecimiento del espacio del espectador, era el modelo teatral preponderante en todo el mundo occidental, a pesar de que John Cage llevara realizando más de quince años sus *events* y sus *pieces*[13]. Los Estados Unidos estaban en la gue-

13 Véase sobre estos dos influyentes acontecimientos: el *Black Mountain Untitled Event* y el concierto *4'33"* (¡los dos realizados en 1952!), entre otros Erika Fischer-Lichte, «Grenzgänge und Tauschhandel. Auf dem Wege zu einer performati-

rra de Vietnam y se estaba formando el movimiento de defensa de los derechos civiles. El *Dionysus in 69*, de Schechner, puede entenderse como una alternativa a estas condiciones estéticas, sociales y políticas y, al mismo tiempo, como una confrontación con ellas. El cambio de roles aspiraba a la utopía de llegar a unas relaciones interhumanas perfectamente simétricas, de hacer realidad las relaciones entre cosujetos –o de explorar al menos, como en *Commune*, los mecanismos de manipulación recíproca– y de abrir al mismo tiempo nuevas posibilidades a la experiencia estética.

En los años noventa quedaba ya muy atrás la performativización de las artes. El arte de la performance pertenecía ya a las artes establecidas y gozaba del reconocimiento general. Entre el teatro y el arte de la performance se producía un intercambio muy dinámico que acercó a ambas artes considerablemente. El teatro venía tomando desde hacía tiempo procedimientos desarrollados en el campo del arte de la performance –como las realizaciones escénicas en lugares inusuales y en nuevos espacios, la exhibición de cuerpos enfermos, demacrados u obesos sobre el escenario, o la autoagresión y otras formas de violencia contra el propio cuerpo por parte de los performadores. Entre tanto, el arte de la performance había empezado a emplear sin mayores problemas procedimientos antes denostados como, por ejemplo, la narración de historias, la creación de ilusión o la inclusión del recurso al «como si». La política oficial en los Estados Unidos perseguía la igualdad para los miembros de minorías étnicas. En ese contexto Fusco y Gómez-Peña emplearon el cambio de roles en *Two Amerindians Visit...* con el fin de conseguir que todos los participantes experimentaran en sus propias carnes, por así decirlo, que la sola mirada por la que percibimos al otro puede degradarlo a objeto o reconocerlo como sujeto. La realización escénica redefinía permanentemente las relaciones entre performadores y espectadores, y entre los

---

ven Kultur», en Uwe Wirth (ed.), *Performanz. Zwischen Sprachphilosophie und Kulturwissenschaften*, Fráncfort, 2002, pp. 277-300 (versión modificada del ensayo del mismo título: Uwe Wirth *et al.* (eds.), *Theater seit den sechziger Jahren*, pp. 1-20); Petra Meyer, «Als das Theater aus dem Rahmen fiel», en Erika Fischer-Lichte *et al.* (eds.), *Theater seit den sechziger Jahren*, pp. 135-195.

espectadores entre sí, y promovía por ello un continuo intercambio no sólo de miradas, también de posiciones e identidades.

Christoph Schlingensief presentó su producción en 1998, que era año de elecciones, ocho después de la reunificación alemana y en el decimosexto de mandato de Helmut Kohl, y lo hizo precisamente en el Volksbühne de Rosa-Luxemburg-Platz. El teatro, en cuyo tejado se exhibe con letras luminosas la inscripción OST [ESTE], es tenido por uno de los más experimentales e innovadores de entre los de lengua alemana. El cambio de roles formaba parte del repertorio habitual de procedimientos que se empleaban en la casa. Schlingensief había presentado cuatro producciones desde 1993 en las que experimentaba con el cambio de roles. Incitar al cambio de roles a los espectadores era también una de las señas de identidad del director artístico del Volksbühne, Frank Castorf. Un año antes de *Chance 2000*, él mismo había montado *Trainspotting*, una versión de la exitosa novela homónima de Irving Welsh que en 1996 ya había sido adaptada al cine por Danny Boyle. La realización escénica tenía lugar sobre el escenario, es decir, el «clásico» espacio de actuación de los actores. Para los espectadores se construyó una estructura de hierro en la parte trasera del escenario sobre la que se pusieron los asientos. Para acceder a ellos, los espectadores tenían que cruzar el escenario principal sobre el que se habían montado unos focos. El espectador que ocupaba su asiento en primer lugar podía observar cómo los siguientes tropezaban al pasar por el escenario y cómo algunos incluso tiraban al suelo algunos de los focos montados, y lo mismo ocurría con los que iban llegando posteriormente. Nada más entrar se jugaba ya con el cambio de roles. Los espectadores que llegaban más tarde tomaban el rol de actores a los ojos de los ya acomodados, lo quisieran o no. Para poder ser espectadores tenían que convertirse primero en actores, aunque después se mantenían en su condición de espectadores, presentes en (la parte trasera de) la escena. Con ello Castorf había ampliado con una interesante variante su amplio repertorio de procedimientos para incitar al cambio de roles, y para llevarlo a cabo. En la producción de Schlingensief el cambio de roles, como tal, no presentaba ninguna innovación estética, aunque sí experimentara considerables modificaciones y variaciones. La producción estaba pensada, entre otras cosas, como un intento de que el ciudadano recuperara el poder que había perdido durante los dieciséis años de mandato de Kohl y para permitirle manifestarse como sujeto activo.

Ciertamente en estos tres casos estamos ante contextos políticos y estéticos distintos. Pero al mismo tiempo presentan un rasgo digno de mención: en todos ellos está en juego algo que podría denominarse procesos de democratización o de redefinición de relaciones entre los miembros de una comunidad. Se trata de hacer realidad los derechos civiles, la eliminación de la discriminación, incluida la latente, y la división equitativa del poder, si es posible entre todos. Tal propósito sólo puede alcanzarse si algunos renuncian al poder y a los privilegios para que otros puedan acceder a ellos. El cambio de roles puede entenderse en este contexto, pues, como un proceso de pérdida y adquisición de poder que concierne tanto a los artistas teatrales como a los espectadores. Los artistas renuncian por sí mismos a su poder como únicos creadores de la realización escénica; se declaran dispuestos a compartir, aunque no sea de manera equitativa, la autoría y el poder de decisión con los espectadores. Esto se consigue sólo por medio de un acto de autoatribución de poder y de incapacitación de los espectadores: los artistas se atribuyen el poder para imponer al espectador nuevos modos de conducta o para hacerle entrar en crisis, y le impiden así mirar cómo ocurre todo, le privan de la posición de observador distante.

Con ello, como se ve en todos los ejemplos aducidos, el cambio de roles revelaba rasgos esenciales de la realización escénica y centraba la atención en ellos, rasgos que son paradigmáticos para el desarrollo de una estética de lo performativo. Por medio del cambio de roles se pone de manifiesto que el proceso estético de la realización escénica se ejecuta siempre como autogeneración, como bucle de retroalimentación autopoiético en continuo cambio. Autogeneración quiere decir que todos los participantes la crean conjuntamente, pero que no puede ser completamente planificada, controlada y, por así decirlo, producida por ninguno de ellos en concreto, que escapa tenazmente al poder de disposición de cada uno de ellos. De ahí que resulte de poca ayuda hablar de productores o receptores. Se trata más bien de cogeneradores que, en distinta medida y de distinta manera, contribuyen a la creación de la realización escénica, aunque sin poder determinarla. En el proceso por el que influyéndose mutuamente crean la realización escénica, es en el que la realización escénica, a su vez, los crea a ellos como actores y espectadores. El actor y el espectador figuran, con sus acciones y modos de comportamiento, como elementos del bucle de retroalimentación, como aquellos que la propia realización escénica genera. De ahí que ésta, en última instancia, tampoco se pueda «entender». No quiero decir con ello que no se les puedan atribuir significados a determinados elementos, secuencias o procedimientos, e interpretar así el cambio de roles, por ejemplo, como el cumplimiento de una relación simétrica entre cosujetos. Lo que de ningún modo es posible es entender la realización escénica como expresión de un sentido o una intención dados de antemano.

Al hablar de indisponibilidad de la realización escénica, tampoco se quiere decir que su existencia sea independiente de los actores y de los espectadores, o que a éstos les sea por definición inaccesible, que es como se suele entender la indisponibilidad de lo «divino» o de lo «sagrado». Se subraya, antes bien, la implicación de todos los participantes de manera expresa, tanto en lo concerniente a la mayor o menor influencia que ejerzan en el desarrollo de la realización escénica como en lo concerniente a la influencia a la que ellos mismos están expuestos, pues en fin de cuentas se trata de una relación de interacción[14]. El bucle de retroalimentación

14 Este aspecto debería ser tratado con más atención en el ámbito de la escenificación política, por ejemplo en el debate sobre las grandes concentraciones de nacionalsocialistas en los *Reichsparteitage* [congresos del NSDAP –Partido Nacionalsocialista Alemán de los Trabajadores– celebrados en distintas ciudades de Alemania entre 1923 y 1938, aunque desde 1929 se celebraran siempre en Nuremberg]. Ya que en estos casos se empleaban estrategias de escenificación que pretendían influir de un modo determinado tanto a los actores como a los espectadores para manipularlos. Pero de ello no se sigue que este efecto se produjera realmente. Lo que ocurría realmente era lo que se producía en el transcurso de la realización escénica. Debería darse más importancia a los tes-

apunta pues a la transformación como una de las categorías fundamentales de una estética de lo performativo.

El concepto de indisponibilidad polemiza en este sentido con la idea de que una realización escénica sea planificable. De ahí que en este contexto sea preciso diferenciar estrictamente entre los conceptos de escenificación *(Inszenierung)* y de realización escénica *(Aufführung)*. El concepto de escenificación implica un plan, una idea escénica que ha elaborado un artista, o varios conjuntamente, y que por regla general se modifica constantemente durante el proceso de ensayos (también aquí vemos en acción un bucle de retroalimentación, aunque de otro tipo). El plan puede prever qué elementos serán empleados, en qué lugares y en qué momentos y de qué modo serán empleados. Pero aunque el plan se siga estrictamente en cada una de las realizaciones escénicas, ninguna de ellas es idéntica a las demás. Pues en cada una de las llamadas repeticiones surgen desviaciones más o menos importantes –como ha mostrado la lupa de aumento del cambio de roles– que no se producen únicamente por el estado de ánimo o por el ambiente en cada caso, sino que su motivo hay que buscarlo en el bucle de retroalimentación autopoiético. Él es responsable de que la realización escénica se produzca cada vez de forma distinta, de que, en este sentido, cada una de ellas sea única e irrepetible.

Podemos, pues, partir de la base de que en una estética de lo performativo los ámbitos del arte, del mundo de la vida y de la política no pueden diferenciarse nítidamente. Una estética de lo performativo fundamentada en el concepto de realización escénica debe, por lo tanto, desarrollar e incluir en los debates teóricos los conceptos, categorías y parámetros adecuados para dar cuenta de esas esquivas transiciones, de esos equívocos rebasamientos de límites y de esas mezclas explosivas.

timonios sobre su desarrollo que a los que nos informan sobre su planificación. También los espectadores eran responsables de lo que tenía lugar en dichas realizaciones escénicas.

2. Comunidad

Una forma posible de crear un bucle de retroalimentación, muchas veces buscada a propósito, tiene que ver con un fenómeno en el que lo estético encuentra un vínculo inmediato con lo social y lo político: la formación de una comunidad de actores y espectadores basada en la copresencia física. Desde principios del siglo veinte se ha discutido y se ha defendido tal posibilidad. La discusión, sostenida por teóricos del teatro y por artistas teatrales, estaba en relación directa con el enardecido debate de los estudiosos del ritual y de los sociólogos sobre cómo puede surgir una comunidad a partir de una concentración de individuos o sobre si, planteado a la inversa, no habría que partir de la idea de que primero es la comunidad y de que más tarde, en su seno, empiezan a diferenciarse los individuos entre sí. En referencia a la teoría del ritual de sacrificio de Robertson Smith escribió Emile Durkheim: «La vida colectiva no ha nacido de la vida individual, sino que, por el contrario, es la segunda la que ha nacido de la primera. Sólo con esta condición se puede explicar la manera cómo la individualidad personal de las unidades sociales ha podido formarse y engrandecerse sin disgregar la sociedad»[15]. Así, al pasar del siglo diecinueve al veinte, la atención empieza a dirigirse a los procesos de formación de las comunidades, en una época en la que el individualismo tenía tal pujanza que, en expresión de Durkheim: «el individuo se convierte en el objeto de una especie de religión»[16], mientras que como consecuencia de la industrialización y la urbanización se constituían masas cada vez más anónimas. En este contexto el teatro les pareció a muchos un lugar en el que estos procesos no sólo se podían observar, sino en el que también se podían poner en práctica en condiciones ideales. Así, Georg Fuchs partía de la idea de que «intérprete y espectador, escenario y platea [...], atendiendo a su origen y a su esencia, no son opuestos sino que forman una uni-

15 Emile Durkheim, *La división del trabajo social*, Madrid, 2001, p. 327.
16 *Ibid.*, p. 205.

dad»[17]. Como muchos vanguardistas y reformadores del teatro, Fuchs era de la opinión de que esta unidad entre actores y espectadores podía restablecerse con la abolición del proscenio que, como lamentaba Meyerhold, «divide el teatro de hoy en dos mundos ajenos entre sí: el de quienes sólo actúan y el de quienes sólo observan»[18]. Los experimentos de Reinhardt con el *hanamichi* y con el teatro-carpa del Circo Schumann buscaban, entre otras cosas, alcanzar esa unidad, hacer que surgiera una comunidad entre actores y espectadores. Carl Vollmoeller, que adaptó la *Orestíada* para Reinhardt, elogió el teatro-carpa con ocasión de la inauguración del Grosses Schauspielhaus, construido a partir de la reforma del Circo Schumann en 1919, acaso como «la asamblea popular de hoy [...]. Lo que la despolitización de nuestro pueblo durante cincuenta años de régimen imperial hacía posible, es hoy posible: la concurrencia de miles de personas en un espacio teatral para formar una comunidad de ciudadanos y compatriotas activos, embelesados y entusiasmados»[19]. Una realización escénica que tenía lugar en un teatro así tenía que ser capaz de transformar a los actores y a los espectadores, en tanto que individuos, en una comunidad.

Los conceptos de comunidad que se tomaron como base en este proceso eran, sin embargo, extraordinariamente diversos. Así Fuchs, en la estela de Nietzsche, esperaba de la nueva manera de construir teatros, y del nuevo arte interpretativo que traería consigo[20], que fuera capaz de poner a los actores y a los especta-

17 Georg Fuchs, *Die Revolution des Theaters. Ergebnisse aus dem Münchener Künstlertheater*, Múnich/Leipzig, 1909, pp. 63 y s.

18 Vsevolod E. Meyerhold, «Zur Geschichte und Technik des Theaters», en *Schriften*, 2 vols., Berlín, 1979, vol. I, p. 131 (esp. «Historia y técnica en el teatro», en Juan Antonio Hormigón (ed.), *Meyerhold: textos teóricos*, Madrid, 1998).

19 Carl Vollmoeller, «Zur Entwicklungsgeschichte des Grossen Hauses», en *Das Grosse Schauspielhaus. Zur Eröffnung des Hauses*, editado por el Deutsches Theater de Berlín, Berlín, 1920, pp. 15-21, p. 21.

20 En un ensayo anterior, *Der Tanz* (Stuttgart, 1906), Fuchs definió este nuevo arte interpretativo como «movimiento rítmico del cuerpo humano proveniente del ímpetu creativo de hacer emerger una sensación usando el propio cuerpo como medio de expresión con la intención de descargar gozosamente precisa-

dores en aquella extraña forma de éxtasis «que nos invade cuando nos sentimos parte de una multitud, de una multitud que se mueve unitariamente. [...] en efecto, nos sacude un escalofrío en cuanto nos sentimos en la descomunal unidad de una pasión con otros, con muchos otros, cuando nos sentimos masa»[21]. Por su parte, Erwin Piscator, que en 1925 presentó en el Grosses Schauspielhaus su revista política *Trotz alledem!* [*¡A pesar de todo!*] y que, a partir de los planes de Walter Gropius para la construcción de un teatro propio, desarrolló la idea del teatro total[22], entendía comunidad como un colectivo político para la lucha de clases[23]. El *Thingspielbewegung** nacionalsocialista entró en esta discusión, que se había prolongado hasta los años treinta, e hizo construir *Thingstätten*, recreaciones de los teatros griegos, en los que empleando, entre otras cosas, estrategias de puesta en escena que habían desarrollado tanto Reinhardt como Piscator transformaban en sus realizaciones escénicas a actores y espectadores en «camaradas compatriotas» con el fin de crear una modélica «comunidad del pueblo»[24].

El nacionalsocialismo desacreditó no sólo los conceptos de comunidad en los que se incorporaba íntegramente al individuo –una comunidad que desprecia su individualidad y que intenta en última instancia anularla–, sino que fue la causa de que, después de la Segunda Guerra Mundial, el término 'comunidad'

---

mente aquel otro ímpetu interno que uno transmite a otras personas para que empiecen a realizar los mismos o similares movimientos, y con ello llevarlas al mismo estado de éxtasis, o a uno similar» (p. 13).

21 Fuchs, *Die Revolution des Theaters*, pp. 4y s.

22 Sobre el teatro total, véase Stefan Woll, *Das Totaltheater. Ein Projekt von Walter Gropius und Erwin Piscator* (= Schriften der Gesellschaft für Theatergeschichte, vol. 68), Berlín, 1984.

23 Véase Erwin Piscator, *Zeittheater. «Das politische Theater» und weitere Schriften von 1915 bis 1966*, Reinbeck bei Hamburg, 1986.

* Véase la nota [*] de la p. 80.

24 Véase sobre su programa el discurso del dramaturgo del Reich Rainer Schlösser ante el Reichsbund: «Vom kommenden Volksschauspiel» (1934), en *Das Volk und seine Bühne*, Berlin, 1935; para el Thingspiel en general, Gaetano Biccari, *«Zuflucht des Geistes»?: konservativ-revolutionäre, faschistische und nationalistische Theaterdiskurse in Deutschland und Italien, 1900-1944*, Tubinga, 2001.

desapareciera del uso de la lengua oficial. El teatro se convirtió de nuevo en espacio artístico –cuando no en templo del arte–, lo que excluía cualquier tipo de contaminación política e incluso social.

Cuando con el giro performativo de las artes en los años sesenta se superaron o eliminaron las fronteras entre arte y no-arte, entre lo estético y lo político, surgió de nuevo la candente discusión sobre la comunidad entre actores y espectadores. A las distintas formas del llamado teatro ritual les correspondió una importante función para el avance de ese proceso. Su punto de partida era una crítica radical a la sociedad industrial en la medida en que priva al individuo de «wholeness, process organic growth, concreteness, religious, transcendental experience»[25]:

> Links must be discovered or forged between industrial societies and non-industrial ones, between individualistic and communal cultures. And a vast reform in the direction of communality –or at least a revision of individualism– is necessary. This reform and revision will leave no aspect of modern society untouched; not economics, government, social life, personal life, aesthetics, or anything else. Theater takes a pivotal position in his movements because the movements are histrionic; a way of focussing attention and demanding change[26].

La creación de comunidades de actores y espectadores debería capacitar a todos los implicados para experimentar lo que antes

25 Schechner, *Enviromental Theater*, p. 197 (esp. «de la integridad, del proceso/crecimiento orgánico, de la concreción [y] de la experiencia religiosa, trascendental», *Teatro ambientalista*, p. 143).

26 *Ibid.* (esp. «Deben descubrirse o forjarse lazos entre las sociedades industriales y las no industriales, entre las culturas individualistas y las comunales. Y es necesaria una vasta reforma encaminada a la comunalidad –o al menos una revisión del individualismo. Esta reforma y revisión no dejará al margen ningún aspecto de la sociedad moderna: la economía, el gobierno, la vida social, la vida personal, la estética o cualquier otro. El teatro ocupa una posición clave en estos movimientos porque todo movimiento es histriónico; se trata de un modo de captar la atención y de exigir cambios», *ibid.*, la trad. ha sido ligeramente modificada).

les estaba vedado e iniciar así los procesos de transformación consiguientes. Propuestas teatrales como las del teatro de orgías y misterios del accionista vienés Nitsch o las del Performance Group de Schechner tomaban el ritual como punto de referencia en su trabajo porque estaban convencidos, como lo estaban ya décadas antes Robertson Smith y Emile Durkheim, de que las comunidades las crea la realización conjunta de rituales. Mientras Nitsch se orientaba a rituales cristiano-católicos y místico-arcaicos –como el ritual de descuartizamiento y resurrección de un dios, que Frazer tenía por universal–, Schechner se centraba en los ritos de paso descritos por Van Gennep. Ambos consideraban importante para la formación de una comunidad un requisito –en realidad su condición de posibilidad–: que actores y espectadores realizaran conjuntamente los ritos, específicamente modificados en cada caso. Para hacerlo posible se servían principalmente de dos estrategias. Por un lado, fomentaban el cambio de roles, sin el que la realización conjunta es impensable. Por otro, evitaban los teatros tradicionales, los templos del arte, y elegían para sus realizaciones escénicas lugares que no estuvieran aislados de la realidad social. Las acciones de descuartizamiento de corderos de Nitsch tenían lugar en su casa o en las de colegas artistas, en galerías y, posteriormente, en las dependencias del Palacio de Prinzendorf. Schechner montó *Dionysus in 69* en el Performance Garage, un antiguo taller que permitía la composición de distintos ambientes.

Por medio de sus realizaciones escénicas redefinieron radicalmente el concepto de comunidad. A diferencia del *Theater der Fünftausend [Teatro para cinco mil]* de Reinhardt, de la *Masse im Rausch* [*Masa en trance*] de Fuchs, del teatro para las masas proletarias de Piscator o del *Theater der Fünfzig bis Hunderttausend [Teatro para entre cincuenta y cien mil]* del *Thingspiel*, en su caso se trataba de un número más bien reducido de personas a partir de las cuales se debía constituir, de manera transitoria, una comunidad. Una comunidad que no forzaba a ninguno de los presentes a que se incorporara singular a ella. Se dejaba al arbitrio de cada cual si se quería pasar a formar parte de ella y, en su caso, cuándo hacerlo. Una comunidad debería posibilitar, como explica Schechner citando a David

Cooper: «a viable dialectic between solitude and being-with-others»[27]. Una comunidad de este tipo, que respeta la individualidad de todos los participantes, una comunidad, pues, de cosujetos, no se podía mantener sino por un muy limitado lapso de tiempo. Nunca llegaba a mantenerse durante todo el transcurso de la realización escénica, sólo en determinados momentos.

Tanto en Nitsch como en Schechner la comunidad debía generarse por la acción y la experiencia conjuntas. En *Dionysus in 69*, por ejemplo, fue la participación en el ritual de nacimiento y de muerte y la danza bacanal con motivo del nacimiento de Dioniso («Together we make a community. We can celebrate together. Be joyous together. So join us in what we do next. It's a circle dance around the sacred spot of my birth».) lo que hizo posible la formación de una comunidad de actores y espectadores. Es decir, que esta comunidad se constituía en un peculiar espacio intermedio. Era una comunidad que se les presentaba a aquellos espectadores que no habían sido incorporados a ella como parte de unos sucesos ficticios, de un *play*, es decir, como una comunidad ficticia y, al mismo tiempo, para aquellos que la ponían por obra, era una comunidad real constituida por la acción conjunta de actores y espectadores. Se originaba, pues, una comunidad que era «real» sólo desde la perspectiva de aquellos que se involucraban en la acción conjunta, aquellos que, en el marco del *play* ficticio, contribuían al nacimiento de Dioniso o a la muerte de Penteo, y creaban así una comunidad no sólo ficticia, sino también real. Es complicado discernir si, desde la perspectiva de los demás, a esta comunidad le correspondía únicamente el estatus de ficción, el de una comunidad meramente escenificada o aparente, o el de realidad. El cambio de roles no sólo para convertirse en un tipo de actor cualquiera, sino para devenir parte activa en el *play*, era el prerrequisito para el cambio de perspectiva y para la consecuente posibilidad de experimentar la comunidad. Se trataba, por lo tanto, de una experiencia que solamente podía darse en la ejecución de las

27 David Cooper, citado en *ibid.*, p. 255 (esp. «una dialéctica viable entre la soledad y el estar-con-otros», p. 182).

acciones, en el proceso de formación de la comunidad. Al respecto queda, por último, sin aclarar qué papel jugaba el «como si» y, si efectivamente tuvo alguno, de qué modo modificó o incluso obstaculizó la experiencia de comunidad vivida por los performadores y los espectadores participantes.

En las acciones de descuartizamiento de corderos que Nitsch llevó a cabo desde comienzos de los años sesenta se daban otras condiciones para la acción conjunta de actores y espectadores. No se realizaban en el contexto de un *play* ficticio, aunque algunos de los elementos que manipulaban tenían una gran carga simbólica. Era muy claro especialmente el caso del elemento central de la acción: el cordero. En la católica Viena de los años sesenta podría muy bien haberse entendido sin más como símbolo del «cordero de Dios», de Jesucristo, y de su sacrificio en la cruz; esta referencia la hacía aún más expresa el hecho de que colgaran al cordero de una cruz. No sorprende, pues, que la frontera entre acción artística y acontecimiento social no siempre pudiera delimitarse claramente, lo que tuvo como consecuencia, entre otras cosas, que Nitsch fuera procesado por blasfemia.

En muchas de las actividades actores y espectadores podían participar si querían: se rociaban mutuamente con sangre, chapoteaban en ella, en agua de fregar y en otros fluidos, toqueteaban vísceras y excrementos, andaban descalzos sobre ellos y destripaban juntos el cordero. Para terminar tenía lugar un banquete colectivo con vino y carne. Los elementos que actores y espectadores manejaban durante sus actividades eran considerados tabú en la cultura occidental de los años sesenta. Las acciones de Nitsch ofrecían a todos los participantes la posibilidad de rebasar abiertamente las fronteras rigurosamente vigiladas y protegidas de ese terreno tabú, de abandonarse junto a otros a impresiones sensibles y de vivir experiencias físicas que por regla general les estaban vedadas y que eran capaces de desencadenar un «exceso originario» (*urexzess*)[28].

28 Herrmann Nitsch, *Das Origen – Mysterien – Theater. Die Partituren aller aufgeführten Aktionen 1960-1979*, Nápoles/Múnich/Viena, 1979, vol. I, p. 87.

Los significados que constituyen el orden simbólico de nuestra cultura se han desvinculado hace tiempo de los objetos concretos y de las experiencias físicas vividas con ellos, es decir, de aquello de lo que una vez partieron los procesos de simbolización. Las acciones de Nitsch brindaban a los participantes la posibilidad de volver a enraizar, en el marco de la actividad colectiva, los procesos de simbolización en las vivencias físicas individuales. Estas acciones lograban al mismo tiempo dos cosas: por un lado, creaban durante el tiempo de su realización conjunta una comunidad de individuos que se habían reunido de manera casual, y que se atrevían, ante los ojos de los demás espectadores, a transgredir abiertamente tabúes vigentes; por otro lado, transformaban de consuno al individuo que las ejecutaba, lo capacitaban para realizar experiencias límite hasta entonces inaccesibles que lo llevaban al exceso y que producían así su catarsis, esto es, el liberador vínculo de la experiencia física y la producción simbólica. La común ingesta de carne y vino renovaba y fortalecía la comunidad de individuos «purificados» por esa misma ingesta. Esto recuerda a la comunión –Nitsch hace referencia explícita a ello–, en la que los creyentes incorporan simbólicamente el cuerpo y la sangre de Cristo, lo cual crea el grupo de feligreses una vez más y lo reafirma como comunidad en Cristo. Y lo mismo ocurre con la comunidad de comensales de Robertson Smith, con la que el grupo de cazadores se convertía primero en una comunidad ritual y luego en una comunidad política[29]. Las comunidades que se creaban en y por las acciones de descuartizamiento de corderos de Nitsch se pueden catalogar en cierto sentido como rituales, sin duda, pero en cualquier caso son comunidades simbólicas y sociales.

Tanto estas acciones de Nitsch como *Dionysus in 69* hacían alusión a rituales de sacrificio en los que la comunidad se creaba y se mantenía por medio del sacrificio de un chivo expiatorio, por la

29 Sobre el teatro de orgías y misterios de Nitsch véase: Erika Fischer-Lichte, «Verwandlung als ästhetische Kategorie», en E. F-L. *et al.* (eds.), *Theater seit den sechziger Jahren*, Tubinga/Basilea, 1998, sobre todo pp. 25-33 y 45-49.

violencia de todos contra uno[30]. Parece claro, no obstante, que las comunidades así creadas no entraban en conflicto con los individuos a partir de los que se constituían –lo cual no excluye conflictos entre ellos–, ni siquiera con aquellos que no querían incorporarse a ellas. Es decir, que no ejercían coacción sobre sus miembros –más bien les ofrecían vivir una experiencia límite, transformadora– ni violencia contra los que se excluían de la comunidad. No parece que se recurriera en estos casos a los mecanismos conocidos de discriminación o de expulsión de individuos. Desde este punto de vista, puede que a las comunidades creadas de este modo performativo les sea inherente un componente utópico. Sin embargo, no se puede pasar por alto que las acciones conjuntas realizadas en estos casos se adecuan sin duda a lo que René Girard llamaba violencia «catártica» ejercida por todos contra uno: el sacrificado. En el caso de las acciones de descuartizamiento de corderos esa violencia se dirigía al cordero, que hacía las veces de sustituto, la clásica víctima y el símbolo de la muerte y sacrificio de Jesucristo. En *Dionysus in 69* se ejerció, de modo ficticio, apelando al «como si», como violencia simbólica, como expulsión de Penteo de una comunidad que él había querido subyugar y dominar.

Aquella comunidad que se ha fraguado por la realización conjunta de acciones no ha de ser entendida como «ficción», sino que hay que entender que surgió en tanto que realidad social, una realidad social que, sin embargo, distinta como es ésta de otras comunidades sociales, tuvo una existencia muy corta en el tiempo. Desaparecía en el instante en el que cesaba las actividades conjuntas. Sus condiciones de éxito no consistían en una serie de disposiciones y convicciones sostenidas largo tiempo que tuvieran que compartir todos los miembros de la comunidad. Únicamente preveían que los miembros de los dos grupos, diferenciados por lo demás claramente por su función –los actores y los espectadores–, realizaran durante un lapso de tiempo previamente determinado por la realización escénica ciertas acciones

30 Véase, al respecto, René Girard, *La violencia y lo sagrado*, Barcelona, 1983.

conjuntas destinadas a contribuir, cada una a su manera, a la constitución de la realización escénica. Este modo de proceder hacía posible que surgiera una comunidad de actores y espectadores al mismo tiempo que ofrecía los motivos por los que al poco tiempo tenía que disgregarse de nuevo[31].

Estas efímeras comunidades teatrales creadas por actores y espectadores son de especial interés con vistas al desarrollo de una estética de lo performativo, sobre todo por dos motivos. En primer lugar, sacan a la luz de manera insoslayable la amalgama, constitutiva de toda realización escénica, entre lo estético y lo social: la comunidad creada a partir de determinados principios estéticos por actores y espectadores es experimentada por sus miembros siempre como una realidad social –por más que los espectadores no involucrados puedan considerarla y entenderla como una comunidad ficticia, puramente estética–. En segundo lugar, se pone de manifiesto que estas comunidades no son sólo el resultado de hábiles estrategias de puesta en escena y de dominación ideadas por individuos de gran inteligencia, como se pensaba en las primeras décadas del siglo veinte, son también el resultado de un particular giro que toma el bucle de retroalimentación autopoiético. Determinadas acciones de los actores pueden encontrar respuesta por parte de algunos espectadores en forma de un cambio de roles –al que sin duda invitan algunas estrategias de puesta en escena–, lo que les da la oportunidad de realizar ciertas acciones con los actores. Ello les proporciona en y con el propio cuerpo –como a los actores– una experiencia de comunidad con personas muy distintas a ellos, con aquellas con las que «realmente», «originariamente» no forman una comunidad. Esta experiencia puede ser anulada en cualquier momento por acciones de los miembros de la comunidad –actores y «espectadores»– o por individuos no involucrados en ella. La comunidad se disgrega. El bucle de retroalimentación da otro giro.

31 Según Vattimo se trata de una característica general de las «comunidades estéticas». Véase G. Vattimo, *La sociedad transparente*, Barcelona, 1998.

En los ejemplos aducidos, la participación activa en el cambio de roles por parte de ciertos espectadores era condición necesaria para el surgimiento de una comunidad de actores y espectadores. Se plantea así la pregunta de si el bucle de retroalimentación puede dar lugar a una comunidad de ese tipo sin cumplir este requisito, es decir, en el ámbito de los microprocesos que, sin que llegue a darse un claro cambio de roles, constituyen una relación de intercambio entre actores y espectadores, un intercambio cuyo potencial efectivo hemos podido ver por primera vez con la ayuda de la lente de aumento del cambio de roles. Nos dedicaremos a esta cuestión examinando el teatro de Einar Schleef.

Desde mediados de los años ochenta hasta su muy prematura muerte en el verano de 2001, Schleef desarrolló y puso a prueba un nuevo teatro coral en el que las comunidades tenían una posición de prominencia, tanto la comunidad del coro como la de actores y espectadores. No obstante, el teatro coral de Schleef se opone radicalmente al teatro de orgías y misterios de Nitsch o al del Performance Group de Schechner. A diferencia de ellos, Schleef se servía para sus realizaciones escénicas de teatros tradicionales que, sin embargo, reformaba a veces considerablemente. Así fue en sus últimos montajes de finales de los años noventa y de principios del siglo veintiuno: *Puntila* en el Berliner Ensemble en 1996, *Sportstück [Pieza deportiva]* en el Burgtheater de Viena en 1998 o *Verratenes Volk [Pueblo traicionado]* en el Deutsches Theater de Berlín en 2002. Además, apenas trabajó con el cambio de roles entre actores y espectadores[32]. Schleef permitía la realización de

32 Una notable excepción fue su *Salome* (Düsseldorf, 1997). En este montaje se fomentaba el cambio de roles haciendo chocar el marco teatral con el vigente en las visitas a museos y galerías de arte. Tras la subida del telón de acero, al público se le presentaba un *tableau vivant* sobre el escenario. Una crepuscular luz azul-grisácea iluminaba todo el espacio escénico, en el que se repartían dieciocho figuras vestidas de negro o gris, perfectamente inmóviles y en actitud y configuración pictóricas. La muy bella imagen, mantenida en un fino difuminado y de perfectas proporciones, se les mostraba a los espectadores durante diez minutos. Después volvía a caer el telón de acero, y se invitaba al público a que saliera para el receso. En la realización escénica a la que yo asistí, que tuvo lugar en el Encuentro Teatral de Berlín en 1998, la imagen fue saludada con algunas entusiastas

acciones conjuntas, a lo sumo, en forma de alusión irónica. Cuando los actores repartían dinero de chocolate, té en vasos de plástico o patatas cocidas entre los espectadores (en *Antes de amanecer*, *Die Schauspieler [Los actores]* y *Götz von Berlichingen* respectivamente, todas ellas montadas en el Schauspielhaus de Fráncfort en 1987, 1988 y 1989 respectivamente), y los invitaban a celebrar un «banquete» conjunto, se percibía la irónica alusión a la comunidad de comensales de Robertson Smith.

Un paralelismo con Nitsch y Schechner puede hallarse quizá en que los tres desarrollaron su novedosa forma de teatro remitiéndose al teatro trágico griego o, al menos, a los mitos griegos: Nitsch apelaba a «la desmembración de dioniso/el deslumbramiento de edipo/[...]/el asesinato de orfeo/[...]/el asesinato de adonis/la castración de atis»[33], Schechner basó *Dionysus in 69* en *Las bacantes* de Eurípides –obra a la que Gilbert Murray se había referido para demostrar que el origen del teatro trágico estaba en el ritual–, y Schleef partía para su primera realización escénica coral, *Die Mütter [Las madres]* (Schauspielhaus Fráncfort, 1986), de las *Suplicantes* de Eurípides y de los *Siete contra Tebas* de Esquilo[34]. En

exclamaciones. Cuando la cosa duraba ya más de un minuto, los espectadores empezaron a mostrar muy distintas conductas. Unos aplaudían, silbaban, gritaban «bravo» o «da capo», es decir, se comportaban de una manera convencional en el teatro. Otros, por el contrario, tomaban el papel de actores, hacían observaciones más o menos agudas y centraban la atención del resto de los espectadores. Había otros que censuraban a estos últimos e insistían a voces en su derecho a sumirse en la observación del *tableau vivant* sin ser molestados por el ruido. Se comportaran como se comportaran los espectadores eran observados por los actores, pues el patio de butacas estaba bien iluminado; aun así éstos no se dejaban arrancar una sonrisa, un carraspeo, ni el más mínimo movimiento. Puesto que, a pesar de todo, estaban presentes en el escenario y no podían, como se ha señalado en varias ocasiones, no reaccionar, fue precisamente su aparente conducta pasiva la que espoleó, la que provocó incluso a algunos espectadores a actuar. También en este caso se puede estudiar, aunque se trate de condiciones muy específicas, el funcionamiento del bucle de retroalimentación.

33 Nitsch, *Das Orgien – Mysterien – Theater*, vol. I, p. 87.

34 Para el significado del teatro griego tras el giro performativo, véase Edith Hall (ed.), *Dionysus since 69: Greek Tragedy and the Public Imagination at the End of the Second Millenium*, Oxford, 2003.

Atenas las realizaciones escénicas del teatro trágico tenían lugar en el contexto de las grandes fiestas consagradas a Dioniso, en las Grandes Dionisias o Dionisias Urbanas. Las fiestas comenzaban con actos rituales conjuntos, como procesiones o sacrificios. Durante la realización escénica propiamente dicha se mantenía, sin embargo, una clara separación entre actores y espectadores, aunque el coro, que danzaba y cantaba por toda la orquesta, la salvaba. Si en el teatro griego se puede hablar de creación de una comunidad entre actores y espectadores, se trataría más bien del fortalecimiento, de la regeneración de una comunidad ya fortalecida y regenerada por procesiones, sacrificios y actos nacionales de autorrepresentación: la comunidad de la polis. El teatro emanaba de la comunidad política, pero no pretendía –como en Nitsch o Schechner– sustituirla ni presentarse como su antítesis o su pre-apariencia *(Vor-Schein)* estético-utópica.

Schleef recurrió al teatro griego más bien en el sentido de Nietzsche. En su obra *El nacimiento de la tragedia en el espíritu de la música* (1872) defendía la tesis de que el teatro trágico tenía su origen en el coro de sátiros cantantes y danzantes. Mientras el principio apolíneo apunta a la individuación, lo dionisíaco la quiebra, precipita a los individuos al éxtasis y los convierte en miembros de una comunidad cantante y danzante. A diferencia de Nitsch y Schechner, en cuyas realizaciones escénicas sólo se creaban comunidades provisionales, aunque en su mayor parte libres de conflictos, para Schleef la comunidad se definía por el permanente conflicto entre individuo y comunidad. En su libro *Droge Faust Parsifal* afirma que:

> La del coro antiguo es una imagen terrorífica: figuras que se arraciman y que se apiñan, que buscan protección unas en otras, a pesar de que se rechazan mutuamente de forma enérgica como si la cercanía de los otros contaminara el aire. De este modo el grupo como tal se pone en peligro y tendrá que ceder ante cualquier ataque; acepta precipitadamente, aterrado, la necesidad de sacrificar a uno de ellos y lo expulsa para comprar su libertad. A pesar de que el coro es consciente de la traición, no corrige su posición, sino que pone a la víctima en la posición de claro culpable. Éste no es

> sólo un aspecto del coro antiguo, es un proceso que se repite diariamente. El enemigo-coro no está en principio constituido por los millones de ignaros, moribundos, saqueadores y asilados, sino por los disidentes, especialmente aquel que habla la propia lengua, a ése es al que hay que eliminar, como sea. Pero hasta que llegue el momento de ese ajuste de cuentas la antigua constelación sigue viva, el coro y el individuo siguen luchando, se deja sentir la relación del individuo con los demás, con los que hasta entonces estaban aislados. Su relación –entre sí y en general– contra el coro, que espera poder mantenerlos a distancia con éxito[35].

La relación que Schleef considera aquí característica de la comunidad del coro vale también para las relaciones entre actores y espectadores.

Para *Die Mütter,* Schleef creó en el Schauspielhaus de Fráncfort un espacio único. Suprimió los asientos del auditorio (a excepción de las tres últimas filas, que estaban reservadas para ancianos y minusválidos). El suelo de la platea se iba elevando gradualmente con la ayuda de escalones que los espectadores iban ocupando poco a poco. Por medio de la platea cruzaba una amplia pasarela que iba desde el escenario hasta el fondo de la sala, y que estaba igualmente inclinada. Por ella se podía llegar a un segundo y estrecho escenario que había detrás de las tres filas de asientos y cuya extensión era de la misma longitud que la última fila. Así pues, el espacio escénico para uso de los actores se encontraba delante, detrás y entre los espectadores, de modo que a menudo eran casi rodeados, e incluso sitiados, por los actores. Sin embargo, la «huida», dado que los pasillos que conducían a las puertas de salida podían ser usados libremente, sí era posible.

En estos espacios escénicos actuaban tres coros de mujeres: el coro de las viudas, que vestían completamente de negro y atacaban a Teseo (Martin Wuttke) empuñando hachas; el coro de las vírgenes, que llevaban vestidos de tul blanco en la primera parte y de tul rojo en la segunda; y el coro de las mujeres, que iban ves-

35 Einar Schleef, *Droge Faust Parsifal*, Fráncfort, 1997, p. 14.

tidas como trabajadoras de una fábrica de munición, con sobretodos negros. Ellas ocupaban y dominaban el espacio: el escenario frente a los espectadores, la pasarela que –especialmente en la segunda parte– recorrían arriba y abajo, que pisoteaban tronantes con sus botas negras de punta y tacón de acero, y el escenario de detrás de los espectadores. Todas las integrantes del coro se movían al mismo ritmo y hablaban, gritaban, vociferaban, chillaban, gemían, lloraban, susurraban y cuchicheaban las mismas palabras al unísono. Sin embargo, el coro no actuaba como un cuerpo colectivo en el que la individualidad de cada integrante desapareciera y confluyera con la de los demás. El coro parecía más bien estar librando una especie de lucha permanente entre el individuo, que se quería incorporar a la comunidad sin renunciar a su singularidad, y la comunidad, que aspiraba a una incorporación total de todos sus integrantes y que amenazaba con expulsar a aquellos que insistían en su individualidad. En el interior del coro se mantenía, pues, una tensión permanente entre sus miembros y la comunidad creada por su actividad conjunta, tanto lingüística como física. Esta tensión ponía al coro en un continuo flujo que tenía como efecto una dinámica transformadora de los individuos con respecto a su posición en la comunidad y a sus relaciones con ella. Esta tensión no cesaba en ningún momento. El coro no se transformaba casi nunca en una comunidad armónica, y la tensión no hacía más que aumentar. Se podía percibir una y otra vez su influjo en tanto que acto de violencia que la comunidad cometía contra el individuo y viceversa.

Esta violencia se manifestaba incluso con más fuerza cada vez que el coro se enfrentaba con un individuo externo –con Teseo o con Eteocles (Heinrich Giskes). El conflicto entre las mujeres de Tebas y Eteocles se desarrollaba, por ejemplo, por medio de un constante cambio de posiciones sobre la pasarela: las mujeres tumbadas en un escalón mientras Eteocles, altivo, se erguía sobre ellas; o Eteocles acurrucado mientras las mujeres se inclinaban hacia él. La lucha de poder entre el individuo masculino y el coro –femenino– se libraba por medio de un incesante cambio de posiciones en el espacio y por medio de la variación de intensidad de las voces. Cuando las mujeres se incorporaban de repente y arrollaban literalmente a Eteocles con la intensidad de sus voces, éste caía de rodillas y se hacía un ovillo.

Una tensión del mismo tipo mantenida durante largo tiempo determinaba también la relación entre actores y espectadores. La disposición espacial, que permitía a los actores rodear a los espectadores o actuar entre ellos, sugería la idea de una unidad esencial entre ambos. Pero esta idea se probó engañosa: cada vez que surgía esta unidad volvía a disolverse de nuevo poco después. En lugar de unidad, los participantes podían percibir dos fuerzas que se combatían mutuamente. Esto se debía en parte a la ambigua disposición del espacio. La pasarela dividía en dos el espacio de los espectadores, lo que posibilitaba a los actores moverse entre ellos. Los espectadores tenían pues que enfrentarse a la constante amenaza de desmembración de su cuerpo colectivo, al que de todas formas ya atravesaba ostensiblemente la pasarela. Además, el dispositivo espacial dejaba a los espectadores desprotegidos ante la violencia que el coro ejercía contra ellos cuando pateaba escalones arriba y abajo y vociferaba directamente sobre sus cabezas o cuando les vociferaba a ellos directamente, de tal manera que los espectadores se sentían atacados físicamente y reaccionaban, por su parte, retirándose o defendiéndose activamente –por ejemplo con pataleos, palmadas rítmicas o haciendo comentarios a voces. También aquí se estaba dando una lucha de poder librada entre actores y espectadores. El coro estático pretendía someter al público, llevarlo también al éxtasis y obligarlo a entrar en su comunidad, contra ello se defendían algunos espectadores con la palabra, con la fuerza de su voz o simplemente abandonando la sala. Otros, en cambio, parecían entregarse atemorizados o ávidos a esta unión con el coro. Pero eran muy pocos los instantes en los que coro y público formaban una comunidad armónica –instantes de transición antes de que la lucha se desatara de nuevo entre ambos grupos y transformara el teatro, por momentos, en un pandemónium–.

Durante estas luchas y alianzas no se realizaban acciones conjuntas entre actores y espectadores ni intrusiones violentas por parte de miembros de un grupo contra los del otro. Con todo, se libraban batallas entre actores y espectadores y, sin embargo, de vez en cuando surgía entre ellos, por un breve espacio de tiempo, una comunidad. En ella los actores seguían siendo actores y los espectadores, espectadores. ¿Cómo era esto posible? Da la impresión de que el bucle de retroalimentación de la influencia recíproca entre las acciones de los actores y la percepción y el comportamiento de los espectadores hubiera liberado en este caso, entre todos los participantes, energías de una naturaleza especialmente propicia para la formación de comunidades. Hay muchos motivos para pensar que el *ritmo* (al que Schleef le daba una especial importancia) tenía una función esencial en este proceso.

Ya Georg Fuchs partía de la base de que «los movimientos rítmicos del cuerpo humano en el espacio» son capaces de poner a «otras personas a realizar los mismos o similares movimientos rítmicos, y con ello llevarlas al mismo estado de éxtasis»[36]. Por eso le parecía que el mejor camino para crear una comunidad entre actores y espectadores era –junto a la eliminación del proscenio– el desarrollo de un nuevo arte de la actuación basado en el principio del ritmo. Sin duda también tenía en mente las energías que liberan los movimientos rítmicos y que son capaces de transmitirlos. Sin embargo, estas energías le interesaban únicamente por su potencial para generar una comunidad de naturaleza extática.

En *Mütter*, por el contrario, no se trataba de generar un éxtasis. El interés se centraba más bien en el proceso de circulación en sí mismo, en el proceso de liberación, transferencia e intercambio de energías, un proceso que no se ponía en marcha únicamente por los movimientos rítmicos de los actores en el espacio, sino también por su hablar rítmico. Ahora bien, la energía que circula por el teatro no puede verse ni oírse. Aun así se percibe. En cuanto al ritmo, se trata de un principio físico, biológico que regula nuestra respiración y el latido de nuestro corazón. El cuerpo humano está en este sentido rítmicamente configurado. De ahí que sea capaz de percibir el ritmo tanto como principio externo cuanto como principio interno. Vemos

36 Fuchs, *Der Tanz*, p. 13.

determinados movimientos, oímos determinadas series de palabras, de sonidos y de realizaciones fonéticas y las percibimos como rítmicas. Como principio energético, pues, el ritmo sólo puede surtir efecto cuando lo sentimos -del mismo modo que lo hacemos con nuestros propios ritmos físicos- físicamente.

Lo que ocurre cuando percibimos el ritmo no sólo con los sentidos de la vista y el oído, sino también con nuestro sentido corporal, es decir, sinestésicamente, era algo que se podía entender muy bien en *Die Mütter*. Las energías liberadas por los movimientos rítmicos y por el hablar rítmico de los actores circulaban entre actores y espectadores, esto es, daban lugar a una liberación mutua y a una intensificación de la energía. Estas energías podían entonces, por así decirlo, encontrarse en tanto que opuestas, de tal manera que desembocaran en una «batalla» entre coro y público; podían también armonizarse y crear, durante algunos momentos de felicidad, una comunidad de la que, no obstante, algunos espectadores podían evadirse. El camino que pudieran tomar no era susceptible de previsión. Dependía, por un lado, de la fuerza de la energía que los actores fueran capaces de movilizar en cada realización escénica y en cada momento de la realización escénica; y por otro lado, de la capacidad de respuesta de cada uno de los espectadores ante la energía fluctuante en el espacio, de su capacidad de experimentarla físicamente y de su disposición para dejarse afectar por ella, y dependía además, entre otros muchos factores, de la relación de fuerzas entre los espectadores predispuestos y los no predispuestos: los que se cerraban a la circulación de energía. En este sentido puede afirmarse que se trata de un modo especial de percepción que mantiene en marcha el bucle de retroalimentación hasta en los niveles más bajos y que capacita al espectador para influir en el curso de la realización escénica. Éste experimenta la energía[37] que, partiendo de los actores, termina siéndole transmitida a él.

37 El concepto de energía no se emplea aquí como un concepto claramente definido, como por ejemplo en la física; se le concederá más bien una cierta vaguedad que se acepta conscientemente en aras de la proximidad a la experiencia cotidiana.

Esta energía no requiere ni siquiera una particular distribución del espacio. Puede circular también si actores y espectadores se encuentran en un teatro a la italiana. Algo que demuestra de manera abrumadora la realización escénica de la obra de Elfriede Jelinek *Sportstück*, montada por Einar Schleef. Con gran intensidad, los actores realizaban durante cuarenta y cinco minutos los mismos ejercicios una y otra vez hasta la extenuación, y además, en el coro, repetían con la misma intensidad una y otra vez las mismas frases en distintos tonos y registros de voz. Se podía sentir cómo se liberaba la energía y circulaba. Algunos espectadores se lo tomaban como algo fuera de toda medida y abandonaban la sala a los pocos minutos. Quien, por el contrario, se exponía a todos estos acontecimientos hasta el final, sentía cómo se formaba un campo energético entre actores y espectadores que se iba intensificando con el paso del tiempo.

Las comunidades teatrales del teatro coral de Schleef le aportan aspectos importantes a una estética de lo performativo. Al estudiarlas se ha mostrado que el bucle de retroalimentación autopoiético no sólo se genera y se mantiene por acciones y modos de comportamiento observables de actores y espectadores, esto es, visibles y audibles, sino también a través de la energía que circula entre ellos. Esta energía no es ninguna quimera, como demostró Hermann Schmitz por primera vez[38]. Es también perceptible, aunque de un modo particular, a saber: a través de la experiencia física.

Mientras que en Nitsch y Schechner las acciones realizadas conjuntamente por actores y espectadores eran las que permitían crear una comunidad, en el caso de Schleef son las percepciones mutuas entre actores y espectadores las que liberan las energías y las hacen circular, las que hacen la comunidad experimentable. En lo que se refiere al cambio de roles son las acciones y los comportamientos observables los que mantienen en movimiento el bucle de retroalimentación. Se suele pasar por alto en este proceso que éstos han de ser en primer lugar percibidos una vez; es

38 Véase Hermann Schmitz, *System der Philosophie*, especialmente II, i, *Der Leib*, Bonn 1965.

decir, que la percepción cumple una importante función en el proceso de autopoiesis del bucle de retroalimentación. Esta función es, en el teatro coral de Schleef, atraer la atención. La percepción del espectador influye desde el primer momento en el transcurso de la realización escénica y afecta, a su vez, tanto a actores como espectadores en la medida en que moviliza energía y la hace circular.

A partir del ejemplo de *Two Amerindians Visit...* se ha mostrado la fuerza transformadora de la mirada sobre el otro. Es capaz de reconocerlo como cosujeto o degradarlo a objeto, puede atribuirle identidades, vigilarlo, controlarlo, codiciarlo. Mientras que la mirada despliega su potencial transformador en la confrontación directa con los otros, el potencial energético no se orienta en una sola dirección. No circula solamente entre el actor X y el espectador Y, sino entre todos los actores y espectadores. En la realización escénica la percepción es, en este sentido (ya sea en tanto que mirada o en tanto que sensación física), inimaginable sin el potencial activo que es capaz de desplegar.

Así pues, el cambio de roles no es estrictamente necesario para que el espectador se convierta en parte activa, en actor. La oposición entre actuar y observar se viene abajo. Como se ha demostrado, en las comunidades teatrales del teatro coral de Schleef el espectador es también, en tanto que espectador, esto es, en tanto que perceptor, un actor que influye en el transcurso de la realización escénica con lo que hace *y* con aquello que le ocurre. Así, las condiciones de percepción que se crean para una realización escénica —ya sea a través de la distribución espacial, ya sea a través de una forma específica de presentación—, son las que preparan y dan lugar a la dinámica del bucle de retroalimentación, aunque sin poder llegar a determinarla.

3. Contacto

Del mismo modo que la copresencia física de actores y espectadores es la condición de posibilidad para la creación de una comunidad formada por ambos grupos, ésta implica también la posibilidad de que un actor toque a un espectador y viceversa. Pese a que a menudo la específica distribución del espacio teatral se interpreta como expresión espacial de la unidad de actores y espectadores (ejemplos de ello serían el teatro-orquesta griego, el escenario de la plaza del mercado medieval, el teatro isabelino o el teatro Kabuki japonés, con el *hanamichi*), la idea de una comunidad entre ambos sólo parece estar legitimada y propiciada por su presencia simultánea en el mismo espacio. Sin embargo, la idea de un contacto recíproco entre actores y espectadores parece, en principio, descabellada. Pues, como sugiere el término 'teatro' (del griego *theatron*: espacio para mirar, de *theasthai*: mirar o *thea*: mirada), se trata de un medio configurado para el sentido de la vista, para ver. De ello son testimonio los gigantescos teatros griegos, algunos con capacidad para más de diez mil espectadores. Esto no excluye que en la historia del teatro europeo pueda haber una serie de ejemplos en los que se pueda especular sobre el contacto entre actores y espectadores. Es, sin duda, imaginable que los actores intentaran tocar a los espectadores, por ejemplo, en algunos de los dramas religiosos medievales que se celebraban con motivo de la Semana Santa, concretamente aquellos en los que, tras la liberación por Cristo de las almas cautivas en el infierno, los diablos se dispersaban para volver a llenarlo de ellas. Es probable que los actores intentaran agarrar, en esa operación, a algún que otro espectador, y quizá llegaran incluso a tocarlos. Faltan, no obstante, testimonios que lo corroboren. No es descartable que Puck, tras las palabras dirigidas al espectador, y con las que termina *El sueño de una noche de verano*: «So good night onto you all./ Give me your hands, if we be friends,/ And Robin shall restore amends» (V, i, 425-427)*, se despidiera de cada uno de los espectadores con un apretón de manos. Pero también esto es incierto. Por otro lado, el hecho de que en algún caso haya habido contactos no modificaría en nada la oposición entre ver y tocar que existe de manera expresa en el teatro.

* «Os doy, pues, las buenas noches. / Vosotros dadme las manos, / si es que quedamos amigos, / y Robin lo arreglará todo».

Una de las causas de esta oposición podría estribar en el hecho de que el teatro se considera un medio público y que el contacto, por el contrario, se suele adscribir a la esfera íntima. Hasta bien entrado el siglo dieciocho los detractores del teatro le reprochaban que, pese a su carácter público, ofreciera a los espectadores la posibilidad del contacto mutuo –y obsceno–, que incluso lo promoviera. Esto no afecta, sin embargo, a la relación entre actores y espectadores durante la realización escénica, sino únicamente a la de los espectadores entre sí[40].

El desarrollo del teatro ilusionista en el siglo dieciocho proporcionó un motivo más para la exclusión del contacto entre actores y espectadores cuyo origen hay que atribuir igualmente a la oposición entre ver y tocar. Como explica Johann Jakob Engel en su *Mimik* (1785/86), la ilusión del espectador se desvanece si no percibe el cuerpo del actor como un signo del personaje, sino como el cuerpo real de un actor por el que empieza a interesarse como tal cuerpo. En caso de haber contacto el peligro se antojaba aún mayor, pues conllevaría la irrupción de lo real en la ficción. La mirada, por el contrario, favorece la generación de ilusión y desencadena emociones en el espectador que valen para el personaje, pero no para el actor. En sus *Elements of Criticism*, aparecidos en 1762 y traducidos al alemán un año después, Henry Home constató que son «el rostro y los gestos», signos visibles en el cuerpo del actor y constituyentes del personaje, los que abren «un camino directo al corazón»[41], es decir, que al verlos suscitan emociones en el espectador dirigidas al personaje de ficción.

Ya en 1751, Denis Diderot da cuenta en su *Carta sobre los sordomudos*, traducida por Lessing al alemán ese mismo año, de un autoexperimento con el que quería probar la función y el significado del sentido de la vista en la generación y el mantenimiento de la ilusión, que es el prerrequisito de las emociones que se

40 Véanse los pertinentes testimonios a los que se refiere Barish: Jonas Barish, *The Antitheatrical Prejudice*, Berkeley/Los Ángeles/Londres, 1981.

41 Henry Home, *Grundsätze der Kritik*, vol. I, Leipzig, 1772, p. 582 (orig. *Elements of Criticism*, 2 vols., Indianápolis, 2005).

orientan hacia los personajes de ficción. Escribe cómo se preocupaba de taparse los oídos en el teatro:

> seguía tapándome los oídos obstinadamente mientras la actuación del actor me parecía acorde con el discurso que yo recordaba. [...] Pero prefiero hablaros de la renovada sorpresa en la que no dejaban de caer los de mi entorno, cuando me veían llorar en las partes patéticas, siempre con los oídos tapados[42].

Tanto en opinión de Diderot como en la de otros importantes teóricos del siglo dieciocho, la ilusión surge precisamente de una forma de mirar el espectador una interpretación del actor que no esté dirigida a acabar con esa misma ilusión, y es también esa forma de mirar la que produce en el espectador las emociones orientadas al personaje. Según esto, el contacto sólo tiene lugar a un nivel metafórico: los pasajes conmovedores y emotivos son los que desencadenan las emociones; son «el rostro y los gestos» del actor los que, mediante la percepción visual, la mirada, son capaces de «tocar» al espectador, suscitando en él un sentimiento de proximidad al personaje de ficción. La cercanía física al actor, el contacto directo con él, haría que el espectador centrara su atención en el actor. Ello daría al traste con la ilusión y con todas las emociones relacionadas con el personaje, incluido el anhelo de tocarlo producido por la mirada. De ahí que el teatro ilusionista descarte un contacto real, un contacto físico directo entre actores y espectadores.

De hasta qué punto era indiscutida la vigencia de esta máxima a principios del siglo veinte dan testimonio las críticas que recibieron la pantomima *Sumurun* de Reinhardt o su montaje de la *Orestíada*. Con motivo de la presentación de *Sumurun* en Nueva York un crítico se sorprendía de que, pese a la proximidad física de los actores a los espectadores, sobre todo cuando interpretaban sobre el *hanamichi*, la ilusión de éstos se mantuviera:

42 Denis Diderot, «Carta sobre los sordomudos», en *«Carta sobre los ciegos» seguido de «Carta sobre los sordomudos»*, Julia Escobar (ed.), Valencia, 2002, p. 94.

> [...] it is all the more tribute to the acting of the German company, who present «Sumurun» and to the staging that although some of the audience could put out their hands and touch the garments of the actors as they passed them, none of the spell that enveloped the actors on the stage left them as they crossed the runaway [...] and made their way back[43].

En la crítica anteriormente citada de Alfred Klaar sobre la *Orestíada* de Reinhardt, montaje que difícilmente puede considerarse ya como perteneciente al teatro ilusionista, el crítico se queja explícitamente de que «esa invasión del patio de butacas por parte de los actores, que con sus trajes ondulantes, sus pelucas y su maquillaje se aproximaban a nosotros [...] no alimenta la ilusión, la extingue»[44].

Ambos críticos –uno en su asombro, el otro en su enfado– parten sin duda del supuesto de que la proximidad física es perjudicial para la ilusión, que la extingue, un supuesto del que se sigue forzosamente la lejanía propia de los grandes espacios en los que el actor mantiene la distancia con el espectador, una distancia que mantiene al espectador alejado del cuerpo del actor y que no le permite ya reconocer elementos tan propios del teatro como los «adornos de los trajes», «las pelucas» y «el maquillaje».

Todos estos ejemplos han mostrado que la dicotomía entre ver y tocar en las realizaciones escénicas parece estar vinculada a otra serie de pares opuestos: publicidad vs. privacidad/intimidad; distancia vs. proximidad; ficción/ilusión vs. realidad. Todos ellos se fundamentan en la oposición supuestamente insalvable entre ver y tocar. Un fundamento que socava Maurice Merleau-Ponty en su escrito inacabado, y publicado póstumamente, «El entrelazo – El quiasmo» cuando afirma que:

43 Joseph Gollomb, *New York City Call*, 4 de febrero de 1912 [«(...) la mayor alabanza a la actuación de la compañía alemana que presentó «Sumurun» y a la puesta en escena es el hecho de que, a pesar de que parte del público podía sacar las manos y tocar las ropas de los actores cuando pasaban a su lado, en ningún momento desapareció el hechizo que envolvía a los actores en escena cuando iban hacia un lado (...) y cuando volvían a pasar de vuelta»].

44 Alfred Klaar, *Vossische Zeitung*, 14 de octubre de 1911.

> [...] la mirada envuelve, palpa y se ciñe a las cosas visibles. [...] Hemos de acostumbrarnos a la idea de que todo lo visible está cincelado a partir de lo tangible, que todo ser táctil está ya en cierta manera pensado para la visibilidad, que no sólo hay superposiciones y rebasamientos entre lo tocado y lo tocante, sino también entre lo tangible y lo visible. En lo visible está incluido lo tangible de igual modo que, a la inversa, lo tangible no carece de visibilidad, de existencia visual. El mismo cuerpo ve y toca, razón por la cual lo visible y lo tangible pertenecen al mismo mundo[45].

No sólo el contacto físico produce proximidad e intimidad, lo hace de igual manera la mirada que se intercambian dos personas. Es la mirada la que provoca el deseo de contacto y la que toca —al escrutarlo— al otro. Si la oposición entre ver y tocar no se sostiene, como sugiere Merleau-Ponty, surge la pregunta de si siguen en pie las demás oposiciones aparentemente asociadas a ella en el contexto de una realización escénica, o al menos de qué ocurre con ellas.

Desde finales de los años sesenta algunas realizaciones escénicas en las que los actores tocan a los espectadores y viceversa han intentado dar una respuesta a esta pregunta. En *Dionysus in 69* había una escena que Schechner describió como *caress-scene* [escena de caricias]. Los performadores se acercaban a los espectadores, se agachaban, se tendían a su lado y empezaban a acariciarlos. Los performadores llevaban muy poca ropa —las mujeres sólo un biquini—. Los espectadores reaccionaban de muy diversas maneras. Algunos —sobre todo mujeres— admitían el afectuoso contacto. Sin embargo, otros espectadores —mayoritaria, si no exclusivamente hombres— respondían activamente al contacto y lo ampliaban a partes del cuerpo que los performadores habían evitado cuidadosamente. Hacían caso omiso de las normas fijadas implícitamente por los performadores y de su propuesta para

45 Maurice Merleau-Ponty, *Le visible et l'invisible; suivi de Notes de travail*, París, 1964, pp. 175 y ss. (esp. «El entrelazo – El quiasmo», en *Lo visible y lo invisible*, Barcelona, 1970).

concretar su relación y de ese modo convertían la situación en una situación íntima que no pertenecía al *play*. Los performadores, por su parte, lo interpretaron como una intrusión impertinente, como una inadecuada interpretación de la situación y se sintieron degradados a objetos de placer. Como quiera que en posteriores realizaciones escénicas tampoco se logró llegar a un acuerdo entre actores y espectadores sobre la determinación de la situación y de la relación, la escena se suprimió.

El contacto produjo ostensibles malentendidos entre actores y espectadores que, era evidente, no se podían integrar de manera productiva en el bucle de retroalimentación. Los performadores tocaban a los espectadores en una «escena» que no presentaba ningún vínculo reconocible con el resto del *play*. El contacto tenía sentido, desde el punto de vista de los actores, en consonancia con sus nuevos principios estéticos: por un lado, tenía que hacer permeables las fronteras entre ficción –el *play*– y realidad y, por otro, pretendía «humanizar»[46] la relación entre actor y espectador, es decir, reconocer expresamente a los espectadores como cosujetos. Para los espectadores, en cambio, la situación era ambigua. La escasa ropa que llevaban los performadores –un claro toque de atención en los puritanos Estados Unidos de finales de los años sesenta– y la manifiesta ausencia de relación entre la *caress-scene* y el resto del *play* hicieron que los espectadores interpretaran el contacto como una irrupción de lo real que centraba su atención exclusivamente en el cuerpo de los performadores; lo tomaron como una propuesta para llegar a una situación de proximidad física, de intimidad.

Por parte de los actores el contacto pretendía ser una tentativa de desestabilizar la relación dicotómica entre realidad y ficción, entre publicidad e intimidad, de llevar a los espectadores más allá de las demarcaciones y los ámbitos conocidos y de brindarles así la oportunidad de tener nuevas experiencias. Los espectadores, por el contrario, entendieron el contacto justamente según esta dicotomía. Les remitía al ámbito, claramente marcado, de una

46 Schechner, *Enviromental Theater*, p. 60 (esp. *Teatro ambientalista*, p. 50).

situación íntima real en la que esperaban poder tener experiencias de modo estereotipado y consabido. Todo ello llevó a los performadores a una situación en la que sentían que efectivamente abusaban de ellos, que los prostituían, que estaban enfrentados a la misma realidad social que pretendían desestabilizar, la que se estructura de acuerdo a esa dicotomía y se sigue, por lo tanto, de ella. La *caress-scene* se vio abocada al fracaso. Y con ella el intento de emplear el contacto en la realización escénica como medio de flexibilizar determinadas dicotomías.

En cambio, en la acción *Celtic +~ ~ ~*, que Joseph Beuys realizó junto a Henning Christiansen el 5 de abril de 1971 en Basilea, parece que sí tuvo éxito, en y por el acto del contacto, la revocación de la oposición entre publicidad e intimidad. La acción tuvo lugar en lo que había sido un búnker. En ella participaron entre 500 y 800 personas –las fuentes difieren al respecto–, las suficientes, en cualquier caso, para que se produjera una aglomeración de enormes proporciones, una cercanía física continua y contactos involuntarios entre los participantes, sobre todo cuando luchaban entre ellos para colocarse en los lugares desde los que se podía ver mejor a Beuys[47]. Ya en las condiciones de partida de la acción –que Beuys no había podido planificar en todos los detalles, pues era imposible prever la cantidad de participantes– se observa una relación extremadamente tensa entre publicidad e intimidad, distancia y proximidad, ver y tocar. En medio de esta muchedumbre Beuys no sólo tenía que hablar constantemente con algunos participantes, también tenía que tocarlos para abrirse paso entre ellos.

El carácter público de la acción estaba garantizado no sólo por el anuncio de que se iba a realizar una acción artística de Joseph Beuys y Henning Christiansen, sino también por la gran cantidad de participantes. Una aglomeración de personas de esa naturaleza parece excluir cualquier tipo de intimidad. No obstante, eran precisamente la estrechez y la proximidad propiciadas

47 Véase al respecto, entre otros, Schneede, *Joseph Beuys – Die Aktionen*, pp. 274-285; Mario Kramer, *Joseph Beuys 'Das Kapital Raum 1970-1977*, Heidelberg, 1992.

las que –como han venido denunciando los detractores del teatro desde tiempos de los Padres de la Iglesia– no sólo dieron lugar al contacto entre participantes, sino que lo hicieron casi inevitable. En una situación tal la publicidad incluía la intimidad. Y en ella se dio un contacto que llegó a los empujones y a los zarandeos por conquistar el mejor sitio posible para ver la acción anunciada. Lo cierto es que había algunos bancos de madera repartidos por el espacio. Pero un sitio en ellos no aseguraba de ninguna manera que se pudieran ver sin limitaciones las acciones del artista. Como Beuys se movía continuamente por el espacio, la multitud estaba también en movimiento permanente, dando lugar una y otra vez a tumultos y aglomeraciones. No era posible ver la acción desde la distancia, únicamente desde lugares próximos –a no ser que se buscara un punto lo más distante posible, se subiera uno a uno de los bancos de madera para evitar a la muchedumbre y se ganara así al menos una perspectiva general de todo lo que ocurría. Para poder ver había que recurrir, pues, al contacto. Dado que los movimientos de todos los participantes por el espacio –no sólo los de ambos artistas– eran también parte constitutiva de la acción, ésta consistió en gran medida en la experimentación de las contradictorias, tensas y, aún así, complementarias relaciones entre publicidad e intimidad, distancia y proximidad, ver y tocar, que en esas circunstancias difícilmente podían entenderse como dicotómicas.

Beuys hizo esta experiencia más intensa y la convirtió en materia de reflexión para los participantes al tocar a algunos de ellos con el claro y deliberado objetivo de que todos los circunstantes lo vieran: les lavó los pies. La acción de lavar los pies es en nuestra cultura una acción altamente simbólica. Representa en primer lugar la realización de una acción a la que una persona de rango más bajo puede estar obligada con respecto a una de rango más alto. Pero dado que Jesús lavó los pies a sus discípulos y el Papa repite esa acción todos los años, ha pasado a entenderse como un simbólico gesto de humildad. No obstante, Beuys no realizó la acción de lavar los pies como un acto simbólico, sino como una auténtica limpieza que llevó a cabo con gran esmero. Se arrodilló delante de uno de los bancos de madera y se dirigió a una mujer joven que llevaba unas altas botas lacadas de las que entonces estaban de moda. Ella sonrió y asintió con la cabeza, a continuación Beuys la descalzó con gran destreza y profesionalidad, casi como un vendedor de zapatos, y sumergió sus pies en una palangana esmaltada llena de agua. Frotó uno de los pies con una pastilla de jabón duro, lo enjabonó completamente y dejó que se deslizara de nuevo en la palangana. Beuys tomó entonces una toalla de lino que llevaba al hombro y frotó el pie hasta secarlo, dedo por dedo. Repitió el procedimiento con el otro pie. Durante la limpieza, Beuys evitaba cualquier contacto visual con la mujer. Mantenía los ojos centrados en los pies que lavaba; de vez en cuando miraba también a los circunstantes, bromeaba y se reía con ellos. Cuando hubo limpiado los dos pies volvió a colgarse la toalla sobre el hombro, tomó la palangana, se levantó, fue hacia la ventana y echó el agua por ella. Con una larga manguera de goma llenó de nuevo la palangana. Repitió la acción de lavar los pies con otros seis participantes según el procedimiento descrito[48].

La acción de lavar los pies era sin duda de carácter público, algo que aun enfatizaba más el hecho de que Beuys mirara continuamente a los participantes que lo rodeaban a él y a la mujer, que hablara y se riera con ellos. Ello estaría en contradicción –según las ideas al uso– con el hecho de que Beuys no realizara la acción de lavar los pies simbólica, sino íntimamente: era una limpieza concienzuda en la que lo que parecía importar era eliminar completamente cualquier tipo de suciedad, sudor u olor de los pies. De ahí que no tuviera carácter erótico, algo que el artista subrayaba al evitar el contacto visual. Así, los participantes la percibieron como una acción singularmente oscilante. La manera específica en la que Beuys la llevó a cabo logró que se desmoronara la dicotomía entre publicidad y privacidad/intimidad y llevó a los participantes a un estado intermedio entre todos los

48 Esta acción quedó registrada en las películas que Bernd Klüser –Super 8, blanco y negro, 25 minutos– y Hans Emmerling –blanco y negro, 40 minutos– rodaron durante la acción. Las películas se pueden ver en el Beuys Medien-Archiv del museo de arte moderno Hamburger Bahnhof en Berlín.

ámbitos y posiciones claramente demarcados, algo que experimentaron en los zarandeos y empujones que dieron o recibieron en la lucha por un sitio, aunque sin dirigir a ello su atención. Durante el lavado de pies, y por medio de él, este estado de «betwixt and between»[49], como lo llamó Victor Turner, se convirtió en el centro de atención de los espectadores: experimentaron algo que, al menos mientras duró la experiencia, los transformó y los liberó de las dicotomías vigentes en nuestra cultura.

Mientras que en la acción de Beuys era el artista el que tocaba a algunos espectadores/participantes, Marina Abramović estaba determinada, como quedó claro en el primer capítulo, a incitar en sus performances a los espectadores/participantes a que la tocaran. En ellas el contacto tenía lugar, como sucedió en *Lips of Thomas*, como consecuencia de una situación liminar: los espectadores no sabían si comportarse estética o éticamente ante las acciones de la artista, o ante las agresiones que sufría por parte de otras personas, como en *Rhythm 0*, una acción celebrada en la Galería Studio Mora de Nápoles en 1974 en la que Abramović dejó que un grupo de gente de la calle, escogida al azar, abusara de ella y la maltratara durante horas. En tanto que miraban, los espectadores se comportaban «estéticamente», lo que se reveló como una actitud voyerista o simplemente sádica. El contacto, en cambio, los ponía en situación de tomar una decisión «ética» o «no-ética»: o bien le causaban dolor y lesiones a la artista o bien ponían fin al tormento, como hicieron algunos participantes en *Lips of Thomas* o en *Rhythm 0*. La oposición entre estética y ética era insostenible en estos casos.

En 1977, en el marco de *La performance oggi: settimana internazionale della performance*, se realizó *Imponderabilia* en la Galleria Communale d'Arte Moderna de Bolonia. En ella Abramović, junto a su compañero Ulay, incitaba a los espectadores a que los tocaran, lo cual, y puesto que daban por supuestos los pares de opuestos público vs. privado y ver vs. tocar, los ponía en un estado de liminaridad: Abramović y Ulay se colocaron de pie desnudos, frente a frente, a

49 Victor Turner, *The Ritual Process – Structure and Anti-Structure*, Londres, 1969, p. 95 (esp. *El proceso ritual: estructura y antiestructura*, Madrid, 1998, p. 101).

ambos lados de la puerta de entrada. El espacio que quedaba entre ellos era tan estrecho que todo el que quería pasar por la puerta tenía que tocar el cuerpo desnudo de Abramović o el de Ulay. Las mujeres se decidían por regla general por tocar a Abramović, mientras que los hombres tendían a abrirse paso en contacto con el cuerpo de Ulay. Los espectadores bajaban la vista al pasar, evitaban cualquier contacto visual con los performadores. Mientras cruzaban la entrada, eran observados por otros visitantes del museo, los que ya habían atravesado el umbral de la puerta o los que todavía dudaban si cruzarla o no. El contacto se llevaba a cabo en tanto que acto público, por más que no pudiera negarse su carácter íntimo –al fin y al cabo se trataba del contacto con un cuerpo desnudo–. La desnudez era pública e íntima al mismo tiempo. El momento en el umbral de la puerta era, a su vez, un «estado umbral», un estado literalmente *betwixt and between* en el que se anulaban las oposiciones dicotómicas vigentes hasta entonces.

Mientras que a finales de los años sesenta y en los setenta el contacto entre actores y espectadores en las realizaciones escénicas teatrales y en las del arte de la performance y de acción contribuyó a desestabilizar y, en última instancia, a terminar con la dicotomía entre publicidad y privacidad surgida con la formación de la sociedad burguesa en el siglo dieciocho, desde finales de los noventa se da sin duda una situación en la que esta dicotomía ha perdido en gran medida su vigencia. En el metro, en el tren, en el aeropuerto y en otros lugares públicos nos vemos continuamente obligados a oír las conversaciones que mantienen nuestros conciudadanos por el teléfono móvil, en voz alta y sin el menor reparo, sobre asuntos privados. Los asuntos más íntimos, como el *affaire* de Bill Clinton con Monica Lewinsky, han pasado a ser de dominio público. Las comparecencias, retransmitidas por televisión y colgadas en internet, daban acceso a cualquiera a todos los detalles del asunto. Nótese que no sólo se discutía públicamente el aspecto moral de la ruptura de un matrimonio, o del engaño a la opinión pública por parte del presidente de los Estados Unidos, se discutían todos los pormenores del *affaire*, incluida la práctica de sexo oral. La frontera entre la esfera pública y la privada, que en los sesenta estaba todavía rigurosamente trazada –a ningún senador ni periodista de entonces se le hubiera ocurrido que las aventuras amorosas de John F. Kennedy eran un asunto público–, se ha venido difuminando progresivamente desde los años noventa.

Esta situación también crea nuevas condiciones para las realizaciones escénicas. Pretender desestabilizar hoy la ya superada oposición entre lo público y lo privado apenas brinda nuevas posibilidades de experimentación. Cuando hoy en día actores y espectadores se tocan mutuamente en una realización escénica lo hacen partiendo del acuerdo de que esta oposición fue suprimida hace mucho y que pertenece al pasado. ¿Qué efectos tiene entonces el contacto hoy en día?

En *Secret Service*[50], de 2002, el coreógrafo berlinés Felix Ruckert, que en los años ochenta trabajó como bailarín con coreógrafos como Jean-François Duroure, Mathilde Mounier y Wanda Golanka, y que entre 1992 y 1994 fue miembro del Tanztheater de Pina Bausch en Wuppertal, ponía a prueba las posibilidades y el potencial del contacto recíproco entre actores y espectadores en una medida increíble y desconocida hasta ese momento. Hasta donde yo sé, era el primer caso en el teatro occidental en el que se privaba del sentido de la vista a los espectadores. Durante todo el transcurso de la realización escénica tenían los ojos vendados. Sólo los actores podían ver.

La pieza constaba de dos partes. Antes de cada una de ellas, una de las bailarinas ponía en conocimiento de los espectadores/participantes las reglas. En cualquier momento de la realización escénica podían hacer una señal a los bailarines indicando que deseaban interrumpirla. El visitante se quitaba los zapatos y los calcetines, la bailarina le ponía la venda en los ojos y lo llevaba de la mano al espacio escénico.

> Pasado un rato, una mano toca de repente mi torso, me empuja hacia el interior de la sala, me toma de la mía, la levanta y la vuelve a soltar. [...] Llevado de la mano doy vueltas en círculo. De

50 El título remite, en su doble sentido, a los «servicios secretos» que se prestan en la prostitución y a los servicios secretos de los Estados, que se encargan de supervisar las más íntimas acciones, y que recurren también a la tortura para ello.

> pronto, alguien me echa en su hombro y mi cuerpo empieza a dar vueltas por la sala. Entonces caigo al suelo y siento pies tocándome y haciendo presión contra mí. Acto seguido alguien se tiende sobre mí y empieza a rodar lentamente sobre mi cuerpo, me agarra los dedos del pie y empieza a hacerme cosquillas en la planta del pie. El espectador forma parte de una precisa coreografía que no puede ver nadie más que los bailarines. [...] ¿Quién es en este caso el sujeto, quién el objeto? La distinción carece de sentido, pues también yo palpo a tientas otros cuerpos al compás de la música tecno, topo con algo, actúo. Y este otro, ¿será uno de los bailarines? ¿O será otro espectador? ¿Es acaso un hombre? A duras penas se puede ir más allá de formular esta última pregunta[51].

En este caso ya no se podía hablar de dicotomía entre lo público y lo privado. Lo íntimo se había convertido en público. Tras la primera parte había un descanso. Al espectador que quería participar también en la segunda parte se le volvían a vendar los ojos en la antesala. Además, se le pedía que se quitara tanta ropa como quisiera. Después era conducido otra vez al espacio escénico. Esta vez, sin embargo, su margen de movimiento se había restringido considerablemente:

> [...] me encadenan, ya con los ojos vendados y en ropa interior, a una estructura metálica. Si la primera parte se centraba sobre todo en la experiencia del movimiento, ahora se trata de una experiencia somática de placer y sufrimiento, una experiencia que va del dolor a las cosquillas y la excitación. Unas manos me acarician todo el cuerpo, mis brazos, mi rostro. Alguien me sopla en el cuello y en el oído. Una pluma me acaricia las axilas. Una mano me palmea los brazos, el pecho, las piernas, el trasero. Después un látigo. Al final, cuando ya hacía mucho que me habían quitado la ropa interior, dos cuerpos me rodean y se estrechan contra mí[52].

51 Peter Boenisch, «ElectrONic Bodies. Corpo-Realities in Contemporary Dance», en manuscrito inédito de 2002, cito aquí por la versión alemana del manuscrito, pp. 10 y ss.

52 *Ibid.*, p. 11.

Aquí, como en los ejemplos anteriormente citados, los espectadores también llevaron a cabo un cambio de roles –aunque en unas condiciones de naturaleza distinta: habían renunciado al sentido de la vista–. Esto no significaba sólo que estuvieran a merced de los demás sentidos: el del oído, el del olfato y, especialmente, el del tacto, también estaban a merced de los actores que, al no estar privados de la vista, podían controlar la acción. La situación de los espectadores era de una liminaridad extrema y suponía un desafío inaudito para ellos. Por un lado, tenían que ponerse en manos de unos actores totalmente desconocidos, entregarse a ellos literalmente en cuerpo y alma sin saber qué les iba a suceder. De esta manera eran arrastrados a una especie de pasividad aún mayor que aquella a la que estaba condenado el público del teatro a la italiana y con proscenio, y que los representantes de las vanguardias históricas criticaron de forma tan elocuente. Por otro lado, se les animaba, se les exigía casi, que influyeran activamente por medio del tacto, del contacto, en el transcurso de la realización escénica. Por medio del tacto, de los empujones, de los pisotones, de las caricias, de los acercamientos, etc., le daban nuevos giros a la realización escénica. Sus reacciones no eran susceptibles de ser planeadas, previstas o controladas por parte de los actores, incluso aunque al ver pudieran seguir el desarrollo de la realización escénica y, en este sentido, supervisarla. Los «espectadores» experimentaban su capacidad para influir físicamente en el desarrollo de la realización escénica como nunca lo habían hecho antes en el teatro, a pesar de no poder controlarla. Es decir, que era justamente el bucle de retroalimentación autopoiético el que producía la realización escénica, el que ponía a los «espectadores» en un estado de liminaridad, en un estado *betwixt and between* de radicalidad apenas imaginable, en un estado que muchos espectadores vivieron, según sus propias palabras, con extraordinario placer[53].

53 Véanse los mensajes colgados por parte de espectadores en http: www.dock11-berlin.de/pressecret02.html. Al hilo de los ejemplos aquí aportados, se puede trazar una interesante línea en el ámbito de lo histórico-cultural tocante al

El contacto entre actores y espectadores en *Secret Service* pone así de manifiesto la misteriosa relación que hay entre el funcionamiento del bucle de retroalimentación autopoiético y la experiencia de liminaridad, que es la que puede conducir a la transformación. Se trata de la aparente contradicción entre la posibilidad de participar activamente en la realización escénica –lo que puede abarcar desde la sensación física de la circulación de energía y de la liberación de la propia energía hasta la participación activa, la «coactuación», etc.– y la experiencia de su indisponibilidad, que pone a los espectadores en un estado de liminaridad que los mantiene durante toda la realización escénica, por así decirlo, en el umbral: ni a un lado ni a otro de él. Ni pueden determinar el transcurso de la realización escénica ni ésta puede realizarse fuera del ámbito de su influencia. Los espectadores oscilan entre todas las posibilidades y posiciones a un lado y a otro, se encuentran *in between*. La copresencia física de actores y espectadores es la que hace posible, condiciona y da origen a este estado.

4. *Liveness* / En vivo

En el marco de la creciente presencia de los medios de comunicación en nuestra cultura resurgió con vigor en los años noventa, especialmente en los Estados Unidos, el debate sobre las particulares condiciones mediáticas de las realizaciones escénicas teatrales, sobre la copresencia física de actores y espectadores, sobre lo

---

cambio en la forma de entender el cuerpo desde los años sesenta hasta nuestros días. Mientras que en los años sesenta no sólo el *going naked* de Schechner, sino cualquier acto de exposición pública del cuerpo era considerado como un acto culturalmente revolucionario en el sentido de Herbert Marcuse y como una *liberation of body* (Herbert Blau), la muy extendida, y narcisista, atención al propio cuerpo y los esfuerzos por modelarlo de acuerdo a los ideales del *fitness* alimentan la necesidad de mostrar en público los resultados de tanto esfuerzo. Una necesidad que *Secret Service* también tenía en cuenta, aunque fuera en la peculiar variante de que el espectador justamente *no* podía ver la reacción de los demás a la mostración de su cuerpo.

que se ha dado en llamar su *liveness*[54*]. De un modo mucho más radical que en anteriores discusiones del mismo tipo se puso en cuestión el potencial efectivo de las realizaciones escénicas basado en la copresencia física de actores y espectadores o, a la inversa, se lo saludó como «salvífico». Es algo más que una mera coincidencia que tal discusión se emprendiera a principios del siglo veinte, en un momento en el que un nuevo medio, el cine, emprendía su marcha triunfal en la cultura occidental. La posibilidad de reproducir en película la interpretación de los actores permitió por primera vez a las categorías «cuerpo real» y «espacio real» –como afirma Max Herrmann, entre otros– avanzar hacia la diferenciación, delimitación y definición de importantes criterios. Y sólo con la posibilidad de registrar técnicamente las realizaciones escénicas –en ello hay que darle la razón a Philip Auslander[55]– tiene sentido hablar de realización escénica en vivo. Antes de la invención y desarrollo de las tecnologías necesarias, no se hablaba de realizaciones escénicas «en vivo», sino meramente de realizaciones escénicas. El concepto sólo tiene sentido cuando hay, además de realizaciones escénicas «en vivo», realizaciones escénicas registradas por medios tecnológicos. En nuestra cultura, en la que los medios tecnológicos tienen un papel tan prominente, se hace pues indispensable una distinción entre ellas. Hoy no hay ya ningún tipo de realización escénica –eventos teatrales o del arte de la performance, conciertos de rock y pop, congresos de partidos políticos, ceremonias de investidura de los presidentes de los Estados Unidos, realizaciones escénicas rituales como la celebración de funerales (por ejemplo, el de Lady Di), la

54 El término '*live*', por su origen televisivo, suele hacer referencia en alemán a las retransmisiones en «tiempo real». Aquí, en cambio, nos referiremos con él a lo que llamamos realización escénica propiamente dicha en contraposición a las realizaciones escénicas filmadas o registradas de alguna manera.

* En español disponemos de la distinción entre las expresiones 'en directo', que se refiere a la mera simultaneidad, y 'en vivo', que implica además la presencia física en el lugar en el que se celebra el acontecimiento.

55 Véase, Philip Auslander, *Liveness – Performance in a mediatized culture*, Londres/Nueva York, 1999, pp. 51 y ss.

bendición del Papa *urbi et orbi* o eventos deportivos como los Juegos Olímpicos– que no sea retransmitido por televisión y sea por ello accesible a millones de espectadores. Parece que ha surgido una nueva oposición: la que distingue entre realizaciones escénicas «en vivo», caracterizadas por la copresencia física de actores y espectadores y generadas a partir del bucle de retroalimentación autopoiético, y las retransmitidas por medios tecnológicos, en las que la producción y la recepción se dan por separado, y en las que por tanto se suprime el bucle de retroalimentación.

Da la impresión de que en los ejemplos del teatro o del arte de acción y de la performance presentados por mí hasta ahora, esta distinción no se consideraba una *quantité negligeable*, más bien parece que la tienen por una distinción fundamental. El cambio de roles entre actores y espectadores, la formación de una comunidad y el contacto entre ellos sólo son posibles «en vivo». Requieren la copresencia física de actores y espectadores. No sorprenderá, pues, que yo afirme que precisamente las realizaciones escénicas de los años sesenta y setenta –las del Performance Group de Schechner o, en Europa, las acciones de Nitsch o Beuys y las performances de Abramović– surgieron como una reacción directa y manifiesta a la creciente preponderancia de los medios de comunicación en la cultura occidental, y que emplearon el postulado de la «inmediatez» y la «autenticidad» como arma para luchar contra ella. Estas realizaciones escénicas hicieron que las dicotomías tradicionales se desmoronaran, pero además parece que tuvieron un papel importante en el surgimiento de una nueva dicotomía en nombre de la lucha crítica contra la industria cultural.

Esta posición artística fue defendida y justificada por teóricos de la performance todavía en los años noventa. Según Peggy Phelan es el carácter de acontecimiento de la realización escénica el que no permite su reproducción por medios tecnológicos.

> Performance cannot be saved, recorded, documented, or otherwise participate in the circulation of representation *of* representations: once it does so, it becomes something other than performance. To the

> degree that performance attempts to enter the economy of reproduction, it betrays and lessens the promise of its own ontology[56].

Phelan atribuye así autenticidad y subversión a las realizaciones escénicas «en vivo». En una cultura totalmente comercializada y sometida a los medios de comunicación las realizaciones escénicas «en vivo» constituyen el último fortín desde el que oponer resistencia al mercado y a los medios, y con ellos a la cultura dominante. Solamente en las realizaciones escénicas «en vivo» aparecen restos de una cultura «auténtica». Es insalvable pues su oposición a la performance retransmitida por medios tecnológicos, que es un producto para la comercialización y que representa los intereses del mercado.

Frente a este punto de vista, Auslander defiende la idea de que la diferencia que Phelan estimaba esencial ha sido ya superada y que la performance «en vivo» hace mucho ya que está integrada en la retransmitida, que se ha desvanecido en ella:

> whatever distinction we may have supposed [...] to be between live and mediatized events is collapsing because live events are becoming more and more identical with mediatized ones. [...] Ironically, intimacy and immediacy are precisely the qualities attributed to television than enabled it to displace live performance. In the case of such large-scale events [...] (like sporting events, Broadway shows and rock concerts) live performance survives as television[57].

56 Peggy Phelan, *Unmarked: The Politics of Performance*, Londres/Nueva York, 1993, p. 146 [«Una performance no puede ser conservada, grabada, documentada ni participar de ninguna manera en la circulación de reproducción *de* reproducciones: tan pronto como se registra se convierte en algo distinto de una performance. Si la performance intenta introducirse en la economía de la reproducción traiciona, y debilita la promesa de su propia ontología»]. Véase al respecto del argumento de Phelan sobre la fugacidad de las performances y sobre el problema de su documentación la introducción al capítulo cuarto de este trabajo.

57 Auslander, *Liveness*, p. 32 [«cualquier distinción que pudiéramos suponer que existía [...] entre acontecimientos en vivo y retransmitidos se desmorona porque los acontecimientos en vivo se están convirtiendo cada vez más en retransmitidos. [...] Irónicamente, intimidad e inmediatez son las cualidades atribui-

Auslander ve el motivo de este desarrollo, en gran medida, en los cambios histórico-culturales que se originaron a raíz de que los medios de comunicación tomaran una posición preponderante que ha conducido a una transvaloración de los valores:

> The ubiquity of reproductions of performances of all kinds in our culture has lead to the depreciation of live presence, which can only be compensated for by making the perceptual experience of the live as much as possible like that of the mediatized, even in cases where the live event provides its own brand of proximity[58].

En las citas de Phelan y Auslander se advierte que en ambos teóricos prima el interés ideológico. Afirman o niegan una oposición esencial entre la realización escénica «en vivo» y la retransmitida con el fin de probar la superioridad cultural de la una o de la otra respectivamente. Auslander está sin duda en lo cierto cuando afirma que es precisamente en la reproducibilidad de las performances *retransmitidas* donde hay que buscar el origen de su amplísima difusión y disponibilidad. De ello no se sigue necesariamente, no obstante, su superioridad cultural, hecho que Auslander da por bueno al menos en los Estados Unidos. Se puede sin duda argüir que justamente porque las experiencias que posibilitan las performances «en vivo» no son reproducibles a voluntad ni accesibles a cualquiera en cualquier momento se les adjudica un prestigio cultural mayor que a las retransmitidas. La supuesta superioridad cultural no se sigue, por lo tanto, de la diferencia negada por Auslander y ensalzada por Phelan.

---

das a la televisión que la capacitan para reemplazar a la realización escénica en vivo. En el caso de acontecimientos de gran escala [...] (como eventos deportivos, espectáculos de Broadway o conciertos de rock) la realización escénica en vivo sobrevive en tanto que televisión»].

58 *Ibid.*, p. 36 [«La ubicuidad de las reproducciones de realizaciones escénicas de todo tipo en nuestra cultura ha conducido a la devaluación de la presencia en vivo, lo cual sólo puede compensarse haciendo que la experiencia perceptiva en vivo y la retransmitida, incluso en los casos en que el acontecimiento en vivo conlleva un modo propio de cercanía, sean lo más semejantes posible»].

Sin embargo, no hay motivos para dar carpetazo al debate sobre la diferencia o no-diferencia entre las realizaciones escénicas «en vivo» y las retransmitidas. Antes al contrario, pues Auslander esgrime dos argumentos cuya consideración no es baladí para el desarrollo posterior de nuestra investigación. Según el primero, la distinción entre una realización escénica «en vivo» y una retransmitida quedaría asumida y suprimida en el contexto de preponderancia general de los medios tecnológicos: «[...] the live event itself is shaped to the demands of mediatization. [...] To the extent that live performances now emulate mediatized representations, they have become second-hand recreations of themselves as refracted through mediatization»[59]. El segundo argumento se refiere al empleo de tecnologías de reproducción: «Almost all live performances now incorporate the technology of reproduction, at the very least in the use of electric amplification, and sometimes to the point where they are hardly live at all»[60]. Es decir, que sería el exagerado empleo de tecnologías de reproducción en las realizaciones escénicas «en vivo» el que limaría sus diferencias con las retransmitidas, si es que no las eliminaría.

Los ejemplos aducidos por mí hasta ahora parecen oponerse diametralmente a la primera tesis de Auslander. En ellos se emplean conscientemente procedimientos que sólo son posibles por la copresencia física de actores y espectadores. Así pues, lo que precisamente constituye su singularidad no puede alcanzarse por medio de la reproducción tecnológica. Tampoco se puede justificar la afirmación de que sean realizaciones escénicas constituidas según el modelo de las realizaciones escénicas retransmitidas, por más laxamente que se interprete ese modelo. Esto no significa, sin

59 *Ibid.*, p. 158 [«[...] es el propio acontecimiento en vivo el que toma la forma exigida para su adaptación a los medios tecnológicos. [...] En la medida en que las performances en vivo emulan hoy a las representaciones retransmitidas por medios tecnológicos, se han convertido en recreaciones de segunda mano de sí mismas en tanto que refractadas tras su paso por los medios»].

60 *Ibid.* [«Casi todas las performances en vivo incorporan hoy en día la tecnología de reproducción, como poco emplean la amplificación eléctrica y a veces llegan hasta un punto en el que ya no cabe hablar de performance en vivo»].

embargo, que las realizaciones escénicas «en vivo» no pudieran ser reacciones a la preponderancia de los medios en nuestra cultura. Como ya se ha señalado, las realizaciones escénicas de los años sesenta y setenta surgieron también como reacción a la creciente preponderancia de los medios de comunicación en nuestra cultura, aunque de ningún modo se agotaran en esa función. En los años cuarenta y cincuenta apenas se había perfilado la distinción entre realización escénica «en vivo» y retransmitida, y mucho menos como una oposición rígida, sobre todo porque al principio la televisión se orientó hacia los hábitos de percepción de los asistentes al teatro a la italiana y se remitía expresamente, por motivos publicitarios, a su parentesco con el teatro. Son muy conocidos esos anuncios en los que una pareja con elegantes trajes de noche ha tomado asiento en su salón frente a la televisión, como hacen los espectadores en su butaca en el teatro. Sin embargo, en el transcurso de su desarrollo posterior empezaron a hacer su aparición cada vez con más fuerza las diferencias entre ambos medios, y las diferencias ideológicas vinculadas a ellas. El giro performativo en las artes por el que se apartaron del artefacto comercializado, de la obra como mercancía, y fueron creando con frecuencia creciente realizaciones escénicas cada vez más fugaces, no fijables ni transmisibles, está sin duda relacionado con este desarrollo. (No me interesa discutir aquí hasta qué punto las realizaciones escénicas «en vivo» pueden convertirse también en «mercancía»). Los ejemplos mencionados de los años sesenta y setenta ponen de relieve expresamente la oposición surgida poco antes en la cultura, y fundamental para ellos, entre realizaciones escénicas «en vivo» y retransmitidas. No obstante, los artistas no tuvieron ningún miedo a los nuevos medios, eran conscientes de las posibilidades que les abrían para la documentación de sus fugaces y efímeras realizaciones escénicas y supieron servirse de ellos. Así surgieron, por ejemplo, documentaciones cinematográficas de *Dionysus in 69* y de *Celtic + ~ ~ ~*, las cuales no sólo nos sirven hoy como importantes fuentes de la historia del teatro, sino que poseen además valor artístico propio en tanto que películas. Dado que los artistas tenían clara conciencia de las diferencias entre las realizaciones escénicas «en vivo» y sus reproducciones, así como de las posibilidades artísticas específicas que resultaban de ellas, supieron servirse de ellas para su actividad artística.

En las realizaciones escénicas de los años noventa esta oposición tenía un carácter más bien lúdico, llegaban incluso a suprimirla –aunque no en el sentido del argumento de Auslander–. Las realizaciones escénicas de Schlingensief y Ruckert, por ejemplo, hacen referencia a la pretendida o real interactividad de los nuevos medios, aunque en buena medida de manera irónica. En programas de televisión como *Gran Hermano* los espectadores tenían la posibilidad de influir con su voto en el desarrollo del programa y de decidir por mayoría qué actor debía abandonar la casa. Pero el espectador no podía intervenir directamente en lo que ocurría, su intervención se limitaba a un único aspecto, que además habían establecido los responsables del programa. A aquellos espectadores que perdían en la votación se les negaba cualquier posibilidad de influencia, los espectadores nunca podían estar seguros de si la decisión había sido el resultado de una votación real o si la habían tomado los responsables del programa mientras les hacían creer que la decisión la tomaban ellos. En cualquier caso, se había creado un dispositivo que, aunque fuera de forma limitada, se proponía lograr la interactividad, y quizá llegaba incluso a lograrla.

En la producción *Bitte liebt Österreich! Erste europäische Koalitionswoche [¡Amad a Austria, por favor! Primera semana de coalición europea]*, realizada con motivo de las Festwochen 2000 en Viena, Schlingensief se servía, con cierta distancia irónica, de este mismo sistema. En la plaza de la Ópera de Viena se construyó una especie de contenedor-vivienda en el que se alojaban solicitantes de asilo que de vez en cuando eran visitados y entrevistados por famosos como el actor Sepp Bierbichler. Lo que ocurría dentro del contenedor se proyectaba en una gran pantalla. Junto al contenedor había una pancarta que rezaba: «*Ausländer raus!*» *[«¡Fuera extranjeros!»]*. Los espectadores/transeúntes podían escoger diariamente a dos habitantes del container a los que después se expulsaría de Austria. Schlingensief mantenía adrede la incertidumbre del público sobre si la deportación se llevaría efectivamente a cabo y sobre si realmente tenía la posibilidad de tomar parte en lo que finalmente ocurría en la realización escénica –lo que en este caso significaba decidir sobre el destino de otras personas–. Lo que está claro es que, en cualquiera de los casos, sí influyeron en el transcurso de la realización escénica. Al igual que en *Chance 2000*, aquí prevalecía también el principio de interactividad. Si es cierto que el teatro y la televisión pueden ser medios interactivos, no lo es menos que el teatro ofrece sin lugar a dudas muchas más posibilidades para la interacción, y más eficaces, que la televisión[61].

Si el ordenador se considera hoy en día el medio interactivo por antonomasia, *Secret Service* de Ruckert demostró palmariamente que las posibilidades de interactuar que ofrecen las realizaciones escénicas «en vivo», con ayuda de todos los sentidos menos el de la vista, están todavía lejos de agotarse y que, en comparación con ellas, las que hasta ahora ofrecen los guantes cibernéticos parecen poca cosa. Ni en el caso de Schlingensief ni en el de Ruckert se trataba de distinguir las realizaciones escénicas «en vivo» de las retransmitidas recurriendo a una supuesta diferencia ontológica entre ellas, ni de aprovecharse de la rivalidad entre el teatro y los medios electrónicos. Muy al contrario, las posibles diferencias eran más bien minimizadas. En estos casos se daba por supuesto que tanto el teatro como los medios electrónicos son medios interactivos y no se postulaba ninguna oposición de principio entre ellos. No se podía pasar por alto, sin embargo, la superioridad de las realizaciones escénicas «en vivo» con respecto a las retransmitidas tocante a la interactividad, de ahí que la evolución de los medios electrónicos en busca de la interactividad pueda tomar elementos y aprender mucho del bucle de retroalimentación autopoiético que se genera en las realizaciones escénicas «en vivo». A la luz de estos ejemplos, no parece muy convincente el primer argumento de Auslander de que la categoría de realización escénica «en vivo» debía ser integrada en el contexto de proponderancia general de los medios de comunicación.

61 Para una comparación de *Gran hermano* con el teatro, véase Schlingensief y Jens Roselt, «*Big Brother*-Zur Theatralität eines Medienereignisses», en Mathias Lilienthat y Claus Philipp (eds.), *Schlingensiefs AUSLÄNDER RAUS*, Fráncfort, 2000, pp. 70-78.

Su segundo argumento se refería a la excesiva utilización de tecnologías de reproducción en las realizaciones escénicas «en vivo» lo que las despoja de su condición de acontecimiento «en vivo» y las convierte en mediatizadas. Frank Castorf es de los directores que usan profusa y frecuentemente las tecnologías de reproducción en sus escenificaciones[62]. En *El idiota*, por ejemplo, montada en 2002, empleó tal cantidad de tecnologías de reproducción que eclipsó todo lo que él mismo había experimentado en ese campo anteriormente y superó de largo las expectativas de los espectadores. Precisamente por ello esta realización escénica es especialmente adecuada para examinar el segundo argumento de Auslander.

El escenógrafo de Frank Castorf, Bert Neumann, creó para la realización escénica de *El idiota* en el Volksbühne una «Ciudad Nueva», un entorno que incluía todo el espacio del teatro, incluido el patio de butacas. En el escenario giratorio se había construido una estructura de hierro de tres pisos en la que habían situado contenedores como los que se usan en las obras para los trabajadores que no viven en la misma ciudad. En ellos había sitio para alrededor de 200 espectadores. Sobre la muy inclinada platea se había construido una gran escalera. Conducía desde el escenario hasta una plataforma en la parte posterior del patio de butacas donde se habían construido un quiosco de bebidas, una

62 En *Trainspotting*, por ejemplo, podían verse en una pantalla que separaba el escenario de la platea fragmentos de vídeo que mostraban imágenes de un paisaje primaveral filmado desde un tren en marcha, o un documental sobre la estrella del grupo The Velvet Underground, Nico Icon. Además, había gran cantidad de vídeos con música de The Velvet Underground, Iggy Popp, Lou Reed, Karel Gott y Arnold Schönberg. En *Endstation Amerika* (versión de *Un tranvía llamado deseo* de Tennessee Williams, 2000) las escenas que tenían lugar en un cuarto de baño cerrado se filmaban con una cámara de vídeo y se mostraban en un monitor. En *Los Demonios* (1999) y *Humillados y ofendidos* (2001) Castorf situó muchas escenas en los interiores de un contenedor-bungalow cuya visibilidad era escasa o nula. Al igual que en *Endstation Amerika* las imágenes eran tomadas por una cámara de vídeo que, junto a otros materiales previamente grabados, eran proyectadas en una pantalla que se había montado sobre el tejado del bungalow.

agencia de viajes y una tienda más bien escasa de mercancías. En la pared del lado derecho del patio de butacas, visto desde el escenario, habían situado una peluquería, a su lado había una entrada con una cartel luminoso en su parte superior: «Kino» [«Cine»]. Sobre los edificios de atrás se veía un moderno *skyline*, que no recordaba a ninguna ciudad concreta, podía ser el de una gran ciudad moderna cualquiera. A ambos lados del escenario se levantaban bloques de apartamentos de varios pisos, la planta baja de uno de ellos cobijaba un bar de nombre «Las Vegas» que no parecía estar pasando por su mejor momento. Al final del escenario, en último término, había una casa oscura de varios pisos –el único edificio que recordaba a Dostoievski y al viejo San Petersburgo–. Antes de que empezara la realización escénica, y durante el descanso, el espectador podía moverse libremente por la «Ciudad Nueva», entrar en los locales construidos en la planta baja y estudiar los detalles de su cuidadosamente elaborada disposición: el dibujo del papel pintado de las paredes, la ropa de cama o la copia del «Cristo» de Holbein. Durante la realización escénica, sentado o bien abajo o bien en uno de los contenedores que habían sido separados de la estructura principal, el espectador daba vueltas alrededor de la Ciudad Nueva en el escenario giratorio.

La visibilidad era más o menos limitada desde todos los asientos. Esto no sólo se debía al hecho de que desde ninguno de ellos fuera posible ver todo lo que se desarrollaba al mismo tiempo en este enorme entorno, o al de que al estar todas las sillas al mismo nivel el espectador de delante no siempre le dejara a uno ver lo que quería. La limitación de la visibilidad tenía su razón, antes bien, en que la mayoría de las escenas no se desarrollaban en los lugares de los edificios que se veían mejor desde los asientos, sino en habitaciones interiores. Como las persianas y cortinas de las habitaciones limitaban aún más la ya muy limitada visibilidad, los cuerpos de los actores escapaban una y otra vez, en parte o completamente, a la mirada de los espectadores. Este perceptible déficit de presencia física de los actores lo compensaba el uso de las tecnologías de reproducción: en la habitación en la que en cada caso se desarrollaba la acción –a menudo visible para los espectadores– estaba el cámara Jan Speckenbach, que filmaba todas las escenas. La grabación se proyectaba simultáneamente –al modo de las retransmisiones en directo– en una serie de pequeños, más bien minúsculos, monitores, que pendían sobre las cabezas de los espectadores y que tenían pantallas de distintos tamaños (la película de la realización escénica se podía seguir íntegramente desde el contenedor superior en una gran pantalla por cinco euros). Así, el espectador veía, a través de una ventana entreabierta, la espalda del príncipe Mishkin (interpretado por Martin Wuttke) o las manos de Yepanchina (a la que interpretaba Sophie Rois), mientras sus rostros los veía en el monitor. Cuanto más avanzaba la realización escénica, más largos eran los periodos de tiempo durante los que se les impedía a los espectadores ver los cuerpos «reales» de los actores –sobre todo completos– y durante los que se tenían que conformar con la imagen parcial del monitor. Durante la última hora los monitores eran la única posibilidad de ver a los actores: las cortinas de las habitaciones en las que tenían lugar las últimas escenas estaban completamente echadas, y las persianas bajadas. La mirada del espectador podía perderse por todo el edificio y centrarse en los demás espectadores. No obstante, para poder seguir la acción había que recurrir a los monitores. ¿Pero podía estar seguro el espectador, dado que se le privaba de toda visibilidad de los espacios interiores, de que el vídeo era «en directo», es decir, de que los actores continuaban actuando y que su actuación se retransmitía de manera inmediata a través de los monitores? ¿No era posible –y quizá incluso probable– que los actores dejaran de actuar y que se les mostrara a los espectadores material grabado? ¿Seguía siendo una realización escénica «en vivo» o se había convertido tiempo atrás, como en la película que veían los espectadores del contenedor superior, en una realización escénica retransmitida?

El final de la realización escénica no coincidía con el final de la retransmisión de la acción por los monitores. Eran los actores los que lo determinaban, pues al terminar la retransmisión a través de los monitores salían a la plaza que estaba frente a los edificios y, siguiendo la convención del marco teatral, hacían una reverencia al público. Pero este gesto ciertamente convencional, buscar el aplauso del público y agradecerlo con una reverencia, adquiría en este caso un carácter completamente nuevo. Tras haberse retirado más de una hora, los actores salían a la luz en su corporalidad, y en esa salida convencional, que se agotaba literalmente en la mostración de sus cuerpos, esos mismos cuerpos sobre los que ahora caía la luz aparecían transfigurados, a pesar de que se trataba más de una luz neutral, de una iluminación sobria en sentido brechtiano, que de un fulgor místico. Su larga ausencia le confería a la mera aparición de sus cuerpos una cualidad nueva.

Sobre todo durante la última hora, se podía observar que los espectadores no anteponían de ninguna manera la filmación a la realización escénica «en vivo». Reaccionaban con creciente rechazo, de manera incluso agresiva. Casi se podría decir que daban síntomas de una especie de síndrome de abstinencia. Cada minuto de proyección aumentaba el deseo de ver los cuerpos «reales» de los actores –un deseo que se veía una y otra vez malogrado, frustrado–. Algunos perdían definitivamente la esperanza del regreso físico de los actores y abandonaban la «Ciudad Nueva». A pesar de que la retransmisión no era propia de amateurs, sino que estaba hecha de manera muy profesional, no en vano mantenía cautivados en sus asientos a los espectadores que la veían desde el piso superior, a los espectadores «en vivo» les parecía insípida, prolija, decepcionante.

En la primera parte de la realización escénica, hasta el descanso, predominaban las escenas en las que el espectador podía efectivamente ver «todo» el cuerpo de los actores o, por lo menos, partes de él. Al completarse la percepción con los rostros que mostraban los monitores, se producían efectos teatrales fascinantes: el espectador, que desde su asiento sólo hubiera podido observar a los actores desde una perspectiva, empezaba a verlos de repente desde diversos ángulos, como si fuera él mismo –y no meramente sus ojos– quien se desplazara a un lado y al otro de la sala. La retransmisión no hacía que nadie se cuestionase en ningún momento si la realización escénica era «en vivo». Tras el descanso, la alternancia entre corporalidad y plasticidad, entre situación «en vivo» y retransmisión, pasó de ser un entretenido juego con los modos de percepción para convertirse en un juego más bien cruel entre concesión y privación. Los actores iban ocultando su corporalidad a la mirada de los espectadores de un modo cada vez más intenso y frecuente. Después de una larga ausencia, a los espectadores se les volvía a dar por un instante la oportunidad de ver a los actores en su presencia física. Después de otra larga fase de ausencia, los actores volvían a aparecer en la plaza frente a los edificios, se dirigían a los espectadores y se mezclaban con ellos. Rápidamente se establecía una situación de proximidad, de intimidad, que en ningún momento habían logrado establecer las imágenes de vídeo. Éstas parecían estériles y no hacían más que alimentar el deseo de ver de nuevo a los actores en persona.

En circunstancias normales, aquel que asiste a una realización escénica teatral da por supuesta la copresencia física de actores y espectadores, mientras que no la echa en falta en el cine o en la televisión. En el caso de esta realización escénica, por el contrario, la retransmisión amenazaba permanentemente con la desaparición de la presencia física de los actores. En esos momentos el bucle de retroalimentación se interrumpía, o parecía al menos interrumpirse: los espectadores tenían unas imágenes de vídeo ante sus ojos en las que sólo podían influir mediatamente, a través de los actores. Lo que los espectadores no podían saber es si los actores estaban en condiciones de percibir las reacciones del público, ni siquiera sabían si se encontraban en las habitaciones interiores o se habían ido al bar o a los camerinos. Para ellos el bucle de retroalimentación se había interrumpido. Su deseo de que los actores regresaran físicamente era también un deseo del mutuo percibir y ser percibido que pone en marcha el bucle de retroalimentación y que, de ese modo, genera la realización escénica.

En *El idiota* se consiguió que la realización escénica incorporara su propia retransmisión, sin que por ello, como afirma Auslander, desapareciera su condición de realización escénica «en vivo». El efecto fue, antes bien, que la progresiva preponderancia de la retransmisión avivaba en los espectadores el deseo de ver físicamente a los actores y les confería un aura a sus «cuerpos reales». Cuando los actores salían finalmente a la luz al final de la realización escénica, era quizá el momento en el que los espectadores podían tener por fin esa experiencia de «trascendencia» que, como lamentaron con amargura muchos críticos de esta versión del texto de Dostoievski, se les había negado ostensiblemente durante toda la realización escénica.

La interrupción del bucle de retroalimentación durante una hora puede entenderse como una dislocación de la influencia mutua entre actores y espectadores, incluyendo entre estos últimos a los que se convirtieron en actores moviendo las sillas, levantándose, abandonando el teatro, bostezando, hablando, etc. Pero como en este caso, a diferencia de lo que ocurrió en *Commune* de Schechner, a los espectadores se les ofrecía otro foco de atención, a saber: los monitores, hay que inclinarse a aceptar que la interrupción del bucle de retroalimentación efectivamente se producía.

Pero esa interrupción no conducía, sin embargo, como se podría suponer a partir del argumento de Auslander, a la disolución de la realización escénica en su retransmisión, a que la realización escénica «en vivo» se convirtiera en mediatizada. Aunque en la última hora pudiera dar esa impresión, ésta se terminaba tornando falsa. Pues lo que en realidad hacía la interrupción era suscitar en el espectador un creciente deseo de que los actores aparecieran físicamente que daba lugar a que en su última aparición, meramente convencional, los viera de una manera distinta.

Fue precisamente este montaje de *El idiota*, que usaba profusamente las tecnologías de reproducción y que, según la tesis de Auslander, debería por ello haberse anulado a sí misma en tanto que realización escénica «en vivo», el que terminó desembocando en una apoteosis de la copresencia física de actores y espectadores. La aparición convencional de los actores al final se vivía como su transfiguración, como celebración de la presencia física. Tras seis horas, los espectadores experimentaban en un instante, y en carne propia, la «iluminación» de que independientemente de qué historia se cuente en una realización escénica y de cómo se haga, es la presencia física de los actores la que tiene un efecto sobre ellos, la que pone en marcha el proceso autopoiético del bucle de retroalimentación, que es el que genera, en última instancia, la realización escénica.

IV. SOBRE LA PRODUCCIÓN PERFORMATIVA DE LA MATERIALIDAD

En el capítulo anterior he mostrado que la autopoiesis del bucle de retroalimentación revela que, tocante a la realización escénica, la distinción, aunque sólo sea heurística, entre estética de la producción y estética de la recepción es de muy poca ayuda. Con ello se problematizaba implícitamente la categoría de estética de la obra, cuyo análisis será uno de los centros de interés de este trabajo. Partiendo del fenómeno de la fugacidad de las realizaciones escénicas, intentaré dar respuesta a las preguntas de cómo se produce performativamente la materialidad en las realizaciones escénicas, de cuál es el estatus que le corresponde a esta materialidad, y de si ese estatus puede ser compatible con el concepto de obra.

Las realizaciones escénicas no son un artefacto material fijable ni transmisible, son fugaces, transitorias y se agotan en su propia actualidad *(Gegenwärtigkeit)*, es decir, en su continuo devenir y desvanecerse, en la autopoiesis del bucle de retroalimentación. Esto no excluye en ningún caso que en ellas algunos objetos materiales –decorado, atrezo, vestuario– tengan su función, que haya objetos que al final de la realización escénica se mantengan como tales, que puedan conservarse como vestigios de ella y exponerse en un museo teatral o en un museo de arte (que es lugar adecuado cuando se trata del arte de acción y de la performance). La realización escénica, no obstante, se pierde irremediablemente al terminar y no se puede repetir nunca de forma idéntica. Como ha señalado acertadamente Peggy Phelan, la realización escénica no es «rescatable» a posteriori. Todo intento de capturarla en un artefacto por medio de un registro magnetofónico o de vídeo está condenado al fracaso, y no hace sino poner aún más claramente de relieve el abismo infranqueable entre una realización escénica y un artefacto fijable o incluso reproducible. Cualquier intento de reproducirla termina convirtiéndose en un intento de documentarla. En este punto hay que contradecir a Phelan cuando afirma que las realizaciones escénicas no pueden documentarse. Precisamente su documentación es la condición de posibilidad para que se pueda hablar de ellas. Es justamente la tensión entre su fugacidad y las constantes tentativas de documentarlas en vídeo, películas, fotografía o descripciones la que pone de relieve su inequívoco carácter efímero y único.

> El discurso sobre la performance da testimonio de un vacío, de una pérdida. Sólo se convierte en un objeto accesible, en un objeto al que nos podemos referir, sobre el que podemos discutir o que podemos juzgar, si pagamos el precio de su desaparición, una experiencia que presupone el reconocimiento de condiciones imposibles. [...] Al arte de la performance no habría que interrogarle por su programa artístico o por la experiencia subjetiva del artista-cuerpo, sino sobre la distancia entre presentación y percepción, que se articula en los documentos y en los testimonios escritos de los observadores[1].

Lo que nos es accesible cuando termina la realización escénica son los documentos que se preparan sobre ella o a partir de ella, pero nunca su materialidad específica. Ésta precisa la transformación en otros medios –en vídeo, fotografía, o descripciones, entre otros– para que nos sea accesible. Esta investigación también tiene que recurrir a documentaciones de este tipo, aunque a

1 Hans-Friedrich Bormann/Gabriele Brandstetter, «An der Schwelle. Performance als Forschungslabor», en Hanne Seitz (eds.), *Schreiben auf Wasser. Performative Verfahren in Kunst, Wissenschaft und Bildung*, Bonn, 1999, pp. 45-55, citas pp. 46 y 50 respectivamente.

veces sean mis propias anotaciones o protocolos de recuerdos. La materialidad específica de la realización escénica escapa a cualquier intento de fijarla. Es la propia realización escénica la que se produce en tanto que actual (*gegenwärtig*) en el proceso de ejecución y la que, precisamente por ello, en el momento que se produce vuelve a anonadarse.

Desde el giro performativo en los años sesenta el teatro y el arte de acción y de la performance han desarrollado gran cantidad de procedimientos que se proponen centrar la atención en la producción performativa de la materialidad en la realización escénica y que destacan y subrayan, tanto en la práctica como en el laboratorio de investigación, diversos factores clave y diversos modos de ejecución. Esto vale tanto para la corporalidad de la realización escénica como para su espacialidad y su sonoridad. Estos procedimientos nos permiten observar, casi al microscopio, el proceso específico de generación que lleva a cabo la realización escénica tocante a la materialidad que le es propia. Ellos serán los que nos permitan orientar el desarrollo de esta investigación, sus líneas maestras.

1. Corporalidad

En las realizaciones escénicas se da el caso de que el artista «productor» no se puede separar de su material. Produce su «obra» —para servirnos una vez más de la expresión— en un material y con un material extremadamente singular, raro incluso: su propio cuerpo o, como lo expresó Helmuth Plessner, «el material de la propia existencia»[2]. En las teorías teatrales y de la actuación se hace referencia a esta singularidad continuamente. Se ha hecho especial hincapié, sobre todo, en la tensión que se da entre el cuerpo fenoménico del actor, su físico estar-en-el-mundo (*In-*

2 Helmuth Plessner, «Zur Anthropologie des Schauspielers», en *Gesammelte Schriften*, Günter Dux, Odo Marquard, Elisabeth Ströker (eds.), Fráncfort, 1982, pp. 399-418, p. 407.

der-Welt-sein) y la interpretación de un personaje. En opinión de Plessner en esta singularidad se expone la distancia esencial del hombre con respecto a sí mismo, razón por la que ve en el actor la condición humana simbolizada de una forma singular. El ser humano *tiene* un cuerpo que puede manipular e instrumentalizar como cualquier objeto. Al mismo tiempo, sin embargo, *es* ese cuerpo, es un sujeto-cuerpo. El actor, al salirse de sí mismo para interpretar un personaje «en el material de la propia existencia», apunta expresamente a la duplicidad y a la distancia esencial que fundan ese mismo personaje. Para Plessner, la tensión entre el cuerpo fenoménico del actor y su interpretación de un personaje es la que le confiere a la realización escénica su profundo significado antropológico y su especial dignidad.

Edward Gordon Craig, por el contrario, ve en esta tensión el principal motivo para desterrar al actor del teatro y reemplazarlo por una Supermarioneta. En efecto, el material actoral no es de acceso libre ni se deja moldear o controlar a voluntad. Está más bien sujeto a las muy específicas condiciones establecidas por la doble condición de ser-cuerpo y tener-cuerpo. Para garantizar el carácter de obra de arte de la realización escénica, según la argumentación de Craig, habría que eliminar al actor del escenario:

> La naturaleza humana tiende a la libertad, por eso el hombre como tal trae la prueba de su inadecuación como *material* para el teatro. En el teatro moderno, puesto que uno utiliza como *material* el cuerpo de hombres y mujeres, todo lo que se representa es de carácter accidental. [...] El arte como lo hemos definido no puede admitir hechos accidentales; por lo tanto, lo que el actor nos ofrece no es una obra de arte[3].

Sin quererle atribuir un significado simbólico a la tensión entre el físico estar-en-el-mundo del actor y su interpretación de

3 Edward Gordon Craig, «The actor and the Über-marionette», en *On the Art of Theater*, Londres, 1912, pp. 54-94, aquí pp. 56 y s. (esp. *El arte del teatro*, México D.F., 1999).

un personaje, como hacía Plessner, por no hablar de la pretensión de Craig de desterrarla del teatro por su inadecuación para el ámbito artístico, sí la entiendo como núcleo y punto de partida para la investigación de la producción de la corporalidad en la realización escénica. Pues en ella veo la condición de posibilidad de la producción performativa de la corporalidad en la realización escénica y para su extremadamente singular percepción por parte de los espectadores. Hay sobre todo dos fenómenos en los procesos de generación y percepción de la corporalidad como factor decisivo y como factor potencial en los que esa tensión se manifiesta de manera peculiar, y en los que, por lo tanto, se centrará nuestra investigación: los procesos de corporización y el fenómeno de la presencia.

Corporización / *Embodiment* *

En la segunda mitad del siglo dieciocho se le dio forma a un nuevo concepto del arte de la actuación que, más tarde, hacia finales del mismo siglo, se vería confirmado con la aparición del término 'encarnación'. Mientras que hasta entonces se solía decir que el actor interpretaba un papel o también, en ocasiones, que lo presentaba, incluso que lo daba o que lo era («Cenie es Madame Hensel», dice Lessing en la vigésima pieza de la *Hamburgische Dramaturgie [Dramaturgia de Hamburgo]*), se empezó entonces a hablar de que el actor «encarnaba» a un personaje. ¿Qué se quería decir con ese concepto?

* El término *Verkörperung* se ha vertido al español tradicionalmente como 'encarnación'. La autora lleva a cabo en este capítulo una redefinición del término alemán, sin sustituirlo, no obstante, por otro. Algo que las implicaciones religiosas, y las puramente semánticas, de la traducción tradicional del mismo al español hacen imposible en nuestro caso. Alternaremos, pues, los términos 'encarnación', cuando la autora se refiera a contextos en los que se pretendía que la corporalidad específica del actor fuera relegada para dar lugar a que el espectador viera en él exclusivamente al personaje, y 'corporización', un término ya común entre nosotros sobre todo a partir de Merleau-Ponty (a cuya filosofía se remite también la autora), para los contextos en los que se hace referencia a las teorías contemporáneas sobre teatro y cultura.

En la segunda mitad del siglo dieciocho, el teatro alemán experimentó dos importantes cambios: la creación de un teatro literario y la evolución de un nuevo arte de la actuación realista-psicológico. Ambos están estrechamente relacionados.

El intento de algunos intelectuales burgueses de terminar con la hegemonía del actor en el teatro tenía por objeto elevar el texto del dramaturgo a instancia de control del teatro. El actor debía dejar de actuar de acuerdo a su capricho, a su talento para la improvisación, a su ingenio, a su genio, incluso a su vanidad o a su intención de agradar. Su tarea debía limitarse a transmitir al público los significados que el autor había expresado en su texto por medios lingüísticos. El arte de la actuación en su performatividad no debía producir significados nuevos, propios, sino que tenía que limitarse a darles expresión a los que el autor había hallado o inventado en su texto.

Para poder cumplir esta función había que modificar radicalmente el arte de la actuación. Había que capacitar al actor para dar expresión en su cuerpo, y con su cuerpo, a los significados que el autor había expresado lingüísticamente en el texto –especialmente los sentimientos, los estados de ánimo, los razonamientos y los rasgos de carácter de las *dramatis personae*–. Debía ayudar al actor a hacer desaparecer su físico estar-en-el-mundo, su cuerpo fenoménico sobre el escenario y transformarlo en un «texto» de signos al servicio de los sentimientos, los estados de ánimo, etc., de un personaje. La tensión entre el cuerpo fenoménico del actor y la interpretación de un personaje dramático debía ser eliminada en beneficio de la interpretación.

Consecuentemente, Johann Jakob Engel reprende a los actores en su *Mimik [Carta sobre el gesto, la pantomima y la acción teatral]* (1785/86) por hacer un uso de su cuerpo que dirigía la atención del espectador hacía su fisicidad e impedía así que pudiera ser percibido como signo de un personaje:

> Ignoro qué demonio hostil posee a nuestros actores, especialmente a los de sexo femenino, que pretenden hacer que tan gran arte caiga, ¿o debiera decir que se derrumbe? Puede verse una Ariadna que, cuando sabe de su desgraciado destino por voz de la divinidad

> de la montaña, cae al suelo todo lo larga que es, más rápido que si hubiera sido alcanzada por un rayo y con una violencia que parece quisiera romperse el cráneo. Si a esta actuación tan poco natural y tan inadecuada sigue una calurosa ovación es porque proviene, sin lugar a dudas, de las manos de los ignorantes que no entienden el verdadero interés de una pieza, que pagaron su entrada sólo para mirar boquiabiertos y que preferirían sentarse en una función de circo o en una corrida de toros. El conocedor, si aplaude, lo hace únicamente por compasiva alegría de que la pobre criatura, que aunque pésima actriz será seguramente una buena chica, haya salido sana y salva del trance. Artificios peligrosos [...] que pertenecen a los números de feria, en los que el mayor interés recae en los seres humanos reales y su destreza física, y cuanto más se incrementa [la atención] más aumenta el riesgo[4].

En el teatro el espectador debía percibir sólo al personaje, sentir sólo a través de él. Si, por el contrario, centraba su atención en el cuerpo del actor como cuerpo fenoménico, como su físico estar-en-el-mundo, de tal manera que no lo percibiera como signo del estado anímico o psíquico de un personaje, entonces empezaba «a tener sentimientos por él», o por ella, lo cual «le arrancaba inevitablemente de la ilusión»[5]. El espectador se veía obligado, pues, a abandonar el mundo ficticio de la obra y a introducirse en el mundo de la corporalidad real.

A partir de la argumentación de Engel queda claro lo que se quería decir con el nuevo concepto de «encarnación». El actor debía transformar su cuerpo sensible y fenoménico en un cuerpo semiótico en una medida tal que estuviera en condiciones de ponerse, en tanto que nuevo portador de signos, al servicio de la expresión de los significados lingüísticos del texto y de hacerlo en tanto que signo material. Los significados que el autor había expresado en el texto debían hallar en el cuerpo del actor un nuevo cuerpo-signo sensible y perceptible en el que desapareciera

4 Johann Jakob Engel, *Ideen zu einer Mimik* (1785/6) en *Schriften*, vols. 7/8, Berlín, 1804, vol. 7, pp. 59 y s.

5 *Ibid.*, p. 58.

o se extinguiera todo lo que no sirviera para la transmisión de estos significados, todo lo que pudiera afectarlos, falsearlos, mancillarlos, contaminarlos o menoscabarlos de cualquier forma.

Esta idea se basa en un concepto del significado fundamentado en una teoría de los dos mundos. En ella los significados se consideran entidades mentales, «espirituales», que sólo pueden manifestarse por medio de la invención de los signos adecuados. Mientras el lenguaje constituye un sistema casi ideal de signos en el que lo mental, es decir, los significados, puede ser expresado de manera «pura», no falsificable, el cuerpo humano se presenta como un medio y un material mucho menos fiable para la constitución de signos. De ahí que Schiller advirtiera expresamente de «los dudosos beneficios de la encarnación en el teatro»[6]. Para que el cuerpo pueda emplearse de esta manera, hay que someterlo primero a una cierta descorporización (*Entleiblichung*): todo lo que remita al cuerpo orgánico del actor, a su físico estar-en-el-mundo, debe ser eliminado de él hasta que quede un cuerpo semiótico «puro». Pues sólo un cuerpo semiótico «puro» estará en condiciones de traer a presencia, sensorialmente perceptibles y sin falsificar, los significados depositados en el texto y de transmitírselos al espectador. La encarnación presupone, pues, una previa descorporización o desencarnación, que además opone también resistencia a la fugacidad de la realización escénica. Los gestos, los movimientos y los sonidos articulados que produce el actor pueden muy bien ser transitorios, pero los significados que se expresan con ellos existen más allá de la fugacidad de esos signos.

Aunque el concepto de significado que está en la base de esta idea hace mucho tiempo que ha quedado obsoleto, aunque ya nadie defiende en serio la idea de que los significados «auténticos» de un texto dramático pueden hallarse en una lectura concienzuda[7], el concepto de encarnación referido a la tarea del

6 Cit. por el *Deutsches Wörterbuch*, Jakob y Wilhelm Grimm (eds.), vols. 1-31, Múnich, 1984, vol. 25, p. 683.

7 Véase Erika Fischer-Lichte (ed.), *Das Drama und seine Inszenierung*, Tubinga, 1983.

actor sigue empleándose aún hoy frecuentemente en el sentido de una descorporización. Así, el teórico de la literatura Wolfgang Iser escribía aún en 1983: «Para producir la determinación de un personaje irreal, el actor debe irrealizarse de manera que la realidad de su cuerpo sea desposeída de su fuerza y se convierta en *analogon*, para que con ello un personaje irreal pueda tener la posibilidad de ganar su presencia real»[8]. En la base de estas palabras están tanto la teoría de los dos mundos como la idea de encarnación como descorporización: el actor encarna al personaje de Hamlet constituido lingüísticamente en el texto en la medida en que su propio cuerpo real «es desposeído de su fuerza y se convierte en *analogon*».

Tal concepción ya había sido impugnada a principios del siglo veinte por Georg Simmel. En su texto póstumo *Zur Philosophie des Schauspielers [Sobre la filosofía del actor]*, de 1923, expone por qué la encarnación de una *dramatis persona* por un actor no puede concebirse y explicarse como una transmisión de significados constituidos lingüísticamente a través de otro medio especialmente enderezado a tal fin, a saber: el cuerpo descorporizado del actor, su cuerpo semiótico. Simmel empieza por explicar las diferencias esenciales entre los significados constituidos lingüísticamente y los constituidos corporalmente:

> El personaje dramático tal y como aparece en el texto no es, por así decirlo, un ser humano completo, no es un ser humano en sentido sensorial, sino el complejo de lo literariamente captable de un ser humano. El autor no puede predeterminar ni la voz, ni la entonación, ni el *ritardando* o *accelerando* del discurso, ni los gestos o la especial atmósfera del personaje carnal, ni tampoco dar directrices unívocas para lograrlo. Le ha conferido, eso sí, en el proceso meramente unidimensional de lo mental, un destino, una apariencia y un alma a ese personaje. En tanto que creación literaria el drama es un todo autosuficiente, con respecto a la totalidad de lo

8 Wolfgang Iser, «Akte des Fingierens oder Was ist das Fiktive im fiktionalen Text?», en D. Henrich y W. Iser (eds.), *Funktionen des Fiktiven*, Múnich, 1983, pp. 121-151, pp. 145 y s.

que realmente termina ocurriendo se queda en símbolo a partir del cual esa totalidad no se puede inferir lógicamente[9].

Mientras que Diderot en su *Carta sobre los sordomudos* (1751) se esforzaba en explicar que todos los enunciados sobre objetos concretos y sobre aquellas ideas que pueden ser expuestas por medio de una denominación transferida pueden formularse con la misma eficacia por medio de signos lingüísticos que por medio de signos gestuales, y que, por lo tanto, los signos lingüísticos pueden ser traducidos sin más a signos gestuales –con lo que se fija el fundamento teórico para el concepto de encarnación–, Simmel hacía hincapié en la distinción entre lenguaje y cuerpo, con lo que convertía en imposible por definición la traducción de los signos lingüísticos a signos gestuales. Por esa razón se muestra tan decididamente contrario a la idea de que:

> [...] el modo ideal de interpretar un papel venga dado inequívoca y necesariamente en el propio papel; como si a partir de las páginas del libro surgiera, sólo para aquel que pudiera ver con la suficiente agudeza y que supiera inferir lógicamente, toda la sensibilización *(Versinnlichung)* teatral de Hamlet; tomado en serio, sería como si existiera una sola interpretación «correcta» de cada papel dramático a la que el actor empírico se aproxima más o menos. Esta idea la refuta el solo hecho de que tres grandes actores interpretaran el papel de tres maneras completamente distintas, todas de un valor equivalente y ninguna «más correcta» que las demás [...] [no] se [puede] interpretar a Hamlet basándose exclusivamente en el texto; éste legitima la concepción de Moisi, como antes había legitimado la de Kainz y la de Salviati (sic)[10].

9 Georg Simmel, «Zur Philosophie des Schauspielers», en *Das individuelle Gesetz. Philosophische Exkurse*, Fráncfort, 1968, pp. 75-95, pp. 75 y s.

10 *Ibid.*, p. 78. Como en tiempos de Simmel no había ningún actor conocido con el nombre de Salviati, doy por supuesto que se refiere a Tommaso Salvini (1829-1915), y que se trata de un error de imprenta.

Simmel habla aquí de distintas «concepciones» del papel por parte de Moissi, Kainz y Salvini. Si se atiende, no obstante, a lo que había dicho poco antes sobre la distinción entre lenguaje y cuerpo, se comprueba que no hay que remitir los distintos Hamlets de los tres actores sólo a sus distintas «concepciones», sino a su muy distinta naturaleza *(physis)*: sus «voces», su «entonación», sus «gestos» y «la atmósfera particular» de sus «figuras carnales». En otras palabras, los Hamlets de Moissi, de Kainz y de Salvini no son una encarnación del papel en tanto que caracterizado por medio de signos lingüísticos en el texto, sino que cada uno es un Hamlet completamente distinto. El Hamlet que corporiza Moissi no existe más que en la interpretación de Moissi –del mismo modo que el Hamlet de Salvini sólo existe en y por su interpretación–. Son sus cuerpos en su especificidad y los actos performativos realizados con y por ellos los que crean el personaje. Por eso el Hamlet de Moissi no puede ser idéntico al Hamlet de Salvini o al de Kainz, ni tampoco al Hamlet del texto literario. El concepto de encarnación tal y como se desarrolló a finales del siglo dieciocho ya no basta.

Ya a principios del siglo veinte fue impugnado con contundencia tanto por teóricos del teatro como por los artistas teatrales. El rechazo del teatro literario y la proclamación del teatro como arte autónomo que ya no se conforma con darle expresión a los significados previamente dados en la literatura, sino que genera por sí mismo significados nuevos, resultaron en una nueva concepción del arte de la actuación como actividad al mismo tiempo corporal y creativa. Suena a réplica directa a Engel la afirmación de Meyerhold referida a las casetas de feria o al circo ambulante, y como a eco sordo el hecho de que algunos críticos se mostraran contrarios a esa nueva forma de emplear el cuerpo en los montajes del *Edipo Rey* y de la *Orestíada* dirigidos por Reinhardt con el argumento de que se trataba de una práctica «circense en el sentido más vulgar» y sólo apta para un público «educado en corridas de toros»[11].

11 Siegfried Jacobsohn, *Das Jahr der Bühne*, p. 49.

En el desarrollo del nuevo arte de la actuación, la reflexión sobre la naturaleza material del cuerpo humano tiene un papel preponderante. Mientras que Craig, por su imprevisibilidad, no lo consideraba apto y quería desterrarlo del escenario, Meyerhold, Eisenstein, Tairov y muchos otros entendían el cuerpo como un material infinitamente moldeable y controlable que el actor podía elaborar creativamente. Meyerhold afirma que:

> En el arte se trata siempre de la organización de material. [...] El arte del actor consiste en la organización de su propio material, es decir, en la capacidad de aprovechar convenientemente los medios expresivos de su cuerpo. En la persona del actor confluyen el organizador y aquello que ha der ser organizado (es decir, el artista y su material). Expresado en una fórmula vendría a ser lo siguiente: $N=A_I+A_2$, donde N es el actor, A_I el constructor, que tiene una intención determinada y que da instrucciones para que se lleve a cabo lo que quiere, y A_2 el cuerpo del actor, que ejecuta y realiza la tarea encomendada por el constructor (A_I). El actor debe adiestrar su material, el cuerpo, de tal manera que pueda ejecutar al punto las tareas encomendadas desde el exterior por el actor o por el director[12].

El actor se libera así de su dependencia con respecto a la literatura. No obstante, el concepto de cuerpo que subyace a este texto presenta, en cierto sentido, llamativas semejanzas con el que era inherente al concepto de encarnación. En ambos casos se supera la tensión entre ser-cuerpo y tener-cuerpo: al sujeto, al que difícilmente se lo podría entender como sujeto-cuerpo, se le atribuye una disponibilidad absoluta sobre el objeto-cuerpo. Mientras que los teóricos del siglo dieciocho confiaban en que todo lo que en el cuerpo es naturaleza humana sensible, precaria y deficiente podría hacerse desaparecer en el proceso de su

12 Vesevolod Meyerhold, «El actor del futuro y la biomecánica», en *La escena moderna: manifiestos y textos sobre el teatro de la época de vanguardias*, José A. Sánchez (ed.), Madrid, 1999, p. 278. [Traducción ligeramente modificada].

semiotización –incluso aunque algunos, como por ejemplo Schiller, albergaran serias dudas al respecto–, en Meyerhold y en otros vanguardistas el cuerpo humano parece concebirse como una máquina infinitamente perfectible que, por medio de intervenciones de su constructor hábilmente calculadas, puede ser mejorada hasta el punto de reducir significativamente su vulnerabilidad y de garantizar un funcionamiento perfecto. En ambos casos topamos con el fantasma del control absoluto del cuerpo. No hay un ser-cuerpo, sino únicamente un sujeto casi omnipotente que no está condicionado ni determinado por su cuerpo, sino que por el contrario puede disponer libremente de él como de un material moldeable a voluntad. Pero hay que hacer una distinción decisiva al respecto: mientras que con el principio de encarnación vigente la corporalidad no se entiende como materialidad, sino como signicidad, es decir, como expresión de los significados depositados en el texto literario del drama, en el caso de Meyerhold y de otros vanguardistas la corporalidad hace su aparición primordialmente como materialidad. Los diversos ejercicios de la biomecánica no estaban pensados en tanto que signos para comunicar significados, sino que hacían hincapié en ciertas posibilidades de movimiento del cuerpo y desviaban la atención hacia su movilidad, hacia su «*excitabilidad refleja*», que «contagia al espectador»[13]. Y es con la materialidad específica de su cuerpo movible y motor con la que el actor afecta de manera inmediata al cuerpo del espectador, lo «contagia»[14], esto es, lo traslada también a él a un estado de excitación. Ello no excluye en ningún caso los procesos de generación de significado. La ostensible enfatización de la materialidad del cuerpo del actor le da la oportunidad de generar, en su percepción o con su percepción, significados completamente nuevos, de convertirse en «*creador de*

13 *Ibid.*

14 También los teóricos del siglo dieciocho partían del supuesto de que el actor «contagia» al espectador, de que suscita sentimientos en él. Pero este «contagio» estaba vinculado a la idea de que el espectador podía percibir el «rostro y los gestos del actor» como expresión de un determinado sentimiento. Véase Erika Fischer-Lichte, «Der Körper als Zeichen und als Erfahrung», en *Theater im Prozess der Zivilisation*, Tubinga/Basilea, 2000, pp. 67-80.

un nuevo sentido»[15]. La corporalidad del actor se produce, en este sentido, como un potencial efectivo a partir del cual pueden ciertamente surgir nuevos significados.

Meyerhold dio forma a su concepto de un nuevo arte de la actuación como antítesis explícita del concepto de encarnación. Mientras que anteriormente el efecto del actor en el espectador sólo parecía posible si éste era capaz de descifrar los movimientos de aquél como signos de determinados significados, Meyerhold parte del supuesto de que el cuerpo del actor, de excitación refleja y responsable de sus propios movimientos, tiene un efecto directo sobre el cuerpo del espectador. Mientras que anteriormente el actor debía ejecutar sus movimientos en tanto que signos de los significados fijados en el texto literario, en Meyerhold los movimientos del actor pasaban a considerarse una especie de estímulo que suscitaba en el espectador la respuesta de la excitación y/o el impulso de generar por su parte nuevos significados. Mientras que anteriormente la performatividad estaba puesta al servicio de la expresividad, ahora se concibe como potencial efectivo. El concepto de Meyerhold de un nuevo arte de la actuación surgió, en cierto modo, como inversión del concepto de encarnación. Lo puso, por así decirlo, patas arriba.

Desde los años sesenta se viene experimentando en las realizaciones escénicas teatrales y del arte de la performance con distintos modos de emplear el cuerpo, y se vienen desarrollando igualmente nuevos modos, que, en lo tocante a su énfasis y a su exposición de la materialidad, entroncan sin duda con conceptos de las vanguardias históricas y los llevan más allá. Aquéllos se distinguen, sin embargo, de éstos en la medida en que no presuponen el cuerpo como material absolutamente moldeable y controlable, sino que, de manera consecuente, parten de la tensión entre ser-cuerpo y tener-cuerpo, entre cuerpo fenoménico y cuerpo semiótico. Tales formas de emplear el cuerpo hallan su fundamento y su

15 Vsevolod Meyerhold, «Rezension des Buches 'Aufzeichungen eines Regisseurs' de A. Ja. Tairov (1921/1922)», en *Vsevolod Meyerhold. Theaterarbeit 1917-1930*, pp. 63-72, p. 72.

justificación en el físico estar-en-el-mundo del actor/performador. Con ello brindan la posibilidad de reintroducir el concepto de encarnación, aunque, eso sí, definido de manera completa y radicalmente nueva [como corporización].

En este contexto se han mostrado particularmente productivos y decisivos cuatro procedimientos entre los que se han empleado o se emplean en los más diversos tipos de realización escénica: 1) la inversión de la relación entre actor y papel; 2) el realce y la exhibición de la singularidad del (cuerpo del) actor; 3) el hincapié en la vulnerabilidad, la fragilidad y la insuficiencia del cuerpo (del actor); 4) el *cross-casting*. Muchas veces se emplean dos o más de estos procedimientos al mismo tiempo.

1) Jerzy Grotowski definió la relación entre actor y papel de un modo completamente nuevo. En su opinión, el actor no puede simplemente estar ahí para interpretar un papel y, en ese sentido, encarnarlo. Entiende más bien el papel fijado en el texto del dramaturgo como una herramienta: «[...] el actor debe aprender a utilizar su papel como el bisturí de un cirujano, para diseccionarse»[16]. El papel deja de ser, pues, el objetivo y la intención última de la actividad del actor y se convierte meramente en un medio para la consecución de otro fin: dejar que el cuerpo mismo aparezca como algo mental, hacer que aparezca como mente corporizada. Con ello se le da carpetazo a la teoría de los dos mundos en la que se basaba el viejo concepto de encarnación. El actor no le presta su cuerpo a una mente, no encarna en este sentido algo mental, esto es, significados preexistentes, sino que hace que la mente aparezca a través de su cuerpo al conferirle capacidad operativa *(agency)* a su cuerpo.

Por ello, para formar actores Grotowski renunciaba a:

> enseñarles algo; tratamos de eliminar la resistencia que su organismo opone a los procesos psíquicos. El resultado es una liberación que se produce en el paso del impulso interior a la reacción externa, de tal modo que el impulso se convierte en reacción

16 Jerzy Grotowski, *Hacia un teatro pobre*, Madrid, 2009, p. 19.

> externa. El impulso y la acción son concurrentes: el cuerpo se desvanece, se quema, y el espectador sólo contempla una serie de impulsos visibles. La nuestra es una *vía negativa*, no una colección de técnicas, sino la destrucción de obstáculos[17].

Para Grotowski tener-cuerpo es indisociable de ser-cuerpo. Para él, el cuerpo no es un instrumento ni un medio de expresión ni un material para la constitución de signos, sino que su «materia» se «quema» en y por la actividad del actor y se transforma en energía. El actor no domina su cuerpo –ni en el sentido de Engel ni en el de Meyerhold–, deja que se convierta él mismo en actor: el cuerpo actúa como una mente corporizada *(embodied mind)*.

Grotowski calificaba al actor que fuera capaz de lograrlo de actor «santo»: «Es un acto solemne y profundo de revelación. [...] Es como un paso hacia lo más alto del organismo del actor en el que la conciencia y los instintos estarán unidos»[18]. La terminología religiosa vincula implícitamente al actor con el Cristo sufriente y resucitado, pues fue por su sufrimiento que adquirió un cuerpo carnal y espiritual al mismo tiempo. El Cristo resucitado figura aquí como símbolo de un nuevo modo de concebir al ser humano, un nuevo modo de concebir lo corporal en el que se supera la antigua escisión entre cuerpo y mente, en el que la mente sólo se puede entender como «corporizada» y el cuerpo como «espiritualizado».

Puede que la interpretación que más se haya acercado a la idea de actor «santo» de Grotowski sea la de Ryszard Cieślak en *El príncipe constante* (1965). Sobre él escribe el crítico Józef Kelera en *ODRA XI* (1965):

> La esencia [...] no reside en realidad en el hecho de que el actor haga un uso sorprendente de su voz, ni tampoco en la manera en que utiliza su cuerpo desnudo para esculpir formas móviles que

17 *Ibid.*, p. 2.
18 *Ibid.*, p. 153.

> son extraordinarias por su expresividad; tampoco reside en lograr que la técnica del cuerpo y de la voz constituyan una unidad durante el largo y cansado monólogo que colinda, física y vocalmente, con la acrobacia. Es cuestión de algo muy diferente. [...] Hasta ahora había aceptado con reserva los términos «santidad secular», «acto de humildad», «purificación», que Grotowski emplea. Acepto hoy que pueden ser aplicados perfectamente al personaje de *El príncipe constante*. Una especie de iluminación psíquica emana del actor. No puedo encontrar otra definición. En los momentos culminantes de su papel, todo lo que es técnica se encuentra iluminado desde dentro, con una luz imponderable en sentido literal. [...] El actor puede levitar en un momento dado... Está en estado de gracia. Y alrededor de él, este «teatro cruel» con sus blasfemias y sus excesos se transforma en un teatro en estado de gracia[19].

El tipo de palabras que escoge el crítico parece apuntar también a que en la realización escénica de *El príncipe constante*, al aparecer el cuerpo del actor como mente corporizada *(embodied mind)*, la teoría de los dos mundos quedaba obsoleta. Los paralelismos entre la práctica teatral de Grotowski y la filosofía del Merleau-Ponty de los últimos años son realmente sorprendentes. Su filosofía de la carne *(chair)* supone un ambicioso intento dirigido a la transmisión de un saber no dualista ni transcendental entre el cuerpo y el alma, entre lo sensible y lo no-sensible. La relación entre ambas dimensiones está pensada de manera asimétrica en beneficio de lo corporal-sensible. Es a través de la carne que el cuerpo está desde el principio vinculado al mundo. Cualquier intervención humana en el mundo se lleva a cabo con el cuerpo, sólo puede llevarse a cabo en tanto que intervención corporizada. Es precisamente por ello que el cuerpo supera en su carnalidad a todas sus funciones instrumentales y semióticas[20].

19 Citado en *ibid.*, p. 76.

20 Véase al respecto Merleau-Ponty, M., *Le visible et l'invisible; suivi de Notes de travail*, París, 1964, pp. 175 y ss. (esp. «El entrelazo – El quiasmo», en *Lo visible y lo invisible*, Barcelona, 1970).

La filosofía de Merleau-Ponty allanó de esta manera el camino para el novedoso empleo del concepto de *Verkörperung* [como corporización] que hoy es común en la antropología cultural, la ciencia cognitiva y los estudios teatrales. La aportación de Merleau-Ponty a la filosofía es sin duda equiparable a la de Grotowski al teatro. Con Ryszard Cieślak aparecía en escena un actor para el que el dualismo entre cuerpo y mente quedaba superado, su cuerpo se presentaba «iluminado» y su mente corporizada. Al invertir en cierta medida la relación entre actor y papel dramático, Grotowski creó las condiciones para una redefinición del concepto de *Verkörperung*[*]. Corporizar significa en este caso hacer que con el cuerpo, o en el cuerpo, venga algo a presencia que sólo existe en virtud de él. Es decir, cuando un personaje –Fernando en *El príncipe constante*– aparece en y a través del cuerpo de Ryszard Cieślak sólo puede hacerlo una sola vez e indisolublemente unido a ese cuerpo en particular. El personaje encuentra en el físico estar-en-el-mundo del actor su fundamento y la condición de posibilidad de su existencia. Únicamente existe, pues, en su ejecución física: llega a existir a partir de sus actos performativos y de la singular corporalidad del actor.

2) El segundo procedimiento, el realce y exhibición de la singularidad (del cuerpo) del actor/performador, explicita esta redefinición al experimentar y clasificar las maneras de llevar a cabo la corporización bajo las condiciones establecidas en el primer procedimiento. Robert Wilson lo pone en práctica de un modo particularmente coherente y ostensible. Toma como punto de partida la singular corporalidad del actor: «Observo al actor, observo su cuerpo, escucho su voz y entonces intento hacer la obra con él»[21]. Desde que comenzó a trabajar a finales de los años sesenta, Wilson se ha fijado en la singularidad de cada uno de los no profesionales, los minusválidos, los aspirantes a actores y performadores o los actores con los que trabaja. Así, al referirse

* Que en español implica la sustitución del término 'encarnación' por el término 'corporización'.

21 Cit. en Otto Riewoldt, «Herrscher über Raum und Zeit. Das Theater Roberts Wilsons», emitido por la estación de radio Südfunk el 3 de junio de 1987.

al trabajo de Christine Oesterlein en *Death, Destruction & Detroit II*, de 1987, lo hizo de este modo:

> Miren, en una actriz como Christine Oesterlein los ojos son de una fuerza expresiva tal, incluso cuando apenas se mueve, que estremece y llega a lo más hondo. [...] A veces, simplemente ahí sentada, tiene tanta fuerza... Pocas personas son capaces de lograr algo así en escena. [...] La mayoría de actores parecerían una estatua, pero ella es siempre vivaz y peligrosa, misteriosa. [...] Hay algo muy especial en ella que sólo consiguen unos pocos. Ya lo sé, ha nacido para ello[22].

Los actores en los que Wilson ha liberado, en expresión de Ivan Nagel, su «genio específico», hacen muy poco en escena según los criterios al uso: aparecen y dan vueltas por el escenario, se quedan de pie o se sientan, permanecen inmóviles en una silla o están colgados de una cuerda; alzan una mano, un brazo, una pierna o hacen un amago de sonrisa. Es decir, que por un lado realizan movimientos que, en cierto sentido, forman parte del vocabulario escénico básico: aparecer, ir por el escenario, estar de pie, colocarse, sentarse, estar sentados, tumbarse, levantarse o irse. Por otra parte, sin embargo, aparecen en posiciones extraordinariamente inusuales: cuelgan de una cuerda, como en *Golden Windows*, en Múnich (1982), o se balancean a un lado y a otro sobre una escalera de mano, como en *the CIVIL warS*, en Colonia en 1984. Todos los movimientos son ejecutados según patrones rítmicos y geométricos, casi siempre de manera muy lenta y, en la mayoría de los casos, repetidamente.

Es sobre todo esta forma de moverse lo que centra la atención del espectador en la singular *physis* del actor. Podría objetarse que los movimientos que siguen estrictos patrones rítmicos y geométricos, y que se realizan además de manera más bien mecánica, eliminan la singularidad del cuerpo y hacen que todos los cuerpos se asemejen. Frente a ello puede alegarse, sin embargo, que

22 *Ibid.*

precisamente la reproducción aparentemente mecánica de un movimiento, realizada por cada cuerpo a voluntad y repetida a voluntad, permite realzar la auténtica singularidad de cada uno de ellos de manera mucho más patente que la llamada expresión individual. En el teatro de Wilson los cuerpos de cada uno de los actores en movimiento en y por el espacio llegan casi a convertirse en el más importante objeto de la realización escénica. La exhibición de su ser específico sobre el escenario consigue lo que Arthur Danto ha denominado «la transfiguración del lugar común»[23]. A través de su exhibirse sobre el escenario los cuerpos de los actores experimentan una transfiguración.

El acto de transfiguración encuentra en el empleo de la luz una forma de realce. En la escenificación de *Hamlet-machine* en el Thalia Theater de Hamburgo (1986), por ejemplo, una mujer que se rascaba la cabeza y sonreía se sentaba en una mesa, mientras que otra (Ofelia) profería las siguientes frases: «Con mis manos ensangrentadas desgarro las fotografías de los hombres que he amado». La luz caía desde arriba sobre la primera mujer. En *Parzival* (Thalia Theater de Hamburgo, 1987), Christopher Knowles aparecía cantando (cantaba una canción de un solo tono), balanceaba una tabla sobre su cabeza y daba vueltas sobre sí mismo; allá donde cantara o diera vueltas le iluminaba una luz proveniente del suelo. En el *Lear* que se montó en 1990 en el Bockenheimer Depot del Schauspielhaus de Fráncfort, en el instante en el que Marianne Hoppe dejaba de hablar y de moverse surgía una luz resplandeciente de gran claridad. La *contre-jour*, la iluminación a contraluz, es la favorita de las empleadas por Wilson, ya que permite presentar el cuerpo de los performadores/actores, sus gestos y movimientos, como si irradiaran luz, hace que sus cuerpos brillen en su singularidad propia.

A ello contribuye otro procedimiento. Wilson trabaja la mayoría de las veces con un fondo de escena plano, con una pantalla que sirve para proyectar imágenes, reflejos de luz o pinturas abs-

23 Arthur Danto, *La transfiguración del lugar común: una filosofía del arte*, Barcelona/Buenos Aires, 2002.

tractas. Prefiere que sus performadores/actores realicen sus movimientos por el escenario y paralelamente al fondo de escena. De este modo se da la impresión de que su corporalidad se terminaría fundiendo con el fondo plano si no fuera porque la iluminación a contraluz y cenital que proyecta sobre ellos simultáneamente realza expresamente su tridimensionalidad. En las realizaciones escénicas de Wilson se crea y se repite una y otra vez el momento en el que el cuerpo del performador se dispone a trasladarse desde el espacio escénico a la pantalla, el momento en el que la tridimensionalidad propia de la absoluta singularidad del cuerpo amenaza con desaparecer en la pantalla, sin que esto termine, no obstante, de pasar nunca.

Estos procedimientos de Wilson para destacar la individualidad del cuerpo del performador –especialmente la lentitud de movimientos y la repetición de su ejecución a partir de patrones rítmicos y geométricos– se han solido interpretar como procedimientos de desemantización y de deconstrucción de la categoría de personaje. Precisamente la *slow motion* y las repeticiones, pero también la realización de los mismos patrones por parte de distintos performadores, ha sido el motivo de que los espectadores ya no perciban los gestos y movimientos de los performadores como signos de los gestos y movimientos de un personaje, ni siquiera como signos de sus estados internos, por más que su vestimenta o la lista del elenco en el programa de mano nos permita relacionar al performador con el personaje. La atención del espectador se centra, en cambio, en el *tempo*, la intensidad, la fuerza, la energía y la dirección de los movimientos, y con ello en la materialidad específica del cuerpo-performador, en la especial singularidad de su corporalidad.

El argumento es tanto más acertado cuanto que en este caso el cuerpo del performador y el personaje no forman una unidad, al menos si entendemos por ello que la singularidad del cuerpo ha de diluirse en el personaje. Ambos están separados con claridad. Es evidente que aquí, como en Grotowski, la tarea del performador no consiste en interpretar a un personaje. Se trata más bien de hacer aparecer su propia corporalidad en una irrebasable individualidad y poner el cuerpo-arte creado por él –con ayuda también del vestuario y el maquillaje– literalmente de relieve. La referencia al personaje parece en este caso más bien accidental. No se recurre a ella como pretexto para la actuación de un performador, que puede actuar con su propio nombre.

Sin embargo, de ello no se puede extraer la conclusión de que los movimientos del performador se hayan desemantizado por completo. Es más bien que ahora significan aquello que realizan: tardar, por ejemplo, cuarenta y cinco segundos en alzar el brazo desde la cintura hasta la altura de los ojos. En este sentido, los movimientos son autorreferenciales y constitutivos de realidad. Asimismo, este proceso de intensificación de la performatividad de los movimientos va acompañado de una pluralización de la oferta de significados. Esos movimientos son capaces de suscitar en el espectador las más diversas asociaciones, recuerdos e imágenes[24].

Por otra parte, tampoco se sigue de ello que la categoría de personaje haya quedado obsoleta: ha sufrido meramente una redefinición, por más radical que sea. El personaje deja de estar determinado a partir de estados internos a los que el actor/performador ha de dar expresión con su cuerpo. El personaje es más bien aquello que se genera y se trae a presencia por medio de los actos performativos por los que el performador genera y trae a presencia su singular corporalidad. Cuando la atención del espectador se centra en la *physis* individual del performador, en su materialidad específica, no se centra sino en la única condición de posibilidad para que en una realización escénica algo así como un personaje pueda hacer acto de presencia. Más allá de la *physis* individual del actor/performador no puede darse eso que llamamos un personaje. Es precisamente esa ostensible separación entre performador y personaje que se da en los trabajos de Wilson la que nos permite ver esta condición como tal y centrar nuestra atención en ella.

3) Mientras que Wilson logra este efecto por medio de la transfiguración del cuerpo-performador, en la compañía Socìetas

24 Véase al respecto el capítulo quinto.

Raffaello Sanzio lo consiguen con la aparición en escena de cuerpos monstruosos, deformes, casi diríamos «malditos», cuerpos que parecen haber salido de un infierno bruegheliano. En sus montajes aparecen actores cuyos cuerpos difieren llamativamente de los cuerpos «normales», ponen ante los ojos la decrepitud, lo efímero y lo excesivo de la existencia física de un modo que produce sudor frío a los espectadores, que hace que les empiecen a temblar las manos, que se les corte la respiración, que se les acelere, que se asusten, que sientan asco, miedo o vergüenza. En el *Giulio Cesare* que presentaron en 1998 en el Hebbel-Theater de Berlín salía a escena un viejo decrépito y lisiado que a duras penas podía sostenerse sobre las piernas y que, en su fragilidad, conmovía y asustaba al mismo tiempo, hacía de César. Uno de los actores/performadores había sido sometido poco antes a una operación de laringe. En lugar de la laringe llevaba un micrófono para hacer audibles sus forzados y afónicos intentos de articulación, con lo que hacía que los espectadores recordaran permanentemente sus heridas, sus carencias, y sus impedimentos, hacía de Marco Antonio. De Cicerón hacía un gigante medio desnudo de las dimensiones de un luchador de sumo. Parecía ahogarse en la obesidad de su cuerpo. Llevaba una media que le cubría el rostro, lo que reforzaba todavía más su apariencia de monstruo sin rostro ni identidad. Además, el elenco lo completaban dos actrices anoréxicas que parecían hallarse en el umbral de la muerte (una de ellas murió inmediatamente antes de que presentaran el montaje en Berlín y fue sustituida por una bailarina muy delgada y frágil). La singular *physis* de los actores tenía un efecto tan inmediato y perturbador en los espectadores que apenas eran capaces de establecer una asociación entre esa *physis* y el personaje que se le había adjudicado a cada uno de los actores o de las actrices. Ello no obsta, en ningún caso, para que a posteriori fueran capaces de adjudicar cada físico concreto de los actores al personaje correspondiente en cada caso. Durante la realización escénica los espectadores difícilmente podían percibir el físico de los actores como signo de un personaje, los percibían sobre todo en su materialidad específica.

Pero aunque resultaba difícil, si es que no era del todo imposible, percibir el cuerpo de los actores como signo de un personaje e interpretarlo como tal, ello no implica que el acto de percepción se realizara libre de atribuciones de significado. La corporalidad que se generaba en este caso parecía estar marcada por la vejez, la falta de salud, la enfermedad crónica, la muerte o el exceso. Precisamente por eso el efecto sobre los espectadores era tan tremendo, precisamente por eso se suscitaban efectos fisiológicos y afectivos inmediatos. La relación interpretativa que se pudiera establecer al terminar la realización escénica entre la singularísima *physis* de cada uno de los actores y el personaje que se le había adjudicado, puede entenderse como un recurso de distanciamiento para intentar controlar a posteriori la amenaza directa que parecía provenir de esos cuerpos o para intentar anularla. El cuerpo fenoménico de los actores durante la realización escénica era solamente semiótico en la medida en que era signo de vejez, enfermedad, muerte y extinción de la individualidad en sí, es decir, en su singular fenomenalidad, y por esa razón infundía terror[25].

Desde la perspectiva del espectador, el cuerpo del actor no se separaba en este caso del personaje debido a un procedimiento performativo específico –como el *slow motion*, la iteración o el seguimiento de patrones geométricos y rítmicos–, sino por la mera presencia del físico estar-en-el-mundo de los actores, que se corporizaba en el acto mismo de su aparición y que no hacía sino reforzarse en todos los procesos de corporización. Ello originaba una especie de círculo vicioso. El físico estar-en-el-mundo del actor, su cuerpo fenoménico, tenía un efecto tan perturbador en el espectador que le resultaba difícil, cuando no imposible, percibirlo al mismo tiempo como cuerpo semiótico que remite a un personaje. Con ello perdía, sin embargo, una ocasión única de crear y mantener una cierta distancia reflexiva entre su cuerpo y el de los actores. Sin esa distancia el espectador estaba a merced del efecto que sus cuerpos fenoménicos causaban. Por ello, el efecto proveniente de los actores no tenía nada que ver con el personaje que interpretaban ni tenía su origen en los procedimientos inter-

25 Véase de nuevo el capítulo quinto al respecto.

pretativos específicos que empleaban, su origen era fundamentalmente la singularidad de cada uno de sus cuerpos fenoménicos y su extraordinaria manera de hacerse presentes.

4) Antes de ocuparme con más detalle del funcionamiento de estos procedimientos en las acciones artísticas y en el arte de la performance, quisiera atender al caso del *cross-casting* como otro método para centrar la atención en el cuerpo fenoménico del actor y para separar al actor y a su cuerpo del personaje.

En su montaje de la obra Zuckmayer *El general del diablo*, presentada en el Volksbühne de la Rosa-Luxemburg-Platz de Berlín en 1996, Frank Casorf cubrió el papel de General Harras con la actriz Corinna Harfouch durante la primera parte de la realización escénica, hasta el descanso, y con Bernhard Schütz en la segunda parte. En su primera aparición, Corinna Harfouch iba vestida con el uniforme de general de las fuerzas aéreas alemanas durante Segunda Guerra Mundial. Bajo la gorra del uniforme lucía una cabeza afeitada. Pronunciaba los discursos del General Harras, tenidos por paradigma de vigor masculino, sin falsear la voz, esto es, con voz femenina, aunque con tono áspero y rudo. Sus movimientos y gestos sí eran de una «masculinidad» muy pronunciada. El público era consciente en todo momento de que el papel del General Harras era «interpretado» por una mujer, pese a que mostraba un comportamiento «típicamente» masculino. Por ello, ya desde el principio, resultaba difícil ver a la actriz Harfouch como el personaje del General Harras.

Las dificultades y la irritación se iban haciendo mayores a medida que avanzaba la realización escénica, por ejemplo, cuando Corinna Harfouch empezaba a desabotonarse y a quitarse el uniforme. Debajo llevaba un body con diversas aberturas que dejaba ver la insoslayable feminidad de su cuerpo. A continuación, se sentaba en el regazo de Hartmann (Kurt Naumann), que le acababa de confesar al general que estaba enamorado de Pützchen, pero que lo había rechazado porque su árbol genealógico era «racialmente» incierto. Las manos de Harfouch tocaban la cintura y las caderas de Naumann, y se iban dirigiendo poco a poco hacia sus muslos. Durante todo ese tiempo pronunciaba uno de los discursos del General Harras sobre Renania como el mejor origen familiar imaginable, como certificado de «pureza racial» (*«Ahnennachweis»*), y Hartmann repetía una y otra vez: *«Ja, Herr General»* [«Sí, mi general»]. La escena era muy irritante. La apariencia externa de la actriz mostraba pocos signos de un personaje masculino. Se trataba sin lugar a dudas de una mujer sentada sobre el regazo de un hombre. No obstante, no daba la impresión de comportarse como una mujer que pretende seducir a un hombre –más bien como alguien que quiere cometer una violación–. Las palabras que Harfouch iba pronunciando contradecían ambas hipótesis. ¿Estaba actuando como el personaje del General Harras, como la actriz Corinna Harfouch o como una actriz que a su vez interpreta otro papel? ¿Se trataba acaso de un personaje masculino de ficción que intentaba violar a otro personaje masculino de ficción? ¿Intentaba Corinna Harfouch seducir a un personaje masculino de ficción o a su compañero Kurt Naumann? ¿O es que la actriz interpretaba otro papel completamente distinto para seducir a cualquier otra persona o para violarla?[26]. Los espectadores no estaban en condiciones de tomar una decisión definitiva al respecto. La indiscutible feminidad del cuerpo de la actriz y su innegable comportamiento masculino, que remitía al personaje del General Harras, se disociaban irremediablemente[27].

En este caso también se trataba de las condiciones en las que se crea un personaje. La feminidad del cuerpo de Harfouch remitía inequívocamente a su físico estar-en-el-mundo. Su cuerpo fenoménico no se podía escindir del artificial cuerpo semiótico que estaba pensado para remitir al personaje del General Harras ni tampoco podía fundirse con él. Esto implica, por

26 Con el *cross-casting*, en este caso, también se insinuaba la latente homosexualidad de los nazis. Pero este aspecto no es de primera importancia para el propósito de esta investigación.

27 Esto no tiene nada que ver con el extrañamiento brechtiano. Pues para alcanzar éste, el actor interpreta, por así decirlo, dos personajes: un personaje asociado con un determinado nombre (por ejemplo, Madre Coraje), y el de la actriz, que se escinde del personaje y comenta su comportamiento (por ejemplo, Helene Weigel). No se puede hablar de tal cosa en este caso.

otro lado, que el personaje tampoco podía escindirse del cuerpo fenoménico del actor: era en ese cuerpo concreto en el que aparecía. Sobre el escenario existía únicamente en esa corporalidad específica, más allá de ella carecía de existencia.

Este fenómeno era todavía más visible tras el descanso, cuando Bernhard Schütz se hacía cargo del papel. El personaje que surgía de su interpretación era completamente distinto. Algo que no estribaba en que la suya y la de Harfouch fueran dos «concepciones» distintas del papel. La única razón era que el cuerpo fenoménico de cada uno de ellos era distinto, algo que las respectivas masculinidad y feminidad de sus cuerpos marcaban aún de manera más clara y drástica.

Pese a las considerables diferencias, los procedimientos descritos hasta el momento coinciden en el hecho de que centran enfáticamente la atención en las impares singularidad e individualidad del cuerpo fenoménico del performador/actor. Con ello el personaje puede llegar a desaparecer transitoriamente, como, por ejemplo, en *Giulio Cesare*, donde se empleaba un procedimiento que de ningún modo se proponía la desaparición del personaje como tal, su fin era más bien irritarnos profundamente en nuestra percepción. Una percepción que oscilaba una y otra vez entre la percepción del cuerpo fenoménico del actor y su remisión a un personaje. Mientras que las técnicas interpretativas y escénicas –o, como en el caso de la compañía Socìetas Rafaello Sanzio, la insoslayable «anormalidad» de los cuerpos de los actores– no sólo pretenden desviar la atención una y otra vez hacia el cuerpo fenoménico del actor, sino fijarla en él, la dramaturgia le brinda la oportunidad a la percepción de saltar al personaje de vez en cuando, con mayor o menor frecuencia dependiendo de la situación y de la realización escénica. Esto es, que la exhibición de la singular e individual corporalidad de cada uno de los actores/performadores crea una situación de multiestabilidad perceptiva del tipo de la que conocemos desde hace tiempo por la multiestabilidad perspectivística: la reversión de figura y fondo (rostro o jarrón) y la ambigüedad del significado (cabeza de liebre o pico de pato, rostro o figura en abrigo de piel)[28]. En ese proceso no queda claro qué causa realmente cada uno de los saltos en la percepción. Qué ocurre cuando un espectador percibe y experimenta un determinado movimiento del actor en su específica energía, intensidad, forma, dirección y *tempo*, ¿lo entiende como el llamamiento, la amenaza u otra señal de un personaje y, al mismo tiempo, lo experimenta intensamente porque le afecta extraordinariamente la corporalidad específica del actor? ¿Está condicionado tal proceso exclusivamente o, al menos, principalmente, por los procedimientos escénicos y dramatúrgicos que pretenden causar el efecto de que la percepción del espectador salte en un determinado momento? ¿Tiene también su importancia en ello –y si es así, en qué medida– la especial disposición del sujeto perceptor a que su percepción –consciente o inconscientemente– se «ajuste» en cada caso? ¿O acaso el salto acontece independientemente de los procedimientos dramatúrgicos y escénicos, sin intención por parte del sujeto perceptor? En cualquier caso, la percepción estética tiene lugar como oscilación entre la focalización en el cuerpo fenoménico y la focalización en el cuerpo semiótico del actor/performador. Sitúa al receptor en una situación de «intersticidad», de *betwixt and between*.

Mientras que en el teatro realista-psicológico desde el siglo dieciocho se defendía insistentemente que el espectador debía percibir el cuerpo del actor únicamente como cuerpo del personaje –lo que, como ya demuestran las consideraciones de Simmel, es una postura cuyas condiciones son imposibles de satisfacer–, en el teatro contemporáneo se juega con la multiestabilidad perceptiva. El interés se centra en el instante en que la percepción del cuerpo fenoménico salta a la percepción del personaje y viceversa, cosa que ocurre según sea el cuerpo del actor o el personaje de ficción el que esté en el primer plano centrando la

28 Véase para este fenómeno Michael Stadler/Peter Kruse, «Visuelles Gedächtnis für Formen und das Problem der Bedeutungszuweisung in kognitiven Systemen», en Siegfried J. Schmidt (ed.), *Gedächtnis. Probleme und Perspektiven der interdisziplinären Gedächtnisforschung*, Fráncfort, 1991, pp. 250-266.

atención. El objetivo es, pues, el momento en el que quien percibe se encuentra en el umbral entre ambas percepciones. Esta oscilación de la percepción en tanto que fenómeno estético –sobre todo con la vista puesta en una estética de lo performativo– se tratará detalladamente más adelante[29].

Nuestro modo de referirnos al personaje, a su heterogénea constitución -lingüística en el texto, por parte del lector en la lectura, por parte de los distintos actores en su interpretación, por parte del espectador en su percepción– y el hecho de que llamemos a todas esas formas de constituirlo por el mismo nombre: Hamlet, Fernando, Cicerón o General Harras, podría ser un indicio de que la teoría de los dos mundos mantiene su vigencia: el personaje se da primero en el texto, donde el lector lo encuentra como ficticio, y ese personaje de ficción se encarna luego en los cuerpos reales de los distintos actores, de tal manera que en las distintas realizaciones escénicas simplemente adopta formas distintas. Hay que admitir, eso sí, que estos personajes a los que designamos con el mismo nombre, pueden tener un cierto aire de familia, para decirlo con Wittgenstein –del mismo modo que a las distintas formas de juego también las llamamos 'juego'–. Sin embargo, frente a la fuerza sugestiva de nuestro modo de hablar hay que aferrarse a la idea de que el cuerpo fenoménico del actor no sirve de medio para el personaje constituido lingüísticamente ni es tampoco signo de él. Antes bien, el personaje que aparece en escena sería impensable en tanto que singular sin el particular estar-en-el-mundo del actor/performador, el personaje no existe más allá del particular cuerpo fenoménico del actor, al que *no* puede de ningún modo suprimir.

Precisamente en esto consiste la radical redefinición del concepto de *Verkörperung* [encarnación-corporización]. Ese nuevo concepto hace hincapié en que el físico estar-en-el-mundo del hombre es la condición de posibilidad para que el cuerpo pueda fungir y ser entendido como objeto, como tema y fuente de constitución de símbolos, como material para la constitución de signos

29 Véase al respecto el capítulo quinto.

y como producto para inscripciones culturales. No sólo los estudios teatrales y la teoría de la literatura han pasado por alto durante mucho tiempo esta palmaria evidencia, o la han dejado de lado, a la hora de formular sus teorías. También lo ha hecho la antropología cultural, que hasta hace poco se ha dedicado preferentemente a estudiar el cuerpo como objeto o tema de sus análisis, o lo ha examinado en tanto que fuente para la constitución de símbolos en discursos de distintos ámbitos culturales como, por ejemplo, la religión o las estructuras sociales. En la antropología cultural prevalecía, consecuentemente, la metáfora explicativa de «cultura como texto». A ella le opone Thomas Csórdas el concepto de *embodiment*/corporización. Lo define como «existential ground of culture and self»[30] y contrapone el concepto de representación (*Repräsentation*) al de la «experiencia vivida», al de «vivencia». Remitiéndose a Merleau-Ponty, Csórdas les reprocha a las definiciones del concepto de cultura propuestas en los estudios culturales que «none have taken seriously the idea that culture is grounded in the human body»[31]. Esta asunción supone para Csórdas la premisa fundamental para tratar cabalmente sobre cultura y cuerpo.

Su idea es concederle al cuerpo una posición de prevalencia paradigmática equivalente a la que tiene el texto, en lugar de subsumirlo al paradigma textual. Algo que debe conseguir el concepto de corporización/*embodiment*, que abre un nuevo campo metodológico en el que el cuerpo fenoménico, el físico estar-en-el-mundo del hombre, figura como condición de posibilidad de cualquier producción cultural. El concepto de corporización debe hacer las veces, por lo tanto, de metódica instancia de corrección frente a la pretensión de elucidar conceptos como como los de texto o representación. Esto vale también para las

30 Thomas J. Csórdas (ed.), *Embodiment and Experience. The existential ground of culture and self*, Cambridge, 1994, p. 6 [«(F)ondo existencial de cultura y yo»]. Sobre la situación en la antropología cultural, véase la introducción: «The body as representation and being in the world», pp. 1-24.

31 *Ibid*. [«(...) que ninguna se haya tomado en serio la idea de que la cultura tiene su fundamento en el cuerpo humano»].

ciencias cognitivas, que han empezado a tomar en consideración el cuerpo en su integridad, y no sólo los datos neurofisiológicos. Las líneas de investigación más importantes hoy: el *enactivism*[32] y el *experimentalism*[33] tienen como fundamento la idea de que la cognición hay que entenderla y estudiarla en tanto que actividad corporizada (*embodied activity*), que la mente siempre está corporizada.

Este concepto de *embodiment*/corporización, como se ha mostrado en el desarrollo de este apartado, es central también para una estética de lo performativo en la medida en que los actos performativos con los que se produce la corporalidad en las realizaciones escénicas son siempre procesos de corporización tal y como ésta se ha definido, y lo son independientemente de que con ellos se produzca también un personaje de ficción, como era el caso de la mayoría de los ejemplos mencionados arriba, o de que no sea así, como es frecuente en el arte de acción y de la performance.

Hasta qué punto tiene un gran valor explicativo el concepto de corporización precisamente cuando consideramos el arte de acción y de la performance, nos lo muestran con especial claridad las performances en las que los artistas se someten a intoxicaciones y lesiones, infligen violencia a su cuerpo de las más variadas maneras o se ponen incluso en peligro de muerte, como Marina Abramović en *Lips of Thomas* o *Rhythm 0*. Independientemente de qué sea lo que los performadores producen en esos casos en y con su cuerpo, lo que producen deja sin duda rastros perceptibles en él que apuntan a un proceso de transformación. Al generar su singular y específica corporalidad, los artistas llevan a cabo procesos con los que corporizan la vulnerabilidad de su cuerpo, su

32 Cfr. Francisco J. Varela/ Evan Thompson/Eleanor Rosch, *The Embodied Mind: Cognitive Science and Human Experience*, Boston, 1991 (esp. *De cuerpo presente*, Barcelona, 1992).

33 Cfr. Mark Johnson/George Lakoff, *Metaphors We Live By*, Chicago/Londres, 1980 (esp. *Metáforas de la vida cotidiana*, Madrid, 2001); Mark Johnson, *The Body in the Mind. The Bodily Basis of Meaning, Imagination and Reason*, Chicago/Londres, 1987 (esp. *El cuerpo en la mente: fundamentos corporales del significado, la imaginación y la razón*, Madrid 1991); George Lakoff, *Woman, Fire and Dangerous Things – What Categories Reveal about the Mind*, Chicago/Londres, 1987.

entrega a la violencia, su vivacidad y la amenaza que surge de ella. El permanente cambio al que está sometido todo organismo vivo se acentúa y se acrecienta en el caso de los performadores con las lesiones que se infligen o que dejan que otros les inflijan; además, con ello lo hacen accesible a la percepción.

El artista de performance americano Chris Burden llevó a cabo, como Marina Abramović, toda una serie de performances de autoexposición al peligro y autoagresión. En su acción *Five-Day-Locker-Piece*, que tuvo lugar en la universidad de Irvine en 1971, se hizo encerrar durante cinco días, tras algunos de ayuno, en una taquilla de 60 cm de alto por 60 de ancho y 90 de profundidad. Encima de ella había una garrafa de quince litros llena de agua de la que salía una manguera que llegaba a la taquilla; desde allí la marquesa llevaba a otra garrafa vacía que estaba debajo de la taquilla, también de quince litros de capacidad. Después de que Burden quedara encerrado, todos los espectadores tuvieron que abandonar la sala. La sala se cerró y no se volvió a abrir hasta pasados los cinco días. En su pieza *Shoot*, del mismo año, Burden se hizo disparar en el brazo izquierdo desde una distancia de cinco pasos. En *Through the Night Softly*, que realizó en la Main Street de Los Ángeles en septiembre de 1973, reptó desnudo con las manos en la espalda sobre quince metros de cristales rotos respirando dificultosamente y sangrando debido a los cortes. Apenas había unos pocos espectadores. La mayoría eran transeúntes que pasaban por allí. (La acción se filmó). *Trans-Fixed* (Venice, California 1974) fue realizada tanto delante como dentro de un pequeño taller en la Speedway Avenue de Venice. Burden colocó los pies en el parachoques trasero de su Volkswagen, se tumbó de espaldas sobre el maletero y el cristal trasero, y extendió los brazos sobre el techo. Le fijaron las manos al techo con clavos. La puerta del taller se abrió y el coche salió a la calle. Mientras aparecía crucificado de esa manera ante los espectadores, el motor subió de revoluciones. Tras dos minutos lo apagaron de nuevo, el coche volvió al taller y la puerta se cerró[34].

34 Véase, para las performances de Burden, Chris Burden/Jan Butterfield,

Tanto en Burden como en Abramović son innegables los rasgos rituales de sus performances. También los encontramos en otros artistas que han creado y desarrollado el «género» de la performance de autoagresión. Michel Journiac, por ejemplo, en *Messe pour un corps* (1969), se sacó sangre en presencia de los espectadores y con ella preparó un pudding que les ofreció para que lo probaran: «Esta es mi sangre...». En *Rituel pour un mort* (1976) se produjo heridas con un cigarrillo encendido. Gina Pane sometió su cuerpo a un tratamiento aún más radical. Desde sus primeros *Projets de silence* (1970) y, sobre todo, tras *Escalade Sanglante* (1971), un trabajo de estudio en el que la artista, con las manos y los pies desnudos, subía por una especie de escalera de mano con peldaños afilados, cortantes. En *Sang, lait chaud* (1972), *Transfert* (1973), *Psyché* (1974) y *Le cas n. 2 sur le ring* (1976) puso en riesgo su cuerpo y su vida repetidas veces: dio buena cuenta de media libra de carne picada podrida mientras miraba las noticias en la televisión en una posición extremadamente incómoda; o se produjo diversas lesiones con una cuchilla de afeitar. Hizo gárgaras con leche durante horas hasta que su sangre se terminó mezclando con el líquido que escupía; masticó cristal o rompió una lámina de vidrio con su cuerpo; anduvo sobre una parrilla bajo la que había un vivo fuego cuyas crecidas llamas quemaban sus pies desnudos, como en una ordalía medieval[35].

Las autoagresiones y la exposición voluntaria al peligro a las que se someten los artistas recuerdan en ciertos aspectos a las prác-

---

«Through the Night Softly», en *The Art of Performance. A Critical Antology*, Gregory Battock y Robert Nickas (eds.), Nueva York, 1982, pp. 222-239; Chris Burden, *Chris Burden. A Twenty Years Survey*. Catálogo de la exposición del museo Newport Harbor, New Port Beach, 1988; *Documentation of Selected Works 1971-1974*, cinta de vídeo (USA 1975), VHS 34 min., A. Wirth (ed.) en colaboración con F. Malch y la unión de artistas de Colonia, Colonia, 1990; Chris Burden, *Beyond the Limits/Jenseits der Grenzen*, P. Noever (ed.), catálogo de la exposición del museo de artes aplicadas, Viena, 1996.

35 Véase el trabajo de François Pluchart, «Risk as Practice of Thought», en G. Battock y R. Nickas (eds.), *The Art of Performance. A critical Anthology*, Nueva York, 1982, pp. 125-134.– Lamentablemente en este texto encontramos muy poca información sobre las reacciones de los espectadores en cada caso.

ticas culturales de monjas, frailes, mártires, santos... y dementes, con las que emulaban en carne propia el sacrificio de Cristo. Sería, no obstante, un error equipararlas a las performances de autoagresión o incluso meterlas en el mismo saco. Pues mientras que para quienes asisten a los rituales de autosacrificio tanto el espanto como la curiosidad sádica o voyerista quedan atenuados o transformados por el hecho de que en la cultura cristiana tales sacrificios son percibidos e interpretados como emulaciones del de Cristo, emulaciones que, de forma efectivamente mágica, parecían garantizar la propia integridad corporal y el bienestar físico, las performances mencionadas carecen, sin embargo, de tal condición. En tanto que performances artísticas pueden muy bien querer aludir a tales prácticas, invocar incluso su contexto, pero desde luego no fueron ni llevadas a cabo ni percibidas en tal contexto.

Las performances lograban su efecto específico precisamente porque les faltaba tal contexto. Exponían a los espectadores a acciones con las que excedían los límites de sus cuerpos, sometían su físico a prácticas violentas, es decir, se hacían lo que los espectadores temían para sí e intentaban evitar, todo ello sin remitirse a otra realidad que las atenuara, que permitiera atribuirles un sentido de orden superior, trascendental, una realidad de la que surgiera la fuerza mágica que evitara que los espectadores sufrieran tal violencia. Lo que ocurría en estos casos es que los espectadores estaban expuestos a esa brutalidad sin protección alguna, lo que los dejaba a merced de su propio espanto y de su propia curiosidad sádica o voyerista. A partir de ello cabe pensar que la percepción iba acompañada de reacciones fisiológicas, afectivas, energéticas y motoras que amenazaban con apoderarse de los espectadores[36].

Un efecto de tal intensidad se debe a que los artistas, con sus autoagresiones, no estaban dando expresión a cualesquiera significados en el sentido al que nos referíamos al hablar de la teoría de los dos mundos, sino que corporizaban, en el sentido literal

36 Véase la nota anterior.

de la palabra, la violencia contra sí mismos. Así pues, si el concepto de corporización según lo hemos definido se refiere a todo lo que se genera en virtud de aquellos actos performativos con los que el performador genera a su vez su propia corporalidad en la realización escénica, entonces es el concepto más adecuado para entender lo que los artistas realizan en las performances de autoagresión.

Grotowski denominaba «actor santo» a aquel capaz de conferirle capacidad operativa *(agency)* a su propio cuerpo, de corporizar tanto en el sentido de ser-cuerpo como en el de tener-cuerpo, mientras que al acto de tal corporización lo denominaba «acto de revelación». El crítico Kelera empleó las expresiones «iluminación» y «estado de gracia» para referirse al trabajo de Ryszard Cieślak. Yo he hablado, al referirme al teatro de Wilson, de cuerpos «transfigurados», de procesos de «transfiguración»; al referirme al *Giulio Cesare* de la Socìetas Raffaello Sanzio he hablado de cuerpos «malditos» que parecían haber salido de un infierno brueghelìano; y he hablado, además, de «violencia ritual» al referirme a las performances de autoagresión. El uso de un vocabulario religioso, o al menos con connotaciones religiosas, está justificado. No se pretende sacralizar el cuerpo del actor/performador, ni tampoco se sugiere. Lo que sí pretende lograr el uso de este vocabulario es poner de relieve el hecho de que el cuerpo humano –como ya había advertido Craig– no es un material como otro cualquiera, un material que pueda trabajarse o moldearse a voluntad, sino un organismo vivo que está siempre deviniendo, en permanente proceso de transformación. El cuerpo humano no posee una esencia invariable, sólo conoce el ser en tanto que devenir, en tanto que proceso, en tanto que cambio. Con cada parpadeo, con cada inspiración, con cada movimiento se genera de nuevo, se convierte en otro, se corporiza como algo nuevo. De ahí que el cuerpo mantenga, en última instancia, su condición de indisponibilidad. El físico estar-en-el-mundo, que no *es*, que *deviene*, contradice palmariamente la idea de obra de arte. El cuerpo humano no puede convertirse en obra hasta que muere, y entonces sólo en tanto que cadáver. Con ello se alcanza al menos provisionalmente una esencia invariable que sólo puede mantenerse con un rápido embalsamamiento. En ese estado, se deja emplear como material, y puede ser trabajado, preparado y moldeado no sólo en rituales, sino también en procesos artísticos –como ha demostrado claramente la exposición «Mundos corporales» de Gunther von Hagens–. Como cuerpo vivo, sin embargo, se resiste obstinadamente a cualquier intento de ser declarado obra, por no hablar de cualquier intento de hacerlo obra. El actor/performador no transforma su cuerpo en una obra, lleva a cabo procesos de corporización en los que el cuerpo deviene otro. Se transforma, se recrea, acontece.

Difícilmente puede ser casual que en las realizaciones escénicas teatrales y del arte de acción y de la performance se haya hecho hincapié una y otra vez desde finales de los años sesenta en que la corporalidad que los actores generan durante la realización escénica no tiene carácter de obra, que es incompatible con cualquier idea de obra. Esto puede explicarse, entre otros motivos, como una reacción a la creciente preponderancia de los medios tecnológicos. Norbert Elias ha descrito el proceso de civilización como un proceso de creciente abstracción en el que la distancia del hombre respecto a su propio cuerpo y al de los demás es cada vez mayor[37]. Con la invención y la propagación de los nuevos medios de comunicación en el siglo veinte, este proceso ha alcanzado su punto culminante: los cuerpos se volatilizan en una reproducción técnica que, pese a la aparente proximidad, aleja e impide cualquier contacto. A la fantasía del cuerpo virtual que suele acompañar a este proceso, del cuerpo astral tecnológicamente reproducible, el teatro y el arte de la performance oponen decididamente el físico estar-en-el-mundo y la idea de mente corporizada *(embodied mind)* ligada a él. El hombre no consigue que su cuerpo se aproxime al cuerpo transfigurado de Dios por medio de la creciente abstracción que logran las imágenes reproducidas

37 Véase Norbert Elias, *Über den Prozess der Zivilisation. Soziogenetische und psychogenetische Untersuchungen*, 2 vols., Fráncfort, 1976 (esp. *El proceso de la civilización. Investigaciones sociogenéticas y psicogenéticas*, México, 1988).

electrónicamente, pues en esa transfiguración sigue siendo «carne» y organismo vivo, sino al generar su cuerpo nuevamente una y otra vez como aquello que constituye su singularidad, como dialéctica entre ser-cuerpo y tener-cuerpo, como organismo vivo dotado de conciencia. Al centrar la atención del espectador en el singular, individual y físico estar-en-el-mundo del actor, en los específicos actos performativos que generan su corporalidad, el teatro y el arte de la performance parecen decir: «mirad esos cuerpos que queréis hacer desaparecer en nombre de otro, mirad su sufrimiento y su luz, y comprenderéis, aparecerán ya como aquello en lo que queríais convertiros: como cuerpos transfigurados». La *promesse de bonheur* de los procesos de civilización se ha cumplido hace mucho en esos cuerpos.

Al cuerpo del actor se le restituye el aura de la que se le había ido privando paso a paso en el proceso de civilización –como cuando Castorf privaba de él a los espectadores en *El idiota*–. A las imágenes de los medios técnicos y electrónicos, reproducidas por millones, el teatro y el arte de la performance les oponen el cuerpo humano –también como sufriente, precisamente como sufriente, enfermo, vulnerable y marcado por la muerte–, el cuerpo humano en su singularidad y su potencial para acontecer, irradiando luz y, pese a su padecimiento, «espléndido como el primer día»*.

Presencia**

Al hilo de esta argumentación surgen una serie de preguntas. ¿Son equiparables la reauratización –en sentido benjaminiano– y la presencia *(Präsenz)*? ¿Nos referimos con 'presencia' a la mera comparecencia *(Anwesenheit)* del cuerpo, sin tener en cuenta los

* Goethe, *Fausto I*, «Prólogo en el cielo» v. 250.

** En este apartado la autora emplea los términos *Präsenz*, *Gegenwärtigkeit* y *Anwesenheit*, que en circunstancias normales traduciríamos sin más por 'presencia'. En lo sucesivo, y para hacer comprensible el contraste entre ellos, verteremos el primero por 'presencia', el segundo por 'actualidad' y el tercero por 'comparecencia'.

procesos de corporización específicos que lleva a cabo una y otra vez en su condición de ser en constante devenir? ¿O con 'presencia' aludimos a procesos de corporización muy concretos, procesos de corporización del ser-cuerpo, por ejemplo? Y en cualquier caso, ¿por qué habría esta presencia de poder cumplir una promesa de felicidad?

En el discurso académico actual en el ámbito de la estética, la presencia se considera una cualidad estética específica no sólo atribuible –mucho menos primordialmente– al cuerpo humano, sino sobre todo, cuando no exclusivamente, a los objetos de nuestro entorno y, en parte también, en el sentido de efectos-presencia *(Präsenz-Effekten)*, a los productos de los medios técnicos y electrónicos. Trataré en lo sucesivo el concepto de presencia exclusivamente en lo que toca al cuerpo del actor, y consideraré, inmediatamente después, si este concepto, ya con tanto bagaje, tiene sentido y es fructífero en el marco de una estética de lo performativo, y si se puede emplear también referido a los objetos de nuestro entorno y a los productos de los medios técnicos y electrónicos.

Mientras que en la estética en general los conceptos de presencia y actualidad *(Gegenwärtigkeit)* no han logrado una posición de preeminencia hasta las últimas décadas, esos conceptos, o sus correspondientes equivalentes históricos, fueron determinantes en los debates sobre teoría del teatro desde sus inicios, sobre todo en los sostenidos por los Padres de la Iglesia y en los que tuvieron lugar en la llamada *Querelle de la moralité du théâtre* en el siglo diecisiete. En su tratado *Le comédien*, que apareció en 1747, Rémond de Sainte Albine resume el estado de la discusión por aquel entonces cuando en una comparación entre la pintura y el teatro escribe a modo de introducción: «El pintor presenta sencillamente un acontecimiento. El actor hace que, en cierto modo, suceda de nuevo»[38]. Doscientos cincuenta años después, el director Peter

38 «Auszug aus dem *Schauspieler* des Herrn Remond von Sainte Albine», en *Lessings Werke*, Robert Boxberger (ed.), Berlín/Stuttgart, 1883-1890, Parte V: *Theatralische Bibliotek*, I. Parte, I. Pieza 1754, pp. 128-159, p. 129.

Stein llega a una conclusión parecida cuando –comparándolo también con la pintura– elogia el «milagro» del teatro, que «todavía hoy a un actor se le dé la oportunidad de decir: soy Prometeo. [...] Si hoy alguien pintara como Piero della Francesa y dijera: uso colores hechos de cáscara de huevo, entonces se trataría, en el mejor de los casos, de una imitación. Pero el actor no imita nada. Es él quien encarna/corporiza *(verkörpert)* el papel como hace 2.500 años»[39].

Sainte Albine y Stein insisten en que lo que sucede en el teatro acontece siempre aquí y ahora, justo delante de los ojos de los espectadores, que lo perciben y se convierten así en testigos. Ambos insisten en la legitimidad del *topos* de la actualidad *(Gegenwärtigkeit)* del teatro.

Con *topos* se quiere decir que el teatro, a diferencia de la epopeya *(epos)*, de la novela o de una sucesión de imágenes, no cuenta una historia que ha ocurrido en otro lugar y en otro tiempo, sino que pone ante los ojos de los espectadores sucesos que acaecen *hic et nunc* y que son percibidos *hic et nunc* por los espectadores. Lo que los espectadores ven y oyen en una realización escénica es, en este sentido, siempre actual. Una realización escénica se vive en tanto que realización, presentación y al mismo tiempo como transcurso del tiempo actual.

El concepto de actualidad, que se puede entender como descriptivo, suele emplearse, sin embargo, en las discusiones sobre teatro como un término con el que hacer juicios de valor sobre la utilidad y las desventajas del teatro, para fundamentar su superioridad sobre otras artes o para defender que se lo sitúe muy por debajo de ellas. De ahí que, precisamente debido a esa actualidad, tanto los Padres de la Iglesia como los participantes en la *Querelle*[40] le atribuyeran al teatro la capacidad de ejercer un efecto sensible

39 Cit. por Peter von Becker, «Die Sehnsucht nach dem Vollkommenen. Über Peter Stein, den Regisseur und sein Stück Theatergeschichte – zum sechzigsten Geburstag», en *Der Tagesspiegel*, 1 de octubre de 1997.

40 Véase al respecto la compilación de los textos de la *Querelle* editada por Laurent Thirouin: Pierre Nicole, *Traité de la comédie et autres pièces d'un procès du théâtre*, París, 1998.

inmediato en los espectadores y de suscitar en ellos afectos intensos, abrumadores incluso. El ambiente del teatro se entiende y se describe como peligrosamente contagioso[41]. Los actores ejecutan sobre el escenario actos apasionados y los espectadores perciben esas acciones, marcadas por su carácter pasional, y se contagian: las pasiones se suscitan también en ellos. El contagio tiene lugar por la vía de la percepción del cuerpo del actor en tanto que actual por parte del espectador, igualmente actual. Sólo por la actualidad de los actores y de los acontecimientos es posible este contagio, es decir, que es la copresencia física de actores y espectadores la que lo hace posible. En eso coinciden los defensores y los detractores del teatro, independientemente de que entiendan la activación de las pasiones como una catarsis terapéutica o –caso de Rousseau aún en la segunda mitad del siglo dieciocho[42]– como uno de los efectos más profundamente perjudiciales para el hombre, un trastorno que lo aleja de sí mismo y de Dios. Ambos ponen de relieve que la actualidad del teatro tiene como consecuencia una transformación del espectador.

Junto a la actualidad de los acontecimientos presentados, los detractores del teatro dieron en la *Querelle* con otra fuente de los efectos de la realización escénica, que localizaron directamente en el cuerpo del actor, independientemente del personaje que interpretara y de las acciones que realizara. Daban por sentado que eran las características corporales de una actriz o de un actor las que ejercían en el espectador del sexo opuesto en cada caso una fuerza de atracción erótica que suscitaba en ellos sentimien-

41 La metáfora del contagio, la experiencia estética entendida como un proceso somático, se emplea con llamativa frecuencia en estos debates. También está experimentando, por cierto, un renacimiento en los debates actuales sobre estética. Véase Erika Fischer-Lichte, «Zuschauen als Ansteckung», en Nicola Suthor y Mirjam Schaub (eds.), *Ansteckung. Zur Körperlichkeit eines ästhetischen Prinzips*, Múnich, 2004.

42 Rousseau maldecía el teatro porque «la constante tensión emocional a la que estamos sometidos [en él][...] enerva y debilita» al espectador y le «incapacita para resistir a las pasiones», amenaza pues con echarlo a perder». Jean-Jacques Rousseau, *Lettre a Mr. D'Alembert sur les spectacles*, M. Fuchs (ed.), Ginebra, 1948, p. 76 (esp. *Carta a d'Alembert sobre los espectáculos*, Madrid, 1994).

tos de insana apetencia, que les incitaba incluso al adulterio, que los pervertía.

Los detractores del teatro distinguían en este sentido entre dos tipos de actualidad en el teatro: la actualidad que crea y posibilita el cuerpo semiótico del actor al interpretar las apasionadas acciones de un personaje y la actualidad como sólo la puede generar el cuerpo fenoménico del actor con su mera comparecencia. Mientras el cuerpo semiótico ejerce una fuerza de contagio[43] sobre el espectador, el cuerpo fenoménico consigue el mismo efecto con la fuerza de atracción erótica que le confieren sus específicas características. Denominaré la referencia al tipo de actualidad que se da con la mera comparecencia del cuerpo fenoménico del actor *concepto débil de presencia*.

Los detractores del teatro dieron muestras de mucha mayor clarividencia que sus defensores. Los teóricos del siglo dieciocho, y en ello su manera de entender el teatro tuvo gran importancia, intentaron que el cuerpo fenoménico del actor se diluyera en su cuerpo semiótico. El «contagio» por medio del cuerpo semiótico, por el personaje interpretado por él, tenía que conservar, aunque modificado, el singular atractivo del actor, pero tenía, eso sí, que dejar de ejercer atracción erótica sobre el cuerpo del espectador. El contagio tenía que percibirse en tanto que fuerza de atracción del personaje, sin duda erótica también, de manera tal que el deseo del espectador se orientara al personaje, no al actor.

Como ya se ha explicado por extenso, estos esfuerzos no lograron nunca, y había buenas razones para que fuera así, que el cuerpo fenoménico del actor se diluyera completamente en su cuerpo semiótico. A esta incongruencia se debe tanto que el concepto de encarnación siguiera gozando de vigencia durante el siglo diecinueve, y en parte durante el siglo veinte –todavía hoy cuenta con partidarios–, como que la distinción entre la actualidad del personaje y la del actor se fuera transformando paulatinamente, y más bien bajo mano, en una distinción entre diversos

43 Véase Erika Fischer-Lichte, «Der Körper als Zeichen und als Erfahrung», en *Theater im Prozess der Zivilisation*, Tubinga/Basilea, 2000, pp. 67-80.

procedimientos artísticos empleados por el actor: aquellos que están al servicio de la exposición del personaje como actual y aquellos que realizan una presentación específica del actor, que ponen de relieve su singular «carisma» independientemente del personaje y más allá de él.

Si nos fijamos en las críticas que se escribieron entre 1922 y 1962 sobre las interpretaciones de Gustaf Gründgens, un decidido partidario del concepto de teatro literario y de la encarnación en el sentido que tenía el término en el siglo dieciocho, encontramos una serie de referencias que apuntan a que la atención de los críticos y de los espectadores no se centraba exclusivamente en el personaje, se centraba en primer lugar en la actualidad del actor. Esto tenía lugar por medio de un doble procedimiento: primero por la ocupación, el dominio casi diríamos, del espacio. Así, en una de las primeras críticas sobre el Marinelli interpretado por Gründgens en *Emilia Galotti*, en el Stadttheater de Kiel en 1922, se dice: «La manera en la que de inmediato domina el espacio, ¡con una libertad de movimientos propia de un bailarín! Sí, ciertamente, eso era lo que primero se le quedaba a uno en la memoria. Sorprendía de tal manera que uno se olvidaba completamente de pensar qué [papel] interpretaba»[44]. Sobre su interpretación de Edipo en el montaje del *Edipo Rey* de Sófocles que él mismo dirigió (Schauspielhaus de Düsseldorf, 1947), escribe Gert Vielhaber: «¿Cómo explicar la corriente de magia que se extendía por la platea en el instante en que aparecía Gründgens? Cuando atraviesa el espacio, moldeándolo [...]»[45]. Ambas críticas, a pesar de los veinticinco años que las separan, destacan el hecho de que Gründgens se apodera del espacio en el instante en que pisa el escenario, y que es precisamente este dominio del espacio el que

44 Florian Kienzl, «Gustaf mit 'f'. Wie Gustaf Gründgens entdeckt wurde», cit. por Dagmar Walach, *«Aber ich habe nicht mein Gesicht». Gustaf Gründgens – eine deutsche Karriere*, libro sobre la exposición homónima en la Staatsbibliothek de Berlín-Preussischer Kulturbesitz, 9 de diciembre de 1999-12 de febrero de 2000, Berlín, 1999, p. 29.

45 Gert Vielhaber, «Oedipus Komplex auf der Bühne», en *Die Zeit*, 2 de octubre de 1947.

ejerce un efecto enorme sobre los espectadores mucho antes de que puedan hacerse una opinión sobre la interpretación del personaje. El actor se hace actual ante los espectadores, insoslayablemente presente por su capacidad para ocupar y dominar el espacio, mucho antes de que tenga la oportunidad de mostrar sus cualidades para interpretar a un determinado personaje. Despliega esa capacidad en cualquier papel, es decir, independientemente del personaje.

El actor lograba no sólo dominar el escenario, sino el teatro entero. Lo dominaba al afectar –de una forma misteriosa, «mágica»– a los espectadores, al hacer que centraran toda su atención en él. Éste parece ser el segundo de los llamativos procedimientos con los que Gründgens se hacía presente al espectador. Así, en la crítica de Herbert Ihering a propósito de la actuación de Gründgens como Mefistófeles en el *Fausto* montado por Lothar Müthels (Staatstheater, Schauspielhaus am Gendarmenmarkt, Berlín 1932) se puede leer: «No es fácil quebrar la reservada actitud de la platea de un *Staatstheater* [teatro estatal]. Este tipo de público ya ha agotado a algunos. Gründgens lo pone todo patas arriba. Se impone. Solivianta. Pero obliga a la gente a escuchar. [...] La quiebra del tedio en el *Staatstheater* es un acontecimiento»[46].

La capacidad de presencia de Gründgens no se contraponía a la interpretación de un personaje, a la actuación. Pero tampoco había que atribuírsela al personaje. Tenía su origen más bien en procesos de corporización con los que el actor no generaba su cuerpo semiótico, sino que generaba, de modo específico, su cuerpo fenoménico.

Sobre este fundamento se impone intentar precisar la definición del concepto de presencia. Un concepto que se refiera al cuerpo fenoménico del actor, no a su cuerpo semiótico. La presencia no es una cualidad expresiva, sino puramente performativa. Se genera por medio de procesos específicos de corporización con los que el actor engendra su cuerpo fenoménico en tanto que dominador del espacio y acaparador de la atención de

46 Herbert Ihering, en *Berliner Börsen-Courier*, 3 de diciembre de 1932.

los espectadores. Cabe suponer que el actor debe su capacidad de presencia a determinadas técnicas que emplea para dar la impresión de presencia cuando quiere y para hacer que los espectadores se muestren receptivos –sea desde la primera aparición en escena y después durante toda la realización escénica, o sea solamente en instantes concretos–. Para el espectador que siente dicha presencia, o mejor, para el espectador al que esa presencia atraviesa como un rayo –«como una corriente de magia»–, aparece de manera imprevista, no de manera violenta, incomprensible pero extremadamente conmovedora. El espectador siente la fuerza que proviene del actor, una fuerza que le obliga a centrar toda su atención exclusivamente en él, una fuerza que, sin embargo, no llega a someterlo. La experimenta como una fuente de fuerza. Los espectadores sienten la inusualmente intensa actualidad del actor, que les confiere la capacidad de sentirse actuales ellos mismos también de manera inusualmente intensa. La presencia acontece para ellos en tanto que intensa experiencia del ahora. Llamaré al domino del espacio por parte del actor y a su capacidad para centrar la atención en sí *concepto fuerte de presencia*.

Esta definición de presencia, todavía en estado embrionario, depende en gran medida de opiniones referidas a la aparición en escena de Gustaf Gründgens, es decir, que no tiene en cuenta el *giro performativo* de los años sesenta y su posterior desarrollo. Por ello sólo está en condiciones de contribuir de manera limitada a la discusión sobre las preguntas formuladas más arriba. Lo que sí hace es explicar la presencia como resultado de determinados procesos de corporización, pero sobre su comportamiento respecto a los procesos de reauratización mencionados en el apartado anterior es difícil ofrecer una explicación satisfactoria partiendo de esta base. Es bien conocido que Benjamin define el aura como «la aparición irrepetible de una lejanía, por cercana que ésta pueda hallarse». Es decir, la auratización produce una especie de rapto, pues aunque un fenómeno aurático se encuentre al alcance de la mano, se resiste a cualquier aproximación, siempre parece lejano. Frente a ello, la presencia se define como un modo particularmente intenso de actualidad. Por otro lado, Benjamin señala: «Ir siguiendo, mientras se descansa, durante una tarde de verano, en el horizonte, una cadena de montañas, o una rama que cruza proyectando su sombra sobre el que reposa: eso significa respirar el aura de aquellas montañas, de esa rama»[47]. El aura se «respira», es decir, se recibe físicamente, como cuando en el caso de la presencia el espectador siente físicamente el efecto de la fuerza proveniente del actor sobre sí. La relación que existe entre aura y presencia requiere una explicación más detallada.

Lo que sigue siendo incomprensible es por qué la presencia definida de este modo supone el cumplimiento de una promesa de felicidad. Martin Seel da en el clavo cuando afirma que «nos hace anhelar un sentido para el ahora de nuestras vidas» y que hace que «queramos experimentar los ahoras en los que nos encontramos como ahoras tangibles»[48]. De estas palabras de Seel se sigue meramente la necesidad de momentos en los que experimentamos la presencia, pero no que la satisfacción de esa necesidad cumpla una promesa de felicidad.

Si no bastara con que la definición de presencia propuesta hasta ahora no puede responder sino de manera rudimentaria las preguntas formuladas al principio, hay que constatar además que plantea preguntas nuevas: ¿Cómo hay que entender la expresión 'corriente de magia' que yo he reformulado ahora como 'fuerza'? Pero sobre todo, ¿qué es lo que viene a presencia cuando el actor aparece como presente: *el* ahora de su cuerpo fenoménico o una cualidad específica de ese cuerpo fenoménico?

Desde los años sesenta los artistas de teatro y del arte de la acción y de la performance han intentado una y otra vez dar respuesta a estas preguntas. Al principio partían de una oposición radical entre presencia y representación/actuación que les permitía aislar el fenómeno de la presencia y, por así decir, «intensificarlo». Las recién surgidas artes de acción y de la performance

47 Walter Benjamin, *Das Kunstwerk im Zeitalter seiner technischen Reproduzierbarkeit*, Frankfurt, 1963, p. 18 (esp. «La obra de arte en la época de su reproductibilidad técnica», en Walter Benjamin, *Obras. Libro I/vol. 2*, Madrid, 2008, p. 16).

48 Martin Seel, «Inszenieren als Erscheinenlassen. Thesen über die Reichweite eines Begriffs», en Josef Früchtl y Jörg Zimmermann (eds.), *Ästhetik der Inszenierung*, Fráncfort, 2001, pp. 48-62, p. 53.

no sólo se posicionaron contra la comercialización del arte y contra el carácter de mercancía de la obra, como se ha destacado en repetidas ocasiones, sino que también se posicionaron vehementemente en contra de la convención teatral de representar como presentes mundos ficticios con personajes ficticios preexistentes en un texto literario. Este tipo de teatro se consideraba el prototipo de la representación, de su actualidad meramente fingida, del «como si». A ello los artistas de acciones y de performance oponían una actualidad «real»: lo que sucedía en una acción o en una performance acontecía siempre *hic et nunc*, en absoluta actualidad.

El teatro consumó la oposición entre representación y presencia al revocar la unidad postulada hasta entonces de común acuerdo –con la excepción de las vanguardias históricas– entre actor y personaje, al separarlos por medio de diversos procedimientos hasta el punto de que en algunos casos el personaje llegaba a desaparecer completamente. Con ello no sólo se redefinió el concepto de *Verkörperung* [pasando de encarnación a corporización], como se ha mostrado en el apartado anterior, sino que se sometió el fenómeno de la presencia a un análisis exhaustivo. Tanto el teatro como el arte de acción y de la performance hicieron importantes aportaciones a la dilucidación de las dos cuestiones planteadas en último lugar.

De la primera se ocupó Eugenio Barba de manera obsesiva no sólo en escenificaciones como *Ornitofilene* (1965/66), *Kaspariana* (1967/68), *Der Milljon* (1978; cuarta versión 1982-84), *Brechts Asche* [*Las cenizas de Brecht*] (1982-84), *Evangelist Oxyrhincus* (1985), que elaboró con su Odin Teatret en Holstebro (el «Nordisk Teaterlaboratorium for Skuespillerkunst») y que realizó en varios lugares del mundo para distintos públicos, sino también en las International Schools of Theatre Anthropology, fundadas y organizadas por él, y cuya celebración tenía lugar en varias ciudades europeas regularmente desde 1980. Barba distingue entre el nivel preexpresivo de la interpretación actoral y el nivel expresivo. Mientras que en el expresivo se representa algo, el preexpresivo está exclusivamente al servicio de la presentación de la actualidad del actor. Barba localiza la presencia en este segundo nivel. Partiendo de la observación de que la «corriente de magia» de la que hablaba Gert Vielhaber a propósito de Gründgens le afectó de manera particularmente intensa en realizaciones escénicas de formas teatrales propias de la India y de Extremo Oriente, Barba estudió las técnicas y las prácticas empleadas en cada caso por los maestros para mostrarse en tanto que presentes. Tras conversar con ellos llegó a la conclusión de que estas técnicas y prácticas tienen por objeto generar energía en el actor para transmitírsela al espectador[49].

Si seguimos a Barba en este aspecto, no sería suficiente definir los procesos de corporización que realiza el actor para generar presencia como la producción de una corporalidad que se adueña del espacio y que acapara la atención del espectador. En los procesos de corporización hay algo mucho más importante, el hecho de que generan energía, es decir, que engendran el propio cuerpo como energético. El actor emplea ciertas técnicas y prácticas de corporización con las que logra generar energía que circula entre él y los espectadores y que tiene un efecto directo sobre ellos.

Así pues, la «magia» de la presencia consiste en la extraordinaria capacidad del actor para generar energía de tal modo que el espectador pueda sentir que circula por toda la sala y que le afecta, que incluso lo tiñe. Esta energía es la fuerza proveniente del actor[50]. En la misma línea se anima también a los espectadores a generar ellos mismos energía, a que sientan al actor como fuente de fuerza para sí mismos, una fuente de fuerza que surge

49 Véase Eugenio Barba, *Jenseits der schwimmenden Inseln. Reflexionen mit dem Odin Teatret. Theorie und Praxis des Freien Theaters*. Con un *post scriptum* de Fernando Taviani, Reinbek bei Hamburg 1985, especialmente pp. 51-174 (esp. *Más allá de las islas flotantes*, México, 1986); véase la entrada «Pre-expressivity», en *A Dictionary of Theatre Anthropology. The Secret Art of the Performer*, Eugenio Barba y Nicola Savarese (eds.), Londres/Nueva York, 1991, pp. 186-204; también la entrada «Energy», *ibid.*, pp. 74-94.

50 A menudo son métodos específicos de entrenamiento los que permiten al actor generar energía. Véase Christel Weiler, «Haschen nach dem Vogelschwanz. Überlegungen zu den Grundlagen schauspielerischer Praxis», en Christel Weiler y Hans-Thies Lehmann (eds.), *Szenarien von Theater (und) Wissenschaft* (= *Theater der Zeit*, Recherchen 15), Berlín, 2003, pp. 204-214.

súbita e inesperadamente, que se derrama entre actores y espectadores y que es capaz de transformarlos.

Barba describe y define como un juego de contrarios las técnicas y prácticas con las que los maestros de las formas teatrales de la India y de Extremo Oriente generan este particular modo de energía que los espectadores sienten como más vivo, que se les aparece en tanto que actual. Así, por ejemplo, todas las posiciones básicas de los actores/bailarines orientales tienen su origen en la alteración del equilibrio que caracteriza la actividad cotidiana del cuerpo. Se busca un nuevo equilibrio que exige un mayor esfuerzo y precisa de una nueva tensión para mantener la verticalidad del cuerpo. Por otro lado, los actores orientales emprenden frecuentemente sus acciones en sentido contrario a su verdadero objetivo: si quieren ir hacia la izquierda, primero dan un paso a la derecha para después, tras un giro repentino, emprender el camino hacia la izquierda[51]. Se trata, pues, de técnicas de uso del cuerpo que no sólo se oponen a sus posturas cotidianas, sino que además tienen un efecto de ruptura –como subraya Barba– en la percepción del espectador y crean nuevas tensiones.

Las técnicas que empleaban los componentes de los coros de Schleef para generar su cuerpo fenoménico como cuerpo energético consistían en movimientos corporales rítmicos y en un modo de hablar rítmico. Producían una energía lo suficientemente intensa como para que los espectadores la sintieran y para que les moviera a generar su propio cuerpo energético. El ritmo producía también un desfase en la percepción del espectador, lo ponía en un estado umbral en el que se originaban permanentemente nuevas tensiones.

En Grotowski era la concurrencia de impulso y reacción la que suscitaba en el espectador la impresión de una singular actualidad y lo capacitaba a su vez para la producción de energía por sí mismo; en Wilson eran las técnicas de *slow motion*, la graduación del ritmo y la repetición. Esto significa que las técnicas y

51 Mientras que Barba parte del hecho de que estas prácticas se basan en leyes universales, en mi opinión son prácticas específicas de una cultura.

prácticas para la separación de actor y personaje, tratadas en el apartado anterior, las empleadas para la ostentación de la singular corporalidad de cada uno de los actores, pueden asimismo describirse como técnicas y prácticas para la generación de presencia. Son las que capacitan al actor para generar su cuerpo fenoménico como cuerpo energético y las que incitan al espectador a sentirse él mismo como cuerpo energético.

El discurso sobre el concepto de presencia que se ha venido desarrollando en los campos del teatro, del arte de acción y de la performance y de la teoría estética desde que se produjo el giro performativo está claramente determinado por la dicotomía cuerpo-mente, preponderante en la tradición occidental. Lo fascinante del fenómeno de la presencia es que los elementos corporales y mentales se combinan e interactúan en él de una manera muy específica. Consecuentemente, se ha insistido una y otra vez en que en el caso de la presencia, aunque tenga efectos a través del cuerpo del actor y sea experimentada físicamente por el espectador, «no se trata primordialmente de un fenómeno físico, sino mental». «El de la comparecencia, el de la presencia, es un proceso «intemporal» de la conciencia, es decir, que tiene lugar a la vez dentro y fuera del transcurrir del tiempo»[52]. A Lehman puede muy bien dársele la razón en que la presencia hay que entenderla como un proceso de la conciencia, pero, eso sí, como un proceso de la conciencia que se articula físicamente y que el espectador experimenta también físicamente. Por ello yo defiendo la tesis de que la presencia es un tipo de fenómeno del que de ningún modo puede darse cuenta recurriendo a las categorías de la dicotomía cuerpo/mente o cuerpo/conciencia; hace, antes bien, que ésta se desmorone, la suprime. Cuando el actor genera su cuerpo fenoménico en tanto que energético y produce así presencia él mismo aparece como *embodied mind*, es decir, como un ser en el que cuerpo y mente o conciencia son absolutamente

52 Hans-Thies Lehmann, «Die Gegenwart des Theaters», en Erika Fischer-Lichte, Doris Kolesch, Christel Weiler (eds.), *TRANSFORMATIONEN. Theater der neunziger Jahre*, Berlín, 1999, pp. 13-26, p. 13.

inseparables, un ser en el que ambos están dados de antemano como uno.

Esto no sólo vale para los actores/bailarines orientales con cuya actuación Eugenio Barba experimentó la presencia de un modo especialmente intenso, o para el actor «santo» Ryszard Cieślak. Puede que en su presencia, particularmente potente e intensa, sean más patentes la supresión de la oposición entre cuerpo y mente o conciencia y la aparición del cuerpo fenoménico de los actores como *embodied mind*. Sin embargo, esto es extensible a todos los actores a los que atribuimos presencia. En presencia del actor el espectador experimenta, siente al actor y, al mismo tiempo, a sí mismo como *embodied mind*, como seres en permanente devenir; la energía circulante es percibida por él como fuerza transformadora y, por lo mismo, como fuerza vital. Llamaré a esto *concepto radical de presencia*.

Este concepto aclara inmediatamente en qué sentido se cumple en la presencia del actor la *promesse de bonheur* del proceso de civilización. El proceso de civilización occidental se erige sobre el antagonismo de cuerpo y mente. Supuestamente avanza con tanto más vigor cuanto mayor es el éxito del hombre en el sometimiento de su cuerpo al control de su mente, cuanto más se abstrae de su cuerpo y cuanto más se libera de las condiciones que dicta su existencia corporal. Al final de este proceso la dicotomía habrá desaparecido y el cuerpo se habrá disuelto completamente en la «mente». Ahora bien, la presencia cumple esta promesa de manera efectiva, suprime la dicotomía entre cuerpo y mente, aunque de un modo muy distinto al que preveía Norbert Elias. Anula la dicotomía al poner las condiciones para que el actor venga a presencia como *embodied mind* y con ello le brinda al espectador la oportunidad de experimentar tanto al actor como a sí mismo como *mentes corporizadas*.

En lugar de aplazar el cumplimiento de la promesa de felicidad hasta el final del proceso de civilización, la presencia del actor la cumple aquí y ahora. Se podría decir aún algo más: en el momento en el que la presencia del actor hace que el espectador se experimente a sí mismo como *embodied mind*, la promesa se revela como cumplida ya de siempre. El ser humano *es embodied mind*. Ni se puede reducir a un cuerpo o a una mente ni puede tampoco definirse como campo de batalla en el que cuerpo y mente luchan por la supremacía. No hay mente sin cuerpo, la mente se articula en el cuerpo y como cuerpo.

Debido a su tradición cultural, el espectador occidental está acostumbrado a dar razón de sí a partir de la dicotomía entre cuerpo y mente, a proyectar la supresión de esa dicotomía en un lejano futuro o a entenderla como una rara gracia que pueden compartir unos pocos elegidos aquí y ahora en virtud de un giro vital, en la mayoría de los casos de naturaleza religiosa. Cuando el espectador siente la presencia del actor, cuando lo experimenta como *embodied mind* y cuando de consuno se genera a sí mismo como *embodied mind*, y lo siente así, lo vive como un momento de felicidad que no puede trasladar a su vida cotidiana. Para hacer que surja de nuevo, precisa de una nueva experiencia de presencia. Esos raros instantes de felicidad, que sólo puede ofrecerle la presencia del actor, pueden llegar a crear adicción en el espectador.

En la presencia no aparece, pues, algo extraordinario, sino que en ella algo perfectamente ordinario se hace patente y deviene acontecimiento: la singularidad de que el hombre es *embodied mind*. Experimentar a los demás y a uno mismo como actuales, como presentes, significa experimentarlos y experimentarse como *embodied mind* y vivir con ello la propia existencia ordinaria como extraordinaria, como transformada, como transfigurada.

Mientras que el concepto de aura enfatiza en esta transformación el momento del rapto, del *noli me tangere*, que al mismo tiempo es percibido físicamente, que «se respira», el concepto de presencia se orienta más a lo llamativo de lo ordinario, a la manera en que lo hace aparecer, algo que se experimenta físicamente y que por ello se convierte en acontecimiento. De ahí que reauratización y presencia no sean equiparables, aunque de ninguna manera se excluyan mutuamente. Se centran en aspectos y momentos distintos del mismo proceso, el proceso en el que el espectador se transforma.

Mientras que el concepto de aura puede aplicarse perfectamente a objetos, sólo los dos primeros conceptos de presencia permiten tal aplicación. Los objetos tienen capacidad para adueñarse del espacio y para acaparar la atención, con lo cual, si esas características se consideran al margen de los procesos de corporización, satisfacen incluso las condiciones del concepto fuerte de presencia. El concepto radical, por el contrario, no se puede aplicar a objetos. Sin duda, los objetos pueden ser también percibidos de una manera muy particular en su actualidad, algo que ocurre con singular frecuencia en realizaciones escénicas teatrales y en performances. Inmediatamente salta a la vista por qué esa actualidad no puede ser descrita como hacer-aparecer-en-tanto-que-*embodied mind*. Y si esta particularidad es el parámetro más importante para el concepto radical de presencia, entonces éste ha de quedar reservado para seres humanos. La actualidad de los objetos se describe más adecuadamente, con Gernot Böhme, como «éxtasis de las cosas». De igual manera que en la presencia el hombre aparece como lo que es ya de siempre, es decir, como *embodied mind*, en ella las cosas aparecen en su éxtasis como lo que son ya de siempre, de una manera que el hombre, que las funcionaliza y las instrumentaliza, no puede percibir en la experiencia cotidiana[53]. Por ello se hace necesario reflexionar sobre las concomitancias entre los conceptos de presencia (del actor) y de éxtasis (de las cosas).

Ninguno de estos conceptos se puede aplicar a productos de medios técnicos y electrónicos, que pueden ser capaces de generar efectos de presencia, pero no presencia. Mientras que el concepto de presencia, al centrarse en el aparecer, hace que la dicotomía entre ser y parecer, esencial e inevitable en los debates estéticos de los pasados siglos, se desmorone, los llamados efectos de presencia de los medios técnicos y electrónicos la dan por supuesta. Hacen que surja la *apariencia* de actualidad sin hacer por ello que los cuerpos, ni los objetos, *aparezcan* realmente como actuales. Con ayuda de determinados procedimientos logran transmitir la promesa de actualidad. Cuerpos humanos, frag-

53 Véase Gernot Böhme, *Atmosphäre. Essays zur neuen Ästhetik*, Fráncfort, 1995, especialmente pp. 31-34, así como el apartado «Atmósferas», en el punto 2, «Espacialidad», de este mismo capítulo.

mentos de cuerpos humanos, cosas o paisajes parecen actuales de una manera particularmente penetrante, aunque de lo que se trata en realidad es de un juego de luces proyectado sobre una pantalla o de una específica combinación de píxeles: ni sobre la pantalla ni sobre el monitor de televisión o del ordenador aparecen realmente como actuales cuerpos humanos, cosas o paisajes. Es precisamente la lograda apariencia de actualidad la que origina los efectos de presencia. Los cuerpos reales, los objetos reales y los paisajes reales se han desvanecido en los juegos de luces y en los píxeles. Éstos son actuales, pero no lo que en y con ellos parece ser actual.

Los medios técnicos y electrónicos buscan cumplir la *promesse de bonheur* del proceso de civilización también por este camino. También ellos aspiran a la supresión de la dicotomía entre cuerpo y conciencia, entre materia y espíritu. El camino que recorren es, sin embargo, diametralmente opuesto al de la presencia. Mientras que en la presencia el cuerpo humano aparece precisamente en su materialidad, también en su materialidad, como cuerpo energético, como organismo vivo, los medios técnicos y electrónicos producen la apariencia de actualidad de los cuerpos humanos al desmaterializarlos, al descorporizarlos. Cuanto más eficazmente logran la supresión de la materialidad de los cuerpos humanos, de las cosas, de los paisajes, cuanto más los anonadan, más intensa y abrumadora es la condición aparente de su actualidad. Con esta apariencia sus productos pueden sin duda, como lo hacía el teatro del siglo dieciocho, conmover al espectador hasta las lágrimas, asustarlo, atemorizarlo de tal manera que se le corte la respiración, rompa a sudar y se le acelere el pulso[54]. A menudo la ilusión que crean es más eficaz incluso que la del teatro ilusionista a la hora de suscitar en el espectador intensas reacciones psicológicas, afectivas, energéticas y motoras. No obstante, no es capaz de que el cuerpo fenoménico del actor aparezca en tanto que actual, no lo hace aparecer como *embodied mind*. Los

54 Véase al respecto el escrito de habilitación de Herrmann Kappelhoff, *Matrix der Gefühle. Das Kino, das Melodrama und das Theater der Empfindsamkeit*, Berlín, 2004.

efectos de presencia y la apariencia de actualidad cumplen la promesa del proceso de civilización sobre todo en la medida en que, siguiendo la lógica de este proceso, inmaterializan la corporalidad real de los actores, los descorporizan y permiten experimentar su actualidad exclusivamente como apariencia estética, completamente escindidos de su corporalidad real, material.

Tanto la presencia como los efectos de presencia pueden ser entendidos como intentos de cumplimiento de la promesa de felicidad implícita en el proceso de civilización. Pero mientras los efectos de presencia de los medios técnicos y electrónicos siguen en ello la lógica del proceso de civilización, en la realización escénica la presencia es capaz de subvertir esa lógica, de acabar con ella y revelar sus carencias precisamente porque no la reconoce.

Una estética de lo performativo es en este sentido una estética de la presencia[55], no de los efectos-presencia, una «estética del aparecer»[56], no una estética de la apariencia.

Cuerpo-animal

Si queremos ocuparnos de la corporalidad en el teatro y en el arte de la performance desde los años sesenta no basta con considerar la corporalidad generada por los actores y los performadores. En sus realizaciones escénicas participan también con frecuencia inusitada animales. Ejemplos especialmente prominentes en los años setenta son los caballos en el montaje de *Las Bacantes* de Grüber en Berlín (1974; Schaubühne am Halleschen Ufer), presentes en escena durante toda la realización escénica, si bien tras un cristal la mayor parte del tiempo, y el coyote de la acción de Beuys *I like America and America likes me* (1974; Galería René Block de Nueva York). En los años noventa, las «apariciones» de animales en escena se hacen mucho más numerosas. Marina Abramović, que, con Ulay, ya en 1978 había hecho participar a una serpiente en una performance, trabajó con serpientes pitón que se enroscaban

55 Véase Lehmann, «Die Gegenwart des Theaters», p. 22.
56 Seel, *Ästhetik des Erscheinens*, Múnich, 2000.

en su cuerpo en *Dragon Heads*, realizada entre 1990 y 1994 en distintos lugares. Jan Fabre, en cuyo *The power of theatrical madness* (1984; Biennale di Venezia) aparecían ya dos papagayos y ranas en escena, dejó salir en *Das Glas im Kopf wird vom Glas [El cristal en la cabeza se hace de cristal]* (1990; De Vlaamse Opera de Amberes) a un «joven con la luna y las estrellas sobre la cabeza» que llevaba sobre el hombro una lechuza africana. En *Sweet Temptations* (1991; Festwochen de Viena) había de nuevo una lechuza africana en escena, esta vez sobre una rama. En *She was and She is, Even* (1991; Felix Meritis Amsterdam) tres arañas aviculares negras se arrastraban por el escenario y Els Deceukelier las rozaba una y otra vez con el bajo de su vestido blanco. En *Faking as it is, un-faked* (1992; Théâtre National Brüssel) aullaban veintiún gatos a los que impedían moverse –algo que ocurrió sólo en el estreno, en realizaciones escénicas posteriores no volvieron a aparecer–. En las escenificaciones de Castorf en el Volksbühne de Berlín suelen deambular animales por el escenario: una pitón en *Pension Schöller* (1994), cabras en *Los tejedores*, de Hauptmann (1997), un caballo en *Stadt der Frauen [La ciudad de las mujeres]* (1995), un mono en *Schmutzige Hände [Manos sucias]* (1998), un pez dorado en *Los Demonios* (1999), un perro en *Vaterland [Patria]* (1999/2000) y en *Humillados y ofendidos* (2001).

La «aparición» de animales en realizaciones escénicas teatrales no es en ningún caso una novedad, pues está documentada suficientemente en los dramas litúrgicos medievales y abrumadoramente en las realizaciones escénicas cortesanas de los siglos dieciséis y diecisiete. Es bien conocido el caso de *El perro de Aubry de Mont-Didier* de Castelli, en la que un perro desempeñaba «el papel protagonista»[57]. Cuando Caroline Jagemann impuso que se invitara a la compañía para que montara la pieza en el Teatro de la

57 En el siglo diecinueve se representaron en toda Europa los llamados «dramas caninos», que estaban escritos especialmente para perros en el papel principal y que rápidamente se convirtieron en una verdadera atracción. Véase Michael Dobson, «A Dog at all Things. The Transformation of the Onstage Canine, 1550-1850», en Alan Read (ed.), *Performance Research. On Animals*, vol. 5, 2, Londres, 2000, pp. 116-124.

Corte de Weimar en 1817, Johann Wolfgang von Goethe, que era su director, dimitió de su cargo por ello.

A los animales se les habían atribuido significados mitológicos en los dramas litúrgicos, simbólico-emblemáticos en las funciones cortesanas de los siglos dieciséis y diecisiete y funciones dramatúrgicas desde el siglo dieciocho, sobre todo en la recreación de ambientes naturalistas e incluso en la generación de atmósferas. Esto último ocurrió en el caso de la *Orestíada* de Reinhardt –a propósito de la cual el crítico Jacobsohn motejó la aparición de los caballos en el *Agamenón* de «circense en el sentido más vulgar» y afirmó que su carnalidad animal buscaba el aplauso de una masa de espectadores «acostumbrada a las corridas de toros.» Sin embargo, en las realizaciones escénicas que venimos comentando, de los años setenta y posteriores, difícilmente encontramos funciones y significados equivalentes[58]. A partir de las palabras de algunos artistas se puede inferir que en estos casos se trata de una nueva forma de comunicación entre el hombre y el animal. Así, Beuys denominó a su acción con el coyote «diálogo de energía»[59] y Marina Abramović describió su interacción con las serpientes pitón de la siguiente manera: «Estoy sentada en una silla, sin moverme, con 5 serpientes pitón a mi alrededor. Las serpientes, de entre tres y cuatro metros y medio de longitud, no han sido alimentadas en las dos semanas previas a la performance. Me rodea un círculo de bloques de hielo. Durante la performance las serpientes se mueven por mi cuerpo en consonancia con mis corrientes de energía»[60].

58 Esto no significa que hoy no se incluyan animales con función dramatúrgica en algunas realizaciones escénicas. Así ocurrió, por ejemplo, con el caniche que aparecía en la escenificación del *Fausto* de Peter Stein (Hannover/Berlín/Viena, 2000/2001) y con la serpiente pitón en la escenificación de Thomas Ostermeier de *Parásitos* de Marius von Mayenburg (Deutsches Schauspielhaus Hamburg/Berliner Schaubühne 2000).

59 Cit. por Caroline Tisdall, *Joseph Beuys Coyote*, Múnich, 1988, p. 13.

60 Cit. por Toni Stooss (ed.), *Marina Abramovic' Artist Body, Performances 1969-1997*, Milán, 1998, p. 326. La performance tuvo lugar en 1992 en el Mediale Deichtorhalle de Hamburgo y duró 60 minutos.

Se trataba en ambos casos de animales salvajes, sin adiestrar. Ello quiere decir que se sabía que su comportamiento era imprevisible, que no se podía predecir ni controlar. Los animales seguían sus propios instintos. Ambos artistas, sin embargo, dijeron haber descubierto una posibilidad de comunicación con ellos que tomaba la forma de un intercambio de energía. En principio suena más bien misterioso. Tomando el caso de la acción de Beuys *Coyote* podrá aclararse lo que querían decir con ello.

La acción, cuidadosamente documentada por la fotógrafa Caroline Tisdall a petición del propio artista, tuvo lugar entre el 23 y el 25 de mayo de 1974 en la René Block Gallery de Nueva York, cada uno de los tres días entre las 10 y las 18 horas[61]. Al llegar al aeropuerto Kennedy, Beuys se hizo envolver en fieltro y fue conducido en ambulancia hasta la galería. Tras la acción abandonaría el país del mismo modo. Los cinco días de su estancia en los Estados Unidos permaneció en la galería. La acción se llevó a cabo en una sala alargada, iluminada por tres ventanas y dividida en dos por una reja que separaba a Beuys y al coyote de los espectadores. En la esquina del fondo había un poco de paja que habían traído junto con el coyote. El artista, por su parte, aportaba dos largas tiras de fieltro, un bastón, unos guantes, una linterna y cincuenta ejemplares del *Wall Street Journal* que le traían diariamente y que colocaba encima de los que habían quedado el día anterior. Beuys mostraba los periódicos al coyote que los olfateaba y orinaba sobre ellos.

El primer día el artista colocó las dos tiras de fieltro en el centro de la sala; con una de ellas hizo un montón, colocó la linterna encima en dirección a los espectadores y la encendió de modo que

61 Originalmente la acción debía tener lugar como inauguración de la Galería René Block, del 21 de mayo a las 10 horas hasta el 25 de mayo a las 18 horas. Pero al llegar Beuys no encontró todo a su gusto, por lo que la acción tuvo que empezar el 23 de mayo. La descripción que sigue se basa en la documentación de Caroline Tisdall, así como en el informe de Uwe M. Schneede, *Joseph Beuys. Die Aktionen*, Ostfildern-Ruit bei Stuttgart 1994, pp. 330-353. Se tendrá también en cuenta la filmación de Helmuth Wietz *Joseph Beuys. I like America and America likes me*, Vertrieb René Block, Berlín, 1974.

los iluminara. Apiló los ejemplares del *Wall Street Journal* en dos montones en la parte delantera de la sala. Con el bastón marrón colgado del brazo se dirigió hacia la segunda tira de fieltro, se puso los guantes marrones y se envolvió completamente en ella. Únicamente sobresalía el bastón por la parte de arriba. La figura fue sufriendo una serie de modificaciones: elevaba la punta del bastón hacia arriba mientras se mantenía de pie muy recta; conformada como una figura cuadrangular dirigía la punta del bastón hacia el suelo; se arrodillaba y se ponía después en cuclillas con el bastón apoyado en el suelo. Además, la figura se movía continuamente sobre su propio eje según los movimientos del coyote. En un momento dado se dejó caer en el suelo, de medio lado, y permaneció estirada. De repente dio un salto repentino, dejó que cayera la funda de fieltro y golpeó tres veces el triángulo colgado de su cuello. Cuando se volvió a hacer el silencio, Beuys hizo sonar durante veinte segundos, al otro lado de la reja, una grabación de turbinas girando. Cuando se hizo de nuevo el silencio, se quitó los guantes y se los lanzó al coyote, que los mordió. Entonces Beuys fue hasta los periódicos, que el coyote había esparcido y, en parte, despedazado, y los ordenó de nuevo en dos pilas. Finalmente se instaló en el montón de paja y se fumó un cigarrillo. Estas acciones las repetía con pequeñas variaciones. Cuando fumaba, el coyote solía aproximarse a él. Por lo demás, el animal prefería reposar sobre el montón de fieltro. El coyote miraba en la misma dirección en la que iluminaba la linterna, no daba jamás la espalda a los espectadores. A menudo rondaba inquieto por la sala, se dirigía hasta una ventana y miraba a través de ella. Entonces volvía de nuevo hacia los periódicos para masticarlos, desparramarlos por la sala o hacer sus necesidades sobre ellos.

Con respecto a la figura de fieltro el coyote mantenía las distancias; de vez en cuando la rodeaba husmeando nervioso; otras veces, le arrancaba el bastón, mordía el fieltro y lo deshacía. Cuando la figura estaba tendida en el suelo estirada, la husmeaba, la empujaba suavemente o le daba un zarpazo, una vez llegó incluso a instalarse junto a ella e intentó arrastrar el fieltro. La mayoría de las veces, sin embargo, se mantenía apartado sin quitarle los ojos de encima. Sólo cuando Beuys fumaba un cigarrillo sobre el montón de paja el coyote solía buscar su cercanía. Una vez terminado el cigarrillo, Beuys se levantaba, ponía en orden las tiras de fieltro y se envolvía de nuevo. A medida que transcurrían los tres días, el hombre y el animal se iban aproximando cada vez más. Agotado el tiempo, Beuys esparció pausadamente la paja por la sala y, como despedida, estrechó al coyote fuertemente contra sí, después abandonó la galería del mismo modo que había llegado a ella.

¿Qué aconteció durante esos tres días entre el hombre y el animal?

Los objetos que Beuys empleó en su acción procedían en su mayoría del ámbito de la vida cotidiana: periódicos, cigarrillos, una linterna, unos guantes, un bastón, paja, una cinta magnética, un triángulo. Con ellos realizó acciones cotidianas: ordenó los periódicos, fumó, puso en marcha el radiocasete. Sin embargo, todos estos objetos y acciones se podían poner en relación con procesos de producción, mantenimiento, transmisión o bloqueo de energía. Así, Beuys empleó el fieltro «como aislante y envoltorio para abrigarse»: «aislamiento de América y transmisión de calor para el coyote»[62]. La linterna hacía el papel de epítome de la energía. «Primero mantiene la energía almacenada y después esa energía va agotándose poco a poco en el transcurso del día hasta que hay que cambiar las pilas»[63]. La linterna estaba cubierta de fieltro para no mostrar su carácter de objeto tecnológico: «Tenía que ser una fuente de luz, un fuego, la incandescencia del sol al ponerse [...] proveniente de un montón de fieltro gris»[64]. El bastón curvado, que Beuys había usado por primera vez en su acción *Eurasia* (1965), representaba para él las corrientes de energía circulantes entre el este y el oeste. Los dos únicos sonidos o ruidos –el del triángulo y el aullido de las turbinas– fueron empleados por Beuys como potencial de energía que no se usa o que no se despliega con un objetivo concreto. Explicó que el

62 Tisdall, *Josep Beuys Coyote*, p. 14.
63 *Ibid.*
64 *Ibid.*, p.15.

sonido de las turbinas era «el eco de la tecnología imperante: energía que no se emplea», mientras que el sonido del triángulo aludía «a la unidad y a lo uno» y estaba pensado como «un impulso de conciencia dirigido al coyote»[65]. Era importante que esos objetos no sólo apuntaran a las mencionadas corrientes de energía, tenían que generarlas y transmitirlas realmente.

Las energías que esos objetos albergaban y transmitían, por ejemplo, cuando el coyote se tendía sobre el fieltro, olfateaba el bastón o escuchaba atentamente el sonido del triángulo, estaban pensadas meramente como apoyo para las energías que liberaba el artista. Beuys no sólo se escenificó en estas acciones como un chamán por sus implícitas alusiones al vestido de los chamanes navajos: su sombrero, la amplia capa, el trocito de piel de liebre en el chaleco, el triángulo, colgado al cuello en lugar del tambor, y el mazo, todos ellos objetos propios de los navajos. Se entendía a sí mismo como chamán, es decir, como una figura dotada de fuerzas espirituales extraordinarias con las que podía ejercer influencia para modificar el mundo del animal y el del hombre, incluso el propio cosmos:

> Adopté efectivamente la figura de un chamán durante la acción... Pero no para defender que volviéramos al mundo en el que la existencia del chamán estaba justificada [...] Al decir que el chamán era el representante de algo capaz de unificar contextos materiales y espirituales, estaba empleando esta vieja figura para expresar algo relativo al futuro[66].

Con la ejecución de las acciones descritas debían liberarse en el artista y en el coyote energías capaces de iniciar transformaciones. La acción tuvo lugar en una especie de contexto mitológico. De acuerdo con la tradición amerindia, el coyote representaba una de sus deidades más poderosas[67]. El coyote era para ellos jus-

65 *Ibid.*

66 Cit. por Schneede, *Joseph Beuys. Die Aktionen*, p. 336.

67 Beuys sigue en gran medida las reflexiones de Frank J. Doble en su libro *The Voice of the Coyote*, Boston, 1949.

tamente la encarnación de la potencia de transformación, era capaz de transformar su estado de físico en espiritual y viceversa. Entendía todas las lenguas, podía incluso hablar con las cercas y hacer que le dejaran pasar. Si su ira se desataba, podía acarrear la desgracia a los seres humanos; si se calmaba, podía ayudarlos a superar la enfermedad. Los chamanes navajos se ponían máscaras de coyote en sus rituales de curación, que duraban nueve noches, para conjurar la fuerza del coyote y emplearla en la curación de los enfermos[68]. La llegada de los blancos cambió el estatus del coyote. Su capacidad inventiva y de adaptación, admirada y venerada por los indios como fuerza subversiva, se quedó en mera astucia. El coyote pasó a convertirse en el *mean coyote*, chivo expiatorio al que se podía cazar y matar.

En palabras de Beuys, el objetivo de su acción era ese «episodio traumático» en la historia americana: «tenemos que arreglar cuentas, por así decirlo, con el coyote. Sólo entonces podrá restañarse la herida»[69]. Es decir, que la acción tenía que cumplir la función de un rito de curación que confiriera tanto al artista como al coyote una fuerza capaz de llevar a cabo una curación.

Para lograrlo Beuys actuó efectivamente como un chamán en varios aspectos. Con su permanente cambio de posición y de relaciones trataba de crear una situación liminar en la que pudiera llevarse a cabo la transformación del coyote, el restablecimiento de su estatus «original». Él mismo se aposentaba en el montón de paja que trajeron junto con el coyote, mientras que el coyote escogía como lugar de reposo el fieltro que Beuys había traído, había acomodado y al que había provisto de una fuente de energía: la linterna. Por un lado, Beuys dejaba que el coyote despedazara e hiciera sus necesidades sobre el *Wall Street Journal*, en el que veía encarnado el «fosilizado *rigor mortis* del pensamiento sobre el CAPITAL»[70]. Por otro lado, permitía que husmeara y mordiera los guantes, la referencia simbólica de las manos huma-

68 Véase Karl W. Luckert, *Coyoteway. A Navajo Holyway Healing Ceremonial*, Tucson/Flagstaff, 1979.
69 Cit. por Tisdall, *Joseph Beuys Coyote*, p. 10.
70 *Ibid.*, p. 16.

nas y de su potencial creador y transformador. Lo exponía tanto al ruido de las turbinas, el «eco de la tecnología imperante», como al sonido del triángulo, que debía tener por objeto inmediato la «conciencia» del coyote. Con este modo de proceder, Beuys invocaba la fuerza que albergaban los objetos que empleaba y liberaba en sí mismo y en el coyote las «fuerzas sanadoras» capaces de lograr una transformación del hombre y del animal. El «diálogo de energía» que Beuys mantuvo con el coyote pretendía liberar las energías de ambos, engendrar fuerzas espirituales que lograran una transformación.

Que el espectador pudiera percibir la acción como un «diálogo de energía» y un rito de curación es más que dudoso. Beuys y el coyote estaban separados de los espectadores por una reja de alambre, igual que las que se emplean en el zoológico o en un número de circo con animales peligrosos. Esta división sólo se suprimía, aunque parcialmente, cuando algún amigo o conocido de Beuys visitaba la galería y el artista se acercaba a la reja para saludarlo. En general, sin embargo, la separación era un elemento constitutivo de la acción, aunque se pueda interpretar también pragmáticamente como una medida de protección para los espectadores. Con ello, los espectadores eran relegados a la posición de *voyeurs* que, desde una distancia segura, observaban al artista en una empresa peligrosa y de gran riesgo para él. ¿Les estaba vedado el potencial de energía que se engendraba en la acción? ¿Les llegaron las corrientes de energía liberadas por él, y que circulaban entre Beuys y el coyote? La extrañeza que suscitaba en el público americano un Beuys llegado en avión desde Europa, y que actuaba como un chamán indio, no sólo no desapareció, sino que la disposición espacial logró que se intensificara aún más.

No obstante, es de suponer que la acción surtió un efecto inusual en el espectador, el causado por las acciones del artista y el comportamiento del animal. Beuys trató al coyote como a un igual. Trataba de influir en él, pero sin recurrir a ningún tipo de violencia –si pasamos por alto, eso sí, el hecho de que el coyote fue capturado para realizar la acción–. Beuys dejó al animal toda la libertad imaginable dentro de los límites establecidos por él, pero válidos para ambos. Incluso aunque el espectador ni supiera ni se percatara de que Beuys atribuía conciencia al coyote, sí percibía que la relación entre hombre y animal no era jerárquica –como en un número de circo con animales–, sino que estaba regulada por procesos de intercambio, que el hombre aceptaba al animal en su indisponibilidad esencial como un parigual con los mismos derechos, lo que seguramente para muchos era muy irritante.

Durante la acción al espectador se le confrontaba con la indisponibilidad del animal, algo en lo que vienen haciendo hincapié reiteradamente desde los años sesenta las realizaciones escénicas de teatro y las performances en las que participan animales. Esta indisponibilidad afecta, por un lado, a la materialidad de las realizaciones escénicas y, por otro, a su desarrollo, al bucle de retroalimentación autopoiético.

En la acción de Beuys el cuerpo-animal apareció como un organismo vigoroso, energético, como un cuerpo-en-devenir. En lo referente a su materialidad, no había ninguna diferencia entre el cuerpo del ser humano y el del animal. Ninguno de ellos es susceptible de ser empleado como material moldeable y controlable a partir del cual se pueda crear una obra. Del mismo modo que el cuerpo humano, el cuerpo del animal sólo se convierte en material con su muerte. Algo que dejan claro acciones como las de Herrmann Nitsch, en las que un cadáver de cordero era «trabajado», rociado con sangre, rellenado de vísceras y atado a una persona. O como ocurre también en performances como *Cleaning the House*, realizada por Marina Abramović en 1995 en la Sean Kelly Gallery de Nueva York. Abramović se sentó en un pequeño taburete rodeado de una inmensa montaña de huesos de vaca crudos. Tomó los huesos uno por uno, les quitó la carne que les quedaba y los lavó. Trabajó los huesos, les quitó los últimos restos de carne, los últimos vestigios de vida del animal, y los transformó en objetos, en materiales, en artefactos.

El cuerpo-animal vivo, sin embargo, sigue siendo indisponible. Igual que en el caso del cuerpo humano, no presenta carácter de obra, tiene carácter de acontecimiento. A este respecto no existe ninguna diferencia entre ser humano y animal. Esta evidencia debió imponérseles a los espectadores de la acción de

Beuys del mismo modo que a los de las demás realizaciones escénicas mencionadas. No podemos más que hacer especulaciones sobre hasta qué punto esta expuesta imposibilidad de diferenciar entre animal y ser humano llevó a los espectadores sólo a cambiar su visión sobre la comparabilidad y la semejanza entre organismos vivos, o si desencadenó en ellos una reacción inmediata, fisiológica, afectiva o energética. No tenemos la menor certeza sobre si en la confrontación directa con el organismo vivo del animal tuvo lugar en el espectador la animalización de la que hablan Deleuze y Guattari[71], o si en ella el espectador se sintió confrontado con su propia animalidad y reaccionó con los correspondientes síntomas físicos. Cabe pensar, sin embargo, que la imposibilidad de diferenciar entre ser humano y animal, una idea opuesta a los hábitos intelectuales y prácticos del hombre occidental durante siglos, y que, en cierta medida, ha confirmado por primera vez la investigación genética más reciente, no dejó indiferente al espectador.

Sin duda, la indisponibilidad de los animales ha sido desde siempre un estímulo especial para el espectador. Pues siempre que salen a escena animales despliegan una «presencia» verdaderamente inquietante en el sentido más literal: parecen llenar todo el espacio escénico y se convierten en el centro de atención. Les roban el protagonismo a los actores, especialmente en las realizaciones escénicas en las que los animales desempeñan una tarea dramatúrgica claramente definida. Pues con el animal –aunque se trate de un animal doméstico o de un caniche adiestrado– irrumpe en escena la «primigenia», «misteriosa» e «imprevisible» naturaleza. En el caso del actor, el espectador asume que actúa según una pauta. En el animal le fascina precisamente la posibilidad, que se abre con su aparición, de que sobre el escenario suceda algo imprevisto en lugar de lo que estaba planeado. La aparición del animal en escena es percibida como la irrupción de lo real en lo ficticio, de lo casual en el orden, de la naturaleza en la cultura. Cuando un animal sale a escena se evoca un momento

71 Véase Gilles Deleuze y Félix Guattari, *¿Qué es la filosofía?*, Barcelona, 2001, p. 151.

crítico –comparable a un huracán o una inundación– en el que todo está en cuestión, en el que el orden humano amenaza con rendirse a la naturaleza, un momento en el que, contrariamente a lo que ocurre en un huracán o en una inundación, la expectativa de que el orden humano sea destruido, esto es, la expectativa de que el animal haga que se desmorone el montaje escénico parece significativamente más ansiada que la esperanza de que todo salga según lo previsto. La salida a escena de animales le confiere a la escenificación un aspecto subversivo que amenaza con dinamitarla, pero que al espectador le produce una gran fascinación.

Esta indisponibilidad de los animales, constantemente temida, es la que vienen persiguiendo, en la que vienen haciendo hincapié desde los años sesenta, los artistas de teatro y de performance. La mayoría de las veces los animales que aparecen en una realización escénica no tienen ninguna tarea especial que cumplir. Basta con que estén presentes en el espacio escénico y se muestren en su indisponibilidad. Hagan lo que hagan se considera un elemento de la realización escénica, y termina siendo parte constitutiva de ella. Así pues, los animales refuerzan la esencial indisponibilidad de la realización escénica, la ponen por primera vez ante los ojos de los espectadores y, en algunos casos, también de los actores. Efectivamente, en toda realización escénica es la interacción entre actores y espectadores, independientemente de qué curso tome, la que hace que el bucle de retroalimentación autopoiético dé giros inesperados. Dado que tanto actores como espectadores están implicados en él, estos giros muchas veces no se perciben en absoluto como emergencias[72]. Los animales, en cambio, que hacen surgir constantemente emergencias con su comporta-

72 Con el concepto de emergencia me refiero a fenómenos surgidos de modo imprevisto e inmotivado que, en algunos casos, parecen enteramente plausibles a posteriori. Para el concepto de emergencia, véase Achim Stephan, *Emergenz. Von der Unvorhersagbarkeit zur Selbstorganisation*, Dresde/Múnich, 1999; y «Emergenz in kognitionsfähigen Systemen», en Michael Pauen/Gerhard Roth (eds.), *Neurowissenschaften und Philosophie*, Múnich, 2001, pp. 123-154; Thomas Wägenbaur (ed.), *Blinde Emergenz? Interdisziplinäre Beiträge zu Fragen kultureller Evolution*, Heidelberg, 2000.

miento, acaparan la atención de ambos y los sensibilizan para el fenómeno. En especial las realizaciones escénicas en las que intervienen animales pueden por ello parecerles a los espectadores uno de esos sistemas naturales sobre los que de ninguna manera se puede decir que funcionen de acuerdo a un «plan» bien concebido, sino uno de aquellos, el inmunológico, por ejemplo, que cuentan de antemano con las emergencias y que tienen que reaccionar ante ellas.

2. Espacialidad

También la espacialidad es fugaz y transitoria. No existe ni antes ni más allá de la realización escénica ni después de ella, sino que —como ocurre con la corporalidad o la sonoridad— sólo tiene lugar en y por la realización escénica. Por eso tampoco hay que equipararla con el espacio en el que acontece.

El espacio en que tiene lugar una realización escénica puede ser entendido, por un lado, como un espacio geométrico. Como tal, viene dado antes del comienzo de la realización escénica y no deja de existir cuando termina. Dispone de una planta determinada, cuenta con una altura, una anchura, una longitud y un volumen concretos; es sólido, estable y, tocante a estas características, permanece inalterable durante un largo periodo de tiempo. Cuando se piensa en el espacio geométrico, surge a menudo la asociación con la idea de contenedor. Se entiende el espacio como una especie de recipiente que, en sus características esenciales, no se ve afectado por lo que acontece en él. Aunque en el suelo aparezcan con el tiempo agujeros e irregularidades, aunque se desgasten los colores o se desconche el enyesado de las paredes, el espacio geométrico sigue siendo el mismo.

Por otro lado, el espacio en el que tiene lugar una realización escénica hay que considerarlo también como espacio performativo. Brinda singulares posibilidades para la relación entre actores y espectadores, para el movimiento y la percepción, que además organiza y estructura. El espacio geométrico, independientemente del uso que se haga de estas posibilidades, de cómo se empleen, se realicen, se traten o se rechacen, terminará repercutiendo en el espacio performativo. Puede modificarlo cualquier movimiento de personas, objetos, luz o cualquier sonido. Es inestable y está en fluctuación permanentemente. La espacialidad de una realización escénica se origina en y a través del espacio performativo y se percibe de acuerdo a las condiciones establecidas por él[73].

Espacios performativos

Los espacios teatrales, tanto si son permanentes como si son construcciones provisionales, son siempre, en este sentido, espacios performativos. La historia de la construcción de teatros y de las técnicas escenográficas se ha escrito primordialmente como historia de espacios geométricos, pero podría escribirse con el mismo derecho como historia de los espacios performativos. Aun así aporta elocuentes testimonios sobre cómo se ha ido concibiendo en cada momento la relación entre actores y espectadores, sobre qué posibilidades de movimiento a través del espacio se preveían para los actores y qué posibilidades de percepción para los espectadores. Nos permite saber si los espectadores se colocaban en círculo alrededor del segmento de espacio previsto para los actores, de modo que prácticamente los rodeaban, o si rodeaban por tres partes un escenario rectangular o cuadrado, si se movían alrededor de él o si se sentaban frente a él separados por el proscenio. En cada uno de esos casos la relación entre actores y espectadores se concebía de modo distinto. Se dan casos en que los actores tienen a su disposición un lugar espacioso y circular, casi vacío, como la orquesta, a veces tienen que actuar en el estrecho espacio que queda delante de la primera pareja de bastidores en un escenario a la italiana, ambas circunstancias conllevan una serie de condiciones que afectan directamente a las posibilidades

73 Véase respecto a las distintos puntos de vista sobre el espacio, como arquitectónico-geométrico y como performativo, el artículo de Jens Roselt, «Wo die Gefühle wohnen – zur Performativität von Räumen», en Hajo Kurzenberger y Annemarie Matzke (eds.), *TheorieTheaterPraxis*, Berlín, 2004.

de movimiento de los actores en cada caso. Tanto si los espectadores pueden dejar que su mirada se pierda por todo el espacio del teatro y por el paisaje circundante, bañado por luz natural y por lo tanto cambiante a lo largo del día, para volver después a centrarla en los actores ante la *skené*, en el coro que está en la orquesta o incluso en los demás espectadores, como si está sentado en un espacio interior iluminado por velas ante un escenario con proscenio construido según el principio de la perspectiva central, si se sienta en una butaca en la que disfruta de un punto de vista ideal o si, por el contrario, se encuentra en un asiento que sólo permite una percepción limitada, pero que cuenta con una mejor perspectiva sobre los palcos fronteros, en cada uno de estos casos, al espectador se le abren distintas posibilidades de percepción.

No obstante, a partir de la peculiaridad de que el lugar de realización escénica organice y estructure de forma distinta en cada caso las relaciones entre actores y espectadores, el movimiento y la percepción, no se puede concluir que esté en condiciones de determinarlas. El espacio performativo brinda posibilidades sin fijar el modo en que se utilizan y se realizan. Además, puede emplearlas de un modo tal que no se puedan planear ni prever. Como quiera que tal utilización del espacio va a contra las costumbres y las opiniones preconcebidas, apenas se lo menciona ocasionalmente, en tanto que acontecimiento extraordinario, en cuadernos de viajes, entradas de diarios, notas autobiográficas, cartas o reportajes periodísticos. Así, nos enteramos de que en el teatro francés del siglo diecisiete algunos espectadores pertenecientes a la nobleza tenían a menudo un sitio reservado sobre el escenario, ocupaban el espacio y hablaban entre ellos en voz alta sin el menor recato. Modificaban así no sólo la relación entre actores y espectadores propuesta por la distribución del espacio, también las posibilidades de movimiento y percepción. Algunos escándalos en el teatro de los siglos dieciocho y diecinueve tuvieron consecuencias similares. Por ejemplo, cuando durante el estreno de *Antes de amanecer,* de Hauptmann, que tuvo lugar en Berlín el 20 de octubre de 1889 bajo los auspicios de la organización Freie Bühne, un espectador se levantó en la platea, que estaba a oscuras, agitó un fórceps sobre su cabeza y ofreció a los actores subir al escenario y asistir como ginecólogo en el parto, a todas luces complicado, que estaba teniendo lugar entre bambalinas, redefinió la relación entre actores y espectadores de un modo radicalmente nuevo. No fue el único. Según algunas reseñas periodísticas, el público brindó «una actuación dentro de la actuación [...]. La lucha entre el entusiasmo y el rechazo, los «bravo» y los «fuera», los silbidos y los aplausos, los gritos, las quejas, la intranquilidad y la excitación que seguían a cada acto, y que llegaron a formar parte de la obra, convirtieron el Teatro Lessing en un local de reunión rebosante de una muchedumbre apasionada e insurgente»[74]. El espacio performativo se distingue precisamente porque posibilita otro empleo además del previsto, aunque muchos participantes puedan considerar ese empleo no previsto como inapropiado e incluso se indignen –como le ocurrió a Claus Peymann en 1965 cuando algunos espectadores asaltaron el escenario en la segunda realización escénica de *Insultos al público*– porque es el modo en el que se emplea en cada caso lo que constituye el espacio performativo y genera una espacialidad específica.

Los movimientos de las vanguardias históricas tuvieron en cuenta este aspecto cuando rompieron radicalmente con la preeminencia del modelo de teatro a la italiana, con proscenio y platea a oscuras. En su lugar experimentaron con distintas formas de espacio teatral que organizaran y estructuraran de otro modo las relaciones entre actores y espectadores, el movimiento y la percepción. Por un lado, recurrieron a diversos modelos históricos para modificarlos mediante métodos específicos, por ejemplo: el escenario de orquesta, la plaza de mercado medieval o el *hanamichi* del teatro Kabuki. Cuando Reinhardt montó el *Edipo Rey* en el Circo Schumann de Berlín y experimentó con las posibilidades de un escenario con orquesta, no tenía la intención de resucitar

74 Curt Baake, *Berliner Volksblatt*, 22 de octubre de 1889, cit. por Norbert Jaron *et al.* (eds.), *Berlin-Theater der Jahrhundertwende. Bühnengeschichte der Reichshauptstadt im Spiegel der Kritik (1889-1914)*, Tubinga, 1986, p. 96.

el teatro griego. Estaba más bien buscando espacios teatrales que posibilitaran a actores y espectadores la formación de una comunidad, quería proporcionar a los actores acostumbrados al teatro a la italiana un nuevo espacio para moverse, y a los espectadores nuevos modos y perspectivas de percepción; algunos críticos lo atacaron duramente por ello. Así, por ejemplo, Alfred Klaar se quejaba de «la distribución de la acción, delante, en medio, debajo y detrás de nosotros; esa incesante necesidad de cambiar de punto de vista»[75].

Por otro lado, los reformadores del teatro y los vanguardistas crearon realizaciones escénicas en espacios y en lugares que tenían relación temática con la obra presentada en cada caso, las montaban, por así decirlo, en sus «ubicaciones originales». Así, Reinhardt montó el *Sueño de una noche de verano* en un pinar cercano al Nikolassee de Berlín (1910), *Das Salzburger große Welttheater [El gran teatro del mundo de Salzburgo]*, de Hofmannsthal, en la Kollegienkirche de Salzburgo (1922) y el *Mercader de Venecia* en el Campo San Trovaso de Venecia (1934). Nikolai Evreinov presentó el espectáculo de masas *Asalto al Palacio de Invierno* en la plaza que está delante del Palacio de Invierno y en sus ventanas (San Petersburgo, 1920), y Sergei Eisenstein escogió como lugar para realizar su montaje de *Máscaras de gas* de Tretiakov (1923) una fábrica de gas de Moscú. Cada uno de estos lugares ofrecía posibilidades específicas para la negociación de las relaciones entre actores y espectadores, para el movimiento y la percepción. Además, estaban acondicionados de una manera que los convertía en ideales para la generación de nuevas posibilidades.

Asimismo, se proyectó finalmente la construcción de nuevos teatros que ofrecieran múltiples posibilidades de utilización del espacio, como hicieron Reinhardt, al convertir el Circo Schumann en el Großes Schauspielhaus, y Piscator que, junto a Gropius, concibió el proyecto de su teatro total.

Los reformadores del teatro en el paso del siglo diecinueve al veinte y los representantes de las vanguardias históricas eran cons-

75 Alfred Klaar, *Vossische Zeitung*, 14 de octubre de 1911.

cientes de la performatividad del espacio. Exploraron las posibilidades que ofrecían los distintos espacios en lo que tocaba a la relación entre actores y espectadores, al movimiento y a la percepción, e intentaron reforzarlas por medio de una con(des)figuración específica según sus repectivos objetivos e ideas, de tal manera que se suscitaran en el espectador determinados modos de percepción y comportamiento. Con estas medidas, los directores de las vanguardias anhelaban, como ya se ha señalado, mantener el control sobre el bucle de retroalimentación autopoiético.

Tras la Segunda Guerra Mundial, en algunos casos ya a finales de los años treinta, el teatro a la italiana con proscenio volvió a ocupar su lugar como modelo dominante. En las numerosas reconstrucciones de teatros en la Alemania de los años cincuenta se siguió, en gran medida, este modelo. Dejaron de construirse teatros con espacios variables. El primer caso que conozco de una nueva edificación o reconstrucción de este tipo es la inauguración del Schaubühne de la Lehniner Platz de Berlín en 1980, al que se puede considerar resultado del giro performativo de los años sesenta.

En los años sesenta volvió a producir un éxodo de los teatros convencionales mucho más masivo y radical que el anterior. Se buscaron nuevos espacios escénicos en antiguas fábricas, mataderos, búnkeres, cocheras de tranvías, mercados, centros comerciales, recintos feriales y estadios deportivos, en calles y plazas, en estaciones de metro y en parques públicos, en puestos de cerveza, en vertederos, en talleres de coches, en ruinas y en cementerios. En la mayor parte de los casos se escogían espacios que no estaban concebidos, construidos ni acondicionados como espacios para realizaciones escénicas, sino que servían o habían servido para usos muy distintos. Presentaban pocas condiciones previas para la relación entre actores y espectadores, no les asignaban a ninguno de los dos grupos un segmento espacial concreto y les brindaban a ambos gran cantidad de posibilidades de movimiento y percepción. Al elegir ese tipo de espacios ponían de manifiesto que es la realización escénica la que determina la relación entre actores y espectadores y la que crea distintas posibilidades de movimiento y percepción, que es la que genera la espacialidad.

Al respecto aparecen sobre todo tres procedimientos con los que se intensifica la performatividad del espacio: 1) la utilización de un espacio (casi) vacío, o bien de un espacio de disposición variable que permite el libre movimiento de actores y espectadores; 2) la creación de configuraciones espaciales específicas que brindan posibilidades desconocidas o no aprovechadas hasta entonces para la negociación de las relaciones entre actores y espectadores, y nuevas posibilidades de movimiento y percepción; y 3) el empleo de espacios ya existentes pero destinados a un uso distinto al escénico cuyas posibilidades escénicas específicas se exploran y se ponen a prueba.

1. En *Celtic + ~~~*, por ejemplo, no había en el búnker otro condicionamiento espacial que los bancos de madera. Beuys y los espectadores se movían en y por todo el espacio. La relación entre ambos sólo la determinaban las acciones de Beuys y las reacciones de los espectadores. Lo que pudiera ser percibido y cómo pudiera serlo dependía de las posiciones, en permanente variación, de cada uno de los participantes –sobre uno de los bancos, quietos en medio de la multitud, al margen de ella, inmediatamente delante del actor, totalmente apartados, etc.–. El actor y los espectadores fueron los que generaron con sus acciones una espacialidad en permanente mudanza.

En *Dionysus in 69* sí había, en cambio, una ordenación espacial determinada. En el centro de un antiguo taller de automóviles, el Performance Garage, había extendidas unas esterillas negras de goma que parecían marcar el espacio de los actores. En las paredes se alzaban estructuras de varios pisos que se unían entre sí por medio de escaleras; desde el suelo se erigía la llamada torre, una construcción de una altura tan considerable que casi llegaba a tocar el techo. Los espectadores podían ocupar la moqueta que rodeaba las esterillas de goma, situarse bajo la estructura metálica o acomodarse en cualquiera de sus pisos. Con ello podían elegir por sí mismos la distancia respecto a la zona central y el ángulo de visión que tendrían sobre lo que allí aconteciera. Las posibilidades que ofrecía la distribución inicial del espacio fueron ampliándose considerablemente en el transcurso de la realización escénica. Los performadores no se limitaban a la zona central, se movían por todo el espacio. El actor que interpretaba a Penteo subió hasta el piso más alto de la torre para dirigir desde allí sus palabras a los ciudadanos de Tebas. En la *caress-scene*, los performadores se distribuían por todo el espacio, llegando incluso hasta los espectadores «escondidos» bajo las estructuras de pisos. Los espectadores, por su parte, tenían el derecho y la posibilidad de moverse libremente durante la realización escénica, de buscar continuamente una nueva ubicación, un nuevo punto de vista, de regular a voluntad la distancia respecto a los performadores y a los demás espectadores y de ocupar ellos mismos la zona central, *to join the story*. Es decir, que no es que los condicionamientos que aparentemente se habían puesto no limitaran a actores y espectadores las posibilidades de moverse y de percibir lo que ocurría con respecto a las que tenían en un espacio vacío, sino que las multiplicaban. En este procedimiento la performatividad del espacio era tanto más intensa cuanto que no favorecía ni excluía de antemano ninguna de las posibilidades. Es indudable que la espacialidad la generaban los movimientos y percepciones de actores y espectadores.

2. El segundo procedimiento, en cambio, favorece determinadas posibilidades y parece excluir otras. Grotowski lo empleó en sus escenificaciones para crear una situación de especial cercanía entre actores y espectadores, para que éstos pudieran sentir la respiración de los actores, para que pudieran oler su sudor. En su escenificación del *Kordian* de Słowacki (1961) hizo colocar literas de hierro en tres puntos de la sala sobre las que tenían que acomodarse los espectadores, no más de 65. Al mismo tiempo las literas hacían las veces de estrados en los que ocurrían los acontecimientos centrales de la realización escénica. Actores y espectadores compartían enfáticamente el mismo espacio. Además, a los espectadores se les trataba como a internos en un manicomio. Por ejemplo, el doctor pedía a los actores y a los espectadores que cantaran una determinada canción. A los espectadores que se negaban los zarandeaba, se plantaba ante ellos, les exigía que hicieran lo que mandaba y les amenazaba con su bastón. Los actores se movían por todo el espacio, mientras que los espectadores estaban, por así decirlo, atados a sus camas. Sus posibilidades de percepción dependían del lugar en el que se encontrara su

litera y de si ocupaban la cama superior o la inferior. De esta manera se generaban espacialidades que exponían a los espectadores a experiencias muy singulares.

Ése fue asimismo el caso del montaje de *El príncipe constante* de Calderón, que Grotowski realizó sobre la versión de Słowacki (1965). En este caso el teatro se conformó como una especie de *theatrum anatomicum*. Los escasos 30 o 40 espectadores estaban de pie en círculos concéntricos y en filas ascendentes alrededor del escenario, cada una de las filas estaba separada de las demás por tabiques que no dejaban ver más que las cabezas de los espectadores y, en algún caso, el pecho. Los espectadores se encontraban, pues, no sólo inmovilizados en buena medida, sino forzados a tomar la posición de *voyeurs* frente a los atroces acontecimientos que sucedían en escena. En ambos casos, la disposición espacial, y los condicionantes que conllevaba cada uno de ellos para la relación entre actores y espectadores, entre movimiento y percepción, tenía la función de canalizar la energía que circulaba por el espacio performativo de tal manera que la espacialidad fuera capaz de desplegar un específico potencial efectivo.

Esto ocurrió asimismo, aunque de una manera completamente distinta, con la disposición espacial que Einar Schleef creó para *Die Mütter* en el grandísimo [teatro] Frankfurter Schauspiel o también en *Götz von Berlichingen*, que tuvo lugar en el Bockenheimer Depot, una antigua cochera de tranvías en forma de nave industrial. En la segunda escenificación, Schleef extendió, a lo largo del eje longitudinal, una amplia pasarela con una especie de piso inferior de la cochera que atravesaba el espacio por la mitad. Llegaba justo hasta una de las puertas traseras, que se abrirían varias veces durante la realización escénica. Los actores se movían —con sus botas de acero— por encima o por debajo de la pasarela y entre los espectadores, esto último mientras repartían patatas cocidas. Los espectadores estaban sentados en filas ascendentes a ambos lados de la pasarela, frente a frente. Mientras que desde las filas superiores tenían una visión reducida de las acciones que sucedían en el piso bajo de la pasarela, a los espectadores situados frente a ellos podían percibirlos con gran detalle. Desde las filas delanteras y centrales, por el contrario, la visión de los asientos ubicados enfrente obstaculizaba su visión de la acción sobre la pasarela. Por otro lado, la proximidad de las filas delanteras a la pasarela era tanta que los espectadores podían oler el sudor de los actores que pasaban corriendo a su lado. Eran estos movimientos sobre la pasarela y por su piso bajo los que iban redefiniendo continuamente la relación entre actores y espectadores, y los que brindaban a éstos nuevas posibilidades de percepción o se las negaban. La espacialidad de la realización escénica así generada variaba constantemente: en un momento favorecía la formación de una comunidad entre actores y espectadores y, al siguiente, volvía a confrontarlos.

3. El tercer procedimiento se centra en las posibilidades que implica, para la generación de espacialidad, la utilización de un espacio que ha sido preparado para cumplir una función escénica, pero que en otros casos, o a veces incluso al mismo tiempo, tiene otras funciones distintas. Klaus Michael Grüber ha empleado con considerable frecuencia este procedimiento. En 1975 montó el *Faust Salpêtrière* (basado en la obra de Goethe) en la Chapelle Saint Louis del Hôpital de la Salpêtrière en París; en 1977 el *Viaje de invierno* en el Estadio Olímpico de Berlín; en 1979 *Rudi* en las ruinas del Hotel Esplanade en Berlín; en 1995 *Pálida madre, tierna hermana* en el cementerio soviético de Oberweimar, en la ladera norte del Palacio de Belvedere, la que fuera residencia de verano del duque Carl August, mecenas de Goethe. Grüber hizo uso de estos espacios no sin modificarlos. Sus escenógrafos (Gilles Aillaud, Eduardo Arroyo o Antonio Recalcati) añadieron en cada ocasión pequeños detalles con los que reforzar la performatividad del espacio y cambiar sus posibilidades de significación, o incluso ampliarlas.

Para *Rudi*, Antonio Recalcati ubicó instalaciones en los espacios del antiguo Grand Hotel Esplanade que no habían sido destruidos, o sólo ligeramente, por las bombas: el vestíbulo, el patio de palmeras, el salón de desayuno y la llamada sala del emperador[76]. Hasta que se construyó el muro de Berlín, que cercaba la plaza de la parte delantera del hotel, con vistas al Tiergarten, estas salas se

76 Hoy pueden visitarse estas salas en el Sony-Center de Postdamer Platz en Berlín, a donde fueron trasladados con medios técnicos muy sofisticados.

habían usado con profusión para veladas de ópera, conferencias de prensa, proyecciones de películas, desfiles de moda o certámenes de belleza. Tras la construcción del muro y hasta los años setenta se celebraron ocasionalmente algunos actos, pese a que las ruinas tenían un aspecto desolador. Ése era precisamente el lugar al que Grüber y Recalcati convocaban para la realización escénica de *Rudi*. En el salón de desayuno estaba sentado el actor Paul Burian leyendo en voz alta y con tono monótono fragmentos de la novela *Rudi* de Bernard von Brentano (del año 1934). Su lectura era recibida en las otras salas, con un cierto desfase temporal, a través de altavoces. Hacían, además, las veces de actores un joven con pelo largo que actuaba en otra sala, llevaba unos pantalones vaqueros, una camisa de talla mucho mayor que la suya y un jersey, y una mujer mayor, gorda y de pelo blanco, que llevaba un vestido y un chaleco negros y que estaba en una silla de ruedas en la misma sala. El espectador podía moverse por todas las salas, quedarse en ellas cuanto quisiera, escuchar atentamente las voces que emitían los altavoces, sentarse, continuar paseando y regresar, si así lo quería, a cualquiera de las salas[77]. Mientras que en el caso de la lectura de Paul Burian el espectador podía estar seguro de que se trataba de un actor, no era así en el caso del joven o de la mujer mayor, ni tampoco en el de otros espectadores que estaban en las salas. Cada uno de los que deambulaban por ellas podía ser considerado un actor o un espectador con los que se establecía un tipo de relación específica –ya fuera siguiendo con especial atención sus movimientos por las salas o ya fuera dirigiéndose a él y preguntándole por sus percepciones, impresiones, sensaciones o simplemente por la hora–. En consecuencia, en *Rudi* la espacialidad la generaban sobre todo los movimientos y las percepciones de los espectadores, aunque no fueran de menor importancia los significados que tenían cada uno de los objetos colocados en el espacio o los que les conferían adicionalmente los fragmentos de texto leídos en

77 Véanse sobre esta realización escénica las ilustrativas reflexiones de Friedemann Kreuder en *Formen des Erinnerns im Theater Klaus Michael Grübers*, Berlín, 2002, especialmente pp. 43-70.

voz alta. Fueron esos significados los que influyeron en su percepción y los que motivaron sus movimientos y acciones, todo lo cual dio lugar a una espacialidad distinta y nueva. Percepción, asociación, recuerdo e imaginación se solapaban, los espacios reales del antiguo Grand Hotel Esplanade se experimentaban simultáneamente como imaginados y como recordados.

El grupo Cornerstone Theater, afincado en Los Ángeles, se sirvió de este procedimiento de un modo completamente distinto cuando realizó su collage de textos de Beckett y Pirandello *Foot/Mouth* (2001) en el Shopping Mall de Santa Mónica. Recibieron a los espectadores en la planta baja, les proveyeron de auriculares y fueron conducidos por uno de los miembros del grupo a una galería de una planta superior, desde la que tenían una buena visibilidad sobre los pisos inferiores. Podían merodear por la galería y también, si les apetecía, por todo el centro comercial. Los actores se movían por todo el Mall, aunque actuaban sobre todo en la galería del piso inferior al de los espectadores, que quedaba casi enfrente de ellos y por la que pasaban los transeúntes. Dado que los espectadores no sabían quiénes eran actores ni de qué dirección venían, en principio cualquier transeúnte se convertía en actor para ellos. Incluso después de haberles aclarado quiénes eran los actores que, en sentido estricto, pertenecían al grupo y quiénes eran sencillamente transeúntes, éstos mantenían su condición de tipo especial de actores y algunos espectadores centraban su atención en ellos de vez en cuando. Algunos transeúntes caminaban pausada o apresuradamente, otros se detenían ante los escaparates de las tiendas, observaban lo expuesto, entraban en las tiendas y, pasado un tiempo más o menos breve, salían de ellas, en la mayor parte de los casos con (nuevas) bolsas. Más de uno se detuvo irritado al ser testigo de cómo una señora mayor (actriz) se inclinaba en la barandilla de tal modo que podía temerse que se arrojase al vacío. Otros transeúntes descubrían a los espectadores con auriculares y permanecían un rato con la mirada clavada en ellos.

En estas circunstancias era difícil saber a quién había que contar entre los actores y a quién entre los espectadores. Cualquiera que pasara por el centro comercial podía convertirse en actor y/o espectador. El tipo de relación que se estableció entre actores y espectadores era distinto en cada caso, dependía de quién veía a quién en qué rol. Todos y cada uno tenían múltiples posibilidades de movimiento y percepción, algo que vale también, y con más motivo, para aquellos que habían comprado una entrada y habían adquirido con ella el singular estatus de espectadores. Independientemente de hacia dónde y de cómo se moviera cada uno de ellos, de adónde dirigiera la mirada, de si se dejaba puestos los auriculares por los que le llegaban las voces de los actores a su oído, o de si se los quitaba de vez en cuando de modo que la algazara y el ajetreo del centro comercial le golpeara en los oídos y ya no pudiera distinguir entre los actores del grupo y los transeúntes, cada vez se originaba una nueva espacialidad en la que la actividad del Mall y la de los actores se solapaban y se superponían de formas cada vez nuevas.

Este principio de generación de espacialidad lo emplea, aunque de forma considerablemente modificada, la compañía «Hygiene heute» en las audioguías que diseña. Hasta hoy se han organizado en Gießen (*Verweis Kirchner [Amonestación Kirchner]* 2000), Fráncfort (*System Kirchner [Sistema Kirchner]* 2000), Múnich (*Kanal Kirchner [Canal Kirchner]* 2001) y Graz (*Kirchners Schwester [La hermana de Kirchner]* 2002). Como ocurre en las audioguías para museos, palacios y otros monumentos históricos, a cada espectador se le entregaba un *walkman* que lo guiaba por un circuito de aproximadamente una hora por la ciudad en cuestión. Se mandaba a los espectadores a realizar el circuito en solitario y en intervalos de quince minutos. La cinta magnetofónica era aparentemente una de las pocas señales de vida que quedaban del bibliotecario Kirchner, que había desaparecido misteriosamente en 1998 sin dejar huella. (En Múnich, según las declaraciones tomadas por la policía, la cinta se encontró en un lavabo público desde el que, como es lógico, daba comienzo el circuito). La voz de la cinta empezaba contando la historia de la desaparición del bibliotecario y envolvía al oyente en una historia en la que era al mismo tiempo perseguidor y perseguido: se encontraba manifiestamente en peligro de caer en una trampa y de ser atrapado por el «caracol». Se convertía así en protagonista de la historia, en el actor principal de la realización escénica. En un enorme aparcamiento subterráneo oía una voz que con respiración acelerada le advertía insistente: «¡Corre! Abre la puerta. El caracol está muy cerca, ¿puedes olerlo? ¡Corre más deprisa, abre la puerta al final del pasillo!». Y en una estación de tranvía la voz le hacía la siguiente advertencia: «Observa a la gente en la parada del tranvía. ¿Ves a los de las maletas?». Dado que en prácticamente todas las paradas de tranvía del centro de la ciudad hay gente con maletas, que en las ciudades hay hombres con camisas azules por todas partes (la voz en Fráncfort aconsejaba precaverse de ellos), que en todos los edificios públicos hay instaladas cámaras de vigilancia (sobre cuya presencia insistía continuamente la voz para aumentar la sensación de persecución), al espectador/actor le resultaba difícil, si no imposible, decidir si eran realmente actores los que pasaban por allí y si hacían el papel de perseguidores. Esta decisión la complicaba todavía más el hecho de que los espectadores/actores que seguían las advertencias de la voz se comportaran de una forma tan llamativa que los transeúntes se detenían y volvían la cabeza hacia ellos. La pregunta era inevitable: los que hacían el papel de perseguidores ¿eran espectadores o también actores? El espectador se convertía en actor sin poder diferenciar entre actores, espectadores y transeúntes.

Al poco tiempo, los espectadores empezaban a percibir con otros ojos la ciudad que tan bien creían conocer. Pasaban por las calles, las plazas, los parques y los edificios que conocían y los experimentaban también como escenarios en los que tenía lugar esa increíble, misteriosa y ficticia historia que le iba contando –con instrucciones, advertencias y aclaraciones– la voz de la cinta magnetofónica, una historia en la que ellos mismos tenían sin duda un papel. Era cada uno de los espectadores el que generaba con sus movimientos por el espacio y con su percepción influida, teñida, por la voz la espacialidad de la ciudad como una curiosa superposición de espacios reales y ficticios, y de personas y acciones reales y ficticias.

Cada uno de los tres procedimientos nos muestra a las claras el espacio performativo como un espacio en continua mudanza en el que la espacialidad tiene su origen en el movimiento y la percepción de actores y espectadores. Mientras que el primer procedimiento se centraba en el proceso por el que la espacialidad se genera a partir del bucle de retroalimentación autopoiético, el segundo dirige su atención al hecho de que a través del espacio performativo circula una energía que es capaz de desplegar un específico potencial efectivo. El tercero, por último, hace que la espacialidad se origine en tanto que superposición de espacios reales e imaginarios, y nos muestra así el espacio performativo como «espacio intermedio».

La espacialidad –como ha quedado claro en los tres casos– no viene dada de antemano, sino que se genera de nuevo permanentemente. El espacio performativo no viene dado –como el geométrico– en tanto que artefacto del que uno o más autores se responsabilizan. No le corresponde el carácter de obra, sino el de acontecimiento.

Atmósferas

El espacio performativo es siempre de por sí un espacio atmosférico. El búnker, la cochera de tranvías, el antiguo Grand Hotel, a cada uno de ellos le corresponde una atmósfera muy especial. La espacialidad no surge únicamente a partir del uso específico que actores y espectadores hacen del espacio, sino también a través de la particular atmósfera que éste parecer irradiar. En el caso del grupo Cornerstone Theater ambos elementos se hallaban vinculados de manera inextricable. Era la posibilidad de moverse por el centro comercial como un *flaneur* y de detenerse en la galería para contemplar lo que ocurría –el ajetreo de un viernes por la tarde en un centro comercial y las situaciones que creaban los actores a partir de los textos de Beckett y de Pirandello, que en esas circunstancias oscilaban constantemente entre realidad y ficción, o las muy variadas reacciones de los transeúntes– la que hacía aflorar la especial atmósfera del centro comercial de una manera tan absolutamente singular y propia que se apoderaba afectivamente de los espectadores que la experimentaban.

Incluso en una distribución convencional del espacio de la que resulte una clara división entre escenario y platea, y que reserve el primero para los actores, la atmósfera contribuye a producir una espacialidad muy particular. Cuando esta espectadora entró en la sala del Volksbühne de Berlín una noche de 1993 en la que se realizaba la pieza *Murx den Europäer! Murx ihn! Murx ihn! Murx ihn! Murx ihn ab!* [*¡Cárgate al europeo! ¡Cárgatelo! ¡Cárgatelo! ¡Cárgatelo! ¡Acaba con él!*], dirigida por Marthaler y con escenografía de Anna Viebrock, la envolvió una atmósfera muy particular. Podríamos describirla como el ambiente propio de una sala de espera, como algo poco acogedor, inquietante, fantasmagórico e irreal. La espectadora vio sobre la escena un espacio que estaba revestido hasta el techo de paneles sintéticos que prolongaban atrozmente el cálido revestimiento de madera de la platea; en el centro había una puerta corredera que daba como a un pasillo, y a derecha e izquierda había sendas puertas de aseos. Sobre la puerta corredera había una especie de reloj de estación parado, y junto a él las palabras: «para que el tiempo no se pare»; en la pared de la derecha había radiadores oxidados y dos enormes estufas de carbón; delante, a la izquierda, había un piano y en medio de la sala dos mesas cuadradas y sillas de plástico dispuestas en dos hileras alineadas sobre las que estaban sentadas, inmóviles, once figuras muy dispares. No era a ninguno de estos elementos tomados individualmente a lo que se debía la especial atmósfera –aunque algunos objetos como el reloj y las estufas de carbón llamaban especialmente su atención–, había que atribuírsela más bien a la impresión de conjunto de todos ellos. Eso fue lo primero que afectó a esta espectadora e influyó en su percepción posterior.

Las atmósferas son atópicas, como explica Gernot Böhme, pero rebosan espacio. No pertenecen ni a los objetos ni a las personas que parecen irradiarlas ni a aquellas personas que entran en la sala y las sienten físicamente. Por regla general son lo primero que atrapa a los espectadores en el espacio teatral, los «tiñe» y hace posible que experimenten la espacialidad de un modo singular. Esto no puede explicarse únicamente recurriendo a elementos concretos del espacio. No son ellos los que crean la atmósfera, sino la conjunción de todos ellos, muy calculada por lo general en las escenificaciones. A Böhme le corresponde el mérito de haber introducido en la estética, partiendo del concepto de aura de Benjamin, aunque modificándolo significativamente, el concepto de atmósfera. Define las atmósferas como «[...] espacios, en la medida en que la presencia de las cosas, de las personas o de las constelaciones que los rodean, esto es, sus «éxtasis», los «tiñen». Ellas mismas son esferas de la presencia de algo, su realidad en el espacio»[78]. Las atmósferas pertenecen, pues, al espacio performativo, no al geométrico:

> [...] no están pensadas como algo que flota libremente, sino, justamente al contrario, como algo que proviene de las cosas, de las personas o de sus constelaciones, y que es creado por ellas. Las atmósferas no se conciben como algo objetivo, como propiedades de las cosas; sin embargo, pertenecen al orden de las cosas, son algo que pertenece a las cosas en la medida en que las cosas, por medio de sus propiedades –consideradas en tanto que éxtasis–, articulan las esferas de su presencia. Las atmósferas tampoco son algo subjetivo, definiciones de un estado mental, por caso. Y, sin embargo, son propias del sujeto, pertenecen a él en la medida en que son sentidas por personas en su presencia física, y en la medida en que, al mismo tiempo, este sentir es para los sujetos un físico encontrarse en el espacio[79].

En esta descripción y definición de atmósfera hay dos aspectos de especial interés para nosotros. Por un lado, Bohme define las atmósferas como «esferas de presencia». Por otro lado, no las localiza ni en las cosas que parecen irradiarlas ni en los sujetos que las experimentan físicamente, sino entre ellos y en ambos al mismo tiempo. Con el concepto «esferas de presencia» se refiere sin duda a una forma específica de actualidad de los objetos. Böhme lo explica como «éxtasis de las cosas», como la forma en que una cosa se hace presente de modo singular a quienes la perciben. Con ello no se quiere decir que el éxtasis sean los colores, los olores o el sonido de una cosa, es decir, sus llamadas cualidades secundarias, sino también sus cualidades primarias, como

78 Böhme, *Atmosphäre. Essays zur neuen Ästhetik*, p. 33.
79 *Ibid.*, pp. 33 y s.

la forma. «La forma de una cosa *opera* [...] también hacia fuera. Irradia en cierta medida todo lo que la rodea, priva al espacio que la rodea de su homogeneidad, lo llena de tensión y sugestiones de movimiento»[80], y de esa manera lo transforma. Lo mismo puede decirse de la extensión y el volumen de una cosa. No deben considerarse sólo como la propiedad de una cosa de ocupar un espacio determinado. «La extensión y el volumen de una cosa [...] pueden sentirse también hacia fuera, le confieren al espacio el peso y la orientación de su presencia»[81].

El éxtasis de las cosas hace que, en tanto que éstas tienen efectos hacia el exterior, aparezcan de modo singular como actuales ante quienes las perciben, y que se apoderen de su atención. El concepto de éxtasis no se refiere exactamente a lo mismo que el de presencia. Ciertamente se orienta también a la actualidad, y no sólo en el sentido del concepto débil de presencia, también en el fuerte. Mientras que en la presencia nos las vemos con procesos energéticos entre personas, a las cosas sólo se les puede atribuir la posesión de energía interna o la capacidad de generarla de forma condicionada. No obstante, de ellas emana algo que no es equiparable a lo que el perceptor pueda ver u oír, algo que, sin embargo, experimenta físicamente al verlo y oírlo, algo que se derrama en el espacio performativo *entre* la cosa y el sujeto que la percibe: una atmósfera específica.

Algo parecido ocurre en el caso del espacio. Cuando el espacio geométrico se convierte en performativo, también sus llamadas cualidades primarias –extensión y volumen– pueden hacerse sentir hacia fuera y tener efectos en quien las percibe.

En una realización escénica, la atmósfera tiene una importancia, tocante a la generación de espacialidad, comparable a la que tiene la presencia para la generación de corporalidad. Para el sujeto que entra en la atmósfera que irradian el espacio y las cosas, éstos se tornan enfáticamente actuales. No es sólo que se le muestren sus llamadas cualidades primarias y secundarias, y que

80 *Ibid.*, p. 33.
81 *Ibid.*

aparezcan ante él en su ser-como-son, llegan incluso a tocar el cuerpo del sujeto perceptor que se encuentra en la atmósfera, a adentrarse en él. El sujeto no se encuentra frente a la atmósfera, no mantiene una distancia con ella, está rodeado y envuelto por ella, sumergido en ella.

Esto es especialmente patente en el caso de los olores que contribuyen a generar las atmósferas. En los teatros nunca faltan los olores –tanto da si son fenómenos indeseados, aunque irremediables, como si son el resultado de una estrategia escénica. Por ello es aún más sorprendente la poca atención que se les ha concedido hasta ahora. Mientras que en el teatro al aire libre son los olores del espacio natural o de la ciudad circundantes los que contribuyen a generar la atmósfera, desde que se generalizaron los teatros cubiertos hasta la invención de la iluminación de gas en los años veinte del siglo diecinueve, los olores provenientes de las velas encendidas, de las lámparas de aceite, y no menos los provenientes del maquillaje, los polvos, el perfume y el sudor de los actores y de los espectadores cumplían la misma función.

Ya en el naturalismo los olores fueron empleados conscientemente para crear determinadas atmósferas. Un apestoso montón de estiércol sobre el escenario y, poco después, el olor a col que se haría proverbial, solían contribuir decisivamente a que los espectadores se dejaran envolver por el ambiente campesino o de pobreza, y a que entraran en contacto físico con él. Max Reinhardt empleó olores para crear distintas atmósferas. Su bosque en *El sueño de una noche de verano* (Neues Theater de Berlín, 1904) no sólo causó sensación porque girara –se trataba de la primera utilización del escenario giratorio desde su invención en 1898, basada en el modelo del teatro Kabuki–, sino también porque el musgo con el que Reinhardt había hecho cubrir el suelo del escenario despedía un olor cautivador que permitía a los espectadores sentir el bosque como actual de un modo muy intenso. Los simbolistas, por su parte, utilizaron olores en el teatro para suscitar determinadas experiencias sinestésicas.

El uso consciente e intencionado de olores partía de la premisa de que éstos se propagan por todo el espacio y dan lugar a efectos físicos intensos en el espectador. Esto se debe sobre todo a que los espacios, los objetos o las personas penetran, con el olor que desprenden, en el cuerpo de quien los huele; el olor se filtra en el cuerpo del sujeto que lo huele. Georg Simmel alude a esta singularidad del olfato cuando escribe:

> Al oler algo absorbemos tan profundamente la impresión o la irradiación del objeto en nosotros, en nuestro centro, la asimilamos, por así decirlo, tan íntimamente mediante el proceso vital de la respiración como ningún otro sentido es capaz de lograrlo con un objeto –si exceptuamos la ingestión. Oler la atmósfera de alguien es la percepción más íntima que podemos tener de él, penetra en nuestra sensibilidad interna, por así decirlo, en forma gaseosa[82].

Desde los años sesenta en el teatro y en el arte de la performance se han empleado los olores en multitud de ocasiones. En el teatro de orgías y misterios de Nitsch era precisamente el olor que despedían el cadáver de cordero, su sangre y sus vísceras lo que hacía que los espectadores se sumergieran en una singular atmósfera, lo que suscitaba en ellos los sentimientos de asco o, en algunos casos, de placer. Grotowski agrupaba a actores y espectadores en un espacio tan pequeño que los espectadores podían oler el sudor de los actores. De esta manera su corporalidad se les hacía presente de un modo tan singular que les hacía sentir intensamente la atmósfera que irradiaban y que se apoderaba del espacio.

Además de los consabidos olores de las máquinas de niebla, son sobre todo los olores a comida los que con más frecuencia se propagan por la sala. En la producción de Johann Kresnik sobre Artaud, *Antonin Nalpas* (Prater, estreno 16 de mayo de 1997), se asaban a la parrilla trozos de un gran pescado. Mientras que su olor despertaba en principio sensaciones agradables, al menos en los espectadores hambrientos, a medida que el proceso iba avanzando y que los trozos de pescado se iban carbonizando, empeza-

82 Georg Simmel, *Soziologie. Untersuchungen über die Form der Vergesellschaftung*, 2. Múnich/ Leipzig, 1922, p. 490 (esp. *Sociología: estudios sobre las formas de socialización*, Madrid, 1986).

ban a extenderse las sensaciones de repugnancia y asco. Algo muy similar les ocurrió a los espectadores de la escenificación de Castorf *Endstation Amerika* [*Última estación: América*] (basada en el texto *Un tranvía llamado deseo*, Volksbühne de Berlín, 2000). Kathrin Angerer se ponía a hacer unos huevos a la plancha que se iban quemando cada vez más y que desprendían el típico olor a clara de huevo carbonizada. En la producción *De Metsiers* del grupo Hollandia (invitados por el Schaubühne de Berlín en 2003), una actriz tomaba una gran botella de cerveza, la abría y rociaba a uno de sus compañeros de arriba a abajo con su contenido. En el suelo del escenario se formaban charcos. Tanto del actor como del suelo del escenario se desprendía un desagradable y penetrante olor a cerveza que rápidamente se extendió por toda la sala. Aunque durante el descanso se limpiaban los charcos de cerveza del escenario, el olor permanecía en la sala hasta el final de la realización escénica y continuaba influyendo en la atmósfera.

Como constató Simmel, sólo ingiriéndolos asimilamos los objetos más intensamente que oliéndolos. Los olores provenientes de la comida y la bebida, al penetrar a través de la respiración, tienen efectos en la producción de saliva en la cavidad bucal y en cierto modo también en las tripas, suscitan intensas sensaciones de placer o de repugnancia. Al asimilarlos, el espectador será consciente de una manera singular de sus procesos físicos internos y se experimentará como un organismo vivo.

El olor es, sin duda, uno de los componentes más esenciales para la generación de atmósferas. Esto tiene que ver también con el hecho de que los olores, una vez se han extendido por el espacio, no pueden ser «retirados» de nuevo, se revelan como elementos de una extraordinaria resistencia. Mucho después de que la niebla se haya disipado del escenario, su olor sigue sintiéndose todavía entre los espectadores. Mucho después de que hayan retirado los huevos calcinados del escenario, su olor permanece en la sala. Y después de haber fregado el escenario, los espectadores, al menos los de las primeras filas, seguían percibiendo en sus narices el olor de la cerveza hasta el final de la realización escénica. El olor se asemeja al famoso genio de la lámpara, que una vez ha salido al mundo es casi imposible de capturar y dominar.

Escapa al control de los actores y de los espectadores y se opone obstinadamente a todo intento de modificar radicalmente la atmósfera.

Ésa es una de las principales razones de que, desde los años sesenta, se haya trabajado tan a menudo con olores en el teatro y en el arte de la performance. Además, se puede constatar que refuerzan también todos los componentes que forman parte de la creación de la atmósfera. Algo que hace posible una especial intensidad en el éxtasis de las cosas, tocante tanto a sus cualidades «primarias» como a sus cualidades «secundarias». Los espacios se emplean de tal modo que incluso su extensión, su volumen y su composición material pueden aflorar vigorosamente, como fue el caso del búnker en *Celtic +~ ~ ~*, de la cochera de tranvías del Bockenheimer Depot en todas las escenificaciones de Einar Schleef o del ábside de hormigón del Schaubühne de Berlín –construido por Mendelssohn– en el *Hamlet* de Grüber (1981) o en *Körper [Cuerpos]* de Sasha Waltz (2000). Además, en algunos casos concretos se instalaron objetos que, precisamente debido a su singular extensión, volumen o composición material, eran capaces de dominar el espacio y la atmósfera, como el gran embudo por el que caía arena en la escenificación de Heiner Goebbels *Die glücklose Landung [El desgraciado aterrizaje]* (1993, TAT/Fráncfort; 1994, Hebbel-Theater de Berlín) o el contenedor de metal que ocupaba el centro del escenario en el más reciente de los montajes de *Hamlet* por parte de Zadek, que se estrenó en el Volkstheater de Viena en mayo de 1999 y que se pudo ver en Berlín, en el Schaubühne de la Lehniner Platz, a partir de septiembre de 1999.

Son sobre todo la luz y el sonido los que contribuyen a la creación de atmósferas y los que pueden modificarlas en una fracción de segundo. Robert Wilson trabaja en sus escenificaciones con una iluminación controlada por computadora que puede realizar más de trescientos ajustes de luz distintos en un intervalo de 120 minutos y cambiar así constantemente la iluminación y los colores. Con ello se modifica al mismo tiempo la atmósfera, aunque debido a la gran velocidad de los cambios de luz esto sucede a menudo por debajo del umbral de la percepción consciente. El hombre no sólo recibe la luz por medio del ojo, lo hace también por la piel. La luz penetra a través de la piel, por así decirlo, en el cuerpo de quien la percibe. El organismo humano reacciona de modo especialmente sensible a la luz. En el caso de un espectador expuesto a continuos cambios de luz, su estado de ánimo puede cambiar muchas veces, y de forma abrupta, sin que él pueda registrarlo conscientemente, y mucho menos controlarlo. La inclinación del espectador a dejarse envolver por la atmósfera durante una realización escénica de Wilson va intensificándose progresivamente debido precisamente a que la ostensible lentitud de movimientos de los actores, que es además conscientemente percibida, desprende una intensa fuerza sugestiva. El espacio performativo aparece aquí sobre todo como un espacio atmosférico.

Los sonidos, los ruidos, los tonos y la música tienen también la capacidad de desarrollar un intenso potencial efectivo atmosférico. Wilson, al que la crítica siempre elogia por la plasticidad de sus imágenes, trabaja en sus escenificaciones con compositores y músicos –Philip Glass, David Byrne, Tom Waits y, sobre todo, Hans Peter Kuhn– que se encargan de que los ruidos, los sonidos, los tonos y la música –desde el sonido de una gota de agua que cae hasta la interpretación de canciones– sean tan decisivos para la atmósfera y sus efectos como la luz.

Los sonidos son comparables con los olores porque rodean al sujeto perceptor, lo envuelven y penetran en su cuerpo. El cuerpo puede convertirse en caja de resonancia de los sonidos que oye, puede resonar con ellos; determinados ruidos pueden incluso causar dolores físicos localizados. El espectador/oyente sólo puede protegerse del sonido si se tapa los oídos. Por lo general está indefenso frente a ellos, como en el caso de los olores. Con ello, los límites corporales se eliminan. Cuando los sonidos, los ruidos o la música convierten el cuerpo del espectador/oyente en su espacio de resonancia, cuando re-suenan en su caja torácica, cuando le causan dolor físico, le ponen la piel de gallina o le revuelven las tripas, el espectador/oyente deja de oírlos como algo externo que se adentra en sus oídos, los siente como un proceso corporal interno que a menudo desencadena una sensación «oceánica». Por medio de los sonidos, la atmósfera se adentra en el cuerpo del espectador y lo abre para ella.

Además de Wilson, Heiner Goebbels y Christoph Marthaler nos dan ejemplos especialmente destacados de ello. En *Murx*, por ejemplo, la atmósfera inicial de miseria y desolación cómico-grotesca cambiaba repentinamente cada vez que los actores se reunían en coro y entonaban una canción. Su canto permitía olvidar el deprimente horror del ambiente de sala de espera, la mezquindad y la hostilidad con las que los personajes se atacaban. Su canto parecía liberarles a ellos, y a los espectadores, de esa deprimente cotidianidad, parecía crear una atmósfera rebosante de abundancia, concordia y armonía, hacía resplandecer la utopía de que liberarse de toda la deprimente adversidad de una cotidianidad nimia e insignificante era posible. Una vez extinguido el sonido del canto, cuando ni siquiera reverberaba su eco en la sala, la atmósfera lúgubre volvía a extenderse por el teatro turbando a los espectadores.

Desde los años sesenta, el teatro y el arte de la performance hacen aflorar enfáticamente el espacio performativo como espacio atmosférico. Con la vista puesta en una estética de lo performativo, resultan especialmente significativos tres aspectos. En primer lugar, queda meridianamente claro que la espacialidad en las realizaciones escénicas no tiene carácter de obra sino de acontecimiento, que es fugaz y transitoria. En segundo lugar, el espectador siente su corporalidad en el espacio atmosférico de un modo muy singular. Se experimenta como un organismo vivo, está en una situación de interacción con su entorno. La atmósfera penetra en su organismo superando las fronteras corporales. Con ello el espacio performativo se define, en tercer lugar, como un espacio liminar en el que tienen lugar transformaciones y se producen modificaciones.

Böhme desarrolló su estética de la atmósfera como antítesis a una estética semiótica. Mientras que la estética semiótica parte del supuesto de que habría que entender el arte como un lenguaje, y que por lo tanto ha de centrarse en procesos de generación de significado, la estética de las atmósferas dirige su atención a la experiencia física. Comparto con Böhme la asunción de que es necesario desplazar el centro de interés de los significados a la experiencia física. Me pregunto, sin embargo, si a partir de la experiencia física, y especialmente a partir de la experiencia de las atmósferas, puede excluirse completamente la dimensión del significado. El efecto de las atmósferas no se puede explicar, a partir del esquema de estímulo-respuesta, como un reflejo fisiológico que se desencadenaría automáticamente en cada sujeto que las percibe, que las siente físicamente, del mismo modo que uno cierra automáticamente los ojos cuando un cuerpo extraño se acerca a ellos. Tanto las cosas –el contenedor en *Hamlet* o las estufas de carbón en *Murx*– como los olores y sonidos que se desprenden de ellas –el olor a pescado asado en *Antonin Nalpas* o el ruido de las gotas de agua cayendo en el *Lear* de Wilson (Schauspielhaus Fráncfort, Bockenheimer Depot 1990)–, así como determinados ajustes de luz –como la luz cegadora que lo invadía todo después de que a Gloucester le sacaran los ojos en el *Lear* de Wilson– pueden poseer una capacidad de significado plena para el espectador, pueden desencadenar, en efecto, contextos y situaciones, o suscitar recuerdos con una fuerte carga emocional para el sujeto que los percibe. Es impensable que esta dimensión significativa de las cosas carezca totalmente de importancia para la capacidad efectiva de las atmósferas. Parto del hecho de que a tales significados les corresponde sin duda una parte en el intenso efecto que producen las atmósferas. De qué modo se relaciona en ellas la materialidad de las cosas, que se manifiesta en sus éxtasis, con los significados que pueden tener para el sujeto perceptor, será algo que discutiremos detalladamente más adelante[83].

3. Sonoridad

Para poder entender la fugacidad de las realizaciones escénicas, la sonoridad es en verdad de primera importancia. ¿Qué puede haber más fugaz que la sonoridad de un sonido? Emerge del silencio del espacio, se expande por él para volver a extinguirse un instante después, se disipa y desaparece. A pesar de esa fugaci-

83 Véase el capítulo quinto «Emergencia de significado».

dad, tiene un efecto inmediato –y a menudo duradero– en quien lo oye. No le transmite sólo una sensación de espacio (recordemos que nuestro sentido del equilibrio se encuentra en el oído), penetra en su cuerpo y a menudo es capaz de desencadenar reacciones fisiológicas y afectivas. Un escalofrío recorre todo el cuerpo del oyente, se le pone la piel de gallina, su pulso se acelera, su respiración se entrecorta y se intensifica; cae en la melancolía, se siente eufórico o se apodera de él un anhelo de *je-ne-sais-quoi*, se le agolpan los recuerdos, etc. A la sonoridad, como se ha explicado en el apartado anterior, le es inherente un intenso potencial efectivo.

El teatro nunca es sólo un espacio visual *(theatron)*, es siempre también un espacio sonoro *(auditorium)*[84]. En él resuenan voces que hablan o cantan, música, ruidos. Ya en el teatro griego se trabajaba con efectos especiales de sonido. Así, se recreaba el ruido del trueno con el *bronteion*, que se construía con un recipiente de algún mineral que se cubría con un trozo de piel en tensión sobre el que, al agitarlo, golpeaban unas bolas de plomo que había en su interior, o simplemente con un recipiente de algún metal que se llenaba con piedras y que se sacudía con fuerza.

Está muy extendida en suplementos culturales, en el mundo académico e incluso en el ámbito de los estudios literarios, la opinión de que el teatro europeo se distingue del de otras culturas por el hecho de que su sonoridad es equiparable en buena medida al lenguaje hablado. De esto se concluye que en la realización escénica la sonoridad como tal no sería en verdad relevante, que sería meramente transmisora de lenguaje, un medio en el que, y a través del que, el lenguaje hace su aparición. Sabemos, sin embargo, que ya en el teatro griego no se limitaban a recitar. Tanto las recitaciones de tetrámetros trocaicos, propias de las tragedias, como las de los largos versos yámbicos y anapésticos de las comedias antiguas se acompañaban con la flauta en el

84 Véase Erika Fischer-Lichte, «Berliner Antikenprojekte», en Doris Kolesch y Christel Weiler (eds.), *Berliner Theater im 20. Jahrhundert*, Berlín, 1998, pp. 77-100, en especial pp. 93-96.

momento de la parabase. Todas las partes de texto de composición lírica se cantaban, en parte alternando con el coro (como en los lamentos por las muertes en la tragedia: el *Commos*), en parte como virtuosos solos de arias. No se puede hablar, pues, de la preeminencia del lenguaje hablado.

Ello es aún más evidente a partir de la invención de la ópera, que surgió a finales del siglo dieciséis como resultado del esfuerzo de la Camerata Florentina para revivir la tragedia griega. Desde entonces, son sobre todo los géneros del teatro musical, precisamente aquellos en los que la sonoridad va más allá de su mera condición de intermediaria del lenguaje, los responsables del gran atractivo y de la positiva acogida que tienen entre un publico muy amplio la ópera, el *Singspiel* alemán, el ballet, más tarde la opereta y, ya por último, el musical. Tampoco en el teatro dramático se tiene por incontestable la preeminencia del carácter lingüístico de la voz. Al margen de la particularidad de que hasta finales del siglo dieciocho las realizaciones escénicas constaban de series de números teatrales que por lo general incluían una pieza musical –a menudo como acompañamiento para el ballet con el que terminan–, la realización escénica de la obra misma la interrumpían también algunas piezas musicales. Durante los entreactos, mientras el encargado de las velas recortaba sus mechas para mantener la cantidad de humo en sala en un nivel soportable, sonaba la llamada música de entreactos. Casi hasta mediados del siglo dieciocho esta música no solía tener nada que ver con la pieza. Sin embargo, a finales de los años treinta de ese siglo la primera actriz Friederike Caroline Neuber y el compositor Johann Adolph Scheibe empezaron a trabajar juntos, una colaboración de la que resultaría el nuevo arte de los entreactos. Scheibe defendía la idea de que entre la música y las acciones de los actores, sus caracteres y sus afectos, debía haber una vinculación[85]. La música tenía que desempeñar, así, una función dramatúrgica que estaba encaminada sobre todo «a conducir a los

85 En el número 67 de la revista *Der Critische Musicus*, que él mismo editaba, Scheibe formula los nuevos principios de la siguiente manera: «La sinfonía de aper-

espectadores, sin que lo notaran, de un estado de ánimo a otro»[86]. Siguiendo este criterio, Scheibe compuso para Neuber la música de *Polyeuctes* y *Mithridates*, que se presentaron en Hamburgo el 30 de abril y el 2 de junio de 1738 respectivamente. Ya a finales del siglo dieciocho, y durante el diecinueve, la música para el teatro dejó de limitarse a los entreactos y empezó a componerse para determinadas partes o secuencias de la obra[87].

En las realizaciones escénicas en las que intervenían los personajes cómicos polichinela o arlequín y, posteriormente, Bernadon (Felix von Kurz, 1717-1784), así como en las realizaciones

tura de una obra dramática [...] tiene que [...] hacer referencia al conjunto de la obra y, al mismo tiempo, preparar para su arranque, consecuentemente tiene que estar en consonancia con la primera salida a escena, [...] Las sinfonías que suenen entre los actos han de orientarse de acuerdo al final del acto previo y al principio del siguiente. Tienen que conectar un acto con el otro y conducir de consuno a los espectadores, sin que lo noten, de un estado de ánimo a otro. Por eso está muy bien dividir las piezas en dos movimientos. En el primero puede uno hacer referencia al acto previo y en el segundo al posterior. Ello es necesario, no obstante, sólo en el caso de que la sentimentalidad de uno y otro sean muy opuestas, si no fuera así se puede escribir un solo movimiento, siempre y cuando tenga la duración suficiente para que se puedan limpiar las luces y para que se hagan, en su caso, los cambios de vestuario necesarios. Cuando se haya llegado al final de la obra, la sinfonía que lo siga habrá de concordar con él hasta en el más mínimo detalle para hacer la vivencia del espectador aún más intensa. ¿Hay algo más ridículo que ver cómo el héroe pierde la vida de forma desgraciada y que acto seguido empiece a sonar una sinfonía alegre y vivaz? ¿Hay algo de peor gusto que ver terminar una comedia de final feliz y que le siga una sinfonía triste y conmovedora?». Johann Adolph Scheibe, *Der Critische Musicus*, Leipzig, 1745, p. 616.

86 *Ibid.*

87 Dado que la música para el teatro se consideraba una especie de «música de consumo», la teoría musical la desatendió durante mucho tiempo. No se ha empezado a estudiar con seriedad hasta hace muy poco. Véase Detlef Altenburg, «Das Phantom des Theaters. Zur Schauspielmusik im späten 18. und frühen 19. Jahrhundert», en Hans-Peter Bayderdörfer (ed.), *Stimmen - Klänge - Töne. Synergien im szenischen Spiel* (=*Forum Modernes Theater* 30), Tubinga, 2002, pp. 183-208; «Von den Schubladen der Wissenschaft. Zur Schauspielkunst im klassisch-romantischen Zeitalter», en Helen Geyer/Michael Berg/Matthias Tischer (eds.), *Denn in jenen Tränen lebt es. Festschrift Wolfgang Marggraf*, Weimar, 1999, pp. 425-449; «Schauspielmusik», en *Die Musik in Geschichte und Gegenwart*, 2ª ed. revisada, Ludwig Finscher (ed.), vol. 8, Kassel, 1998, pp. 1046-1049.

escénicas del Volkstheater de Viena, incluso en las obras de Raimund y Nestroy, abundaban las canciones y el acompañamiento musical –al principio se trataba de «arias», después serían «cuplés»–. Fue Nestroy el que introdujo en Viena el nuevo género teatral de la opereta que, en cierto modo, debía reemplazar al teatro popular. El 16 de octubre de 1858 se estrenó *Hochzeit bei Laternenschein [Boda a la luz de las farolas]* de Jacques Offenbach en el Carltheater, que dirigía el propio Nestroy. Con ello daba comienzo la marcha triunfal de la opereta en Viena. En la opereta *Orpheus in der Unterwelt [Orfeo en el inframundo]*, que Nestroy estrenó en el Carltheater en 1860 según la traducción que Ludwig Kalischs había preparado para su realización escénica en Breslau en 1859, él mismo hacía el papel de Pan: «Nestroy, haciendo de Pan, ha ampliado el repertorio de sus creaciones cómicas con una interpretación magistral. Ha sido una interpretación, una forma de hablar y de cantar de irresistible comicidad»[88].

Ya en el siglo veinte, siguió empleándose la música en el teatro –a veces incluso de manera exagerada–. Reinhardt hacía que compusieran música para cada una de sus escenificaciones –y no solamente, ni mucho menos, en el caso de las pantomimas como *Sumurun*–. Además, introducía ruidos a propósito, sobre todo para la creación de determinadas atmósferas. Así, la realización escénica de *El mercader de Venecia* (Deutsches Theater de Berlín, 1905) se abría con un preámbulo que Engelbert Humperdinck había compuesto a partir de diversos ruidos. Al principio se oían voces de animales, luego un traqueteo, un martilleo y un tableteo seguidos de gritos de gondoleros. Se iban añadiendo más voces, cada vez más hasta que todas se confundían en el ruido de la muchedumbre: la ciudad se acababa de despertar. Sonaban un canto y lejanas notas de violín que, casi imperceptibles al principio, terminaban convirtiéndose en música militar. Sobre esta composición escribe Bruno Walter: «una marcial marcha militar [...] de la que el oyente no es en absoluto consciente y que, sin

88 *Blätter für Theater, Musik und Kunst*, Viena, 5 de marzo de 1861, p. 75.

embargo, eleva a los cielos –precisamente de manera inconsciente– incluso al ánimo más alegre e intenso»[89].

Como muestra este breve panorama, en el teatro europeo la generación de la sonoridad no era en ningún caso responsabilidad exclusiva, ni siquiera primordial, de las voces lingüísticas, del lenguaje hablado. El teatro como espacio sonoro lo constituyen más bien, en una proporción que, no obstante, varía según el género y la época: la música, las voces –hablando, cantando, riendo, sollozando, gritando– y distintas clases de ruidos. En ese proceso, la voz de los actores tiene una importancia crucial. A partir de este hallazgo surgen sobre todo dos preguntas para el estudio de la sonoridad en las realizaciones escénicas desde los años sesenta: 1) ¿Qué tipo de espacio sonoro se genera en ellas? 2) ¿En qué aspectos de la vocalidad hay que centrar la atención?

Espacios sonoros

Los ejemplos históricos aducidos evidencian que no fue hasta el siglo dieciocho que se consideraron como constitutivos del espacio sonoro teatral únicamente aquellos sonidos, tonos y ruidos que los artífices del teatro –actores, músicos y técnicos– producían durante la realización escénica. En efecto, había clara conciencia de que también el público generaba ruidos continuamente, algo que generaba un creciente disgusto. Se consideraba que entorpecía la realización escénica y, consecuentemente, se intentaba combatir. Así Reichard, el editor del *Theater-Kalender* de Gotha, se lamentaba en la edición de 1781 del ruido que producían los espectadores: «Para los oyentes y espectadores atentos es un tormento que el resto se dedique a hacer un ruido tal con la bocaza, con los pies o con el bastón que no se puede entender nada de lo que dicen los actores»[90]. «La muchedumbre y el

89 Bruno Walter en «Gespräch über Reinhardt mit Hugo von Hofmannsthal, Alfred Roller und Bruno Walter (1910)», en Max Reinhardt, *Schriften. Briefe, Reden, Aufsätze, Interviews, Gespräche und Auszüge aus den Regiebüchern*, Hugo Fetting (ed.), Berlín, 1974, p. 383.

90 Heinrich August Ottokar Reichard (ed.), *Theater-Kalender auf das Jahr 1781*, Gotha, 1781, pp. 57 y s.

ruido» importunaban a Reichard de tal modo que propuso publicar en los programas de mano lo siguiente a modo de amenaza: «Todo aquel que moleste a los demás espectadores con ruidos o con un comportamiento impropio será expulsado de la sala»[91]. Quejas muy parecidas se pudieron oír hasta bien entrado el siglo diecinueve. Así protestaba el director de teatro de Hamburgo Friedrich Ludwig Schmidt: «los retrasos, el tableteo de los asientos y el crujir de los vestidos son habituales entre la mayoría de los espectadores, los mismos que –como se pierden partes esenciales de la obra– más tarde se sorprenden cuando no pueden seguirla»[92]. Había que disciplinar al público, hacer que permaneciera en su asiento quieto y en silencio, que prestara atención, sin distraerse, a lo que ocurría sobre el escenario, a los sonidos que emitían los actores. Un proyecto que no llegó a completarse jamás. A la altura de los años cincuenta del siglo veinte, sin embargo, el público había interiorizado estas exigencias hasta el punto de que se esforzaba con ahínco en no hacer ruido, a pesar de que los estornudos y los movimientos de los pies nunca se llegaban a reprimir del todo.

El 29 de abril de 1952 tuvo lugar en el Maverick Hall de Woodstock (Nueva York) el estreno de *4'33"*, la primera *Silent Piece* de John Cage. La pieza constaba de tres movimientos. El pianista David Tudor apareció en escena con un frac negro y se sentó frente al piano. Abrió la tapa y permaneció un rato ante el piano abierto, sin tocarlo. Cerró la tapa. Treinta y tres segundos después la abrió de nuevo. Poco más tarde volvió a cerrar la tapa y la abrió otra vez después de dos minutos y cuarenta segundos. Cerró la tapa una tercera vez, en esta ocasión durante un minuto y veinte segundos. Entonces la abrió por última vez. La pieza había terminado. David Tudor no había tocado una sola nota al piano. Se levantó e hizo una reverencia al público.

91 *Ibid.*, p. 58.

92 Friedrich Ludwig Schmidt, *Denkwürdigkeiten des Schauspielers, Schauspieldichters und Schauspieldirectors Friedrich Ludwig Schmidt (1772-1841)*, Herrmann Uhde (ed.), 2 vols., Stuttgart, 1878, vol. 2, p. 175.

El artista participó en la generación del espacio sonoro únicamente con el ruido de sus pasos y con los sonidos de la tapa del piano al cerrarlo. Es decir, que el espacio sonoro, en gran medida, no lo generó el artista, sino los ruidos que, provenientes del exterior o producidos por el público, se oían en la sala. Surgió no como consecuencia de sonidos que se hubieran producido con la intención de crear la sonoridad de la realización escénica, sino que emergió a partir de la combinación o de la sucesión de sonidos que se oían de manera casual, como los del viento, la lluvia o el del disgusto de algunos espectadores. Los espectadores/oyentes no los entendieron, sin embargo, como pertenecientes a la realización escénica. Dado que el pianista no había tocado, creían no oír nada más que un silencio que los irritaba. En cualquier caso, no se sintieron animados a participar, es decir, a escuchar el silencio y a percibir los ruidos que surgieran casualmente, o incluso a añadir algunos propios conscientemente. A los ojos de Cage «la mayoría de la gente no entendió lo esencial. El silencio no existe. Lo que les parecía silencio rebosaba de ruidos azarosos, algo que los oyentes no entendieron porque les faltaba capacidad auditiva para ello. Durante el primer movimiento [en el estreno] se podían oír los aullidos del viento en el exterior. Durante el segundo, la lluvia golpeaba el tejado, y durante el tercero el público realizó todo tipo de ruidos interesantes al hablar o al abandonar la sala»[93].

El espacio sonoro de la realización escénica, su sonoridad, lo generó precisamente todo aquello que hasta entonces se creía debía mantenerse lo más lejos posible: los sonidos que se colaban desde fuera y los ruidos que hacía el público al toser, al arrastrar los pies, al hablar, al levantarse, o al abrir y cerrar las puertas de la sala. La sonoridad no había sido planificada, no era previsible ni dependiente de la intervención de una sola persona. Por un lado, se debía al bucle de retroalimentación autopoiético, es decir, que la generaron las acciones del actor y de los espectadores que en gran medida no eran ni planificables ni previsibles.

93 John Cage, en Richard Kostelanetz, *Cage im Gespräch*, Colonia, 1989, p. 63.

Por otro lado, se debía a sonidos que no tenían su origen en ninguno de los participantes en la realización escénica, sonidos cuyo origen había que buscarlo en sucesos que tenían lugar fuera del espacio escénico, que no se podían calcular y sobre los que no se podía ejercer influencia: las sacudidas del viento o la caída del agua. Se hacía evidente, pues, la indisponibilidad de la sonoridad, que escapaba a las intenciones, los planes y las maquinaciones de los individuos y que acontecía imprevisiblemente. Diversos sonidos se hacían presentes en la sala, se propagaban por ella en intervalos de tiempo desiguales, sonaban al tiempo y, cada uno distinto a los demás, volvían a desvanecerse. La sonoridad cambiaba permanentemente, se transformaba continuamente. Es obvio que no tenía carácter de obra, sino de acontecimiento*.

Además, la generación del espacio sonoro tuvo como resultado un ensanchamiento de los límites del espacio performativo. El espacio sonoro se expande por el espacio geométrico en el que tiene lugar la realización escénica, conquista el espacio circundante. El espacio performativo pierde así sus fronteras, que se abren a espacios «externos». La frontera entre dentro y fuera se hace permeable. El espacio circundante penetra en el espacio performativo a través de sonidos y ruidos, y lo amplía de manera insospechada: todo lo que azarosamente se oiga pasa a formar parte de la realización escénica y está en condiciones de modificar el espacio performativo.

Cage califica esta experiencia como experiencia expresamente teatral: «pienso que lo que diferenciaba mi trabajo del de otros [...][94], lo que lo hacía distinto, es que era más teatral. Mis experiencias son teatrales»[95]. Precisamente son la carencia de intención y de planificación, la apertura a lo que pueda acontecer, la

* El artista de performance berlinés Jörg Laue trabaja según este principio con su grupo «Lose Combo». Véase al respecto Christel Weiler, «Bilderloses Licht. *Mythos Europa* von Jörg Laue», en *Theater der Zeit*, mayo/junio 1999, pp. 48 y ss.

94 Se refiere a Earle Brown, Morton Feldman, Christian Wolff y David Tudor, con los que Cage colaboró estrechamente en los años cincuenta.

95 John Cage, cit. por William Furlong, *Audio Arts*, Leipzig ,1992, p. 91.

indisponibilidad, el azar, la fugacidad y el carácter de constante alteración sin intervención externa, lo que define el concepto de teatro de Cage. Es por ello que la realización de *4'33"* le pareció el epítome de lo teatral: «qué podría tener más que ver con el teatro que una pieza silenciosa, que alguien aparezca en escena y no haga absolutamente nada»[96]. Se limitó a dejar que ocurriera lo que tuviera que ocurrir, pero sin que él pudiera intervenir.

Aunque la *Silent Piece* pueda suponer un caso extremo en algunos aspectos, los principios en los que estaba basada siguieron siendo fundamentales para los posteriores trabajos teatrales de Cage. Para asegurar su validez y eficacia incluso en los casos en los que los actores tenían que hacer algo –algo incluso preparado, planificado–, Cage introdujo las operaciones casuales y los segmentos temporales *(time brackets)*. Para las *Europeras I & II* (Fráncfort, 1987), por ejemplo, Cage eligió mediante operaciones casuales sesenta y cuatro óperas que no estuvieran protegidas por derechos de autor de la lista de las disponibles en la Metropolitan Opera, y las combinó sobre la base del libro chino *I Ching*, o *Libro de las transformaciones*. Con este procedimiento se estableció de qué ópera tomaría su parte cada instrumento. Por medio de unas operaciones casuales aún más precisas, se determinó qué fragmentos se iban a tocar finalmente. Los segmentos temporales indicaban el instante inicial y final de cada fragmento. Cada miembro de la orquesta ensayaba su parte al margen de los demás. Los diecinueve cantantes, provenientes de las más diversas especialidades: ópera dramática, lírica y bufa, cubrían todos los registros vocales. Cantaban, en los segmentos temporales previstos, arias que habían escogido ellos mismos de su repertorio.

El espacio escénico se dividió, de acuerdo con lo previsto en el *I Ching*, en 64 partes. En este espacio se les asignaban sus respectivas posiciones a los cantantes y a sus «asistentes» (bailarines y tramoyistas) mediante un programa de ordenador diseñado por el compositor Andrew Culver para generar combinaciones casua-

96 John Cage en Kostelanetz, *Cage im Gespräch*, p. 95.

les y se decidían las acciones que cada uno de ellos tenía que llevar a cabo, así como la ubicación de los miembros de la orquesta y de la utilería. Los instrumentistas estaban repartidos por todo el espacio escénico, incluido el foso de la orquesta. Cuatro grupos de músicos con instrumentos de viento, metal y cuerda, de cuatro miembros cada uno, estaban colocados en las cuatro esquinas de la sala a modo de grupos de música de cámara. Los encargados de los instrumentos de percusión estaban de pie o sentados en el foso de la orquesta. En el escenario y en la platea se instalaron altavoces por los que sonaba un mix de ciento una óperas realizado en Nueva York según un cronograma establecido por medio de operaciones casuales.

La utilización de las operaciones casuales garantizaba que ningún material empleado en la realización escénica fuera planificado o elegido con una intención específica. De ello se seguía que los elementos seleccionados no tuvieran nada que ver entre sí, no había entre ellos ningún tipo de referencia o relación buscadas. Además, a los «asistentes» se les pedía que registraran con micrófonos de contacto los posibles sonidos y ruidos que se produjeran en el teatro y que, tanto si provenían de la platea como si habían entrado desde el exterior, los hicieran audibles para los actores y el resto de los espectadores. De este modo a los espectadores se les devolvían, intensificados, los ruidos que ellos mismos habían hecho, se les hacía conscientes de que también ellos, como espectadores, tomaban parte en la generación del espacio sonoro, de la sonoridad de la realización escénica.

Dado que los segmentos temporales señalaban meramente el inicio y el final de las acciones y que la duración de los materiales musicales –ganados por medio de las operaciones casuales y hechos audibles por ellas, o de las arias escogidas por los cantantes– no coincidían en absoluto con la mayor duración posible prevista, en todas las realizaciones escénicas se producían desfases que no estaban planeados ni acordados. Asimismo, el espacio sonoro que surgía en cada realización escénica era distinto cada vez –sobre todo porque los ruidos provenientes de la platea y del exterior eran distintos cada día–. La casualidad, el carácter fugaz e indisponible de la sonoridad, su carácter de acontecimiento se hacía presente de forma enfática. El espacio performativo se modificaba continuamente justamente en tanto que espacio sonoro, sus límites se disipaban y se expandía más allá del espacio geométrico en el que la realización escénica tenía lugar.

Voces

La sonoridad genera siempre espacialidad y, como hemos visto, no sólo en el sentido de espacio atmosférico. La vocalidad, además, produce siempre corporalidad. Con y en la voz se originan los tres tipos de materialidad: la corporalidad, la espacialidad y la sonoridad. La voz suena al arrancársele al cuerpo y vibra en el espacio, razón por la que es audible tanto para el cantante/hablante como para los demás. La estrecha relación entre cuerpo y voz se manifiesta sobre todo al gritar, suspirar, gemir, sollozar o reír. Todas esas actividades se producen en procesos que, innegablemente, afectan a todo el cuerpo, que se dobla, se contorsiona o se tensa al máximo. Asimismo, estas expresiones de la voz exentas de palabras pueden conmover corporalmente hasta lo más profundo a quien las oye. Quien oye el grito de una persona, quien la oye suspirar, gemir, sollozar o reír, percibe procesos de corporización específicos, es decir, percibe procesos por los que se genera la singular corporalidad de cada cual. Se percibe a la persona en cuestión en su físico estar-en-el-mundo, lo cual afecta al mismo tiempo de manera inmediata a quien lo percibe en su propio físico estar-en-el-mundo, pues al oír el grito, el sollozo o la risa, la voz que grita, solloza o ríe penetra en su cuerpo, re-suena en él, es recibida por él[97]. Los momentos en los que, durante una realización escénica, un actor profiere un grito, suspira, gime o ríe, pueden ser considerados y experimentados, por lo tanto, como momentos en los que el actor hace audible su voz en su singular fisicalidad, en la sensibilidad que le es propia[98].

97 Véase al respecto Helmuth Plessner, «Lachen und Weinen», en Günter Dux (ed.), *Philosophische Anthropologie*, Fráncfort, 1970, pp. 11-171 (esp. *La risa y el llanto: investigación sobre los límites del comportamiento humano*, Madrid, 2007).

98 Véase Clemens Risi, «Die bewegende Sängerin. Zu stimmlichen und körper-

Ahora bien, en una realización escénica oímos sobre todo voces que cantan o hablan, voces que tienen un vínculo indisoluble con el lenguaje. Desde el siglo diecisiete, tanto en la retórica como en las lecciones de declamación, que por algo provienen de ella, se entendía que en ese vínculo el lenguaje tenía prevalencia. El actor ha de emplear su voz de modo que, tocante a lo enunciado, cumpla una función parasintáctica, parasemántica y pragmática. Es decir, que en primer lugar la voz tenía que hacer explícita la estructura sintáctica de lo enunciado; en segundo lugar, tenía que poner de relieve y subrayar su significado; y, por último, tenía que intensificar el efecto que lo enunciado quería causar en el oyente. Así, Goethe explica en sus *Regeln für Schauspieler [Reglas para actores]* (1803) que:

> Cuando, en primer lugar, entiendo el sentido de las palabras completamente y lo he interiorizado en su integridad, debo intentar acompañarlas del tono de voz adecuado y pronunciarlas con más o menos fuerza y con más velocidad o lentitud, según lo requiera el sentido de cada frase. Por ejemplo:

La multitud murmura	debe pronunciarse en tono medio, murmurando.
Nombres resuenan	debe pronunciarse con claridad, resonante,
El tenebroso olvido	} debe pronunciarse de manera
extiende sus alas	} ronca
negras como la noche	} profunda
sobre linajes enteros	} escalofriante

> Y en el siguiente fragmento:
>
> *«Arrojado súbitamente de mi corcel*
> *me apresuro tras él...»*

lichen Austauschprozessen in Opernaufführungen», en Christa Brüstle / Albrecht Rietmüller (eds.), *Klang und Bewegung. Beitrage zu einer Grundkonstellation*, Aquisgrán, 2003.

con otro tempo, mucho más rápido que en el fragmento anterior, pues es el propio contenido de las palabras el que lo requiere[99].

En efecto, la voz debía ponerse, sin la menor reserva, al servicio de lo enunciado. Según esta concepción, su única tarea era facilitar la comprensión de las palabras.

Con el naturalismo se introdujo una modificación importante. El vínculo entre voz y lenguaje, hasta entonces indisoluble, se distiende. La voz podía emplearse de modo que ya no tuviera que coincidir –en entonación, prosodia, tono o volumen– con las palabras que pronunciara: mientras que las palabras parecían denotar un cálido saludo, de la voz –así como también, en su caso, de la expresión del rostro, de los gestos, de los movimientos– podía inferirse temor o incluso agresividad. Se produjo así una ruptura que remitía a la contradicción entre la conducta voluntaria y consciente y la actitud que se mostraba en realidad, y que quizá fuera meramente inconsciente: mientras que el lenguaje puede mentir, el cuerpo se considera sincero y auténtico. Asimismo, la voz, como las demás manifestaciones corporales, revela el «verdadero» estado de ánimo del personaje, incluso aunque se le oculte a él mismo. En este caso, la voz y el lenguaje se desvinculan. Aunque esta desvinculación ha de ser interpretada y entendida con miras al personaje.

Muy distinta es, por el contrario, la tensión que parece existir desde la invención de la ópera entre voz y lenguaje. Los eslóganes cambian una y otra vez: «*Prima la musica/la voce, poi le parole*» o «*Prima le parole, poi la musica/la voce*». Pero esta relación, a pesar de que cuando se inventó la ópera se les dio prevalencia a las palabras sobre la voz con pautas como *parlar cantando* o *recitativo*, se invirtió –pese a las repetidas exigencias en contra– durante el desarrollo posterior de la ópera, que forzaba a tonos cada vez más altos. Efectivamente, cuanto más alto fuera el tono en el que había que cantar, más se escindía la voz del lenguaje. En los tonos más altos no se puede articular inteligiblemente:

99 Johann Wolfgang von Goethe, «Regeln für Schauspieler», en *Sämtliche Werke in 18 Bänden*, 14, Schriften zur Literatur, Zúrich, 1977, pp. 72-90, pp. 77 y s.

> Es más probable que el público comprenda mejor a un cantante cuando la mayor parte de su tesitura (el rango de frecuencias que puede ser emitido sin dificultad) se encuentra en una zona de inteligibilidad óptima; en otras palabras, por debajo de 312 Hz. No debe sorprendernos el hecho de que un bajo sea más fácilmente comprensible que una soprano, pues hay que tener en cuenta que toda la tesitura del bajo está en la zona de inteligibilidad óptima, mientras que sólo la cuarta parte de la tesitura de la soprano, y únicamente una quinta parte de la tesitura de la coloratura soprano (la voz femenina más alta), cae dentro de esta zona[100].

Y es precisamente cuando la voz de la cantante llega a esas alturas en las que las palabras no pueden ya entenderse, cuando causa un escalofrío de placer en el oyente que se convierte en un escalofrío de espanto a medida que el canto se aproxima al grito. Hay que tener en cuenta que de ningún modo es la imposibilidad de comprender el texto cantado como tal la que causa este efecto. Éste es más bien debido a la paulatina escisión con respecto al significado que culmina en las coloraturas o al alcanzar una determinada altura de tono, cuando la voz deja atrás cualquier tipo de significado y le habla al oyente «con el grito del ángel» (Poizat 1986). Se trata de la inexplicable e increíble combinación entre sensualidad y transfiguración que desencadena en el oyente un efecto igualmente inexplicable e increíble: el mayor de los placeres y el más profundo de los miedos.

En su ensayo sobre la *Ópera burguesa* (1955) Adorno resalta esta singularidad del canto operístico:

> [...] la ópera [...] tiene que ver con los hombres empíricos, y ciertamente con aquellos que están reducidos a su mera esencia natural. Esto explica el carácter peculiar de su vestuario: los mortales se visten como si fueran héroes o dioses, y este atuendo es de la misma

100 Nicole Scotto di Carlo, «Travaux de l'Institut de phonétique d'Aix-en-Provence», en *La Recherche*, mayo, 1978, cit. por Michel Poizat, en *L'Opéra ou le cri de l'ange: essai sur la jouissance de l'amateur d'opéra*, París, 1986, p. 68.

> naturaleza que lo que cantan. El canto los eleva y transfigura. [...] Aunque el gesto de las personas dramáticas al cantar engaña en el hecho de que, por más que ya estilizadas, tienen pocas razones para cantar como lo hacen a la mínima oportunidad, ahí resuena algo de la esperanza en la reconciliación con la naturaleza: el canto, utopía de la existencia prosaica, es también al mismo tiempo el recuerdo de la situación prelingüística, indivisa, de la creación [...] El canto de la ópera es el lenguaje de la pasión: prevalece no sólo la exagerada estilización de la existencia, sino también la expresión de que la naturaleza persiste en el hombre contra toda convención y mediación, una invocación de la inmediatez pura[101].

En su canto, especialmente en los tonos más altos, la cantante logra lo que he denominado presencia: la irradiación de una fuerza inmensa que se extiende por el espacio por medio de su voz apoderándose físicamente del oyente. Escindida del lenguaje, la voz aparece como lo otro del logos, como lo que le ha arrebatado su hegemonía, como peligro y tentación que no augura la caída y la muerte, como en el caso de las sirenas, sino que ofrece la experiencia, tan placentera como temible, de vivir la propia corporalidad como sensible y *al mismo tiempo* como capaz de transfiguración.

Es con esta escisión de la voz respecto al lenguaje con la que vienen experimentando una y otra vez el arte de la performance y el teatro desde los años sesenta. En las llamadas performances autobiográficas de Spalding Grey, Laurie Anderson, Rachel Rosenthal y Karen Finley y, sobre todo, en las de Diamanda Galás y David Moss se busca y se alcanza una y otra vez ese instante en el que la voz –que habla o que canta– deja de articular de modo comprensible y se convierte en grito, tonos altos, risa, gemido o

101 Theodor W. Adorno, «Bürgerliche Oper», en *Gesammelte Schriften*, Rolf Tiedemann con la colaboración de Gretel Adorno, Susan Buck-Morss y Klaus Schultz (eds.), vol. 16, *Misikalische* Schriften, Fráncfort, 1978, pp. 24-39 (esp. «Ópera burguesa», en *Escritos musicales I-III* (Obra completa, 16), Madrid, 2006, pp. 25-40, aquí 35 y s. Trad. ligeramente modificada).

distorsión. Tales momentos son posibles no sólo en virtud de determinadas técnicas vocales, sino también –especialmente en el caso de Anderson, Galás y Moss– por el empleo de medios electrónicos que pueden elevar el volumen de la voz, reproducirla, extenderla por el espacio, fragmentarla y deformarla, sin que ello comporte su desmaterialización (como en el caso del cine o del vídeo, que producen una desmaterialización del cuerpo filmado). La voz aparece polimorfa. Pierde toda marca que permita identificar el sexo, la edad, la pertenencia étnica u otros rasgos. El espacio sonoro que genera se experimenta como espacio liminar, como un espacio de continuas transiciones, mudanzas y transformaciones.

Esta experiencia también es posible en el caso de los artistas mencionados cuando articulan de modo comprensible. Aunque en esos casos la voz que canta o habla esté vinculada al lenguaje, no deja de tener vida propia y de atraer la atención del oyente hacia esa vida propia. Los artistas no ponen la voz al servicio del lenguaje, no la emplean como medio para hacer audible el lenguaje. Más bien se da el caso de que su voz se hace audible, en primer lugar, como voz en sí misma. Ello no implica necesariamente una desemantización, a pesar de que a menudo se afirme lo contrario. El polimorfismo de la voz da lugar a la pluralidad de significados de los enunciados lingüísticos, dificulta la comprensión unívoca, pero no la comprensión lingüística en general. Lo que sí hace la voz en esos casos es centrar siempre la atención de quien la oye en sus propias y singulares cualidades, exhaladas en y con la respiración, unas cualidades en las que el físico estar-en-el-mundo de lo proferido-a-sí-mismo-vocalmente se hace audible para los demás.

En estas performances se da una constante tensión entre voz y lenguaje. Ello lleva a que la voz nunca desaparezca tras el lenguaje, a que pueda tener su propia vida y a que se haga audible a través de ella. Este tipo de tensión es característico de muchas realizaciones escénicas desde los años sesenta. Peter Stein, en su *Orestíada* (Schaubühne de Berlín, 1980), configuró explícitamente el espacio como espacio sonoro dejándolo casi a oscuras en las dos primeras partes. De la oscuridad surgían voces. Articulaban extraños sonidos que no podían identificarse como lingüísticos. Así, por ejemplo, los viejos del coro producían un inquietante murmullo con los labios cerrados que se tornaba en silbido gimoteante. O sonaba el *ololygmos*, el «grito de júbilo», «un sonido gritado, cantado y entonado con lengua vibrante y en falsete, mitad canto de grillo, mitad trino de pájaro»[102]. Las voces, sin embargo, articulaban sobre todo sonidos lingüísticos. Uno de los viejos murmuraba una frase; otros, repartidos por la sala, la retomaban y la repetían en distintos volúmenes, tonos y tempos, con lo que se subrayaba la diferencia entre las voces. Desde distintos puntos llegaban a los oídos de los espectadores las frases del coro, entonadas de manera distinta por cada voz. Después surgía, no se sabía de dónde, una palabra griega que complementaba el sonido de la articulación en alemán a modo de contraste. Se hacía audible la singular materialidad de las voces que articulaban sonidos lingüísticos; las singulares sonoridades de la voz y del lenguaje no sonaban, ni mucho menos, al unísono, estaban en una tensa relación entre sí[103].

Muy distinto es el procedimiento que emplea Robert Wilson en sus escenificaciones para generar tensión entre voz y lenguaje. Lo consigue, por un lado, empleando frases hechas del lenguaje cotidiano a modo de *ready mades* lingüísticos. Además, fragmenta las palabras o las unidades fonéticas, las alterna, y hace que las pronuncien, y en la mayoría de los casos que las repitan, dos o más actores. La parte alemana del proyecto internacional *the CIVIL warS* (Schauspielhaus de Colonia, 1984), que integraban cuatro miembros más, comenzaba con el siguiente «discurso alterno» entre una mujer en una escalera (1) y un hombre en otra (2):

102 Rolf Michaelis, «Die Geburt des Rechtsstaates im Regen», en *Die Zeit*, 24 de octubre de 1980.

103 Ésta fue, en realidad, la única escenificación de Peter Stein –junto a *Übungen für Schauspieler [Ejercicios para actores]* en *Antikenprojekt* del Schaubühne (1974)– en la que se enfatizaba de tal modo la tensión entre voz y lenguaje.

1 estás
2 e
1 estás
2 estás
1 tú
2 bien
1 estás bien
2 estás bien
1 estás tú
2 estás bien tú
2 E AHORA
1 hay
2 no hay
1 no hay nada
2 hay
1 hay
2 no hay nada a
1 estás bien
[...][104]

Las voces resonaban a través de micrófonos portátiles y producían una especie de reverberación esférica. Iban acompañadas de sonidos en *off* y de música, y formaban un collage de sonidos que conseguía que parecieran casi escindidos de las palabras o de los sonidos articulados, lo que producía un efecto asombroso.

En las escenificaciones de Einar Schleef se creaba una fuerte tensión entre voz y lenguaje, especialmente en las muy dominantes partes del coro. La tensión la generaban las múltiples repeticiones con las que se enunciaba cada frase, la superposición de voces individuales, los susurros o, a veces, el altísimo, casi doloroso, volumen que llegaba hasta el grito –como en *Die Mütter*– y en el que la voz terminaba escindiéndose del lenguaje.

El momento en el que la voz se escinde del lenguaje supone el último paso o el punto de inflexión de la tensión entre ambos. Es

104 Robert Wilson, *the CIVIL warS, a tree is best measured when it is down*, Fráncfort, 1984, p. 72.

entonces cuando la tensión se desvanece, pues la voz se ha convertido ella misma en lenguaje. Ya no transmite lenguaje, es el lenguaje en el que un físico estar-en-el-mundo se pronuncia y en el que interpela al oyente. Es pura proferencia e interpelación. En la materialidad de la voz no se hace presente únicamente toda la materialidad de la realización escénica –como sonoridad, porque la voz suena; como corporalidad, porque escapa del cuerpo con la respiración; como espacialidad, porque se expande por el espacio y penetra tanto en el oído del oyente y en el de quien la profiere–. La voz es en su materialidad ya lenguaje sin tener que ser antes significante.

La voz es desde muchos puntos de vista un material muy valioso, incluso raro. No sólo por el hecho de que no está dada hasta que suena, hasta que no se la hace sonar; no sólo porque no perdura más allá de la expiración con la que abandona el cuerpo y porque tiene que ser generada cada vez de nuevo; es, pues, un material que únicamente se da como «éxtasis». No sólo porque en ella se aúnen sonoridad, corporalidad y espacialidad de tal manera que en ella la materialidad de la realización escénica aparece siempre como algo que siempre se genera de nuevo. Además, en el caso de la voz, estamos ante un material que puede ser lenguaje sin ser significante –lo cual contradice todos los principios y reglas semióticos–. En ella se pronuncia el físico estar-en-el-mundo del que la profiere, interpela a quien la oye en tanto que físico estar-en-el-mundo. Llena el espacio entre los dos, los pone en relación, crea un vínculo entre ellos. Quien la hace audible conmueve con la voz a quien la oye.

4. Temporalidad

Ciertamente la temporalidad no se puede subsumir –como la corporalidad, la espacialidad y la sonoridad– en la categoría de materialidad de la realización escénica. En realidad es la condición de posibilidad para que ésta aparezca en el espacio. Pues la materialidad de la realización escénica no viene dada sin más, como ya hemos visto, se genera en el transcurso, y con ella vuelve a desaparecer. Los sujetos individuales participan en su generación, aunque sin poder determinarla o tenerla a su disposición. Deben estar dispuestos, en cambio, a dejarse hasta cierto punto determinar por ella.

Dado que las realizaciones escénicas acontecen en el tiempo –aunque su duración puede extenderse desde, por ejemplo, cuatro minutos treinta y tres segundos hasta varias horas o incluso varios días–, requieren determinados procedimientos que regulen la duración y la sucesión de la aparición de los distintos materiales así como la relación que mantienen entre ellos. A estos procedimientos pertenecen tradicionalmente la subida y la bajada del telón, además de los descansos, pero sobre todo la dramaturgia del desarrollo de la acción y la psicología de los personajes. Desde los años sesenta, y con la excepción de las realizaciones escénicas operísticas, se ha dejado de emplear prácticamente el telón, incluso en los teatros a la italiana. Además, muchas realizaciones escénicas transcurren sin intermedio. En los años setenta, en los que se produjeron montajes de varias horas, e incluso de varios días de duración –como *KA Mountain Guardenia Terrace*, que se estrenó en 1972 en el festival de Shiraz/Persia, y que duraba siete días –, Wilson defendía con ahínco la opinión de que no es necesaria ninguna pausa, ya que cada espectador puede elegir por sí mismo cuándo desea tomar parte en la realización escénica y cuándo no.

Sin duda la renuncia al telón y a los descansos tiene que ver tanto con el realce del bucle de retroalimentación autopoiético como con la emergencia de la materialidad. Si la realización escénica es generada por la constante influencia mutua entre las acciones de los actores y los espectadores, y si su materialidad en este proceso se origina y viene a presencia como fenómeno emergente, entonces la bajada del telón, o incluso los descansos, se revelan como contraproducentes. Los descansos no son el resultado de los efectos del bucle de retroalimentación: interrumpen el constante proceso de intercambio, de autoestabilización y de desaparición de los materiales –salvo en el caso en el que se consideren parte del proceso, como en el montaje de *Salomé* que hizo Schleef[105].

105 Al respecto véase, en el capítulo tercero, la nota 32.

Si la atención ha de dirigirse al fenómeno de la emergencia, hay que descartar aquellos procedimientos de la estructuración temporal que pretendan remitir a algún origen concreto el surgimiento de un elemento e identificarlo como eslabón de una cadena causal, como ocurre cuando se invoca la sucesión de los acontecimientos dramáticos o la psicología de los personajes. Se han mencionado dos de los procedimientos que intentan evitar esto mismo, pero aún no se ha investigado su eficacia respecto a la sensibilización de los espectadores/oyentes de cara a la emergencia de la materialidad. Me refiero a los segmentos temporales, mencionados en el apartado anterior, y al ritmo, al que me referí en el apartado «Comunidad».

Segmentos temporales *(Time brackets)*

Cage introdujo por primera vez segmentos temporales en *Untitled Event*, que tuvo lugar en el marco de la escuela de verano del Black Mountain College en 1952. El «acontecimiento» se celebró en el comedor de la universidad. Tanto en las paredes más largas como en las más cortas se habían colocado las sillas para los espectadores en cuatro triángulos cuyas puntas estaban dirigidas al centro de la sala, aunque sin llegar a tocarse. En el centro quedaba, por lo tanto, un gran espacio libre en el que, sin embargo, se llevaba a cabo muy poca actividad. Hacía más bien las veces de zona de paso. Entre los triángulos se habían dejado amplios pasillos libres que se cruzaban en diagonal en el centro de la sala y que iban de un lado a otro de ella. Sobre cada asiento habían puesto una taza blanca. A los espectadores no se les dio ninguna explicación sobre su posible utilidad, algunos las emplearon incluso a modo de cenicero. Del techo colgaban pinturas de Robert Rauschenberg, sus *white paintings*.

Además de Cage y Rauschenberg, participaban David Tudor, el compositor Jay Watts, el bailarín Merce Cunningham y los poetas Charles Olsen y Mary Caroline Richards. Cage, con traje negro y corbata, se subió a una tarima y leyó un texto sobre la relación entre la música y el budismo zen así como extractos de los escritos del Maestro Eckhart. Después interpretó una composición con una radio. Simultáneamente Rauschenberg ponía discos antiguos en un gramófono manual junto al que había un perro sentado. David Tudor elaboraba un *prepared radio*; luego comenzó a trasvasar agua de un cubo a otro, mientras Olsen y Richard recitaban sus propios poemas –algunos en medio de los espectadores, otros desde una escalera que estaba apoyada en una de las paredes cortas–. Cunningham y otros bailarines bailaban por los pasillos y por entre los espectadores perseguidos por el perro que, con todo el alboroto, había enloquecido. Rauschenberg proyectaba sobre el techo y sobre una de las paredes largas diapositivas abstractas (formadas por la pulverización de gelatinas de colores entre dos placas de vidrio) y fragmentos fílmicos que primero mostraban al cocinero del *college* y después, a medida que la proyección se iba desplazando del techo a la pared, una puesta de sol. En una esquina de la sala el compositor Jay Watts tocaba varios instrumentos. La realización escénica finalizó cuando cuatro jóvenes vestidos de blanco sirvieron café en las tazas, las hubieran usado los espectadores a modo de cenicero o no.

La preparación de la realización escénica empezó cuando Cage repartió a cada uno de los participantes una especie de partitura en la que había introducido segmentos temporales. Con ello quedaba establecido con qué frecuencia debía intervenir cada uno de los participantes y cuánto podían durar como máximo sus intervenciones. Cada uno de los artistas tenía total libertad para elegir qué tipo de acción quería ejecutar y cuándo quería empezarla y terminarla, eso sí, dentro del segmento temporal asignado. Los artistas habían quedado en no informarse de antemano sobre ninguna de las acciones escogidas, y mucho menos en ponerse de acuerdo sobre ellas. Los segmentos temporales suponían para los artistas tanto restricción como libertad. Restricción en cuanto a que eran los únicos periodos de tiempo en los que podían ejecutar sus acciones. Los artistas no podían excederlos en ningún caso. La duración de la intervención tenía que ser, pues, controlada por cronómetro para cumplir este requisito. La restricción se aplicaba igualmente al comienzo y al final de cada una de las acciones. El artista tenía que prestar atención al reloj para no empezar antes de tiempo o acabar más tarde de lo previsto. En lo concerniente a todo lo demás disfrutaba de absoluta libertad: podía hacer lo que quisiera sin tener en consideración lo que hicieran los demás. No tenía que bajar el volumen del gramófono para que el espectador pudiera oír las recitaciones; no tenía que ponerse de acuerdo con los demás sobre el traje que llevaba ni sobre los objetos que empleaba ni tenía que remitirse tampoco, a la hora de hacer su elección, a una «idea» o «intención» de rango superior.

Por ello lo que ocurrió, todo lo que se pudo ver u oír, al espectador le parecía completamente inmotivado. Ninguna acción se infería o resultaba de otra y, cuando era capaz de establecer algún vínculo entre dos de ellas, no se debía más que a la casualidad o a condiciones subjetivas muy particulares. Cada una de las acciones tenía autonomía propia. Surgía en un momento concreto, imprevisto, se estabilizaba por un instante en su permanente transformación y, en un instante igualmente imprevisible, cesaba y desaparecía. Así, el espectador podía centrar su atención a voluntad en cualquier acción hasta que otros sonidos o movimientos, surgidos de forma repentina, la requirieran para sí.

Mientras que el seguimiento de una trama coherente –aunque siga el patrón «clásico» de planteamiento, desarrollo, clímax, giro, catástrofe/desenlace– y el desarrollo psicológico de los personajes hacen experimentable el tiempo como un continuo estructurado en el que todo lo que ocurre se sigue de lo anterior comprensiblemente de modo tal que tanto el establecimiento del principio como el del final está justificado, el *Untitled Event* generó una temporalidad totalmente distinta. Ni el comienzo ni el final de la realización escénica estaban motivados por la sucesión de las acciones, estaban establecidos como cortes arbitrarios que muy bien podían haber sucedido de otra manera. Esto dio lugar a una experiencia de a-temporalidad, esto es, se sentía el tiempo por medio de la emergencia y la desaparición de algo que, mientras duraba su aparición, era capaz de absorber la atención. No se originaba una sensación de continuidad en la que el tiempo, con sus distintos tempo, ritmo e intensidad, a diferencia del tiempo mensurable, avanzara imparable. Con el recurso al tiempo mensurable, al imponer los segmentos temporales, se originaba una sensación de islas temporales, cada una de las cuales seguía su propio ritmo, tempo e intensidad, sin que por ello la aparición o percepción sucesivas de las distintas islas temporales fuera capaz de suscitar una sensación de continuidad.

Se podría decir que las islas temporales estaban situadas, en cierto modo, unas junto a otras, que con ellas el tiempo se espacializaba. Surgía una isla temporal cuando algo venía a presencia, es decir, cuando se extendía por el espacio. Y desaparecía cuando lo que había venido a presencia desaparecía del espacio y con ello de la percepción. En *Europeras 1 & 2* esa sensación se intensificó aún más, en ellas todos los materiales empleados, las imágenes (como «decoración»), la utilería, los trajes, las acciones de los cantantes y de sus «asistentes», así como el material musical para cada uno de los instrumentos, se escogieron por medio de operaciones casuales. Además, la elección de las arias que debían interpretar los cantantes se dejó al criterio de cada uno. Las fotografías se seleccionaron de entre las del fondo de la biblioteca municipal y universitaria de Fráncfort. Se exhibían fotografías de distintos siglos en las que se podía ver a compositores y cantantes, así como animales y paisajes de épocas distintas. En un segundo paso, se volvieron a seleccionar, también por medio de operaciones casuales, los fragmentos de las fotografías que se mostrarían y se fijó su tamaño definitivo. Un plano espacio-temporal elaborado de antemano regulaba sus movimientos en el espacio desde su aparición hasta su desaparición. Cage escogió asimismo los trajes para los cantantes por medio de operaciones casuales de entre la inmensa cantidad de exquisitos figurines de distintas épocas y países que incluía la enciclopedia de trajes históricos del Fashion Institute de Nueva York, que consta de varios volúmenes. Las acciones asignadas a los cantantes –que realizaban, en caso de que fueran demasiado complicadas para ellos, bailarines y a veces tramoyistas–, se seleccionaron al azar a partir de entradas del *Dictionary of the English Language* de Webster, por ejemplo: bailes de claqué, tejer, desmontar un juego de construcción para niños y volver a montarlo, nadar sobre el escenario como una platija. El tiempo disponible para su realización se estableció asimismo mediante operaciones casuales, mientras que el primer momento posible para el comienzo y el último para la finalización se estableció por medio de segmentos temporales.

De este modo el principio de incoherencia se radicalizó: «Todo está separado, absolutamente *todo de todo*. La escena no está concebida de modo que los distintos elementos teatrales se apoyen o se apuntalen entre sí, o de tal manera que estén relacionados, sino que cada uno tiene su propio estatus, sus propias condiciones de actividad totalmente independientes»[106].

Cada uno formaba su propia isla temporal separada de las demás, cada uno disponía de su propia temporalidad. Del mismo modo que un organismo unicelular, un ser humano, una cadena montañosa o el universo tienen sus respectivas temporalidades, así las tenían también las fotografías, los trajes, las acciones, las arias y las secuencias tonales de los distintos instrumentos en *Europeras 1 & 2*. El logro de los segmentos temporales, especialmente en combinación con las operaciones casuales, es crear islas temporales, posibilitar su emergencia específica y no únicamente realzarlas, sino exponerlas y hacerlas experimentables para el espectador de este modo.

Ritmo

Al ritmo se le concede hoy una especial relevancia en la organización y estructuración del tiempo de muchas realizaciones escénicas. Es el ritmo el que establece una relación entre la corporalidad, la espacialidad y la sonoridad, y el que regula tanto su aparición en el espacio como su desaparición. Pero no es –a diferencia de los segmentos temporales– un invento nuevo. En realidad, una realización escénica en la que el ritmo no participe de algún modo en la estructuración del tiempo es de todo punto impensable. Incluso aunque el desarrollo de la acción y la evolución de los personajes aporten los principios estructuradores, el

106 John Cage, en *Die Opernzeitung Frankfurt*, octubre/noviembre 1987, n. 1/2, Fráncfort, 1987, p. 11.

ritmo sigue siendo de una importancia crucial en la sucesión de las escenas: al hablar, en los movimientos, dentro de cada una de las escenas, incluso fuera del ámbito del teatro musical y la danza. En estos casos, sin embargo, el ritmo está subordinado a principios rectores básicos, les sirve de apoyo en la estructura que proponen. Desde los años sesenta, por el contrario, en muchas realizaciones escénicas de teatro y del arte de la performance el ritmo aparece como el principio rector, prevalente, cuando no único, en la organización y estructuración del tiempo.

Por ritmo entiendo, en este contexto, un principio ordenador que, a diferencia del compás y el metro, tiene por objetivo la regularidad, no la proporción. Como explica Hanno Helbling, se trata de un principio dinámico que «está siempre *en camino* y como tal permanece: siempre ocupado en la producción y la presentación de determinadas relaciones y siempre capaz de rediseñarlas»[107]. Lo previsible y lo imprevisible interactúan en el ritmo. Se origina por la repetición *y* la divergencia de lo repetido. De la sola repetición no resulta el ritmo. El ritmo puede describirse, en este sentido, como un principio ordenador que presupone una permanente transformación y progresa en su propia actividad[108].

Si el ritmo ha llegado a convertirse en el principio ordenador más importante, si no en el único, es porque entre corporalidad, espacialidad y sonoridad se establecen relaciones que cambian continuamente, y porque la aparición y desaparición de éstas la regulan o determinan la repetición y la divergencia.

Robert Wilson perseguía con su empleo del ritmo –sobre todo en sus trabajos anteriores a la mitad de los años ochenta– un efecto comparable al que Cage alcanzó con los segmentos temporales. Cada sistema de elementos teatrales sigue su propio ritmo: la luz, que cambia en una fracción de segundo; los movimientos

107 Hanno Helbling, *Rhythmus. Ein Versuch*, Fráncfort, 1999, p. 18.

108 Véase al respecto Clemens Risi, «Rhythmen der Aufführung. Kollidierende Rhythmen bei Steve Reich und Heiner Goebbels», en Erika Fischer-Lichte, Clemens Risi, Jens Roselt (eds.), *Kunst der Aufführung – Aufführung der Kunst*, Berlín, 2004, pp. 165-177.

de los actores, que se ejecutan en *slow motion*; las voces, los ruidos, la música y los sonidos, que se trenzan para formar un collage sonoro que suena con un ritmo totalmente autónomo. El ritmo desjerarquiza los elementos, los aísla entre sí, los hace aparecer como incoherentes. Crea para cada uno de ellos una estructura temporal propia que difiere perceptiblemente de la de los demás. El espectador experimenta distintas temporalidades simultáneamente. Su percepción se des-sincroniza y se sensibiliza para el efecto específico de cada uno de los elementos. La variedad de ritmos le dificulta el establecimiento inmediato de vínculos entre la corporalidad, la espacialidad y la sonoridad, la fijación de relaciones de subordinación o prevalencia o el descubrimiento de concomitancias significativas entre ellas. La singularísima temporalidad que crea el ritmo no aporta una conexión entre los distintos elementos, más bien los deja estar en igualdad de condiciones junto a los demás y da lugar a que se despliegue y muestre la importancia de la dinámica que les es propia. Si al final el espectador termina estableciendo relaciones entre ellos, será, igual que en las piezas de Cage, porque las establece él.

Schleef empleaba el ritmo de forma muy distinta. Respecto a sus coros se podría tener en principio la impresión de que la corporalidad, la espacialidad y la sonoridad estuvieran totalmente sincronizadas rítmicamente. No obstante, una mirada y una audición más atentas revelaban rápidamente la falsedad de esa impresión. Eran precisamente los continuos desfases rítmicos del movimiento y del habla los que permitían apreciar su condición de campo de batalla en el que no se combatía solamente entre individuo y comunidad, sino también entre cuerpo y lenguaje. El ritmo de enunciación de las frases pretendía imponerse al cuerpo, forzarlo a realizar movimientos a su ritmo y subordinarlo al orden lingüístico en tanto que organismo en movimiento, subsumirlo a él. Los cuerpos, por su parte, no sólo se defendían frente a tales intentos, sino que perseguían transmitir el ritmo de sus movimientos por medio de la voz al lenguaje –un ritmo que rompía el orden sintáctico del lenguaje, que lo distorsionaba de tal manera que las frases perdían su significado y se tornaban incomprensibles. La voz se escindía del lenguaje y su orden simbólico de éste quedaba desbaratado por el ritmo de los movimientos corporales que se apoderaban de la voz. En ocasiones la voz se doblegaba al ritmo que fijaba el orden sintáctico y semántico de lo enunciado y lo transmitía a los movimientos corporales, un instante después los cuerpos imponían su ritmo a las voces, con lo que el ritmo desbarataba el sentido del lenguaje, y con él su significado.

En esta lucha no había vencedores ni vencidos, como tampoco los había en la que se libraba entre el individuo y la comunidad. Era el ritmo el que identificaba el lenguaje y el cuerpo como fuerzas opuestas que tienen que interactuar y al mismo tiempo combatir de modo irreconciliable. Los coros de Schleef recuerdan así a la idea fundamental de Nietzsche sobre el nacimiento de la tragedia en el espíritu de la música. En ellos combatían el principio dionisíaco, tal y como lo encarnaban los cuerpos extáticos, derribados, caídos, y el principio apolíneo, representado por el orden simbólico del lenguaje. El resultado de esta lucha no era nunca predecible. En los coros de Schleef era el ritmo el que establecía una relación, más tensa que armónica, entre la corporalidad, la espacialidad y la sonoridad. Este ritmo intentaba permanentemente establecer una jerarquización entre ellos y lo que conseguía, en cambio, era una constante desjerarquización. Cada elemento disponía de su propia temporalidad, y con su ritmo era siempre capaz de transmitírsela provisionalmente a otro.

Los trabajos de Wilson y Schleef serían los dos extremos de una escala que fuera desde una total ausencia de relación entre los elementos teatrales (movimientos corporales, luz, sonidos) hasta la generación permanente de una relación entre ellos. Es el ritmo el que constituye cada vez las relaciones o la ausencia de ellas. Con ello alcanza además otro logro que vincula incluso, pese a las diferencias, los trabajos de Schleef y Wilson: no permite ninguna relación jerárquica entre los elementos. Se los considera a todos del mismo valor e importancia. La atención se centra, pues, en su materialidad específica, en su singular aparecer en el espacio.

El ritmo es además el principio que funda la dramaturgia de las realizaciones escénicas –no sólo en los casos de Wilson y

Schleef, sino también en los de Jan Fabre, Jan Lauwers, el Wooster Group, Heiner Goebbels, Christoph Marthaler y muchos más–. Qué elementos aparecen, cuándo, en qué forma y por cuánto tiempo lo hacen depende básicamente del ritmo de cada realización escénica. Consecuentemente se trabaja muy a menudo con repeticiones en las que el elemento que aparece diverge de lo que se repite, aunque a veces sea sólo mínimamente. Así, algunas escenificaciones de Marthaler como *Murx, Die Stunde Null oder die Kunst des Servierens [La hora cero o el arte de servir]* (Deutsches Schauspielhaus de Hamburgo, 1995) o *La bella molinera* (Schauspielhaus de Zúrich, 2002) parecen consistir, por formularlo de una manera algo exagerada, casi exclusivamente en repeticiones: se introduce un elemento que se repite en el transcurso de la velada siempre con nuevas variaciones; luego se añade un segundo elemento con el que ocurre lo mismo, después un tercero y así sucesivamente. Las variaciones van desde divergencias mínimas hasta golpes *(coups)* abrumadores. En ese proceso puede muy bien ocurrir que lo uno produzca el efecto de lo otro.

En *Murx* –que se ha mantenido hasta hace poco en la programación del Volksbühne– se dan repeticiones con pequeñas variaciones como, por ejemplo, el intento de Susanne Düllmann de entrar en el aseo masculino, que Jürgen Rothert acierta siempre a impedir variando en cada ocasión las palabras, el tono o la disposición sintáctica. Otra sería la historia de Ueli Jäggi sobre el curso de cocina al que no puede asistir: *Backen ohne Mehl [Pastelería sin harina]*; razón por la que acaba en el curso *Ficken ohne Frau [Fornicar sin mujer]*. Se trata de repeticiones que, a medida que transcurre la velada, terminan reconociéndose con una sonrisa cansada. Por el contrario, la mínima divergencia con la que se cantaban, se entonaban y eran acompañadas al piano por Jürg Kienberger las dieciséis estrofas del canto de iglesia «Danke»[109] [«Gracias»] causaban un enorme efecto. En cada nueva estrofa se subía medio tono

109 Agradezco la constatación de que se trata de dieciséis estrofas, algo de lo que no me di cuenta las dos veces que asistí a la realización escénica, a Robert Sollich, quien no sólo contó las estrofas, sino que además realizó un brillante análisis de la realización.

más, lo que al llegar a las últimas, cuando las cuerdas vocales de los cantantes amenazaban con romperse, causaba una carcajada compulsiva, apenas contenible, en un público que ya no podía moderarse.

Ruedi Häusermann se dirigía en intervalos de tiempo determinados a los grandes hornos, los abría y hurgaba dentro de ellos con unas tenazas. Sus movimientos apenas variaban de una vez a otra. En el último tercio de la realización escénica se producía, sin embargo, una tremenda divergencia. Desde el interior del horno abierto sonaba el himno de la antigua RDA [República Democrática Alemana], lo que generaba un efecto abrumador.

Una y otra vez en el transcurso de la realización escénica los actores, sin razón aparente ni motivo comprensible, se encontraban cantando todos juntos. Era el ritmo en el que se repetía el canto coral –es decir, la sucesión temporal– lo que motivaba su aparición. Las divergencias –en algunos casos de importancia– resultaban de la selección de canciones que se hacía en cada caso, para la que tampoco se daba ningún motivo. El repertorio iba desde el *Kühlem Grunde [En el fresco hondón]* de Eichendorff, pasando por la pieza folcórica del año 1650 *Sichres Deutschland schläfst du noch [Aún duermes confiada Alemania]*, cuyo estribillo reza *Wach auf, du deutsches Reich [Despierta, Imperio alemán]*, el *Glühwürmchenidyll [El idilio de la luciérnaga]* de Paul Lincke, y llegaba hasta el éxito pop alemán *Ich lass mir meinen Körper schwarz bepinseln [Me hago pintar el cuerpo de negro]*.

El ritmo de la realización escénica que surge de tal manera no es una mera sucesión de «números» en la que unos siguen a otros caprichosamente. Aparecen distintos elementos que tienen lugar simultánea o sucesivamente, en principio de forma inconexa, pero que en el desarrollo posterior de la realización escénica, por mor de las repeticiones que los van modificando constantemente, se engolfan los unos en los otros de manera que sólo el ritmo puede establecer vínculos entre ellos. La primera aparición de los elementos que en conjunto constituyen el material de la realización escénica ocurre no sólo de modo injustificado e inmotivado, sino también de forma totalmente independiente de los demás. Cada elemento aparece inopinadamente en un determinado momento durante las dos horas y media que dura la realización escénica. Pero no es hasta que ha hecho su aparición que cada elemento se expande y se modifica continuamente de un modo más o menos claramente perceptible. Sin embargo, esto no ocurre de manera ininterrumpida –únicamente la presencia de los once actores en el espacio produce continuidad y es un signo de ella–. Sus acciones, por el contrario, que no presentan ningún tipo de concomitancia entre sí, son tan fugaces que, en su ejecución, parecen desvanecerse sin dejar rastro. Pero entonces reaparecen con ligeras variaciones en un momento posterior. El presupuesto se invierte: ninguna acción parece desvanecerse sin dejar huella. Sólo cuando ha aparecido una vez en el mundo puede volver a aparecer, aunque nunca igual a sí misma. La razón de su transformación es incierta y queda inexplicada, igual que la de su primera aparición. Parece que esa transformación sólo es debida al ritmo y que, a su vez, sólo a través de ella se le presta atención al ritmo. Las repeticiones dan lugar a una especie de bucle de retroalimentación que convierte en fútil la pregunta por la causa y el efecto. El ritmo se presenta como un principio organizador que regula la aparición y la desaparición de elementos, de materialidades, sin remitirse a otros principios o sistemas. Una vez puesto en marcha, da la impresión de que fuera a partir de él que los elementos aparecen y vuelven a desaparecer. El que marca el tiempo para la aparición y desaparición de materialidades en la realización escénica es en este caso el ritmo[110].

Así pues, como ya se ha señalado en el apartado «Comunidad», el ritmo es un principio que se establece con el cuerpo humano. No sólo los latidos del corazón, la circulación sanguínea y la respiración siguen su propio ritmo, no sólo realizamos rítmicamente los movimientos que nuestro cuerpo lleva a cabo al caminar, bailar, nadar, escribir, etc., y producimos sonidos rítmicamente cuando hablamos, cantamos, reímos o lloramos. También los movimientos que se producen en el interior de nuestro cuerpo, y que no somos capaces de percibir, se realizan

110 O bien aquel que, cuando es posible, fija el ritmo. Véase al respecto el apartado «Escenificación» en el capítulo séptimo.

rítmicamente[III]. El cuerpo humano está configurado, en efecto, rítmicamente.

Por eso somos capaces de percibir ritmos de una forma tan singular y de «acomodarnos» a ellos. En las realizaciones escénicas en las que la temporalidad se organiza y se estructura esencialmente a través del ritmo confluyen distintos «sistemas rítmicos»: el de la realización escénica y el de los espectadores, aunque hay que tener en cuenta que el ritmo de cada espectador es distinto. Es decir, que para el bucle de retroalimentación autopoiético es particularmente relevante, en tanto que tiene lugar en la realización escénica, el modo en que se realiza la armonización rítmica: depende de si la realización escénica es capaz, y si lo es hasta qué punto, de hacer entrar a los espectadores en el ritmo establecido por ella, aunque su «acomodo» les transmita después nuevos impulsos a los actores; de si varios espectadores con ritmos semejantes son capaces de influir en los demás o en los actores, y si lo son hasta qué punto, y así sucesivamente. Independientemente de cómo transcurra este proceso en cada caso, podemos partir de la base de que el bucle de retroalimentación autopoiético se autorregula en buena medida a través de desfases, modificaciones y cambios rítmicos. Éste se realiza por medio de «acomodos» alternos en los ritmos de otros y por la interacción física directa entre actores y espectadores. Es decir, una estructuración rítmica le proporciona al bucle de retroalimentación autopoiético condiciones especialmente favorables para su ejecución. Además, dirige la atención de los espectadores a este proceso.

Al organizar y estructurar la generación performativa de la materialidad, el ritmo hace aparecer, de consuno y como factor efectivo para el bucle de retroalimentación autopoiético, el material performativamente generado. En el ritmo se ponen en relación y se hacen productivos recíprocamente de un modo perceptible para el espectador la generación performativa de la materialidad y el bucle de retroalimentación autopoiético.

III Véase entre otros, Gerold Baier, *Rhythmus. Tanz in Körper und Gehirn*, Reinbeck bei Hamburgo, 2001.

V. EMERGENCIA DE SIGNIFICADO

Cuando Max Herrmann desarrolló su concepto de realización escénica, se ocupó en detalle de la medialidad, la materialidad y la esteticidad de las realizaciones escénicas. A su semioticidad, sin embargo, no atendió con igual interés. El motivo de ello estriba en que en su época la semioticidad de las realizaciones escénicas se equiparaba a la de los textos dramáticos. Críticos de teatro y estudiosos de la literatura partían del supuesto de que en y con la realización escénica los significados «extraídos» al texto se expresaban con medios teatrales y se transmitían al público. En su opinión, la performatividad de la realización escénica estaba subordinada a su expresividad. En cuanto a la relación entre actores y espectadores, sólo les preocupaba la cuestión de si los actores eran capaces de expresar «adecuadamente» los significados «correctos» y de transmitírselos al espectador. Max Herrmann, por el contrario, entendía la copresencia física de actores y espectadores como constitutiva de la realización escénica. En la medida en que la semioticidad de las realizaciones escénicas dependiera del texto literario del drama y fuera valorada a partir de él, el concepto carecía de interés para él.

Con el rechazo del teatro literario tal y como lo pusieron por obra los representantes de las vanguardias históricas –sobre todo Craig, los futuristas, los dadaístas, los surrealistas, Meyerhold, el teatro de la Bauhaus y Artaud–, la remisión a los significados del texto literario quedó obsoleta. Incluso se pidió repetidas veces que el teatro cesara de comunicar significados y que se propusiera en su lugar la tarea de suscitar reacciones. Como modelo contrapuesto tanto al teatro literario como al psicológico y realista recurrieron al teatro de variedades y al circo. Los futuristas italianos habían proclamado con sus dos manifiestos «El teatro de variedades» (1913) y «El teatro futurista sintético» (1915) que querían transformar el teatro, de acuerdo a los principios de las *varietés* y del circo, en «un teatro de la fantasía pura, del récord y de la fisicofolía»[1]. En los primeros años de la Unión Soviética hubo una gran cantidad de intentos de crear un nuevo teatro recurriendo al circo, un teatro que no pretendiera transmitir significados. Sergei Radlov, que entre 1913 y 1916 había trabajado en el estudio de Meyerhold, fundó un teatro circense en el que aparecían, junto a los actores, payasos, acróbatas y malabaristas, e incluso hacían de actores. Su objetivo era fundar, de esa manera, un nuevo teatro cómico popular (en 1922, no obstante, Radlov tuvo que cerrar su teatro, pues el público, que al principio acudía masivamente, dejó de hacerlo.) En los años 1922 y 1923 la llamada FEKS *(Fabrik des exzentrischen Schauspieler [Fábrica del actor excéntrico])* experimentó también con el circo y las *varietés*.

Especialmente relevantes al respecto fueron los intentos de Meyerhold para hacer del circo algo fecundo para el teatro. El resultado de sus esfuerzos que disfrutó de más éxito y celebridad fue la escenificación, en 1922, de la obra de teatro grotesco de Sukhovo-Kobylin *La muerte de Tarelkin*, en la que también participó Sergei M. Eisenstein. Éste hizo asimismo la escenificación de la comedia de Ostrovski *Todos los hombres son bastante sencillos* sobre la base del modelo circense. Pues en su opinión, como subraya en su escrito *Método* (1943-1947) veinte años después,

> el de las funciones de circo [...] [es] un caso en el que nos las vemos con un subgénero artístico en el que sólo se ha mantenido el

1 Marinetti, «El teatro futurista sintético», en *La escena moderna. Manifiestos y textos sobre el teatro de la época de las vanguardias*, José A. Sánchez (ed.), Madrid, 1999, pp. 121-127, aquí: p. 125.

> componente sensorial de forma pura..., que en los demás casos es meramente una forma de corporización de algunos contenidos ideal-materiales. Por eso el circo hace las veces, necesariamente, de un singular baño sensitivo-tonificante. [...] Por ese motivo el circo no abriga esperanzas de ningún tipo en cuanto a la constitución de sentido o a su empleo como transmisor de sentido[2].

Aunque Meyerhold coincidía con Eisenstein en que la sensorialidad del circo no persigue la transmisión de significados, sino causar reacciones inmediatas, razón por la que parece un modelo tan particularmente adecuado para un nuevo teatro, la conclusión que extraía de ello era algo distinta. En su opinión, uno de los efectos que tenía que operar el teatro consistía precisamente en que el espectador se considerara «partícipe y creador de un nuevo sentido». Mientras que los actores tenían que renunciar a transmitir significados al espectador y centrar su tarea en generar sensorialidad, materialidad, la de cada uno de los espectadores debía ser generar nuevos significados remitiéndose a esa materialidad, cada espectador tenía que convertirse en creador de un nuevo sentido.

Desde los años sesenta, los artistas de teatro y de performance, como los ya mencionados representantes de las vanguardias históricas, parten de la premisa de que la función de las realizaciones escénicas no puede ser transmitir al grupo de los espectadores los significados que ha generado el grupo de sus participantes –actores, director, escenógrafo, compositor o incluso el autor de una obra. Las realizaciones escénicas no han de estar al servicio de la transmisión de significados o, en expresión de Eisenstein, de la transmisión de sentido. De ello surgen problemas similares a aquellos con los que las vanguardias históricas tuvieron que enfrentarse. Entre ellos se cuentan la pregunta por la relación entre materialidad y signicidad, así como la de la relación entre efecto y significado. Los representantes de las vanguardias históricas cuyo obje-

2 Cit. por Viatcheslav V. Ivanov, *Einführung in allgemeine Probleme der Semiotik*, Tubinga, 1985, p. 248.

tivo era una nueva estética del efecto las respondieron claramente: la reducción de los medios teatrales a su materialidad/sensorialidad impide la constitución de significado a través de los actores, pero les da la posibilidad a los espectadores de generar también significados. La constitución de significado por los actores excluye el efecto sobre los espectadores. Una estética del efecto exige, pues, la renuncia de los actores a cualquier tipo de constitución de significado.

Los artistas de teatro y de performance de los últimos treinta o cuarenta años, por el contrario, no han encontrado una respuesta unívoca a estas preguntas. Como hemos visto hasta ahora, tampoco parecen tener especial interés en respuestas de ese tipo. En absoluto dan por supuesta la mutua exclusión de materialidad y signicidad, de efecto y significado. En general, no dan por supuestas las relaciones dicotómicas *per se*. Se plantean más bien la pregunta de cómo dichas categorías se relacionan entre sí y tratan de indagar en sus distintas posibilidades en cada una de las realizaciones escénicas. Así, han centrado su atención en cómo se originan los significados en las realizaciones escénicas, cuál es su papel en ellas y qué efectos producen. En este capítulo intentaré explicitar las respuestas a estas preguntas que las distintas realizaciones escénicas mencionadas hasta ahora han dado, o han formulado al menos de forma implícita, con el fin de poder discutirlas en el contexto de una estética de lo performativo y, más en concreto, en lo que concierne a la específica semioticidad de las realizaciones escénicas.

1. Materialidad, significante, significado

Las realizaciones escénicas desde los años sesenta han ido escindiendo cada uno de los medios teatrales de los contextos de orden superior a los que antes se remitían. No sólo han dejado de subordinarlos a la lógica de la acción o a la psicológica, sino que han intentado liberarlos de cualquier tipo de encadenamiento causal. Siguiendo determinados parámetros geométricos y rítmicos, o por medio de operaciones casuales, los elementos surgen en el espacio, se estabilizan durante un periodo de tiempo –de la más diversa duración–, en algunos casos también en constante transformación, y vuelven a desaparecer en algún momento sin que se pueda dar una explicación comprensible o una motivación concreta para su aparición o desaparición. Parece que en la aparición de cada uno de los elementos se trata mayormente, si no exclusivamente, de fenómenos emergentes.

Su emergencia tiene como consecuencia un fenómeno que en principio puede parecer contradictorio, un fenómeno de la mayor importancia para la semioticidad de las realizaciones escénicas. Por un lado, los elementos emergentes, que han sido aislados de esta manera, aparecen en cierto modo desemantizados, son percibidos en su materialidad específica y no como portadores de significados; no se ponen ni en relación con otros elementos ni se trasladan a otro contexto. En este sentido no tienen contenido significativo, no tienen significado.

Por otro lado, sin embargo, son precisamente los fenómenos aislados, emergentes y percibidos en su materialidad, los que pueden suscitar en el sujeto perceptor gran cantidad de asociaciones, ideas, pensamientos, recuerdos, sentimientos y brindarle la posibilidad de ponerlos en relación con otros fenómenos. Sin duda, son percibidos como significantes que se pueden referir a los distintos fenómenos, trasladarse a diversos contextos y ponerse en relación con los más diversos significados, lo que conlleva una enorme pluralización de las posibilidades de significación.

¿Cómo puede aclararse esta contradicción?

Ya en el capítulo anterior me he referido brevemente a la tesis de la desemantización y he intentado mostrar en qué medida puede estar justificada, a saber: en tanto que se oriente a la lógica de la acción y a la lógica de una psicología de orden superior en la que a cada elemento le correspondan uno o varios significados. Además, he intentado mostrar los motivos de su corto alcance. Al hablar del recurso a la *slow motion* en el caso de Wilson explicaba que ese procedimiento no desemantiza el gesto, sino que lo hace aflorar en su autorreferencialidad. El gesto significa precisamente aquello que realiza; es percibido como un movimiento del brazo que se flexiona para ir de la cintura a la altura de los ojos. Lo explicado a partir de este ejemplo sirve igualmente para todos los demás casos en los que la tesis de la desemantización ha encontrado una aplicación. Si el gesto de Marina Abramović de tallarse una estrella de cinco puntas en la piel es percibido simplemente como tal –y no, por ejemplo, como una acción simbólica que haría referencia a la inscripción del símbolo estatal en los cuerpos de cada uno de sus miembros–, entonces no será percibido como in-significante, sino precisamente como aquello que el gesto realiza. Si el espectador no percibe el cuerpo obeso, desbordado, de Giancarlo Paludi como signo del cuerpo del personaje de Cicerón, sino como un cuerpo casi deforme que llena el espacio, entonces lo percibe como aquello que aparece, lo percibe en su ser fenoménico.

Lo que acabo de explicar a propósito de cuerpos y gestos es igualmente válido en los casos de espacios, cosas, colores, sonidos, etc. Percibir los elementos teatrales en su materialidad específica significa, pues, percibirlos como autorreferenciales, percibirlos en su ser fenoménico. ¿Puede esto querer decir que se los percibe como carentes de contenido significativo? ¿Se seguiría de ello la equiparación de la percepción de objetos en su materialidad específica con la percepción de éstos como no significativos, como fenómenos puramente «sensibles»?

Cuando percibo el cuerpo del actor como cuerpo singular o la sangre con la que se salpicaba a los actores y a los espectadores en las acciones de Nitsch, cuando la considero en su rojo específico, cuando saboreo su extraño dulzor o siento las vísceras bajo los pies en su singular consistencia y elasticidad, estoy percibiendo todos estos fenómenos *como algo*. No se trata de una sensación inconcreta, sino de la percepción de algo como algo. Las cosas significan aquello que son o aquello como lo que aparecen. Así pues, percibir algo como algo quiere decir percibirlo como significativo. En la autorreferencialidad coinciden materialidad, significante y significado. La materialidad no funciona como un significante al cual puede atribuírsele este o aquel significado. Más bien hay que entender la materialidad como el significado que, para el sujeto que la percibe como tal, viene dado con ella.

La materialidad de la cosa recibe el significado, tautológicamente hablando, de su materialidad en la percepción del sujeto, esto es, en la percepción de su ser fenoménico. El objeto que es percibido como algo significa aquello como lo que es percibido.

Esto sirve únicamente, claro está, para la percepción consciente. Percibir algo conscientemente significa percibirlo como algo. Ciertamente tenemos que tener en cuenta las percepciones que no llegan al umbral de la conciencia y que, sin embargo, pueden influir en nuestro comportamiento[3]. Pero, dado que no somos conscientes de ellas, para el sujeto perceptor carecen de significado, y como nadie puede decir nada sobre ellas, quedan forzosamente desatendidas –aunque no, por cierto, las conductas observables desencadenadas por ellas. Éstas son sin duda parte integrante del bucle de retroalimentación autopoiético.

Dado que en el caso del fenómeno del que pretende dar cuenta la tesis de la desemantización se trata en sentido estricto de autorreferencialidad, este fenómeno puede explicarse de manera más convincente como el proceso de una constitución de significado muy específica. Este proceso se realiza mediante la percepción de algo como algo. No es que se perciba primero algo como algo y que luego, en un segundo paso, a eso se le atribuya un significado. Más bien es que el significado se origina en el acto de percepción y como acto de percepción.

El repentino e inmotivado aparecer de un fenómeno dirige la atención del espectador a este gesto concreto, a esa determinada cosa o a aquel cierto sonido. En ese proceso su percepción puede adquirir una cualidad muy especial: la de descartar la pregunta por posibles significados ulteriores, potenciales funciones, formas de aplicación o por un contexto de aparición distinto. La percepción se realiza como una suerte de inmersión contemplativa en ese gesto, esa cosa, o esa serie de sonidos en la que los objetos percibidos se le muestran al sujeto como lo que son: revelan su «significado propio». Esto ocurre cuando el que per-

3 Véase Gerhard Roth, *Fühlen, Denken, Handeln. Wie das Gehirn unser Verhalten steuert*, Fráncfort, 2001, pp. 217 y ss.

cibe experimenta la presencia de un actor o el éxtasis de una cosa. Es el instante en el que parece revelársele un misterio: el significado secreto, el significado «dado» en el ser fenoménico (y en tanto que ser fenoménico) de lo percibido es «desvelado» o, mejor dicho, producido en el acto de la percepción.

No se trata, pues, de un proceso de desemantización, sino de autorreferencialidad. En ésta se elimina una distinción fundamental para las vanguardias históricas de la que parten también muchas teorías estéticas: la distinción entre la percepción sensible de un objeto, que se entiende como un proceso más bien psicológico, y la atribución de significado, que se tiene por un acto mental.

Permítaseme recurrir a uno de mis ejemplos predilectos para aclarar esta idea: si la percepción del rojo de un semáforo sobre el que cae la lluvia como un rojo muy singular, que cambia continuamente e irisa en los más variados matices, me fascina tanto que me hace sumergirme en su observación, es porque lo percibo como algo distinto de cuando lo percibo como una señal de parar. En ambos casos la percepción da lugar a un significado específico –en el primero, el de una impresión sensible particularmente fascinante; en el segundo, el de una instrucción práctica–. Expresado de manera más incisiva, y quizá para algunos provocadora: la percepción consciente genera siempre significado y es por ello que las «impresiones sensibles» se pueden describir de manera más adecuada como aquel tipo de significados que se convierten en impresiones sensibles conscientes para mí. De ello no se sigue, no obstante, que se puedan expresar sin más lingüísticamente. En efecto, puede que tenga dificultades para expresarlas con palabras, puedo llegar incluso a la convicción de que se resisten a la expresión lingüística, y que por lo tanto no pueden describirse o parafrasearse sino de forma muy insatisfactoria. Este hecho pone de manifiesto que los significados pueden muy bien equipararse a estados de conciencia, pero no a significados lingüísticos.

Al haberse ido eliminando en las realizaciones escénicas de los últimos treinta años los elementos teatrales pertenecientes a cualquier tipo de contexto de orden superior, al hacer que estos elementos aparezcan y desaparezcan –a menudo con numerosas repeticiones– sin referirlos o subordinarlos a conexión causal alguna, al presentarlos de manera explícita como fenómenos emergentes que no remiten más que a sí mismos, se ha preparado al espectador para la idea de que el de percepción y el de generación de significado son uno y el mismo proceso.

Asimismo, el repentino, injustificado e inmotivado aparecer de un fenómeno es la premisa para que pueda darse una nueva manera de percibirlo. Si bien en primer lugar se lo percibe en su ser fenoménico, después, tan pronto como la atención deja de centrarse en lo percibido, empieza, por así decirlo, a divagar, se convierte en un significante con el que se vinculan las más diversas asociaciones –ideas, recuerdos, sensaciones, emociones, pensamientos– en calidad de sus objetos de denotación. ¿De acuerdo a qué reglas surgen esas asociaciones? ¿A qué dan lugar?

Si un espectador hubiera padecido de fobia a los caballos –como el pequeño Hans de Freud–, a las arañas o a las serpientes, habría una cierta probabilidad, aunque no tendría por qué ser así necesariamente, de que en *Las Bacantes* de Grüber, en *She was and She is, Even* de Fabre o en *Dragon Heads* de Abramović la fobia lo dominara. Aparte de estos ejemplos, parece del todo imposible predecir a qué tipo de asociaciones puede dar lugar la percepción de un objeto, aunque quien percibe pueda detectar posteriormente vínculos razonables para sí.

Como muestra el que posiblemente sea el ejemplo más famoso de la literatura, el caso de la magdalena de Proust, cuyo aroma y sabor liberaron en él un torrente de recuerdos, se puede producir una conexión entre el aroma y el sabor de algo y los recuerdos a los que dan lugar, a pesar de que éstos no sean deducibles con necesidad, ni siquiera con una cierta probabilidad, a partir de aquéllos. Emergen en la conciencia del perceptor sin que haya un mecanismo que lo fuerce y sin que el perceptor pretenda conscientemente suscitarlos o invocarlos –el aroma y sabor de una magdalena mojada en té, cuando Proust los percibe, no dan lugar siempre a los mismos recuerdos–.

La supresión de los fenómenos emergentes de contextos dados de antemano crea sin duda una situación favorable para poner al perceptor en un estado comparable con el de Proust al oler y saborear la magdalena mojada en té. Estos fenómenos pueden incluirse casi en cualquier contexto que queramos, pueden establecer un vínculo con él repentinamente o a través de toda una serie de mediaciones. Este vínculo raramente se establece de manera consciente e intencionada, como, por ejemplo, cuando un espectador que percibe el horno en *Murx* trata de acordarse de dónde ha visto antes un horno así, y en esa búsqueda termina llegando a una situación autobiográfica determinada. Las asociaciones, por el contrario, acontecen sin que se las invoque o se las busque. Se regulan por sí mismas, se le imponen a aquel en cuya conciencia surgen al percibir un determinado objeto.

Estas asociaciones hacen referencia –en tanto que recuerdos– a lo vivido, aprendido o experimentado, a vivencias muy concretas, únicas, subjetivas, y a códigos culturales intersubjetivos vigentes. Junto a ellas pueden suscitarse también asociaciones que surjan como intuiciones repentinas, nuevas ideas, pensamientos nunca antes pensados. En este último caso pueden suponer una mayor sorpresa para el sujeto perceptor que todas las demás, pues no puede saber qué pueda tener que ver el pensamiento repentinamente surgido con la percepción de ese objeto concreto.

En ambos casos, los significados emergen sin que el sujeto perceptor lo haya pretendido. No aparecen ni como consecuencia de un nexo causal establecido de la manera que sea ni debido a la intención del sujeto en cuestión. Su aparecer es, en este sentido, injustificado e inmotivado. El proceso de generación de significado como asociación se diferencia en este aspecto de un proceso de dilucidación e interpretación ejecutado claramente de manera intencionada. Mientras que en éste se buscan significados que –independientemente los criterios en cada caso– «encajen» los unos con los otros (aunque su accesibilidad en ningún caso esté siempre en poder de quien interpreta), en aquél, en cambio, los significados emergen ajenos a la voluntad o a los empeños del sujeto perceptor en cuestión, a veces incluso emergen en contra de su voluntad. Los significados que se generan en ese proceso pueden entenderse como emergencias.

Siempre y cuando sean pensamientos, las asociaciones se mantienen, por así decirlo, en la conciencia. Ello es así tanto si son recuerdos como si son nuevos significados, a menos que a la persona en cuestión la novedad de su pensamiento le produzca una excitación tal que termine articulándose físicamente (como taquicardia, sudoración o desasosiego físico), con lo que puede ser percibida por los demás, o que desee anotar sus pensamientos, lo que conducirá a una acción perceptible. Las sensaciones y las emociones que surgen en ese proceso se articulan, por el contrario, físicamente, y a menudo de manera que los demás pueden percibirlas. Así, por ejemplo, pueden articularse como temblor o sollozo, pero sobre todo como desasosiego físico. Tan pronto como otros espectadores y/o los actores pueden percibirlos, es decir, cuando son vistos, oídos, olidos o sentidos, se convierten en parte integrante del bucle de retroalimentación autopoiético. Los significados que surgen en la conciencia del sujeto perceptor como contenidos significativos del objeto percibido como significante pueden sin duda tomar parte en el bucle de retroalimentación autopoiético, sea porque se articulan físicamente, y son por ello perceptibles para otros, sea porque conllevan reacciones físicas perceptibles para otros.

Así pues, la desvinculación de los elementos teatrales de contextos dados de antemano, su aislamiento, tiene como consecuencia dos tipos muy distintos de percepción y de generación de significado. En ambos casos la materialidad, el significante y el significado están en relaciones distintas. En el primero, el fenómeno es percibido como lo que aparece, es decir, en su ser fenoménico. En este sentido materialidad, significante y significado coinciden. En el segundo caso, por el contrario, se separan claramente. El fenómeno es percibido como un significante que puede vincularse a los más diversos significados. Los significados que se le atribuyen en este proceso no dependen de la voluntad del sujeto, surgen injustificada e inmotivadamente en su conciencia –aunque a menudo de forma que posteriormente puede plausiblemente explicarse. Mientras que los primeros significados surgidos de esta manera pueden, al menos a posteriori, ser puestos en relación con el objeto percibido, los que aparecen después apenas tienen relación con él. En este caso son los significados ya generados los que generan los siguientes significados. Ambos modos de generación tienen en común, sin embargo, que no se realizan sobre la base de un código intersubjetivo vigente, de una atribución convencionalmente fundamentada.

Existe un sorprendente paralelismo entre estos dos modos de percepción y de constitución de significado y los conceptos de símbolo y alegoría en la teoría estética de Benjamin. Es posible que tal paralelismo haya sido eclipsado por el hecho de que la teoría estética de Benjamin está fundamentada en su teoría lingüística y se desarrolla en el contexto de una particular concepción de la filosofía de la historia. Pese a ello, se impone establecer aquí esa relación. Benjamin le da forma a su concepto de símbolo partiendo de la teoría del símbolo de Goerres, «que pone el acento sobre lo que de semejante a la naturaleza de las montañas y las plantas hay en el crecimiento del símbolo»[4]. Por otro lado, Benjamin se remite a la *Mitología* de Creuzer, en la que los símbolos son caracterizados como «lo momentáneo, lo total, lo insondable de su origen y lo necesario»[5]. «La medida temporal de la experiencia simbólica es el instante místico *[Nu]*, en el que el símbolo da acogida al sentido en su interior oculto e incluso boscoso, si es que puede decirse de ese modo»[6]. El símbolo es concebido de tal manera que niega cualquier tipo de participación de un sujeto generador de significado, pues ya ha acogido a su significado en su «interior». Se remite a un significado intrínseco, a su significado intrínseco. Aunque el símbolo lo cree un sujeto –como es el caso, por nombrar uno, en un símbolo artístico–, en él la subjetividad tiende a borrar sus huellas, a diluirse y a desaparecer. De ahí que parezca que el símbolo se sustrae a cualquier acto de concesión de significado, sea por parte del artista que lo crea o por parte del intérprete que lo explica. Sólo puede ser percibido. El símbolo creado por un sujeto ha de comprehender

4 Walter Benjamin, *Ursprung des deutschen Trauerspiels*. Rolf Tiedemann (ed.), Fráncfort, 1972, p. 182 (esp. *El origen del 'Trauerspiel' alemán*, en Walter Benjamin, *Obras. Libro I/vol. I*, Madrid, 2006, pp. 217-459, p. 382).

5 Friedrich Creuzer, citado por Benjamin, *Ursprung des deutschen Trauerspiels*, p. 179 (esp. *ibid.*, p. 380).

6 Benjamin, *Ursprung des deutschen Trauerspiels*, p. 182 (esp., p. 382).

y revelar su significado del mismo modo que lo hicieron las cosas con los significados que Dios les había otorgado antes del inicio de la Historia, en el Paraíso: materialidad, significante y significado coinciden. Por ello el significado del símbolo no aparece ni como algo arbitrario ni como una relación creada subjetivamente, sino como algo dado en él.

El símbolo niega así la participación efectiva de la subjetividad e intenta excluirla de su significado. Con ello se convierte, en la filosofía de la historia de Benjamin, en una anticipación de lo por venir. Y al igual que el símbolo oculta su significado en su interior y también lo desvela, así también la naturaleza, el Día de la Redención, revelará «en *Nu*» el significado oculto en ella. Por ello, el símbolo apunta al Final de la Historia, que él mismo simboliza de consuno porque en él «con la transfiguración de la caducidad el rostro transfigurado de la naturaleza se revela fugazmente a la luz de la redención»[7].

La similitud entre ambas concepciones salta a la vista. Tanto en la una como en la otra se trata de la coincidencia de materialidad, significante y significado, y tanto aquí como allí, en el caso del símbolo y en el de la autorreferencialidad, puede hablarse de significado intrínseco. Sin embargo, no se pueden pasar por alto las importantes diferencias, que en lo fundamental se basan en la concepción de la filosofía de la historia de Benjamin. Pues en el caso de la autorreferencialidad no se niega en absoluto la participación del sujeto perceptor. Es más bien su percepción del fenómeno en su ser la que permite que hablemos de significado intrínseco. Es el acto de percepción de un sujeto el que por primera vez genera el significado del objeto percibido como su ser fenoménico.

Pese a estas diferencias puede concluirse, en mi opinión, que al escindir los fenómenos emergentes de los contextos dados de antemano, los artistas de teatro y de performance han creado las condiciones para que en ellos pueda surgir algo así como el sím-

7 *Ibid.* (esp., p. 383).

bolo benjaminiano tanto en el aparecer de las cosas en el espacio como en el acto de su percepción.

Benjamin contrapone al símbolo así concebido la alegoría como «prehistoria del significar». La alegoría se enfrenta al fenómeno del significado tal y como viene dado en el mundo histórico, esto es, en el periodo que va desde el pecado original hasta la salvación. Parte del supuesto de que naturaleza y lenguaje se han disociado por el mutismo de aquélla y por la consecuente necesidad de que el ser humano se ve obligado a atribuirle continuamente nuevos significados. El significado alegórico es el resultado de una configuración subjetiva que en última instancia es arbitraria.

Benjamin describe la alegoría como un procedimiento de generación de significado que remite explícitamente a esa arbitrariedad, es decir, que al mismo tiempo remite también a la participación de la subjetividad. «Cada personaje, cada cosa y cada situación puede significar cualquier otra»[8]. En el mundo histórico las cosas han dejado de tener un significado en sí. Por ello cualquier objeto que queramos puede emplearse, independientemente de su materialidad específica, como signo de cualquier otro. Materialidad, significante y significado divergen.

Los objetos de los que se apodera el alegórico dejan de tener significado, carecen de contenido significativo. Cualquier significado que pueda atribuírseles se lo deben a la configuración subjetiva que les impone el alegórico. El objeto «yace ante el alegórico, enteramente entregado a merced suya. Lo que significa que a partir de ahora es totalmente incapaz de irradiar un significado ni un sentido; de significado le corresponde lo que le confiere el alegórico, que se lo mete dentro. [...] En sus manos la cosa se convierte en algo distinto»[9]. La acción del alegórico convierte a las cosas en carentes de significado y en significativas a la vez: carentes de significado porque la intención de su subjetividad les priva de la posibilidad, que quizá aún tengan y que les era originalmente inherente, de revelar los significados conferidos por

8 *Ibid.*, p. 193 (esp., p. 393).

9 *Ibid.*, pp. 204 y s. (esp., pp. 402 y s.).

Dios; y significativas, porque justamente ese acto de subjetividad intencional les vuelve a dotar de significado.

Al convertir las cosas, lo significado originalmente, en significativas, el significado en significante, el alegórico les procura la posibilidad de que por primera vez en el mundo histórico vuelvan a ser algo significado, algo con contenido significativo. Pues las cosas que han devenido significantes pueden remitir las unas a las otras, en un proceso teóricamente infinito, de igual forma que remiten a su contenido significativo.

La contemplación alegórica en un objeto concreto sólo puede considerar el objeto como un fragmento, es decir, como una cosa arrancada a cualquier tipo de contexto, y sólo puede remitir al hecho de la fragmentariedad. Sólo en tanto que fragmento puede la cosa, en el acto alegórico y en virtud de la arbitrariedad subjetiva, ser dotada de un nuevo significado. Benjamin entiende este procedimiento de atribución de significado a las cosas en tanto que fragmentadas, en tanto que aisladas, como su «salvación». Pues de otro modo terminarían siendo insignificantes, mudas, serían destruidas por su transitoriedad. El significado que atribuye el alegórico a una cosa no tiene nada en común –como es obvio– con su significado primigenio, aquel que podía expresar sin intermediación antes del pecado original. Pero puesto que en cualquier caso es un significado, el procedimiento alegórico anticipa el estado de redención alegóricamente, el estado en el que las cosas podrán volver a revelar su significado intrínseco[10].

Para la dotación de significado alegórica es condición necesaria la escisión de los contextos predeterminados, como lo es para la generación de significado asociativa en nuestro segundo caso. Tanto en la alegoría como en la asociación cualquier forma de atribución o de generación de significado se lleva a cabo en con-

10 Véase para un análisis más detallado de la teoría del arte de Benjamin, Fischer-Lichte, *Bedeutung – Probleme einer semiotischen Hermeneutik und Ästhetik*, especialmente pp. 180-206; Fischer-Lichte, «Die Allegorie als Paradigma einer Ästhetik der Avantgarde. Eine semiotische *re-lecture* von Walter Benjamins *Ursprung des deutschen Trauerspiels*», en *Ästhetische Erfahrung. Das Semiotische und das Performative*, Tubinga/Basilea, 2001, pp. 121-137.

diciones que dependen exclusivamente de la subjetividad del perceptor. En esa medida se puede decir que prevalece una llamativa concordancia. La diferencia crucial, sin embargo, estriba en que para el significado alegórico lo decisivo es la sola intención del autor de la alegoría, es él quien le atribuye voluntariamente ese significado a la cosa percibida. En el caso de las asociaciones, por el contrario, los significados surgen en la conciencia del sujeto perceptor sin que este proceso pueda controlarse a voluntad, sin que se tenga completa potestad sobre los significados.

Símbolo y alegoría se oponen, parecen excluirse mutuamente. Los separa el abismo de la historia, aunque ambos remiten al estado de salvación mesiánica en el que las cosas pueden revelar de nuevo su significado primigenio, el otorgado por Dios. En las realizaciones escénicas analizadas, los dos tipos de percepción y de generación de significado que se hacían posibles por medio del aislamiento de los elementos teatrales de contextos predeterminados, por medio de la emergencia, están, sin embargo, en otra relación entre sí. En cualquier momento el uno puede convertirse en el otro: lo que ahora tiene lugar como percepción de algo, como su ser fenoménico, se convierte de repente en su percepción en tanto que significante al que se le pueden referir los más diversos significados –la percepción de algo como «símbolo» puede convertirse en cualquier instante en su percepción como «alegoría». También para este fenómeno se encuentra un paralelismo en el marco de la filosofía de la historia de Benjamin: pues en la alegoría «la caducidad no es significada, no es alegóricamente representada, tanto como es significante y ofrecida como alegoría. Alegoría de la resurrección. En las señales de muerte del Barroco, la consideración de lo alegórico [...] acabaría por cambiar de rumbo. [...] El alegórico despierta de este modo en el mundo de la divinidad»[11].

He mencionado la teoría del arte y del significado de Benjamin para incidir una vez más en un aspecto de la semioticidad de las realizaciones escénicas al que se le ha dado una y otra vez un

11 Benjamin, *Ursprung des deutschen Trauerspiels*, pp. 263 y s. (esp., p. 456).

papel decisivo desde los años sesenta: la oscilación entre dos modos completamente distintos de generación de significado, el significado dado, casi «objetivo», como en el símbolo en Benjamin, y las asociaciones, cuya emergencia depende de condiciones que al parecer establece el sujeto perceptor, razón por la que sin duda pueden compararse con la alegoría en Benjamin. En ninguno de los dos casos se genera el significado sobre la base de un código intersubjetivo vigente.

En este contexto me gustaría volver a insistir en que en los significados generados en los casos que aquí nos ocupan –a diferencia de lo que ocurre en Benjamin– no se trata, en su mayoría, de significados lingüísticos. Es mucho más frecuente que sean significados que se resisten tenazmente a las fórmulas verbales. El proceso por el que tratamos de «traducirlos» a lenguaje entra en juego siempre a posteriori, cuando queremos reflexionar sobre ellos o transmitírselos a otros.

2. «Presencia» y «representación»

En el capítulo sobre la materialidad de las realizaciones escénicas introduje el concepto de multiestabilidad perceptiva y lo expliqué refiriéndome al ejemplo de los saltos de atención entre la singularidad corporal del actor y el personaje que interpreta. Partiendo de este ejemplo quiero discutir en primer lugar la relación entre los conceptos de presencia y representación/exposición (*Repräsentation/Darstellung*), para, sobre esta base, pasar después a ocuparme de la pregunta por la repercusión de los significados en la dinámica de los procesos de percepción y de la pregunta por su función en las realizaciones escénicas.

En las teorías estéticas los de presencia y representación fueron considerados largo tiempo como conceptos antagónicos. Presencia se equiparaba a inmediatez, a experiencia de plenitud y totalidad, a autenticidad. Representación, por el contrario, se relacionaba con los *grands récits* [metarrelatos] que servían de instancia de poder y control; se entendía que su significado había sido establecido sólidamente, que como tal era rígida y parecía, por lo tanto, un concepto problemático sobre todo porque su signicidad sólo permitía un acceso mediato al mundo. Aplicada a las realizaciones escénicas esta oposición significaba –justamente en los años sesenta y principios de los setenta– que el cuerpo del actor era el epítome de la presencia, en muchas ocasiones sólo el cuerpo desnudo. El personaje dramático, por el contrario, aparecía como epítome de la representación. Predeterminado por la «instancia de poder y control» del texto literario, reproducido o imitado por el actor con su cuerpo como representación de lo allí «prescrito», se consideraba al personaje sobre el escenario como prueba de la represión que el texto ejercía sobre el actor, y especialmente sobre su cuerpo. El cuerpo del actor tenía pues que ser liberado de las cadenas de la representación, de su control absoluto, para ayudar a abrirse paso a la espontaneidad, a la autenticidad de su existencia física.

Como se ha mostrado en el apartado «Corporización», no se pueden seguir entendiendo los conceptos de presencia y representación de esa manera, como si estuvieran en una relación de antagonismo. Tanto la presencia como el personaje se generan a través de procesos de corporización específicos. Así pues, el personaje no se origina como reproducción o imitación de algo dado de antemano, sino que sólo pueden generarlo determinados procesos de corporización. El personaje generado en cada caso está vinculado a la corporalidad específica del actor que lo genera. El cuerpo fenoménico del actor, su físico estar-en-el-mundo constituye el fundamento existencial para el surgimiento del personaje. Al margen del cuerpo individual el personaje no existe.

Cuando el actor interpreta un personaje, no reproduce algo dado en otra parte –en el texto de la obra–, sino que crea algo completamente nuevo, algo único que sólo puede existir de esa manera en virtud de su corporalidad individual. Si queremos mantener el concepto de representación para explicar el proceso de generación de un personaje, tenemos que redefinirlo radicalmente. Representación y presencia son el resultado, tal y como se originan en la percepción, de procesos de corporización específicos. De ello no se sigue, sin duda, que se haya eliminado toda diferencia entre los conceptos de presencia y representación.

Pues incluso si en ambos casos se tratara de los mismos procesos de corporización –un caso que, sin duda, puede darse, que se da incluso a menudo, a saber: cuando un actor aparece en todo momento de la interpretación como presente cuando «interpreta» a un personaje–, los resultados que se originan en la percepción de cada uno son considerablemente distintos. Esto se evidencia sobre todo en el fenómeno de la multiestabilidad perceptiva.

Como se ha explicado, la percepción puede dar un giro en el mismo acto de percibir. Lo que en un momento se percibe como presencia del actor, puede percibirse como personaje un instante después y viceversa. No es un trabajo de la naturaleza de éste el lugar adecuado para dar con una explicación psicológica para este fenómeno[12]. Para lo que aquí interesa, y ya que no se puede dar razón del salto perceptivo, basta con constatar que en estos casos se trata sin duda de emergencias. Nuestros intentos de tratar de explicarlo como consecuencia de determinados procedimientos dramatúrgicos o escénicos han fracasado hasta el momento. Aunque en una realización escénica no se establezca un vínculo perceptible entre los personajes y los actores mencionados en el programa de mano, siempre habrá algunos espectadores que consideren al actor, pese a todo, como personaje. Asimismo, en una realización escénica psicológico-realista que sea consecuente los espectadores sentirán permanentemente la presencia del actor. Por ello deberíamos conformarnos, en este punto, con la conclusión de que en el estado actual de nuestros conocimientos, el caso de los saltos perceptivos es un fenómeno de emergencia.

Para lo que a nosotros nos ocupa es mucho más interesante la pregunta por los efectos de la multiestabilidad perceptiva en una realización escénica. Como ya habíamos visto, en las realizaciones escénicas posteriores a los años sesenta se han empleado una gran

12 Para una aclaración, véase Michael Stadler/Peter Kruse, «Zur Emergenz psychischer Qualitäten. Das psychologische Problem im Lichte der Selbstorganisationstheorie», en Wolfgang Krohn y Günter Küppers, *Emergenz: Die Entstehung von Ordnung. Organization und Bedeutung*, Fráncfort, 1992, pp. 134-160.

cantidad de procedimientos que parecen posibilitar la irrupción de la multiestabilidad perceptiva en mucha mayor medida que en el caso de las realizaciones escénicas psicológico-realistas. Los montajes de Wilson, Castorf y Fabre, entre otros, parecen efectivamente buscar su aparición. Sin duda se proponen que se produzca el salto perceptivo una y otra vez. Pues en ese instante se produce una fractura, una discontinuidad. Se altera el orden de percepción vigente hasta entonces, se abandona y se establece uno nuevo. Percibir el cuerpo del actor como su físico estar-en-el-mundo instaura un orden de percepción específico; percibir, en cambio, el cuerpo del actor como signo de un personaje instaura un orden distinto. Mientras que el primer orden genera significado como ser fenoménico de lo percibido, aunque este significado puede generar gran cantidad de nuevos significados, que en su mayoría no tendrán relación con lo percibido, el segundo produce significados que, en su totalidad, constituyen al personaje. Al primer tipo de orden de percepción podemos denominarlo, en el sentido del concepto débil de presencia, orden de la presencia y, al segundo, orden de la representación.

¿Qué sucede entonces en el instante del salto, es decir, en el momento en el que se altera el orden de percepción vigente pero aún no se ha establecido uno nuevo, el instante en el que se pasa del orden de la presencia al orden de la representación y viceversa? Se origina un estado de inestabilidad que pone al perceptor entre dos órdenes, en un estado *betwixt and between*. Se encuentra justo en el umbral que constituye la transición de un orden al otro, en un estado liminar.

Si durante una realización escénica la percepción salta continuamente, al espectador se le pone entre dos órdenes de percepción, y como consecuencia de ello la diferencia entre órdenes se va haciendo cada vez menos importante y la atención del perceptor se concentra en las transiciones, en la alteración de la estabilidad, en el estado de inestabilidad y en la creación de una estabilidad nueva. Cuanto más frecuentes sean los saltos, más frecuentemente se convertirá el perceptor en errante entre dos mundos, entre dos órdenes de percepción. En ese proceso se hace cada vez más consciente de que las transiciones escapan a su control. Puede intentar, eso sí, «ajustar» su percepción al orden de la presencia o al orden de la representación. En ese momento experimenta su propia percepción como emergente, como algo que escapa a su voluntad y a su control, como algo de lo que no tiene disponibilidad absoluta y libre, pero que ejecuta al mismo tiempo conscientemente.

Son percepciones conscientes, aunque no tengan origen voluntario. Los significados que se generan en esas percepciones y con esas percepciones tampoco hay que pensarlos como generados intencionalmente. Surgen súbitamente en la conciencia en el acto de la percepción.

Al respecto se suscita la pregunta de si los significados generados en el ámbito de ambos órdenes de percepción –primero en el acto perceptivo y después a partir de los significados generados en ese mismo acto– son de naturaleza esencialmente distinta. El orden de percepción de la presencia ¿produce como significados sobre todo sensaciones, representaciones mentales (*Vorstellungen*) y emociones que pueden articularse físicamente y ser percibidas por los demás como reacciones psicológicas, afectivas, energéticas o motoras? Y en el orden de percepción de la representación ¿se originan sobre todo pensamientos, representaciones mentales y emociones que sólo se articulan en el interior del cuerpo y que en muy pocas ocasiones llegan a ser tan intensos como para apoderarse del perceptor, de tal manera que siempre se puede mantener una cierta distancia con lo percibido? Las realizaciones escénicas a las que me he referido hasta ahora parecen sugerir esta conclusión. Una conclusión que parece tanto más plausible cuanto que los significados generados en el primer caso se consideran significados constitutivos de realidad, mientras que en el segundo erigen un mundo ficticio o un orden simbólico. Sin embargo, sabemos por la historia del teatro, especialmente la de los siglos diecisiete y dieciocho, que precisamente significados de ese tipo han dado lugar a emociones de gran intensidad. No se pueden extraer por lo tanto conclusiones de validez general en lo que concierne a esta cuestión. Si nos limitamos exclusivamente a las realizaciones escénicas analizadas hasta ahora, la conclusión parece sin duda lícita.

Cada uno de los dos órdenes de percepción genera sus significados de acuerdo a principios distintos, que se convierten en dominantes cuando un orden se estabiliza. En el orden de la representación, por ejemplo, todo lo que se percibe, se percibe en relación con el personaje, con un determinado mundo ficticio o un determinado orden simbólico. Los significados así generados, generan a su vez al personaje, el mundo ficticio o el orden simbólico en cuestión en su integridad. En estos casos, el objetivo de crear un personaje, un mundo ficticio, etc., es el que guía sin duda el proceso de percepción. Los elementos percibidos que no hayan de fungir como signos del personaje son desatendidos en los posteriores procesos de generación de significado. Los significados generados en cada caso, los que crean al personaje, tienen una influencia en la dinámica del proceso de percepción de manera que ésta selecciona sólo aquellos elementos que el sujeto en cuestión puede percibir en aras de la constitución de ese personaje. El proceso se realiza en este sentido con una finalidad clara y es por ello, hasta cierto punto, predecible.

Éste es el orden de la percepción al que aspiraban los teóricos del siglo dieciocho. Pero, como ya ellos mismos pudieron comprobar, el orden de la percepción no se puede estabilizar de esa manera. En un momento dado la percepción salta, el orden de la representación se altera y se da lugar –aunque sólo sea provisionalmente– a otro orden, el orden de la presencia.

En el orden de percepción de la presencia rigen principios muy distintos. El significado del ser fenoménico del cuerpo o del objeto percibidos genera a su vez significados asociativos que no tienen por qué tener relación con lo percibido. Cuando el orden de percepción de la presencia se estabiliza, el proceso de percepción y de generación de significado transcurre de manera totalmente imprevisible, es, por así decirlo, «caótico». Nunca se puede prever qué significados se van a generar por asociación, nunca se puede saber de antemano qué significado guiará a la percepción a qué elemento teatral. La estabilidad en el caso de este orden implica un alto grado de imprevisibilidad[13]. En este

13 Esto tiene considerables consecuencias teóricas que hay que tener en cuenta,

sentido, el proceso de percepción se lleva a cabo como un proceso completamente emergente. Es el orden de la presencia, la autorreferencialidad, el que genera significados sólo como emergentes, significados sobre los que el perceptor no tiene ninguna potestad.

La multiestabilidad perceptiva, que da lugar al salto de la percepción de un orden al otro, es la responsable de que ninguno de los dos órdenes pueda estabilizarse de manera perdurable. La dinámica del proceso de percepción da un nuevo giro en cada transición, en cada estado de inestabilidad. Pierde el carácter azaroso y se orienta a un objetivo, o bien pierde su carácter de proceso orientado a una finalidad y empieza a descontrolarse. Cada giro conduce, con una alta probabilidad, a la percepción de algo distinto –a saber: la de aquello que se puede insertar en el orden recién estabilizado y que contribuye a su estabilización–, y con ello a la generación de significados distintos en cada caso.

Además, el salto perceptivo, como se ha descrito más arriba, dirige la atención del perceptor al proceso de percepción en sí y a su dinámica específica. El perceptor empieza a percibirse a sí mismo como perceptor, lo que genera significados específicos que a su vez generan otros significados que influyen en la dinámica del proceso de percepción.

Cuanto más frecuentemente pasa la percepción del orden de la presencia al orden de la representación, es decir, de procesos de percepción y de generación de significado «azarosos» a procesos predecibles, mayor es el grado de imprevisibilidad general y más intensamente se centra la atención del sujeto perceptor en el proceso de percepción en sí. Se hace cada vez más consciente de que los significados no le son transmitidos, sino que es él quien los genera y que, por lo tanto, podría haber generado otros significados muy distintos dependiendo, por ejemplo, de si la transición de un orden a otro hubiera tenido lugar en otro momento o con mayor o menor frecuencia.

---

sobre todo respecto a las posibilidades y métodos de análisis de realizaciones escénicas.

Aunque los procesos de percepción y de generación de significado han de ser considerados subjetivos, no por ello hay que considerarlos procesos solipsistas. Lo cierto es que participan activamente en la autopoiesis del bucle de retroalimentación. Se comunican con los demás, con los actores y con el resto de espectadores, ya sea porque articulan en sí físicamente determinadas sensaciones o emociones de forma perceptible, ya porque de ellas se siguen acciones igualmente perceptibles. ¿Pero cómo se configura en este proceso la relación entre significado y efecto, dos conceptos que los representantes de las vanguardias históricas entendían y defendían como opuestos?

3. Significado y efecto

Los vanguardistas insistieron una y otra vez en que las realizaciones escénicas tenían que lograr dos tipos de efectos: shocks o cualquier otro tipo de emociones y acciones impactantes. En lo tocante al primer tipo de efectos, los artistas de las vanguardias se adherían, a pesar de que la mayoría de ellos la desconocía, a una larga y venerable tradición. Desde la *Poética* de Aristóteles hasta la estética del efecto en las postrimerías del siglo dieciocho, la excitación de pasiones, emociones y afectos es el efecto primordial de las realizaciones escénicas teatrales. Era este efecto en el que se basaban primordialmente su valor y el riesgo que pudiera provenir de ellas. En ese caso se partía del supuesto de que era la interpretación de pasiones por parte del actor –o sea, un modo específico de significarlas– la que suscitaba a su vez pasiones en el espectador, aunque no fueran necesariamente las interpretadas por el actor, sino muchas veces otras muy distintas. En este caso, el significado estaba al servicio del efecto. Se pensaba que sólo cuando se les transmitían a los espectadores ciertos significados de una manera determinada –una manera que prescribían las reglas de la actuación actoral– se podían suscitar en ellos los efectos deseados en ellos. La posibilidad de reconocer de inmediato y con exactitud la emoción presentada en cada caso se consideraba la premisa más importante para que afloraran las emociones en el espectador. A esta premisa se remitía el código gestual del teatro barroco según lo estableció Franciscus Lang en su *Dissertatio de actione scenica* (1727), así como el código de un arte de la actuación «natural», cuyo estadio de desarrollo en su época fue resumido por Johan Jakob Engel en su *Mimik* (1785-1786)[14]. La transmisión precisa de un significado específico era tenida por la condición de posibilidad para que la realización escénica fuera eficaz, para que se desencadenaran los afectos del espectador.

Por el contrario, los representantes de las vanguardias históricas, que se posicionaron contra la estética representacional del teatro psicológico-realista del siglo diecinueve y que proclamaron una nueva estética del efecto, consideraban el significado, por un lado, como un fenómeno puramente intelectual que sólo puede poner en marcha procesos intelectuales, pero no emociones, y lo entendían, por otro, en el sentido de un mensaje en el que se formulaba una ideología, la burguesa, que rechazaban. Consideraban las reacciones físicas intensas que pueden ser percibidas por otros, del modo en que las describe y exige Marinetti en «El teatro de variedades», como efectos que no se pueden escindir de los significados. En su opinión, reacciones de este tipo sólo podían suscitarse por medio de acciones que supusieran un ataque directo al cuerpo del espectador y que carecieran de significado en el sentido mencionado más arriba.

Que consideremos los conceptos de significado y efecto como opuestos o como mutuamente condicionados depende, por una parte, de cómo entendamos el uno y el otro, y por otra parte, de la teoría psicológica de la que se parta en cada caso. Así pues, el problema de la relación entre significado y efecto sólo puede tratarse cabalmente en el contexto de los presupuestos teóricos de los que se parta.

En la medida en que defino los significados en general como estados de conciencia, entiendo que las sensaciones y las emocio-

14 Véase al respecto Erika Fischer-Lichte, *Semiotik des Theaters*, vol. 2, *Vom «künstlichen» zum «natürlichen» Zeichen. Theater des Barock und der Aufklärung*, Tubinga, 1983, 3.ª ed. 1995 (esp. *Semiótica del teatro. Libro II: del signo 'artificial' al 'natural'. Teatro del Barroco y de la Ilustración*, Madrid, 1999, pp. 295-510).

nes son significados[15]. Cuando hablamos de sensaciones y emociones, estamos también ante significados que se articulan físicamente y que sólo pueden llegar a ser conscientes por medio de ese articularse físicamente y como ese articularse físicamente. Es decir, que las articulaciones físicas concretas –respiración entrecortada, sudoración, piel de gallina, etc.– no hay que entenderlas como síntomas, como signos que remitieran a un sentimiento localizado en otra parte –en el «interior» de la persona, en su alma– y que el cuerpo se limitara a expresar, una idea sostenida por los teóricos del siglo dieciocho. Parto de la tesis de que las emociones se generan corporalmente y de que sólo pueden ser conscientes en tanto que articulaciones físicas. Las emociones son, pues, significados que, porque son articulados físicamente, pueden ser percibidos por otros y, en este sentido, pueden sin duda serles transmitidos sin que haya que «traducirlos» a palabras.

Si queremos arrojar más luz sobre la relación entre significado y efecto, la estrategia más prometedora parece la de centrarse, en primer lugar, en un determinado tipo de significados: en las emociones. Pues en la medida en que se articulan físicamente de modo perceptible, pueden ser registradas también por otros e intervenir así en la autopoiesis del bucle de retroalimentación. Si se entiende efecto como influencia en el proceso de autoorganización del bucle de retroalimentación, de ello se sigue que los significados, en la medida en que intervienen en el bucle de retroalimentación, pueden ser considerados como efectos. La cuestión que hay que aclarar al respecto es la siguiente: ¿cómo pueden los significados intervenir en el bucle de retroalimentación autopoiético?

En el primer apartado se ha mostrado que, si consideramos las percepciones, en tanto que estados de conciencia, como significados, serán significados que en general den lugar a nuevos significados. En el segundo apartado ha quedado claro hasta qué punto otros significados pueden intervenir en la percepción.

15 Véase al respecto las pp. 281-285. De esta definición de significado se derivan importantes consecuencias para la semiótica en las que no podemos entrar aquí.

Ahora bien, el sujeto perceptor no es una *tabula rasa* cuando asiste a una realización escénica. Ha generado durante toda su vida gran cantidad de significados de los que tiene memoria. Por ello hay que partir del supuesto de que la «primera» percepción que surja durante una realización escénica también habrá sido generada por significados previos que pueden ser puramente subjetivos o adquiridos en el ámbito de un código cultural.

Si nos referimos a emociones suscitadas en la realización escénica, se sigue que cuando la percepción de un elemento teatral genera emociones hay que dar por supuesto que éstas remiten a significados generados anteriormente. Esto quiere decir, como muestra el ejemplo de las fobias, que aquel que sufra de fobia a las serpientes, cuando perciba una lo hará presa del temor. La fobia es, en este sentido, parte integrante del significado que el objeto serpiente tiene para él. Así pues, lo primero que genera el miedo no es la percepción de la serpiente. Es porque la fobia pertenece al significado del objeto serpiente y porque ése es el significado que genera la percepción como significado, por lo que la percepción de la serpiente suscita miedo en ese momento.

Las fobias son significados absolutamente subjetivos que tienen su origen en la biografía individual. Hay, sin embargo, objetos y procesos cuya percepción puede desencadenar parecidas emociones, de alto contenido afectivo, en un gran número de integrantes de una misma cultura. Al escindir los elementos teatrales de contextos específicos dados, contextos que llegado el caso podían influir sobre ellas de tal manera que atenuara el componente emocional de su significado, si es que no llegaba a neutralizarlo, las realizaciones escénicas consideradas hasta ahora creaban condiciones favorables para que un elemento teatral eventualmente cargado emocionalmente pudiera tener un impacto tal que suscitara emociones de gran intensidad.

Cuando se quebranta un tabú sólidamente enraizado, se desencadenan emociones muy similares en muchos espectadores. Así parece que ocurrió en *Lips of Thomas* o en *Giulio Cesare*, por referirnos a dos ejemplos muy claros.

En nuestra cultura impera el culto obsesivo a la juventud, a la delgadez y la buena forma física. Los cuerpos que se oponen rotundamente a este ideal son estigmatizados apelando al expediente de anomalía y excluidos en lo posible del ámbito público. La enfermedad y la muerte en nuestra sociedad no es que sean un tabú, es que son anatema. Los cuerpos que nos recuerdan a ellas suscitan aversión, repugnancia, asco, miedo y vergüenza. Al presentar precisamente tales cuerpos en escena, sin justificar especialmente su desviación de la normalidad –porque así lo exigía algún papel, por ejemplo–, la Socìetas Raffaelo Sanzio exponía a los espectadores «desprotegidos» a la visión de tales cuerpos. Los significados que, en nuestra sociedad, y consecuentemente en el caso de la mayoría de sus miembros, se les atribuyen a tales cuerpos, generaban en los perceptores las mismas emociones que articulaban físicamente de manera claramente perceptible. En este caso eran, sin duda, los significados culturales que les habían sido transmitidos a los miembros de una cultura los que daban lugar a la percepción de determinadas –e intensas– emociones.

Procesos similares tuvieron lugar en muchas performances de Abramović, como *Lips of Thomas* o *Rhythm 0*. Ambas atacaban un tabú sólidamente arraigado. En nuestra cultura la vida de los individuos y su integridad física se consideran el bien más preciado. Quien hiere el cuerpo de otro, amenaza su vida o llega incluso a matarlo se convierte en culpable del peor crimen imaginable, un crimen que sólo puede ser castigado con la pena más dura y la exclusión de la sociedad. Pero también quien se hiere a sí mismo o intenta suicidarse se pone al margen de la sociedad. Pasa a ser considerado un enfermo, se le pone en observación, se le vigila y se le impide agredirse. A ambos tipos de personas se les aparta de la sociedad, de la mirada de otras personas y del contacto con ellas. La violencia contra los demás y contra uno mismo es un fuerte tabú en nuestra sociedad. Mientras que la violencia contra los miembros de la propia comunidad parece ser un tabú en todas las sociedades, algo que ha señalado sobre todo Girard en su teoría del sacrificio, el rechazo de la violencia contra uno mismo no era absoluto en la cultura cristiana –sobre todo cuando se ejercía como emulación del sufrimiento de Cristo, como era el caso de la autoflagelación de frailes y monjas desde el siglo XI o el de las flagelaciones masivas en el siglo XVI–. En la sociedad actual, por el contrario, estas prácticas también son consideradas tabú. Sobre los tabúes se puede decir que en general, para los miembros de la sociedad en la que están vigentes, están cargados de intensas emociones y, la mayoría de las veces, de un alto grado de ambivalencia. El deseo de romperlos suele ser tan ferviente como desmesurada es la avidez de ver cómo se castiga y se excluye de la sociedad a quien lo hace.

En *Lips of Thomas* y *Rythm 0* Marina Abramović contravino ambos tabúes. Cuando los espectadores de *Lips of Thomas* fueron testigos de cómo Abramović se hería, de cómo se tallaba en la piel una estrella de cinco puntas, se fustigaba la espalda hasta sangrar y se tendía en una cruz hecha de bloques de hielo, o cuando presenciaron en *Rhythm 0* cómo otros la herían, la atormentaban, la hacían sufrir y le infligían violencia, muchos de ellos manifestaron emociones de gran intensidad. Ahora bien, esas emociones no eran consecuencia de un reflejo fisiológico, como cuando cerramos los ojos al sentir la presencia de un cuerpo extraño, ni del dolor físico que pueden causar algunos ruidos estridentes. Se generaron, más bien, porque las lesiones causadas a uno mismo o a otros estaban cargadas para los espectadores, ya antes de la realización escénica, de emociones de gran intensidad y tenían para ellos un significado acorde con ellas.

Estos significados adquiridos previamente eran los que influían en la dinámica del proceso de percepción: en el acto de la percepción se generaban significados que se articulaban físicamente como emociones de gran intensidad. Por un lado, estas emociones revelaron que no hay que entender los significados como fenómenos meramente «mentales» para cuya explicación haya que recurrir a una teoría de los dos mundos. Teniendo en cuenta el concepto de ser humano como *embodied mind*, los significados hay que entenderlos como corporizados, como algo que se articula corporalmente –aunque no siempre sea perceptible para los demás–. En el ejemplo de las emociones que se articulan físicamente queda claro hasta qué punto los significados que genera el espectador pueden influir en la autopoiesis del bucle de retroalimentación, hasta qué punto los significados producen efectos. Pues las articulaciones físicas que los demás espectadores o los actores ven, oyen, huelen o sienten, suscitan en quien las percibe modos de comportamiento y acciones observables, y así sucesivamente.

Las emociones pueden intervenir en la autopoiesis del bucle de retroalimentación aún de otra manera: como han demostrado las últimas investigaciones neuropsicológicas, nuestras acciones no se pueden explicar tanto a partir de la reflexión serena, a partir de nuestra concepción de la naturaleza del mundo o de cualquier otro tipo de convicciones que sostengamos, como a partir de nuestras emociones, en las que se originan las motivaciones más decisivas para dar razón de ellas[16].

Como se pudo observar en las performances de Abramović, eran las emociones generadas en la percepción las que motivaron impulsos activos. En *Lips of Thomas*, los espectadores se aproximaron a la artista que se mantenía impertérrita en la cruz de hielo, la bajaron de allí y se la llevaron. En *Rhythm 0* algunos de los espectadores impidieron a otros que prosiguieran con el martirio de la artista. Pero también en los casos en los que las realizaciones escénicas no pudieron terminar por acciones de los espectadores debidas a emociones, éstas influyeron igualmente en la autopoiesis del bucle de retroalimentación. Cuando algunos espectadores de las escenificaciones de Schleef abandonaban la sala despotricando y dando un portazo, le daban al bucle de retroalimentación un nuevo giro. Esto es aplicable a toda acción con la que un espectador se convierta en actor llevando a cabo un cambio de roles, como se mostró en el tercer capítulo. Lo que interesa en el contexto de la semioticidad de las realizaciones escénicas es la pregunta de hasta qué punto tales acciones son desencadenadas por significados. Como se ha mostrado en el ejemplo de las emociones, son los significados los que en realidad producen el impulso para actuar. Si estos impulsos se cohíben –y las emociones suscitadas por ellos no se articulan físicamente de manera

16 Véanse, entre otros, Luc Ciompi, *Die emotionalen Grundlagen des Denkens. Entwurf einer fraktalen Affektlogik*, Gotinga, 2.ª ed., 1999; Antonio R. Damasio, *Descartes' Error: Emotion, Reason, and the Human Brain*, Nueva York, 1994 (esp. *El error de Descartes: la emoción, la razón y el cerebro humano*, Barcelona, 2006); Roth, Gerhard, *Fühlen, Denken, Handeln*, Fráncfort, 2001; Ronald de Soussa, *The Rationality of Emotion*, MIT, 1987.

perceptible–, los significados carecen de relevancia para la autopoiesis del bucle de retroalimentación. Si, por el contrario, tales impulsos se siguen, esos significados generados por lo espectadores contribuyen decisivamente al desarrollo de la realización escénica. Ciertamente, cada individuo genera significados acordes con sus condiciones subjetivas. Asimismo, vale también respecto a la generación de significado lo que hemos dicho de la autopoiesis del bucle de retroalimentación, que todos lo determinan y al mismo tiempo son determinados por él, sin que ninguno tenga potestad absoluta sobre él.

Así pues, el efecto no es concebido unilateralmente, como era el caso en las «viejas» y en las «nuevas» estéticas del efecto: las vigentes hasta finales del siglo dieciocho y las de las vanguardias históricas respectivamente. En estos casos estaban por un lado los significados transmitidos por la realización escénica, que pretendían suscitar en el espectador efectos determinados –como lamentos, estremecimientos, admiración, temor, compasión, entre otros– y estaban, por otro lado, los «ataques» físicos a los que se exponía a los espectadores y que tenían la intención de moverlos a la acción o transformarlos. Eran los actores en escena, y detrás de la escena, los que se servían de determinados medios para lograr determinados efectos.

En las realizaciones escénicas posteriores a los años sesenta, por el contrario, el efecto es concebido como bilateral. Los actores traen algo a presencia que los espectadores perciben como algo. Los significados generados en el acto de la percepción, o en actos subsiguientes a él, pueden incluso influir a su vez en otros espectadores y en los actores, siempre que se articulen físicamente de modo perceptible, y así sucesivamente hasta el final de la realización escénica. Son pues los significados generados por el espectador los que pueden intervenir en la autopoiesis del bucle de retroalimentación y dar lugar a efectos.

No sólo se muestra en ello, aunque en ello lo haga con especial claridad, lo inadecuado de entender la semioticidad de una realización escénica en contraposición a su performatividad, aunque mucho más lo es tratar ambos conceptos como si estuvieran en contradicción; la semioticidad hay que entenderla en el contexto de una estética de lo performativo, un contexto en el que la emergencia de significados se revela como un elemento de importancia crucial. El proceso de generación de significados que tiene lugar en la realización escénica muestra una serie de semejanzas significativas con el bucle de retroalimentación autopoiético. Lo mismo que les ocurre a todos y cada uno de los participantes en la realización escénica, que toman parte en su determinación tanto como son determinados por ella, le ocurre al sujeto en los procesos de generación de significado que lleva a cabo. Los determina siempre que sigue, por ejemplo, el orden de la representación, es decir, cuando percibe de una manera orientada a un fin y produce significados de acuerdo a esa orientación. Y es determinado por ellos, por el contrario, cuando se dedica a hacer sus propias asociaciones, de las que surgen sensaciones, representaciones mentales o pensamientos que emergen en su conciencia sin que nadie las haya invocado y cuya emergencia no es capaz de impedir. En los procesos de generación de significado llevados a cabo por él mismo el sujeto no se experimenta tanto de manera activa como de manera pasiva, ni como un sujeto autónomo ni como un sujeto a merced de poderes insondables. Tal oposición ya no sirve.

Tras esta afirmación surge de manera perentoria una pregunta, una pregunta que desde el comienzo del capítulo estaba, por así decir, emboscada y al acecho: ¿se trata en el caso de este sujeto de un sujeto hermenéutico, es decir, un sujeto que genera significados para entender la realización escénica –sin que nos importe ahora si pretende efectivamente entenderla o si, en el transcurso del proceso, ha llegado a la conclusión de que el objetivo de entenderla está condenado al fracaso? Para dar respuesta a esta pregunta debemos ocuparnos de nuevo de los procesos de generación de significado, de los que ya hemos hablado en este capítulo, para dilucidar si se pueden subsumir al paradigma de una estética hermenéutica[17].

17 Para el concepto de estética hermenéutica, véase Fischer-Lichte, *Bedeutung – Probleme einer semiotischen Hermeneutik und Ästhetik*, Múnich, 1979.

4. ¿Se pueden entender las realizaciones escénicas?

Para los procesos de generación de significado en las realizaciones escénicas –y no sólo desde los años sesenta– goza de amplia aceptación la tesis de que el espectador no los realiza a distancia, sino en la medida en que toma parte en ellas, en la medida en que se implica. Aunque «internamente» mantenga una distancia con la realización, se recline aburrido en su butaca e incluso cierre los ojos, o aunque exprese su desafecto con comentarios irónicos en voz alta, con ello toma también parte en ella, es decir, interviene en la autopoiesis del bucle de retroalimentación. Mientras permanezca en la sala no puede no tomar parte. La distancia que puede mantener al observar un cuadro o al leer un poema es inviable en una realización escénica, le está vedada.

Al espectador no le es posible en ningún momento tener ante sus ojos la realización escénica en su totalidad, como si fuera un cuadro, y poder así relacionar con esa totalidad los elementos teatrales que percibe tomados por separado. Tampoco puede pasar las páginas ni hacia delante ni hacia atrás, como si de un libro se tratara. Sólo puede establecer conexiones entre los elementos nuevos que aparecen en cada momento, los ya aparecidos y los que aún recuerda. Así sucede también cuando vuelve a asistir a una misma escenificación. Pues dado que la realización escénica se origina cada vez de un modo nuevo y distinto en virtud de la autopoiesis del bucle de retroalimentación, el espectador no se encuentra nunca en una realización escénica exactamente igual, aunque se trate sin duda de la misma escenificación. Se constata, pues, de nuevo la necesidad de distinguir entre realización escénica y escenificación. En realidad, la condición más importante para que el espectador genere significado en la realización escénica estriba en la notable particularidad de que él mismo es a la vez parte y generador del proceso que pretende entender.

Una condición que no pierde su vigencia hasta que no termina la realización escénica. Es entonces, a posteriori, cuando el espectador puede intentar poner en relación con la totalidad cada uno de los detalles percibidos que mantenga en el recuerdo y conectar unas cosas con otras para, de esa manera, entender la realización escénica, o fracasar en el intento. Sin embargo, esa tentativa de comprender lo ocurrido a posteriori ya no forma parte del proceso estético, que termina con la realización escénica. En efecto, una tentativa de esa naturaleza no puede ser integrada en la experiencia estética como tal, que sólo tiene lugar durante la realización escénica. Sólo puede ser entendida como premisa para otro tipo de experiencia estética, para saber cómo se experimenta en sucesivas realizaciones escénicas. La cuestión que en realidad nos interesa es si los procesos de generación de significado, de los que me vengo ocupando en este capítulo, se pueden entender y explicar como procesos hermenéuticos.

¿Qué puede entenderse, por ejemplo, en la oscilación entre símbolo y alegoría? ¿Qué procesos de comprensión se llevan a cabo en ella? La percepción de un objeto (cuerpo, movimiento, cosa, color, sonido, etc.) como aquello que viene a presencia en el acto de percepción produce una rara «amalgama» entre el objeto percibido y el sujeto perceptor que no debe confundirse con la fusión de horizontes de Gadamer. La mirada del perceptor palpa el objeto, como lo expresó Merleau-Ponty, lo toca, o tiene lugar –como en las realizaciones escénicas teatrales de Felix Ruckert– un contacto físico real entre dos cuerpos. El sonido, la luz y el olor penetran en virtud del acto de percepción en el cuerpo del perceptor, le influyen, lo transforman. ¿Podría decirse que el sujeto perceptor entiende la extensión del objeto en el espacio que observa, en el olor que inhala, en el sonido que resuena en su caja torácica o en la resplandeciente luz que le deslumbra? Difícilmente. Más bien los experimenta en su ser fenoménico, que acaece en el acto de percepción. El espectador es afectado físicamente por la percepción, esto es, por lo percibido. Pero no lo «entiende». Esto no sólo se debe, pese a la reiterada insistencia de las teorías estéticas en lo contrario, a que la compresión llegue a sus límites, a que sea radicalmente cuestionada tan pronto la materialidad se sitúa en primer plano y acapara la atención del perceptor, como es aquí el caso[18]. Ello tiene su razón de ser, prin-

18 Véase respecto a este problema, entre otros, Jacques Derrida, «Restitucio-

cipalmente, en que aquí materialidad, significante y significado coinciden, con lo que queda vedada cualquier posibilidad de «desciframiento» del significado. El significado no puede escindirse de la materialidad, entenderse como un concepto. El significado es idéntico al aparecer material del objeto.

Las asociaciones de los más diversos tipos a que pueda dar lugar la percepción de un objeto, en concreto en quien lo percibe, pueden sin duda entenderse como respuesta (*respons*): responden al desafío que origina el aparecer del objeto, pero difícilmente pueden entenderse como un intento de entenderlo. Aquel en quien estas asociaciones surgen podría en todo caso intentar entender por qué aparecen precisamente en él esas asociaciones, y por qué precisamente ésas. En este sentido es sin duda pensable que en el caso de determinadas asociaciones el espectador en cuestión emprenda un intento de hermenéutica de la autocomprensión, que se esfuerce por desentrañar qué función ha tenido ese objeto en el desarrollo de su identidad personal y en el transcurso de su vida. La percepción no conduce, pues, al intento de comprender la realización escénica, sino al de entenderse uno mismo y la propia vida[19]. Pero un intento así será con toda probabilidad abortado muy pronto. Nuevos fenómenos aparecen en el espacio, son percibidos –aunque quizá al principio sólo de modo subliminal– y atraen la atención del mismo espectador que poco antes reflexionaba sobre sí mismo y sobre su historia vital.

De los procesos de generación de significado que son llevados a cabo oscilando entre símbolo y alegoría, entre autorreferencialidad y asociación, difícilmente puede decirse que sean procesos hermenéuticos orientados a la comprensión de la realización escénica. Se trata más bien, como se ha explicado, de procesos

---

nes», en *La verdad en pintura*, Buenos Aires, 2005; Christoph Menke, *Die Souveränität der Kunst*, Fráncfort, 1998.

19 Para una hermenéutica de la comprensión de sí y de la comprensión del otro véanse, entre otros, Alfred Lorenzer, *Kritik des Psychoanalytischen Symbolbegriffs*, Fráncfort, 1970 (esp. *Crítica del concepto psicoanalítico de símbolo*, Buenos Aires, 1976); *Zur Begründung einer materialistischen Sozialisationstheorie*, Fráncfort, 1972 (esp. *Bases para una teoría de la socialización*, Buenos Aires, 1976).

que intervienen en la autopoiesis del bucle de retroalimentación y que toman parte así en la génesis de la realización escénica.

Muy distintos son los problemas que surgen respecto a la multiestabilidad perceptiva, al salto repentino e imprevisible de la percepción del orden de la representación al de la presencia, y viceversa. Se puede sin duda partir de que, mientras el perceptor siga en el orden de la representación, genera significados con los que de consuno lleva a cabo procesos hermenéuticos. Cuando constituye un personaje, o cuando erige un mundo ficticio o un orden simbólico, podemos ciertamente afirmar que se trata, siempre que se den ciertas condiciones, de un intento por su parte de entender al personaje, el mundo ficticio o el orden simbólico en cuestión. Dado que en el teatro le está vedada la perspectiva global, el espectador puede entender al personaje mientras lo constituye justamente hasta el punto hasta el que llegue esa constitución suya. Su entender provisional opera entonces como una hipótesis tentativa orientada a la posterior constitución del personaje que va llevando a cabo a medida que avanza la realización escénica. Si el actor en cuestión realiza procesos de corporización que contradicen las hipótesis elaboradas hasta el momento por el espectador, entonces éste las reformulará y pondrá las nuevas hipótesis reformuladas como base para la reconstitución del personaje, y así sucesivamente hasta el final de la realización escénica[20]. Y lo mismo vale para la construcción de un mundo ficticio o de un orden simbólico. En esa medida sí se puede hablar, en efecto, de procesos hermenéuticos que forman parte de la experiencia estética, que contribuyen a constituirla.

En mi descripción de este proceso he desatendido hasta ahora un aspecto importante, a saber: los saltos perceptivos. La percep-

20 Véase para este proceso Erika Fischer-Lichte, *Semiotik des Theaters*, vol. 3, *Die Aufführung als Text*, Tubinga, 1983, 4.ª ed., 1999, especialmente 1.4 «Hermeneutik des theatralischen Textes», pp. 54-68, y 2. «Verfahren der Bedeutungs-und Sinnkonstitution», pp. 69-118 (esp. *Semiótica del teatro. Libro III, La representación como texto*, especialmente 1.4, «Hermenéutica del texto teatral», pp. 567-586, y 2. «Procedimientos de constitución de significado y sentido como métodos de análisis de textos teatrales», pp. 587-651).

ción salta de repente del orden de la representación al orden de la presencia. Se percibe un elemento teatral emergente en su ser fenoménico que afecta físicamente al perceptor. Como consecuencia de ello se interrumpe abruptamente el proceso de constitución de un personaje, de un mundo ficticio o de un orden simbólico. En su lugar aparece una amalgama de sujeto perceptor y objeto percibido y, como consecuencia de ella, una focalización en la corriente de asociaciones que emergen en el perceptor o incluso una reflexión acerca de su propia vida. Cuando la percepción vuelve a saltar un instante después al orden de la representación, el perceptor difícilmente estará en condiciones de proseguir con la constitución del personaje en el punto en que la dejó, en el punto del que fue arrancado abruptamente. Deberá retomarla, quiera o no, en cualquier otro punto que recuerde, de tal manera que el intento de generar significados como resultado de un proceso hermenéutico se revela como un auténtico trabajo de Sísifo.

El salto acontece y pone al perceptor en un estado de inestabilidad. La experiencia estética vendrá esencialmente troquelada por la experiencia de la inestabilidad, la experiencia de encontrarse *betwixt and between* entre los dos órdenes de percepción, sin poder proporcionarles estabilidad permanente a ninguno de los dos de manera intencionada. El perceptor puede modificar esta experiencia por medio de una reflexión sobre el estado de inestabilidad, y sobre la experiencia de liminaridad que resulta de él, antes de que un nuevo fenómeno haga su aparición en el espacio, le afecte físicamente y lo vuelva a subyugar. Los procesos hermenéuticos que rudimentariamente pueda realizar, cuando quiera que su percepción siga el orden de la representación, son más bien marginales para la experiencia estética comparados con el estado de inestabilidad. A ésta la determina menos la tentativa de comprensión que la experiencia de la intersticidad, la liminaridad, la inestabilidad y la indisponibilidad de lo que acontece. En este contexto cumple igualmente tener en cuenta la disposición del espectador. Si el fracaso en la comprensión se vive como una experiencia frustrante, la inestabilidad se experimenta sobre todo como una crisis.

Lo específico de la experiencia estética se muestra también cuando tenemos en consideración las emociones que se suscitan en el acto de percepción, o como consecuencia de él. Son significados que, como hemos visto, pueden tener en algunas ocasiones una intervención decisiva en la autopoiesis del bucle de retroalimentación, ya sea porque se articulen físicamente de modo claramente perceptible para otros, ya sea porque desencadenen impulsos activos que motiven acciones. Ya expliqué esto mismo recurriendo al ejemplo de la ruptura de un tabú por medio de las emociones que se originan en la percepción de acciones o de modos de comportamiento y emergencia. El espectador vive la infracción del tabú como una crisis. Como se expuso en el primer capítulo en referencia al caso de *Lips of Thomas*, el espectador se encontraba de pronto en una situación en la que las normas, las reglas y las convicciones válidas hasta ese momento dejaban de tener vigencia. Hasta entonces el espectador consideraba que su papel en el teatro o en una galería consistía en observar y mirar, incluso en el caso en el que, sobre el escenario, un personaje (Otelo), se dispusiera a matar a otro (Desdémona). Sabe bien que la muerte es «interpretada», que la actriz que se encarga del papel de Desdémona va a sufrir con la muerte de su personaje lo mismo que su compañero cuando muera Otelo, y que ambos saldrán al final a saludar, harán una reverencia y agradecerán los aplausos del público. En la vida cotidiana, sin embargo, sigue vigente la regla de intervenir de inmediato cuando alguien amenaza con infligirse daño o infligírselo a los demás, incluso aunque uno tenga que poner en riesgo su propia integridad.

¿Qué norma debía seguir el espectador en la performance de Abramović? Se hirió, en efecto, a sí misma y estaba dispuesta a prolongar indefinidamente la autotortura. Si hubiera hecho lo mismo en cualquier lugar público, es probable que el espectador no hubiera vacilado demasiado tiempo en intervenir. Pero en este caso, ¿exigía el respeto a la artista que se la dejara llevar a cabo lo que parecían ser su plan y su intención artísticos? ¿No se corría el riesgo de arruinar su «obra»? Y por otro lado, ¿es compatible con criterios humanitarios y con la compasión humana contemplar tranquilamente cómo la artista se infligía lesiones? ¿Quería relegar al espectador al papel de *voyeur*? ¿O pretendía ponerlo a prueba para saber hasta qué punto debía llegar para que algún espectador pusiera fin a su tortura?

La situación que creó Abramović con su infracción del tabú puso al espectador en un estado de un radical *betwixt and between*, y en este sentido lo precipitó a una crisis. Ahora bien, aparentemente el espectador no puede superar una crisis de este tipo formulándose las preguntas mencionadas e intentando, por medio de una reflexión, entender la situación en la que está inmerso. Lo que hace es responder a ella con una emoción que puede llegar a ser tan intensa como para estar por encima de cualquier reflexión, una emoción que no dé siquiera lugar a que surja la tentativa de comprensión. La experiencia estética se vive en este caso como una experiencia de crisis que no puede superarse por medio de la reflexión sosegada o de la mera contemplación.

¿Cómo encuentra el espectador una salida a esta situación de liminaridad, incluso aunque sea al precio de meterse en otra? La emoción es tan intensa, se ha dicho ya, que puede desencadenar impulsos para la acción. Si el sujeto que la siente no sigue este impulso, queda atrapado en la situación, se sigue encontrando en el umbral, sin utilizar los espacios libres ni su capacidad de maniobra para enfrentarse a la crisis estableciendo un nuevo orden. Aquellos espectadores que, por el contrario, siguieron su impulso de intervenir y bajaron a la artista de la cruz de hielo, crearon ese nuevo orden. Suprimieron la dicotomía establecida entre el ámbito de lo estético y el de lo ético y crearon un nuevo vínculo entre ellos. Fue la intervención de los espectadores, motivada por el sentimiento, la que redefinió la situación y superó la crisis, aunque fuera al precio de que con ello, de acuerdo a la voluntad de la artista, que hasta entonces no conocían, la performance se acabara. No fueron ni la reflexión sobre la situación ni el intento de entenderla los que permitieron superar la crisis – o los que quizá desencadenaron otra–, sino una acción a la que llevó un impulso cuyo origen era el sentimiento. Los procesos hermenéuticos no tuvieron papel alguno en ello.

La gran mayoría de los procesos de generación de significado, a los que me he dedicado en este capítulo, no se llevan a cabo como procesos hermenéuticos. Ha quedado claro que en ellos lo esencial no es entender la realización escénica, sino posibilitar determinadas experiencias. Sin duda, los procesos hermenéuticos pueden incorporarse en parte a la experiencia estética, pero su papel no deja de ser meramente marginal. Las realizaciones escénicas a las que he hecho referencia no piden ser entendidas, piden ser experimentadas. No se pueden subsumir, por tanto, al paradigma de una estética hermenéutica.

Sólo cuando la realización escénica ha terminado se puede empezar a hacer esfuerzos orientados a comprenderla a posteriori. Sin embargo, esos esfuerzos hay que situarlos fuera de los límites de la experiencia estética, no pueden tomar parte en su constitución. En tanto que tentativas de entender la realización escénica a posteriori, quien las emprende se expone a problemas muy específicos. Dos de ellos son especialmente graves. El primero consiste en que el intento de comprensión depende del recuerdo, de la memoria. Quien quiera entender una realización escénica a posteriori, tiene que recordarla. El segundo surge del hecho de que tal proceso se realiza lingüísticamente, mientras que los significados generados durante la realización escénica son en gran medida significados no-lingüísticos. Así pues, quien quiera entender una realización escénica a posteriori tiene que «traducir» los significados no-lingüísticos que recuerde a significados lingüísticos, una tarea que presenta dificultades casi insuperables.

En este intento de comprensión a posteriori de una realización escénica son especialmente relevantes la memoria episódica y la semántica[21]. La memoria episódica me permite recordar los

21 Véase al respecto Daniel L. Schacter, *Wir sind Erinnerung. Gedächtnis und Persönlichkeit*. Reinbeck bei Hamburg, 1999 (esp. *En busca de la memoria :el cerebro, la mente y el pasado*, Barcelona, 1999. Orig. *Searching for memory. The brain, the mind, and the past*. Nueva York, 1996). Schacter distingue entre tres tipos de memoria: «la memoria *episódica*, con cuya ayuda recordamos algunos sucesos de nuestro pasado personal; la memoria *semántica*, que es la vasta red de asociaciones y conceptos que está en la base de nuestro conocimiento general del mundo; y la memoria *procedimental*, que nos permite adquirir destrezas que nos enseñan a realizar tareas cotidianas» (p. 222 de la trad. al.). Con el concepto memoria *procedimental* se refiere a funciones memorísticas que nos permiten adquirir

detalles del espacio escénico, la posición de los actores sobre el escenario, su movimiento a través del espacio en el instante en que entra la música, la melodía y el ritmo de ésta, el singular modo en que la luz caía sobre el escenario y lo iba tiñendo de azul, la consonancia o disonancia entre el ritmo de la enunciación y el de los movimientos, etc. La memoria episódica nos permite, pues, recordar las innumerables apariciones concretas en una realización escénica.

La memoria semántica, por el contrario, recuerda los significados lingüísticos –esto es, tanto las palabras pronunciadas durante la realización escénica como mis pensamientos e interpretaciones sobre ellas durante esa misma realización escénica–. A ellos pertenecen igualmente las traducciones efectuadas ya durante la realización escénica –por ejemplo, que he identificado un determinado color como rojo, un movimiento como abrupto, o una atmósfera como lúgubre–. La memoria episódica, por su parte, recuerda los matices de ese rojo, la dirección específica del movimiento y su singular rastro, del que fui consciente cuando entré en la sala, o el espacio concreto con todos los detalles que esa atmósfera parecía irradiar. Por lo general ambos tipos de memoria interactúan y se prestan apoyo mutuo. Así, por ejemplo, los recuerdos sobre el desarrollo de la acción y los significados lingüísticos que se constituyeron en su transcurso pueden motivar a la memoria episódica a recordar los procesos y los detalles complementarios. Dado que las realizaciones escénicas a las que me vengo refiriendo no siguen en su mayoría una lógica de la acción ni responden a ningún otro nexo causal, en el intento de entenderlas a posteriori la memoria episódica adquiere una especial relevancia. Ahora bien, para las apariciones surgidas en la

---

nuevos patrones motores, como montar en bicicleta, nadar, bailar, jugar al tenis, etc. La memoria *procedimental* se consolida por medio de la repetición. Esta memoria –que también puede llamarse «memoria corporal»– es de especial relevancia para el actor/performador. En el intento de entender una realización escénica a posteriori, sin embargo, tiene un papel más bien marginal –por ejemplo, repetir el movimiento de un actor para recordarlo–. Por ello pasaré por alto este tercer tipo de memoria en lo que sigue.

realización escénica que se recuerden de forma inconexa o aislada pueden buscarse nuevas concomitancias y establecer así relaciones que las situarán en un contexto completamente nuevo.

Al hacerlo es preciso, sin embargo, tener en consideración otro problema. Los últimos estudios sobre la memoria centrados en la experiencia cotidiana han corroborado que, en muchos aspectos, nuestra memoria es «poco fiable». No funciona como una estructura de almacenamiento que conserva fielmente los objetos del pasado que depositamos en ella como lo haría una casa de empeño, sino que construye el pasado de forma nueva y distinta según la situación y el contexto. Y por si eso no fuera suficiente, puede incluso producir vivos recuerdos de acontecimientos que jamás han ocurrido[22]. Además, es frecuente que se niegue a suministrarnos determinados recuerdos que le solicitamos. Esta «falla» de nuestra memoria tampoco puede remediarla la asistencia reiterada a la misma escenificación. Pues, por una parte, en cada nueva visita el espectador percibe apariciones que hasta entonces le habían pasado por alto y que ahora tiene que añadir a las que necesita recordar. Y, por otro lado, el recuerdo de la primera se infiltra en la percepción de la segunda y la modifica. Con ello disminuye sobre todo el grado de novedad, que en la primera visita puede ser considerable, de tal manera que lo percibido influye en el espectador de forma distinta a como lo hizo la primera vez. No en vano cada una de las veces se trata de una realización escénica distinta, por lo que, por definición, aquello que hay que recordar puede ser percibido de forma distinta cada vez[23].

Así pues, el primer requisito para la compresión a posteriori, el recurso a los propios recuerdos, no parece estar libre de problemas, incluso dejando al margen la cuestión de si se entiende «correcta» o «incorrectamente». No muy distinta es la situa-

22 Véase al respecto la obra citada en la nota anterior.

23 Sobre el problema de cómo se recuerdan las realizaciones escénicas véase también Christel Weiler, «Am Ende/Geschichte. Anmerkungen zur theatralen Historiographie und zur Zeitlichkeit theaterwissenschaftlicher Arbeit», en Fischer-Lichte, Weiler (eds.), *TRANSFORMATIONEN*, pp. 43-56.

ción con el segundo requisito, la traducción a significados lingüísticos. Como se ha señalado reiteradas veces, hay un sinnúmero de significados generados por el sujeto perceptor en el transcurso de una realización escénica, algunos de los cuales recuerda posteriormente, que no son equiparables a significados lingüísticos. Tanto las representaciones mentales, las imágenes, las fantasías o los recuerdos no-lingüísticos como los estados de ánimo, las sensaciones y los sentimientos, que se articulan corporalmente y que llegan así a ser conscientes, difícilmente se pueden «traducir» a lenguaje. Pues al signo lingüístico le corresponde siempre una cierta abstracción, la misma que lo capacita para la producción de relaciones y conexiones. Por el contrario, a los cuerpos, objetos, sonidos y luz concretos que percibo sólo les puedo arrebatar su singular ser fenoménico, la forma en la que vienen a presencia, si trato de reducirlos a posteriori, o incluso durante la realización escénica, a conceptos. Ni la descripción lingüística más exacta lo lograría nunca. Lo más que podrá hacer será poner en marcha en aquel que oiga o lea productos de la imaginación que apenas divergirán de la percepción que se está describiendo. La descripción lingüística tiene un acceso muy limitado a lo que se recuerda por medio de la memoria episódica. Lo que se recuerda, en cambio, mediante la memoria semántica está estructurado *per se* lingüísticamente y puede por lo tanto expresarse lingüísticamente. No hay que pasar por alto, sin embargo, las deformaciones que establecen los límites del lenguaje, concretamente en todos los casos en los que la memoria semántica recuerda conceptos y descripciones que tenían su origen en procesos de traducción que se remontan a la propia realización escénica.

Todo intento de comprender está pensado para superar los límites que le establece el lenguaje, sin que esto pueda llegar a pasar nunca en realidad. Pues el lenguaje, como el medio especial que es, dispone de su propia materialidad, que sólo es de él, y como sistema sígnico también especial dispone de sus propias reglas específicas, sólo aplicables a él. Al tener como base de cualquier descripción esas reglas, o al seguirlas, el proceso de escritura asume su condición de proceso autónomo, desarrolla su propia dinámica, que puede llevarle sin duda a aproximarse con cierto grado de exactitud a las percepciones recordadas, pero tiene que continuar necesariamente a partir de ellas. Cualquier descripción lingüística, cualquier interpretación, es decir, cualquier intento de entender la realización escénica a posteriori, contribuye a la producción de un texto que sigue sus propias reglas, que se autonomiza en el proceso de su generación y que se aleja progresivamente de su punto de partida: el recuerdo de la realización escénica. De este modo, el intento de entender una realización escénica a posteriori genera un texto autónomo que, a su vez, pide ser entendido. La realización escénica, por el contrario, difícilmente puede comprenderse a posteriori de esta manera.

VI. LA REALIZACIÓN ESCÉNICA COMO ACONTECIMIENTO

Cuando en el cambio del siglo diecinueve al veinte Peter Behrens y Georg Fuchs proclamaron que el teatro debía convertirse «de nuevo» en una fiesta, y cuando poco después Max Herrmann creyó haber encontrado el «sentido originario» del teatro en la *Theater-Fest [Fiesta-teatro]*, en cuya constitución participaban actores y espectadores, todos ellos tenían en mente la condición de acontecimiento de la realización escénica. Veían en ella el fundamento de su esteticidad. Con ello se posicionaban contra los presupuestos tradicionales de una estética centrada en la obra y le abrían nuevas perspectivas al debate en los ámbitos de la estética y de la teoría del arte.

Durante mucho tiempo la obra fue el centro de atención de ese debate, y con ella su creador, el gran artista, el genio. Así, la producción de la obra era a menudo concebida o descrita –aunque más tarde sólo en sentido metafórico– como analogía de la creación del mundo por Dios: del mismo modo que Dios ha creado el mundo como una obra completa y cerrada, así produce el artista su obra. Y así como en la obra de Dios descansa la eterna verdad divina que se le revela a quien sabe leer el libro del mundo, la obra del artista alberga también verdad en sí. Quien se sumerja en ella y emprenda cuidadosamente la tarea de su desciframiento, podrá, como recompensa a sus esfuerzos, participar del conocimiento. Desde el momento en que empezó a extenderse el culto al genio, a finales del siglo dieciocho, no antes, al artista se lo considera un sujeto autónomo que crea una obra autónoma en la que está contenida la verdad. La idea de que la obra de arte era baluarte de la verdad, que en ella la verdad se ponía a la obra, como lo expresó Heidegger*, ha estado vigente en la estética filosófica –con la notable excepción de Nietzsche– desde Hegel hasta Adorno. Esta idea caracteriza asimismo la manera en la que Gadamer entiende la obra clásica, y ello a pesar de que en su hermenéutica no cabe un supuesto de esa naturaleza.

Más tarde, esa pretensión de verdad de la obra fue no sólo relativizada, sino incluso categóricamente rechazada tanto por la estética estructuralista como por la estética de la recepción. Sin embargo, ello no ponía en cuestión la idea de que la obra tenía que seguir ocupando el lugar más importante en la reflexión estética. Pues incluso aunque al receptor se lo incluye en el papel de cocreador, aunque se lo entiende como el que genera, en el proceso de recepción, los significados y el sentido de la obra, ésta sigue siendo el punto de referencia para cualquier reflexión estética, el objeto sobre el que el receptor lleva a cabo sus operaciones hermenéuticas. La obra se crea como una «cosa» (*«Ding»*), una condición que no puede exceder, está ahí como un artefacto que se mantiene igual a sí mismo independientemente de la intervención de un receptor; como mucho experimenta los cambios propios del paso del tiempo: se oscurecen los colores, amarillean los recortes de periódico, etc. El artefacto es accesible a distintos receptores de distintas épocas, sea una escultura, un monumento o una partitura, y en el caso de estas últimas y de los textos en general es accesible incluso en distintos lugares. En el transcurso de su vida un receptor puede volver a ver una misma obra una y otra vez, y descubrir cada vez nuevas particularidades y posibilidades, puede establecer conexiones entre algunos de sus elementos concretos y otros, o puede establecerlas con estructuras extratextuales, de tal manera que siempre se generan nuevos significados

* Martin Heidegger, «Der Ursprung des Kuntswerkes», en *Holzwege*, GA 5, Fráncfort, 1984, p. 44 (esp. «El origen de la obra de arte», en *Caminos de bosque*, Madrid, 1998, p. 41).

de la misma. En este sentido uno puede mantener un diálogo con una obra durante toda su vida.

Dada la larga y venerable historia del concepto de obra, puede parecer casi un sacrilegio que Behrens, Fuchs y Herrmann lo negaran implícitamente y defendieran en su lugar el concepto de acontecimiento (aunque ellos, como hemos visto, siguieran empleándolo y de ninguna manera lo rechazaran referido al teatro). Era un sacrilegio en la medida en que afirmaban que dos de las premisas fundamentales para que en el teatro se pueda hablar de obra y para que se pueda hablar de arte no se daban, y era un sacrilegio porque además insistían en que el teatro tenía que ser considerado como un arte: por un lado negaban que hubiera tal artefacto, y ponían en su lugar fenómenos fugaces, únicos e irrepetibles, y por otro relativizaban la división fundamental entre productores y receptores, si es que no la suprimían. De estos supuestos es de los que parten justamente las estéticas de la obra, de la producción y de la recepción, cuyos parámetros y categorías ya no era razonable seguir aplicando a la realización escénica. La consecuencia de ello es que el carácter artístico de la realización escénica, su esteticidad específica, debía resultar solamente de su carácter de acontecimiento.

Lo que algunos teóricos defendían a finales del siglo diecinueve y principios del veinte para fundar un nuevo teatro –y un nuevo campo de estudio–, se aplicó a las realizaciones escénicas de teatro y del arte de la performance desde los años sesenta como una *conditio sine qua non*. Uno de los impulsos para el surgimiento del arte de acción y de performance partía directamente de la decidida voluntad de algunos artistas de no crear obras –es decir, lo que ahora son artefactos comercializables o mercancías–, sino acontecimientos fugaces que nadie puede adquirir mediante la compra, meterlos en su caja fuerte o colgarlos en su sala de estar. La fugacidad del acontecimiento, su carácter único e irrepetible pasó entonces a ocupar la posición de mayor relevancia.

Como se ha mostrado al analizar su medialidad, su materialidad y su semioticidad, las realizaciones escénicas se caracterizan esencialmente por su naturaleza de acontecimiento. No sólo es que la realización escénica en su integridad acaece en la autopoiesis del bucle de retroalimentación, sino que con todos los elementos que la integran ocurre otro tanto. Su materialidad no se genera, pues, como artefacto o en un artefacto, sino que tiene lugar al generarse performativamente la corporalidad, la espacialidad y la sonoridad. La presencia de los actores, el éxtasis de los objetos, las atmósferas y la circulación de energía acontecen igual que los significados que se generan durante la realización escénica, ya sea como percepciones, ya como emociones, representaciones mentales o pensamientos suscitados por ellas. Las acciones de los espectadores acontecen como respuestas a lo percibido del mismo modo que las de los actores responden a lo que ellos perciben –lo que ven, oyen o sienten– de los comportamientos y actividad de los espectadores. La esteticidad de las realizaciones escénicas la constituye obviamente su carácter de acontecimiento.

Para poder describirla y definirla con más precisión no quiero partir, en consonancia con mi manera de proceder hasta el momento, de conceptos de acontecimiento dados previamente, como los de Heidegger, Derrida o Lyotard. Prefiero referirme a los resultados de mis análisis sobre medialidad, materialidad y semioticidad de las realizaciones escénicas, e intentar, sobre esta base, dar razón de la específica esteticidad de las realizaciones escénicas desde los años sesenta. Se ha comprobado que son especialmente tres aspectos los que están más inmediatamente vinculados a la condición de acontecimiento de la realización escénica, tres aspectos que son de gran importancia para su singular esteticidad. Nos referimos, en primer lugar, a la autopoiesis del bucle de retroalimentación, que hace que la realización escénica se origine, y al fenómeno de la emergencia; en segundo lugar, a la desestabilización, cuando no desmoronamiento, de las oposiciones dicotómicas; y, en tercer lugar, a las situaciones de liminaridad que experimentan los participantes en la realización escénica, y las transformaciones vinculadas a ellas. Mi tesis es que de un análisis más detallado de estos tres aspectos obtendremos resultados que nos permitirán arrojar luz sobre la singular esteticidad de las realizaciones escénicas.

1. Autopoiesis y emergencia

Como hemos visto en el tercer capítulo, es el bucle de retroalimentación autopoiético entre las acciones y comportamientos de actores y espectadores el que origina la realización escénica. La idea del artista como sujeto autónomo creador de una obra autónoma que los receptores pueden muy bien interpretar de maneras diversas, pero cuya materialidad no pueden modificar, ha dejado de ser operativa, pese a que en la conciencia de gran parte del público aún no sea así.

Ante una conclusión de esta naturaleza surgen una serie de preguntas. ¿Se puede poner realmente en pie de igualdad a actores y espectadores? ¿No habría que aceptar que la participación de los artistas que preparan el montaje debería determinar el camino que toma la realización escénica y que los espectadores deben como mucho poder reaccionar a todo ello? Y, ¿cómo se puede conciliar la afirmación de que hay que olvidarse del artista como sujeto autónomo con las reiteradas quejas desde finales de los años sesenta sobre la arbitrariedad del director, que se comporta como si fuera omnipotente?

Respecto a estas preguntas quiero en primer lugar diferenciar entre las realizaciones escénicas del arte de la performance, a las que da inicio un único performador, y las realizaciones escénicas de teatro, preparadas conjuntamente por el director, el escenógrafo, el compositor, los actores, los músicos, etc.

El artista de performance crea una situación específica en y con su performance a la que se exponen tanto él mismo como otros: los espectadores. Cuando Beuys convivió tres días con un coyote o Abramović se sometió a la violencia de otros o dejó que enroscaran serpientes pitón alrededor de su cuerpo, ambos artistas estaban renunciando voluntariamente a controlar, dentro de lo posible, el transcurso de la realización escénica. Crearon una situación que hacía difícil, si no imposible, predecir su desarrollo. Éste no dependía únicamente del artista en cuestión, sino que dependía también de forma decisiva de otros: de los espectadores y de los animales. Es decir, que los artistas no sólo se exponían a sí mismos a una situación, también exponían a todos los demás participantes en su creación. Esto exigía de los espectadores que no se consideraran meros espectadores cuya conducta es irrelevante para el desarrollo de la realización escénica. Tenían muy claro que eran también responsables de él. Una conducta que influyera negativamente en el coyote o en las serpientes podría haber acarreado graves consecuencias para el artista en cuestión. Dejar entrar a un grupo de transeúntes tomados al azar no parecía menos irresponsable. En lo que se refiere a los animales, su comportamiento era del todo impredecible. Todos los demás participantes, sobre todo los artistas, pero también los espectadores, tenían que adaptarse a lo que hicieran.

Es cierto que cada una de las situaciones las crea también el artista, y no lo es menos que en el caso de un comportamiento inadecuado por parte de un espectador, es él quien tiene que afrontar las más graves consecuencias. Sin embargo, en ello se evidencia hasta qué punto el artista depende de los espectadores, cuán necesitado está de que éstos asuman también su responsabilidad en una situación que no han creado ellos, pero en la que, por su participación en la performance, se ven involucrados.

Así pues, en esas performances se articula una nueva comprensión de sí de los artistas. Ya no crean una obra a la manera divina, sino que producen una situación específica, como lo haría el responsable de un experimento, a la que se exponen ellos mismos y los demás. Lo único que el artista puede hacer es reservarse el derecho de dar por terminada la realización escénica en el momento que elija, aunque sin estar nunca seguro de que eso signifique que ha terminado realmente, como se ha demostrado en el caso de Schlingensief.

La intensa preparación de una realización escénica, que puede durar varias semanas y a veces varios meses, algo normal en el teatro, debe ser claramente diferenciada de la realización escénica como tal. La preparación tiene una gran importancia para el desarrollo de la realización escénica: en ella se decide qué elementos teatrales aparecerán, en qué forma lo harán, en qué momento y en qué lugar deben emerger en el espacio. Además, en ella se establecen especificaciones muy importantes para la percepción del espectador en la realización escénica. Aunque la decisión definitiva le corresponde al director, su función no es equiparable a la del autor de un poema, que crea su obra en solitario. Los demás artistas, en algunos casos incluso los técnicos o los tramoyistas, presentan ideas y propuestas, participan también en el avance del proceso de ensayos y en el trabajo conjunto de escenificación[1]. En general se considera, sin embargo, que para la autopoiesis del bucle de retroalimentación sólo es relevante lo que, independientemente de lo que se hubiera discutido, establecido o proyectado anteriormente, termina apareciendo realmente en el transcurso de la realización escénica.

Como, por regla general, el director no participa en la realización escénica, no puede, a diferencia de los actores, técnicos o tramoyistas, intervenir directamente en el bucle de retroalimentación autopoiético, a no ser que participe como espectador. A partir de su experiencia como espectador puede efectuar, sin duda, modificaciones en la escenificación al finalizar la realización escénica y establecer nuevas pautas para la siguiente. Pero sobre la realización escénica como tal no tiene ningún control. Mientras que cada actor, técnico o tramoyista interviene continuamente en la autopoiesis del bucle de retroalimentación –y puede hacerlo incluso de forma no acordada de antemano–, el director queda excluido de él al no poder participar en la realización escénica ni como actor ni como espectador. Es decir, que en este caso no está en condiciones de influir en el acontecimiento que es la realización escénica mientras ésta tiene lugar.

Las realizaciones escénicas de teatro a las que me he referido pueden compararse, en este sentido, con las performances en la medida en que es la escenificación la que crea una determinada situación a la que están expuestos todos los participantes y a la que pueden reaccionar de modo distinto. También en este caso nos las vemos con ajustes experimentales a los que se puede reaccionar de diversas maneras, sean las pautas que impuso Schechner para la participación del espectador, la disposición espacial en el

1 Para el concepto de escenificación, véase el apartado correspondiente en el capítulo séptimo.

Frankfurter Depot en las escenificaciones de Schleef o el empleo del vídeo por parte de Castorf.

Al centrar su atención –por medio del cambio de roles, de la formación de comunidades, etc.– en la autopoiesis del bucle de retroalimentación que actúa en cada una de ellas, las realizaciones escénicas posteriores a los años sesenta dirigían su interés al mismo tiempo a que en ellas se articulara una nueva imagen del artista, si es que no pretendían dar forma a una nueva imagen del ser humano y de la sociedad, aunque en este último caso es cuestionable que hayan tenido una repercusión efectiva en ella. La efectividad del bucle de retroalimentación autopoiético se opone a la idea de un sujeto autónomo. Se trata más bien de que tanto el artista como todos los participantes son sujetos que determinan a otros y que son, a su vez, determinados por ellos. Contradice la idea de un sujeto que, en virtud de su libre albedrío, decide de manera soberana lo que hace y lo que deja hacer, que se puede desarrollar como aquel que quiere ser independientemente de los demás y al margen de «directrices externas». Asimismo, se opone diametralmente a la idea de un ser humano totalmente determinado por lo externo, y al que precisamente por esa determinación no se le puede atribuir responsabilidad por sus acciones. La perceptible autopoiesis del bucle de retroalimentación, que se hace presente con especial claridad tan pronto se da cualquier forma de cambio de roles entre actores y espectadores, brinda a todos los participantes la posibilidad de experimentarse durante la realización escénica como un sujeto que puede participar en la determinación de las acciones y los comportamientos de otros, y cuyas acciones y comportamiento pueden ser a su vez determinados por ellos, como un sujeto que no es ni autónomo ni está totalmente determinado externamente y que asume la responsabilidad de una situación que no ha creado, pero en la que se ve involucrado. Esta experiencia es uno de los componentes esenciales de la experiencia estética que hace posible la autopoiesis del bucle de retroalimentación.

Este bucle funciona como un sistema que se reorganiza a sí mismo, un sistema en el que constantemente hay que integrar elementos recién surgidos, no planeados y, por ello, no predecibles. Para los actores, entre estos elementos se cuentan los comportamientos y las acciones mostradas por los espectadores, sus propias reacciones ante ellas, las de sus compañeros. En algunos casos hay que añadir acontecimientos imprevistos sobre el escenario como un tropiezo repentino, un foco que cae, un olvido en el atrezo, etc., o el comportamiento impredecible de los animales que participan: el mono que muerde a Kathrin Angerer, el caballo que defeca en el escenario o el perro que de pronto irrumpe ladrando en el patio de butacas. Desde el punto de vista del espectador, en cambio, todos los elementos que integran la autopoiesis del bucle de retroalimentación son fenómenos emergentes. Pues dado que en las realizaciones escénicas en cuestión la aparición y la desaparición de las emergencias no se rige por una lógica de la acción o de la psique predecible, ni tampoco obedece a nexos causales, sino que depende de parámetros rítmicos, segmentos temporales u operaciones casuales, entre otros, esas emergencias son tan poco previsibles para los espectadores como el comportamiento de otros espectadores o como sus propias reacciones. En efecto, todo debe parecerles emergente.

Este hecho tiene consecuencias de gran alcance para la percepción de una realización escénica. En la medida en que se da por sentada la lógica de una determinada sucesión de acontecimientos o una determinada psicología de los personajes –que en algunos casos pueden ser conocidas de antemano–, a la percepción le vienen dados ciertos principios de selección. Es decir, que la atención del espectador no se centrará del mismo modo en todo lo que aparece en el espacio, sino solamente en aquello que le ayude a seguir el desarrollo de una trama y le sirva para entender el comportamiento de los personajes. Cuando fallan esos principios de selección, la economía de la atención –de la que tanto se habla hoy–[2] debe organizarse, en la realización escénica como en la vida cotidiana, de acuerdo a otros criterios. Entre

2 Véase Georg Franck, *Ökonomie der Aufmerksamkeit*, Múnich, 1998.

ellos están el grado de intensidad de la aparición, su divergencia, la sorpresa que produzca o su vistosidad[3].

Si les aplicamos estos criterios a las realizaciones escénicas que venimos estudiando, nos encontraremos en serias dificultades. Pues a las apariciones que emergen en ellas se les puede aplicar, por regla general, al menos uno de ellos, si no varios. El criterio de intensidad de la aparición abarcaría, por ejemplo, la presencia del actor, el éxtasis de los objetos o la atmósfera, a la cual contribuyen en considerable medida la presencia y el éxtasis. Así, el concepto fuerte de presencia requiere que la aparición física del actor ocupe el espacio y fuerce a los espectadores a centrar su atención en él. El actor presente libera energías en sí y en el espectador que circulan por el espacio y que se pueden sentir físicamente. En su éxtasis, los objetos dejan de estar dados en su cerrada completud. Salen de sí mismos, se muestran, vienen a presencia de un modo tan particularmente intenso que acapara la atención del espectador. Esto es aplicable sobre todo a las llamadas cualidades secundarias de las cosas: sus colores, olores o sonidos. Dado que tanto la presencia del actor como el éxtasis de los objetos son los que constituyen las atmósferas, éstas aparecen con singular intensidad ante el perceptor; lo envuelven, se sumerge en ellas, penetran en su cuerpo en forma de luz, sonido u olor.

Tal y como he explicado, desde los años sesenta se han desarrollado en teatro y en el arte de la performance gran cantidad de procedimientos cuyo objetivo era hacer que aparecieran el actor como presente, las cosas en su éxtasis y generar densas atmósferas. La intensa experiencia que posibilitan no es, obviamente, una experiencia ocasional, sino que puede prolongarse durante toda la realización escénica. En la realización escénica del montaje *Sportstück [Pieza deportiva]* de Schleef, por ejemplo, el coro se empleaba con gran intensidad en la parte inicial, que duraba cuarenta y cinco minutos, una intensidad que no sólo se mante-

3 Véase sobre estos criterios Walter Seitter, «Aufmerksamkeitskorrelate auf der Ebene der Erscheinungen», en Aleida Assman y Jan Assman (eds.), *Aufmerksamkeiten. Archäologie der literarischen Kommunikation*, Múnich, 2000, pp. 171-182.

nía a lo largo del tiempo, sino que se iba incrementando. Si nos centramos sólo en el criterio de la intensidad habría que concluir que las realizaciones escénicas exigen del espectador un alto grado de atención durante un largo periodo de tiempo, cuando no durante todo su desarrollo.

Asimismo, el criterio de divergencia/sorpresa puede aplicarse a cualquier realización escénica durante casi toda su duración. Pues en las realizaciones escénicas en las que la sucesión temporal se organiza por medio de segmentos temporales o del ritmo, la divergencia es un principio fundamental. En el caso de cada uno de los segmentos temporales, el comienzo y el final de cada actividad puede establecerse de manera distinta en cada caso. Al ritmo lo define precisamente la divergencia. Pues ninguna repetición repite exactamente aquello a lo que se refiere exactamente de la misma manera, como ocurrió, por ejemplo, en los *Nô-walks* de los *Knee plays* de Wilson, en las distintas partes del coro en *Murx*, o en la elevación de medio tono en cada nueva estrofa de «Danke». Lo que caracteriza precisamente a las realizaciones escénicas de las que venimos hablando es que son capaces de dirigir la atención del espectador incluso a las mínimas desviaciones, a las «menos aparentes», las que nos pasarían inadvertidas en nuestra vida cotidiana. En este caso son el foco de atención. Las realizaciones escénicas mantienen su ritmo precisamente por el hecho de introducir algo y hacerlo aparecer poco después con una variación, y así sucesivamente. Es decir, que el espectador, que sin duda espera una divergencia, está, por así decirlo, siempre al acecho para terminar pese a todo dejándose sorprender por una divergencia que no esperaba que fuera *así*. El principio de la divergencia/sorpresa se mantiene durante toda la realización escénica. Supone un especial desafío para la atención del espectador.

Apliquemos, por último, el criterio de la vistosidad. Por un lado encontramos en las realizaciones escénicas una gran cantidad de apariciones que llamarían la atención también en la vida cotidiana, un ejemplo serían las performances de autoagresión. Éstas se basan en que el artista realiza en ellas acciones que no sólo causarían gran expectación en el mundo cotidiano, sino también en el marco de eventos que pretenden atraer la atención de los espectadores apelando a las sensaciones. En el marco de una performance o de una realización escénica de teatro tales acciones resultan sin duda llamativas. Como habíamos visto, entre las apariciones llamativas se cuentan siempre las de animales, ya sean salvajes, como serpientes, coyotes, monos, lechuzas africanas o tarántulas, que también atraen la atención en el zoo; o domésticos, como perros, gatos, caballos, canarios o peces, que en general apenas llaman la atención en la vida cotidiana. Por otro lado, las realizaciones escénicas logran una y otra vez que lo cotidiano aparezca como extraordinario. Cuando el actor llama la atención del espectador con su presencia como *embodied mind*, cuando una estufa de carbón normal y corriente reclama toda su atención o cuando el sonido de una melodía conocida es capaz de absorber totalmente al espectador, sucede lo que Arthur Danto ha llamado la transfiguración del lugar común: lo cotidiano aparece transfigurado y se convierte en algo llamativo. Así, para el espectador, la propia percepción será uno de los centros de atención durante la realización escénica; por ejemplo, con los constantes saltos de atención entre el orden de la presencia y el de la representación. El arte de la realización escénica consiste, sin duda, en convertir en llamativo todo lo que aparece en ella. Y como todo lo que aparece en ella es impredecible, aparece tan sorprendente como llamativo.

Así pues, en las realizaciones escénicas que he tomado en consideración, se satisfacen los tres criterios para atraer la atención no sólo de manera ocasional, sino durante toda su duración. Es decir, que en estos casos no se puede hablar de una economía de la atención en sentido estricto. Nos las vemos más bien con un exceso de atención, con el «derroche» de un recurso tan apreciado. Y esto no vale sólo para los actores, a los que suponemos de antemano en un estado de permanente atención, dirigida tanto a su propia actividad como a la de otros: los espectadores y los demás actores. Vale igualmente para los espectadores, de quienes lo que va emergiendo en el espacio reclama toda su atención. Cabe sin duda pensar que cada espectador tiene su propia economía de la atención, que no en todos los casos puede mantener el mismo nivel de atención en todo momento. En el caso de los espectadores se puede observar un aumento de la atención en momentos concretos. Tanto para los actores como para los espectadores se puede decir que su atención se dirige tanto al propio cuerpo como al ajeno.

Si no los limitamos a la definición de atención de Seitter, que la entiende como «una inclinación de relativa intensidad de la conciencia hacia un objeto o contenido del tipo que sea»[4], sino que partimos con Csórdas de que la atención abarca «more bodily and multisensory engagement than we usually allow for psychological definitions of attention» y que «[s]omatic modes of attention are culturally elaborated ways of attending to and with one's body in surroundings that include the embodied presence of others»[5], entonces se aclara el sentido profundo de ese «derroche». El estado de permanente e intensiva atención permite al sujeto preceptor experimentarse de manera singular como *embodied mind*. Es, sin la menor duda, otro de los componentes esenciales de la experiencia estética que se da en la realización escénica.

El estado de permanente e intensiva atención, de la manera que puede producirlo, o al menos reclamarlo, la emergencia de fenómenos en las realizaciones escénicas es un estado no cotidiano, es un estado excepcional. Por el contrario, las demás experiencias que posibilitan la emergencia y la autopoiesis del bucle de retroalimentación se corresponden muchas veces con experiencias de nuestro día a día. Así, la experiencia de no disponer libremente de los sucesos o asuntos en los que uno está involucrado, de poder, sí, influir en ellos hasta cierto punto, pero de estar también determinados por ellos, se puede ciertamente considerar una experiencia cotidiana, ordinaria, incluso trivial. En

4 *Ibid.*, p. 171.

5 Thomas J. Csórdas, «Somatic Modes of Attention», en *Cultural Anthropology 8*, 1993, pp. 135-156, p. 138 [«más implicación corporal y multisensorial de la que normalmente aceptamos en las definiciones psicológicas de atención» [...] y que «los modos somáticos de atención son procedimientos culturalmente elaborados de prestar atención al cuerpo y con el cuerpo en ámbitos que incluyen la presencia corporizada de otros»].

nuestra vida diaria, en contextos sociales o políticos, o en procesos históricos, nos enfrentamos una y otra vez a la experiencia de que lo que ocurre no había sido planeado ni era previsible, y que el curso de los acontecimientos siempre podría haber tomado otro camino. La razón por la que finalmente toman un camino u otro es inexplicable, por más que nos esforcemos continuamente en buscarle explicaciones. También en nuestra vida diaria nos encontramos de vez en cuando con personas que parecen poseer un extraordinario poder de fascinación, personas de las que surge algo que se transmite a los demás; cuando estas personas tienen una posición de prominencia social o política, hablamos de personalidades carismáticas sin que por ello podamos explicar el porqué de su carisma. Para mencionar un último ejemplo: también en nuestra vida diaria podemos experimentar el éxtasis de los objetos. Algo que ocurre también, y entonces es especialmente llamativo, en el caso de objetos poco aparentes que adquieren para quien los percibe, por los motivos que sea, un valor especial, un aura.

Se trata ciertamente de experiencias que todos hemos tenido alguna vez, pero que, sin embargo, suelen quedar excluidas del discurso oficial. En la medida en que éste está determinado por el ideal de la Ilustración, no puede admitirlas, tiene que combatirlas allá donde se articulen y desenmascararlas por estar basadas en falsas premisas: el ser humano en tanto que sujeto autónomo es soberano respecto a su destino. Es capaz de planificar racionalmente los procesos en los que está involucrado y de cumplir consecuentemente sus previsiones. Cuando emerge un nuevo fenómeno –en el cosmos o en la cultura–, siempre hay una explicación plausible para ello. Y cuando algo nuevo surge en el mundo es porque, en la mayoría de los casos, resulta de actos perfectamente planeados. Dado que todos los seres humanos son iguales, no puede darse ninguna personalidad carismática. Si algunas personas se lo parecen a otros se debe a que éstas, como los actores, se han servido de ciertas técnicas y prácticas –«trucos»– con los que se puede dar la apariencia de carisma. Tocante al aura de los objetos, ésta sólo se origina en psiques enfermas. Las cosas están ahí con algún fin que cumplen o no cumplen, si lo uno hay que conservarlas, si lo otro se puede uno deshacer de ellas. Más allá de ahí no se les puede atribuir influencia sobre el hombre.

No es, sin embargo, el discurso de la Ilustración el único que niega esas experiencias, el postmoderno hace lo mismo desde la perspectiva opuesta. Dado que hay que entender al sujeto como un ente descentrado, la sola idea de que pueda participar en la determinación de algo se considera como una mera ilusión. En su lugar aparece como objeto del efecto de entidades abstractas como el lenguaje o el contexto cultural: el sujeto no habla, no emplea el lenguaje, sino que es hablado por el lenguaje. La dialéctica entre ser-cuerpo y tener-cuerpo se revela como una quimera. El cuerpo se entiende como una superficie pasiva para inscripciones culturales. Y como todo es, como cada una de las experiencias es, en última instancia, una construcción subjetiva, no puede concluirse que haya sujetos que puedan constituir la experiencia del carisma de otras personas o del aura de las cosas.

El discurso determinado por los criterios de la Ilustración moteja estas experiencias cotidianas de reliquias y residuos de un pensamiento preilustrado, las entiende como propias de una conciencia influida por la religión, o incluso por la magia. Pues este tipo de conciencia asume la existencia de misteriosos e indomeñables poderes o fuerzas sobre las que el hombre no tiene ninguna influencia, razón por la que tiene que dejarse dominar por ellas siempre que intervienen en procesos en los que él está involucrado. Estas fuerzas tienen como efecto, además, que surjan de repente nuevos e inexplicables fenómenos y son asimismo capaces de actuar sobre personas o cosas, haciéndolas aparecer como carismáticas o auráticas respectivamente.

El discurso postmoderno, por el contrario, moteja estas experiencias cotidianas de ilusiones o quimeras en las que, por un lado, siguen aún rondando conceptos ilustrados como el del sujeto autónomo y en las que, por otro, sigue influyendo la idea romántica de un mundo encantado.

Ambos discursos desprecian esas experiencias cotidianas. Desde los años sesenta, las realizaciones escénicas de teatro y del arte de la performance intentan, por el contrario, devolverles su valor, ennoblecerlas incluso por medio de la emergencia y la autopoiesis del bucle de retroalimentación. El estado no-cotidiano de permanente e intensiva atención convierte esas experiencias en componentes de la experiencia estética. Con ello tiene lugar también una transfiguración del lugar común.

2. Oposiciones que se desploman

Recordémoslo: después de que Austin introdujera en un principio el par de conceptos constatativo-performativo, y explicara con su ayuda que el concepto de lo performativo –a diferencia precisamente del de lo constatativo– se refería a actos de habla autorreferenciales y constitutivos de realidad, fue él mismo quien abandonó esta distinción. Su forma de actuar da pie a sospechar que lo performativo puede poner en marcha una dinámica que lleva al desmoronamiento de las oposiciones conceptuales y, como escribe Sybille Krämer, «conduce a la desestabilización de la idea misma de esquema conceptual dicotómico»[6].

El estudio de las realizaciones escénicas de las que me he venido ocupando no ha hecho más que corroborar esta sospecha. Como se ha mostrado, son las parejas de conceptos que precisamente se entienden como dicotómicas, y que además son centrales en nuestra cultura: arte y realidad, sujeto y objeto, cuerpo y mente, animal y ser humano, significante y significado, las que tras nuestra investigación empiezan a perder solidez, a dinamizarse y a oscilar, si es que no se desmoronan completamente. ¿En qué medida es esta dinámica constitutiva de la condición de acontecimiento de la realización escénica? ¿Cómo repercute en su esteticidad?

Desde la Antigüedad la distinción entre arte y realidad ha sido fundamental para la teoría del arte. En su larga historia no ha cesado de concebir y definir la obra de arte a partir de esta diferencia. Esta determinación ha sido la base de cualquier valora-

6 Krämer/Stahlhut, «Das 'Performative' als Thema der Sprach-und Kulturphilosophie», p. 56.

ción y ha sido considerada, fijada y empleada como criterio para la esteticidad de cada una de las obras. Independientemente de si el arte se entiende como mímesis de una realidad dada, preexistente o, por el contrario, como creación de una realidad independiente, de una realidad *sui generis* que sólo puede hallarse de esa manera en la obra de arte, la diferencia de base entre arte y realidad sigue dándose por supuesta sin mayores cuestionamientos. Este hecho sorprende aún más si tenemos en cuenta que la obra de arte es –aunque de naturaleza muy singular– una «cosa» entre otras, y que por lo tanto pertenece, del mismo modo que las demás cosas creadas por el hombre, una cuchara, una mesa o una casa, a la llamada realidad objetiva. Esto es así tanto si la realidad se considera como la cantidad de materia dada, como aquello que percibo o como una construcción subjetiva de mi percepción. La obra de arte se diferencia de las otras cosas producidas por el hombre, como mucho, en el hecho de que no ha sido creada para un uso cotidiano determinado. Mientras que yo vivo en una casa, me siento a una mesa y puedo comer sopa con una cuchara, las obras de arte difícilmente se pueden emplear –a excepción quizá de con fines decorativos– en la vida cotidiana. Mientras que en épocas anteriores y en otras culturas estaban pensadas para emplearse en contextos políticos y religiosos, a partir de la proclamación de la autonomía del arte fueron disociándose de todos los contextos cotidianos –aunque nunca de las coerciones económicas–. Los artistas son pagados por sus obras del mismo modo que el fabricante de porcelana o de máquinas de vapor. Mientras que hasta finales del siglo dieciocho era quien la encargaba el que en casi todos los casos determinaba el valor de la mercancía que era la obra de arte, desde el siglo diecinueve esta tarea la lleva a cabo el mercado.

El reconocimiento general y público de esa separación entre arte y realidad protegía a los artistas de la persecución en caso de que sus obras fueran impopulares y les evitaba al mismo tiempo a las obras el paso por la censura. Pues con autonomía no sólo se quería decir que la obra, escindida de todas sus conexiones con los usos cotidianos y convertida en un valioso recipiente para la verdad, se declarara una especie de grial, o que llegara incluso a convertirse en objeto de veneración, que el arte fuera adquiriendo progresivamente el estatus de sustituto de la religión y que fuera adorada en sus templos. Con autonomía se quería decir también, y sobre todo, que la verdad de las obras nunca aparece en lo que dicen o muestran, sino que está tras ello, que se oculta, por así decirlo, en lo más profundo de ellas. Las obras de arte nunca quieren decir lo que muestran o dicen. No pueden ser malinterpretadas como las declaraciones políticas o morales, ni considerarse blasfemia o pornografía, aunque a primera vista pueda dar la impresión de que incitan a dar golpes de Estado o a provocar revoluciones, que glorifican el asesinato, el adulterio o el robo; aunque ofendan a Dios o muestren a personas desnudas. Significan algo completamente distinto. Están separadas por un abismo insondable de la realidad en la que se incita al golpe de Estado o a la revolución, o en la que el crimen, la blasfemia y la pornografía están a la orden del día. La autonomía del arte da por supuesta la esencial diferencia entre arte y realidad, la postula y la afirma.

A esta afirmación se han opuesto decidida y vehementemente las realizaciones escénicas de teatro y del arte de la performance desde los años sesenta. A ellas no se les aplica –o sólo en parte– la idea de que no quieren decir lo que muestran y dicen. Pues en ellas se realizan permanentemente acciones que son autorreferenciales y constitutivas de realidad. Cuando Marina Abramović rompió la copa de vino con su mano y ésta empezó a sangrar, su acción significaba precisamente que la artista había roto la copa de vino en su mano y que ésta había comenzado a sangrar. Esta acción constituyó la realidad de una copa rota y una mano que sangraba. En el marco de esa realización escénica no podía constatarse, por lo tanto, ninguna diferencia decisiva entre arte y realidad. Todo lo que en ella se hizo y se mostró significaba aquello que se hizo y se mostró, y constituyó así la correspondiente realidad.

La condición de autorreferenciales y de constitutivas de realidad es común a todas las realizaciones escénicas. Cuando un actor que interpreta a Hamlet atraviesa la escena su acción significa, primordialmente, el andar del actor sobre la escena y constituye la realidad de dicho andar. El actor no hace como si anduviera.

Anda en efecto y cambia con ello la realidad. Ésta es la condición necesaria para que, llegado el caso, el andar pueda interpretarse como otra cosa –por ejemplo, como el llegarse de Hamlet hasta la habitación de Gertrudis–. Como observa acertadamente Max Herrmann, las realizaciones escénicas de teatro tratan siempre de «personas reales» en «espacios reales». Cuando los actores se mueven en y a través del espacio modifican realmente la posición de sus cuerpos, y con ello el espacio performativo. La generación performativa de la materialidad de las realizaciones escénicas tiene como consecuencia que todo lo que aparece en ellas acontece realmente, aunque a eso que aparece también puedan atribuírsele significados adicionales.

La oposición entre arte y realidad ha generado gran cantidad de nuevas oposiciones dicotómicas como las de lo estético *vs.* lo social, lo estético *vs.* lo político y lo estético *vs.* lo ético. Como se ha mostrado, las realizaciones escénicas desde los años sesenta han conducido al desmantelamiento de todas esas oposiciones de manera ostensible. El cambio de roles y la formación de comunidades revelan con particular claridad que las realizaciones escénicas son siempre una situación social, una forma de sociabilidad. Lo que acontece en una realización escénica entre actores y espectadores, o entre espectadores, se lleva a cabo siempre como un proceso social específico, constituye una realidad social específica. Tales procesos se convierten en políticos si entra en juego el poder a la hora de negociar las relaciones o de fijar las posiciones. Siempre que un individuo, o un grupo, intenta imponer a otros determinadas posiciones, modos de comportamiento, acciones o ideas, estamos ante procesos de naturaleza política. Siempre que James Griffith, en *Commune*, instaba a los espectadores a entrar en el círculo para hacer de habitantes del pueblo de My Lai, estaba llevando a cabo un acto político. Siempre que Schlingensief, en *Chance 2000*, amenazaba a los espectadores con expulsarlos de la realización escénica, su acto era también político. Cuando los «no-creyentes», en *Two Amerindians Visit...*, se reían de los «creyentes» e intentaban convencerles de la insostenibilidad de sus ideas, también era un acto político. La dimensión política se muestra con total nitidez sobre todo cuando algo parece «salirse de madre», cuando algo fracasa porque otro no ha querido tomar parte en el juego propuesto: cuando algunos participantes se negaban a entrar en el círculo, cuando se solidarizaban con los espectadores amenazados por Schlingensief, cuando se defendían de los «no-creyentes». La contraposición de lo estético y lo político, en este como en otros muchos casos, no se sostiene. La disposición elegida por los artistas, la situación que habían creado y a la que exponían a los demás participantes y a sí mismos, era siempre estética y política al mismo tiempo. Separar lo estético de lo político, o contraponerlos, parecía del todo imposible.

Cuando, en su famoso discurso en la Kurfürstliche Deutsche Gesellschaft de Mannheim, Schiller definió el teatro como una institución moral, porque la escena «más que cualquier otra institución pública [...] es una escuela de sabiduría práctica, una guía para la vida social, una llave infalible para llegar a los rincones más secretos del alma humana»[7], y cuando Brecht, por su parte, sugería al público que encontraran por sí mismos una solución a los problemas presentados en la escena («¡estimado público, vamos, busca la clave/tiene que haber una buena, tiene, tiene que haberla!»)[8], ambos estaban considerando el teatro como un espacio no apto para la acción. No era la realización escénica el lugar donde el espectador tenía que intervenir, sino en las relaciones sociales y políticas externas al teatro. La realización escénica debía proveerlo de imágenes que lo sacudieran, que lo movieran a reflexión sobre la situación política y social, y lo guiaran en ellas, unas imágenes a partir de las cuales fuera el espectador el que actuara en la realidad social y política. Lo estético se concebía, pues, como opuesto a lo ético. Si tenemos en cuenta muchas de las realizaciones escénicas de teatro y del arte de la performance

7 Friedrich Schiller, «Was kann eine gute stehende Schaubühne eigentlich wirken?» (1784), en *Schillers Werke*, Nationalausgabe, vol. 20, Weimar, 1962, pp. 87-100, p. 95.

8 Bertolt Brecht, *Der gute Mensch von Sezuan*, en: *Gesammelte Werke*, Fráncfort, 1967, vol. 2, p. 1607 (esp. *La buena persona de Sezuan*, en Bertolt Brecht, *Obra*, México, 1972).

llevadas a cabo desde los años sesenta, tal oposición tampoco puede sostenerse. Una y otra vez al espectador se lo involucra en una situación en la que debe tomar decisiones, en la que tiene que actuar. Comparte, asimismo, la responsabilidad respecto a la situación creada, que ya no es sólo cosa de los artistas.

Da la impresión de que en los últimos años se hubieran invertido las relaciones. Mientras que en la «vida real» las personas adoptan cada vez más a menudo el papel de espectadores cuando son testigos de actos violentos y es evidente que no se sienten obligados a intervenir, a actuar –incluso aunque su intervención se limite a llamar por el móvil a la policía–, los artistas trabajan para exponerlos, en las realizaciones escénicas, a situaciones en las que no se pueden limitar a considerarse espectadores, y a comportarse como tales, situaciones en las que se sienten incitados a intervenir, a actuar. Al estar dispuestos a llegar a lo más extremo, a llegar incluso a traspasar el límite del peligro de muerte, los artistas incluyen a los espectadores entre los responsables, les hacen sentir responsables, sentir que tienen que decidir y actuar.

En tales realizaciones escénicas lo estético es impensable sin lo ético. Lo ético es más bien una dimensión constitutiva de lo estético. Por eso las realizaciones escénicas de este tipo suponen un gran desafío: exigen una revisión de los fundamentos de la relación entre lo estético y lo ético, una nueva y radical conceptualización de la misma.

¿Se puede extraer del hecho de que las realizaciones escénicas analizadas lleven al desmoronamiento de la contraposición entre arte y realidad en sus distintas manifestaciones y formulaciones, la conclusión de que en esas realizaciones escénicas ya no cabe la distinción entre arte y realidad, que equiparan lo uno con lo otro y que con ello terminan cuestionando la autonomía del arte, o incluso negándola? Antes de dar por buena una conclusión como ésta, habría que tener en cuenta que, en las realizaciones escénicas de este tipo, los artistas pretenden crear intencionadamente, y sirviéndose de medios artísticos –que en algunos casos requieren laboriosas preparaciones y meses de ensayos–, una situación que se asemeje a las situaciones de la vida cotidiana, pero que en realidad es una situación de laboratorio. Y de igual manera que no equipararíamos una situación de laboratorio con una de la vida diaria –incluso aunque con ello ampliemos nuestro conocimiento sobre el comportamiento humano–, tampoco podemos equiparar una realización escénica artística con una situación cotidiana. No obstante, la una no se contrapone a la otra, aunque en algunos aspectos sean distintas.

A la luz de este análisis se impone una reconsideración del concepto de autonomía del arte. De las realizaciones escénicas aquí analizadas, en cualquier caso, no se puede dar cuenta adecuadamente con ayuda de ese tipo de pares de conceptos antagónicos basados en la diametral oposición entre lo estético y lo no-estético. En ellas se puede ver que lo estético es al mismo tiempo social, político y ético. Lo que los conceptos formados de acuerdo a esta dicotomía pretenden estrictamente separado, se encuentra en las realizaciones escénicas unido sin más, es incluso impensable sin lo que supuestamente se le opone: lo uno es ya de siempre lo otro, lo que aparentemente se le oponía, lo que lo contradecía. Esto es lo que constituye, entre otras cosas, la singularidad de la experiencia estética en dichas realizaciones escénicas. En ellas es lo estético lo que sabe adaptarse de manera portentosa, por no decir mágica, a su opuesto en cada caso: lo social, lo político, lo ético. Lo estético se fusiona con lo no-estético, la frontera entre los dos ámbitos se diluye. La autonomía del arte se convierte en objeto de autorreflexión de las realizaciones escénicas, incluso cuando llevan al desplome una y otra vez a las oposiciones entre arte y realidad, entre lo estético y lo no-estético. Precisamente el desmantelamiento de estas contraposiciones, su amalgamamiento, se puede considerar como uno de los resultados de las reflexiones sobre la autonomía del arte llevadas a cabo por las realizaciones escénicas, en las que de consuno se cuestiona radicalmente esa misma autonomía.

Al derribar las parejas de conceptos dicotómicos arte/realidad y estético/no-estético, al hacer que su desplome tenga lugar, las realizaciones escénicas reflexionan también sobre su propia condición de posibilidad como acontecimientos artísticos. No se conforman con derribar los pares de conceptos referidos a ellas en tanto que acontecimientos artísticos. También desestabilizan otras dicotomías que desde la Antigüedad han sido fundamentales en la cultura occidental, a saber: sujeto *vs.* objeto, cuerpo *vs.* mente, signo *vs.* significado. ¿Qué sucede cuando éstas se desmoronan o cuando empiezan, al menos, a oscilar?

También en estos casos es manifiesto que no estamos ante una disyunción exclusiva, sino ante una conjunción. En el bucle de retroalimentación autopoiético cada uno de los participantes es al mismo tiempo sujeto *y* objeto: le da un nuevo giro a su desarrollo con el que se determina tanto a sí mismo como a lo que perciben los demás y, al tiempo, se ve determinado por el desarrollo de la realización escénica y por los giros que le dan los demás. Esto es especialmente visible en el cambio de roles, en todas las modalidades de participación del espectador, y rige también en lo concerniente a la percepción del participante. Lo que aparece se convierte en objeto de su percepción. Desde este punto de vista el espectador es sujeto de la percepción y objeto percibido. Ahora bien, lo percibido puede afectar al perceptor de distintas maneras. Traspasa los límites corporales del perceptor, penetra en su cuerpo en forma de olor, sonido o luz. El espectador inhala el olor quiera o no; la voz del otro, del actor o del cantante, resuena en su caja torácica. Entre el perceptor y lo percibido tiene lugar un incesante intercambio, es decir, que la diferencia entre sujeto y objeto, una oposición que en la filosofía y en la historia del pensamiento occidental en general se ha tenido por fundamental, aquí no lo parece de ninguna manera. El bucle de retroalimentación autopoiético oscila, como la percepción, entre las posiciones de sujeto y objeto, se desliza constantemente entre una y otra. «Sujeto» y «objeto» dejan de constituir una oposición, marcan meramente distintos estados o posiciones del perceptor y de lo percibido que pueden ser adoptados sucesiva o, en algunos casos, simultáneamente. Esto puede ocurrir también en el caso de una percepción cotidiana. Pero no somos conscientes de ello sino en virtud de la atención con la que percibimos las realizaciones escénicas. En ellas nos experimentamos en el acto de la percepción al mismo tiempo como perceptores activos y como afectados por lo que percibimos, es decir, como sujeto y objeto.

El tratamiento que se le da en las realizaciones escénicas al antagonismo entre cuerpo y mente es aún más radical. No sólo desequilibran el par de conceptos antagónicos, sino que lo suprimen sin contemplaciones. Las realizaciones escénicas se originan a partir de procesos de corporización que son capaces de generar tanto el cuerpo de quien actúa como significados. Por ello he definido corporización, a diferencia del uso que se hacía del término desde finales del siglo dieciocho [entendiéndolo como encarnación], no como expresión de algo preexistente, dado de antemano, como sugiere la teoría de los dos mundos, sino como un proceso de generación. Según este concepto, la mente no se puede entender como opuesta, o sólo como opuesta, al cuerpo. La mente halla en el cuerpo su base existencial, es generada por él, y viene a presencia en tanto que *embodied mind*. El fenómeno de la presencia revela la dicotomía entre cuerpo y mente como un instrumento totalmente inapropiado para la descripción del ser humano.

En opinión de Schiller, al hombre ordinario se lo podía describir efectivamente a partir de la oposición entre cuerpo y mente, entre naturaleza sensible y razón. A él oponía el ser humano ideal, en el que estas dos fuerzas en eterna contradicción se concilian y están en una relación equilibrada. Esto sería posible en el mundo histórico, sólo en el ámbito del arte. En él se unen el impulso de lo material y el de lo formal para dar lugar al impulso de juego. Las palabras, tantas veces citadas, de las *Cartas sobre la educación estética del hombre* (1795): «El hombre sólo debe jugar con la belleza, y debe jugar sólo con la belleza. Pues [...] el hombre sólo juega cuando es hombre en el pleno sentido de la palabra, y sólo es enteramente hombre cuando juega»[9], apuntan expresamente a que la oposición sólo se puede suprimir en el arte. Al arte se le concede su prominente posición precisamente

9 Friedrich Schiller, «Briefe über die ästhetische Erziehung des Menschen», en *Schillers Werke*, Nationalausgabe, vol. 20, Weimar, 1962, pp. 309-412, p. 359 (esp. *Cartas sobre la educación estética del hombre*, en *Kallias. Cartas sobre la educación estética del hombre*, Barcelona, 1990, pp. 110-381, aquí p. 241).

porque sólo en su ámbito el ser humano puede ser llevado, al menos provisionalmente, a un estado en el que el concepto de hombre adquiera su significado pleno, a un estado estético. Sólo en él encontramos conciliados el cuerpo y la mente del hombre, su naturaleza y su razón, el impulso formal y el material.

Este breve excurso ha dejado claro que el concepto de hombre como *embodied mind* no es equiparable a la conciliación de pares antagónicos propuesta por Schiller –ni a su síntesis *(Aufhebung)*, si lo queremos decir con Hegel–. Pues el concepto de mente corporizada implica que en el cuerpo humano entendido como un organismo vivo la mente viene ya de siempre dada. Con esto no nos remitimos a un lejano ideal, sino que describimos al ser humano común. Así, quien aparece en las realizaciones escénicas es el ser humano común, aunque transfigurado por el fenómeno de la presencia. Es la presencia la que hace que esta condición de común se note, y la que la hace, de ese modo, consciente.

Esta concepción del ser humano relativiza también otro antagonismo, el que hay entre ser humano y animal. Cuando Beuys entabló un diálogo de energía con el coyote y Abramović se comunicó con las serpientes a través de sus corrientes energéticas, ambos estaban presuponiendo la condición de generador de energía tanto en la persona como en los animales, con lo que la oposición, que parecía fundamental, se quedaba en una mera diferencia gradual. Hay diferencias, sí, pero no una oposición radical. También en esta dirección apuntan expresamente las realizaciones escénicas.

Hay muchos otros pares de conceptos dicotómicos que pierden su vigencia en las realizaciones escénicas, como se ha mostrado en el transcurso de este estudio. Aquí me ocuparé solamente del par significante *(Signifikant)*/significado *(Signifikat)*. En las realizaciones escénicas la oposición entre ambos se trata de dos maneras absolutamente distintas: por un lado, en virtud del fenómeno de la autorreferencialidad –que en ellas tiene una posición prominente– niegan no sólo su condición de elementos antagónicos, niegan que haya cualquier tipo de diferencia entre ambos. Lo percibido significa justamente aquello como lo que viene a presencia en el acto de percepción. Por otro lado, la oposición se refuerza aparentemente aún más cuando, como en el caso de las asociaciones, se le atribuyen un gran número de posibles significados a un significante, de tal manera que cada significante puede significar cualquier objeto, o cualquier otro significante que se quiera. No hay que pasar por alto, sin embargo, que este «refuerzo» de la oposición entre significante y significado encuentra su fundamento precisamente en su negación. Pues tampoco aquí estamos ante una disyunción exclusiva, sino ante una conjunción. Precisamente porque el fenómeno percibido significa aquello como lo que aparece en el acto de la percepción, puede también significar lo que se quiera. Así pues, se niega tanto la oposición entre significante y significado como cualquier posibilidad de correspondencia uno a uno entre significado y significante.

Las realizaciones escénicas que dan lugar al colapso de pares de conceptos dicotómicos de este tipo, que derrumban los antagonismos, constituyen una realidad en la que uno puede simultáneamente aparecer como otro, una realidad de la inestabilidad, de lo difuso, de lo ambiguo, de lo transitorio, una realidad en la que se suprimen las fronteras. Uno no puede aproximarse a la realidad de la realización escénica sirviéndose de construcciones dicotómicas. Dado que las realizaciones escénicas hacen hincapié en las experiencias cotidianas, en lo ordinario, dado que dirigen su atención a ello y pueden así transfigurarlo, surge la pregunta de si no darán pie, puesto que han mostrado la inadecuación de esos conceptos dicotómicos para describirlas, a la duda de en qué medida esas parejas conceptuales dicotómicas puedan ser instrumentos heurísticos adecuados para la descripción de la realidad extraestética[10]. Al desestabilizar el esquema de formación de conceptos dicotómicos con los que estamos acostumbrados a entender y describir la realidad, las realizaciones escénicas alimentan la sospecha de que tales parejas de conceptos sirven para construir una realidad que contradice nuestra experiencia cotidiana. Pues postulan un «lo uno o lo otro» en vez de un «tanto lo uno

10 La distinción entre realidad estética y extraestética pertenece también a las dicotomías que ha derruido la estética de lo performativo. Las realizaciones escénicas prestan atención a ambas realidades.

como lo otro», que sería mucho más apropiado. Por este motivo no son adecuadas ni como instrumentos heurísticos para el conocimiento y la descripción de la realidad, ni como pautas para nuestro comportamiento y nuestra actividad. Si las realizaciones escénicas se aproximan a la vida también en el sentido en que son tan imprevisibles e imponderables como ella, entonces hay una cierta probabilidad de que los parámetros que no pueden aplicarse a ellas tampoco puedan aspirar a tener validez para el conocimiento y la descripción de la vida.

3. Liminaridad y transformación

Cuando dos contrarios coinciden, de modo que uno puede ser al mismo tiempo el otro, la atención se dirige a la transición entre los dos estados. Se abre el espacio entre los contrarios, sus intersticios. La intersticidad asciende de este modo a categoría predilecta. Se ha demostrado repetidamente que la experiencia estética que posibilitan las realizaciones escénicas puede considerarse por encima de todo una experiencia umbral, una experiencia que puede llevar a cabo una transformación en quienes la experimentan. Para una estética de lo performativo esta forma de experiencia estética es, sin duda, de una gran importancia, pues está estrechamente relacionada con el carácter de acontecimiento de la realización escénica.

El concepto de «liminaridad», que es central en este contexto, no proviene de la teoría del arte ni de la estética filosófica, sino de los estudios sobre el ritual. Dicho concepto fue acuñado por Victor Turner –que trabajaba en estrecha colaboración con Schechner– aunque con la vista puesta en la obra de Arnold van Gennep. Éste había compilado en su estudio *Los ritos de paso* (1909) gran cantidad de materiales etnológicos que demostraban que el ritual está vinculado a una experiencia del límite y del paso de gran carga simbólica. Los ritos de paso se dividen en tres fases:

1.– Fase de separación, en la que el sujeto que va a sufrir la transformación es apartado de su vida cotidiana y distanciado de su entorno social.

2.– Fase del umbral o de la transformación, en la que el sujeto que va a sufrir la transformación es llevado a un estado «entre» todos los ámbitos posibles, lo que le proporciona experiencias totalmente nuevas y, en algunos casos, perturbadoras.

3.– Fase de incorporación, en la que el sujeto ya transformado es reintegrado en la comunidad y es aceptado con su nuevo estatus y su identidad modificada.

De acuerdo con Van Gennep, esta estructura puede observarse en las culturas más diversas. Las diferencias aparecen cuando entramos en su contenido, que sí es específico de cada cultura. Victor Turner denominó el estado que se crea en la fase del umbral estado de liminaridad (del lat. *limen* – límite, umbral) y precisó su definición al calificarlo de estado de una lábil existencia intermedia «betwixt and between the positions assigned and arrayed by law, custom, convention, and ceremonial»[11]. Turner explica que la fase del umbral abre espacios culturales de actuación para la experimentación y la innovación y explica cómo lo hace en la medida en que «[i]n liminality, new ways of acting, new combinations of symbols, are tried out, to be discarded or accepted»[12]. Los cambios que resultan de la fase umbral afectan normalmente, según Turner, tanto al estatus social de aquellos que se someten al ritual como a la sociedad en su conjunto. Referido a individuos esto significa que los muchachos se transforman en guerreros, una mujer y un hombre solteros, en un matrimonio, un enfermo, en sano, etc. En lo referente al conjunto de la sociedad, Turner considera los rituales como un medio para la renovación y el asentamiento de grupos en tanto que comunidades. A este respecto Turner identifica la influencia de dos mecanismos: el primero es el aspecto de *communitas* generado en el

11 Turner, *The Ritual Process. Structure and Anti-Structure*, p. 95 (esp. *El proceso ritual. Estructura y antiestructura*: «en una especie de limbo entre las posiciones asignadas por las leyes, las costumbres, las convenciones y el ceremonial», p. 102).

12 Turner, «Variations on a Theme of Liminality», en Sally F. Moore & Barbara C. Myerhoff (eds.), *Secular Rites*, Assen, 1977, pp. 36-57, p. 40 [«en el estado de liminalidad, se prueban nuevos modos de actuación, nuevas combinaciones de símbolos, para ser descartados o aceptados»].

ritual, que describe como un intenso sentimiento de comunidad que elimina las barreras que separan a los individuos; el segundo es un empleo específico de símbolos que los hace aparecer como compactos y polisémicos portadores de significados y que permite tanto a actores como espectadores establecer varios marcos de interpretación.

En su aceptación crítica de este enfoque, Rao y Köpping subrayan por una parte la ambigüedad de los rituales y, por otra, su performatividad específica, su carácter de realización escénica. Los definen como acontecimientos por ser «actos transformadores [...] a los que se les atribuye el poder» de «*transformar* en cualquier sentido posible todos los contextos de acción y significado, todos los marcos y todos los elementos y personas que los constituyen; de este modo, les confieren un nuevo estatus a las personas y a los símbolos»[13]. Por ello parten de la tesis de que la fase umbral no sólo conduce hacia un cambio del estatus social de las personas implicadas, sino a su transformación «en cualquier sentido posible», lo cual concierne a su percepción de la realidad.

Si califico de experiencia umbral la experiencia estética que hacen posible las realizaciones escénicas de teatro y del arte de la performance, de ello no se sigue que esté equiparando las realizaciones escénicas artísticas con las rituales. Es, en efecto, difícil dar con criterios para una clara delimitación entre ellas. También está claro que en las realizaciones escénicas artísticas, como se ha mostrado en los casos de Abrámovic, Beuys, Nitsch, Schechner y Schleef, entre otros, tales delimitaciones son puestas en cuestión y burladas una y otra vez. Tanto las realizaciones escénicas artísticas como las rituales son el resultado de meticulosas escenificaciones, en ambos casos se puede trabajar con guión, con ensayos o por medio de improvisaciones, ambas pueden constituir realidad y entretener también al público. Ambas prevén tanto para los actores como para los espectadores la posibilidad de cambiar sus roles.

13 Ursula Rao, Klaus-Peter Köpping, «Die 'performative Wende': Leben – Ritual – Theater», en Klaus-Peter Köpping y Ursula Rao (eds.), *Im Rausch des Rituals. Gestaltung und Transformation der Wirklichkeit in körperlicher Performanz*, Múnich/Hamburgo/Londres, 2000, pp. 1-31, p. 10.

A este respecto no sirven de nada las etiquetas del tipo: «esto es una realización escénica de teatro» y «esto es un ritual», porque la distinción puede ser salvada, como hemos visto, por cualquiera de los participantes, tanto actores como espectadores. Hay una diferencia que, no obstante, se mantiene. Mientras que en el ritual la experiencia del umbral, por la que pasa un participante, puede llevar a la transformación de su estatus social y de su identidad reconocida, en la experiencia estética propia de las realizaciones escénicas es muy discutible que ocurra tal cosa.

A lo largo de mi estudio he mostrado en múltiples ocasiones, con ayuda de ejemplos concretos, cuándo y cómo se origina un estado de liminaridad y la posibilidad que conlleva, para quien se encuentra en él, de sufrir una transformación. Si echamos la mirada atrás, podremos comprobar que hay dos factores por encima de los demás que son capaces de producir experiencias liminares: la autopoiesis y la emergencia, por un lado, y el desplome de las oposiciones, por otro. Las experiencias posibilitadas por ellos son también siempre experiencias umbral.

Parece que es sobre todo el desmantelamiento de la oposición entre arte y realidad, así como todas las demás oposiciones que se derivan de ella, el que pone a los participantes en un estado umbral. Esto se puso de manifiesto con particular claridad en el caso de las performances de autoagresión. En ellas se infringían reglas y normas vigentes hasta entonces y creaban así para todos los participantes –también para los artistas que se estaban agrediendo– un estado de radical *betwixt and between*. En dichas situaciones, un comportamiento puramente «estético» habría dado en voyerismo o sadismo; uno ético habría comportado el riesgo de contravenir la intención del artista. Estas performances precipitaban al espectador a una crisis para cuya superación no podía recurrir a patrones de comportamiento convencionalmente admitidos. Los estándares válidos hasta el momento dejaban de serlo y los nuevos no se habían formulado todavía. El espectador estaba en una situación liminar, se hallaba en una fase umbral. La crisis sólo podía superarse si se buscaban y probaban –a pesar del peligro amenazante de un posible fracaso– nuevos modos de comportamiento.

Ese tipo de situación surgía una y otra vez en las realizaciones escénicas de Schechner, Castorf o Schlingensief, o también en performances de Coco Fusco y Guillermo Gómez-Peña, es decir, en realizaciones escénicas que acaban con las contraposiciones entre lo estético y lo social y lo estético y lo político. Mientras que en el caso de Schechner el espectador oscilaba constantemente entre su estatus de espectador y su participación en el *play*, en el de Castorf estaba expuesto a menudo a la incertidumbre sobre si en un momento dado tenía que actuar como espectador o como actor, sobre si tenía que seguir los acontecimientos como observador no observado o debía convertirse en objeto de observación; si percibía a un personaje dramático o a un actor que se salía del papel y hablaba en nombre propio, si lo insultaba y amenazaba como Frank o como Hendrik Arnst, como Puntila o como Michael Wittenborn; si se confrontaba con un mundo «ficticio» o si se movía en la «realidad», o si era incluso él mismo un personaje de ficción en un mundo ficticio. En estos casos se juega a un juego con el espectador que éste no siempre es capaz de descubrir, un juego que lo pone en una situación liminar con la que puede tener un trato lúdico.

Schlingensief juega a un juego parecido, aunque en algunos casos menos lúdico y en otros verdaderamente brutal. Priva al espectador de cualquier base sobre la que pueda decidir con un mínimo de certeza en qué tipo de *cultural performance* participa, en qué marco lo sitúan, a qué reglas, normas y estándares de comportamiento debe atenerse. Empuja al espectador a un estado de profunda inseguridad que tiene que ver cómo superar por sí mismo. Schlingensief, en cualquier caso, no actúa como un chamán bienintencionado que acompaña al espectador a través de las turbulencias y trastornos, y que lo ayuda a encontrar una nueva orientación para percibir el mundo y a sí mismo de una manera nueva. Eso es algo de lo que debe ocuparse cada espectador, incluso aunque el intento de superación de la crisis dé en la mayoría de los casos en el surgimiento de una nueva situación liminar que se anuncia como una nueva crisis.

Puesto que las parejas conceptuales dicotómicas no sólo sirven como instrumentos para la descripción del mundo, sino también como reguladoras de nuestras acciones y comportamientos, su desestabilización, su derrumbe, implica no sólo la desestabilización de la percepción del mundo, de uno mismo y de los demás, sino también una oscilación de las reglas y normas que rigen nuestra conducta. A partir de los pares de conceptos se infieren distintos procedimientos para el establecimiento de marcos como: «esto es teatro/arte» o «esto es una situación social o política». Estos marcos dan pautas para un comportamiento adecuado en la situación que demarcan. Al hacer que marcos aparentemente opuestos, o simplemente distintos, choquen, las realizaciones escénicas ponen al espectador *entre* todas las reglas, normas y órdenes que emanan de ellos. A algunos este estado puede no parecerles «propio del arte». Así, los organizadores de las Festwochen de Viena, frustrados por las reacciones del público, intentaron sacar de este estado a los participantes en *Bitte liebt Österreich! [¡Amad a Austria, por favor!]* repartiendo octavillas en las que se leía: «Dies ist Kunst!» *[«¡Esto es arte!»]*. Había que marcar una frontera clara para hacer posible una reacción «adecuada», «estética», para evitar la intervención. ¿Pero qué es una reacción «adecuada» en este tipo de acontecimiento? En este caso se trataba de un dispositivo para la experimentación, para poder llevar a cabo un experimento con los espectadores y los transeúntes cuyo objeto era preguntarse por la motivación del comportamiento justamente en la frontera entre lo estético y lo ético. De más está añadir que Schlingensief retiró las octavillas distribuidas entre el público.

El estado de *betwixt and between*, la experiencia de crisis, se vive en primer lugar como transformación física, como modificación del estado psicológico, energético, afectivo y motor. Y a la inversa, puede ser la conciencia de los cambios físicos la que sea capaz de producir un estado umbral, a veces incluso en forma de crisis. Esto es aplicable sobre todo a las sensaciones y emociones intensas tal y como se suscitan en el sujeto perceptor en y por el acto de la percepción de un fenómeno surgido repentinamente en el espacio, por ejemplo, los sentimientos de compasión, miedo u horror que podían asaltar al espectador al observar los cuerpos frágiles y moribundos de *Giulio Cesare*, o la risa convulsa que causaba la subida de medio tono en cada nueva estrofa de «Danke», en *Murx*. Como habíamos visto, son precisamente las emociones intensas las que desencadenan un impulso activo que puede llevar a la intervención; con ella se adquiere un nuevo estatus, el de parte activa, se establecen nuevas normas y se experimenta con ellas. En una estética de lo performativo, la generación de emociones y la precipitación a un estado liminar son impensables por separado.

La experiencia estética como experiencia umbral en una realización escénica se debe, en última instancia, a la actividad y a los efectos del bucle de retroalimentación autopoiético. La situación liminar no sólo se da a partir de las experiencias de la indisponibilidad o de la transición permanente y alterna entre las posiciones de sujeto y objeto. Hay que entender más bien que cada giro que toma el bucle de retroalimentación supone una transición y, con ella, una situación umbral. Cada uno de los pasos por el «umbral» crea un estado de inestabilidad a partir del cual puede surgir algo imprevisible, algo que alberga el riesgo del fracaso, pero también la oportunidad de una transformación exitosa. Esto se puede comprobar con especial claridad en las realizaciones escénicas aquí estudiadas en la medida en que en ellas las transiciones no suelen llevarse a cabo de modo suave o imperceptible, sino abruptamente, de tal manera que se marcan insoslayablemente. La ejecución del bucle de retroalimentación autopoiético puede ser entendida y descrita como una sucesión de transiciones cada una de las cuales alberga un elevado potencial de liminaridad que libera precisamente en la ejecución.

El comienzo y el final de una realización escénica, que coinciden con el inicio y la interrupción del bucle de retroalimentación autopoiético, son un tipo muy especial de transición. Puesto que las realizaciones escénicas aquí consideradas no tuvieron lugar en su mayor parte en edificios de teatro tradicionales o, cuando fue así, no siguieron las normas y reglas vigentes, la transición del mundo cotidiano a la realización escénica, la escisión del espectador de su medio habitual y su entrada en la realización escénica, la transformación de conciudadano en espectador, no se antojaba carente de problemas. Esta transición estaba visiblemente marcada en cada una de ellas, como lo estaba la del final de la realización escénica, la salida del espectador de ésta.

Schechner desarrolló para esas dos transiciones, en consonancia con los ritos de separación y de reintegración de los que había hablado Van Gennep, una especial ceremonia de apertura (cada espectador debía entrar solo en el espacio escénico atravesando un pasillo semioscuro) y un rito de incorporación específico (la procesión conjunta por las calles de Nueva York). Su función era garantizar una transición segura en las fases especialmente peligrosas: la transformación del visitante en participante y su incorporación, ya transformado por las experiencias por las que había pasado en la realización escénica, a la sociedad. Con ello le daban a la realización escénica en su integridad carácter de fase umbral y de transformación.

En *Secret Service,* de Ruckert, la separación de la vida cotidiana y la transición a la realización escénica la llevaba a cabo un miembro de la compañía, que ponía a cada visitante una venda en los ojos y lo acompañaba al espacio escénico, cruzaba un umbral con él o bien, en el caso de la segunda parte, lo acompañaba además mientras se despojaba de su ropa –un procedimiento frecuente en los rituales–. La acción de desvestirse y volver a vestirse simboliza la separación del entorno cotidiano y la posterior reincorporación. La transición de la realización escénica al exterior se ejecutaba a la inversa: cada participante era acompañado hacia el exterior del espacio escénico, se le quitaba la venda y se ponía de nuevo su ropa. Sin duda, en este caso se le daba también una importancia crucial a la seguridad de las transiciones. Pues lo que acontecía durante la realización escénica tenía el fin de hacer posibles experiencias muy poco comunes y ciertamente irritantes a quien había venido como espectador y se le había transformado en un participante «ciego». También en este caso las transiciones, realizadas y declaradas como transgresión de límites, le dieron a toda la realización escénica como tal carácter de fase umbral y de transformación.

Castorf procedió de modo muy distinto en *Trainspotting*. Al espectador lo recibía un empleado del teatro en el vestíbulo, lo saludaba y le pedía que esperara delante de cierta puerta. Cuando se había reunido un grupo de espectadores, el empleado les conducía a través de los tortuosos y laberínticos pasillos del teatro, escaleras arriba y escaleras abajo, al espacio escénico, al que entraban uno por uno por una puerta estrecha y cruzando el escenario. Cuando sus ojos se habían acostumbrado a la tenue luz y habían reconocido la grada de metal que había detrás del escenario, los espectadores se dirigían a sus asientos. Durante un buen rato los que ya estaban sentados podían observar cómo los espectadores recién llegados tropezaban al pasar por el escenario, sin estar seguros de si la transición se había llevado a cabo, es decir, sin saber si la realización escénica había empezado ya, o si se encontraban todavía en el umbral. La inseguridad que por principio alberga toda transición se hacía más intensa. La transición se experimentaba, pues, como una fase desorientadora, como una situación liminar extrema. Lo mismo ocurría en la transición hacia el exterior. Dado que los actores regresaban una y otra vez al escenario, paraban a los espectadores que querían irse e intentaban establecer un diálogo con ellos sobre la realización escénica, y como además volvían después a despedirse de algunas espectadoras con un formal beso en la mano, el espectador que abandonaba la sala no podía tener la certeza de que la realización escénica hubiera terminado, la verdad es que continuaba hasta que el último espectador abandonaba la sala. Todo lo que sucedía entre el momento en que el espectador se encontraba en el vestíbulo y el momento en que regresaba a él, se experimentaba como fase umbral y de transformación.

Abramović y Ulay obraron de manera especialmente radical en su performance *Imponderabilia*. Toda la performance consistía en que los espectadores, uno a uno, tenían que atravesar la puerta principal del museo entre los dos artistas, que la flanqueaban completamente desnudos: entrar en el umbral, cruzarlo y volverlo a abandonar, es decir, que toda la realización escénica era la propia transición. Es difícil expresar de forma más gráfica que en las realizaciones escénicas lo esencial es el paso por fases umbral y de transformación.

Es pues la autopoiesis del bucle de retroalimentación la que, al producir la realización escénica, genera simultáneamente liminaridad. La liminaridad está, pues, estrechamente relacionada con la autopoiesis, proviene de su condición de acontecimiento. El bucle de retroalimentación autopoiético pone al espectador en un estado que lo aparta de su entorno cotidiano y de las normas y reglas que lo rigen –incluso aunque las experiencias que viva durante su transcurso puedan coincidir con ciertas experiencias cotidianas–, sin indicarle cómo podría lograr reorientarse. Este estado puede experimentarse como un suplicio o como una vivencia placentera.

Las transformaciones que tienen lugar en él son sobre todo transitorias y sólo perduran mientras lo hace la realización escénica, o a veces sólo durante algunas partes de ella. Entre ellas se cuentan los cambios psicológicos, afectivos, energéticos y motores (en el cuerpo), pero a veces también se logran cambios de estatus, como el de espectador a actor, o incluso la formación de una comunidad. Si las experiencias de desestabilización de la percepción de uno mismo, de los demás o del mundo, y la de la obsolescencia de normas y reglas vigentes conducen realmente a una reorientación y transformación del sujeto en cuestión, de su percepción de la realidad y de su percepción de sí mismo, es algo que sólo se puede saber examinando cada caso particular. Puede también ocurrir que, tras el abandono del espacio escénico, el espectador rechace su desestabilización transitoria por absurda e injustificada, y que intente volver a su antiguo orden de valores, o también que después de la realización escénica se mantenga largo tiempo en estado de desestabilización y que, mucho más tarde, reflexionando, logre reorientarse. Esto no afecta en absoluto al hecho de que haya vivido la participación en la realización escénica como una experiencia umbral. Esta experiencia se diferencia de la experiencia umbral en un ritual por dos criterios que sólo se dan en este segundo tipo, a saber: 1) el de la durabilidad (irreversibilidad) y 2) el del reconocimiento social.

La experiencia estética no se produce solamente a partir de acontecimientos excepcionales, sino también a partir de la percepción de lo ordinario. He insistido con diversos argumentos en que durante las realizaciones escénicas se tienen experiencias que coinciden en algunos aspectos con vivencias cotidianas del espectador, a pesar de que tales experiencias están al margen del discurso oficial; he insistido en que en ellas se perciben cuerpos, acciones, movimientos, objetos, sonidos y olores cotidianos que al mismo tiempo aparecen como extraordinarios, como transfigurados; he insistido en que lo singular de las realizaciones escénicas es precisamente su capacidad de convertir lo ordinario en llamativo, como en el caso de las *silent pieces* de Cage, en las que se hacía audible el silencio. Cuando lo cotidiano se convierte en extraordinario, las dicotomías se desmoronan y las cosas se transforman en su opuesto, el espectador experimenta entonces la realidad como «encantada». Es este encantamiento el que lo pone en un estado de liminaridad que puede transformarlo.

VII. EL REENCANTAMIENTO DEL MUNDO

Lo que acontece en las realizaciones escénicas se puede describir concisamente como un reencantamiento del mundo y como una transformación de los que participan en ellas. Su carácter de acontecimiento se articula y se manifiesta en la copresencia física de actores y espectadores, en la producción performativa de la materialidad y en la emergencia de significado, que son los procesos que posibilitan y llevan a cabo los procesos de transformación. La singularidad de las realizaciones escénicas de teatro y del arte de la performance desde los años sesenta ha sido haber expuesto una y otra vez de manera enfática estas condiciones de su configuración –así como los procesos de transformación vinculados a ellas–, haber jugado con ellas y haber reflexionado sobre ellas. Con ello han permitido una consideración más incisiva de la idea de que estas condiciones se aplican a todas las realizaciones escénicas, del tipo o de la época que sean. A ellas se refiere la estética de lo performativo que aquí se viene desarrollando.

Cuando nos planteamos sus pretensiones de validez tenemos que establecer una limitación y eliminar otra. Una estética de lo performativo *no pretende* reemplazar a las estéticas tradicionales de la obra, de la producción y de la recepción. Allá donde tenga lugar, o haya tenido lugar, un proceso artístico que se pueda entender y describir adecuadamente con los conceptos de «obra», «producción» y «recepción» no hay la menor necesidad de sustituirlas por una estética de lo performativo, aunque la posibilidad de complementarlas con ella sea muy prometedora. Una estética de lo performativo se orienta más bien a aquellos procesos artísticos para los que los conceptos de «obra», «producción» y «recepción» nunca fueron adecuados; procesos que por lo tanto no eran accesibles en el marco de las estéticas tradicionales o que, cuando se los consideraba, eran distorsionados, como es el caso de las realizaciones escénicas.

Puesto que desde los años sesenta del siglo veinte, y en algunos casos ya en el movimiento de las vanguardias históricas entre 1900 y 1930, las formas artísticas «no teatrales» también tienden a dar relieve a su naturaleza escénica y de acontecimiento, parece urgente, dado el desarrollo de las artes tras el giro performativo, la formulación de una estética de lo performativo no sólo para el teatro, sino para todas las artes.

Como en este caso su fundamento es el concepto de realización escénica, su pretensión de validez es ampliable a todo tipo de realización escénica artística, pertenezca al arte que pertenezca. Desde los años sesenta, es decir, con el giro performativo y con la generalización de los nuevos medios de comunicación, se han desarrollado en nuestra cultura una gran cantidad de nuevos modos de realización escénica en los ámbitos de la política, el deporte, el espectáculo y las fiestas o festivales. Estas realizaciones escénicas, que no tienen la pretensión de ser arte, son, sin embargo, organizadas y percibidas como nuevas posibilidades de teatralización y estetización de nuestro entorno, como caminos o medios de llevar a cabo un reencantamiento del mundo[1]. Puesto

1 A partir de este desarrollo no se puede extraer la conclusión inversa de que el proceso de desencantamiento del mundo durante la Ilustración estuviera vinculado a una regresión o a una degeneración de las realizaciones escénicas. Si es cierto que durante el siglo diecinueve se dejaron de llevar a cabo algunas realizaciones escénicas –como las ejecuciones públicas–, también lo es que han surgido nuevos géneros de realización escénica como el circo, las exposiciones etnológicas y coloniales o los espectáculos de *strip-tease*. (Los grandes almacenes podrían, por algunas de sus características, incluirse también en esta categoría). Con ellas ocurría que o bien desde instancias oficiales se les atribuía una función instructiva o didáctica, o bien se toleraban tácitamente como com-

que una estética de lo performativo ha de ser aplicable también a ellas, se antoja como un marco particularmente adecuado para discutir la oscilante relación entre lo estético y lo no-estético, entre lo artístico y lo no-artístico, y para retomar la pregunta por la autonomía del arte en nuestros días.

En el transcurso de nuestro estudio, aunque sobre todo en el capítulo anterior –dedicado al carácter de acontecimiento de las realizaciones escénicas–, he empleado repetidamente dos conceptos que sin duda están estrechamente relacionados con los procesos de reencantamiento del mundo y de transformación de los participantes en la realización escénica. Sin embargo, no me he ocupado de explicar por extenso estos dos conceptos tan fundamentales para una estética de lo performativo, me refiero al de escenificación y al de experiencia estética. Ambos tienen su origen en el siglo diecinueve y han sufrido una serie de modificaciones desde su acuñación. Hasta los años setenta del siglo veinte tenían un alcance limitado, aunque por motivos de muy diversa índole. Mientras que el concepto de escenificación se empleaba hasta entonces sólo en el ámbito del teatro, las tradiciones que influían en el desarrollo del concepto de experiencia estética se interrumpieron de forma abrupta con la Segunda Guerra Mundial. En los años setenta, la estética filosófica (sobre todo Rüdiger Bubner) y la nueva estética de la recepción, todavía en estado embrionario, volvieron a vincularse a esa tradición y desarrollaron el concepto con la mirada puesta en la singular relación entre el sujeto receptor y la obra de arte, el recipiente. Aunque en los setenta hubo algunos precursores, no fue, sin embargo, hasta los años ochenta que el concepto de escenificación pasó de ser un concepto meramente teatral a tener un lugar entre los conceptos estéticos generales. En este empleo ha seguido gozando hasta hoy de una coyuntura muy favorable.

pensación por las pérdidas que acarreaba la progresiva imposición del proceso de Ilustración. Puede asumirse que cada uno de los participantes de estas realizaciones escénicas las vivía de modo muy distinto. Tocante a las exposiciones etnológicas, véase Peter Altenberg, *Ashantee* (1898), Berlín, 1987.

No parece casual que ambos conceptos fueran retomados y redefinidos en el transcurso del giro performativo a finales de los años sesenta o principios de los setenta, o como consecuencia de él, y que desde entonces hayan tenido una amplia difusión. En efecto, el giro performativo ha contribuido, si es que no ha sido el principal causante, a una relajación de las fronteras entre las artes entre sí, y entre lo que es arte y lo que no lo es. Con ello se estaba poniendo de relieve la necesidad de desarrollar complejos conceptuales que, por un lado, fueran aplicables a los más diversos tipos de arte y que, por otro, fueran capaces de dar cabida a lo estético también en fenómenos y procesos no-artísticos. Para ello nuestros dos conceptos parecían especialmente adecuados. Así, el de escenificación se emplea hoy no sólo en referencia a las distintas artes, sino también a las realizaciones escénicas no artísticas y a todos los procesos de teatralización y estetización de nuestro entorno cotidiano. El de experiencia estética, por su parte, comprehende no sólo las experiencias que hacen posibles las diversas artes, sino también experiencias específicas. Aquellas que hacen posibles todos los fenómenos y procesos a los que se les puede atribuir una función estética, incluso aunque pertenezcan a los ámbitos de la moda, el diseño, la cosmética, la publicidad, el deporte, el diseño urbano o de jardines, o a los fenómenos y procesos naturales.

Mientras que el concepto de obra pedía ser complementado por los de producción y recepción, el concepto de acontecimiento en procesos estéticos se complementa con los de escenificación y experiencia estética. Esta tríada de conceptos constituye el armazón conceptual para una estética de lo performativo. Antes de discutir, en la parte final, el alcance y el rendimiento de una estética de este tipo, quiero explicar los conceptos de «escenificación» y «experiencia estética» que, a pesar de haber sido empleados profusamente en este estudio, todavía no habían sido definidos explícitamente.

1. Escenificación

Aunque el término escenificación fue acuñado en el siglo diecinueve, el proceso al que se refiere es antiquísimo, tanto que está presente siempre que una realización escénica tiene lugar. Sin duda, cualquier realización escénica en la que tomen parte varias personas precisa de preparación y, en algunos casos, incluso de un minucioso y elaborado estudio previo. En Atenas, las realizaciones escénicas de tragedias tenían lugar en el marco de las fiestas más grandes y representativas de la polis, las grandes Dionisias, de las que eran también parte integrante. De acuerdo con fuentes dignas de crédito, sus preparativos tenían lugar a lo largo de varios meses. La responsabilidad de cada realización escénica recaía normalmente en una sola persona, que redactaba el texto y estudiaba sus respectivas partes con los miembros del coro y con los actores. (De la financiación de los preparativos no se encargaba esa persona, sino un ciudadano ateniense rico). El trabajo previo con los ciudadanos que debían formar parte del coro –cantando y bailando– solía ser lo que más tiempo y energía requería. Los responsables de cada una de estas obras, entre los que conocemos sobre todo a Esquilo, Sófocles y Eurípides, dedicaban mucha atención y muchos esfuerzos a los preparativos, al proceso de escenificación. Esto era así porque los autores exitosos, aquellos que alcanzaban repetidamente el triunfo en el agón trágico, obtenían un gran prestigio y un excepcional aprecio en el ámbito público de la polis. Un poeta/director exitoso disfrutaba de tal consideración entre sus conciudadanos que se convertía en uno de los candidatos predilectos para cargos políticos y militares. Sófocles, que entre 468 a.C. (el año de su primera participación) y 406 a.C. (año de su fallecimiento) obtuvo veinte victorias en el agón trágico, fue elegido en 443/442 a.C. helenotamia (algo así como encargado de la comisión principal de finanzas del Estado); entre 441 y 439 a.C. se le encargó, junto a Pericles, la estrategia en la guerra de Samos –debido, como consta por escrito, al extraordinario efecto de la realización escénica de su *Antígona*–. En 428 fue responsable de nuevo, esta vez junto a Tucídides, de la estrategia militar y, finalmente, fue nombrado próbulo en el año 411. No es una prueba de nada, pero sí impresiona el hecho de que la capacidad para desarrollar estrategias escénicas que terminan dando lugar a una realización escénica impactante, pudiera ser tenida como cualificación relevante para el desempeño de cargos políticos y militares.

Las realizaciones escénicas son inconcebibles sin escenificación. No obstante, la palabra fue acuñada por vez primera como término específico en el siglo diecinueve. En lengua alemana se introdujo a principios de ese siglo. August Lewald explica el término en su ensayo de 1837 *In die Szene setzen [Poner en escena]*:

> Recientemente ha sido introducida la expresión «poner en escena» en todos los teatros alemanes; yo la oí por primera vez en el otoño del año 1818 en Viena, y en ese momento no supe muy bien qué pensar de ella. El señor Carl Blum, al que me encontré por la calle, me dijo que permanecería en Viena hasta que se hubiera puesto en escena su último ballet *Aline*. Suena ciertamente más elegante que: dar o realizar la pieza, y nosotros nos la hemos apropiado claramente del francés. Los franceses también dicen la «mise en scène», la «puesta en escena», un término que para nosotros no es corriente[2].

Durante el proceso de corrección de pruebas para la publicación, Lewald añadió una nota a pie de página: «Recientemente la palabra *Inscenierung* [escenificación] se ha hecho popular». Después Lewald se esfuerza por definir más detalladamente el concepto: «'Poner en escena' significa hacer visible un texto dramático en su integridad para complementar con medios externos la intención del autor e intensificar el efecto del drama»[3]. El concepto se empleaba pues referido al teatro literario y había surgido en el contexto de la teoría de los dos mundos. Sin embargo, abarca algo más que el proceso de «traducción» al que se orien-

2 August Lewald, «In die Scene setzen», en Klaus Lazarowicz y Christopher Blame (eds.), *Texte zur Theorie des Theaters*, Stuttgart, 1991, pp. 306-311, pp. 306 y s.

3 *Ibid.*, p. 306.

taban los teóricos del siglo dieciocho, el de verter lo expresado con signos lingüísticos, y los significados transmitidos con ellos, a signos teatrales. Le daba especial relevancia al hecho de que sobre el escenario algo se tenía que hacer visible, algo tenía que ser traído a presencia, a saber: lo expresado lingüísticamente en el texto del drama, algo que por su condición sólo podía aparecer como presente –en virtud de la imaginación– en forma de ilusión mental.

Como ya señaló Lewald, el término 'poner en escena'/'escenificación', con el significado que él le atribuía, había sido tomado del francés[4]. De la aparición de la expresión '*mise en scène*' no tenemos testimonios anteriores a 1800, y sabemos que su uso no se generalizó hasta después de 1835. Fue empleada con el significado de «dispositions prises pour mettre une pièce en état d'être representée»[5] o en el sentido de «transformer (un texte dramatique) en spectacle»[6]. Consecuentemente, el significado de la expresión «*mettre en scène*» se modificó también con ella. Estos términos pertenecen asimismo al ámbito del teatro literario. En su empleo se parte del supuesto de que lo primordial, lo dado, es el texto literario del drama, y que hay que transformarlo por medio de un proceso específico –la *mise en scène*– en una realización escénica. La introducción del término demuestra que la ejecución de este proceso de transformación no podía seguir dándose por supuesta y considerándose carente de problemas, sino que se era cada vez más consciente de que requería el desarrollo de determinadas estrategias de representación.

4 Ya a partir de 1660 se había generalizado en Francia la expresión «*metre quelqu'un, quelque chose sur la scène*» –aunque con un significado totalmente distinto, se refería a «ubicar a alguien o algo en una obra literaria o artística», por ejemplo en un cuadro–. Fue reemplazada a finales del siglo dieciocho por la expresión «*mettre sur scène*». La palabra aparece por primera vez en *Salons*, de Diderot, en el año 1765, referida a la pintura.

5 *Französisches etymologisches Wörterbuch*, vol. 11, Basilea, 1964, p. 294 [«disposiciones que se toman para poner una pieza en condiciones de ser representada»].

6 *Dicctionnaire historique de la langue française*, vol. 2, París, 1994, p. 1892 [«transformar (un texto dramático) en espectáculo»].

La noción de '*mise en scène*'/'escenificación' surgió en un tiempo en el que se anunciaban cambios fundamentales para el teatro, sobre todo el ascenso del director de organizador a artista, a creador de la «obra de arte» que es la realización escénica. Ciertamente Goethe ya había asumido esta nueva función de director en muchos aspectos durante sus años en la dirección del Teatro de la Corte de Weimar (1791-1817): introdujo sesiones de lectura en los ensayos, a partir de las cuales los actores conocían la obra completa y se familiarizaban con su papel (hasta entonces los actores, por lo general, sólo conocían su parte del texto); discutía detalladamente sobre los decorados con el pintor y ajustaba cuidadosamente los colores de las pinturas y los trajes de los actores, fijaba las posiciones y las posturas, ensayaba con ellos la declamación, los gestos y los movimientos, y escogía un acompañamiento musical «apropiado». Éstas son precisamente las tareas que tanto Lewald como el *Allgemeine Theater-Lexikon* del año 1846 incluían en la voz *Inscenesetzen* [poner en escena][7]. De todas formas, en este aspecto el Teatro de la Corte de Weimar era más una excepción que la regla general. No fue hasta los años cuarenta que empezó a considerarse en un ámbito más general que la tarea del director era, en palabras de ese mismo diccionario: «la disposición del personal y del material necesarios para todo lo que conlleva la representación de un texto dramático». Justo en ese momento empezó también a generalizarse la costumbre de mencionar el nombre del director en el cartel.

En los años cuarenta no había todavía, ni mucho menos, un acuerdo sobre si la actividad de «poner en escena» podía calificarse como artística, y el proceso correspondiente como estético, o si se trataba de una tarea meramente técnica. Lewald insistía, ciertamente, al igual que el autor de la entrada del *Allgemeinen Theater-Lexicon,* en que dicha actividad requería una serie de conocimientos y capacidades que no se limitaban a las distintas artes –poesía, arte de la actuación, pintura, música–, sino que incluía

7 Véase el *Allgemeine Theater-Lexicon oder Encyclopädie alles Wissenswerten für Bühnenkünstler, Dilettanten und Theaterfreunde*. K. Herlossohn, H. Marggraff *et al.* (eds.), 3 vols., nueva ed., Altenburg, Leipzig, 1846, p. 284.

también la posesión de conocimientos sobre los distintos estilos arquitectónicos y los modos de vestir históricos «para evitar anacronismos»[8]. Aunque Lewald describa la «puesta en escena» como un asunto de la mayor dificultad, cuya importancia para el teatro no se puede ponderar lo suficiente, en ningún momento la califica de actividad artística. Franz von Akáts, que en su tratado *Kunst der Scenik in ästhetischer und ökonomischer Hinsicht [El arte escénico desde una perspectiva estética y económica]* (1841), divide el «arte escénico» en «ordenación y decoración» y «ordenación de lo vivo», clasifica ciertamente la «escenificación» entre las artes visuales porque se propone «la representación de ideas estéticas mediante imágenes», pero le niega expresamente el estatus de «creación propiamente dicha»[9]. El arte escénico, al que entiende como una mera técnica, lo explica también sobre la base de la teoría de los dos mundos, según la cual en un lado está el mundo de las ideas estéticas y en el otro el de las imágenes creadas por la escenificación para representarlas, para traerlas a presencia. En el siglo diecinueve la noción de escenificación mentaba el traer a presencia algo dado previamente y que existía «en otro lugar» –en el texto literario del drama o en el mundo de las ideas estéticas–, un lugar en el que todavía no se le había dado sentido de manera vívida, un lugar en el que solamente tomaba «forma» en la imaginación o en el pensamiento. La tarea y función de la escenificación era hacer que viniera a presencia. Con escenificación se hacía referencia a las estrategias de representación necesarias para ello.

Esta definición del concepto no se modificó hasta que la escenificación, en el cambio del siglo diecinueve al veinte, pasó a considerarse una actividad artística y dejó de referirse al texto literario de un drama. Así, los movimientos de las vanguardias históricas declararon el teatro una forma artística autónoma e independiente de la literatura. Edward Gordon Craig constataba en su escrito *El arte del teatro*, de 1905, que:

8 Lewald, «In die Szene setzen», p. 308.

9 Franz von Akáts, *Kunst der Scenik in ästhetischer und ökonomischer Hinsicht*, Viena, 1841, p. IV.

> [...] el arte del teatro no es ni la actuación ni el drama, tampoco la escenografía o la danza, sino que consta de todos los elementos de que se componen éstas: acción, que es el espíritu mismo de la actuación; palabras, que son el cuerpo del drama; línea y color, que son el corazón mismo de la escenografía; ritmo, que es la esencia misma de la danza[10].

Consecuentemente, la realización escénica no se creaba como la transformación de un texto literario, sino como la selección, combinación y presentación de hasta sus más mínimos elementos constitutivos. El director lleva a cabo estos procedimientos y «en tanto que artista [...] domina los usos de las acciones, palabras, línea, color y ritmo»[11]. Con ello se le da a la realización escénica, como explica Lothar Schreyer en su escrito *Das Bühnenkunstwerk* [*La obra de arte escénica*] (1916), el marchamo de «obra de arte autónoma» y al teatro el de «arte autónomo»[12]. La tarea del director, la puesta en escena, se convierte en una actividad creadora. La actividad de la escenificación deja de verse solamente como un «hacer visible un texto dramático en su integridad, para [...] complementar la intención del autor e intensificar el efecto del drama», como escribía Lewald. Cuando Craig la define como aquello que debería hacer visible lo «invisible»[13], da la impresión, sin embargo, de que recurre a la teoría de los dos mundos, como si la escenificación tuviera que traer a presencia algo que existe «en otra parte», en «el reino de lo invisible». Las aclaraciones subsiguientes de Craig parecen poner en duda esta conclusión:

> Hay algo que el hombre todavía no ha aprendido a controlar; algo que el hombre no soñaba con alcanzar y que sin embargo anhelaba;

10 Craig, *On the Art of the Theater*, Londres, 1912, p. 138 (esp. *El arte del teatro*, México D.F., 1999).
11 *Ibid.*, p. 148.
12 Véase Lothar Schreyer, «Das Bühnenkunstwerk», en *Der Sturm* 7, 5 (agosto de 1916), pp. 50-51, p. 50.
13 Craig, *On the Art of the Theater*, p. 46.

> algo invisible y presente al mismo tiempo; algo de una magia abrumadora y susceptible de desaparecer en cualquier momento, algo a la espera de que lo alcancen los hombres adecuados para elevarse junto a ellos a través de todas las esferas más allá de la tierra: el movimiento[14].

La labor de la escenificación consiste, pues, en hacer aparecer el movimiento, en hacerlo actual. En realidad, el movimiento es siempre actual, pero a menudo permanece «invisible». Cuando la escenificación pone las bases para traerlo a presencia, esto significa que el movimiento viene a presencia en tanto tal en virtud de la escenificación. Mientras que en los casos de Lewald, del *Theater-Lexicon* y de Akáts la escenificación era entendida como un traer a presencia algo otro, en hacerlo visible en el sentido de una representación, en Craig se entiende como el empleo de todos los medios artísticos y técnicos con objeto de traer algo a presencia en tanto tal. Según esto, no sólo es que ese algo se percibe, sino que se percibe en su «magia abrumadora», es decir, en su relevancia para el perceptor, como algo que puede «hechizar» su mundo, que puede cambiarlo: la escenificación no se refiere pues a una estrategia de representación, sino una estrategia de generación. Produce la actualidad de lo que muestra.

Junto a esta nueva definición de escenificación se ha mantenido durante mucho tiempo con distintas modificaciones y variaciones –en parte hasta hoy– la definición que Lewald había hecho del concepto, y ello a pesar de que en el siglo veinte había ya un acuerdo general respecto al carácter artístico de la escenificación. Así, Jacques Copeau, en un artículo sobre dirección y escenificación para la *Encyclopédie Française* (París, 1936), definía esta última como «la suma de los procesos artísticos y técnicos con cuya ayuda la obra creada por un autor como texto escrito es transferida de una existencia puramente mental y oculta a su real y actual existencia teatral»[15], con lo que se considera el texto una entidad

14 *Ibid.*, pp. 46 y s.
15 Cit. por Lazarowicz/Balme (eds.), *Texte zur Theorie des Theaters*, p. 341.

«mental» dada que se transforma en el proceso de escenificación en presencia sensible y que toma apariencia física.

Esta definición, y con ella la validez de la teoría de los dos mundos que lleva implícita, está también en la base de la ampliación del concepto de escenificación, de concepto estético a concepto antropológico, que llevó a cabo Wolfang Iser remitiéndose a la teoría de Plessner de la distancia esencial del hombre con respecto a sí mismo. Para él el fin de la escenificación es «hacer aparecer aquello que no puede hacerse actual». Consecuentemente debe:

> haber algo previo [...] que en virtud de ella viene a presencia. Este algo previo no puede nunca tener cabida íntegramente en la escenificación, si así fuera la escenificación sería su propio algo previo. Visto desde otra perspectiva podría decirse que toda escenificación vive a partir de aquello que no es. Pues todo lo que se materializa en ella está al servicio de algo ausente que, en virtud de lo presente, puede visualizarse, pero no hacerse presente ello mismo[16].

Como se ha mostrado sobre todo en el cuarto capítulo, desde finales de los años sesenta se trabaja en casi todos los casos con una noción de escenificación que no remite a algo previo ni necesita de la teoría de los dos mundos. La escenificación se entiende, como en el caso de Craig, como una estrategia de generación. Cuando los medios artísticos y técnicos se emplean de tal modo que los actores aparecen entendidos en tanto que presentes y los objetos aparecen entendidos en tanto que en éxtasis, cuando los emplean de tal manera que dirigen la atención del espectador a su ser fenoménico, a su llamativo ser fenoménico, entonces lo que viene a presencia en o a través del cuerpo del actor, en o a través de las cosas, no es algo distinto a ellos, sino ellos mismos en su fugaz actualidad. Los actores o performadores generan presencia y se muestran a los espectadores en esa presen-

16 Wolfgang Iser, *Das Fiktive und das Imaginäre. Perspektiven einer literarischen Anthropologie*, Fráncfort, 1991, pp. 505 y 511.

cia generada por ellos. Al aparecer las personas y las cosas como presentes, como sí mismas, el mundo aparece como encantado. Es decir, que el encantamiento se origina en el núcleo de la autorreferencialidad como liberación de su función secundaria respecto al entendimiento, como desvelamiento del «significado propio» del hombre y de la cosa.

Es en el proceso de escenificación en el que se ensaya y se establece, y en algunos casos después de la realización escénica se modifica, el modo en que la producción performativa de la materialidad ha de llevarse a cabo. La escenificación ha de ser concebida como un proceso intencional en la medida en que, por medio de los procedimientos más variados –incluso por medio de operaciones casuales–, se establecen los elementos que han de ser producidos performativamente, es decir, en qué momento de la realización escénica y en qué punto del espacio aparecen, de qué modo se mueven por él y, en su caso, se modifican, y en qué momento y en qué lugar han de desaparecer de nuevo. La escenificación puede, pues, describirse como el proceso en el que se desarrollan y ensayan paulatinamente las estrategias para decidir qué, cuándo, dónde y cómo algo debe venir a presencia ante los espectadores. Se puede definir, pues, como una estrategia de generación según la cual la actualidad de las apariciones en la realización escénica ha de ser presentada y producida performativamente como fugaz y efímera en una sucesión temporal determinada y en una determinada constelación espacial.

Este fenómeno es el que satisface de modo más aproximado la definición del concepto de escenificación como la ha planteado Martin Seel. La define como: «escenificación de actualidad. Es el llamativo producir y poner de relieve la actualidad de algo que ocurre aquí y ahora, y que por ello, porque es actual, escapa a cualquier fijación intelectual de su integridad, por más aproximada que quiera ser»[17]. La escenificación hace aparecer el ahora. Seel identifica una diferencia importante entre escenificaciones

17 Martin Seel, «Inszenieren als Erscheinenlassen. Thesen über die Reichweite eines Begriffs», en Früchtl/Zimmermann, *Ästhetik der Inszenierung*, p. 53.

artísticas y no-artísticas. Las escenificaciones artísticas las define, en total consonancia con mi exposición en el cuarto capítulo, como «presentaciones en un sentido peculiar. No sólo se limitan a producir y a poner de relieve una singular actualidad, ofrecen actualidad. [...] no sólo *producen* presencia, *presentan* la presencia [...] Son ahoras efímeros de la vida humana. Son aquello que muestran»[18].

Seel menciona de modo explícito que las escenificaciones son «procesos sensibles introducidos o realizados con un claro propósito y *que se presentan ante un público*»[19]. Lo que no hace, sin embargo, es distinguir entre escenificación y realización escénica. En su definición coinciden los planes preparatorios, la concepción de la realización escénica, con la realización escénica en sí. Su frase «son ahoras efímeros de la vida humana. Son aquello que muestran», que él refería a la escenificación, define a mi entender más bien la realización escénica, y además con mucha exactitud, pero no a la escenificación. Por ello me gustaría insistir de nuevo en este punto en la distinción entre escenificación y realización escénica, y fundamentarla aún más sólidamente.

Puesto que las definiciones de escenificación citadas no la distinguen de la realización escénica, y parecen por lo tanto dar por supuesto que aquello que se planea y establece de antemano se repite todas las noches de manera exacta, el resultado es que pasan por alto el efecto del bucle de retroalimentación autopoiético, sin el cual no hay generación de la realización escénica. Ahora bien, la escenificación, como señala expresamente Seel, se prepara con la vista puesta en la percepción del espectador. Es decir, que el propio proceso de escenificación ya presupone la distinción entre escenificación y realización escénica en el sentido de que son primordialmente la percepción del espectador y su reacción ante lo percibido –la copresencia física de actores y espectadores– las que crean la realización escénica. En la medida

18 *Ibid.*, pp. 58 y s. Para la distinción entre escenificaciones artísticas y no-artísticas véase el tercer apartado de este capítulo.

19 *Ibid.*, p. 50.

en que el proceso de escenificación parte de estos supuestos y los toma en cuenta, a la hora de definir el concepto éstos han de ser también considerados.

Vuelvo, por ello, a la propuesta que he hecho en los capítulos anteriores. Al ensayar, concebir y establecer en el proceso de escenificación cómo ha de llevarse a cabo la producción performativa de la materialidad, se crea una situación en la que se incluye tanto a los actores como a los espectadores. Se trata de una situación abierta por definición, pues no es predecible la manera en la que responderán los espectadores y cómo reaccionarán ante ello los actores. Es decir, que el proceso de escenificación deja siempre espacios libres y margen de maniobra para que lo no planificado, lo no escenificado, lo imprevisible pueda acontecer en la realización escénica, incluso aunque algunas escenificaciones tanto artísticas como no-artísticas puedan intentar limitar todo lo posible los espacios libres y el margen de maniobra. La historia del teatro y de la cultura ofrece gran cantidad de ejemplos en los que las realizaciones escénicas no transcurren de acuerdo a lo planeado y en las que los participantes aprovechan los espacios libres y el margen de maniobra que se les ofrecen para llevar la realización escénica por un camino muy distinto al planeado.

Defino, por tanto, escenificación como el proceso de planificación, ensayo y establecimiento de estrategias de acuerdo a las que ha de generarse la materialidad performativa de la realización escénica. Por medio de ellas los elementos materiales pueden aparecer como presentes, venir a presencia en su ser fenoménico; además, se crea una situación que abre espacios libres y da margen de maniobra para acciones, modos de comportamiento y acontecimientos no escenificados. La escenificación da pautas muy importantes, decisivas, para la realización escénica, para la autopoiesis del bucle de retroalimentación. No está en condiciones, sin embargo, de establecer de manera definitiva su transcurso ni de predecir o controlar el proceso de autopoiesis. Así pues, el concepto de escenificación tiene que incluir siempre la reflexión sobre sus propios límites.

De ello no se sigue que dichos límites deban ser claramente reconocibles por cada uno de los participantes. Si durante una realización escénica cae al suelo un foco, los espectadores suelen dar por supuesto que ha tenido lugar un accidente, que ha sucedido algo no planificado, previsto ni escenificado. Sólo quien asiste a la realización escénica por segunda vez y es testigo de cómo cae el foco otra vez, se apercibirá de que se trata de un acontecimiento escenificado. Aquel que dé por supuesto que es un actor haciendo su papel el espectador que desde la fila diez, a intervalos regulares, hace comentarios más o menos ingeniosos en voz alta a los que los actores reaccionan encantados, no podrá descubrir hasta la segunda visita, en la que buscará en vano al supuesto actor, que la vez anterior los comentarios eran reacciones «espontáneas» de un espectador con las que quizá quería hacerse notar, pero que, sin embargo, no estaban ni planificadas ni escenificadas por los artistas, como tampoco lo estaban las reacciones de los actores a los comentarios. Los actores, en cambio, eran conscientes en el primer ejemplo de que se trataba de un acontecimiento escenificado; en el segundo caso, quizá ni ellos mismos estaban muy seguros de si se trataba de una acción planeada por un espectador o de si se trataba de un colega al que no conocían. Así pues, los límites de la escenificación los establece siempre la percepción de los sujetos participantes.

El concepto de escenificación que aquí se propone está estrechamente relacionado con el de acontecimiento. En la escenificación se diseña una situación en la que algo puede acontecer. En ese sentido, es del todo incomprensible que se afirme que una estética del acontecimiento no debería ser compatible con una estética de la escenificación, como hacen los defensores de un concepto enfático de acontecimiento. No pasa inadvertido el tono de disgusto en su voz cuando pronuncian la palabra escenificación. En él se perciben todavía las consecuencias de un debate que se desarrolló en los años sesenta y setenta en los campos de la historia y de la teoría del arte. Así, Michael Fried, para referirse al proceso de escenificación en sus escritos, usa los términos '*theatre*', '*theatrical*' y '*theatricality*' como los miembros negativos de unos pares conceptuales antagónicos cuyos términos positivos serían '*objecthood*', '*absorption*' y '*authenticity*'. En los años sesenta, es decir, en el momento en que se ocupaba de la recepción de la segunda generación de las vanguardias americanas, Fried se centraba en las propiedades fenoménicas fundamentales de las obras. En este contexto exigía *objecthood* «*to defeat theatre*»[20]. La teatralidad como escenificación implica aquí una crisis en la definición del objeto arte.

En su libro sobre la pintura francesa del siglo dieciocho *Absorption and Theatricality. Painting and Beholder in the Age of Diderot* (Berkeley, 1980), Fried subraya como aspecto negativo de la escenificación que sea llevada a cabo en función de la percepción ajena. En este sentido, aplica el concepto *theatrical* a los personajes que pueden verse en la pintura. A las poses de las figuras que con sus colores de intenso tintado parecen ser conscientes de que el pintor las está pintando las califica de *theatrical*; su actitud le parece «escenificada», por ello las tiene por menos que las figuras que muestran una actitud de intensa absorción –juegan o trabajan– y que no parecen percibir al pintor como espectador de su actividad.

Es obvio que el par de conceptos antagónicos autenticidad-escenificación es precisamente el que se desmorona en las realizaciones escénicas que hemos venido considerando hasta ahora. La escenificación es la que crea los espacios libres y la que da margen de maniobra para que pueda acontecer lo imprevisible y lo impredecible. Cuando los defensores de un concepto enfático de acontecimiento quieren desarrollar una estética del acontecimiento en sustitución de una estética de la escenificación, o en contraposición a ella, dan pie a la sospecha de que conciben su estética del acontecimiento como un residuo de la idea de sacralidad del arte, de la idea del arte como religión. Es lo divino, lo numinoso por antonomasia, lo que aquí tiene lugar en el encuentro con el arte[21]. Una idea así no tiene cabida, como hemos visto, en una estética de lo performativo. En ella las estéticas del acontecimiento y de la escenificación están estrechamente relacionadas, son indisolubles.

20 Michael Fried, «Art and Objecthood», en Gregory Battock (ed.), *Minimal Art*, Nueva York, 1969, pp. 116-147, p. 139 [«para vencer al teatro»].

21 Véase al respecto, entre otros, Dieter Mersch, *Aura und Ereignis*, Fráncfort, 2002.

A la definición de «escenificación» que venimos proponiendo le falta todavía un componente esencial del que me he ocupado en los capítulos anteriores. La escenificación es también la que diseña estrategias para estimular y dirigir la atención. Se encarga de que la materialidad de la realización escénica se genere de modo performativo, de manera que los elementos que en cada caso aparezcan, atraigan la atención del espectador y la dirijan de consuno al acto mismo de la percepción. Es la escenificación la que tiene por objeto que, por un lado, lo que aparezca, incluidos los elementos poco aparentes u ordinarios, se convierta en llamativo, que aparezca transfigurado; por otro lado, pretende que el perceptor se percate de cómo, en el acto de la percepción, los movimientos, la luz, los colores, los sonidos, los olores, etc., le afectan y le transforman. En este sentido, la escenificación puede también definirse y describirse como un procedimiento encaminado al reencantamiento del mundo y a la transformación de los participantes durante la realización escénica.

También en este aspecto vale lo que decía con respecto a la relación entre escenificación y realización escénica en general. La escenificación puede tener el objetivo de dirigir la atención del espectador hacia un elemento concreto. No está en condiciones, sin embargo, de influir y controlar que el espectador se centre efectivamente en ese elemento. Lo que se planifica en la escenificación y lo que termina ocurriendo en la realización escénica a menudo no coinciden. Y esto de ninguna manera es porque las estrategias de escenificación escogidas no fueran las adecuadas. Pueden haber demostrado con creces su adecuación en realizaciones escénicas anteriores de la misma escenificación. No obstante, en el transcurso de la realización escénica en cuestión pueden darse circunstancias que debiliten su eficacia, por ejemplo, porque la «parte del público poco sensible», sobre la que hablaba Herrmann, si es mayoría, «contagie» al resto de los espectadores de un modo que los inmunice contra la influencia de las estrategias de escenificación. Que el reencantamiento del mundo tenga lugar en todas las realizaciones escénicas y que todos los espectadores la experimenten es algo sobre lo que la escenificación no tiene ningún control, de garantizarlo ni hablemos. A fin de cuentas, su éxito –a pesar del empleo de aplicación de estrategias de escenificación escogidas a base de muchas pruebas por su eficacia– no deja de ser un fenómeno emergente.

La definición del concepto de escenificación desarrollada hasta ahora vale, desde mi punto de vista, para todo tipo de escenificaciones, sean artísticas o no-artísticas, es decir, para escenificaciones de realizaciones escénicas de teatro y del arte de la performance, para exposiciones, instalaciones, conciertos, así como para las escenificaciones de rituales, fiestas, espectáculos, eventos deportivos y mítines políticos, entre otras. El concepto de escenificación abarca, pues, el trabajo estético en todas las formas posibles de realización escénica. Como categoría estética, la escenificación siempre está en relación con el concepto de percepción en un sentido muy específico que aún no hemos explicado.

Es posible diferenciar las escenificaciones atendiendo al criterio de si son percibidas como escenificaciones o no. Mientras que para las escenificaciones artísticas se entiende en la mayoría de los casos que sólo pueden ser eficaces a condición de que sean percibidas como escenificaciones –una condición que Schlingensief, por ejemplo, evita cumplir conscientemente–, esta premisa no se cumple, ni mucho menos, en otros tipos de escenificación. Cuando alguien que está de paseo encuentra «natural» un jardín inglés, o cuando en un diálogo encontramos igualmente «natural» la conducta, cuidadosamente escenificada, de quien habla con nosotros, en ambos casos se perciben el paisaje y la conducta de acuerdo a las estrategias de escenificación, pero no se perciben como escenificados. Es decir, que en esos casos la escenificación puede ser eficaz precisamente porque no es percibida como tal. La impresión de autenticidad surge precisamente como resultado de una escenificación especialmente cuidadosa. Junto a éstas, se dan en la vida social gran cantidad de situaciones en las que las escenificaciones de un *environment*, de un fenómeno o de una conducta son sin duda percibidas como escenificaciones, y están hechas para que sean admiradas como tales, sin que por ello pierdan eficacia. De hecho, en esos casos es frecuente que sólo puedan desplegar toda su eficacia si se da esta condición. De ello se infiere que el criterio de que la escenificación sea percibida como tal o no, difícilmente puede servir para distinguir entre escenificaciones artísticas y no-artísticas. La cuestión de si se pueden encontrar, como quería Seel, otros criterios prácticos para diferenciarlas será algo que discuta en el último apartado de este capítulo. Como se ha mostrado, el objetivo del proceso de escenificación, tanto en un caso como en el otro, es el reencantamiento del mundo.

2. Experiencia estética

Para lograr este reencantamiento del mundo no basta únicamente con la escenificación, es necesario también un tipo especial de percepción por parte del espectador, la que ha de llevarle a su transformación. En el capítulo anterior he definido la experiencia estética en las realizaciones escénicas de teatro y del arte de la performance desde finales de los años sesenta del siglo veinte como una experiencia umbral, como una experiencia de liminaridad que puede llevar a una transformación o que, en sí misma, se experimenta ya como una transformación. Además, he sostenido que este tipo de experiencia estética es central en una estética de lo performativo. Puesto que defiendo la tesis de que tal estética tiene validez para todas las realizaciones escénicas, surge la pregunta de si la definición de la experiencia estética como experiencia umbral tiene también validez para realizaciones escénicas de teatro de otras épocas –o incluso de otras culturas–, así como para todas las formas de realizaciones escénicas no-artísticas que cumplan una función estética.

Disponemos de textos, en la cultura occidental ya desde la Antigüedad griega y, en la India, desde la época que va aproximadamente de los siglos primero al tercero después de Cristo, en los que se trata con detalle la experiencia que les brindan las realizaciones escénicas a espectadores y a actores. Aunque el concepto de experiencia estética fue acuñado por primera vez en el transcurso del proceso de proclamación de la autonomía del arte, o como consecuencia inmediata de él, la cuestión sobre las singulares cualidades de esa experiencia, tal y como la hace posible la realización escénica, se remonta a los orígenes de la teoría estética o de la reflexión estética en la cultura occidental y en la de la India. Para describirla se acuñaron diversos términos, como el de catarsis, por parte de Aristóteles, o el de *rasa*, propuesto en el libro indio de aprendizaje de teatro *Natyasastra*. A continuación examinaré someramente en qué medida estos conceptos, reflexiones o tesis son compatibles con la definición de experiencia estética como experiencia umbral. Llama la atención que las obras y los autores mencionados, a pesar de las diferencias de detalle en la definición, parezcan partir de una misma idea básica, la de que las realizaciones escénicas de teatro poseen potencial transformador, que implican procesos que pueden llevar a la transformación de los que participan en ellas: los actores y los espectadores.

Cuando Aristóteles describe en su *Poética* el efecto del teatro trágico como la capacidad de suscitar ἔλεος y φόβος, desolación y estremecimiento*, alude a un estado afectivo poco común que se produce en o por la realización escénica, que se articula físicamente y que altera a quien afecta. Para definir el fin del teatro trágico, a saber: la purificación precisamente de esas emociones introduce el concepto de catarsis, en cuyo origen son innegables las fuentes rituales, sobre todo los ritos de curación. Mientras que el desencadenamiento de las emociones pone al espectador en un estado liminar, la transformación se lleva a cabo por medio de la catarsis. La experiencia que hacen posible las realizaciones escénicas del teatro trágico, la catarsis, es una experiencia liminar y transformadora[22]. El concepto de catarsis ha influido de forma decisiva en el debate sobre la experiencia estética en las realizacio-

* La autora se adhiere a la propuesta de Gadamer de traducir los términos griegos aludidos por 'desolación' *(Jammer)* y 'estremecimiento' *(Schauder)* respectivamente, en lugar de los habituales, también en español, 'compasión' *(Mitleid)* y 'temor' *(Furcht)*. Gadamer explica su postura en *Verdad y Método I*, Salamanca, 1999 [1.ª ed., 1977], pp. 176 y s.

22 Véanse Elizabeth S. Belfiore, *Tragic Pleasures. Aristotle on Plot and Emotion*, Princeton, 1992; y Fortunat Hoessly, *Katharsis. Reinigung als Heilverfahren. Studien zum Ritual der archaischen und klassischen Zeit*, Gotinga, 2001.

nes escénicas de teatro hasta el final del periodo de vigencia de la estética del efecto, es decir, hasta finales del siglo dieciocho.

El concepto de *rasa* como está desarrollado en el *Natyasastra* ha disfrutado de una influencia comparable. Este «manual de teatro» centra sus esfuerzos en indagar la singularidad de la experiencia que suscitan las realizaciones escénicas tanto en los bailarines/actores como en los espectadores. *Rasa* es un término difícil de traducir; en alemán se suele verter como *Geschmack* [gusto], *Saft* [jugo] o *Gefühlszustand* [estado emocional]; en inglés, se recurre a las expresiones *sentiment*, *aesthetic rapture* o *emotional consciousness*. Se distingue entre ocho tipos de *rasa* –entre ellos la *rasa* erótica o la heroica–, que se corresponden con determinados modos de ser o disposiciones sentimentales que se dan por supuestos en todo ser humano. Suscitada por medio de gestos, vestidos, música, etc., tanto en los actores como en los espectadores, la *rasa* convierte la disposición en un estado físico y espiritual. En esa medida, el concepto de *rasa* también hace referencia a una experiencia de liminaridad y transformación[23].

Cuando en la Antigüedad tardía los Padres de la Iglesia, como harían otros detractores del teatro en la Edad Media y en la primera Modernidad, advertían del peligro que entraña para la salud del alma la asistencia a realizaciones escénicas teatrales; o, al revés, cuando en 1609 el médico de cámara del Káiser le recomendaba expresamente frecuentar el teatro, porque las comedias «abren la mente y el corazón y producen bienestar general»[24], los unos y el otro tenían en mente el potencial transformador de las realizaciones escénicas, en el primer caso para evitarlo y en el segundo para aprovecharlo. Al respecto es interesante que la

23 Véase especialmente L. Bansat-Brudon, *Poétique du théâtre indien: Lecture du Natyashastra*, París, 1992; Edwin Gerow, «Rasa as a category. What are the limits of its applications?», en Rachel van Baumer, James Brandon (eds.), *Sanskrit Drama in Performance*, Honolulu, 1981, pp. 226-257; J. L. Masson, M. V. Patwardhan, *Aesthetic rapture – The Rasadhy-ya of Natyasastra*, Poona, 1970; además, Richard Schechner, «Rasaesthetics», en *TDR*, 45. 3 (T171), Fall ,2001, pp. 27-50.

24 Cit. por Willi Flemming, Barockdrama. Vol. 3, *Das Schauspiel der Wanderbühne*, 2.ª Edición ampliada, Hildesheim, 1965, p. 14.

transformación, se considere como peligro o como oportunidad, se localice siempre en las singulares condiciones de mediación de la realización escénica, es decir, en la copresencia física de actores y espectadores. Es por ello que la manera en la que los actores emplean su cuerpo abre la posibilidad a esa transformación, o la conjura. Así, el padre Franciscus Lang, que compendió en su *Dissertatio de actione scenica* las reglas más importantes que había desarrollado el teatro jesuita en el transcurso del siglo diecisiete para poder influir en el espectador, escribe que «un afecto aún más intenso se apodera de los espectadores, tanto más fuerte cuanto más intenso, vivaz y absorbente es el arte interpretativo de quien está en escena. Los sentidos son la puerta del alma, a través de ella penetran los fenómenos de las cosas en la residencia de los afectos»[25].

La idea que está en la base de estas palabras, la de que es la percepción de los afectos que el actor hace aparecer por medio de su arte interpretativo la que desencadena a su vez afectos en el espectador, seguiría vigente hasta bien avanzado el siglo dieciocho. Henry Home escribió en sus *Elements of Criticism*, obra publicada en 1762, que «el rostro y los gestos [...] abren un camino directo al corazón»[26], y todavía en 1792 Sulzer afirmaba en su *Allgemeine Theorie der schönen Künste [Teoría general de las bellas artes]*: «Es cierto que no hay ninguna otra circunstancia en la que el hombre pueda experimentar y sentir de manera más vivaz que en la interpretación. [...] No hay nada en el mundo más contagioso y ni nada que tenga un efecto más intenso que las sensaciones percibidas en una multitud de personas simultáneamente»[27]. Es el fenómeno del *contagio* el que por vía de la percepción traslada las sensaciones percibidas en el cuerpo del actor al del espectador y hace posible de esa manera el efecto de la realización escénica. El

25 P. Franciscus Lang, *Abhandlung über die Schauspielkunst*, Aleksander Rudin (ed. y trad.), Múnich, 1975, p. 200.
26 Home, *Grundsätze der Kritik*, p. 582 (orig. *Elements of Criticism*, Indianapolis, 2005).
27 Johan Georg Sulzer, *Allgemeine Theorie der schönen Künste*, vol. 4, reedición Leipzig, 1794, p. 254.

término 'contagio' designa lo que es prácticamente un estado liminar «clásico», un estado intermedio, de transición entre la salud y la enfermedad. Con el «contagio de emociones» las realizaciones escénicas demuestran su fuerza transformadora. Mientras que Rousseau condena el teatro precisamente por este poder transformador, y por lo tanto amenazante para la identidad del espectador, porque «la constante tensión emocional a la que estamos sometidos [en él] [...] enerva y debilita» al espectador y le «incapacita para resistir a las pasiones»[28], porque lo pone en un estado umbral que amenaza con la autodisolución del sujeto, Diderot, Lessing, Lichtenberg, Engel y muchos otros teóricos del siglo dieciocho promovieron las realizaciones escénicas de teatro precisamente por su fuerza transformadora, por su capacidad «de hacernos sentir de tal manera que el desgraciado nos conmoverá y nos conquistará en cualquier momento y en cualquier forma que aparezca»[29], como escribe Lessing en una carta a Friedrich Nicolai en la que intenta definir con más precisión el poder transformador del teatro.

Con el postulado de la autonomía del arte, de la autonomía del desarrollo de los conceptos de lo estético y de la experiencia estética, así como con el fin de la estética del efecto, la idea de teatro como performance transformadora va quedando paulatinamente obsoleta en el paso del siglo dieciocho al diecinueve, o al menos va siendo cada vez más marginal. Sin embargo, no parece del todo errado ver una variante de esta idea en el concepto de *Bildungstheater* [teatro formativo] desarrollado por Goethe y Schiller, sobre todo si nos centramos en el *Wilhelm Meister* y en las *Cartas sobre la educación estética del hombre*. El concepto de juego, central en las *Cartas*, puede sin duda interpretarse en el sentido de un *betwixt and between*, de una experiencia umbral. Pues en el juego el ser humano común, aquel en el que se oponen y están en perma-

28 Jean-Jacques Rousseau, *Lettre a Mr. D'Alembert sur les spectacles*, M. Fuchs (ed.), Ginebra, 1948, p. 76 (esp. *Carta a d'Alembert sobre los espectáculos*, Madrid, 1994).

29 Véase la carta de Lessing a Nicolai de noviembre de 1756 en G. E. Lessing, *Werke*, Herbert G. Göpfert (ed.), 8 vols., Múnich, 1970-1979, vol. 4, p. 163.

nente lucha el impulso material y el formal, la naturaleza sensible y la racional, se transforma de manera provisional en el hombre ideal –en el que ambos ámbitos aparecen conciliados–, es decir, lo hace mientras dura el «juego», mientras dura la experiencia estética.

A principios del siglo diecinueve también perdió vigencia la idea de la percepción en las realizaciones escénicas como fenómeno de contagio somático. En su lugar surgió el concepto de empatía *(Einfühlung)*[30]. Ahora bien, en este caso también se puede argumentar que el concepto de empatía de ninguna manera entra en contradicción con la idea del poder transformador de las realizaciones escénicas de teatro. Pues la empatía, sobre todo la empatía entre distintas personas, como se da en el transcurso de una realización escénica, puede entenderse como un tentativo adoptar o exteriorizar nuevos roles e identificaciones y, en ese sentido, como una experiencia umbral. Sin embargo, los primeros teóricos de la empatía no parece que la concibieran así. Friedrich Theodor Vischer define el concepto en su *Ästhetik [Estética]* (1846-1858) como mirada de concesión *(leihendes Anschauen)*[31] y posteriormente en su ensayo «Symbol» (1887) como acto de cesión anímica *(Akt der Seelenleihung)*[32]. Su hijo Robert describe este acto del siguiente modo: «mi yo sensible-mental se traslada al interior del objeto y siente su carácter formal de dentro afuera»[33]. No parece que en esta definición se haya tenido en cuenta la posibilidad de una transformación del sujeto observador por medio del acto de cesión anímica, pero tampoco se excluye categóricamente. Sin embargo, en la medida en que se pretende que se trate de una articulación física de emociones perceptible, recibe el más inmisericorde de los veredictos, como se puede leer

30 Véase para el concepto de empatía *(Einfühlung)* Martin Fontius, «Einfühlung/Empathie/Identifikation», en Karlheinz Barck (ed.), *Ästhetische Grundbegriffe*, vol. 2, Stuttgart, 2001, pp. 121-142.

31 Friedrich Theodor Vischer cit. por *ibid.*, p. 130.

32 Vischer, *Kritische Gänge*, vol. 4, p. 435.

33 Robert Vischer, «Der ästhetische Akt und die reine Form» (1874), en *Drei Schriften zum ästhetischen Formproblem*, Halle, 1927, pp. 45-54, p. 48.

en las observaciones sobre el Théâtre de la Porte St. Martin de París extraídas de una popular guía de la ciudad de los años setenta del siglo diecinueve: «En pleno siglo diecinueve uno se encuentra aún seres primitivos que no pueden contener las lágrimas cuando presencian los infortunios de una heroína a manos de un traidor. No acudan a estos teatros, a no ser que deseen experimentar la candidez lacrimógena de estos obreros de buen corazón, de estos honrados burgueses»[34].

Con el giro performativo que supuso el paso del siglo diecinueve al veinte y con la proclamación de la cultura del cuerpo, vuelve al discurso teórico sobre las realizaciones escénicas de teatro, después de haber quedado en el siglo diecinueve sino totalmente arrumbada sí al menos marginada, la idea de teatro como performance transformadora. En clara alusión a Nietzsche, que en su obra *El nacimiento de la tragedia en el espíritu de la música* (1872) habla de «la esperanza [...] de un renacimiento de Dionisos, que ahora nosotros llenos de presentimientos hemos de concebir como el fin de la individuación»[35], y que en los años posteriores emprendió una reformulación de la estética del efecto[36], Georg Fuchs le exigía al teatro la transformación del individuo burgués en un ser humano «nuevo» y transindividual. Fuchs veía la posibilidad de transformación, en consonancia con los teóricos anteriores al final del siglo dieciocho, en la copresencia física de actores y espectadores. Pues ésta hacía posible que los movimientos rítmicos de los actores se transmitieran a los espectadores y los pusieran en un «estado de embriaguez».

Es de especial interés para el tema que nos ocupa el hecho de que Fuchs reincorporara la idea del potencial transformador de las realizaciones escénicas al debate sobre el teatro al ponerlo en

34 Pierre Véron, *Paris s'amuse*, París, 1874, p. 36.

35 Friedrich Nietzsche, *Die Geburt der Tragödie aus dem Geist der Musik*, en *Sämtliche Werke*. Kritische Studienausgabe en 15 vols., edición de G. Colli y M. Montinari, Múnich, 1988, vol. I, pp. 9-156, p. 72 (esp. *El nacimiento de la tragedia*, Madrid, 1973, p. 100.)

36 Véase Helmut Pfotenhauer, *Kunst als Physiologie. Nietzsches ästhetische Theorie und literarische Produktion*, Stuttgart, 1985.

relación con un género de realización escénica en el que diversos estudios habían ya descubierto ese potencial transformador, hablamos del ritual. Como ya se ha mostrado, con la llegada del siglo veinte el ritual llegó a convertirse en el epítome de la performance transformadora. Si las realizaciones escénicas de teatro querían recuperar el potencial transformador que aparentemente habían perdido durante el siglo diecinueve, tenían que orientarse hacia el paradigma del ritual y hacer posibles experiencias como las que tienen lugar en el ámbito del ritual, experiencias umbral.

Esta idea está también en la base de las consideraciones de Artaud para la consecución de un cambio radical en el teatro. Artaud parte, igual que Fuchs aunque sus objetivos difieran, de una crítica a la cultura contemporánea europea. En su opinión, entre las ideas sobre la vida que nos ha dejado el Renacimiento[37] las más terriblemente destructivas y erradas, y a pesar de ello imperantes, son el logocentrismo, el racionalismo y el individualismo. Para superarlos, el teatro tenía que poner al individuo occidental en contacto con sus orígenes prelógicos, prerracionales y preindividualistas. Debía suscitar en el espectador «estados de trance»[38] –es decir, «clásicos» estados umbral– y, mediante una influencia directa sobre su inconsciente, «capacitarlo para cobrar conciencia y hacerse con el control de ciertas fuerzas dominantes [...] que todo lo dirigen»[39]. La realización escénica de teatro tenía que convertirse en un «ritual mágico» que llevara a cabo un exorcismo en el espectador, que le hiciera experimentar un *rito de paso*. Debía sanar al hombre occidental, enfermo de civilización, restableciendo en el espectador «la vida» y «el hombre»[40], pero «no al hombre psicológico, con sus bien definidos sentimientos y rasgos de carácter», y tampoco «el social, el

37 Veáse Antonin Artaud, *Messages révolutionnaires*, en *Oeuvres complètes*, tomo VIII, París, 1971, pp. 169-315, aquí p. 198 (esp. *Mensajes revolucionarios*, Madrid, 2002).

38 Antonin Artaud, *Le théâtre et son double*, en *Oeuvres complètes*, tomo IV, París, 1964, pp. 9-171, aquí p. 96 (esp. *El teatro y su doble*, Madrid, 1996).

39 *Ibid.*, p. 96.

40 Artaud, *Messages révolutionnaires*, pp. 200 y s.

sometido a leyes y deformado por las prescripciones religiosas», sino «al hombre total»[41]. Artaud insite una y otra vez en que las realizaciones escénicas han de perseguir el estado umbral. «El teatro, como la peste, es una crisis que se resuelve en la muerte o en la curación»[42]. Con la imagen de la peste Artaud reincorpora otro viejo concepto al discurso sobre el teatro, el del contagio. «Es importante sobre todo la confesión de que el juego teatral es, como la peste, un furor y que tiene efecto contagioso»[43]. En tanto que «contagioso» no sólo afecta al «alma» del espectador, sino que tiene un efecto inmediato también en su cuerpo y cambia su estado[44].

El teatro en tanto que arte autónomo, como nos lo legaron el teatro literario, el pedagógico y el empático en el siglo diecinueve, no parece que posea potencial transformador en opinión de Fuchs y de Artaud. Para ellos, tiene que convertirse en ritual si quiere recobrarlo. Cuando se dice teatro como ritual, se quiere decir un teatro que haya recuperado la potencia transformadora que hasta finales del siglo dieciocho le atribuían tanto sus detractores como sus partidarios. No sólo el llamado teatro ritual de un Grotowski, de un Nitsch o de un Schechner, sino muchas realizaciones escénicas de teatro y del arte de la performance desde los años sesenta han puesto de relieve una y otra vez este potencial transformador y lo han tenido siempre por esencial. Tras haber recuperado de este modo la idea de teatro como performance transformadora para el discurso teatral, se antoja no sólo poco útil sino incluso contraproductivo, sobre todo teniendo en cuenta las realizaciones escénicas de las que aquí hemos hablado, entender la singular expe-

41 Artaud, *Le théâtre et son double*, p. 147.
42 *Ibid.*, p. 38.
43 *Ibid.*, p. 33.
44 Para el concepto de teatro de Artaud, véanse Doris Kolesch, «Der magische Atem des Theaters. Ritual und Revolte bei Antonin Artaud», en Franz Norbert Mennemeier y Erika Fischer-Lichte (eds.), *Drama und Theater der europäischen Avantgarde*, Tubinga/Basilea, 1994, pp. 231-254; y «'Listen to the radio': Artauds Radio-Stimme(n)», en *FORUM MODERNES THEATER*, vol. 14, H. 2, 1999, pp. 115-143.

riencia que hacen posible las realizaciones escénicas, la experiencia de liminaridad, como experiencia ritual. Es mucho más pertinente reclamar para ella el concepto de experiencia estética y redefinirlo con referencia a él, como estamos haciendo aquí.

Aunque la visión del teatro como performance transformadora, como ha mostrado esta breve digresión histórica, ha imperado entre teóricos y artífices del teatro desde la Antigüedad hasta el siglo dieciocho, y después en el siglo veinte, hay que tener muy en cuenta las específicas condiciones históricas, culturales y estéticas en las que las realizaciones escénicas de teatro podían desplegar en cada caso su potencial transformador, y distinguir entre ellas. En todas las épocas los espectadores abandonan sus casas y se reúnen en el lugar en el que tiene lugar la realización escénica. En algunos casos, dependiendo de su ubicación y del trayecto que haya que hacer para llegar hasta allí, puede muy bien significar el abandono del entorno cotidiano. Sin embargo, los personajes y las historias, los recursos escénicos y las estrategias de escenificación con los que se ha de alejar al espectador de su cotidianidad y se le ha de brindar la ocasión de tener nuevas experiencias, serán distintos en cada caso[45]. Así, puede que alrededor del año 1800 fuera la «satisfacción desinteresada y libre», aquella que se orienta a la utilidad formal de lo percibido, la condición de posibilidad para que el espectador pudiera abandonar su entorno cotidiano, para que se le empujara a experiencias en las que, a diferencia de lo que ocurre en la vida cotidiana, «no hay interés *alguno*, *ni* el de los sentidos *ni* el de la razón, que arranque el aplauso»[46], y que de ese modo pudiera dar lugar a su transformación. Al respecto me atrevería a afirmar que tanto la estética de la autonomía como el concepto de experiencia estética fueron

45 En esto estriba precisamente el problema del concepto de transformación, en que se refiere, por un lado, a modos muy diversos de modificación, pero en que a la vez *no* hay manera de seleccionar los únicos tipos concretos de modificación a los que debería referirse el concepto.

46 Immanuel Kant, *Kritk der Urteilskraft*, en *Werke in zehn Bände*, vol. 8, Wilhelm Weischedel (ed.), Darmstadt, 1975, p. 287 (esp. *Crítica del Juicio*, Madrid, 1991, p. 140).

desarrollados para poder describir un modo nuevo y esencialmente distinto de experiencia umbral que, en tanto que escindido en aspectos básicos del que nos había llegado a través de los rituales, no se asemejaba a él. Era esa «satisfacción desinteresada y libre» la que el sujeto sentía al percibir obras de arte –o la naturaleza–, la que le brindaba la oportunidad de experimentarse como subjetividad libre.

En el paso del siglo veinte al veintiuno se dan unas condiciones completamente distintas. En tiempos de una estetización rampante del entorno vital, en una situación en la que priman la cultura del ocio y del entretenimiento, la «satisfacción desinteresada y libre» no es ciertamente la sensación adecuada para poner al sujeto en un estado umbral. Para ello es necesaria la alteración tanto de los «sentidos» como de la «razón». Para llevar a cabo la tarea, parecen mucho más eficaces estrategias como la irritación, el choque de marcos, la desestabilización de la percepción de uno mismo, del otro y del mundo, esto es, el desencadenamiento de crisis. Éstas dan lugar a experiencias profundamente turbadoras que, precisamente por ello, pueden llevar a la transformación de quien las vive.

Como ha puesto de manifiesto este breve examen, las realizaciones escénicas de teatro no sólo son siempre resultado de una escenificación, sino que además su capacidad para dar lugar a experiencias umbral se considera uno de sus rasgos esenciales, y ello a pesar de que en cada caso los estados liminares se definen de manera distinta y se logran por distintos medios. Al igual que la escenificación de las realizaciones escénicas teatrales tiene como fin, en tanto que intencionada producción performativa de su materialidad, el reencantamiento del mundo, la experiencia estética, en tanto que experiencia umbral, aspira a una transformación de los participantes en la realización escénica. La transformación se confirma así como una categoría fundamental de una estética de lo performativo.

Sin duda, puede parecer obvia la afirmación de que el teatro ha sido considerado predominantemente como una performance transformadora y la de que a las realizaciones escénicas teatrales se les haya atribuido, consecuentemente, capacidad transformadora. ¿Pero qué ocurre con otros tipos de realización escénica? ¿Qué tipo de experiencia hacen posibles los rituales, las fiestas, los espectáculos, las competiciones deportivas, las asambleas políticas, por nombrar únicamente los géneros de realización escénica (*cultural performance*) en los que los representantes de las vanguardias históricas querían transformar el teatro? ¿No es obvia la suposición de que consideraron y proclamaron estos géneros como modelo de las realizaciones escénicas de un nuevo teatro porque en ellos veían en acción el poder transformador que echaban en falta en el teatro del cambio de siglo, porque le atribuían la capacidad de poner a todos los participantes en un estado umbral? La nueva estética del efecto a la que aspiraban las vanguardias históricas apunta sin duda en esta dirección. Pues en las insistentes demandas de transformar el teatro en un ritual o en una fiesta, en primer plano estaba el deseo de experimentar nuevas formas de comunidad en el teatro. Dirigían su atención a la función fundamentadora, fortalecedora y mantenedora de la comunidad que tenían los rituales y las fiestas. Y lo mismo vale para los eventos políticos. También en ellos se trataba de producir y afirmar determinadas comunidades políticas, que precisamente tenían que ser generadas o fortalecidas por ellas al realizar acciones conjuntamente, y dar lugar a vivencias específicas. Por el contrario, las referencias al circo o al deporte se explicaban por su efecto, en palabras de Eisenstein, como «tonificante baño para los sentidos», por su negativa a transmitir significados, por su capacidad para suscitar en el espectador sentimientos de sorpresa, estupefacción, horror, shock, y por la posibilidad, por ello mismo, de influir corporalmente en él de manera directa. Las experiencias umbral en las que venimos insistiendo concernían por un lado al proceso de transformación del individuo en miembro de una comunidad, es decir, a su transformación social; y, por otro, al proceso de su cambio somático –psicológico, afectivo–. Las realizaciones escénicas de teatro tenían que aproximarse en sus efectos a esos otros tipos de realización escénica.

No es posible entrar aquí en el análisis histórico de la relación entre las realizaciones escénicas teatrales y otros tipos de realización escénica, por más interesante que esa empresa pueda parecer desde el punto de vista de la historia cultural. En una estética de lo performativo que se ha desarrollado partiendo del análisis de realizaciones escénicas teatrales y del arte de la performance desde los años sesenta, interesa sobre todo la pregunta de cómo se ha configurado la relación entre las realizaciones escénicas artísticas y las no-artísticas a partir del giro performativo. Es decir, la pregunta de si hay una diferencia específica entre las experiencias que hoy hacen posibles las fiestas, las competiciones deportivas, los distintos tipos de actos políticos, entre otros tipos de realización escénica, y la experiencia estética definida aquí como experiencia umbral; la de si esas experiencias se pueden considerar igualmente como experiencias umbral y, llegado el caso, si se pueden incluir en la categoría de experiencia estética.

Ahora bien, desde los años noventa se viene señalando reiteradamente que a partir del giro performativo no sólo se han creado nuevos tipos de realización escénica, sino que estamos ante una estetización y teatralización general de las realizaciones escénicas no-artísticas. Como consecuencia de este fenómeno se han ido desdibujando, si es que no se han eliminado completamente, las fronteras entre realizaciones escénicas artísticas y no-artísticas. Esto es especialmente evidente en fiestas que tienen lugar en espacios públicos, como la Love Parade, el Christopher Street Day o el Carnaval de las Culturas del Mundo de Berlín, que se realizan a modo de desfiles o procesiones, y que no se limitan a ocupar el espacio público, sino que lo transforman en un espacio liminar. ¿Dónde puede situarse la frontera entre esas fiestas y las realizaciones escénicas de teatro que han decidido abandonar los edificios de teatro tradicionales, como las realizaciones escénicas llevadas a cabo por el Cornerstone Theater o por Hygiene heute, realizaciones en las que se trabaja en espacios públicos atendiendo a la especificidad de cada uno? Tanto los festivales como las realizaciones escénicas de teatro no sólo transforman el espacio público en liminar, en un espacio de transición, sino que además convierten el tiempo cotidiano en tiempo de transición y hacen posibles experiencias umbral para los participantes[47]. En realizaciones escé-

47 Véanse Klaus-Peter Köpping, «Fest», en Christopher Wulf (ed.), *Der Mensch. Handbuch Historische Anthropologie*, Weinheim/Basilea, 1997, pp. 1048-1065; Joa-

nicas como las escenificaciones de ciudades, que se han ido extendiendo más y más en los últimos años, es donde la realización escénica teatral y la fiesta se aproximan hoy en día cada vez más. Así, en el décimo Documenta se utilizó la ciudad de Kassel como un gran espacio para exposiciones, espectáculos y fiestas en el que se insertaban las realizaciones escénicas del programa adaptándose a sus peculiaridades como, por ejemplo, *15 minutes to comply*, del grupo de performance Gob Squad, que tuvo lugar en una parada de tranvía, o la escenificación de Heiner Goebbels *Landschaft mit dem von der Schlange getöteten Mann* [*Paisaje con el hombre al que mató la serpiente*], que lo hizo bajo un gran puente[48]. En los últimos diez años la compañía italiana Teatro Potlach ha venido realizando con regularidad ese tipo de escenificaciones bajo el título *Città invisibile* en ciudades como Fara Sabina, Farfa, Klagenfurt, Cardiff o en la isla de Malta. En Fara Sabina, por ejemplo, los habitantes de la ciudad cedieron sus sótanos y patios durante una semana para que artistas de teatro de todo el mundo, sobre la base de la novela de Italo Calvino *La ciudad invisible*, pudieran remodelarlos en función de su fantasía. Una vez transformada de esa manera, la ciudad se abrió al público. ¿Se trataba de una fiesta o de una realización escénica de teatro? Difícilmente puede responderse a esta pregunta de manera categórica. En cualquier caso, se trataba de la transformación de espacios no-públicos de la ciudad en espacios públicos que, acondicionados convenientemente, brindaban a quien los visitaba la posibilidad de tener una experiencia umbral[49].

---

chim Küchenhoff, «Das Fest und die Grenzen des Ich – Begrenzung und Entgrenzung im 'vom Gesetz gebotenen Exzess'», en Walter Haug y Rainer Warning (eds.), *Poetik und Hermeneutik XIV*, Múnich, 1989, pp. 99-119; Wolfgang Lipp, «Feste heute: Animation, Partizipation und Happening», en *Drama Kultur*, Berlín, 1994, pp. 523-547.

48 Véase para esta realización escénica Christel Weiler «Heiner Goebbels *Landschaft mit dem von der Schlange getöteten Mann*», en *Theater der Zeit*, sept/oct. 1997, Spezial «Theaterskizzen zur Dokumenta X», Siglos XIII-XVI.

49 Véase Christian Horn, Sandra Umathum, Matthias Warstat, «Auswählen und Versäumen. Wahrnehmungsmodi zwischen Fernsehen und Theater», en Erika Fischer-Lichte, Christian Horn, Sandra Umathum y Matthias Warstat (eds.), *Wahrnehmung und Medialität* (= *Theatralität*, vol. 3), Tubinga/Basilea, 2001, pp. 143-158.

Mientras que las fiestas modernas también se asemejan a las realizaciones escénicas de teatro en que sólo pueden crear comunidades de manera ocasional o, en el mejor de los casos, durante la duración de la fiesta, de tal manera que la comunidad vuelve a disolverse cuando termina la realización escénica, los actos políticos contemporáneos tienen como fin, por regla general, la fundación y el fortalecimiento de comunidades cuya duración exceda a la de la realización escénica en cuestión. Esta función también ha sido puesta en práctica en actos políticos de épocas pasadas recurriendo a la estetización y teatralización, como se puede ver con especial claridad en celebraciones políticas, ya sean las fiestas cortesanas de los siglos dieciséis y diecisiete, las de la Revolución Francesa o las del movimiento obrero de los años veinte del pasado siglo[50]. Por eso resulta aún más sorprendente que hoy se expresen tantos lamentos por la teatralización de los eventos políticos y que esto se considere el abominable origen de la decadencia de nuestra cultura política. Cuando en 1998, con ocasión del congreso del SPD* en Leipzig, se incluyó por error en el dossier de prensa el plan de iluminación, se desató una tormenta de rechazo e indignación sobre los organizadores. En una serie de periódicos se daba detallada cuenta del plan para darle solidez a la crítica de que el congreso del partido se había presentado como un «acontecimiento escenificado». Heribert Prantl, redactor jefe de la sección de política nacional del *Süddeutsche Zeitung*, explicó la crítica como «una reacción alérgica a la sensación de estar siendo usado como mera decoración»[51]. En el ámbito de la política alemana contemporánea se tenía sin duda conciencia de la importancia de las escenificaciones, especialmente las que se hacen pensando en los medios de comunicación, como prueban,

50 Véase Christian Horn, *Der aufgeführte Staat. Zur Theatralität höfischer Repräsentation unter Kurfürst Johann Georg II. von Sachsen*, Tubinga/Basilea, 2004; Inge Baxmann, *Die Feste der Französischen Revolution*, Weinheim/Basilea, 1989; Matthias Warstat, *Theatrale Gemeinschaften. Zur Festkultur der Arbeiterbewegung 1918-1933*, Tubinga/Basilea, 2004.

* Partido Socialdemócrata Alemán *(Sozialdemokratische Partei Deutschlands)*.

51 Heribert Prantl, «Wir denken zu sehr in PR-Kategorien», en *Sage & Schreibe* 9/1998, pp. 44-45 (entrevista con R. Schatz), p. 45.

por ejemplo, las muy eficaces escenificaciones de Kohl y Mitterand en el campo de batalla de Verdun, o la de Klaus Toepfer atravesando el Rin a nado como Ministro de Medio Ambiente. Pero en el caso de las escenificaciones en congresos de partidos políticos, se consideraba una estrategia típica de la política norteamericana. Se pasaba por alto que ese tipo de realización escénica siempre requiere una puesta en escena. El desarrollo y la organización de los congresos de partidos políticos persigue, sirviéndose de las emociones y las vivencias comunes, no sólo el surgimiento de un sentimiento colectivo, sino la creación de una comunidad política con voluntad de victoria. El congreso del SPD empezó con la entrada de Gerhard Schröder y Oskar Lafontaine. Entraron en el pabellón agitando los brazos entre las fanfarrias de un himno compuesto precisamente para la ocasión. El himno, que tenía un fuerte componente emocional y que pretendía transmitir sentimientos como el espíritu optimista, la confianza o la certeza en la victoria, los suscitó efectivamente a juzgar por las caras de los delegados allí presentes. La música se combinaba con el lenguaje corporal de ambos protagonistas y transmitía su estado de ánimo al resto de los delegados. Tenía un efecto «contagioso». El objetivo de lo que quedaba de congreso no era distinto: transformar a los delegados en una comunidad de personas con voluntad de vencer y con la certeza de poder hacerlo[52].

Lo dicho sobre el congreso del SPD en Leipzig puede aplicarse *mutatis mutandis* a otros actos políticos. Hacen posibles gestos, acciones y vivencias conjuntos que persiguen la formación de una comunidad cuya duración debe exceder a la del evento[53]. En eso se diferencian de las realizaciones escénicas de teatro.

52 Véase al respecto Carsten Brosda y Christian Schicha, «Politikvermittlung als Event Marketing», en Erika Fischer-Lichte *et al.* (eds.), *Performativität und Ereignis* (= *Theatralität*, vol. 4), Tubinga/Basilea, 2003, pp. 319-338.

53 Véase Thomas Meyer/Martina Kampmann, *Politik als Theater. Die neue Macht der Darstellungskunst*, Berlín, 1998; Herfried Münkler, «Die Theatralisierung der Politik», en Früchtl/Zimmermann (eds.), *Ästhetik der Inszenierung*, pp. 144-163; Hans Georg Soeffner/Dirk Tänzler (eds.), *Figurative Politik. Zur Performanz der Macht in der modernen Gesellschaft*, Opladen, 2002.

Pero ¿qué sucedió en el caso de *Chance 2000* de Schlingensief? ¿No se superaba esa diferencia? ¿No se pretendía acaso la fundación de un nuevo partido político: «Chance 2000»? En ese caso también se trataba –¿presuntamente?– de la formación de una comunidad cuya duración fuera más allá de la de la realización escénica, aunque de lo que realmente se trataba era de incidir en la difuminación y la nivelación de las diferencias entre realización escénica teatral y evento político, o por lo menos de suscitar incertidumbre sobre el fundamento de su diferencia. Por otro lado, se observa que los actos políticos cada vez tienen menos éxito a la hora de conseguir que las comunidades que crean perduren más allá del propio evento. Parece que en su caso nos las vemos, cada vez más, con comunidades estéticas en el sentido que Vattimo le da al término[54].

También en las competiciones deportivas se trata en muchos casos de la creación y consolidación de comunidades, de la transformación de los individuos en miembros de comunidades de aficionados. Por medio de los cánticos, de los gestos, de las acciones conjuntas y de todas las emociones que viven juntos, los hinchas de los equipos de fútbol se transforman en miembros de comunidades de aficionados o en miembros de una comunidad nacional, en el caso de las competiciones futbolísticas internacionales. En lo tocante a ciertos equipos de fútbol o a las selecciones nacionales, antes del partido se dan ya ciertas relaciones afectivas y de identificación. Pero no es hasta que éste da comienzo que se origina, al intensificarse y consolidarse esas relaciones, la comunidad.

Los partidos de fútbol son un tipo de realización escénica que genera emociones de especial intensidad en actores y espectadores; entre los espectadores que rodean el terreno de juego y los jugadores que actúan en él parecen crearse campos energéticos de gran intensidad. En algunos casos se produce una tensión tan difícil de soportar que tiene que descargarse por medio de reacciones explosivas de los espectadores. Este estado emocional fuera de lo común, la entrada en una comunidad, la paradójica combi-

54 Véase Vattimo, *La sociedad transparente*.

nación de lo reglado y lo excesivo que caracteriza tanto a las competiciones deportivas como a las fiestas, pone a todos los participantes en un estado de radical *betwixt and between* y hace posible que tengan experiencias umbral.

Puesto que las competiciones deportivas se basan en un principio agonal, la formación de una comunidad entre todos los actores y espectadores es por principio imposible. Se forman comunidades, sí, pero antagónicas. El que pertenece a una comunidad queda inmediatamente excluido de la otra. Así pues, estas comunidades no sólo se conforman y consolidan por las vivencias y acciones conjuntas, sino también porque dirigen emociones y acciones *contra* el otro grupo. Las explosiones de violencia durante el juego o inmediatamente después de que termine, como puede observarse en muchas competiciones internacionales, no sólo se deben a la paradójica combinación de lo reglado y lo excesivo, como es el caso de las fiestas, en cuyo transcurso la violencia puede desatarse en cualquier momento. En el fútbol puede explicarse también por el hecho de que una comunidad se reafirma como tal precisamente infligiendo violencia sobre los miembros de la otra comunidad. En ambos casos, en el del fútbol y en el de las fiestas (o también en realizaciones escénicas artísticas como *Kukei, akopee – Nein!, Braunkreuz, Fettecken, Modellfettecken [Kukei, akopee ¡No!, cruz parda, esquinas de grasa, esquinas de grasa modelo]*, de Beuys, en Aquisgrán), el estado de liminaridad es el que desencadena la violencia, la cual, por su parte, hace posibles determinadas experiencias umbral.

La formación de comunidades, un aspecto tan primordial en las competiciones futbolísticas y en las de otros juegos de equipo –a cada una de las comunidades de jugadores se adhiere la comunidad de los espectadores aficionados–, tiene un papel secundario, o no lo tiene en absoluto, en el caso de otros eventos deportivos. El patinaje artístico, la gimnasia, y muchas disciplinas del atletismo: las carreras, el salto de longitud o de altura son percibidos por los espectadores más bien como un espectáculo –como pasa con el circo–. Las emociones que se suscitan entre los espectadores son preferentemente el asombro y la admiración ante las excepcionales capacidades de los atletas. Asimismo, el espectador disfruta de la percepción de cuerpos más jóvenes, más bellos, más fuertes, más capaces, cuerpos que –en oposición radical a los que se podían ver en el caso de la Socìetas Raffaello Sanzio: marcados por la vejez, la enfermedad, la fragilidad y la muerte– suscitan primordialmente sentimientos positivos. El espectador, al observar cómo se mueven los deportistas en y a través del espacio, percibe cómo crean un mundo nuevo y bello en y con sus movimientos. Un mundo definido por la juventud, la belleza, el erotismo, la buena forma física, la justicia, el afán de superación y la voluntad de victoria –en suma: un mundo de la presencia en el sentido débil del concepto y, sobre todo, en el fuerte, un mundo en el que prevalece el principio de eficacia y que, de consuno, le permite al espectador dejar atrás su vida cotidiana y vivir experiencias completamente nuevas[55]–.

Independientemente de que tratemos de fiestas, de actos políticos o de competiciones deportivas, estamos en todos los casos ante realizaciones escénicas que brindan la oportunidad de vivir experiencias umbral. Esto no puede sorprender si tenemos en cuenta que toda realización escénica se produce como resultado de la autopoiesis del bucle de retroalimentación y que, como he mostrado, es precisamente esta autopoiesis, que tiene su base en la copresencia física de actores y espectadores, la que genera la liminaridad. Aunque he definido la experiencia estética como experiencia umbral y he afirmado que todos los géneros de realización escénica hacen posibles experiencias umbral, de ello no se debe inferir en ningún caso que todas las formas de experiencia umbral puedan subsumirse en la categoría de experiencia estética. Mientras que a una experiencia umbral que se caracteriza por que su fin es su camino la califico de experiencia estética, a una que se orienta a «otro» objetivo la tengo por no-estética. Cuando hablo de objetivos, me refiero a cambios de estatus socialmente reconocidos, a la generación de vencedores y vencidos, a la formación de comunidades, a la legitimación de aspira-

55 Véase respecto a los eventos deportivos Gunter Gebauer, *Sport in der Gesellschaft des Spektakels*, Sankt Augustin, 2002.

ciones de poder, al establecimiento de un compromiso social o al entretenimiento, entre otros. Es decir, cuando hablamos de experiencia estética, nos referimos a experimentar el umbral, la transición, el paso en sí mismos, nos referimos al proceso de transformación. En las experiencias umbral no-estéticas, por el contrario, se trata de la transición *a* algo, de la transformación *en* esto o *en* aquello.

Con ello queda inmediatamente claro que esta distinción no está pensada como un criterio con cuya ayuda podamos diferenciar las realizaciones escénicas artísticas de las que no lo son. Pues las experiencias estéticas y no-estéticas pueden alternarse en el transcurso de una misma realización escénica. Depende de la percepción de cada espectador, de si se concentra en el estado liminar en el que le ha puesto su percepción, o de si lo considera o lo vive como la transición hacia otro fin. Esta oscilación puede darse, y cambiar minuto a minuto, tanto en la performance *Lips of Thomas* como en la final Alemania-Brasil en el Campeonato Mundial de Fútbol de 2002.

No podemos pasar por alto que los artistas son precisamente los que aspiran siempre a traspasar, difuminar o suprimir las fronteras entre arte y no-arte, entre lo estético y lo no-estético. Una y otra vez crean situaciones que le dificultan al espectador, cuando no se lo imposibilitan, considerar la experiencia umbral como fin en sí mismo, situaciones que le fuerzan a tomar decisiones encaminadas a acciones con un objetivo. No obstante, la experiencia estética, es decir, la experiencia umbral como tal, es la que regula y, llegado el caso, integra las experiencias umbral no-estéticas.

Por otro lado, se multiplican las fiestas, los actos políticos y las competiciones deportivas –algo que se puede observar sobre todo en los Juegos Olímpicos– entre cuyas posibilidades inherentes está el concentrarse en las experiencias umbral, y que entienden por lo tanto el estado de liminaridad como un fin en sí mismo. Eso es lo que se quiere decir cuando se habla –en algunos casos peyorativamente– de la estetización y la teatralización de las realizaciones escénicas no-artísticas. Sin embargo, como criterio para distinguir las realizaciones escénicas artísticas de las no-artísticas no sirve la diferencia entre la experiencia estética como forma particular de experiencia umbral y las demás experiencias umbral. Cuando las realizaciones escénicas de hoy pretenden rebasar las fronteras y llegar a eliminarlas, es esto precisamente lo que tienen en mente. En todos los tipos de realización escénica la percepción puede deslizarse, oscilante, entre la experiencia estética y la experiencia no-estética. Que la realización escénica artística se pueda diferenciar de la no-artística por ello, porque en ella predomina la experiencia estética, es, a la luz de lo que vengo sosteniendo, extremadamente dudoso. Ni las performances de Abramović ni las realizaciones de Schlingensief nos permiten suponer tal cosa. ¿Cómo pueden distinguirse las realizaciones escénicas artísticas de las no-artísticas? Y si eso no es posible, o sólo lo es gradual o parcialmente, ¿se puede seguir sosteniendo la autonomía del arte?

3. Arte y vida

Ni el concepto de escenificación ni el de experiencia estética nos proporcionan criterios con los que distinguir las realizaciones escénicas artísticas de las no-artísticas. A pesar de que Seel opina que las escenificaciones artísticas se caracterizan por que no sólo producen presencia, sino que la presentan, eso mismo se puede decir de las escenificaciones deportivas, por dar un solo contraejemplo. Las escenificaciones deportivas no se limitan a producir presencia, sino que la presentan y la ofrecen también en tanto que presencia. En cuanto al concepto de experiencia estética, se ha mostrado que puede aplicarse tanto a realizaciones escénicas artísticas como a no-artísticas.

Richard Shusterman, que evita conscientemente en todos sus escritos dar una definición esencialista de arte con la que se pueda distinguir claramente, y de una vez por todas, entre arte y no-arte, se propuso la tarea de formular una definición que sirviera como instrumento heurístico «para destacar determinados rasgos del arte a los que no se ha atendido suficientemente»[56]. Su pro-

56 Richard Shusterman, «Tarot: Kunst als Dramatisieren», en Früchtl/Zimmermann (eds.), *Ästhetik der Inszenierung*, pp. 126-143, p. 128.

puesta de entender y de definir el arte como dramatización apunta a dos aspectos en los que el arte se diferencia de la realidad ordinaria: «el poner en escena o el enmarcar escenas» y «la mayor viveza de la experiencia y la acción»[57]. Ahora bien, no estamos sino ante un rasgo que les podemos adjudicar a todas las realizaciones escénicas, independientemente de su condición de artísticas. También en un partido de fútbol, en una sesión parlamentaria, en un juicio, en una misa, en una boda, en un entierro y en otros tipos de *cultural performances* «se dramatiza» en este sentido: se enmarcan determinadas escenas, y se separa con ello lo enmarcado de aquello que el marco no incluye; además, en todas ellas se les confiere una gran viveza a las experiencias y a las acciones. Este pudo ser el motivo que llevó a Milton Singer a acuñar el término *cultural performance* a finales de los años cincuenta. Lo definió como la unidad observable más pequeña de una estructura cultural en la que se articula la imagen y la idea que la cultura en cuestión tiene de sí, y en la que se les presenta y se les expone tanto a sus miembros como a quienes no lo son[58]. Es precisamente la «dramatización» la que distingue las *cultural performances*, esto es, las realizaciones escénicas del mundo cotidiano, de la «realidad ordinaria». Parece por ello ocioso continuar buscando rasgos que pudieran servir como criterio para diferenciar las realizaciones escénicas artísticas de las no-artísticas.

A pesar de que no parece que pueda haber un criterio de ese tipo, es curioso que no tengamos la menor dificultad en atribuirles la condición de realizaciones escénicas artísticas a los descuartizamientos de corderos de Nitsch, al *Dionysus in 69* de Schechner, al *Coyote* de Beuys, a las distintas performances de autoagresión, al *Sportstück* de Schleef o al *Bitte liebt Österreich!* de Schlingensief, ni para clasificar, a su vez, a la Love Parade como festival, al congreso del SPD en Leipzig como acto político o a los Juegos Olímpicos como evento deportivo, es decir, como realizaciones escénicas no-artísticas. Si, por un lado, las realizaciones escénicas artísticas

57 *Ibid.*, p. 136.

58 Véase Milton Singer, *Traditional India – Structure und Change*, Filadelfia, 1959, pp. XII y s.

se esfuerzan por rebasar la frontera que las separa de las no-artísticas y éstas, por otro lado, se van acercando constantemente y cada vez más a las realizaciones escénicas artísticas en virtud de la estetización y la teatralización, tal clasificación no debería ser posible. No obstante, se hace constantemente, aunque sólo sea para sumir a los participantes en la incertidumbre sobre el género de realización escénica en la que han ido a parar como transeúntes que paseaban por un lugar público, o para darles indicaciones sobre el modo de comportamiento «adecuado», como pasó en Festwochen de Viena en el año 2000. Sólo la pertenencia a una determinada institución permite hacer ese tipo de clasificación. Una realización escénica se considera artística cuando tiene lugar en el marco de la institución arte; del mismo modo, se clasifica como realización escénica no-artística cuando tiene lugar en el marco de la institución Política, Deporte, Derecho, Religión, etc. Lo esencial para distinguir las realizaciones escénicas artísticas de las no artísticas no es ni el específico carácter de acontecimiento de cada una de ellas, ni las estrategias escénicas en las que se basen ni la experiencia estética que hagan posible. Es el marco institucional el que permite decidir si hay que clasificarlas como artísticas o como no-artísticas.

Aunque los artistas se esfuercen por traspasar, difuminar o incluso anular las fronteras entre arte y vida, entre lo estético y lo social, lo político o lo ético, las realizaciones escénicas que ponen en marcha están en condiciones de reflexionar sobre la autonomía del arte, pero no de suprimirla. Las instituciones artísticas le sirven de garantía. Cada uno de los gestos iconoclastas de los artistas, cada una de las acciones dirigidas a desmantelar la institución arte tiene lugar, sin embargo, dentro del marco de la institución arte, y con ello topa con sus límites. Al respecto nada puede hacer una estética de lo performativo.

La institución arte se constituyó en el propio proceso de exigencia de autonomía del arte y como consecuencia de él. En lugar de la estética del efecto, que iba de la mano de una estética normativa, y que aspiraba al cumplimiento de ciertos fines religiosos o morales, surgió una estética autónoma. Es decir, que el arte debía establecerse desde ese momento como un ámbito propio e independiente de presiones e intereses extraartísticos, fueran sociales o económicos, y desarrollarse de acuerdo a sus propias normas y reglas. No hay que olvidar que esta autonomía surgió sin duda para ponerse al servicio de un fin «más elevado»: la «formación» y el perfeccionamiento del hombre. No es el escrito de Schiller *Sobre la educación estética del hombre* el único testimonio elocuente de este «objetivo último» de la autonomía del arte, la teoría de la obra de arte total de Wagner, desarrollada a mediados del siglo diecinueve, sería otro ejemplo. En el caso de la autonomía se trataba de la compensación de una pérdida, del «restablecimiento» de la «integridad» del hombre, de la «recuperación» de una totalidad perdida en el mundo histórico y, sobre todo, en la sociedad burguesa. Estrechamente vinculada al establecimiento de este fin estaba la aspiración de que con su autonomía se le transmitiera al arte la exigencia de verdad.

Habida cuenta de la enorme relevancia que con ello ganaba el arte, se creyó que no se podía dejar solamente en manos de los artistas, esos misteriosos y geniales creadores de las obras de arte. Así pues, un ejército en permanente crecimiento de críticos, teóricos, administradores, censores y agentes, entre otros, velaba por el mantenimiento de la autonomía del arte. Dirigían su interés no sólo a que el ciudadano pudiera formarse mediante el «placer» proporcionado por el arte autónomo, sino que se preocupaban sobre todo de que no se pervirtieran sus nobles pretensiones de verdad y de totalidad con tomas de partido, con su intervención en cuestiones políticas, religiosas o de moralidad pública. Como resultado de la cooperación de todos los implicados surgió la institución arte, que ha permanecido estable hasta hoy.

Si el teatro quería estar a la altura de su nueva aspiración de formar a los espectadores, es decir, de contribuir al desarrollo de su personalidad, una aspiración formulada en primer lugar por Goethe y Schiller, y mantenida consecuentemente después, en primer lugar tenía que hacer que su público dejara de considerar el espacio teatral como espacio social, que empezara a entenderlo como un espacio que exigía una extrema atención. A tal fin debían servir, en la primera mitad del siglo diecinueve, las normas teatrales que se promulgaron por doquier, pero que en muy pocos casos se cumplieron. Ya en la segunda mitad del siglo se impondría el oscurecimiento de la platea, que fue mucho más eficaz. Pese a estos esfuerzos, en las realizaciones escénicas teatrales continuó habiendo infracciones. Así, nos consta que hubo un alboroto durante la realización escénica de *La muda de Portici* de Auber en la Ópera de Bruselas, hubo un alboroto que desembocó en la sublevación que dio lugar a la separación de Bélgica de los Países Bajos y a la fundación del Estado belga. Aunque no tuvieran tan graves consecuencias, vale la pena mencionar en este contexto las muchas realizaciones escénicas del Volkstheater de Viena en las que actuó Nestroy. Sus improvisaciones verbales y gestuales, que incluían invectivas contra el gobierno y la Iglesia o ataques contra las normas morales vigentes, daban lugar a la intervención de la policía teatral, presente en la realización escénica, que le exigía el pago de una multa en mitad de la función. Asimismo cabe destacar al respecto el estreno de *Antes de amanecer* de Hauptmann, ya mencionado a otro propósito; en él, según un crítico, la sala de teatro se convirtió en un local de reuniones. Como se observa, el teatro no siempre cumplía su cometido educativo en los términos deseados. El bucle de retroalimentación autopoiético, el «contagio» de los espectadores por parte de los actores o de otros espectadores, obstaculizaba en todos estos casos las aspiraciones de verdad y de formación pretendidas por la autonomía del arte, algo que tanto en el campo de la literatura como en el de las artes visuales, dadas sus muy distintas condiciones de recepción y producción, se pudo imponer de manera mucho más consecuente.

A principios del siglo veinte los movimientos vanguardistas expresaron la exigencia de una aproximación entre el arte y la vida y proclamaron una nueva estética del efecto, pues no podían creer por más tiempo ni en la pretensión de verdad ni en la tarea educativa de un arte autónomo. Defendían como fin del arte, en cambio, su total escisión respecto a la vida. Cuando Marcel Duchamp colocó en un museo una bicicleta, una caja de botellas o un urinario con la firma R. Mutt, cuando el Superdadá Johannes Baader impidió que el predicador Dryander diera el sermón en una misa matutina en noviembre de 1918 en la catedral de

Berlín, o cuando un año después él mismo interrumpió una sesión parlamentaria en la Asamblea Nacional de Weimar lanzando octavillas desde la tribuna que llevaban el título de *Die grüne Leiche [El cadáver verde]*, y en las que, entre otras cosas, se podía leer: «Wir werden Weimar in die Luft sprengen. Berlin ist der Ort DA-DA» [«Haremos saltar Weimar por los aires. Berlín es el lugar DA-DÁ»], estaban contribuyendo, como harían a partir de los años sesenta muchos otros artistas, a suprimir la diferencia entre realizaciones escénicas artísticas y no-artísticas, entre el arte y la vida. Pero para entonces la institución arte se había consolidado de tal manera que todos los ataques contra ella, o contra la autonomía del arte, no sólo resultaban vanos, sino que terminaban integrados en ella. No es de extrañar, por tanto, que tanto Baader entonces como Hermann Nitsch cuarenta años después, fueran absueltos de la acusación de blasfemia apelando a la autonomía del arte.

En la medida en que la autonomía del arte está garantizada por la institución arte, una estética de lo performativo no está en condiciones de ponerla seriamente en cuestión, y mucho menos de acabar con ella. En la medida en que implica la escisión del arte de todos los contextos que tienen que ver con la vida, muchos artistas se esfuerzan desde los años sesenta por suprimirla efectivamente. Así, practican el arte como arte del rebasamiento de fronteras. Como hemos visto, es precisamente la frontera establecida en la cultura occidental a partir de finales del siglo dieciocho entre arte y no-arte, entre arte y «realidad», entre arte y vida, la que esos artistas han estado rebasando, difuminando y anulando permanentemente. En esta dirección no apuntan solamente las realizaciones escénicas de teatro y del arte de la performance, también las realizaciones escénicas de otras artes, sobre todo las exposiciones que se dedican mucho menos a exponer el arte que a ponerlo por obra. Ejemplos prominentes de ello son las dos últimas exposiciones *Documenta*, cuyos comisarios Catherine David (Documenta X) y Okwui Enzor (Documenta XI) formularon de manera programática su pretensión no sólo de que las obras presentadas en ellas mostraran «imágenes críticas del mundo de hoy y de los fenómenos que lo mueven y lo modifican»[59], sino también la de que *Documenta* hiciera las veces de «plataforma» en la que «se entrecruzan las ideas teóricas y la práctica»[60]. La exposición que con motivo del festival «Theater der Welt 2002» fue puesta en marcha y organizada por el Museum Ludwig de Colonia y por el «Theater der Welt» en un trabajo conjunto llevaba a modo de afirmación programática el título *I promise it's political. Performativität in der Kunst [Prometo que es político. Performatividad en el arte]*. En un concepto de exposición aplicado de esa manera se evidencia «el modo en que han llegado a surgir términos imprecisos como 'teatro', 'arte' y 'mundo'»[61]. La exposición se organizó de tal manera que pudiera producir «nuevas formas de mutualidad, [...] es decir, relaciones que ya no fueran (sólo) entre observadores y objetos, sino entre observadores y espacios», de tal manera que en «los procesos de percepción surgiera un nuevo 'NOSOTROS'»[62], esto es, de tal modo que la exposición pudiera desplegar el consiguiente potencial transformador.

Una estética de lo performativo tiene por objeto de estudio ese arte del rebasamiento de fronteras. Trabaja incesantemente para superar fronteras establecidas a finales del siglo dieciocho y asumidas desde entonces como inamovibles e insuperables, divisiones que se tenían casi por naturales, es decir, que se entendían como establecidas por naturaleza: nos referimos a la división entre arte y vida, entre alta cultura y cultura popular, entre el arte de la cultura occidental y el de aquellas otras culturas para las que es extraño el concepto de la autonomía del arte. Con ello, una estética de lo performativo se propone también la redefinición del concepto mismo de frontera. Mientras que hasta ahora, entre los aspectos decisivos para el arte, la separación, la delimitación y las diferencias de principio eran los que más importancia tenían,

59 Catherine David, *Stand der Dinge*, Teil I, Katalog Kunstwerke, Berlín, 2000.

60 Platform I, *Documenta XI: Democracy Unrealized*, Begleitheft, Kassel/Berlín, 2001.

61 Matthias Lilienthal im Vorwort zum Katalog *I promise it's political. Performativität in der Kunst*, Colonia, 2002, p. 5.

62 Irit Rogoff, «WIR. Kollektivitäten, Mutualitäten, Partizipationen», en *I promise it's political*, pp. 52-60, p. 53.

en una estética de lo performativo se enfatizan el rebasamiento y la transición. La frontera se convierte en umbral, que no separa dos ámbitos, sino que los vincula. En lugar de oposiciones infranqueables surgen diferencias graduales. Una estética de lo performativo no sigue pues los pasos de un proyecto de indiferenciación, lo que según la teoría del sacrificio de Girard conduciría inevitablemente a una eclosión de violencia. Más bien trata de superar las oposiciones rígidas, de convertirlas en distinciones dinámicas. Nos hemos acostumbrado a entender que el empleo de parejas conceptuales antitéticas es la garantía de un proceder racional que se corresponde con el desencantamiento del mundo llevado a cabo por la Ilustración y a que este proceder es el que mejor describe ese proceso. Por ello es oportuno entender el proyecto de una estética de lo performativo –que demuele precisamente tales dicotomías y que, en vez de proceder argumentalmente con un «lo uno o lo otro», lo hace con un «tanto lo uno como lo otro»– como una tentativa de reencantamiento del mundo, como un intento de transformar en umbrales las fronteras establecidas en el siglo dieciocho.

Tanto la frontera como el umbral poseen un cierto potencial de riesgo. La violación de lindes va a menudo acompañada de sanciones. Quienquiera que instituye una frontera se encarga de protegerla y vigilarla, y decreta normas y leyes que detallan las condiciones, siempre excepcionales, en las que se permite su rebasamiento, leyes que intentan evitar todo intento de que se crucen ilícitamente. Pero el traspaso de umbrales conlleva también múltiples peligros y riesgos, porque no puede saberse lo que le espera a uno al otro lado ni con qué fenómenos, desafíos o incertidumbres deberá uno enfrentarse allí. Los monstruos que se han dejado a este lado del umbral pueden volver a acechar al otro lado. La diferencia entre frontera y umbral no puede definirse, por tanto, a partir de los peligros de su traspaso. Más bien está en el conjunto de connotaciones, incluso de asociaciones, que rodean a ambos conceptos. El concepto de frontera implica más bien exclusión, delimitación, punto final. Aquel que llega a su límite, no puede continuar, permanece quieto, está al final. La frontera marca una clara diferencia; más allá de ella está lo anhelado, lo deseado, la libertad, el paraíso, o lo aborrecible, lo temido, el infierno. Cruzar la frontera legalmente exige procesos a menudo complicados, justificaciones, determinados documentos, pasaportes, permisos de salida, etc. Atravesarla ilegalmente es un acto peligroso, clandestino, subversivo; quebrantarla abiertamente es un acto de insurrección, revolucionario, heroico, o incluso un acto de agresión por parte del enemigo, un ataque.

Muy distintas son las connotaciones del concepto de umbral. No tiene el aroma de lo prohibido, de lo protegido por la ley. Mientras la frontera está ahí para impedir su traspaso, el umbral parece invitar a ello. Puesto que muchas veces uno no puede saber lo que acontecerá al otro lado del umbral, su traspaso exige ciertas medidas de precaución y de protección. Los umbrales son a menudo lugares mágicos, incluso a veces de mala reputación. Conjurar su magia, transformar su vileza en bendición exige capacidades y conocimientos especiales. Si el umbral ha sido mancillado, ha de ser purificado antes de pasarlo. Pese a todas las posibles dificultades, riesgos y peligros inherentes al paso del umbral, éste promete, si se ejecuta de modo adecuado, todo tipo de bondades: el restablecimiento de la salud, la misericordia de los dioses, la adquisición de un nuevo estatus social, de una posesión valiosa, de una capacidad que no tiene precio, de conocimientos secretos, etc. Si, por el contrario, al cruzarlo se dan pasos en falso, el resultado puede ser desastroso: la persona en cuestión se hunde en una ciénaga o cae en una trampilla secreta, es asaltado por fantasmas o bestias salvajes, puede ser empujada a la locura, atormentada o lacerada hasta la muerte, puede ser despedazada..., es decir, que le puede acontecer todo aquello que sucede en los casos desgraciados. El umbral es de una gran ambivalencia.

Mientras que la frontera está relacionada con la ley, el umbral remite más bien a la magia. Mientras que la frontera es concebida como una línea que incluye algo y excluye otra cosa, el umbral es concebido como un espacio intermedio en el que puede ocurrir cualquier cosa. Mientras que la frontera lleva a cabo una clara división, el umbral se abre como lugar de posibilitación, de capacitación, de transformación. No obstante, no se puede pasar por alto en esta tentativa de distinción entre frontera y umbral, que tanto la una como el otro son fenómenos de percepción: lo que a uno le parece una frontera –quizá insuperable– es percibido por otro como un umbral que invita a traspasarlo. Además, es frecuente que las fronteras no se experimenten como tales hasta el momento mismo de su rebasamiento, es decir, cuando se descubre el error de haberlas creído umbral.

En las realizaciones escénicas es el bucle de retroalimentación autopoiético generado por ellas el que transforma las fronteras en umbrales, la frontera entre escenario y platea, por ejemplo, entre actores y espectadores, entre individuo y comunidad, o entre arte y vida. Como hemos visto, se debe al empleo de determinadas estrategias de escenificación el que las fronteras se perciban menos como tales y más como umbrales. Cuando he afirmado que una estética de lo performativo tiene por objeto de estudio el arte del rebasamiento, quería decir con ello que su objeto de estudio es la transformación de fronteras en umbrales, que se dedica al arte de la transición, del paso de umbrales.

Con ello las realizaciones escénicas dirigen su atención también a las condiciones antropológicas en las que se basan. Como ha mostrado Plessner, el hombre necesita del umbral que ha de cruzar en el proceso de distanciamiento esencial de sí si se quiere (re)encontrar a sí mismo en tanto que otro. Como organismo vivo dotado de conciencia, como *embodied mind*, únicamente puede llegar a ser él mismo cuando se genera continuamente de un modo nuevo, cuando se transforma incesantemente, cuando cruza umbrales una y otra vez, y eso es algo que las realizaciones escénicas hacen posible, algo que le exigen. La realización escénica ha de ser concebida desde este punto de vista, y dicho con toda claridad, como la vida misma y como su modelo: como la vida misma, en tanto que consume efectivamente tiempo de la vida de los que participan en ella, actores y espectadores, y porque les da la oportunidad de generarse a sí mismos permanentemente; y como su modelo, en la medida en que realiza estos procesos con una intensidad y una vistosidad extraordinarias, de tal manera que dirige la atención de los que participan en ella a esos procesos, que son así percibidos por ellos. Es nuestra vida la que aparece, se hace presente y pasa en la realización escénica.

Una formulación así recuerda a la vieja metáfora *theatrum vitae humanae*. En ella el teatro se concibe como emblema e imitación de la vida humana. Dado que la realización escénica es tan ilusoria y efímera como la vida humana, está en condiciones de remitir a esos atributos en tanto que perfecto emblema de ella. Toda realización escénica hace conscientes a los espectadores del carácter ilusorio y efímero de su propia vida y los pone en un estado propicio para que se aparten de lo terrenal y busquen la verdad y la eternidad en la fe en Dios. La metáfora *theatrum vitae humanae* sólo tiene sentido en el marco de una cosmovisión cristiana.

En una estética de lo performativo se trata, por el contrario, de la aparición de personas y cosas, no de su condición ilusoria, de la fugacidad de su aparecer y no de su caducidad. No califica las realizaciones escénicas ni de emblema ni de imitación de la vida humana, sino que las entiende como vida humana propiamente dicha y, al mismo tiempo, como su modelo. Es la vida de cada uno de los que participan en una realización escénica la que tiene lugar en ella y, además, literalmente, no en sentido metafórico. Difícilmente puede el arte vincularse de manera más profunda con la vida dc lo que lo hace en una realización escénica, aproximarse más a ella.

El reencantamiento del mundo que se lleva a cabo en esta imbricación de arte y vida, que es el objeto de estudio de una estética de lo performativo, no ha de ser confundido con una vuelta a la cosmovisión religiosa del siglo diecisiete ni tampoco con la conciencia mágica de aquellos lejanos tiempos en los que el desear aún servía de algo. El hechizo inherente al mundo tal y como Dios lo creó, entretejido por fuerzas invisibles provenientes de ÉL, y que entrelazaban todo con todo, ese hechizo es desde la época de la Ilustración irrecuperable. Tampoco las artes pueden ya invocarlo e insuflarle de nuevo vida. Hemos de aceptar su pérdida como irreparable.

En su lugar, ha surgido durante la segunda mitad del siglo veinte un nuevo hechizo que, por muy sorprendente que pueda sonar, ha de ser entendido como un descendiente «directo», aunque lejano, de la Ilustración. Pues no son sino las ciencias modernas y el desarrollo cultural, tecnológico y social que éstas han hecho posible los que lo han liberado. Los resultados de sus investigaciones nos convencen cada vez más de que el mundo está efectivamente atravesado por fuerzas invisibles que nos influyen sin que podamos verlas u oírlas, pese a que podemos sentir físicamente sus efectos; de que en la naturaleza y en las sociedades surgen fenómenos que escapan a toda intencionalidad, planificación y cálculo previo; de que todo está conectado con todo y que el aleteo de una mariposa en un hemisferio puede desencadenar o evitar un tornado en el otro; de que las sociedades –especialmente en el marco de la globalización– se han hecho tan complejas que no se pueden hacer previsiones fiables sobre los posibles efectos de los cambios introducidos, y de que, pese a todo, hay que actuar de alguna manera; de que el yo, como ya dijera Freud, no es dueño y señor ni siquiera en su propia casa, sino que, antes bien, como defienden algunos de los principales representantes de la investigación neurológica actual, las decisiones se toman mucho antes de que sean conscientes; la convicción, en fin, de que también al hombre lo determinan fuerzas misteriosas que escapan a sus conscientes querer y saber.

Ahora bien, ni en el caso de las emergencias ni en el de las fuerzas invisibles que parecen afectar a los seres humanos y a la naturaleza se puede hablar de fuerzas mágicas. Se puede dar una explicación racional de ellas, que de todas formas no llega a convertirlas en disponibles. Mientras que en el mundo occidental previo a la Ilustración el hombre creía tener cierta influencia –mediante plegarias, penitencia, o cambiando su forma de vivir, etc.– sobre la salud, el bienestar, las cosechas, etc., y creía poder evitar epidemias, granizos o guerras, nosotros le concedemos hoy un poder análogo a la ciencia a pesar de que, en este sentido, se ha mostrado tan insuficiente como las plegarias o los ejercicios de penitencia. Cuanto mayores son los avances de la ciencia, cuanto más espectaculares son sus resultados –por ejemplo, en la genética o en la neurología–, más se desvanece, paradójicamente, la ilusión creada por la Ilustración, la ilusión de la infinita perfectibilidad del hombre y del mundo. Hoy son precisamente las ciencias, las investigaciones sobre el caos o las que se llevan a cabo en el campo de la microbiología, por ejemplo, las que hacen aflorar cada vez con más claridad el convencimiento de que el mundo está, en el sentido en el que venimos empleando la expresión, «encantado» y que escapa una y otra vez –muy probablemente para bien del hombre– a toda tentativa de la ciencia y la tecnología de someterlo, que es tan indisponible como el bucle de retroalimentación autopoiético en las realizaciones escénicas. Al fin y al cabo, el hombre no está en condiciones de someter a las «las fuerzas invisibles» que atraviesan el mundo. Aunque intente dominarlas y definirlas, al final siempre termina siendo dominado y determinado por ellas.

Mientras que esta asunción no ha sido general hasta las postrimerías del siglo veinte –de manera individual se defendió con anterioridad–, sí está en la base de las artes ya desde el giro performativo en los años sesenta. Lo que muchos científicos no se atrevían a pensar o a aceptar durante mucho tiempo, y lo que aún hoy muchos siguen negando, lo habían intuido décadas atrás los artistas y lo habían puesto por obra en su actividad artística. En sus acciones, performances, instalaciones y otras realizaciones escénicas han hecho experimentable y vivible precisamente ese reconocimiento de la misteriosa indisponibilidad tanto para sí como para los espectadores. En las realizaciones escénicas, ambos grupos podían experimentar y vivir el mundo como encantado y concebirse a sí mismos como en proceso de transformación, como seres en transición.

Aunque una estética de lo performativo haga posible la experimentación y la vivencia del reencantamiento del mundo al hacer hincapié en la autorreferencialidad y al renunciar a los resultados de la comprensión, no se la puede calificar de tendencia contraria a la Ilustración. Precisamente al demarcar los límites de la Ilustración, que necesita recurrir a parejas de conceptos antitéticos para la descripción y el sometimiento del mundo, al hacer que el hombre venga a presencia como *embodied mind*, se manifiesta como consecuencia de una «nueva» Ilustración: no llama ni incita al hombre al sometimiento de la naturaleza –ni a la suya ni a la de lo que le rodea–, sino que le alienta a que intente establecer una nueva relación consigo mismo y con el mundo, una relación no de disyunción exclusiva sino de conjunción, lo anima a que se realice en la vida como en las realizaciones escénicas artísticas.

BIBLIOGRAFÍA

ADORNO, Theodor W., «Bürgerliche Oper», en *Gesammelte Schriften*, Rolf Tiedemann con la colaboración de Gretel Adorno, Susan Buck-Morss y Klaus Schultz (eds.), vol. 16, *Musikalische Schriften*, Fráncfort, 1978, pp. 24-39 (esp. «Ópera burguesa», en *Escritos musicales I-III. Obra completa 16*, Madrid, 2006, pp. 25-40).

AKÁTS, Franz von, *Kunst der Scenik in ästhetischer und ökonomischer Hinsicht*, Viena, 1841.

ALBERS, Irene, «Scheitern als Chance: Die Kunst des Krisenexperiments», en Johannes Finke y Matthias Wulff (eds.), *Chance 2000. Die Dokumentation – Phänomen, Materialien, Chronologie*, Neuweiler, 1998.

ALTENBURG, Detlef, «Das Phantom des Theaters. Zur Schauspielmusik im späten 18. und frühen 19. Jahrhundert», en Hans-Peter Bayerdörfer (ed.), *Stimmen – Klänge – Töne. Synergien im szenischen Spiel* (=*Forum Modernes Theater* 30), Tubinga, 2002, pp. 183-208.

—, «Schauspielmusik», en *Die Musik in Geschichte und Gegenwart*, 2. Ludwig Fenscher (ed.), Sachteil, vol. 8, Kassel, 1998, pp. 1046-1049.

—, «Von den Schubladen der Wissenschaft. Zur Schauspielmusik im klassisch-romantischen Zeitalter», en Helen Geyer, Michael

Berg y Matthias Tischer (eds.), *Denn in jenen Tränen lebt es. Festschrift Wolfgang Marggraf*, Weimar, 1999, pp. 425-449.

Allgemeines Theater-Lexicon oder Encyclopädie alles Wissenswerthen für Bühnenkünstler, Dilettanten und Theaterfreunde, K. Herloßsohn, H. Marggraff *et al.* (eds.), 3 vols., nueva ed., Altenburg/Leipzig, 1846, entrada: «Inscenesetzen».

Ancelet-Hustache, Jeanne, «Les 'Vitae sororum' d'Unterlenden. Edition critique du manuscript 508 de la bibliothèque de Colmar», en *Archives d'histoire doctrinale et littéraire du Moyen Âge* (1930), pp. 317-509.

Artaud, Antonin, *Messages révolutionnaires*, en *Oeuvres complètes*, tomo VIII, París, 1971, pp. 169-315 (esp. *Mensajes revolucionarios*, Madrid, 2002).

—, *Le théâtre et son double*, en *Oeuvres complètes*, tomo IV, París, 1964, pp. 9-171 (esp. *El teatro y su doble*, Barcelona, 2006).

Auslander, Philip, *Liveness – Performance in a mediatized culture*, Londres/Nueva York, 1999.

Austin, John L., «Emisiones realizativas», en L. M. Valdés Villanueva (ed.), *Los caminos del significado*, Barcelona, 2000.

—, *Cómo hacer cosas con palabras: palabras y acciones*, Barcelona, 2008.

Baier, Gerold, *Rhythmus. Tanz in Körper und Gehirn*, Reinbek bei Hamburg, 2001.

Bansat-Boudon, Lynde, *Poètique du théâtre indiens: Lecture du Natyashastra*, París, 1992.

Barba, Eugenio, *Jenseits der schwimmenden Inseln. Reflexionen mit dem Odin Teatret. Theorie und Praxis des Freien Theaters.* Con una posdata de Ferdinando Taviani, Reinbek bei Hamburg, 1985 (esp. *Más allá de las islas flotantes*, México, 1986).

Bateson, Gregory, «A Theory of Play and Phantasy» (1955), en *Steps to an ecology of mind*, Chicago, 2000, pp. 177-193 (esp. *Pasos hacia una ecología de la mente*, Buenos Aires, 1972).

Baxmann, Inge, *Die Feste der Französischen Revolution*, Weinheim/Basilea, 1989.

Beck, Julian, *The Life of the Theatre*, San Francisco, 1972.

Beck/Malina, J., *Paradise Now*, Nueva York, 1971.

Becker, Peter von, «Die Sehnsucht nach dem Vollkommenen. Über Peter Stein, den Regisseur und sein Stück Theatergeschichte – zum sechzigsten Geburtstag», en *Der Tagesspiegel*, n.º 16, 1 de octubre de 1997.

BELFIORE, Elizabeth S., *Tragic Pleasures. Aristotle on Plot and Emotion*, Princeton, 1992.

BENJAMIN, Walter, *Das Kunstwerk im Zeitalter seiner technischen Reproduzierbarkeit*, Fráncfort, 1963 (esp. «La obra de arte en la época de su reproductibilidad técnica», en Walter Benjamin, *Obras. Libro I/vol. 2*, Madrid, 2008).

—, *Ursprung des deutschen Trauerspiels*. Ed. de Rolf Tiedemann, Fráncfort, 1972 (esp. *El origen del 'Trauerspiel' alemán*, en Walter Benjamin, *Obras. Libro I/vol. I*, Madrid, 2006, pp. 217-459).

BICCARI, Gaetano, *«Zuflucht des Geistes»?: konservativ-revolutionäre, faschistische und nationalistische Theaterdiskurse in Deutschland und Italien, 1900-1944*, Tubinga, 2001.

Blätter für Theater, Musik und Kunst, Leopold Alexander Zellner (ed.), Viena, 5 de marzo de 1861.

BOENISCH, Peter, «ElectrONic Bodies. Corpo-Realities in Contemporary Dance Performance», en *Moving Bodies*. Performance Research 8.4, D. Williams y R. Allsop (eds.), Londres/Nueva York, 2003, pp. 33-41.

BÖHME, Gernot, *Atmosphäre. Essays zur neuen Ästhetik*, Fráncfort, 1995.

BORMANN, Hans-Friedrich/BRANDSTETTER, Gabriele, «An der Schwelle. Performance als Forschungslabor», en Hanne Seitz (ed.), *Schreiben auf Wasser. Performative Verfahren in Kunst, Wissenschaft und Bildung*, Bonn, 1999, pp. 45-55.

BRECHT, Bertolt, *Der gute Mensch von Sezuan*, en *Gesammelte Werke*, Fráncfort, 1967, vol. 2, pp. 1478-1607 (esp. *La buena persona de Sezuan*, en *Obra*, México, 1972).

BROSDA, C., y SCHICHA, Ch., «Politikvermittlung als Event Marketing», en Erika Fischer-Lichte *et al.* (eds.), *Performativität und Ereignis* (= *Theatralität*, vol. 4), Tubinga/Basilea, 2003, pp. 319-338.

BRÜSTLE, Christa, «Performance/Performativität in der neuen Musik», en Erika Fischer-Lichte und Christoph Wulf (eds.), *Theorien des Performativen* (=*Paragrana*, Vol. 10, H. 1), Berlín, 2001, pp. 271-283.

Chris Burden. Beyond the limits / Jenseits der Grenzen, P. Noever (ed.),

Catálogo de la exposición en el Museo de Artes Aplicadas de Viena, 1996.

Chris Burden. A Twenty Years Survey. Catálogo de la exposición del Newport Harbor Museums, New Port Beach, 1988.

BURDEN, Chris/BUTTERFIELD, Jan, «Through the Night Softly», en *The Art of Performance. A Critical Anthology*, Gregory Battock y Robert Nickas (eds.), Nueva York, 1982, pp. 222-239.

BUTLER, Judith, *Gender Trouble*, Nueva York, 1990 (esp. *El género en disputa: el feminismo y la subversión de la identidad*, Barcelona, 2008).

—, «Actos perfomativos y constitución de género: un ensayo sobre fenomenología y teoría feminista». *Debate feminista* 9.18, octubre 1998, pp. 296-314.

CARLSON, Marvin, *Performance. A critical introduction*, Londres/Nueva York, 1996.

CARTER, Huntly, *The Theatre of Max Reinhardt*, Nueva York, 1914.

CIOMPI, Luc, *Die emotionalen Grundlagen des Denkens. Entwurf einer fraktalen Affektlogik*, Gotinga, 2.ª ed. 1999.

CRAIG, Edward Gordon, «The actor and the Über-marionette», en *On the Art of Theater*, Londres, 1912, pp. 54-94.

—, *On the Art of Theater*, Londres, 1912 (esp. *El arte del teatro*, México D.F., 1999).

CSÓRDAS, Thomas J. (ed.), *Embodiment and Experience. The existential ground of culture and self*, Cambridge, 1994.

—, «Somatic Modes of Attention», en *Cultural Anthropology* 8, 1993, pp. 135-156.

DAMASIO, Antonio R., *Descartes' Error: Emotion, Reason, and the Human Brain*, 1994 (esp. *El error de Descartes: la emoción, la razón y el cerebro humano*, Barcelona, 2006).

DANTO, Arthur, *La transfiguración del lugar común: una filosofía del arte*, Barcelona/Buenos Aires, 2002.

DAVID, Catherine, *Stand der Dinge*, Teil 1, Katalog Kunstwerke, Berlín, 2000.

DELEUZE, Gilles/GUATTARI, Félix, *¿Qué es la filosofía?*, Barcelona, 2001.

DERRIDA, Jacques, «Restituciones», en *La verdad en pintura*, Buenos Aires, 2005.

Deutsches Wörterbuch, Jakob y Wilhelm Grimm (eds.), Múnich, 1984, vol. 25.

Dictionnaire de spiritualité 3, París, 1957, entrada: «Discipline» de E. Bertaud.

Dictionnaire historique de la langue française, vol. 2, París, 1994, entrada: «mise en scène».

A Dictionary of Theatre Anthropology. The Secret Art of the Performer, ed. de Eugenio Barba y Nicola Savarese, Londres/Nueva York ,1991, entradas: «Energy», pp. 74-94, y «Pre-expressivity», pp. 186-204.

DIDEROT, Denis, «Carta sobre los sordomudos», en *«Carta sobre los ciegos» seguido de «Carta sobre los sordomudos»*, Julia Escobar (ed.), Valencia, 2002.

DOBLE, Frank J., *The Voice of the Coyote*, Boston, 1949.

DOBSON, Michael, «A Dog at all Things. The Transformation of the Onstage Canine, 1550-1850», en Alan Read (ed.), *Performance Research. On Animals,* vol. 5, n.º 2, Londres, 2000, pp. 116-124.

DÜLMEN, Richard van, *Theater des Schreckens. Gerichtspraxis und Strafrituale der frühen Neuzeit*, Múnich, 1988.

DURKHEIM, Émile, *La division del trabajo social*, Madrid, 2001.

EISENSTEIN, Sergei M., «El montaje de atracciones (1923)», en S. M. Eisenstein, *El sentido del cine*, Madrid, 1999.

ELIAS, Norbert, *Über den Prozeß der Zivilisation. Soziogenetische und psychogenetische Untersuchungen*, 2 vols., Fráncfort, 1976 (esp. *El proceso de la civilización. Investigaciones sociogenéticas y psicogenéticas*, México, 1988).

ENGEL, Johann Jakob, *Ideen zu einer Mimik* (1785/6), en *Schriften*, vol. 7/8, Berlín, 1804.

FELMAN, Shoshana, *The Literary Speech Act. Don Juan with J. L. Austin or Seduction in Two Languages*, Ithaca/Nueva York, 1983.

FISCHER-LICHTE, Erika, «Grenzgänge und Tauschhandel. Auf dem Wege zu einer performativen Kultur», en Uwe Wirth (ed.), *Performanz. Zwischen Sprachphilosophie und Kulturwissenschaften*, Fráncfort, 2002, pp. 277-300.

—, «Die Allegorie als Paradigma einer Ästhetik der Avantgarde. Eine semiotische *re-lecture* von Walter Benjamins *Ursprung des deutschen Trauerspiels»*, en *Ästhetische Erfahrung. Das Semiotische und das Performative*, Tubinga/Basilea, 2001, pp. 121-137.

—, «*Rite de passage* im Spiel der Blicke», en Kersten Gernig (ed.), *Fremde Körper. Zur Konstruktion des Anderen im europäischen Diskurs*, Berlín, 2001, pp. 297-315.

—, «Der Körper als Zeichen und als Erfahrung», en *Theater im Prozeß der Zivilisation*, Tubinga/Basilea, 2000, pp. 67-80.

—, «Verwandlung als ästhetische Kategorie. Zur Entwicklung einer neuen Ästhetik des Performativen», en VV.AA. (eds.), *Theater seit den sechziger Jahren*, Tubinga/Basilea, 1998, pp. 21-91.

— (ed.), *Das Drama und seine Inszenierung*, Tubinga, 1983.

—, *Semiotik des Theaters*, 3 vols., Tubinga, 1983 (esp. *Semiótica del Teatro*, Madrid, 1999).

—, *Bedeutung – Probleme einer semiotischen Hermeneutik und Ästhetik*, Múnich, 1979.

FLEMMING, Willi, *Barockdrama*, vol. 3, *Das Schauspiel der Wanderbühne*, 2.ª ed. Hildesheim, 1965.

FONTIUS, Martin, «Einfühlung/Empathie/Identifikation», en Karlheinz Barck (ed.), *Ästhetische Grundbegriffe*, vol. 2, Stuttgart, 2001, pp. 121-142.

FRANK, Georg, *Ökonomie des Aufmerksamkeit*, Múnich, 1998.

Französisches etymologisches Wörterbuch, Basilea, 1964, vol. II, entrada: «mise en scène».

FRIED, Michael, «Art and Objecthood», en Gregory Battock (ed.), *Minimal Art*, Nueva York, 1969, pp. 116-147.

FUCHS, Georg, *Die Revolution des Theaters. Ergebnisse aus dem Münchener Künstlertheater*, Múnich/Leipzig, 1909.

—, *Der Tanz*, Stuttgart, 1906.

FURLONG, William, *Audio Arts*, Leipzig, 1992.

FUSCO, Coco, «The Other History of Cultural Performance», en *The Drama Review* 38, 1 (primavera 1994), pp. 145-167.

GALLESE, Vittorio y GOLDMAN, Alvin, «Mirror neurons and the simulation theory of mind-reading», en *Trends in Cognitive Sciences*, vol. 2, n.º 12, diciembre de 1998, pp. 493-501.

GEBAUER, Gunter, *Sport in der Gesellschaft des Spektakels*, Sankt Augusten, 2002.

GEROW, Edwen, «Rasa as a category. What are the limits of its applications?», en Rachel van Baumer y James Brandon (eds.), *Sanskrit Drama en Performance*, Honolulu, 1981, pp. 226-257.

«Gespräch über Reinhardt mit Hugo de Hofmannsthal, Alfred Roller und Bruno Walter (1910)», en Max Reinhardt, *Schriften. Briefe, Reden, Aufsätze, Interviews, Gespräche und Auszüge aus den Regiebüchern*, Hugo Fetting (ed.), Berlín, 1974, pp. 380-384.

GIRARD, René, *La Violence et le sacré*, París, 1972 (esp. *La violencia y lo sagrado*, Barcelona, 1983).

GOFFMAN, Erving, *Frame analysis :an essay on the organization of experience*, Nueva York, 1974 (esp. *Frame analysis. Los marcos de la experiencia*, Madrid, 2006).

GOETHE, Johann Wolfgang von, «Regeln für Schauspieler», en *Sämtliche Werke in 18 Bänden*, vol. 14, *Schriften zur Literatur*, Zúrich, 1977, pp. 72-90.

GOLLOMB, Joseph, «Sumurun», en *New York City Call*, 4 de febrero de 1912.

GRONAU, Barbara, «Zeitfluß und Spur – Kunstbeschreibung en der Theaterwissenschaft zwischen Erinnerung und Imagination», en Heiko Wandhoff (ed.), *Ekphrasis. Kunstbeschreibung und virtuelle Räume im medialen Wandel*, Berlín, 2004.

GROTOWSKI, Jerzy, *Hacia un teatro pobre*, Madrid, 2009.

HALL, Edith (ed.), *Dionysus since 69: Greek Tragedy and the Public Imagination at the End of the Second Millenium*, Oxford, 2003.

HELBLING, Hanno, *Rhythmus. Ein Versuch*, Fráncfort, 1999.

HERRMANN, Max, «Das theatralische Raumerlebnis», en *Bericht vom 4. Kongreß für Ästhetik und Allgemeine Kunstwissenschaft*, Berlín, 1930.

—, «Über die Aufgaben eines theaterwissenschaftlichen Instituts», Conferencia del 27 de junio de 1920, en Helmar Klier (ed.), *Theaterwissenschaft im deutschsprachigen Raum*, Darmstadt, 1981, pp. 15-24.

—, «Bühne und Drama», en *Vossische Zeitung* 30 de julio de 1918 – Respuesta al Prof. Dr. Klaar.

—, *Forschungen zur deutschen Theatergeschichte des Mittelalters und der Renaissance*, Berlín, 1914, Teil II.

HOESSLY, Fortunat, *Katharsis. Reinigung als Heilverfahren. Studien zum Ritual der archaischen und klassischen Zeit*, Gotinga, 2001.

HOME, Henry, *Grundsätze der Kritik*, vol. 1, Leipzig, 1772 (orig. *Elements of criticism*, Indianápolis, 2005).

HORN, Christian, *Der aufgeführte Staat. Zur Theatralität höfischer Repräsentation unter Kurfürst Johann Georg II. de Sachsen*, Tubinga/Basilea, 2004.

HORN, Ch., UMATHUM, Sandra y WARSTAT, Matthias, «Auswählen und Versäumen. Wahrnehmungsmodi zwischen Fernsehen und Theater», en Erika Fischer-Lichte, Christian Horn, Sandra Umathum y Matthias Warstat (eds.), *Wahrnehmung und Medialität*. = Theatralität vol. 3, Tubinga/Basilea, 2001, pp. 143-158.

HYMES, Dell, «Breakthrough into Performance», en Dan Ben-Amos y Kenneth S. Goldstein (eds.), *Folklore: Performance and Communication*, La Haya, 1975, pp. 11-74.

ISER, Wolfgang, «Akte des Fingierens oder Was ist das Fiktive im fiktionalen Text?», en Dieter Henrich y Wolfgang Iser (eds.), *Funktionen des Fiktiven*, Múnich, 1983, pp. 121-151.

—, *Das Fiktive und das Imagenäre. Perspektiven einer literarischen Anthropologie*, Fráncfort, 1991.

IVANOV, Viacheslav Vsevolodovich, *Einführung in die allgemeine Problematik der Semiotik*, Tubinga, 1985.

JACOBSOHN, Siegfried, *Das Jahr der Bühne*, vol. 1, Berlín, 1912.

—, *Die Schaubühne* 46, 17 de noviembre de 1910.

JARON, Norbert *et al.* (eds.), *Berlin-Theater der Jahrhundertwende. Bühnengeschichte der Reichshauptstadt im Spiegel der Kritik (1889-1914)*, Tubinga, 1986.

JOHNSON, Mark y LAKOFF, George, *Metaphors We Live By*, Chicago/Londres, 1980 (esp. *Metáforas de la vida cotidiana*, Madrid, 2001).

JOHNSON, Mark, *The Body in the Mind. The Bodily Basis of Meaning, Imagination, and Reason*, Chicago/Londres, 1993 (esp. *El cuerpo en la mente: fundamentos corporales del significado, la imaginación y la razón*, Madrid, 1991).

KANT, Immanuel, *Werke in zehn Bände*, vol. 8: *Kritk der Urteilskraft*, Wilhelm Weischedel (ed.), Darmstad,t 1975, p. 287 (esp. *Crítica del Juicio*, Madrid, 1991).

KAPPELHOFF, Herrmann, *Matrix der Gefühle. Das Kino, das Melodrama und das Theater der Empfindsamkeit*, Berlín, 2004.

KIPPENBERG, Hans G., *Die Entdeckung der Religionsgeschichte, Religionswissenschaft und Moderne*, Múnich, 1997.

KLAAR, Alfred, «Bühne und Drama. Zum Programm der deutschen dramatischen Gesellschaft de Prof. Max Herrmann», en *Vossische Zeitung*, 18 de julio de 1918.

KOLESCH, Doris, «Der magische Atem des Theaters. Ritual und Revolte bei Antonin Artaud», en Franz Norbert Mennemeier y Erika Fischer-Lichte (eds.), *Drama und Theater der europäischen Avantgarde*, Tubinga/Basilea, 1994, pp. 231-254.

—, «'Listen to the radio': Artauds Radio-Stimme(n)», en *FORUM MODERNES THEATER*, vol. 14, H.2, 1999, pp. 115-143.

KÖPPING, Klaus-Peter, «Fest», en Christoph Wulf (ed.), *Der Mensch. Handbuch Historische Anthropologie*, Weenheim/Basilea, 1997, pp. 1048-1065.

KÖPPING, K-P./ RAO, Ursula, «Die 'performative Wende': Leben – Ritual – Theater.», en Klaus-Peter Köppeng y Ursula Rao (eds.), *Im Rausch des Rituals. Gestaltung und Transformation der Wirklichkeit in körperlicher Performanz*, Münster/Hamburgo/Londres, 2000, pp. 1-31.

KOSTELANETZ, Richard, *Conversing with Cage*, Nueva York/Londres, Routledge, 2.ª ed. 2003.

KRÄMER, Sibylle y STAHLHUT, Marco, «Das 'Performative' als Thema der Sprach- und Kulturphilosophie», en Erika Fischer-Lichte y Christoph Wulf (eds.), *Theorien des Performativen* (= *Paragrana*, vol. 10, H. 1), Berlín, 2001, pp. 35-64.

KRAMER, Mario, *Joseph Beuys 'Das Kapital Raum 1970-1977'*, Heidelberg, 1992.

KREUDER, Friedemann, *Formen des Erinnerns im Theater Klaus Michael Grübers*, Berlín, 2002.

KÜCHENHOFF, Joachim, «Das Fest und die Grenzen des Ich – Begrenzung und Entgrenzung im 'vom Gesetz gebotenen Exzeß», en Walter Haug y Rainer Warneng (eds.), *Poetik und Hermeneutik XIV*, Múnich, 1989, pp. 99-119.

LAKOFF, George, *Woman, Fire and Dangerous Things – What Categories Reveal about the Mind*, Chicago/Londres, 1987.

LANG, P. Franciscus, *Abhandlung über die Schauspielkunst*, Alexander Ruden (ed. y trad.) Múnich, 1975.

LARGIER, Niklaus, *Lob der Peitsche. Eine Kulturgeschichte der Erregung*, Múnich, 2001.

LAZAROWICZ, Klaus y BALME, Christopher (eds.), *Texte zur Theorie des Theaters*, Stuttgart, 1991.

LEHMANN, Hans-Thies, «Die Gegenwart des Theaters», en Erika Fischer-Lichte, Doris Kolesch y Christel Weiler (eds.), *TRANSFORMATIONEN. Theater der neunziger Jahre*, Berlín, 1999, pp. 13-26.

—, *Postdramatisches Theater*, Fráncfort, 1999.

LESSING, Gotthold Ephraim, «Brief an Nicolai vom November 1756», en *Werke*, Herbert G. Göpfert (ed.), 8 vols., Múnich, 1970-1979, vol. 4.

LEWALD, August, «In die Szene setzen», en Klaus Lazarowicz y Christopher Balme (eds.), *Texte zur Theorie des Theaters*, Stuttgart, 1991, pp. 306-311.

LIPP, Wolfgang, «Feste heute: Animation, Partizipation und Happening», en: *Drama Kultur*, Berlín, 1994, pp. 523-547.

LORENZER, Alfred, *Kritik des psychoanalytischen Symbolbegriffs*, Fráncfort, 1970 (esp. *Crítica del concepto psicoanalítico de símbolo*, Buenos Aires, 1976).

—, *Zur Begründung einer materialistischen Sozialisationstheorie*, Fráncfort, 1972 (esp. *Bases para una teoría de la socialización*, Buenos Aires, 1976).

LUCKERT, Karl W., *Coyoteway. A Navajo Holyway Healeng Ceremonial*, Tucson/Flagstaff, 1979.

MARINETTI, Filippo Tommaso, «El teatro de variedades», en *La escena moderna: manifiestos y textos sobre el teatro de la época de vanguardias*, José A. Sánchez (ed.), Cuenca, 1997, pp. 114-122.

MASSON, Jeffrey y PATWARDHAN, M. V., *Aesthetic rapture – The Rasadhy-ya of Natyasastra*, Poona, 1970.

MATURANA, Humberto R. y VARELA, Francisco J., *El arbol del conocimiento: las bases biológicas del entendimiento humano*, Santiago de Chile, 1984.

MCKENZIE, Jon, *Perform – or else. From discipline to performance*, Londres/Nueva York, 2001.

MENKE, Christoph, *Die Souveränität der Kunst*, Fráncfort, 1988.

MERLEAU-PONTY, Maurice, *Le visible et l'invisible ; suivi de Notes de travail*, París, 1964 (esp. «El entrelazo – El quiasmo», en *Lo visible y lo invisible*, Barcelona, 1970).

MERSCH, Dieter, *Aura und Ereignis*, Fráncfort, 2002.

MEYER, Petra Maria, «Als das Theater aus dem Rahmen fiel», en Erika Fischer-Lichte *et al.* (eds.), *Theater seit den sechziger Jahren*, Tubinga/Basilea, 1998, pp. 135-195.

MEYER, Thomas y KAMPMANN, Martena, *Politik als Theater. Die neue Macht der Darstellungskunst*, Berlín, 1998.

MEYERHOLD, Vsevolod E., «Der Schauspieler der Zukunft und die Biomechanik», en *Vsevolod Meyerhold. Theaterarbeit 1917-1930*, ed. de Rosemarie Tietze, Múnich, 1974, pp. 72-76.

—, «Rezension des Buches 'Aufzeichnungen eines Regisseurs' von A. Ja. Tairov (1921/1922)», en *Vsevolod Meyerhold. Theaterarbeit 1917-1930*, Rosemarie Tietze (ed.), Múnich, 1974, pp. 63-72.

—, «Zur Geschichte und Technik des Theaters», en *Schriften*, 2 vols., Berlín, 1979, vol. I (esp. «Historia y técnica en el teatro», en *Meyerhold: textos teóricos,* ed. de Juan Antonio Hormigón, Madrid, 1998, pp.138 y ss.).

MICHAELIS, Rolf, «Die Geburt des Rechtsstaates im Regen», en *DIE ZEIT* 35, 24 de octubre de 1980.

MÜNKLER, Herfried, «Die Theatralisierung der Politik», en Josef Früchtl y Jörg Zimmermann (eds.), *Ästhetik der Inszenierung*, Fráncfort, 2001, pp. 144-163.

MÜNZ, Rudolf, «'Theater – eine Leistung des Publikums und seiner Diener'. Zu Max Herrmanns Vorstellungen de Theater», en Erika Fischer-Lichte *et al.* (eds.), *Berliner Theater im 20. Jahrhundert*, Berlín, 1998, pp. 43-52.

NICOLE, Pierre, *Traité de la comédie et autres pièces d'un procès du théâtre*, Laurent Thirouen (ed.), París, 1998.

NIETZSCHE, Friedrich, *Die Geburt der Tragödie aus dem Geist der Musik*, en *Sämtliche Werke*, Kritische Studienausgabe en 15 vols., edición de G. Colli y M. Montinari, Múnich, 1988, vol I, pp. 9-156 (esp. *El nacimiento de la tragedia*, Madrid, 1973).

NITSCH, Hermann, *Das Orgien – Mysterien – Theater. Die Partituren aller aufgeführten Aktionen 1960-1979*, Nápoles/Múnich/Viena, 1979, vol. I.

PFOTENHAUER, Helmut, *Kunst als Physiologie. Nietzsches ästhetische Theorie und literarische Produktion,* Stuttgart, 1985.

PHELAN, Peggy, *Unmarked: The Politics of Performance*, Londres/Nueva York, 1993.

PISCATOR, Erwin, *Zeittheater. «Das Politische Theater» und weitere Schriften von 1915 bis 1966*, Reinbek bei Hamburg, 1986.

Plattform 1, Documenta 11: Democracy Unrealized, cuadernillo, Kassel/ Berlín, 2001.

PLESSNER, Helmuth, «Lachen und Weinen», en *Philosophische Anthropologie*, ed. de Günter Dux, Fráncfort, 1970, pp. 11-171 (esp. *La risa y el llanto: investigación sobre los límites del comportamiento humano*, Madrid, 2007).

—, «Zur Anthropologie des Schauspielers», en Günter Dux, Odo Marquard y Elisabeth Ströker (eds.), *Gesammelte Schriften*, Fráncfort, 1982, pp. 399-418.

PLUCHART, François, «Risk as Practice of Thought», en G. Battock y R. Nickas (eds.), *The Art of Performance. A Critical Anthology*, Nueva York, 1982, pp. 125-134.

POIZAT, Michel, *L'Opéra ou le cri de l'ange: essai sur la jouissance de l'amateur d'opéra*, París, 1986.

PRANTL, Heribert, «Wir denken zu sehr in PR-Kategorien», en *Sage & Schreibe* 9/1998, pp. 44-45 (entrevista con R. Schatz).

RAPP, Uri, *Handeln und Zuschauen. Untersuchungen über den theatersoziologischen Aspekt in der menschlichen Interaktion*, Darmstadt/Neuwied, 1973.

REICHARD, August Ottokar (ed.), *Theater-Kalender auf das Jahr 1781*, Gotha, 1781.

RISCHBIETER, Henning, «EXPERIMENTA. Theater und Publikum neu defeniert», en *Theater heute* 6, julio de 1966, pp. 8-17.

RISI, Clemens, «Die bewegende Sängerin. Zu stimmlichen und körperlichen Austauschprozessen in Opernaufführungen», en Christa Brüstle/Albrecht Riethmüller (eds.), *Klang und Bewegung. Beiträge zu einer Grundkonstellation*, Aquisgrán, 2003.

—, «Rhythmen der Aufführung. Kollidierende Rhythmen bei Steve Reich und Heiner Goebbels», en Erika Fischer-Lichte, Clemens Risi y Jens Roselt (eds.), *Kunst der Aufführung – Aufführung der Kunst*, Berlín, 2004.

ROGOFF, Irit, «WIR. Kollektivitäten, Mutualitäten, Partizipationen», en *I promise it's political. Performativität in der Kunst*, Ausstellungskatalog, Colonia, 2002, pp. 53-60.

ROSELT, Jens, «*Big Brother* – Zur Theatralität eines Medienereignisses», en Matthias Lilienthal y Claus Philipp (eds.), *Schlingensiefs AUSLÄNDER RAUS*, Fráncfort, 2000, pp. 70-78.

—, «Wo die Gefühle wohnen – zur Performativität von Räumen», en Hajo Kurzenberger y Annemarie Matzke (eds.), *TheorieTheaterPraxis*, Berlín, 2004.

ROTH, Gerhard, *Fühlen, Denken, Handeln. Wie das Gehirn unser Verhalten steuert*, Fráncfort, 2001.

ROSENTHAL, Rachel, «Performance and the Masochist Tradition», en *High Performance*, invierno 1981/2.

ROUSSEAU, Jean-Jacques, *Lettre a Mr. D'Alembert sur les spectacles*, ed. de M. Fuchs, Ginebra, 1948 (esp. *Carta a d'Alembert sobre los espectáculos*, Madrid, 1994).

RÜHLE, Günther, *Theater für die Republik*, 2 ed., Fráncfort, 1988, vol. 2, 1926-1933.

SAINTE ALBINE, Rémonde de, «Auszug aus dem *Schauspieler* des Herrn Remond de Sainte Albine», en *Lessings Werke*, Robert Boxberger (ed.), Berlín/Stuttgart, 1883-1890, V. Teil: *Theatralische Bibliothek*, 1. Teil, 1. Stück 1754, pp. 128-159.

SCHACTER, Daniel L., *Wir sind Erinnerung. Gedächtnis und Persönlichkeit*, Reinbek bei Hamburg, 1999.

SCHECHNER, Richard, *Dionysus in 69*, Nueva York, 1970.

—, *Enviromental Theater*, Nueva York, 1973 (esp. *El teatro ambientalista*. México D.F., 1988).

—, «Rasaesthetics», en *TDR*, vol. 45, n.º 3 (T171), otoño, 2001, pp. 27-50.

SCHEIBE, Johann Adolph, *Der Critische Musicus*, Leipzig, 1745.

SCHILLER, Friedrich, «Was kann eine gute stehende Schaubühne eigentlich wirken?» (1784), en *Schillers Werke*, Nationalausgabe, vol. 20, Weimar, 1962, pp. 87-100.

—, «Briefe über die ästhetische Erziehung des Menschen», en *Schillers Werke*, Nationalausgabe, vol. 20, Weimar 1962, pp. 309-412 (esp. *Cartas sobre la educación estética del hombre*, en *Kallias. Cartas sobre la educación estética del hombre*, ed. bilingüe, Barcelona, 1990, pp. 110-381.)

SCHLEEF, Einar, *Droge Faust Parsifal*, Fráncfort, 1997.

SCHLÖSSER, Rainer, «Vom kommenden Volksschauspiel», en *Das Volk und seine Bühne*, Berlín, 1935.

SCHMIDT, Friedrich Ludwig, *Denkwürdigkeiten des Schauspielers, Schauspieldichters und Schauspieldirectors Friedrich Ludwig Schmidt (1722-1841)*, Hermann Uhde (ed.), 2.ª ed., Stuttgart, 1878, vol. 2.

SCHMITZ, Hermann, *System der Philosophie*, II, 1: *Der Leib*, Bonn, 1965.

SCHMITZ-EMANS, Monika, «Labyrinthbücher als Spielanleitungen», en Erika Fischer-Lichte y Gertrud Lehnert (eds.), *[(v)er]SPIEL[en] Felder – Figuren – Regeln* (=*Paragrana*, Vol. 11, H. 1), Berlín, 2002, pp. 179-207.

SCHNEEDE, Uwe M., *Joseph Beuys – Die Aktionen*, Kommentiertes Werkverzeichnis mit fotografischer Dokumentation, Ostfildern-Ruit bei Stuttgart, 1994.

SCHREYER, Lothar, «Das Bühnenkunstwerk», en *Der Sturm* 7, 5 (agosto 1916), pp. 50 y ss.

SEEL, Martin, *Ästhetik des Erscheinens*, Múnich, 2000.

—, «Inszenieren als Erscheinenlassen. Thesen über die Reichweite eines Begriffs», en Josef Früchtl y Jörg Zimmermann (eds.), *Ästhetik der Inszenierung*, Fráncfort, 2001, pp. 48-62.

SEITTER, Walter, «Aufmerksamkeitskorrelate auf der Ebene der Erscheinungen», en Aleida Assmann y Jan Assmann (eds.), *Aufmerksamkeiten. Archäologie der literarischen Kommunikation*, Múnich, 2002.

SHUSTERMAN, Richard, «Tatort: Kunst als Dramatisieren», en Josef Früchtl y Jörg Zimmermann (eds.), *Ästhetik der Inszenierung*, Fráncfort, 2001, pp. 126-143.

SIMMEL, Georg, «Zur Philosophie des Schauspielers», en *Das individuelle Gesetz. Philosophische Exkurse*, Fráncfort, 1968, pp. 75-95.

—, *Soziologie. Untersuchungen über die Form der Vergesellschaftung*, 2ª. ed., Múnich/Leipzig, 1922 (esp. *Sociología: estudios sobre las formas de socialización*, Madrid 1986).

SINGER, Milton, *Traditional India – Structure and Change*, Filadelfia, 1959.

SMITH, William Robertson, *Lectures on the Religion of the Semites*, First Series: *The Fundamental Institutions* (Burnett Lectures 1888/9), Londres, 1894.

SOEFFNER, Hans Georg y TÄNZLER, Dirk (eds.), *Figurative Politik. Zur Performanz der Macht in der modernen Gesellschaft*, Opladen, 2002.

STADLER, Michael y KRUSE, Peter, «Visuelles Gedächtnis für Formen und das Problem der Bedeutungszuweisung in kognitiven Systemen», en Siegfried J. Schmidt (ed.), *Gedächtnis. Probleme und Perspektiven der interdisziplinären Gedächtnisforschung,* Fráncfort, 1991, pp. 250-266.

STADLER, M., «Zur Emergenz psychischer Qualitäten. Das psychophysische Problem im Lichte der Selbstorganisationstheorie», en Wolfgang Krohn y Günter Küppers (eds.), *Emergenz: Die Entstehung de Ordnung, Organisation und Bedeutung,* Fráncfort, 1992, pp. 134-160.

STEINWEG, Reiner, «Ein 'Theater der Zukunft'. Über die Arbeit von Angelus Novus am Beispiel von Brecht und Homer», en *Falter,* Ausgabe 23, 1986.

STEPHAN, Achim, *Emergenz. Von der Unvorhersagbarkeit zur Selbstorganisation,* Dresde/Múnich, 1999.

—, «Emergenz in kognitionsfähigen Systemen», en Michael Pauen y Gerhard Roth (eds.), *Neurowissenschaften und Philosophie,* Múnich, 2001, pp. 123-154.

STOSS, Toni (ed.), *Marina Abramovic Artist Body, Performances 1969-1997,* Milán, 1998.

SOUSSA, Ronald de, *Die Rationalität des Gefühls,* Fráncfort, 1997.

SULZER, Johann Georg, *Allgemeine Theorie der schönen Künste,* vol. 4, nueva 2.ª ed., Leipzig, 1794.

TISDALL, Carolene, *Joseph Beuys Coyote,* Múnich, 3.ª ed., 1988.

TURNER, Victor, *The Ritual Process – Structure and Anti-Structure,* Londres, 1969 (esp. *El proceso ritual: estructura y antiestructura,* Madrid, 1988).

—, «Variations on a Theme of Limenality», en Sally F. Moore y Barbara C. Myerhoff (eds.), *Secular Rites,* Assen, 1977, pp. 36-57.

VARELA, Francisco J., THOMPSON, Evan y ROSCH, Eleanor, *The Embodied Mind: Cognitive Science and Human Experience,* Boston, 1991 (esp. *De cuerpo presente,* Barcelona, 1992).

VATTIMO, Gianni, *La sociedad transparente,* Barcelona, 1998.

VÉRON, Pierre, *Paris s'amuse,* París, 1874.

VIELHABER, Gert, «Oedipus Komplex auf der Bühne», en *DIE ZEIT,* 2 de octubre de 1947.

VISCHER, Friedrich Theodor, «Das Symbol» (1887), en *Kritische Gänge IV*, Robert Vischer (ed.), Múnich, 1922, pp. 420-456.

—, *Ästhetik* (1846-1858), vol. 2, Múnich, 1922.

VISCHER, Robert, «Der ästhetische Akt und die reine Form» (1874), en *Drei Schriften zum ästhetischen Formproblem*, Halle, 1927, pp. 45-54.

VOLLMOELLER, Carl, «Zur Entwicklungsgeschichte des Großen Hauses», en *Das Große Schauspielhaus. Zur Eröffnung des Hauses*, Deutschen Theater Berlin (ed.), Berlín, 1920, pp. 15-21.

WÄGENBAUR, Thomas (ed.), *Blinde Emergenz? Interdisziplinäre Beiträge zu Fragen kultureller Evolution*, Heidelberg, 2000.

WARSTAT, Matthias, *Theatrale Gemeinschaften. Zur Festkultur der Arbeiterbewegung 1918-1933*, Tubinga/Basilea, 2004.

WEILER, Christel, «Heiner Goebbels *Landschaft mit dem von der Schlange getöteten Mann*», en *Theater der Zeit*, sept./oct. 1997, Spezial «Theaterskizzen zur Dokumenta X», pp. XIII-XVI.

—, «Bilderloses licht. *Mythos Europa* von Jörg Laue», en *Theater der Zeit*, mayo/junio 1991, pp. 48 y ss.

—, «Am Ende Geschichte. Anmerkungen zur theatralen Historiographie und zur Zeitlichkeit theaterwissenschaftlicher Arbeit», en Erika Fischer-Lichte, Doris Kolesch y Christel Weiler (eds.), *TRANSFORMATIONEN. Theater der neunziges Jahre*, Berlín, 1999, pp. 43-56.

—, «Haschen nach dem Vogelschwanz. Überlegungen zu den Grundlagen schauspielerischer Praxis», en Christel Weiler y Hans-Thies Lehmann (eds.), *Szenarien von Theater (und) Wissenschaft* (= Theater der Zeit, Recherchen 15), Berlín, 2003, pp. 204-214.

WILSON, Robert, *the CIVIL warS, a tree is best measured when it is down*, Fráncfort, 1984.

WOLL, Stefan, *Das Totaltheater. Ein Projekt von Walter Gropius und Erwen Piscator* (= *Schriften der Gesellschaft für Theatergeschichte e.V.*, vol. 68), Berlín, 1984.

Documentación de audio y fílmica

BURDEN, Chris, *Documentation of Selected Works 1971-1974*, cinta de vídeo (USA 1975), VHS 34 min., ed. de A. Wirths en colaboración con F. Malsch y la Kunstverein de Colonia, Colonia, 1990.

EMMERLING, Hans, documentación fílmica sobre la acción de Beuys *Celtic + ~~~*, en Medien-Archiv im Hamburger Bahnhof-Museum für Moderne Kunst, Berlín.

KLÜSER, Bernd, documentación fílmica sobre la acción de Beuys *Celtic + ~~~* , en Medien Archiv Hamburger Bahnhof – Museum für Moderne Kunst, Berlín.

RIEWOLDT, Otto, «Herrscher über Raum und Zeit. Das Theater Robert Wilsons», emitido por Südfunk el 3 de junio de 1987.

WIETZ, Helmuth, *Joseph Beuys. I like America and America likes me*, Film-Dokumentation, Vertrieb René Block, Berlín, 1974.

ÍNDICE